£1.99   £2.99

Phillip Margolin is a retired criminal defence lawyer in Oregon where he has tried many high profile cases. He is married with two children.

(f)

D0595655

41

GONE, BUT NOT FORGOTTEN
and
AFTER DARK

Omnibus

Two Novels in One Volume

PHILLIP MARGOLIN

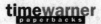

A *Time Warner* Paperback

First published in this omnibus edition
in 2002 by Time Warner Paperbacks

Gone, But Not Forgotten and After Dark Omnibus
Copyright © 2002 by Phillip M. Margolin
Gone, But Not Forgotten
Copyright © 1993 by Phillip M. Margolin
After Dark Copyright © 1995 by Phillip M. Margolin

The moral right of the author has been asserted.

A CIP catalogue record for this book
is available from the British Library.

ISBN 0 7515 3306 8

Typeset by M Rules
Printed and bound in Great Britain by
Clays Ltd, St Ives plc

Time Warner Paperbacks
An imprint of
Time Warner Books UK
Brettenham House
Lancaster Place
London WC2E 7EN

www.TimeWarnerBooks.co.uk

GONE, BUT NOT FORGOTTEN

PART ONE

WAKE-UP CALL

Chapter One

1

'Have you reached a verdict?' Judge Alfred Neff asked the eight men and four women seated in the jury box.

A heavy-set, barrel-chested man in his mid-sixties struggled to his feet. Betsy Tannenbaum checked the chart she had drawn up two weeks ago, during jury selection. This was Walter Korn, a retired welder. Betsy felt uncomfortable with Korn as the foreman. He was a member of the jury only because Betsy had run out of challenges.

The bailiff took the verdict form from Korn and handed it to the judge. Betsy's eyes followed the folded square of white paper. As the judge opened it and read the verdict to himself, she watched his face for a tell-tale sign, but there was none.

Betsy stole a glance at Andrea Hammermill, the plump, matronly woman sitting beside her. Andrea stared straight ahead, as subdued and resigned as she had been throughout her trial for the murder of her husband. The only time

Andrea had shown any emotion was during direct examination when she explained why she shot Sidney Hammermill to death. As she told the jury about firing the revolver over and over until the dull click of hammer on steel told her there were no more bullets, her hands trembled, her body shook and she sobbed pitifully.

'Will the defendant please stand,' Judge Neff said.

Andrea got to her feet unsteadily. Betsy stood with her, eyes forward.

'Omitting the caption, the verdict reads as follows: "We the jury, being duly impaneled and sworn, do find the defendant, Andrea Marie Hammermill, not guilty . . ." '

Betsy could not hear the rest of the verdict over the din in the courtroom. Andrea collapsed on her chair, sobbing into her hands.

'Its okay,' Betsy said, 'it's okay.' She felt tears on her cheeks as she wrapped a protective arm around Andrea's shoulders. Someone tapped Betsy on the arm. She looked up. Randy Highsmith, the prosecutor, was standing over her holding a glass of water.

'Can she use this?' he asked.

Betsy took the glass and handed it to her client. Highsmith waited a moment while Andrea regained her composure.

'Mrs Hammermill,' he said, 'I want you to know that I prosecuted you because I believe you took the law into your own hands. But I also want you to know that I don't think your husband had the right to treat you the way he did. I don't care who he was. If you had come to me, instead of shooting him, I would have done my best to put him in jail. I hope you can put this behind you and go on with your life.

You seem like a good person.'

Betsy wanted to thank Highsmith for his kind words, but she was too choked up to speak. As Andrea's friends and supporters started to crowd around her Betsy pushed away from the throng to get some air. Over the crowd she could see Highsmith, alone, bent over his table, gathering law books and files. As the assistant district attorney started toward the door, he noticed Betsy standing on the fringe of the crowd. Now that the trial was over, the two lawyers were superfluous. Highsmith nodded. Betsy nodded back.

2

With his back arched, his sleek muscles straining and his head tipped back, Martin Darius looked like a wolf baying over fallen prey. The blonde lying beneath him tightened her legs around his waist. Darius shuddered and closed his eyes. The woman panted from exertion. Darius's face contorted, then he collapsed. His cheek fell against her breast. He heard the blonde's heart-beat and smelled perspiration mingled with a trace of perfume. The woman threw an arm across her face. Darius ran a lazy hand along her leg and glanced across her flat stomach at the cheap digital clock on the motel end-table. It was two PM. Darius sat up slowly and dropped his legs over the side of the bed. The woman heard the bed move and watched Darius cross the room.

'I wish you didn't have to go,' she said, unable to hide her disappointment.

Darius grabbed his kit off of the low-slung chest of drawers and padded toward the bathroom.

'I've got a meeting at three,' he answered, without looking back.

Darius washed away the sheen of sweat he had worked up during sex, then toweled himself roughly in the narrow confines of the motel bathroom. Steam from the shower misted the mirror. He wiped the glass surface and saw a gaunt face with deep-set blue eyes. His neatly trimmed beard and mustache framed a devil's mouth that could be seductive or intimidating. Darius used a portable dryer, then combed his straight black hair and beard. When he opened the bathroom door, the blonde was still in bed. A few times, she had tried to lure him back into bed after he was showered and dressed. He guessed she was trying to exercise sexual control over him and refused to give in.

'I've decided we should stop seeing each other,' Darius said casually as he buttoned his white, silk shirt.

The blonde sat up in bed, a shocked expression on her normally confident, cheer-leader face. He had her attention now. She was not used to being dumped. Darius turned slightly so she would not see his smile.

'Why?' she managed as he stepped into his charcoal-gray suit trousers. Darius turned to look at her, so he could enjoy the play of emotions on her face.

'To your credit, you are beautiful and good in bed,' he said, knotting his tie, 'but you're boring.'

The blonde gaped at him for a moment, then flushed with anger.

'You shit.'

Darius laughed and picked up his suit jacket.

'You can't mean it,' she went on, her anger passing quickly.

'I'm very serious. We're through. It was nice for a while, but I want to move on.'

'And you think you can use me, then toss me away like a cigarette,' she said, the anger back. 'I'll tell your wife, you son-of-a-bitch. I'll call her right now.'

Darius stopped smiling. The expression on his face forced the blonde back against the headboard. Darius strolled around the bed slowly, until he was standing over her. She cowered back and put her hands up. Darius watched her for a moment, the way a biologist would study a specimen on a slide. Then he grabbed her wrist and twisted her arm until she was bent forward on the bed, her forehead against the crumpled sheets.

Darius admired the curve of her body from her backside to her slender neck as she knelt in pain. He ran his free hand along her rump, then applied pressure to her wrist to make her body quiver. He liked watching her breasts sway rapidly as she jerked to attention.

'Let me make one thing very clear to you,' Darius said in the same tone he might use with a recalcitrant child. 'You will never call my wife, or me, ever. Do you understand?'

'Yes,' the blonde gasped as he twisted her arm behind her, pushing it slowly up toward her shoulder.

'Tell me what you will never do,' he commanded calmly, releasing the pressure for a moment and stroking the curve of her buttocks with his free hand.

'I won't call, Martin. I swear,' she wept.

'Why won't you call my wife or bother me?' Darius asked, putting pressure on the wrist.

The blonde gasped, twitching with the pain. Darius fought back a giggle, then eased up so she could answer.

'I won't call,' she repeated between sobs.

'But you haven't said why,' Darius responded in a reasonable tone.

'Because you said I shouldn't. I'll do what you want. Please, Martin, don't hurt me anymore.'

Darius released his hold and the woman collapsed, sobbing pitifully.

'That's a good answer. A better one would be that you won't do anything to annoy me, because I can do far worse to you than I just have. Far, far worse.'

Darius knelt by her face and took out his lighter. It was solid gold with an inscription from his wife. The bright orange flame wavered in front of the blonde's terrified eyes. Darius held it close enough for her to feel the heat.

'Far, far worse,' Darius repeated. Then he closed the lighter and walked across the motel room. The blonde rolled over and lay with the white sheet tangled around her hips, leaving her slender legs and smooth back exposed. Each time she sobbed, her shoulders trembled. Martin Darius watched her in the motel mirror as he adjusted his wine-red tie. He wondered if he could convince her this was all a joke, then get her to submit to him again. The thought brought a smile to his thin lips. For a moment, he toyed with the image of the woman kneeling before him and taking him in her mouth, convinced that he wanted her back. It would be a challenge to get her on her knees after the way he had crushed her spirit. Darius was confident he could do it, but there was a meeting to attend.

'The room's paid for,' he said. 'You can stay as long as you want.'

'Can't we talk? Please, Martin,' the woman begged, sitting up and turning on the bed so that her small, sad breasts were exposed, but Darius was already closing the motel-room door.

Outside, the sky looked ominous. Thick, black clouds were rolling in from the coast. Darius unlocked the door of his jet-black Ferrari and silenced the alarm. In a short while, he would do something that would increase the woman's pain. Something exquisite that would make it impossible for her to forget him. Darius smiled in anticipation, then drove off without the slightest suspicion that someone was photographing him from the corner of the motel parking lot.

Martin Darius sped across the Marquam Bridge toward downtown Portland. The heavy rain kept the pleasure-boats off of the Willamette River, but a rusty tanker was pushing through the storm toward the port at Swan Island. Across the river was an architectural mix of functional, gray, futuristic buildings linked by sky bridges, Michael Graves' whimsical, post-modern Portland Building, the rose-colored US Bank skyscraper, and three-story historical landmarks dating back to the eighteen hundreds. Darius had made his fortune adding to Portland's skyline and rebuilding sections of the city.

Darius changed lanes just as a reporter began the lead story on the five o'clock news.

'This is Larry Prescott at the Multnomah County Court-house speaking with Betsy Tannenbaum, the attorney for

Andrea Hammermill, who has just been acquitted in the shooting death of her husband, City Commissioner Sidney Hammermill.

'Betsy, why do you think the jury voted "not guilty"?'

'I believe it was an easy choice once the jurors understood how battering affects the mind of a woman who undergoes the frequent beatings and abuse Andrea suffered.'

'You've been critical of this prosecution from the start. Do you think the case would have been handled differently if Mr Hammermill was not a Mayoral candidate?'

'The fact that Sidney Hammermill was wealthy and very active in Oregon politics may have influenced the decision to prosecute.'

'Would it have made a difference if District Attorney Alan Page had assigned a woman deputy to the case?'

'It could have. A woman would have been able to evaluate the evidence more objectively than a man and might have declined prosecution.'

'Betsy, this is your second acquittal in a murder case using the battered wife defense. Earlier this year, you won a million-dollar verdict against an anti-abortion group and *Time* magazine listed you as one of America's up-and-coming female trial lawyers. How are you handling your new-found fame?'

There was a moment of dead air. When Betsy answered she sounded uncomfortable.

'Believe me, Larry, I'm much too busy with my law practice and my daughter to worry about anything more pressing than my next case and tonight's dinner.'

The car-phone rang. Darius turned down the radio.

The Ferrari purred as it pulled away from the traffic. Darius glided into the fast lane, then picked up on the third ring.

'Mr Darius?'

'Who is this?'

Only a few people knew the number of his car-phone and he did not recognize the voice.

'You don't need to know my name.'

'I don't need to speak to you, either.'

'Maybe not, but I thought you'd be interested in what I have to say.'

'I don't know how you got this number, but my patience is wearing thin. Get to the point or I'll disconnect.'

'Right. You're a businessman. I shouldn't waste your time. Still, if you hung up now, I can guarantee I'd be gone, but not forgotten.'

'What did you say?'

'Got your attention, huh?'

Darius took a deep, slow breath. Suddenly, there were beads of perspiration on his brow and upper lip.

'Do you know Captain Ned's? It's a seafood place on Marine Drive. The bar's pretty dark. Drive there now and we'll talk.'

The connection was broken. Darius lowered the phone on to its cradle. He had slowed without realizing it and there was a car on his bumper. Darius crossed two lanes of traffic and pulled on to the shoulder of the road. His heart was racing and there was a shooting pain in his temples. Darius closed his eyes and leaned back against the headrest. He willed his breathing back to normal and the pain in his temples eased.

The voice on the phone was rough and uncultured. The man would be after money, of course. Darius smiled grimly. He dealt with greedy men all the time. They were the easiest to manipulate. They always believed the person they were dealing with was as stupid and frightened as they were.

The pain in his temples was gone now and Darius was breathing easily again. In a way he was grateful to the caller. He had grown complacent, believing he was safe after all these years, but you were never safe. He would consider this a wake-up call.

3

Captain Ned's was weathered wood and rain-spattered glass jutting out over the Columbia River. The bar was as dark as the voice promised. Darius sat in a booth near the kitchen, ordered a beer and waited patiently. A young couple entered, arm in arm. He dismissed them. A tall, balding salesman in a disheveled suit sat on a stool at the bar. Most of the tables were taken by couples. Darius scanned the other booths. A heavy-set man in a trench-coat smiled and stood up after Darius fixed on him.

'I was waiting to see how long it would take you,' the man said as he slipped into the booth. Darius did not reply. The man shrugged and stopped smiling. It was unsettling to sit opposite Martin Darius, even if you thought you held the winning hand.

'We can be civilized about this or you can be bitchy,' the man said. 'It don't matter to me. In the end, you'll pay.'

'What are you selling and what do you want?' Darius answered, studying the fleshy face in the dim light.

'Always the businessman, so let's get down to business. I've been to Hunter's Point. The old newspapers were full of information. There were pictures, too. I had to look hard, but it was you. I got one here, if you'd like to see,' the man said, sliding his hand out of his coat pocket and pushing a photocopy of a newspaper front page across the table. Darius studied it for a moment, then slid it back.

'Ancient history, friend.'

'Oh? You think so? I have friends on the force, Martin. The public don't know yet, but I do. Someone has been leaving little notes and black roses around Portland. I figure it's the same person who left 'em in Hunter's Point. What do you think?'

'I think you're a very clever man, Mr . . .?' Darius said, stalling for time to dope out the implications.

The man shook his head. 'You don't need my name, Martin. You just have to pay me.'

'How much are we talking about?'

'I thought two hundred and fifty thousand dollars would be fair. It'd cost you at least that much in attorney fees.'

The man had thinning, straw-colored hair. Darius could see flesh between the strands when he bent forward. The nose had been broken. There was a gut, but the shoulders were thick and the chest heavy.

'Have you told the people who hired you about Hunter's Point?' Darius asked.

There was a brief flicker of surprise, then a flash of nicotine-stained teeth.

'That was terrific. I ain't even gonna ask how you figured

it out. Tell me what you think.'

'I think you and I are the only ones who know, for now.'

The man did not answer.

'There is one thing I'd like to know,' Darius said, eyeing him curiously. 'I know what you think I've done. What I'm capable of doing. Why aren't you afraid I'll kill you?'

The man laughed.

'You're a pussy, Martin, just like the other rape-os I run into in the joint. Guys who were real tough with women and not so tough with anyone else. You know what I used to do to those guys? I made 'em my girls, Martin. I turned 'em into little queens. I'd do it to you, too, if I wasn't more interested in your money.'

While Darius considered this information, the man watched him with a confident smirk.

'It will take me a while to come up with that much money,' Darius said. 'How much time can you give me?'

'Today is Wednesday. How's Friday?'

Darius pretended to be considering the problems involved with liquidating stocks and closing accounts.

'Make it Monday. A lot of my holdings are in land. It will take me until Friday to arrange for loans and sell some stock.'

The man nodded. 'I heard you didn't believe in bullshit. Good. You're doing the right thing. And, let me tell you, friend, I'm not someone to fuck with. Also, I'm not greedy. This'll be a one-shot deal.'

The man stood. Then he thought of something and grinned at Darius.

'Once I'm paid, I'll be gone *and* forgotten.'

The man laughed at his little joke, turned his back and

left the bar. Darius watched him go. He did not find the joke, or anything else about the man, amusing.

4

A hard rain hit the windshield. Big drops, falling fast. Russ Miller switched the wiper to maximum. The cascade still obliterated his view of the road and he had to squint to catch the broken, center line in the headlight beams. It was almost eight, but Vicky was used to late suppers. You put in the hours at Brand, Gates and Valcroft if you expected to get anywhere. Russ grinned as he imagined Vicky's reaction to the news. He wished he could drive faster, but a few more minutes would not make much difference.

Russ had warned Vicky he might not be home on time as soon as Frank Valcroft's secretary summoned him. At the advertising firm, it was an honor to be asked into Valcroft's corner office. Russ had been there only twice before. The deep, wine-colored carpets and dark wood reminded him of where he wanted to be. When Valcroft told him he was going to be in charge of the Darius Construction account, Russ knew he was on his way.

Russ and Vicky had been introduced to Martin Darius this summer at a party Darius hosted to celebrate the opening of his new mall. All the men who worked on the account were there, but Russ had this feeling that Darius had singled him out. An invitation to join Darius on his yacht arrived a week later. Since then, he and Vicky had been guests at two house parties. Stuart Webb, another account executive at Brand, Gates, said he felt like he was standing in a chill wind when he was with Darius, but Darius was the most dynamic human being Russ had ever met and he had a knack for making Russ feel like the most important person on Earth. Russ was certain that Martin Darius was responsible for making him the team leader of the Darius Construction account. If Russ was successful as team leader, who knew what he would be doing in the future. He might even leave Brand, Gates and go to work for the man himself.

As Russ pulled into his driveway the garage door opened automatically. The rain pounding on the garage roof sounded like the end of the world and Russ was glad to get inside the warm kitchen. There was a large, metal pot on the stove, so he knew Vicky was making pasta. The surprise would be the sauce. Russ shouted Vicky's name as he peeked under the cover of another pot. It was empty. There was a cutting board covered with vegetables, but none of them were sliced. Russ frowned. There was no fire under the large pot. He lifted the lid. It was filled with water, but the pasta was lying, uncooked, next to the pasta maker he had bought Vicky for their third anniversary.

'Vick,' Russ shouted again. He loosened his tie and took off his jacket. The lights were on in the living-room. Later, Russ told the police he had not called sooner because everything looked so normal. The TV set was on. The Judith Krantz novel Vicky was reading was open and face down on the end-table. When he realized Vicky was not home, he assumed she was over at one of the neighbors.

The first time Russ went into the bedroom, he missed the rose and the note. His back was to the bed when he stripped off his clothes and hung them in the closet. After that, he slipped into a warm-up suit and checked the cable guide to see what was on TV. When fifteen more minutes passed without Vicky, Russ went back into the bedroom to phone her best friend, who lived down the block. That was when he saw the note on the pillow on the immaculately made bed. There was a black rose lying across the plain, white paper. Written in a careful hand were the words, 'Gone, But Not Forgotten'.

Chapter Two

As Austin Forbes, the President of the United States, walked toward United States Senator Raymond Francis Colby he passed through the rays of sunlight streaming through the high French windows of the Oval Office, creating the impression that God was spotlighting a chosen son. Had he noticed, the diminutive Chief Executive would have appreciated the vote of confidence from above. The results of his earthly polls were not nearly as complimentary.

'Good to see you, Ray,' Forbes said. 'You know Kelly Bendelow, don't you?'

'Kelly and I have met,' Colby said, remembering the in-depth interview the President's troubleshooter had conducted just two weeks before.

Senator Colby sat in the chair the President indicated and glanced out the east windows toward the rose garden. The President sat in an old armchair that had graced his

Missouri law office and followed him up the ladder of power to the Oval Office. He looked pensive.

'How's Ellen?' Forbes asked.

'She's fine.'

'And are you fine? You're in good health?'

'Excellent health, Mr President. I had a thorough physical last month,' Colby answered, knowing that the FBI would have furnished Forbes with his doctor's report.

'No personal problems? Everything's going well at home? Your finances are sound?'

'Ellen and I are celebrating our thirty-second anniversary next month.'

Forbes stared hard at Colby. The good old boy vanished and the hard-nosed politician who had carried forty-eight states in the last election took his place.

'I can't afford another fiasco like this Hutchings thing,' Forbes said. 'I'm telling you this in confidence, Ray. She lied to me. Hutchings sat where you're sitting and lied. Then that reporter for the *Post* found out and . . .'

Forbes let the thought trail off. Everyone in the room was painfully aware of the blow that had been dealt to Forbes' prestige when the Senate voted against confirming the nomination of Mabel Hutchings.

'Is there anything in your past that can cause us problems, Ray? Anything at all? When you were CEO of Marlin Steel did you ever pay a corporate bribe? Did you use marijuana at Princeton or Harvard Law? Did you knock up some girl in high school?'

Colby knew the questions were not ridiculous. The aspirations of Presidential hopefuls and Supreme Court nominees had run aground on just such rocky shoals.

'There will be no surprises, Mr President.'

The silence in the Oval Office grew. Then, Forbes spoke.

'You know why you're here, Ray. If I nominate you to be Chief Justice of the United States Supreme Court, will you accept?'

'Yes, Mr President.'

Forbes grinned. The tension in the room evaporated.

'We make the announcement tomorrow. You'll make a great Chief Justice.'

'I'm indebted to you,' Colby said, not trusting himself to say more. He had known the President would make the offer when he was summoned to the White House, but that did not keep him from feeling as light as a free-floating cloud.

Raymond Colby sat up as quietly as possible and shuffled his feet along the carpet until he found his slippers. Ellen Colby stirred on the other side of their king-size bed. The Senator watched the moonlight play on her peaceful features. He shook his head in amazement. Only his wife could sleep the sleep of angels after what had happened today.

There was a liquor cabinet in the den of Colby's Georgetown town house. Colby fixed himself some bourbon. On the upper landing the antique grandfather clock ticked away the seconds, each movement of the ancient hands perfectly audible in the stillness.

Colby rested his glass on the fireplace mantel and picked up a framed and fading black and white photograph that had been taken the day his father argued a case before the United States Supreme Court. Howard

Colby, a distinguished partner in Wall Street's most prestigious law firm, died at his desk two months after the photograph was taken. Raymond Colby may have been first at Harvard Law, CEO of Marlin Steel, the Governor of New York and a United States Senator, but he always saw himself in relationship to his father as he had been that day on the steps of the Court, a ten-year-old boy under the protection of a wise and gruff giant whom Raymond remembered as the smartest man he had ever known.

There were fifty-three broad steps leading from the street to the entrance to the Court. Raymond had counted as he climbed them, hand in hand with his father. When they passed between the columns supporting the west portico, his father had stopped to point out 'Equal Justice Under Law' engraved in the bone-white marble of the Great Hall.

That's what they do here, Raymond. Justice. This is the court of last resort. The final place for all lawsuits in this great country.'

Massive oak doors guarded the Court's chambers, but the courtroom was intimate. Behind a raised mahogany bench were nine high-backed chairs of various styles. When the Justices filed to their seats, his father stood. When Howard Colby addressed the Court, Raymond was surprised to hear respect in the voice of a man who commanded the respect of others. These men in black, these wise men who towered over Howard Colby and commanded his respect, left a lasting impression. On the train-ride back to New York, Raymond swore silently to sit some day upon the bench of the nation's highest court. His dream would come true when the President made his announcement at tomorrow's press conference.

The waiting had begun Friday when a White House source told him that the President had narrowed his choice to the Senator and Alfred Gustafson of the Fifth Circuit Court of Appeals. This afternoon, during their meeting in the Oval Office, the President told Colby it was his membership in the Senate that made the difference. After the disastrous defeat of Mabel Hutchings, his first nominee, the President wanted a sure thing. The Senate was not going to reject one of its own, especially someone with Colby's credentials. All he need do now was pass through the nominating process unscathed.

Colby put down the photograph and picked up his drink. It was not only the excitement of the nomination that kept him from sleep. Colby was an honest man. When he told the President that there was no scandal in his past, he was telling the truth. But there *was* something in his past. Few people knew about it. Those who did could be trusted to keep silent. Still, it concerned him that he had not been entirely candid with the man who was fulfilling his greatest dream.

Colby sipped his drink and stared at the lights of the Capitol. The bourbon was doing its job. His tense muscles were relaxing. He felt a bit sleepy. There was no way to change history. Even if he knew what the future would bring, he was certain he would have made no other choice. Worrying now would not change the past and the chances of his secret surfacing were very small. Within the hour the Senator was sound asleep.

Chapter Three

1

The pathetic thing was that after the affairs and the lies, not to mention the divorce settlement, which left Alan Page living in the same type of shabby apartment he had lived in when he was a law student, he still loved Tina. She was what he thought about when he was not thinking about work. Going to a movie did not help, reading a book did not help, even bedding the women with whom his well-meaning friends fixed him up did not help. The women were the worst, because he always found himself comparing and they never stacked up. Alan had not been with a woman in months.

The District Attorney's mood was starting to affect his staff. Last week, Randy Highsmith, his chief deputy, had taken him aside and told him to shape up, but he still found it hard to cope with bachelorhood after twelve years of what he thought was a good marriage. It was the sense of betrayal that overwhelmed him. He had never cheated on

Tina or lied to her and he felt that she was the one person he could trust completely. When he found out about her secret life, it was too much. Alan doubted he would ever fully trust anyone ever again.

Alan pulled into the City garage and parked in the spot reserved for the Multnomah County District Attorney, one of the few things Tina hadn't gotten in the divorce, he mused bitterly. He opened his umbrella and raced across the street to the court-house. The wind blew the rain under the umbrella and almost wrenched it from his hand. He was drenched by the time he ducked inside the gray, stone building.

Alan ran a hand through his damp hair while he waited for the elevator. It was almost eight. Around him, in the lobby, were young lawyers trying to look important, anxious litigants hoping for the best and dreading the worst, and a bored-looking judge or two. Alan was not in the mood for aimless social chatter. When the elevator came, he pushed six and stepped to the rear of the car.

'Chief Tobias wants you to call,' the receptionist told him as soon as he entered the District Attorney's Office.

'He said it was important.'

Alan thanked her and pushed open the low gate that separated the waiting area from the rest of the offices. His private office was the first on the right along a narrow hall.

'Chief Tobias called,' his secretary said.

'Winona told me.'

'He sounded upset.'

It was hard to imagine what could upset William Tobias. The slender Police Chief was as unflappable as an accountant. Alan shook out his umbrella and hung up his raincoat, then sat behind his large desk and dialed across the street to police headquarters.

'What's up?' Alan asked.

'We've got another one.'

It took a moment for Alan to figure out what Tobias was talking about.

'Her name is Victoria Miller. Twenty-six. Attractive, blonde. Housewife. No kids. The husband is with Brand, Gates and Valcroft, the ad agency.'

'Is there a body?'

'No. She's just missing, but we know it's him.'

'The same note?'

'On the bed on the pillow. "Gone, But Not Forgotten". And there's another black rose.'

'Was there any sign of a struggle this time?'

'It's just like the others. She could have disappeared in a puff of smoke.'

Both men were silent for a moment.

'The papers still don't know?'

'We're lucky there. Since there aren't any bodies, we've been handling them like missing persons cases. But I don't know how long we can keep this quiet. The three husbands aren't going to just sit around. Reiser, the lawyer, is on the phone every day, two or three times a day, and Farrar, the accountant, is threatening to go public if we don't come up with something soon.'

'Do you have anything?'

'Not a thing. Forensics is stumped. We've got no unusual fibers or hairs. No fingerprints. You can buy the notepaper at any Payless. The rose is an ordinary rose. Ditto the black dye.'

'What do you suggest?'

'We're doing a computer search on the MO and I've got Ross Barrow calling around to other police departments and the FBI.'

'Are you looking into possible connections between the victims?'

'Sure. We've got lots of obvious similarities. The three women are around the same age, upper middle-class, child-less, housewives with executive-type husbands. But we've got nothing connecting the victims to each other.'

Tobias could have been describing Tina. Alan closed his eyes and massaged the lids.

'What about health clubs, favorite stores, reading circles? Do they use the same dentist or doctor?' Alan asked.

'We've thought of all those and a dozen more.'

'Yeah, I'm sure you have. How far apart is he working?'

'It looks like one a month. We're into what? Early October? Farrar was August and Reiser was September.'

'Christ. We better get something going soon. The press will eat us alive once this breaks.'

'Tell me about it.'

Alan sighed. 'Thanks for calling. Keep me up to date.'

'You got it.'

Alan hung up and swiveled his chair so he could look out the window. Man, he was tired. Tired of the rain and this asshole with the black rose and Tina and everything else he could think of. More than anything, he wanted to be by himself on some sun-soaked beach where there were no women and no phones and the only decision he would have to make was about the strength of his sun-tan lotion.

2

No one ever called Elizabeth Tannenbaum stunning, but most men found her attractive. Hardly anyone called her Elizabeth, either. An 'Elizabeth' was regal, cool, an eye-catching beauty. A 'Betsy' was pleasant to look at, a tiny bit overweight, capable, but still fun to be with. Betsy suited her just fine.

A Betsy could also be a bit frazzled at times and that was how Betsy Tannenbaum felt when her secretary buzzed her just as she was stuffing the papers in the Morales case into her briefcase so she could work on them at home this evening, after she picked up Kathy from day care and cooked dinner and straightened the house and played with Kathy and . . .

'I can't take it, Ann. I'm late for day care.'

'He says it's important.'

'It's always important. Who is it?'

'He won't say.'

Betsy sighed and looked at the clock. It was already four-thirty. If she got Kathy by five and rushed to the store, she would not be done cooking until six. On the other hand, if she did not keep bringing in clients she would have all day to shop. Betsy stopped pushing papers into her briefcase and picked up the phone.

'Betsy Tannenbaum.'

'Thank you for taking the call. My name is Martin Darius.' Betsy caught her breath. Everyone in Portland knew who Darius was, but he did not call many of them. 'When does your staff leave?'

'Around five, five-fifteen. Why?'

27

'I need to speak to you this evening and I don't want anyone to know about it, including your secretary. Would six be convenient?'

'Actually, no. I'm sorry. Is there any way we can meet tomorrow? My schedule is pretty open then.'

'How much is your normal fee, Mrs Tannenbaum?'

'One hundred dollars an hour.'

'If you'll meet me at six tonight, I'll pay you twenty-five hundred dollars for the consultation. If I decide to hire you, you will be extremely pleased by the fee.'

Betsy took a deep breath. She dreaded doing it, but she was going to have to call Rick. She simply could not afford to turn down that kind of money or such a high-profile client.

'Can I put you on hold, Mr Darius? I have another obligation and I want to see if I can get someone else to take care of it.'

'I can hold.'

Betsy dialed Rick Tannenbaum on the other line. He was in a meeting, but his secretary put her through.

'What is it, Betsy? I'm very busy,' Rick said, making no attempt to hide his annoyance.

'I'm sorry to bother you, but I have an emergency. A client needs to meet me at six. Can you get Kathy at day care?'

'What about your mother?'

'She's playing bridge and I don't have the number at her friend's house.'

'Just tell the client you'll meet him tomorrow.'

'He can't. It has to be tonight.'

'Damn it, Betsy, when we separated, you promised you

wouldn't do this to me.'

'I'm really sorry,' Betsy said, as angry at herself for begging as she was at Rick for making this so difficult. 'I rarely ask you to pick up Kathy, but I need you, this once. Please.'

Rick was silent for a moment.

'I'll do it,' he answered angrily. 'When do I have to be there?'

'They close at six. I really appreciate this.'

Betsy hung up quickly, before Rick could change his mind.

'Six will be fine, Mr Darius. Do you know the address of my office?'

'Yes,' Darius said and the line went dead. Betsy put the phone down and sank into her chair, wondering what business a man like Martin Darius could possibly have with her.

Betsy glanced at her watch. It was six thirty-five and Darius had not arrived. She was annoyed that he had kept her waiting after she had put herself out, but not annoyed enough to jeopardize a twenty-five-hundred-dollar fee. Besides, the wait had given her time to work on the Morales case. She decided to give Darius another half-hour.

Rain spattered against the window behind her. Betsy yawned and swiveled her chair so she could look out into the night. Most of the offices in the building across the way were deserted. She could see cleaning women starting to work. By now, her own building was probably deserted, except for the night people. The silence made her a little uncomfortable. When she swiveled back, Darius was standing in the doorway. Betsy started.

29

'Mrs Tannenbaum?' Darius said, as he entered the room. Betsy stood. She was almost five foot eleven, but she had to look up at Darius. He extended his hand, exposing the exquisite gold cufflinks that secured his French cuffs. His hand was cold and his manner distant. Betsy did not believe in auras, but there was definitely something about the man that did not come across on television or in newspaper photos.

'I'm sorry to be so mysterious, Mrs Tannenbaum,' Darius said when they were seated.

'For twenty-five hundred dollars you can wear a mask, Mr Darius.'

Darius grinned. 'I like an attorney with a sense of humor. I haven't met too many of them.'

'That's because you deal with business lawyers and tax attorneys. Criminal lawyers don't last long without a sense of humor.'

Darius leaned back in his chair and looked around Betsy's cluttered office. It was her first and it was small and cramped. She had made just enough money this year to think about moving to larger quarters. If she ever collected the verdict in the abortion case she would definitely move, but that case was bogged down in the appellate courts and she might never see a penny.

'I was at a charity affair for the Portland Opera the other night,' Darius said. 'Do you go?'

'I'm afraid not.'

'Too bad. It's quite good. I had an interesting discussion with Maxine Silver. She's on the staff. A very strong-minded woman. We were discussing Greig's book. Have you read it?'

'The novel by the serial killer?' Betsy asked, puzzled by the direction the conversation was taking.

Darius nodded.

'I've seen a few reviews, but I don't have time to read anything but legal periodicals. It's not my kind of book, anyway.'

'Don't judge the book by its author, Mrs Tannenbaum. It's really a very sensitive work. A coming-of-age story. He handles the subject of his protagonist's abuse with such tenderness that you almost forget what Greig did to those children. Still, Maxine felt it shouldn't have been published, solely because Greig wrote it. Do you agree with her?'

Darius's question was strange but Betsy decided to play along.

'I'm opposed to censorship. I would not ban a book because I disapproved of the person who wrote it.'

'If the publisher bowed to pressure from, say, women's groups and withdrew the book from circulation, would you represent Greig?'

'Mr Darius . . .'

'Martin.'

'Is there a point to these questions or are you just making small-talk?'

'Humor me.'

'I could represent Greig.'

'Knowing that he's a monster?'

'I would be representing a principle, Mr Darius. Freedom of speech. *Hamlet* would still be *Hamlet*, even if Charles Manson wrote it.'

'Well put,' Darius laughed. Then he took a check out of his pocket.

'Tell me what you think, after reading this,' he said, placing the check on the desk between them. The check was made out to Elizabeth Tannenbaum. It was for $58,346.47. Something about the figure was familiar. Betsy frowned for a moment, then flushed when she realized the sum was her exact gross income for the previous year. Something Darius would know only if he had access to her tax returns.

'I think someone has been invading my privacy,' Betsy snapped, 'and I don't like it.'

'Twenty-five hundred dollars of this is your fee for this evening's consultation,' Darius said, ignoring Betsy's anger. 'The rest is a retainer. Place it in trust and keep the interest. Someday, I may ask you to return it. I may also ask you to represent me, in which case you may charge me whatever you believe the case is worth over and above the retainer.'

'I'm not certain I want to work for you, Mr Darius.'

'Why? Because I had you investigated? I don't blame you for being angry, but a man in my position can't take chances. There is only one copy of the investigative report and I'll send it to you no matter how our meeting concludes. You'll be pleased to hear what your colleagues have to say about you.'

'Why don't you give this money to the firm that handles your business affairs?'

'I don't wish to discuss this matter with my business lawyers.'

'Are you being investigated in connection with a crime?'

'Why don't we discuss that if it becomes necessary.'

'Mr Darius, there are a number of excellent criminal

defense attorneys in Portland. Why me?'

Darius looked amused. 'Let's just say that I believe you are the most qualified person to handle my case, should representation become necessary.'

'I'm a little leery of taking a case on this basis.'

'Don't be. You're under no obligation. Take the check, use the interest. If I do come to you and you decide you can't represent me, you can always give the money back. And, I can assure you, if I'm accused I will be innocent and you will be able to pursue my defense with a clear conscience.'

Betsy studied the check. It was almost four times the largest fee she'd ever earned and Martin Darius was the type of client a sane person did not turn down.

'As long as you understand I'm under no obligation,' Betsy said.

'Of course. I'll send you a retainer agreement that spells out the terms of our arrangement.'

They shook hands and Betsy showed Darius out. Then she locked the door and re-entered her office. When Betsy was certain Darius was gone, she gave the check a big kiss, gave a subdued whoop and whirled around. A Betsy was allowed to indulge in immature behavior from time to time.

Betsy was in a terrific mood by the time she parked her station wagon in her carport. It was not so much the retainer but the fact that Martin Darius had chosen her over all the other attorneys in Portland. Betsy was building a reputation with cases like *State* v. *Hammermill*, but the big money clients were still going to the big name criminal defense attorneys. Until this evening.

Rick Tannenbaum opened the door before Betsy fished her key out of her purse. Her husband was slender and an inch shorter than Betsy. His thick black hair was styled to fall across his high forehead and his smooth skin and clear blue eyes made him look younger than thirty-six. Rick had always been overly formal. Even now, when he should be relaxing, his tie was still knotted and his suit coat was on.

'Damn it, Betsy, it's almost eight o'clock. Where were you?'

'My client didn't come until six-thirty. I'm sorry.'

Before Rick could say anything else Kathy came tearing down the hall. Betsy dumped her briefcase and purse on a chair and scooped up their six-year-old daughter.

'I made a picture. You have to come see,' Kathy yelled, fighting to get down as soon as she received a hug and kiss from her mother.

'Bring it to the kitchen,' Betsy answered, lowering Kathy to the ground and taking off her jacket. Kathy streaked down the hall toward her bedroom with her long, blonde hair flying after her.

'Please don't do this to me again, Betsy,' Rick said, when Kathy was far enough away so she wouldn't hear. 'I felt like a fool. I was in a meeting with Donovan and three other lawyers and I had to tell them I couldn't participate any longer because I had to pick up my daughter from day care. Something we agreed is your responsibility.'

'I'm sorry, Rick. Mom wasn't available and I had to meet this client.'

'I have clients too and a position to maintain in my firm.

I'm trying to make partner and that's not going to happen if I get a reputation as someone who can't be relied on.'

'For Christ's sake, Rick. How many times have I asked you to do this? She's your daughter, too. Donovan understands you have a child. These things happen.'

Kathy rushed into the kitchen and they stopped arguing.

'This is the picture, Mom,' Kathy said, thrusting forward a large piece of drawing paper. Betsy scrutinized the picture while Kathy looked up at her expectantly. She was adorable in her tiny jeans and striped, long-sleeve shirt.

'Why Kathy Tannenbaum,' Betsy said, holding the picture at arm's length, 'this is the most fantastic picture of an elephant I have ever seen.'

'Its a cow, Mom.'

'A cow with a trunk?'

'That's the tail.'

'Oh. You're sure it's not an elephant?'

'Stop teasing,' Kathy said seriously.

Betsy laughed and returned the picture with a hug and kiss. 'You are the greatest artist since Leonardo da Vinci. Greater even. Now let me get dinner ready.'

Kathy ran back to her room. Betsy put a frying pan on the stove and took out a tomato and some lettuce for a salad.

'Who is this big client?' Rick asked.

Betsy didn't want to tell Rick, especially since Darius wanted his visit kept secret. But she felt she owed Rick the information.

'This is very confidential. Will you promise not to breathe a word if I tell you?'

'Sure.'

'Martin Darius retained me, tonight,' she said, breaking into a huge grin.

'Martin Darius?' Rick answered incredulously. 'Why would he hire you? Parish, Marquette and Reeves handles his legal work.'

'Apparently he thinks I'm also capable of representing him,' Betsy answered, trying not to show how much Rick's reaction hurt her.

'You don't have a business practice.'

'I don't think it's a business matter.'

'Then what is it?'

'He didn't say.'

'What's Darius like?'

Betsy thought about the question. What was Darius like?

'Spooky,' Betsy answered just as Kathy hurtled back into the kitchen. 'He likes to be mysterious and he wants you to know how powerful he is.'

'What are you cooking, Mom?'

'Roast little girl,' Betsy said, picking up Kathy and nibbling her neck until she squealed. 'Now buzz off or I'll never get dinner ready.'

Betsy lowered Kathy to the floor. 'Do you want to stay for dinner?' she asked Rick. He looked uncomfortable and checked his watch

'Thanks, but I've got to get back to the office.'

'Alright. Thanks again for picking up Kathy. I do know how busy you are and I appreciate the help.'

'Yeah, well . . . Sorry I jumped down your throat. It's just . . .'

'I know,' Betsy said.

Rick looked like he was going to say something, but went to the closet instead and got his raincoat.

'Good luck with Darius,' Rick told her as he was leaving. Betsy shut the door behind him. She had heard the hint of jealousy in his voice and regretted telling Rick about her new client. She should have known better than to say anything that would let him know how well she was doing.

' "But it takes time to make a raft, even when one is as industrious and untiring as the Tin Woodsman, and when night came the work was not done. So they found a cozy place under the trees where they slept well until the morning. And Dorothy dreamed of the Emerald City, and of the good Wizard Oz, who should soon send her back to her own home again."

'And now,' Betsy said, closing the book and laying it on Kathy's bed, 'it's time for my little wizard to hit the hay.'

'Can't you read one more chapter?' Kathy begged.

'No, I cannot read another chapter,' Betsy said, giving Kathy a hug. 'I already read you one more than you were entitled to. Enough is enough.'

'You're mean, Mommy,' Kathy said with a smile Betsy could not see, because her cheek was against Kathy's baby-soft hair.

'That's tough. You're stuck with the world's meanest mommy and there's nothing you can do about it.' Betsy kissed Kathy's forehead, then sat up. 'Now get to bed. I'll see you in the morning.'

'Night, Mom.'

Kathy rolled on to her side and wrestled Oliver, an over-sized, stuffed skunk, into position against her chest.

'Night, hon.'

Betsy closed the door of Kathy's room behind her and went into the kitchen to wash the dishes. Although she would never admit it to her feminist friends, Betsy loved washing dishes. It was perfect therapy. A lawyer's day was littered with stressful situations and insoluble problems. Washing dishes was a finite task that Betsy could do perfectly every time she tried. Instant gratification from a job well done, over and over again. And Betsy needed some instant gratification after being with Rick.

She knew why he was so angry. Rick had been a super-star in law school and Donovan, Chastain and Mills had lured him to their two-hundred-lawyer sweat shop with a large salary and glowing promises of a fast track to a part-nership. The firm had worked him like a dog, constantly holding the partnership just out of reach. When he was passed over last year, just as her career was starting to take off, it had been a crushing blow to his ego. Their ten-year-old marriage had not been able to withstand the strain.

Two months ago, when Rick told her he was leaving, Betsy was stunned. She knew they had problems, but she never believed he would walk out on her. Betsy had searched her memory for a clue to Rick's jealousy. Had he changed or was he always so self-centered? Betsy had trouble believing that Rick's love was too fragile to withstand her success, but she was not willing to give up her career to appease his ego. Why should she? The way she saw it, it was a matter of Rick accepting her as an equal. If he couldn't do that then she could never stay married to him. If he loved her, it should not be such a hard thing to do. She was proud of his achievements. Why couldn't he be proud of hers?

Betsy poured herself a glass of milk and turned off the light. The kitchen joined the rest of the house in soothing darkness. Betsy carried her glass to the kitchen table and slumped into a chair. She took a sip and gazed sleepily out the window. Many of the houses in the neighborhood were dark. A street-light cast a pale glow over a corner of the front yard. It was so quiet with Rick gone and Kathy asleep. No traffic sounds outside, no television on. None of the little noises people make shuffling around a house.

Betsy had handled enough divorces to know that many estranged husbands would never have done what Rick had done for her tonight. He had done it for Kathy, because he loved her. And Kathy loved Rick. The separation was very hard on their daughter. There were times, like now, when the house was quiet and Betsy was alone, that she missed Rick. She was not certain she loved him any more, but she remembered how good it had been. Sleeping alone was the hardest thing. She missed the lovemaking, but she missed the cuddling and the pillow-talk more. Sometimes she thought they might get back together. Tonight, before Rick left, she was certain that there was something he wanted to tell her. What was he about to say? And if he said he wanted her back, what would she say? After all, he was the one who had walked out on ten years of marriage, a child, their life together. They were a family and Rick's actions told her that meant nothing to him.

The night Rick walked out, alone in bed, when she

couldn't cry any more, Betsy had rolled on her side and stared at their wedding picture. Rick was grinning. He had told her he had never been so happy. She had been so filled with joy, she was afraid she could not hold all of it. How could a feeling like that disappear?

Chapter Four

1

'Late night?' Wayne Turner's secretary asked, trying, unsuccessfully, to conceal a grin.

'It shows, huh?'

'Only to those who know how perky you usually look.'

The night before, Turner, Senator Raymond Colby's Administrative Assistant, had gotten stinking drunk celebrating the Senator's nomination to the Supreme Court. This morning, he was paying for his sins, but he didn't mind. He was happy for the old gent, who had done so much for him. His only regret was that Colby had not run for President. He would have made a great one.

Turner was five foot nine and slender. He had a narrow face, high cheek bones, close-cropped, kinky black hair that was graying at the temples and brown skin a few shades darker than his tan suit. Turner weighed about what he had when he first met Colby. He hadn't lost his intensity, but the scowl that used to be a permanent feature had wilted over the years.

Turner hung his jacket on a hook behind the door, lit his fourth Winston of the day and sat behind his cluttered desk. Framed in the window at his back was the shining, white dome of the Capitol Building.

Turner shuffled through his messages. Many were from reporters who wanted the inside scoop on Colby's nomination. Some were from AAs for other senators who were probably calling about Colby's crime bill. A few were from partners in prestigious Washington law firms, confirmation that Turner need not be worried about what he would do after the Senator became Chief Justice. Washington power-brokers were always interested in someone who had the ear of a powerful man. Turner would do all right, but he would miss working with the Senator.

The last message in the stack caught Turner's eye. It was from Nancy Gordon, one of the few people whose call he would have returned yesterday afternoon if he had made it back to the office. Turner assumed she was calling about the nomination. There was a Hunter's Point, New York number on the message slip.

'It's Wayne,' he said when he heard the familiar voice at the other end. 'How you doin'?'

'He's surfaced,' Gordon answered without any preliminaries. It took Turner a few seconds to catch on, then he felt sick.

'Where?'

'Portland, Oregon.'

'How do you know?'

She told him. When she was through, Turner asked, 'What are you going to do?'

'There's a flight to Portland leaving in two hours.'

'Why do you think he started again?'

'I'm surprised he held out for so long,' Gordon answered.

'When did you get the letter?'

'Yesterday, around four. I just came on shift.'

'You know about the Senator?'

'Heard it on the news.'

'Do you think there's a connection? The timing, I mean. It seems odd it would be so soon after the President made the announcement.'

'There could be a connection. I don't know. And I don't want to jump to conclusions.'

'Have you called Frank?' Turner asked.

'Not yet.'

'Do it. Let him know.'

'All right.'

'Shit. This is the absolute worst possible time for this to happen.'

'You're worried about the Senator?'

'Of course.'

'What about the women?' Gordon asked coldly.

'Don't lay that trip on me, Nancy. You know damn well I care about the women, but Colby is my best friend. Can you keep him out of it?'

'I will if I can.'

Turner was sweating. The plastic receiver was uncomfortable against his ear.

'What will you do when you find him?' he asked nervously. Gordon did not answer immediately. Turner could hear her breathing deeply.

'Nancy?'

'I'll do what I have to.'

Turner knew what that was. If Nancy Gordon found the man who had haunted their dreams for the past ten years, she would kill him. The civilized side of Wayne Turner wanted to tell Gordon that she should not take the law into her own hands. But there was a primitive side of Wayne Turner that kept him from saying it, because everyone, including the Senator, would be better off if the man Homicide Detective Nancy Gordon was stalking died.

2

The microwave buzzed. Alan Page backed into the kitchen, keeping one eye on the television. The CBS anchorman was talking about the date that had been set for Raymond Colby's confirmation hearing. Colby would give the Supreme Court a solid conservative majority and that was good news, if you were a prosecutor.

Alan took his TV dinner out of the microwave, giving the food the briefest of glances. He was thirty-seven, with close-cropped black hair, a face that still bore the scars of acne and a sense of purpose that made most people nervous. His rail-thin body suggested an interest in distance running. In fact Alan was thin because he had no use for food and ate the bare minimum that would keep him going. It was worse now that he was divorced. On a good day breakfast was instant coffee, lunch a sandwich and more black coffee and dinner a pizza.

A reporter was interviewing someone who knew Colby when he was CEO of Marlin Steel. Alan used the remote to jack up the volume. From what he was hearing, there was nothing standing in the way of Colby's confirmation as Chief Justice of the United States Supreme Court. The doorbell rang just as the Colby story ended. Alan hoped it wasn't business. There was a Bogart classic on at nine that he'd been looking forward to all day.

The woman standing on Alan's doorstep held a briefcase over her head to shield herself from the rain. A small, tan valise stood beside her. A taxi was waiting at the curb, its wipers swinging back and forth and its headlight beams cutting through the torrent.

'Alan Page?'

He nodded. The woman flipped open a leather case she was clutching in her free hand and showed Alan her badge.

'Nancy Gordon. I'm a homicide detective with the Hunter's Point PD in Hunter's Point, New York. Can I come in?'

'Of course,' he said, stepping back. Gordon signaled the taxi, then ducked inside. She held the briefcase at arm's length, shook off the water on the welcome mat, then pulled in the valise.

'Let me take your coat,' Alan said. 'Can I get you something to drink?'

'Hot coffee, please,' Gordon answered, as she handed him her raincoat.

'What's a detective from New York doing in Portland, Oregon?' Alan asked, as he hung the coat in the hall closet.

'Does the phrase "Gone, But Not Forgotten" mean anything to you, Mr Page?'

Alan stood perfectly still for a second, then turned around. 'That information hasn't been released to the public. How do you know about it?'

'I know more than you can imagine about "Gone, But Not Forgotten", Mr Page. I know what the note means. I know about the black rose. I also know who took your missing women.'

Alan needed a moment to think.

'Please sit down and I'll get your coffee,' he told Gordon.

The apartment was small. The living-room and kitchen were one space divided by a counter. Gordon chose an arm chair near the television and waited patiently while Alan mixed water from a tea kettle with Folger's instant. He handed the cup to the detective, turned off the set, then sat opposite her on the couch. Gordon was tall with an athlete's body. Alan guessed she was in her mid-thirties. Her blonde hair was cut short. She was attractive without working at it. The most striking thing about the detective was her utter seriousness. Her dress was severe, her eyes were cold, her mouth was sealed in a straight line and her body was rigid, like an animal prepared to defend itself.

Gordon leaned forward slightly. 'Think of the most repulsive criminals, Mr Page. Think of Bundy, Manson, Dahmer. The man leaving these notes is smarter and far more dangerous than any of them, because they're all dead or in prison. The man you're after is the man who got away.'

'You know who he is?' Alan asked.

Gordon nodded. 'I've been waiting for him to surface for ten years.'

Gordon paused. She looked into the steam rising from her cup. Then she looked back at Alan.

'This man is cunning, Mr Page, and he's different. He's

not human, the way we think of human. I knew he wouldn't be able to control himself forever and I was right. Now he's surfaced and I can catch him, but I need your help.'

'If you can clear this up, you've got all the help you want. But I'm still confused about who you are and what you're talking about.'

'Of course. I'm sorry. I've been involved with this case so long, I forget other people don't know what happened. And you'll need to know it all or you won't understand. Do you have the time, Mr Page? Can I tell you now? I don't think we can wait, even until morning. Not while he's still out there, free.'

'If you're not too tired.'

Gordon stared into Alan's eyes with an intensity that forced him to look away.

'I'm always tired, Mr Page. There was a time when I couldn't sleep without pills. I'm over that, but the nightmares haven't stopped and I still don't sleep well. I won't until he's caught.'

Alan did not know what to say. Gordon looked down. She drank more coffee. Then, she told Alan Page about Hunter's Point.

PART TWO
HUNTER'S POINT

Chapter Five

1

The sprawling, two-story colonial was in the middle of a cul-de-sac, set well back from the street. A large, well-tended lawn created a wide buffer zone between the house and those on either side. A red Ferrari was parked in the driveway in front of a three-car garage.

Nancy Gordon knew it was going to be bad as soon as she saw the stunned expressions on the faces of the neighbors, who huddled just outside the police barriers. They were shocked by the presence of police cars and a morgue wagon in the quiet confines of The Meadows, where the houses started at half a million and crime was simply not permitted. She knew it was going to be really bad when she saw the grim faces of the two homicide detectives who were talking in low tones on the lawn near the front door.

Nancy parked her Ford behind a marked car and squeezed through the saw horses. Frank Grimsbo and Wayne Turner stopped their conversation when they saw

51

her. She was dressed in jeans and a tee-shirt. The call had come while she was sprawled in front of the TV in a ratty nightgown, sipping a cheap white wine and watching the Mets smoke the Dodgers. The clothes were the first thing she could find and the last thing she thought about.

'Newman said there's a body this time,' she said excitedly. 'Two.'

'How can we be sure it's him?' Nancy asked.

'The note and the rose were on the floor near the woman,' Grimsbo answered. He was a big man with a beer gut and thinning black hair, who wore cheap plaid jackets and polyester slacks.

'It's him all right,' said Turner, a skinny black man with close-cropped hair and a permanent scowl who was in his second year in night law school. 'The first cop on the scene was smart enough to figure out what was going on. He called me right away. Michaels did the note and the crime scene before anyone else was let in.'

'That was a break. Who's the second victim?'

'Melody Lake,' Grimsbo answered. 'She's six years old, Nancy.'

'Oh, fuck.' The excitement she felt at finally getting a body disappeared instantly. 'Did he . . . Was there anything done to her?'

Turner shook his head. 'She wasn't molested.'

'And the woman?'

'Sandra Lake. The mother. Death by strangulation. She was beaten pretty badly, too, but there's no evidence of sexual activity. 'Course, she hasn't been autopsied.'

'Do we have a witness?'

'I don't know,' Grimsbo answered. 'We have uniforms

talking to the neighbors, but nothing yet. Husband found the bodies and called it in to 911 about eight-fifteen. He says he didn't see anyone, so the killer must have left way before the husband got home. We got a cul-de-sac here and it leads into Sparrow Lane, the only road out of the development. The husband would have seen someone coming in or out.'

'Who's talked to him?'

'I did, for a few minutes,' Turner answered. 'And the first cops on the scene, of course. He was too bent out of shape to make any sense. You know him, Nancy.'

'I do?'

'It's Peter Lake.'

'The attorney?'

Grimsbo nodded. 'He defended Daley.'

Nancy frowned and tried to remember what she could about Peter Lake. She had not done much in the Daley investigation. All she recalled about the defense attorney was his good looks and efficient manner. She was on the stand less than a half-hour.

'I better go in,' Nancy said.

The entryway was huge. A small chandelier hung overhead. A sunken living-room was directly in front of her. The room was spotless. She could see a small man-made lake out back through a large picture-window. Strategically placed around the room, most probably by an interior decorator, were bleached oak tables with granite tops, chairs and a sofa in pastel shades and macramé wall hangings. It looked more like a showroom than a place where people lived.

A wide staircase was off to the left. A polished wood

banister followed the curve of the stairs to the second floor. The posts supporting the banister were closely spaced. Through the spaces, halfway up the stairs, Nancy could see a small lump covered by a blanket. She turned away.

Lab technicians were dusting for prints, taking photographs and collecting evidence. Bruce Styles, the deputy medical examiner, was standing with his back to her in the middle of the entryway between a uniformed officer and one of his assistants.

'You finished?' Nancy asked.

The doctor nodded and stepped aside. The woman was face down on the white shag carpet. She was wearing a white cotton dress. It looked well suited for the heat. Her feet were bare. The woman's head was turned away. Blood matted her long brown hair. Nancy guessed she had been brought down by a blow to the head, and Styles confirmed her suspicion.

'I figure she was running for the door and he got her from behind. She could have been partly conscious or completely out when he strangled her.'

Nancy walked around the body so she could see the woman's face. She was sorry she looked. If the woman had been attractive, there was no way to tell now. Nancy took a couple of deep breaths.

'What about the little girl?' she asked.

'Neck broken,' Styles answered. 'It would have been quick and painless.'

'We think she was a witness to the mother's murder,' Turner said. 'Probably heard her screaming and came down the steps.'

'Where's the husband?' Nancy asked.

'Down the hall in the den,' Turner said.

'No sense putting it off.'

Peter Lake slumped in a chair. Someone had given him a glass of scotch, but the glass was still more than half full. He looked up when Nancy entered the den and she could see he had been crying. Even so, he was a striking man, tall with a trim, athletic build. Lake's styled, gold-blond hair, his pale blue eyes, and sharp, clean-shaven features were what won over the women on his juries.

'Mr Lake, do you remember me?' Nancy asked.

Lake looked confused.

'I'm a homicide detective. My name is Nancy Gordon. You cross-examined me in the Daley case.'

'Of course. I'm sorry. I don't handle many criminal cases anymore.'

'How are you feeling?' Nancy asked, sitting across from Lake.

'I'm numb.'

'I know what you're going through . . .' Nancy started, but Lake's head jerked up.

'How could you? They're dead. My family is dead.'

Lake covered his eyes with his hands and wept. His shoulders trembled.

'I do know how you feel,' Nancy said softly. 'A year ago, my fiancé was murdered. The only good thing that came out of it was that I learned how victims really feel, and sometimes I can even help them get through the worst of it.'

Lake looked up. He wiped his eyes. 'I'm sorry,' he said. 'It's just so hard. They meant everything to me. And Melody . . . How could someone do that to a little girl? She couldn't hurt anybody. She was just a little girl.'

'Mr Lake, four women have disappeared in Hunter's Point in the past few months. A black rose and a note, identical to the ones you found, were left at each home. I know how much you're grieving, but we have to act fast. This is the first time we have actually found a victim. That could mean you surprised the killer before he had time to take your wife away. Anything you can tell us would be deeply appreciated, and may help us catch this man before he kills again.'

'I don't know anything. Believe me, I've thought about it. I was working late on a case. I called to let Sandy know. I didn't see anything unusual when I drove up. Then I . . . I'm really not too clear on what I did after I . . . I know I sat down on the bottom step.'

Lake paused. He breathed deeply, trying to keep from crying again. His lip trembled. He took a sip of his scotch.

'This is very hard for me, Detective. I want to help, but . . . Really, this is very hard.'

Nancy stood up and placed a hand on Lake's shoulder. He began to weep again.

'I'm going to leave my card. I want you to call me if I can do anything for you. Anything. If you remember something, no matter how insignificant you may believe it to be, call me. Please.'

'I will. I'll be better in the morning and I'll . . . It's just . . .'

'It's all right. Oh, one other thing. The media will be after you. They won't respect your privacy. Please don't talk to them. There are many aspects of this case we are not going to release to the public. We keep back facts to help us eliminate phoney confessions and to identify the real killer. It's very important that you keep what you know to yourself.'

'I won't talk to the press. I don't want to see anyone.'

'Okay,' Nancy said kindly. 'And you're going to be all right. Not one hundred percent, and not for a long time, but you'll deal with your grief. It won't be easy. I'm still not healed. But I'm better and you'll be better, too. Remember what I said about calling. Not the police business. You know, if you just want to talk.'

Lake nodded. When Nancy left the den, he was sprawled in the chair, his head back and his eyes closed.

2

Hunter's Point was a commuter suburb with a population of 110,000, a small downtown riddled with trendy boutiques and upscale restaurants, a branch of the State University, and a lot of shopping centers. There were no slums in Hunter's Point, but there were clusters of Cape Cods and garden apartments on the fringe of the downtown area that housed students and families unable to afford the high-priced developments, like The Meadows, where the commuting lawyers, doctors and businessmen lived.

Police headquarters was a dull, square building on the outskirts of town. It sat in the middle of a flat, black-topped parking lot surrounded by a chain-link fence. The lot was filled with police cars, unmarked vehicles and tow trucks.

The rose killer task-force was housed in an old storage area in the back of the building. There were no windows, and the fluorescent lights were annoyingly bright. A water cooler was squeezed between two chest-high filing cabinets. A low wood table stood on rickety legs against a cream-colored wall. On the table sat a coffee maker, four coffee mugs, a sugar bowl and a brown, plastic cup filled with several packets of artificial creamer. Four gunmetal-gray, government-issue desks were grouped in the center of the room. Bulletin boards with pictures of the victims and information about the crimes covered two walls.

Nancy Gordon hunched over her reports on the Lake murders. The flickering fluorescents were starting to give her a headache. She closed her eyes, leaned back and pinched her lids. When she opened her eyes, she was staring at the photographs of Samantha Reardon and Patricia Cross that Turner had tacked to the wall. The photos had been supplied by their husbands. Samantha on the deck of a sailboat. A tall woman, the wind blowing her flowing brown hair behind her, a smile of genuine happiness brightening her face. Pat in shorts and a halter top on a beach in Oahu, very slender, too thin actually. Her friends said she was overly conscious of her figure. Except for Reardon, who had been a nurse, none of the women had ever held a meaningful job, and Reardon stopped working soon after her marriage. They were happy housewives living in luxury, spending their time at golf and bridge. Their idea of contributing to the community was raising money for charity at country club functions. Where were these women now? Were they dead? Had they died quickly, or slowly, in agony? How had they held up? How much of their dignity were they able to retain?

The phone rang. 'Gordon,' she answered.

'There's a Mr Lake at the front desk,' the receptionist

said. Nancy straightened up. Less than seventy-two hours had passed since her visit to the crime scene.

'I'll be right out,' Gordon said, dropping her pen on a stack of police reports.

Inside the front door of the police station was a small lobby furnished with cheap chairs upholstered in imitation leather and outfitted with chrome arm rests. The lobby was separated from the rest of the building by a counter with a sliding glass window and a door with an electronic lock. Lake was seated in one of the chairs. He was dressed in a dark suit and solid, maroon tie. His hair was carefully combed. The only evidence of his personal tragedy was red-rimmed eyes that suggested a lack of sleep and a lot of mourning. Nancy hit the button next to the receptionist's desk and opened the door.

'I wasn't certain you'd be here,' Lake said. 'I hope you don't mind my showing up without calling.'

'No. Come on in. I'll find us a place to talk.'

Lake followed Nancy down a hall that reminded him of a school corridor. They walked on worn green linoleum that buckled in places, past unpainted brown wood doors. Chipped flakes of green paint fell from spots on the walls. Nancy opened the door to one of the interrogation rooms and stood aside for Lake. The room was covered with white, sound-proof tiles.

'Have a seat,' Nancy said, motioning toward one of the plastic chairs that stood on either side of a long wooden table. 'I'll grab us some coffee. How do you take yours?'

'Black,' Lake answered.

When Nancy returned with two Styrofoam cups, Lake was sitting at the table with his hands in his lap.

'How are you feeling?' she asked.

'I'm very tired, and depressed. I tried going to work today, but I couldn't concentrate. I keep thinking about Melody.'

Lake stopped. He took a deep breath. 'Look, I'll get to the point. I can't work, and I have a feeling I'm not going to be able to work for quite a while. I sat down with the papers on a real-estate closing this morning and it seemed so . . . It just didn't mean anything to me.

'I have two associates who can keep my practice going until I'm able to cope, if that ever happens. But now all I want to do is find out who killed Sandy and Melody. It's all I can think about.'

'Mr Lake, it's all I can think about, too. And I'm not alone. I'm going to tell you some things. This is highly confidential. I'll need your promise to keep it confidential.'

Lake nodded.

'There were four disappearances before your wife and daughter were killed. None of those women have been found. It took us a while to catch on, because there were no bodies. At first, we treated them like missing persons. But a note with "Gone, But Not Forgotten" and a black rose was left at each crime scene, so after the second one we knew what we were dealing with. The Chief has put together a task-force to work on the cases . . .'

'I'm sure you're working very hard,' Lake interrupted. 'I didn't mean to be critical. What I want to do is help. I want to volunteer to be part of the task-force.'

'That's out of the question, Mr Lake. You aren't a police officer. It also wouldn't be advisable. You're too emotionally involved to be objective.'

'Lawyers are trained to be objective. And I can add something to the investigation – the unique insight into the criminal mind that I developed as a defense attorney. Defense attorneys learn things about the way criminals think that the police never know, because we have the criminal's confidence. My clients know they can tell me anything, no matter how horrible, and I will respect their privacy. You see criminals when their false face is on. I see them the way they really are.'

'Mr Lake, police officers get a real good look at the criminal mind – too good. We see these guys on the street, in their homes. You see them cleaned up, in your office, a long way from their victims and after they've had time to rationalize what they've done and cook up a sob story or a defense. But none of that matters, because you simply cannot work on this case. As much as I appreciate the offer, my superiors wouldn't allow it.'

'I know it sounds strange, but I really do think I could contribute. I'm very smart.'

Nancy shook her head. 'There's another good reason you shouldn't get involved in this investigation – it would mean reliving the death of your wife and daughter every day, instead of getting on with your life. We have their autopsy photos lying around, their pictures posted on the wall. Do you want that?'

'I have their pictures all over my house and office, Detective Gordon. And there isn't a minute I don't think about them.'

Nancy sighed. 'I know,' she said, 'but you have to stop thinking about them that way or it will kill you.'

Lake paused. 'Tell me about your fiancé,' he asked

quietly. 'How . . . how did you stop thinking about him?'

'I never did. I think about Ed all the time. Especially at night, when I'm alone. I don't want to forget him and you won't want to forget Sandy and Melody.

'Ed was a cop. A drunk shot him. He was trying to calm down a domestic dispute. It was two weeks before our wedding date. At first, I felt just like you do. I couldn't work. I could barely make it out of bed. I . . . I was racked with guilt, which is ridiculous. I kept on thinking there was something I could have done, insisted he stay home that day, I don't know. I wasn't really making much sense.

'But it got better, Mr Lake. Not all better, not even mostly better. You just get to a point where you face the fact that a lot of the pain comes from feeling sorry for yourself, for what you've lost. Then you realize that you have to start living for yourself. You have to go on and keep the memories of the good times. If you don't, then whoever killed your little girl and your wife will have won. They will have killed you, too.'

Nancy reached across the table and put her hand on Peter Lake's arm.

'We'll get him, Mr Lake. You have so much to deal with, you don't want to get involved with this, too. Let us handle it. We'll get him, I promise.'

Lake stood up. 'Thank you, Detective Gordon.'

'Nancy. Call me Nancy. And give me a call any time you want to talk.'

3

A week later, Hunter's Point Chief of Police John O'Malley entered the task-force office. He was usually in shirt sleeves with his tie askew and his top button open. This morning, O'Malley wore the navy blue suit he saved for Rotary Club speeches and meetings with the city council.

The Chief had the broad shoulders and thick chest of a middleweight boxer. His nose had been broken by a fleeing burglar when he still worked in New York's South Bronx. His receding red hair revealed an old scar, a memento of one of many gang fights he had been in as a youth in Brooklyn. O'Malley would have stayed in New York City if a heart attack hadn't forced him to pursue police work in a less stressful environment.

Walking behind O'Malley was a huge man dressed in a tan, summer-weight suit. Nancy guessed that the suit was custom tailored, because it fit perfectly even though the man was oddly oversized like a serious bodybuilder.

'This is Dr Mark Klien,' O'Malley said. 'He's a psychiatrist who practices in Manhattan, and an expert on serial killers. Dr Klien was consulted in the Son of Sam case, the Atlanta child murders, Bundy. He's worked with VICAP. I met him a few years ago when I was still with the NYPD and working a serial case. He was very helpful. Dr Klien's seen a full set of reports on these disappearances and the deaths of Melody and Sandra Lake.

'Dr Klien,' O'Malley said, pointing to each member of the task-force in turn, 'this is Nancy Gordon, Frank Grimsbo, Wayne Turner and Glen Michaels. They've been on this case since it started.'

Dr Klien was so massive, he filled the entrance to the office. When he stepped into the room to shake hands, someone else followed him in. O'Malley looked uncomfortable.

'Before Dr Klien gets started, I want to explain why Mr Lake is here. Yesterday, the Mayor and I met. He explained that Mr Lake was volunteering to assist the task-force in finding the killer of his wife and daughter.'

Nancy Gordon and Frank Grimsbo exchanged worried glances. Wayne Turner's mouth opened and he stared at O'Malley. O'Malley flushed angrily, stared back and continued.

'The Mayor feels that Mr Lake brings a unique insight into the criminal mind, developed as a defense attorney, that will give us a fresh perspective on the case.'

'I hope I'll be of use,' Peter Lake said, smiling apologetically. 'I know I'm not a trained policeman, so I'll try to keep out of the way.'

'Dr Klien has a busy schedule,' O'Malley said, ignoring Lake. 'He has to take a two-fifty shuttle back to the city, so I'm going to let him take over.'

Lake took a seat behind everyone in the back of the room. Frank Grimsbo shook his head slowly. Wayne Turner folded his arms across his chest and stared accusingly at O'Malley. Nancy frowned. Only Glen Michaels, the chubby, balding criminologist O'Malley had assigned to do the forensic work for the task-force, seemed uninterested in Lake. He was riveted on Mark Klien who went to the front of the room and stood before a wall covered with victim information.

'I hope what I have to say is of some use to you,' Klien

said, talking without notes. 'One disadvantage a small department like Hunter's Point has in these cases is its inexperience with crimes of this type. Although, even larger departments are usually at a loss, since serial killers, for all the suffering they cause and all the publicity they receive, are, fortunately, rare birds. Now that the FBI has established the Violent Crime Apprehension Program in Quantico, small departments, like yours, can forward a description of your case to VICAP and learn if any similar murders have taken place in other parts of the country. VICAP uses a computer program to list violent crimes and their descriptions throughout the country, and can hook you up with other police agencies where similar crimes may have occurred, so you can coordinate your investigation.

'What I want to do today is give you a profile of the serial killer in order to dispel any stereotypes you may have and list some common factors you can look for. The FBI has identified two separate categories: the disorganized asocial and the organized non-social. Let's discuss the latter type first. The organized non-social is a sexual psychopath and, like any psychopath, he is unable to empathize, to feel pity or caring for others. His victims are simply objects he uses as he wishes to serve his own perverted needs. Venting his anger is one of these needs, whether through mutilation or debasing the victim. The Boston Strangler, for example, placed his victims in a position so that the first sight anyone had of them as they entered the room was to see them with their legs spread apart. Another killer mailed the foot of his victim to her parents in order to expand the pain and misery he had already caused.'

'Excuse me, Dr Klien,' Wayne Turner said. 'Is it possible that our killer is leaving the notes to torment the husbands?'

'That's a good possibility. The cruelty in torturing a victim's loved ones, and thereby creating more victims, would be very attractive to a sexual psychopath, since he is unaffected by any moral code and has no sense of remorse. He is capable of any act. Preserving body parts and eating them is not unusual, and having sex with the corpse of a victim is even less rare. Lucas decapitated one of his victims and had oral sex with the head for a week until the odor became so extreme he had to dispose of it.'

'Is that the type of crazy bastard we're dealing with here?' Grimsbo asked.

'Not "crazy", Detective. In spite of the extremes of their behavior, these people are not legally insane. They are well aware of what is morally and legally right and wrong. The terrifying thing is that they do not learn from their experiences, so neither treatment nor imprisonment is likely to alter their behavior. In fact, because of the compulsiveness associated with these sexual acts, it is most likely that they will kill again.'

'What does the black rose mean?' Nancy asked.

'I don't know, but fantasy and compulsion are very much a part of these killers' actions, and the rose could be part of the killer's fantasy. Prior to the killing, they fantasize about it in great detail, planning very specifically what they will do. This increases their level of excitement or tension so that ultimately their act is one of compulsion. When the murder is completed there is a sense of relief until the tension builds up again, starting the cycle anew. Son of Sam talked of the great relief he felt after each killing, but he also demonstrated his faulty judgment when he said he did not know why his victims struggled so much, since he was only going to kill them, not rape them.

'Since fantasy is so much involved in their behavior, these killers often take a specific body part or item of clothing with them. They use it to relive the act. This heavy use of fantasy also results in the crimes being very well planned. The Hillside Strangler not only brought a weapon, he brought plastic bags to help him dispose of the bodies. This could account for the absence of forensic evidence at your crime scenes. I would guess that your killer is very knowledgeable in the area of police investigation. Am I correct that an analysis of the notes and the roses have yielded no clues, and that the crime scenes haven't turned up so much as a fiber or hair that's been of use?'

'That's pretty much true,' answered Glen Michaels. 'We did get a print from the Lake note, but it turned out to be the wife's. All the other notes were spotless and there was nothing unusual about the paper or the ink. So far, the lab hasn't picked up a thing we can use.'

'I'm not surprised,' Klien said. 'There is a peculiar interest among these men with police and police work. Some of them have even been involved on the fringes of law enforcement. Bundy attended FBI lectures and Bianchi was in security work and in the police reserve. That means they may be aware of the steps they must take to avoid detection. Their interest in police work may also lie in a need to know how close the police are to catching them.

'Let's talk about the victims. Usually, they're accidental, in that the killer simply drives around until he fixes on someone. Prostitutes make easy victims, because they'll get in a car or even allow themselves to be tied up. The victim is generally not from the killer's home turf and is usually a stranger, which makes apprehension much more difficult.'

'Do you see that as being true in our case?' Nancy asked. 'I mean, these women all fit a pattern. They're married to professionals, they don't have regular jobs, and except for Mrs Lake they were all childless. They're also from the same town. Doesn't that show advance planning? That he's looking for a particular victim who fits into his fantasy, rather than grabbing women at random?'

'You're right. These victims don't seem to fit the usual pattern of random selection. It's pretty clear that your killer is stalking a particular type of woman in a particular area, which suggests he may live in Hunter's Point.'

'What I don't understand is how he gets to them,' Wayne Turner said. 'We're dealing with educated women. They live in upscale neighborhoods where the residents are suspicious of strangers. Yet, there's no sign of a struggle at any home but the Lakes' and, even there, the crime scene was relatively undisturbed.'

Klien smiled. 'You've brought us to one of the major misconceptions about serial killers, Detective Turner. In the movies, they're portrayed as monsters, but in real life they fit into the community, and do not look suspicious. Typically, they're bright, personable, even good-looking men. Bundy, the I-5 Bandit, the Hillside Strangler, Cortez – they're all respectable-looking men. So, our killer is probably someone these women would let into their homes without fear.'

'Didn't you say there were two types of serial killers?' Grimsbo asked.

'Yes, there's also the disorganized asocial killer, but in this case we're not dealing with someone who fits that category. That's unfortunate, because they're easier to catch. They're psychotic loners who relate quite poorly to others and don't have the charm or ability to melt into the community. Their acts are impulsive and the weapon is usually whatever is at hand. The body is often mangled or blood smeared and they frequently get blood all over themselves. The crime scenes can be very gruesome. They're also not mobile, like the organized non-socials. Their homicides often take place close to their homes and they often return to the scene of the crime, not to check up on the investigation, but to further mutilate the body or relive the killing. Rarely do they penetrate the body sexually. They usually masturbate on it or in the immediate area, which can be helpful, now that we have workable DNA testing. But your boy is much too clever to be a disorganized asocial.'

'Why haven't we found the bodies?' Turner asked.

'He's obviously hiding them, like the Green River Killer. Chief O'Malley tells me there's a lot of farm-land and forest in this area. Someday, a hiker is going to stumble on a mass grave and you'll have your bodies.'

'What will they look like, Dr Klien?' Nancy asked.

'It won't be pretty. We're dealing with a sexual sadist. If he has his victim isolated and he has time . . . You see, these men are expressing their rage toward their women victims. The mutilation and murder increases their sexual stimulation. In some instances, where the killer is usually impotent, the violence makes sex possible. The fantasy and the torture are the foreplay, Detective. The killing is the penetration.

Some of these men ejaculate automatically at the moment they kill.'

'Jesus,' Grimsbo muttered. 'And you say these guys aren't crazy.'

'I said they weren't crazy, but I didn't say they were human. Personally, I see the man you're looking for as less than human. Somewhere along the way, some of the things that make us human were lost, either because of genetics or environment or . . . Well,' Klien shrugged, 'it really doesn't matter, does it, because he's beyond hope and must be stopped. Otherwise he'll go on and on and on, as long as there are women out there for him to feed on.'

4

Nancy Gordon, Wayne Turner, Frank Grimsbo and Glen Michaels were waiting in O'Malley's office when he returned from dropping Dr Klien at the airport.

'I sort of expected this,' he said, when he saw them.

'Then please explain to us what the fuck is going on,' Turner demanded.

'There's no way to sugar-coat it,' O'Malley said. 'I argued with the Mayor and lost, period. We're stuck with Lake.'

'You're shitting me,' Grimsbo said.

'No, Frank, I'm not shitting you. I'm telling you the facts of political life.'

'The guy's a potential suspect,' Grimsbo said.

'Let's get this on the table, boys and girls, because I might be able to dump him, if it's true.'

'I don't think it is, John,' Nancy said. 'I've met with him

a few times and he's pretty broken up about losing his wife and kid.'

'Yeah,' Turner countered, 'but he says he didn't see anyone coming from the house. Where did the killer go? There's only one road out of that development from the cul-de-sac.'

'The neighbors didn't see anyone, either,' Nancy said.

'No one saw anyone at the scene of any of the disappearances, Wayne,' said Glen Michaels.

'What I want to know is what a civilian is doing on a police investigation,' Grimsbo said.

O'Malley sighed. 'Lake's fixed politically. He's known as a criminal lawyer because he won that insanity defense for that fruit-cake Daley. But the guy's specialty is real-estate law and he's made a few million at it, some of which he has contributed to the Mayor's campaign chest. He's also a major contributor to the Governor and he serves on some land-use planning counsel in Albany. The bottom line is the Governor called the Mayor yesterday, who then called me to explain how Lake's experience as a criminal lawyer will be invaluable in the investigation and how lucky we are to have him on our team. The press is already on the Mayor's ass for keeping the disappearances quiet until the Lake murders forced his hand. He's desperate for results and he's not going to buck a request from the Governor or a major campaign contributor.'

'I don't trust him,' Turner said. 'I had a case with Lake a few years back. We served a warrant on this guy and found a kilo of coke in his room. There was a pregnant woman at the house with no record. She swore the coke was hers and the guy was doing her a favor by letting her stay in his room while she was expecting. The defendant beat the case and the DA didn't even bother to indict the chick. I could never prove it, but I heard rumors that Lake paid the woman to perjure herself.'

'Anyone else heard anything like that?' O'Malley asked.

Michaels shook his head. 'He's cross-examined me two or three times. My impression is that he's very bright. He did an excellent job in a case involving blood-spatter evidence. Really had me going up there.'

'I've heard he's a smart guy,' Grimsbo said, 'but I've heard those rumors about the fix, too, and a few of the lawyers I know don't like Lake's ethics. He's still a suspect, even if he's a long-shot, and I just don't like the idea of a citizen working on something this sensitive.'

'Look, I agree with you, Frank,' O'Malley said. 'It stinks. But it doesn't matter. Until I can convince the Mayor otherwise, Lake stays. Just try to keep him out from under our feet. Give him lots of busy work, make him read all the reports. If something comes up you don't want him to see, or there's trouble, come to me. Any questions?'

Turner muttered something about the Mayor and Grimsbo shook his head in disgust. O'Malley ignored them.

'Okay, get outta here and back to work. You all heard Klien. We have to stop this psycho fast.'

5

Nancy Gordon's stomach growled. She guessed it was a little after six. Her watch said it was almost seven. She had been writing reports and lost track of time. On the way out of the station, she walked by the task-force office and noticed the lights were still on. Peter Lake was in shirt sleeves, his feet up on the corner of the desk. Near his elbow were a large stack of reports and a yellow pad. He was making notes as he read.

'You're not going to solve this case in one night,' Nancy said quietly. Lake looked around, startled. Then, he grinned sheepishly.

'I always work this hard. I'm compulsive.'

Nancy walked over to Lake's desk. 'What are you doing?'

'Reading about the Reardon and Escalante disappearances. I had an idea. Do you have time?'

'I was going to eat. Want to join me? Nothing special. There's an all-night coffee shop over on Oak.'

Lake looked at the stack of reports and the clock.

'Sure,' he said, swinging his legs off of the desk and grabbing his jacket. 'I didn't realize how late it was.'

'I was caught up in something, too. If my stomach hadn't yelled at me, I'd still be at my desk.'

'You must like your work.'

'Sometimes.'

'How did you get into it?'

'You mean, what's a nice girl like me doing in a job like this?'

'That never occurred to me.'

'That I was a nice girl?'

Lake laughed. 'No. That you're not suited for police work.'

Nancy checked out at the front desk and followed Lake outside. After sundown Hunter's Point was a ghost town, except for a few spots that catered to the college crowd. Nancy could see the marquee of the Hunter's Point Cinema and the neon signs outside a couple of bars. Most of the stores were shuttered for the night. The coffee shop was only a block and a half from the station. An oasis of light in a desert of darkness.

'Here we are,' Nancy said, holding open the door of Chang's Cafe. There was a counter, but Nancy led Lake to a booth. Chang's wife brought them menus and water.

'The soup and the pies are good and the rest of the menu is edible. Don't look for anything resembling Chinese. Mr Chang cooks Italian, Greek and whatever else strikes his fancy.'

'You're not from Hunter's Point originally, are you?' Lake asked, after they ordered.

'How could you tell?'

'You don't have the accent. I'm a transplanted westerner myself. Let's see. I'd guess Montana.'

'Idaho,' Nancy said. 'My parents still live there. They're farmers. My brother is a high-school teacher in Boise. Me, I didn't love Idaho and I wanted to see the world. Fortunately, I run a mean 800 meters and the U offered the best scholarship. So, I ended up in Hunter's Point.'

'Not exactly Paris,' Lake commented.

'Not exactly Paris,' Nancy repeated with a smile. 'But it *was* New York, and without the scholarship there was no way I could afford college. By the time I realized New York City and Hunter's Point, New York were worlds apart I was enjoying myself too much to care.'

'And the police work?'

'My major was Criminal Justice. When I graduated the

Hunter's Point PD needed a woman to fill its affirmative action quota.'

Nancy shrugged and looked at Lake, as if expecting a challenge.

'I bet you made detective on merit,' he said.

'Damn straight,' Nancy answered proudly, just as Mrs Chang arrived with their soup.

'How did you end up here?' Nancy asked, as she waited for her minestrone to cool.

'I'm from Colorado,' Lake said, smiling. 'I went to Colorado State undergraduate, then I served a hitch in the Marines. There was a guy in JAG who went to law school here and suggested I apply. I met Sandy at the U.'

Lake paused and his smile disappeared. He looked down at his plate. The action had an unnatural quality to it, as if he suddenly realized that a smile would be inappropriate when he was discussing his dead wife. Nancy looked at Lake oddly.

'I'm sorry,' he apologized. 'I keep thinking about her.'

'That's okay. There's nothing wrong with remembering.'

'I don't like myself when I'm maudlin. I've always been a person in control. The murders have made me realize that nothing is predictable or permanent.'

'If it's taken you this long to figure that out, you're lucky.'

'Yeah. A successful career, a great wife and kid. They blind you to the way the world really is, don't they? Then, someone takes that away from you in a second and...and you see...'

'You see how lucky you were to have what you had, while it lasted, Peter. Most people never have in their life-time what you and I had for a little while.'

Lake looked down at the table top.

'At the station, you said you had an idea,' Nancy said, to break his mood.

'It's probably just playing detective,' he answered, 'but something struck me when I was going through the reports. The day Gloria Escalante disappeared, a florist's truck was delivering in the area. A woman would open the door to a man delivering flowers. She would be excited and wouldn't be thinking. He could take the woman away in the back of his truck. And there's the rose. Someone who works in a florist's would have access to roses.'

'Not bad, Peter,' Nancy said, unable to hide her admiration. 'You might make a good detective, after all. The delivery man was Henry Waters. He's got a minor record for indecent exposure and he's one of our suspects. You probably haven't gotten to Wayne's report, yet. He's been doing a background check on Waters.'

Lake flushed. 'I guess you were way ahead of me.'

'Peter, did Sandy have any connection with Evergreen Florists?'

'Is that where Waters works?'

Nancy nodded.

'I don't think so. But I can look at our receipts and the check-book to see if she ever ordered anything from them. I'm pretty certain I never did.'

Their dinner arrived and they ate in silence for a few minutes. Nancy's spaghetti was delicious, but she noted that Lake just picked at his food.

'Do you feel like talking about Sandy?' Nancy asked. 'We're trying to cross-reference the activities of the victims. See if they belonged to the same clubs, subscribed to the same magazines. Anything that gives us a common denominator.'

'Frank asked me to do that the night of the murder. I've been working on it. We were members of the Delmar Country Club, the Hunter's Point Athletic Club, the Racquet Club. I've got a list of our credit cards, subscriptions, everything I can think of. I'll complete it by the end of the week. Is Waters your only suspect?'

'There are others, but nothing solid. I'm talking about known sex offenders, not anyone we've linked to any of the crimes.'

Nancy paused. 'I had an ulterior motive for asking you to eat with me. I'm going to be totally honest with you. You shouldn't be involved in this investigation. You have pull with the Mayor, so you're here, but everyone on the task-force resents the way you forced yourself on us.'

'Including you?'

'No. But that's only because I understand what's driving you. What you don't understand is how self-destructive your behavior is. You're obsessed with this case because you think immersing yourself in detective work will help you escape from reality. But you're stuck in the real world. Eventually, you'll have to come to terms with it and the sooner you do that the better. You've got a good practice. You can build a new life. Don't put off coming to grips with what's happened by continuing to work on the murders.'

Nancy was watching Lake as she spoke. He never took his eyes off her. When she was finished speaking he leaned forward.

'Thank you for your honesty. I know my intrusion into the task-force is resented and I'm glad you told me how everyone feels. I'm not worried about my practice. My associates will keep it going without me and I've made so much money that I could live nicely without it. What matters to me is catching this killer before he hurts someone else.'

Lake reached across the table and covered Nancy's hand with his.

'It also matters to me that you're concerned. I appreciate that.'

Lake stroked Nancy's hand as he spoke. It was a sensual touch, clearly a come-on, and Nancy was struck by the inappropriateness of his action, even if Lake was not.

'I'm concerned for you as a person who is the victim of a horrible crime,' Nancy said firmly, as she slid her hand out from under Lake's. 'I am also concerned that you might do something that would jeopardize our investigation. Please think about what I've said, Peter.'

'I will,' Lake assured her.

Nancy started to open her purse, but Lake stopped her.

'Dinner's on me,' he smiled.

'I always pay my own way,' Nancy answered, laying the exact amount of her dinner on top of the check and putting a dollar tip under her coffee cup. Nancy slipped out of the booth and started toward the door. Peter placed his money next to hers and followed her outside.

'Can I give you a lift home?' he asked.

'My car's in the lot.'

'Mine, too. I'll walk you back.'

They walked in silence until they reached the police station. The lot was dimly lit. Patches were in shadow. Nancy's car was toward the back of the station where the windows were dark.

'It could have happened someplace like this,' Lake mused, as they walked.

'What?'

'The women,' Lake said. 'Walking alone at night in a deserted parking lot. It would be so easy to approach them. Didn't Bundy do that? Wear a false cast to elicit sympathy. They would be in the killer's trunk in a minute and it would all be over for them.'

Nancy felt a chill. There was no one in the lot but the two of them. They entered an unlit area. She turned her head so she could see Lake. He was watching her, thoughtfully. Nancy stopped at her car.

'That's why I wanted to walk with you,' Lake continued. 'No woman is safe until he's caught.'

'Think about what I said, Peter.'

'Good night, Nancy. I think we work well together. Thanks again for your concern.'

Nancy backed her Ford out of its space and drove off. In the rear-view mirror she could see Lake watching her.

6

Nancy stood in the dark and pumped iron, following the routine she and Ed had worked out. Now, she was doing curls, with the maximum weight she could manage. Her forearm arced toward her shoulder, slowly, steadily, as she muscled up the right dumbbell, then the left. Sweat stained her tank top. The veins stood out on her neck.

Something was definitely wrong. Lake had been coming on to her. When Ed died, she had lost all interest in sex for months. It had hurt just to see couples walking hand in hand. But when Lake held her hand, he had stroked it, the way you would caress a lover's hand. When he said he thought they worked well together, it was definitely a proposition.

Nancy finished her curls. She lowered the weights to the floor and took a few deep breaths. It was almost six. She had been up since four-thirty, because a nightmare woke her and she couldn't get back to sleep.

Frank had considered Lake a suspect and she had disagreed. Now she was beginning to wonder. She remembered what Dr Klien had said. Lake was bright and personable. It would have been easy for him to gain the confidence of the victims. They were the type of women he met every day at his clubs, and he was the type of man the victims encountered at theirs.

The organized non-social was a psychopath who could not feel pity or care for others. The type of person who would have to fake emotions. Had Lake been caught off-guard in the coffee shop between remembering his first meeting with Sandra Lake and making the appropriate reaction to that memory? There had been a brief moment when Lake's features had been devoid of emotion.

Klien had also said that these killers were interested in police work. Lake, an experienced criminal defense attorney, would know all about police procedure. Nancy dropped to the floor and did fifty push-ups. What was normally an easy set was difficult. She couldn't focus. Her head filled with a vision of Lake, alone in the shadows of the parking lot, waiting. How did he know about Bundy's fake cast? Dr Klien had not mentioned it.

After the weights, she and Ed would run a six-mile loop through the neighborhood. Ed was stronger than Nancy, but she was the faster runner. On Sundays, they raced the loop. The loser cooked breakfast. The winner decided when and how they made love.

Nancy could not touch the weights or run the loop for two months after the shooting.

One hundred crunches. Up, down, up, down. Her stomach tight as a drum head. Her thoughts in the dark, in the parking lot with Lake. Should she tell Frank and Wayne? Was she just imagining it? Would her suspicions sidetrack the investigation and let the real killer escape?

It was six-fifteen. The weights were in a small room next to the bedroom. The sun was starting its ascent over the wealthy suburbs to the east. Nancy stripped off her panties and top and dropped them in the hamper. She had put on weight after Ed died. Except for a month when she was recovering from a hamstring pull in her sophomore year, it was the first time since junior high that she had not worked out regularly. The weight was off now and she could see the ridged muscles of her stomach and the cords that twisted along her legs. Hot water loosened her up. She shampooed her hair. All the time, she was thinking about Peter Lake.

Why were there no bodies found before? Why were the Lake murders different from the others? Sandra Lake had apparently been killed quickly, suddenly. Why? And why would Peter have killed her? Had she discovered something that would link him to the other murders and confronted him with the evidence? And that still left the hardest question of all, was Lake such a monster that he would kill his own daughter to cover his crimes?

As she dressed, Nancy tried to find one concrete fact that she could present to the other detectives. One piece of evidence that linked Peter to the crimes. She came up dry. For the moment, she'd have to keep her feelings to herself.

9

Frank Grimsbo ran a forearm across his forehead, staining the sleeve of his Madras jacket with sweat. He was wearing a short-sleeve, white shirt and brown polyester pants, and had jerked his paisley-print tie to half-mast after unbuttoning his top button. The heat was killing him and all he could think about was cold beer.

Herbert Solomon answered the door on the third ring. Wearily, Grimsbo held up his shield and identified himself.

'This is about the Lakes, right?' asked Solomon, a stocky man of medium height who sported a well-groomed beard and was dressed in loose, green and red checked Bermuda shorts and a yellow tee-shirt.

'That's right, Mr Solomon. My partner and I are canvassing the neighborhood.'

'I already spoke to a policeman on the evening it happened.'

'I know, sir. I'm a detective on the special task-force that's investigating all of the killings, and I wanted to go into a little more detail with you.'

'Have there been other murders? I thought these women just disappeared.'

'That's right, but we're assuming the worst.'

'Come on in out of the heat. Can I get you a beer, or can't you drink on duty?'

Grimsbo grinned. 'A beer would be great.'

'Wait in there and I'll grab one for you,' Solomon said, pointing to a small front room. Grimsbo pulled his shirt away from his body as he walked toward the den. Thank God they were canvassing in The Meadows, where everyone had air conditioning.

'I hope this is cold enough for you,' Solomon said, handing Grimsbo a chilled Budweiser. Grimsbo placed the cold bottle against his forehead and closed his eyes. Then, he took a sip.

'Boy, that hits the spot. I wish they could think up a way to air-condition the outside.'

Solomon laughed.

'You an accountant?'

'A CPA.'

'I figured,' Grimsbo said, pointing his beer at two large bookcases filled with books about tax and accounting. A desk stood in front of the only window in the room. A computer and printer sat in the center of the desk next to a phone. The window looked out at Sparrow Lane across a wide front lawn.

'Well,' Grimsbo said, after taking another swig from the bottle, 'let me ask you a few questions and get out of your hair. Were you around the night Mrs Lake and her daughter were murdered?'

Solomon stopped smiling and nodded. 'Poor bastard.'

'You know Peter Lake?'

'Sure. Neighbors and all. We have a homeowners

committee in The Meadows. Pete and I are on it. We play doubles together in the tennis tournament. Marge – that's my wife – she and Sandy were good friends.'

'Is your wife home?'

'She's at the club, playing golf. I didn't feel like it in this heat.'

Grimsbo put down the beer and took a pad and pen out of his inside jacket pocket.

'About what time did you get home on the night it happened?'

'It had to be about six.'

'Did you see anything unusual that night?'

'Not a thing. I was in the dining-room until we finished dinner. The dining-room looks out into the backyard. Then I was in the living-room for a few minutes. It's in the back of the house, too. After that I was in here working on the computer with the blinds drawn.'

'Okay,' Grimsbo said, reluctantly ready to wrap up the interview and trudge back out into the heat.

'One thing I forgot about when the officer talked to me the night of the murder. There was so much excitement and Marge was hysterical. I did see Pete come home.'

'Oh yeah. When was that?'

'I can get pretty close there. The Yankees played a day game and I caught the score on Headline Sports. CNN runs the sports scores twenty after and ten to the hour. I went into the den right after the score, so figure seven twenty-two or so. I saw Pete's Ferrari when I closed the blinds.'

'He was heading home?'

'Right.'

'And you're certain about the time.'

'Twenty after the hour, every hour. So it had to be about then, give or take a minute.'

'Did you notice a florist's truck at any time that night, near The Meadows or in it?'

Solomon thought for a second. 'There was a TV repairman at the Osgoods'. That's the only unusual vehicle I saw.'

Grimsbo levered himself out of his seat and extended his hand.

'Thanks for the beer.'

Wayne Turner was leaning against the car, looking so cool in his tan suit and dark brown tie that it pissed Grimsbo off.

'Any luck?' Turner asked as he pushed off the car.

'Nada. Oh, Solomon, the last guy I talked to, saw Lake driving home past his house about seven-twenty. Other than that, I don't have a thing that wasn't in the uniforms' reports.'

'I struck out, too, but I'm not surprised. You get a development like The Meadows, you get houses with land. They're not leaning over each other. Less chance anyone will see what's going on at the neighbors'. And with heat like this, everyone's either inside with the air conditioning on or out at their country club.'

'So, what do we do now?'

'Head back in.'

'You get a hit on a florist's truck?' Grimsbo asked, when he had the car started.

'There was a cable TV repairman at the Osgoods', but no florist.'

'Yeah, I got the TV guy, too. What do you think of Waters?'

'I don't think anything, Frank. You seen him?'

Grimsbo shook his head.

'Our killer's got to be high IQ, right? Waters is a zero. Skinny, pimple-faced kid. He's got this little wisp of a beard. If he's not retarded, he's not far from it. Dropped out of school in the tenth grade. He was eighteen. Worked as a gas-station attendant and a box boy at Safeway. He lost that job when he was arrested for jacking off outside the window of a sixteen-year-old neighbor girl. The girl's father beat the crap out of him.'

'He sounds pretty pathetic,' Grimsbo observed.

'The guy's got no life. He lives with his mother. She's in her late sixties and in poor health. I followed him for a few days. He's a robot. Every day, it's the same routine. He leaves work and walks to the One Way Inn, this bar that's half-way to his house. Orders two beers, nurses 'em, doesn't say a word to anyone but the bartender. Forty-five minutes after he goes in, he leaves, walks straight home and spends the evening watching TV with his mother. I talked to his boss and his neighbors. If he's got any friends, no one knows who they are. He's held this delivery-boy job with Evergreen Florists longer than any of his other jobs.'

'You writing him off?'

'He's a weeny waver. A little twisted, sure, but I don't make him for our killer. He's not smart enough to be our boy. We don't have anything with Waters.'

'We don't have anything, period.'

Glen Michaels walked into the task-force office just as Grimsbo and Turner were finishing the reports on their interviews in The Meadows.

'Whatcha got?' Grimsbo asked. He had shucked his jacket and parked himself next to a small fan.

'Nothing at all,' Michaels said. 'It's like the guy was never there. I just finished all the lab work. Every print matches up to the victims, Lake or one of the neighbors. There's nothing to do a DNA test on. No unusual hairs, no fibers, no semen. This is one smart cookie, gentlemen.'

'You think he knows police procedure?' Turner asked.

'I have to believe it. I've never seen so many clean crime scenes.

'Anyway,' Michaels said, heading for the door, 'I'm out of here. This heat is boiling my blood.'

Turner turned to Grimsbo. 'This perp is starting to piss me off. Nobody's that good. He leaves no prints, no hairs, no one sees him. Christ, we've got a development full of people and no one reports an unusual occurrence. No strangers lurking around, not a single odd car. How does he get in and out?'

Grimsbo didn't answer. He was frowning. He levered himself out of his chair and walked over to the cabinet where they kept the master file on the case.

'What's up?' Turner asked.

'Just something . . . Yeah, here it is.'

Grimsbo pulled a report out of the file and showed it to Turner. It was the one-page report of the dispatcher who had taken the 911 call from Peter Lake.

'You see it?' Grimsbo asked.

Turner read the report a few times and shook his head.

'The time,' Grimsbo said. 'Lake called in the 911 at eight-fifteen.'

'Yeah? So?'

'Solomon said he saw Lake driving by at seven-twenty. He was certain he'd just heard the sports scores. CNN gives them at twenty after.'

'And the bodies were in the hall,' Turner said, suddenly catching on.

'How long does it take to park the car, open the door? Let's give Lake the benefit of the doubt and assume Solomon is a little off. He's still gonna be inside by seven-thirty.'

'Shit,' Turner said softly.

'Am I right, Wayne?' Grimsbo asked.

'I don't know, Frank. If it was your wife and kid . . . I mean, you'd be in shock.'

'Sure the guy's knocked out. He said he sat down on the stairs for a while. You know, gathering himself. But for forty-five minutes? Uh-uh. Something doesn't wash. I think he spent the time cleaning up the crime scene.'

'What's the motive? Jesus, Frank, you saw her face. Why would he do that to his own wife?'

'You know why. She knew something, she found some-thing, and she made the mistake of telling Lake. Think about it, Wayne. If Lake killed them it would explain the absence of clues at the crime scene. There wouldn't be any strange cars in the neighborhood or prints that didn't match the Lakes or the neighbors.'

'I don't know . . .'

'Yes you do. He killed that little girl. His own little girl.'

'Christ, Frank, Lake's a successful lawyer. His wife was beautiful.'

'You heard Klien. The guy we're looking for is a monster, but no one's gonna see that. He's smooth, handsome, the type of guy these women would let in their house without a second thought. It could be a successful lawyer with a beautiful wife. It could be anyone who isn't wired right and is working in some psycho world of his own where this all makes sense.'

Turner paced around the room while Grimsbo waited quietly. Finally, Turner sat down and picked up a picture of Melody Lake.

'We aren't going to do anything stupid, Frank. If Lake is our killer, he is one devious motherfucker. One hint that we're on to him and he'll figure a way to cover this up.'

'So, what's the next step? We can't bring him in and sweat him and we know there's nothing connecting Lake to the other crime scenes.'

'These women weren't picked at random. If he's the killer, they've all got to be connected to Lake somehow. We have to reinterview the husbands, go back over the reports and recheck our lists with Lake in mind. If we're right, there's going to be something there.'

The two men sat silently for a moment, figuring the angles.

'None of this goes in a report,' Turner said. 'Lake could stumble across it when he's here.'

'Right,' Grimsbo answered. 'I'd better take Solomon's interview with me.'

'When do we tell Nancy and the Chief?'

'When we have something solid. Lake's very smart and he's got political connections. If he's the one, I don't want him beating this, I want him nailed.'

8

Nancy Gordon was deep in a dreamless sleep when the phone rang. She jerked up in bed, flailing for a moment, before she realized what was happening. The phone rang again before she found it in the dark.

'Detective Gordon?' the man on the phone asked.

'Speaking,' Nancy said as she tried to orient herself.

'This is Jeff Spears. I'm a patrolman. Fifteen minutes ago we received a complaint about a man sitting in a car on the corner of Bethesda and Champagne. Seems he's been parked there for three successive nights. One of the neighbors got worried.

'Anyway, Officer DeMuniz and I talked to the guy. He identified himself as Peter Lake. He claims he's working on the task-force that's looking into the murders of those women. He gave me your name.'

'What time is it?' Nancy asked. The last thing she wanted to do was turn on the light and scorch her eyeballs.

'One-thirty,' Spears said, apologetically. 'Sorry about waking you.'

'No, that's okay,' she answered as she located the digital clock and confirmed the time. 'Is Lake there?'

'Right beside me.'

Nancy took a deep breath. 'Put him on.'

Nancy heard Spears talking to someone. She swung her legs over the side of the bed, sat up and rubbed her eyes.

'Nancy?' Lake asked.

'What's going on?'

'Do you want me to explain with the officer standing here?'

'What I want is to go back to bed. Now, what's this about you sitting in a parked car in the middle of the night for three straight nights?'

'It's Waters. I was staking out his house.'

'Oh, fuck. I don't believe this. You were staking him out? Like some goddamn movie? Peter, I want you at Chang's in twenty minutes.'

'But . . .'

'Twenty minutes. This is too stupid for words. And put Spears back on.'

Nancy heard Lake calling to the officer. She closed her eyes and turned on the bedside lamp. Then she raised her lids slowly. The light burned and her eyes watered.

'Detective Gordon?'

'Yeah. Look, Spears, he's okay. He is working on the task-force. But that was heads-up work,' she added, since he sounded young and eager and the compliment would mean something.

'It sounded suspicious. And, with the murders . . .'

'No, you did the right thing. But I don't want you to mention this to anyone. We don't want what we're doing getting around.'

'No problem.'

'Thanks for calling.'

Nancy hung up. She felt awful, but she had to find out what Lake was up to.

Lake was waiting for her in a booth when Nancy arrived at Chang's. The little cafe stayed open all night for cops, truckers and an occasional college student. It was a safe place to meet. There was a cup of coffee in front of Lake. Nancy told the waitress to make it two.

'Why don't you clue me in on what you thought you were doing, Peter,' Nancy said, when the waitress left.

'I'm sorry if I was out of line. But I'm certain Waters is the killer. I've been tailing him for three days. Believe me, I did a great job. He has no idea he was followed.'

'Peter, this isn't how things are done. You don't go running off with some half-baked idea you picked up from Magnum, PI. The task-force is a team. You have to run your ideas by everyone before you make a move.

'More important, you don't know the first thing about surveillance. Look how easily you were spotted by the neighbor. If Waters saw you, and it spooked him, he might go to ground and we'd lose him forever. And, if he is the killer, you could have been in danger. Whoever killed your wife and daughter has no conscience and he has no compunction about taking a human life. Remember that.'

'I guess I was foolish.'

'There's no "guess" about it.'

'You're right. I apologize. I never thought about blowing the case or the danger. All I thought about was . . .'

Lake paused and looked down at the table.

'I know you want him, Peter. We all do. But if you don't do this right, you'll ruin the case.'

Lake nodded thoughtfully. 'You've gone out of your way to help me, Nancy, and I appreciate it. I'm finally starting to cope with losing Sandy and Melody and you're one of the reasons.'

Lake smiled at her. Nancy did not return the smile. She watched Lake carefully.

'I've decided to go back to work. This little incident

tonight has convinced me I'm not very valuable to the investigation. I thought I could really help, but that was ego and desperation. I'm not a cop and I was crazy to think I could do more than you're doing.'

'Good. I'm glad to hear you say that. It's a healthy sign.'

'That doesn't mean I'm going to abandon the case altogether. I'd like copies of all the police reports sent to my office. I still might spot something you miss or offer a different perspective. But I'll stop haunting the station house.'

'I can have the reports sent, if O'Malley says it's okay. But you'll have to keep them strictly to yourself. Not even your associates should see them.'

'Of course. You know, you've really taken good care of me,' Lake said, smiling again. 'Do you think we could have dinner sometime? Just get together? Nothing to do with the case.'

'We'll see,' she said, uneasily.

Lake checked his watch. 'Hey, we'd better get going. We're going to be dead tired in the morning. I'm paying this time, no arguments.'

Nancy slid out of the booth and said goodbye. It was late and she'd had little sleep, but she was wide awake. There was no question about it now. With his wife dead less than three weeks, Peter Lake was coming on to her. And that wasn't the only thing bothering her. Nancy wanted to know the real reason Peter Lake was tailing Henry Waters.

9

'Dr Escalante,' Wayne Turner said to a heavy-set, dark-complected man with the sad eyes and weary air of someone who has given up hope, 'I'm one of the detectives working on your wife's disappearance.'

'Is Gloria dead?' Escalante asked, expecting the worst.

They were sitting in the doctor's office at the Wayside Clinic, a modern, two-story building located at the far end of the Wayside Mall. Escalante was one of several doctors, physical therapists and health-care specialists who made up the staff of the clinic. His specialty was cardiology and he had privileges at Hunter's Point Hospital. Everyone spoke highly of Dr Escalante's skills. They also thought he was one hell of a nice guy, who was unfailingly cheerful. Or, at least, he had been until a month and a half ago, when he came home to his Tudor-style house in West Hunter's Point and found a note and a black rose.

'I'm afraid we have no more information about your wife. We assume she's alive, until we learn otherwise.'

'Then why are you here?'

'I have a few questions that may help us with the case.'

Turner read off the names of the other missing women and their spouses, including the Lakes. As he read the names, Turner placed photographs of the victims and their husbands face up on Escalante's desk.

'Do you or your wife know any of these people in any capacity whatsoever, Doctor?' Turner asked.

Escalante studied the photographs carefully. He picked up one of them.

'This is Simon and Samantha Reardon, isn't it?'

Turner nodded.

'He's a neurosurgeon. I've seen the Reardons at a few Medical Association functions. A few years ago, he spoke at a seminar I attended. I don't recall the topic.'

'That's good. Were you friendly with the Reardons?'

Escalante laughed harshly. 'People with my skin color don't travel in the same social circles as the Reardons, Detective. I don't suppose you were permitted to interview the esteemed doctor at the Delmar Country Club.'

Wayne nodded.

'Yeah. Well, that's the type of guy Simon Reardon is . . .'

Escalante suddenly remembered why Turner was interested in Samantha Reardon and his wife.

'I'm sorry. I should be more charitable. Simon is probably going through the same hell I am.'

'Probably. Any of the others ring a bell?'

Escalante started to shake his head, then stopped.

'This one is a lawyer, isn't he?' he asked, pointing at Peter Lake's photograph.

'Yes, he is,' Turner answered, trying to hide his excitement.

'It didn't hit me until now. What a coincidence.'

'What's that?'

'Gloria was chosen for jury duty six months ago. She sat on one of Lake's cases. I remember because she said she was glad it wasn't a medical malpractice or she would have been excused. It didn't matter though. The lawyers settled the case half-way through, so she didn't vote on it.'

'You're certain it was Peter Lake's case?'

'I met her after court. We were going to dinner. I saw him.'

'Okay. That's a big help. Anyone else look familiar?' Turner asked, although, at this point, he really didn't care.

'It's Lake, Chief,' Frank Grimsbo told O'Malley. 'We're certain.'

'Are we talking hard evidence?' O'Malley asked.

'Not yet. But there's too much circumstantial to look the other way,' Wayne Turner answered.

'How do you two feel about this?' O'Malley asked Glen Michaels and Nancy Gordon.

'It makes sense,' Michaels responded. 'I'm going back over the evidence in all of the cases tomorrow to see if I have anything I can tie to Lake.'

O'Malley turned toward Nancy. She looked grim.

'I'd reached the same conclusion for other reasons, Chief. I don't know how we can nail him, but I'm certain he's our man. I talked to Dr Klien, this morning, and ran Lake's profile by him. He said it's possible. A lot of sociopaths aren't serial killers. They're successful businessmen or politicians or lawyers. Think of the advantage you have in those professions if you don't have a conscience to slow you down. In the past few days, I've been talking to people who know Lake. They all say he's charming, but none of them would turn their back on him. He's supposed to have the ethics of a shark and enough savvy to stay just this side of the line. There have been several Bar complaints, but none that were successful. A few malpractice suits. I talked to the lawyers who represented the plaintiffs. He skated on every one of them.'

'There's a big difference between being a sleazy lawyer and killing six people, including your own daughter,'

O'Malley said. 'Why would he endanger himself by getting so close to the investigation?'

'So he can see what we've got,' Grimsbo said.

'I think there's more to it, Chief,' Nancy said. 'He's up to something.'

Nancy told O'Malley about Lake's stakeout.

'That doesn't make sense,' Turner said. 'Waters isn't really a suspect. He just happened to be around the Escalante house the day she disappeared. There's no connection between Waters and any other victim.'

'But there is a connection between Lake and every victim,' Grimsbo cut in.

'Let's hear it,' O'Malley said.

'Okay. We have Gloria Escalante sitting on one of his juries. He and the Reardons belong to the Delmar Country Club. Patricia Cross and Sandra Lake were in the Junior League. Anne Hazelton's husband is an attorney. He says they've been to Bar Association functions the Lakes attended.'

'Some of those connections are pretty tenuous.'

'What are the odds on one person being linked to all six victims?' Turner asked.

'Hunter's Point isn't that big a place.'

'Chief,' Nancy said, 'he's been coming on to me.'

'What?'

'It's sexual. He's interested. He's let me know.'

Nancy recounted the way Lake acted during their two meetings at Chang's.

O'Malley frowned. 'I don't know, Nancy.'

'His wife died less than a month ago. It's not normal.'

'You're attractive. He's trying to get over his grief. Maybe he and Mrs Lake didn't get along that well. Did you find any of that when you talked to the neighbors?'

Grimsbo shook his head. 'No gossip about the Lakes. They were a normal couple according to the people I talked to.'

'Same here,' Turner said.

'Doesn't that undercut your theory?'

'Dr Klien said a serial killer can have a wife and family, or a normal relationship with a girlfriend,' Nancy answered.

'Look at the Lake murders,' Turner offered. 'We know from one of his associates, who was working late, that Lake was at his office until shortly before seven. The neighbor sees him driving toward his house at seven-twenty, maybe a little after. There's no 911 call until forty-five minutes later. What's he doing inside with the dead bodies? If they're dead, that is.

'We think he came in and his wife confronted him with something she'd found that connected him to the disappearances.'

'But they weren't news. No one knew about them,' O'Malley said.

'Oh, shit,' Michaels swore.

'What?'

'The note. It was the only one with prints on it.'

'So?' Grimsbo asked.

'The other notes had no fingerprints on them, but the note next to Sandra Lake's body had her prints on it. According to the autopsy report, Sandra Lake died instantly or, at least, she was unconscious as soon as she was hit on the back of the head. When did she touch the note?'

'I still don't . . .'

'She finds the note or the rose or both. She asks Lake what they are. He knows the story will break in the paper eventually. No matter what he tells her now, she'll know he's the rose killer. So, he panics, kills her and leaves the rose and the note next to the body to make us think the same person who's taken the other women also killed his wife. And that explains why only Lake's note has a print and why it's Sandra Lake's print,' Michaels said. 'She was holding it before she was killed.'

'That also explains why no one saw any strange vehicles going in or out of The Meadows.'

O'Malley leaned back in his chair. He looked troubled.

'You've got me believing this,' he said. 'But theories aren't proof. If it's Lake, how do we prove it with evidence that's admissible in court?'

Before anyone could answer, the door to O'Malley's office opened.

'Sorry to interrupt, Chief, but we just got a 911 that's connected to those women who disappeared. Do you have a suspect named Waters?'

'What's up?' Grimsbo asked.

'The caller said he talked with a guy named Henry Waters at the One Way Inn and Waters said he had a woman in his basement.'

'Did the caller give a name?'

The officer shook his head. 'Said he didn't want to get involved, but he kept thinking about the little kid who was murdered and his conscience wouldn't leave him alone.'

'When did this conversation at the bar take place?' Nancy asked.

'A few days ago.'

'Did Waters describe the woman or give any details?'

'Waters told him the woman had red hair.'

'Patricia Cross,' Turner said.

'This is Lake's doing,' Nancy said. 'It's too much of a coincidence.'

'I'm with Nancy,' Turner said. 'Waters just doesn't figure.'

'Can we take the chance?' Michaels asked. 'With Lake, all we have is some deductive reasoning. We know Waters was around the Escalante residence near the time she disappeared and he has a sex-offender record.'

'I want you four out there, pronto,' O'Malley ordered. 'I'd rather be wrong than sit here talking when we might be able to save one of those women.'

Henry Waters lived in an older section of Hunter's Point. Oak trees shaded the wide streets. High hedges gave the residents privacy. Most of the homes and lawns were well kept-up, but Waters' house, a corner plot, was starting to come apart. The gutters were clogged. One of the steps leading up to the shaded front porch was broken. The lawn was overgrown and full of weeds.

The sun was starting to set when Nancy Gordon followed Wayne Turner and Frank Grimsbo along the slate walk toward Henry Waters' front door. Michaels waited in the car in case he was needed to process a crime scene. Three uniformed officers were stationed behind the house in an alley that divided the large block in two. Two officers preceded the detectives up the walk and positioned themselves, guns drawn but concealed, on either side of the front door.

'We take it easy and we are polite,' Turner cautioned. 'I want his consent or the search- and seizure-issues could get sticky.'

Everyone nodded. No one cracked a joke about Turner and law school, as they might have under other circumstances. Nancy looked back at the high grass in the front yard. The house was weather-beaten. The brown paint was chipping. A window screen was hanging by one screw outside the front window. Nancy peeked through a crack between a drawn shade and the window-sill. No one was in the front room. They could hear a television playing somewhere toward the back of the house.

'He'll be less fearful if he sees a woman,' Nancy said. Grimsbo nodded and Nancy pressed the doorbell. She wore a jacket to conceal her holster. There had been some respite from the heat during the day, but it was still warm. She could feel a trickle of sweat work its way down her side.

Nancy rang the bell a second time and the volume of the TV lowered. She saw a vague shape moving down the hall through the semi-opaque curtain that covered the glassed upper half of the front door. When the door opened, Nancy pulled back the screen door and smiled. The gangly, loose-limbed man did not smile back. He was dressed in jeans and a stained tee-shirt. His long, greasy hair was unkempt. Waters' dull eyes fixed first on Nancy, then on the uniformed officers. His brow furrowed, as if he were working on a calculus problem. Nancy flashed her badge.

'Mr Waters, I'm Nancy Gordon, a detective with the Hunter's Point PD.'

'I didn't do nothin',' Waters said defensively.

101

'I'm certain that's true,' Nancy answered in a firm but friendly tone, 'but we received some information we'd like to check out. Would you mind if we came in?'

'Who is it?' a frail female voice called from the rear of the house.

'That's my mom,' Waters explained. 'She's sick.'

'I'm sorry. We'll try not to disturb her.'

'Why do you have to upset her? She's sick,' Waters asked, his anxiety growing.

'You misunderstood me, Mr Waters. We are *not* going to bother your mother. We only want to look around. May we do that? We won't be long.'

'I ain't done nothin',' Waters repeated, his eyes shifting anxiously from Grimsbo to Turner, then to the uniformed officers. 'Talk to Miss Cummings. She's my PO. She'll tell you.'

'We did talk to your probation officer and she gave you a very good report. She said you cooperated with her completely. We'd like your cooperation, too. You don't want us to have to wait here while one of the officers gets a search warrant, do you?'

'Why do you have to search my house?' Waters asked angrily. The officers tensed. 'Why the hell can't you leave me be? I ain't looked at that girl no more. I'm workin' steady. Miss Cummings can tell you.'

'There's no need to get upset,' Nancy answered calmly. 'The sooner we look around, the sooner we'll be out of your hair.'

Waters thought this over. 'What do you want to see?' he asked.

'The basement.'

'There ain't nothin' in the basement,' Waters said, seeming genuinely puzzled.

'Then we won't be here long,' Nancy assured him.

Waters snorted. 'The basement. You can see all the basement you want. Ain't nothin' but spiders in the basement.'

Waters pointed down a dark hall that led past the stairs toward the rear of the house.

'Why don't you come with us, Mr Waters. You can show us around.'

The hall was dark, but there was a light in the kitchen. Nancy saw a sink filled with dirty dishes and the remains of two TV dinners on a Formica-topped table. The kitchen floor was stained and dirty. There was a solid wood door under the staircase next to the entrance to the kitchen. Waters opened it. Then, his eyes widened and he stepped back. Nancy pushed past him. The smell was so strong it knocked her back a step.

'Stay with Mr Waters,' Nancy told the officers. She took a deep breath and flicked the switch at the head of the stairs. There was nothing unusual at the bottom of the wooden steps. Nancy held her gun with one hand and the rickety railing with the other. The smell of death grew stronger as she descended the stairs. Grimsbo and Turner followed. No one spoke.

Half-way down, Nancy crouched and scanned the basement. The only light came from a bare bulb hanging from the ceiling. She could see a furnace in one corner. Odd pieces of furniture, most with a broken look, were stashed against a wall surrounded by cartons of newspapers and old magazines. A back door opened into a concrete well at the back of the house near the alley. Most of the corner near the door was in shadow, but Nancy could make out a human foot and a pool of blood.

'Fuck,' she whispered, sucking air.

Grimsbo edged past her. Nancy followed close behind. She knew nothing in the basement could hurt her, but she was having trouble catching her breath. Turner aimed a flashlight at the corner and flicked it on.

'Jesus,' he managed in a strangled voice.

The naked woman was sprawled on the cold concrete, swimming in blood and surrounded by an overpowering fecal smell. She had not been 'killed' or 'murdered'. She had been defiled and dehumanized. Nancy could see patches of charred flesh where the skin was not stained with blood or feces. The woman's intestines had burst through a gaping hole in her abdomen. They reminded Nancy of a string of bloated sausage. She turned her head aside.

'Bring Waters down here,' Grimsbo bellowed. Nancy could see the tendons in his neck stretching. His eyes bulged.

'You don't lay one hand on him, Frank,' Turner managed between gasps.

Nancy grabbed Grimsbo's massive forearm. 'Wayne's right. I'm handling this. Back off.'

A uniform hustled Waters down the steps. When Waters saw the body, he turned white and fell to his knees. He was mouthing words, but no sound came out.

Nancy closed her eyes and gathered herself. The body wasn't there. The smell wasn't in the air. She knelt next to Waters.

'Why, Henry?' she asked softly.

Waters looked at her. His face crumpled and he bleated like a wounded animal.

'Why?' Nancy repeated.

'Oh, no. Oh, no,' Waters cried, holding his head in his hands. The head snapped back and forth with each denial, his long hair trailing behind.

'Then who did this? She's here, Henry. In your basement.'

Waters gaped at Nancy, his mouth wide open.

'I'm going to give you your rights. You've heard them before, haven't you?' Nancy asked, but it was clear Waters was in no condition to discuss constitutional rights. His head hung backward and he was making an inhuman baying noise.

'Take him to the station,' she ordered the officer who was standing behind Waters. 'If you, or anyone else, asks this man one question, you'll be scrubbing toilet bowls in public rest-rooms. Is that understood? He hasn't been Mirandized. I want him in an interrogation room with a two-man guard inside and another man outside. No one, including the Chief, is to talk to him. I'll call from here to brief O'Malley. And send Michaels in. Tell him to call for a full forensic team. Post a guard on the stairs. No one else comes down here unless Glen says it's okay. I don't want this crime scene fucked up.'

Grimsbo and Turner had drawn closer to the body, making certain to stay outside the circle of blood that surrounded it. Grimsbo was taking short, deep breaths. Turner willed himself to look at the woman's face. It was Patricia Cross, but barely. The killer's savage attack had not been limited to the victim's body.

The young uniformed officer was also riveted on the body. That was why he was slow to react when Waters leaped up. Nancy was half turned and saw the action from the corner of her eye. By the time she turned back, the cop was sprawled on the floor and Waters was bolting up the stairs, screaming for his mother.

The officer who was watching the cellar door heard Waters' scream. He stepped in front of the entrance to the basement, gun drawn, as Waters barrelled into him.

'Don't shoot,' Nancy screamed just as the gun exploded. The officer stumbled backwards, crashing into the wall opposite the cellar door. The shot plowed through Waters' heart and he tumbled down the stairs, cracking his head on the cement floor. Waters never felt the impact. He was dead by then.

10

'It was on the late news. I can't believe you caught him,' Nancy Gordon heard Peter Lake say. She was alone in the task-force office, writing reports. Nancy swiveled her chair. Lake stood in the doorway of the office. He wore pressed jeans and a maroon and blue rugby shirt. His styled hair was neatly combed. He looked happy and excited. There was no indication that he was thinking of Sandra or Melody Lake. No sign of grief.

'How did you crack it?' Lake asked sitting in the chair opposite Nancy.

'An anonymous tip, Peter. Nothing fancy.'

'That's terrific.'

'It looks like you were right.'

Lake shrugged his shoulders, stifling a smile. 'Say,' he asked sheepishly, 'you didn't tell anyone about my stake-out, did you?'

'That's our little secret.'

'Thanks. I feel like a fool, going off on my own like that. You were right. If Waters caught on, he probably would have killed me.'

'You must feel relieved, knowing Sandy's and Melody's killer has been caught,' Nancy said, watching for a reaction.

Lake suddenly looked somber.

'It's as if an enormous weight was taken off my shoulders. Maybe now, my life can go back to normal.'

'You know, Peter,' Nancy said casually, 'there was a time when I tossed around the possibility that you might be the killer.'

'Why?' Peter asked, shocked.

'You were never a serious suspect, but there were a few inconsistencies in your story.'

'Like what?'

'The time, for instance. You didn't call 911 until eight-fifteen, but a neighbor saw you driving toward your house around seven-twenty. I couldn't figure out why it took you so long to call the police.'

'You've got to be kidding.'

Nancy shrugged.

'I was a suspect because of this time thing?'

'What were you doing for almost an hour?'

'Jesus, Nancy, I don't remember. I was in a daze. I mean I might have blacked out for a bit.'

'You never mentioned that.'

Lake stared at Nancy, open-mouthed.

'Am I still a suspect? Are you interrogating me?'

Nancy shook her head. 'The case is closed, Peter. The Chief is going to hold a press conference in the morning. There were three black roses and another one of those notes on a shelf in the basement. And, of course, there was poor Patricia Cross.'

'But you don't believe it? You honestly think I could have . . .?'

'Relax, Peter,' Nancy answered, closing her eyes. 'I'm real tired and not thinking straight. It's been one very long day.'

'I can't relax. I mean, I really like you and I thought you liked me. It's a shock to find out you seriously thought I could do something . . . something like what was done to that woman.'

Nancy opened her eyes. Lake looked distant, like he was visualizing Patricia Cross's eviscerated body. But he had not been to the crime scene or read an autopsy report. The media had not been told the condition of Patricia Cross's body.

'I said you were never a serious suspect and I meant it,' Nancy lied with a forced smile. 'If you were, I would have told Turner and Grimsbo about the stake-out, wouldn't I?'

'I guess.'

'Well, I didn't and you can't be a suspect any more, what with Waters dead, can you?'

Lake shook his head.

'Look,' Nancy told him, 'I'm really whacked out. I have one more report to write and I'm gone. Why don't you go home, too, and start getting on with your life.'

Lake stood. 'That's good advice. I'm going to take it. And I want to thank you for everything you've done for me. I don't know how I would have gotten through this without you.'

Lake stuck out his hand. Nancy stared at it for a second. Was this the hand that ripped the life out of Patricia Cross and Sandra and Melody Lake, or was she crazy? Nancy shook Lake's hand. He held hers a moment longer than necessary, then released it after a brief squeeze.

'When things get back to normal for both of us, I'd like to take you to dinner,' Lake said.

'Call me,' Nancy answered, her stomach churning. It took every ounce of control to keep the smile on her face.

Lake left the room and Nancy stopped smiling. Waters was too good to be true. She did not believe he was responsible for the carnage in his basement. Lake had to know about the alley and the back door. With Waters at work and the mother an invalid, it would have been simple to drive behind the house without being seen, put the body in the basement and butcher it there. Lake was the anonymous caller, she was certain of it. But she had no proof. And O'Malley would soon tell the world that Henry Waters was a serial killer and the case of the missing women was closed.

PART THREE
CLEAR AND CONVINCING EVIDENCE

Chapter Six

'And that's what happened, Mr Page,' Nancy Gordon said. 'The case was closed. Henry Waters was officially named as the rose killer. Shortly after, Peter Lake disappeared. His house was sold. He closed his bank accounts. His associates were handed a thriving business. And Peter was never heard from again.'

Page looked confused. 'Maybe I'm missing something. Your case against Lake was purely circumstantial. Unless there was more evidence, I don't understand why you're so certain Peter Lake killed those women and framed Waters.'

Gordon took a newspaper clipping and a photograph of a man leaving a motel room out of her briefcase and laid them side by side.

'Do you recognize this man?' she asked, pointing to the photograph. Page leaned over and picked it up.

'This is Martin Darius.'

'Look carefully at this newspaper picture of Peter Lake and tell me what you think.'

Page studied the two pictures. He imagined Lake with a

beard and Darius without one. He tried to judge the size of the two men and compare builds.

'They could be the same person,' he said.

'They are the same person. And the man who is murdering your women is the same man who murdered the women in Hunter's Point. We never released the color of the rose or the contents of the notes. Whoever is killing your women has information known only by the members of the Hunter's Point task-force and the killer.'

Gordon took a fingerprint card from the briefcase and handed it to Page.

'These are Lake's fingerprints. Compare them to Darius's. You must have some on file.'

'How did you find Lake here?' Page asked.

Gordon took a sheet of stationery out of her briefcase and laid it on the coffee table next to the photograph.

'I've had it dusted for prints,' she said. 'There aren't any.'

Page picked up the letter. It had been written on a word processor. The stationery looked cheap, probably the type sold in hundreds of chain stores and impossible to trace. The note read, 'Women in Portland, Oregon are "Gone, But Not Forgotten" '. The first letters of each word were capitalized like those in the notes found in the homes of the victims.

'I received this yesterday. The envelope was postmarked from Portland. The photograph of Darius and an *Oregonian* profile of him were inside. I knew it was Lake, the minute I saw the picture. The envelope also contained a clipping about you, Mr Page, your address and a ticket for a United Airlines flight. No one met me at the airport, so I came to see you.'

114

'What do you suggest we do, Detective Gordon? We certainly can't bring Darius in for questioning with what you've given me.'

'No!' Gordon said, alarmed. 'Don't spook him. You have to stay away from Martin Darius until your case is airtight. You have no idea how clever he is.'

Page was startled by Gordon's desperation.

'We know our business, Detective,' he assured her.

'You don't know Peter Lake. You've never dealt with anyone like him.'

'You said that before.'

'You must believe me.'

'Is there something else you aren't telling me?'

Gordon started to say something, then she shook her head.

'I'm exhausted, Mr Page. I need to rest. You don't know what this is like for me. To have Lake surface after all these years. If you had seen what he did to Patricia Cross . . .'

There was a long pause and Page said nothing.

'I need a place to stay,' Gordon said abruptly. 'Can you suggest a motel? Some place quiet.'

'There's the Lakeview. We keep out-of-town witnesses there. I can drive you.'

'No, don't. I'll take a cab. Can you call one for me?'

'Sure. My phone book is in my bedroom. I'll be right out.'

'I'll leave you the fingerprint card, the photograph and the newspaper clipping. I have copies,' Gordon said, as she gathered up the note.

'You're certain you don't want me to drive you? It's no trouble.'

Gordon shook her head. Page went into the bedroom and

called for a cab. When he returned to the living-room, Gordon was slumped on the couch, her eyes closed.

'They'll be here in ten minutes,' he said.

Gordon's eyes snapped open. She looked startled, as if she had drifted off for a few minutes and had been scared awake.

'It's been a long day,' the detective said. She looked embarrassed.

'Jet lag,' Page said to make conversation. 'I hope you're right about Darius.'

'I am right,' Gordon answered, her features rigid. 'I am one hundred percent right. You believe that, Mr Page. The lives of a lot of women depend on it.'

Chapter Seven

1

Something was definitely wrong with Gordon's story. It was like a book with a great plot and a flat ending. And there were inconsistencies. The way Gordon told it, she, Grimsbo and Turner were dedicated detectives. If they were convinced Lake murdered six women and framed Waters, how could they simply let the case go? And why would Lake suddenly leave a thriving practice and disappear if he thought he was in the clear? Had he ever followed up on his romantic interest in Gordon? She hadn't mentioned any contact after the night of Waters' arrest. Finally, there was the question Page had forgotten to ask. What about the women? Gordon had not told him what happened to the missing women.

While he waited for someone in the Hunter's Point Detective Bureau to pick up the phone, Page listed these points on a yellow legal pad. Rolling black storm-clouds were coming in from the west. Page was awfully tired of the rain. Maybe these clouds would give him a break and float across the city before dropping their load. Maybe they would leave a space for the sun to shine through when they left.

'Roy Lenzer.'

Page laid his pen down on the pad.

'Detective Lenzer, I'm Alan Page, the Multnomah County District Attorney. That's in Portland, Oregon.'

'What can I do for you?' Lenzer asked cordially.

'Do you have a detective in your department named Nancy Gordon?'

'Sure, but she's on vacation. Won't be back for a week or so.'

'Can you describe her?'

Lenzer's description matched the woman who had visited Page's apartment.

'Is there something I can help you with?' he asked.

'Maybe. We have an odd situation here. Three women have disappeared. In each case, we found a note in the bedroom pinned down by a rose. Detective Gordon told me she was involved with an identical case in Hunter's Point, approximately ten years ago.'

'It seems to me I heard something about the case, but I've only been on the force for five years. Moved here from Indiana. So I wouldn't be much help.'

'What about Frank Grimsbo or Wayne Turner? They were the other detectives.'

'There's no Grimsbo or Turner in the department now.'

Page heard a rumble of thunder and looked out the window. A flag on the building across the way was snapping back and forth. It looked like it might rip off of the pole.

'I don't suppose there's any chance I can get a copy of the file. The guy who was eventually arrested was Henry Waters . . .'

'W-A-T-E-R-S?'

'Right. He was shot resisting. I think there were six dead women. One of them was named Patricia Cross. Then there was Melody Lake, a young girl, and Sandra Lake, her mother. I don't remember the names of the others.'

'If this happened ten years ago, the file is in storage. I'll get on it and let you know when I find it. What's your address and phone number?'

Page was telling them to Lenzer when Randy Highsmith, the Chief Criminal Deputy, opened the door for William Tobias, the Chief of Police, and Ross Barrow, the detective in charge of the black-rose case. Page motioned them into seats, then hung up.

'We may have a break in the case of the missing women,' Page said. He started relating Gordon's version of the Hunter's Point case.

'Before the body was found at Waters' house, the chief suspect was Peter Lake, a husband of one of the victims,' Page concluded. 'There was enough circumstantial evidence to raise the possibility that Lake framed Waters. Shortly after the case was officially closed, Lake disappeared.

'Two days ago, Gordon received an anonymous note with the words "Women in Portland, Oregon are 'Gone, But Not Forgotten' ". The first letter in each word was capitalized, just the way our boy does it. Enclosed was a photograph of Martin Darius leaving a motel room. Martin Darius may be Peter Lake. Gordon thinks he's our killer.'

'I know Martin Darius,' Tobias said incredulously.

'Everyone knows Darius,' Page said, 'but how much do we know about him?'

Page pushed the photograph of Darius and the newspaper with Lake's picture across the desk. Barrow, Tobias and Highsmith huddled over them.

'Boy,' Highsmith said, shaking his head.

'I don't know, Al,' Tobias said. 'The news photo isn't that clear.'

'Gordon left me Lake's prints for comparison. Can you run them, Ross?'

Barrow nodded and took the print card from Page.

'I'm having a hard time buying this,' Tobias said. 'I'd like to talk to your detective.'

'Let me call her in. I'd like you to hear her tell the story,' Page said, not revealing his doubts, because he wanted them to have an open mind when they heard Gordon.

Page dialed the number for the Lakeview Motel. He asked to be connected with Gordon's room, then leaned back while the desk clerk rang it.

'She's not? Well, this is very important. Do you know when she left? I see. Okay, tell her to call Alan Page as soon as she gets back.'

Page left his number and hung up. 'She checked in last night around one, but she's not in now. It's possible she's having breakfast.'

'What do you want to do, Al?' Highsmith asked.

'I'd like a twenty-four-hour surveillance on Darius, in case Gordon is right.'

'I can do that,' Barrow said.

'Make sure you use good people, Ross. I don't want Darius to suspect we're watching him.

'Randy, run a background check on Darius. I want his life story as quickly as you can get it.'

Highsmith nodded.

'As soon as Gordon calls, I'll get back to you.'

Highsmith led Tobias and Barrow out of the office and closed the door. Page thought of dialing the Lakeview again, but it was too soon after the first call. He swiveled toward the window. It was pouring.

Why hadn't he spotted the flaws in Gordon's story last night? Was it Gordon? She seemed barely in control, on edge, as if electrical charges were coursing through her. He could not take his eyes off of her when she talked. It was not a physical attraction. Something else drew him to her. Her passion, her desperation. Now that she was out of sight, he could think more clearly. When she was near him, she created a disturbance in the field, like the lightning flashing over the river.

2

Betsy scanned the restaurant for single women as she followed the hostess between a row of tables. She noticed a tall, athletic woman wearing a bright yellow blouse and a navy blue suit seated in a booth against the wall. As Betsy drew near, the woman stood up.

'You must be Nora Sloane,' Betsy said, as they shook hands. Sloane's complexion was pale. So were her blue eyes. She wore her chestnut-colored hair short. Betsy noticed a few gray streaks, but she guessed they were about the same age.

'Thank you for meeting me, Mrs Tannenbaum.'

'It's Betsy and you're a good saleswoman. When you called this morning and mentioned a free lunch, you hooked me.'

Sloane laughed. 'I'm glad you're this easy, because a free lunch is about all you're going to get out of me. I'm writing this article on spec. I got the idea when I covered your suit against the anti-abortion protestors for the Arizona Republic.'

'You're from Phoenix?'

'New York, originally. My husband got a job in Phoenix. We separated a year after we moved. I was never crazy about Arizona, especially with my ex living there, and I fell in love with Portland while I was covering your case. So, a month ago, I quit my job and moved. I'm living on savings and looking for a job and I decided now was as good a time as any to write this article. I ran the idea by Gloria Douglas, an editor at *Pacific West* magazine. She's definitely interested, but she won't commit until she sees a draft of the article.'

'What exactly will the article cover?'

'Women litigators. And I want to use you and your cases as the centerpiece.'

'I hope you're not going to make too much of me.'

'Hey, don't get bashful on me,' Sloane said with a laugh. 'Until recently, women attorneys were relegated to the probate department or handled divorces. Stuff that was acceptable as "woman's work". My whole point is that you're at the vanguard of a new generation of women who are trying murder cases and getting million-dollar verdicts in civil cases. Areas that have traditionally been male-dominated.'

'It sounds interesting.'

'I'm glad you think so, because people want to read about you. You're really the hook for the article.'

'What will I have to do?'

'Not much. Mostly, it will be talking to me about Hammermill and your other cases. On occasion, I may want to tag along when you go to court.'

'That sounds okay. Actually, I think talking through my cases might help me to put them in perspective. I was so close to what was happening when they were going on.'

The waiter arrived. Sloane ordered a Caesar Salad and a glass of white wine. Betsy ordered Yellow Fin Tuna on pasta, but passed on the wine.

'What did you want to do today?' Betsy asked, as soon as the waiter left.

'I thought we'd go over some background material. I read the piece in *Time*, but I felt it was superficial. It didn't tell me what made you the way you are today. For instance, were you a leader in high school?'

'God, no,' Betsy laughed. 'I was so shy. A real gawk.'

Sloane smiled. 'I can understand that. You were tall, right? I had the same problem.'

'I towered over everyone. In elementary school, I walked around with my eyes down and my shoulders hunched, wishing I could disappear. In junior high, it got worse, because I had these Coke-bottle glasses and braces. I looked like Frankenstein.'

'When did you start to feel self-confident?'

'I don't know if I ever feel that way. I mean, I know I do a good job, but I always worry I'm not doing enough. But, I guess it was my senior year in high school that I started believing in myself. I was near the top of my class, the braces were gone, my folks got me contacts and boys started noticing me. By the time I graduated Berkeley I was much more outgoing.'

'You met your husband in law school, didn't you?'

Betsy nodded. 'We're separated now.'

'Oh. I'm sorry.'

Betsy shrugged. 'I really don't want to talk about my personal life. Will that be necessary?'

'Not if you don't want to. I'm not writing this for the *Enquirer*.'

'Okay, because I don't want to discuss Rick.'

'I understand you one hundred percent. I went through the same thing in Phoenix. I know how difficult it can be. So, let's move on to something else.'

The waiter arrived with their food and Sloane asked Betsy some more questions about her childhood while they ate.

'You didn't go into private practice right out of law school, did you?' Sloane asked after the waiter cleared their plates.

'No.'

'Why not? You've done so well at it.'

'That's been all luck,' Betsy answered, blushing slightly. 'I never thought of going out on my own, back then. My law-school grades were all right, but not good enough for a big firm. I worked for the Attorney General doing environmental law for four years. I liked the job, but I quit when I became pregnant with Kathy.'

'How old is she?'

'Six.'

'How did you get back into law?'

'I was bored sitting home when Kathy started pre-school. Rick and I talked it over and we decided I would practice out of our home, so I would be there for Kathy. Margaret McKinnon, a friend of mine from law school, let me use her conference room to meet clients. I didn't have much of a case-load. A few court-appointed misde-meanors, some simple divorces. Just enough to keep me busy.

'Then, Margaret offered me a windowless office about the size of a broom closet, rent free, in exchange for twen-ty hours of free legal work, each month. I agonized over that, but Rick said it was okay. He thought it would be good for me to get out of the house, as long as I kept my case-load low enough to pick up Kathy at day care and stay home with her if she got sick. You know, still be a mom. Anyway, it worked out fine and I started picking up some felonies and a few contested divorces that paid better.'

'The Peterson case was your big break, right?'

'Yeah. One day, I was sitting around without much to do and the clerk who assigns court-appointed cases asked me if I'd represent Grace Peterson. I didn't know much about the battered woman's syndrome, but I remembered see-ing Dr Lenore Walker on a TV talk show. She's the expert in this area. The court authorized the money and Lenore came out from Denver and evaluated Grace. It was pretty horrible, what her husband did. I'd led a sheltered life, I guess. No one where I grew up did things like that.'

'No one you knew about.'

Betsy nodded sadly. 'No one I knew about. Anyway, the case attracted a lot of publicity. We had the support of some women's groups and the press was behind us. After the acquittal, my business really picked up. Then Andrea hired me because of the verdict in Grace's case.'

The waiter arrived with their coffee. Sloane looked at her watch. 'You said you had a one-thirty appointment, didn't you?'

Betsy glanced at her own watch. 'Is it one-ten already? I really got wrapped up in this.'

'Good. I was hoping you'd be as excited about the project as I am.'

'I am. Why don't you call me and we can talk again soon?'

'Great. I'll do that. And thanks for taking the time. I really appreciate it.'

3

Randy Highsmith shook the rain off his umbrella and laid it on the floor under the dashboard as Alan Page drove out of the parking garage. The umbrella hadn't helped much in the gusting rain and Highsmith was cold and wet.

Highsmith was slightly overweight, studious-looking, a staunch conservative and the best prosecutor in the office, Page included. While earning a law degree from

Georgetown he'd fallen in love with Patty Archer, a congressional aide. He then fell in love with Portland when he traveled there to meet Patty's family. When her congressman decided not to run for re-election, the newly-weds moved west, where Patty opened a political consulting firm and Randy was snapped up by the Office of the Multnomah County District Attorney.

'Tell me about Darius,' Page said, as they got on the freeway.

'He moved to Portland eight years ago. He had money to start with and borrowed on his assets. Darius made his name, and increased his fortune, by gambling on the revitalization of downtown Portland. His first big success was the Couch Street Boutique. He bought a block of dilapidated buildings for a song, converted them to an indoor mall, then changed the area surrounding the Boutique into the trendiest section in Portland by leasing renovated buildings to upscale shops and restaurants at low rents. As business increased, so did the rents. The upper floors of a lot of the buildings were converted to condos. That's been his pattern. Buy up all the buildings in a slum area, set up a core attraction, then build around it. Recently, he's branched out into suburban malls, apartment complexes, and so on.

'Two years ago, Darius married Lisa Ryder, the daughter of Oregon Supreme Court Justice Victor Ryder. Ryder's old firm, Parish, Marquette and Reeves, handles his legal work. I talked to a few friends over there in confidence. Darius is brilliant and unscrupulous. Half the firm's energy is spent keeping him honest. The other half is spent defending lawsuits when they fail.'

'What's "unscrupulous" mean? Law violations, ethics, what?'

'Nothing illegal. But he has his own set of rules and a total disregard for the feelings of others. For instance, earlier this year he bought up a street of historically significant houses over in the Northwest so he could tear them down and build townhouses. There were several citizen groups up in arms. They got a temporary injunction and were trying to get the houses landmark status. A smart young lawyer at Parish, Marquette convinced the judge to drop the injunction. Darius moved bulldozers in at night and leveled the block before anyone knew what was going on.'

'A guy like that must have done something illegal.'

'The closest I've got is a rumor that he's friendly with Manuel Ochoa, a Mexican businessman who the DEA thinks is laundering money for a South American drug cartel. Ochoa may be lending Darius money for a big project downstate that was risky enough to scare off some of the banks.'

'What about his past?' Page asked as they drove into the parking lot of the Lakeview Motel.

'Doesn't have one, which makes sense if he's Lake.'

'Did you check newspaper stories, profiles?'

'I did better than that. I spoke to the *Oregonian's* top business reporter. Darius does not give interviews about his private life. For all anyone knows, he was born eight years ago.'

Page pulled into a parking spot in front of the motel office. The dashboard clock read five twenty-six.

'Stay here. I'll see if Gordon's back.'

'Okay. But there's one other thing you should know.'

Page waited with the car door half open. 'We've got a link between our missing women and Darius.'

Page closed the door. Highsmith smiled.

'I saved the best for last. Tom Reiser, the husband of Wendy Reiser, works for Parish, Marquette. He's the lawyer who convinced the judge to drop the injunction. Last Christmas, the Reisers attended a party at the Darius estate. This summer, they were invited to a bash to celebrate the opening of a mall, two weeks before the disappearances started. Reiser has had numerous business dealings with Darius.

'Larry Farrar's accounting firm has Darius Construction for a client. He and Laura Farrar were at the party for the mall opening, too. He's done a lot of work for Darius.

'Finally, there's Victoria Miller. Her husband, Russell, works for Brand, Gates and Valcroft. That's the advertising firm that represents Darius Construction. Russell was just put in charge of the account. They've been on Darius's yacht and to his house. They were also at the mall-opening party.'

'That's unbelievable. Look, I want a list of the women at that party. We've got to alert Bill Tobias and Barrow.'

'I already have. They're putting a second team on Darius.'

'Good work. Gordon could be the key to wrapping this up.'

Highsmith watched Page duck into the manager's office. A chubby man in a plaid shirt was standing behind the counter. Page showed the manager his ID and asked him a question. Highsmith saw the manager shake his head. Page said something else. The manager disappeared into a back room and reappeared in a raincoat. He grabbed a key from a hook on the wall. Page followed the manager outside and gestured to Highsmith.

Highsmith slammed the car door and raced under the protection afforded by the second-floor landing. Gordon's room was around the side of the motel on the ground floor. He arrived just as the manager knocked on the door and called out Gordon's name. There was no answer. A window faced into the parking lot. The green drapes were closed. There was a 'Do Not Disturb' sign hanging from the door knob.

'Miss Gordon,' the manager called again. They waited a minute and he shrugged. 'She hasn't been in all day, as far as I know.'

'Okay,' Page said. 'Let us in.'

The manager opened the door with his key and stood aside. The room was dark, but someone had left the bathroom light on and it cast a pale glow over the empty motel room. Page flipped the light switch and looked around the room. The bed was undisturbed. Gordon's tan valise lay open on a baggage stand next to the dresser. Page walked into the bathroom. A toothbrush, a tube of toothpaste and make-up were set out on the bathroom counter. Page pulled back the shower curtain. A bottle of shampoo rested on a ledge. Page stepped out of the bathroom.

'She unpacked in here. There's a shampoo bottle in the bathtub. It's not a motel sample. Looks like she was planning to take a shower as soon as she unpacked.'

'Then someone interrupted her,' Highsmith said,

pointing at a half-opened dresser drawer. Some of Gordon's clothes lay in it, while others remained in the valise.

'She had a briefcase with her when we talked at my place. Do you see it?'

The two men searched the room, but they did not find the briefcase.

'Look at this,' Highsmith said. He was standing next to the night table. Page looked at a note pad with the motel logo that was next to the phone.

'Looks like directions. An address.'

'Let's not touch it. I want a lab tech to dust the room. Treat it as a crime scene, until we know better.'

'There's no sign of a struggle.'

'There wasn't any at the homes of the missing women, either.'

Highsmith nodded. 'I'll call from the manager's office, in case there are prints on the phone.'

'Do you have any idea where this is?' Page asked, as he reread the notes on the pad.

Highsmith's brow furrowed for a moment, then he frowned.

'As a matter of fact, I do. Remember I told you about the houses Darius bulldozed? This sounds like the address.'

'What's there now?'

'A block-wide empty lot. As soon as the neighbors saw what Darius did, they went nuts. There have been protests, lawsuits. Darius went ahead with construction anyway and had three units built, but someone torched them. Construction's been halted ever since.'

'I don't like this. How would anyone know where Gordon was? I'm the one who suggested the Lakeview.'

'She could have phoned someone.'

'No. I asked the manager. There weren't any outgoing calls. Besides, she doesn't know anyone in Portland. That's why she came to my place. She assumed the person who sent her the anonymous letter would meet her at the airport, but no one showed. A clipping about me and my address were in with the note. If she knew anyone else, she would have spent the night with them.'

'Then someone must have followed her from the airport to your place and from your place here.'

'That's possible.'

'What if that person waited until she was in the room, then phoned Gordon and asked her to come to the construction site.'

'Or came here and talked Gordon into going with him or took her by force.'

'Gordon's a detective,' Highsmith said. 'I mean, you'd think she would have enough sense to be careful.'

Page thought about Gordon. Her edge, the tension in her body.

'She's driven, Randy. Gordon told me she stayed a cop so she could track down Lake. She's been on this case for ten years and she dreams about it. Gordon's smart, but she might not be smart where this case is concerned.'

The building site was larger than Page had imagined. The houses Darius had destroyed were built along a bluff overlooking the Columbia River. The land included a steep, wooded hill that angled down toward the water. A high, chain-link fence surrounded the property. A 'Darius Construction – Absolutely No Trespassing' sign was fastened to the fence. Page and Highsmith huddled under their umbrellas, the collars of their raincoats turned up around their cheeks, and studied the padlock on the gate. The moon was full, but storm-clouds scudded across it with great frequency. The heavy rain made the night as dark as it would have been with no moon.

'What do you think?' Highsmith asked.

'Let's walk along the fence to see if there's another entrance. There's no sign she came in here.'

'These are new shoes,' Highsmith complained.

Page started off along the periphery without answering. The ground had been stripped bare of grass during construction. Page felt the mud oozing around his shoes. He peered through the fence as he walked, occasionally shining his flashlight inside the site. Most of the land was empty and flat where the bulldozers had done their work. At one point, he saw a shack. At another, his beam highlighted broken and burned timbers that had once been the framework of a Darius townhouse.

'Al, bring your light here,' Highsmith shouted. He had walked ahead and was pointing at a section of fence that had been sheared through and folded back. Page ran over. He paused just before he reached Highsmith. A gust of cold wind struck his face. Page turned away for a second and clutched his collar closer to his neck.

'Look at this,' Page said. He was standing under an ancient oak tree pointing the flashlight beam toward the ground. Tire tracks had gouged out the mud where they were standing. The canopy formed by the leaves covered the tracks. Page and Highsmith followed them away from the fence.

'Someone drove off the road across the field in this mud,' Page said.

'Not necessarily tonight, though.'

The tracks stopped at the street and disappeared. The rain would have washed away the mud from the asphalt.

'I think the driver backed up to the fence, Al. There's no sign that he turned around.'

'Why back up? Why drive over to the fence at all and risk getting stuck in the mud?'

'What's in the back of a car?'

Page nodded, imagining Nancy Gordon folded in the confined space of a car trunk.

'Let's go,' he said, heading back toward the hole in the fence. In his heart, Page knew she was down there, buried in the soft earth.

Highsmith followed him through. As he ducked, he snagged his coat on a jagged piece of wire. By the time he freed himself, Page was well ahead, obscured by the darkness, only the wavering beam of the flashlight showing his location.

'Do you see any tracks?' Highsmith asked when he caught up.

'Look out!' Page cried, grabbing Highsmith by his coat. Highsmith pulled up. Page shone his light down. They were on the edge of a deep pit that had been gouged out of the earth for a foundation. Muddy walls sloped down toward the bottom, which was lost in darkness. Suddenly, the moon appeared, bathing the bottom of the pit in a pale glow. The uneven surface cast shadows over rocks and mounds of dirt.

'I'm going down,' Page said, as he went over the rim. He

edged along the wall of the pit sideways, leaning into the slope and digging in with the sides of his shoes. Half-way down, he slipped to one knee and slid along the smooth mud, stopping his descent by grabbing a protruding root. The root had been severed by a bulldozer blade. The end came free of the mud, but Page slowed enough to dig in and stop his slide.

'You okay?' Highsmith called into the wind.

'Yeah. Randy, get down here. Someone's been digging recently.'

Highsmith swore, then started edging down the slope. When he reached the bottom, Page was wandering slowly over the muddy ground, studying everything that entered the beam of his flashlight. The ground looked as if it had been turned over recently. He examined it as closely as he could in the dark.

The wind died suddenly and Page thought he heard a sound. Something slithering in the shadows just out of his line of sight. He tensed, trying to hear above the wind, peering helplessly into the darkness. When he convinced himself he was the victim of his imagination, he turned around and shone the light near the base of a steel girder. Page straightened suddenly and took a step back, catching his heel on a timber half concealed in the mud. He stumbled and the flashlight fell, its beam fanning out over the rain-soaked earth, catching something white in the light. A rock or a paper cup. Page knelt quickly and recovered the flashlight. He walked over to the object and squatted next to it. His breath caught in his chest. Protruding from the earth was a human hand.

*

The sun was just coming up when they dug the last body out of the ground. The horizon took on a scarlet tinge as two officers lifted the corpse on to a stretcher. Around them, other officers walked slowly over the muddy floor of the construction site in search of more graves, but the area had been scoured so thoroughly that no one expected to find one.

A prowl car perched on the edge of the pit. The door on the driver's side was open. Alan Page sat in the front seat with one foot on the ground, holding a paper cup filled with scalding black coffee, trying not to think about Nancy Gordon and thinking of nothing else.

Page rested his head against the back of the seat. As the darkness retreated, the river began taking on dimension. Page watched the flat black ribbon turn liquid and turbulent in the red dawn. He believed Nancy Gordon was in the pit, buried under layers of mud. He wondered if there was something he could have done to save her. He imagined Gordon's frustration and rage when she died at the hands of the man she had sworn to stop.

The rain had ended shortly after the first police car arrived. Ross Barrow took charge of the crime scene, after consulting with the lab techs about the best way to handle the evidence. Flood lights shone down on the workers from the rim of the pit. Designated search-areas were fenced off with yellow tape. Saw horses had been erected as barriers against the curious. As soon as Page was certain Barrow could get along without him, he and Highsmith had grabbed a quick dinner at a local restaurant. By the time they returned, Barrow had positively identified Wendy Reiser's body and an officer had located a second grave.

Through the windshield, Page watched Randy Highsmith trudge toward the car. He had been in the pit observing while Page took a break.

'That's the last one,' Highsmith said.

'What have we got?'

'Four bodies and positive IDs on Laura Farrar, Wendy Reiser and Victoria Miller.'

'Were they killed like Patricia Cross?'

'I didn't look that closely, Al. To tell the truth, I almost lost it. Dr Gregg is down there. She can give you the straight scoop when she comes up.'

Page nodded. He was used to dealing with the dead, but that didn't mean he liked looking at a corpse any more than Highsmith.

'What about the fourth woman?' Page asked hesitantly. 'Does she match my description of Nancy Gordon?'

'It's not a woman, Al.'

'What!'

'It's an adult male, also naked and his face and fingertips were burned away with acid. We'll be lucky to identify him.'

Page saw Ross Barrow slogging through the mud and got out of the car.

'You're not stopping, Ross?'

'There's nothing more down there. You can look if you want.'

'I was sure that Gordon . . . It doesn't make sense. She wrote the address.'

'Maybe she met someone here and left with them,' Barrow suggested.

'We didn't find any footprints,' Highsmith reminded him. 'She may not have found a way in.'

'Did you find anything down there that'll help us figure out who did this?'

'Not a thing, Al. I'm guessing all four were killed elsewhere and transported here.'

'Why's that?'

'Some of the bodies are missing organs. We haven't found them or any pieces of bone or excess flesh. No one could clean the area that thoroughly.'

'Do you think we have enough to arrest Darius?' Page asked Highsmith.

'Not without Gordon or some solid evidence from Hunter's Point.'

'What if we don't find her?' Page asked anxiously.

'In a pinch, you could swear to what she told you. We might get a warrant out of a judge with that. She's a cop. She'd be reliable. But, I don't know. With something like this, we shouldn't rush.'

'And we don't really have a solid connection between Darius and the victims,' Barrow added. 'Finding them at a site owned by Darius Construction doesn't mean a thing. Especially when it's deserted and anyone could have gotten in.'

'Do we know if Darius is Lake?' Page asked Barrow.

'Yeah. The prints match.'

'Well, that's something,' Highsmith said. 'If we can get a match between those tire tracks and one of Darius's cars . . .'

'And, if we can find Nancy Gordon,' Page said, staring into the pit. He desperately wanted Gordon to be alive, but he had been in the business of violent death and lost hopes too long to grasp at straws.

Chapter Eight

1

'Detective Lenzer, this is Alan Page from Portland, Oregon. We talked the other day.'

'Right. I was going to call you. That file you asked for is missing. We switched to computers seven years ago, but I did a search anyway. When I couldn't find it listed, I had a secretary go through the old files in storage. There's no file card and no file.'

'Did someone check it out?'

'If they did, they didn't follow procedure. You're supposed to fill in a log sheet in case someone else needs the file, and there's no log entry.'

'Could Detective Gordon have checked it out? She had a fingerprint card with her. It probably came from the file.'

'The file isn't with her stuff in the office and it's against departmental policy to take files home unless you log them out. There's no record showing anyone logged it out. Besides, if there were six dead women it would be the highest victim count we've ever had here. We're probably talking about a file that would take up an entire shelf. Maybe more. Why would she be lugging around something that big? Hell, you'd need a couple of suitcases to get it home.'

Page thought that over. 'You're certain it's not in storage and just misplaced?'

'The file's not in storage, believe me. The person who looked for it did a real thorough job and *I* even went down there for a while.'

Page was silent for a moment. He decided to tell Lenzer everything.

'Detective Lenzer, I'm pretty sure Nancy Gordon's in danger. She may even be dead.'

'What?'

'I met her for the first time two nights ago and she told me about the Hunter's Point murders. She was convinced the man who committed them is living in Portland under a different name, committing similar crimes here.

'Gordon left my apartment a little after midnight and took a cab to a motel. Shortly after checking in, she left in a hurry. We found an address on a pad in her motel room. It's a construction site. We searched it and discovered the bodies of three missing Portland women and an unidentified man. They were tortured to death. We have no idea where Gordon is, and I'm thinking she was right about your killer being in Portland.'

'Jesus. I like Nancy. She's a little intense, but she's a very good cop.'

'The key to this case could be in the Hunter's Point files. She may have brought them home. I would suggest searching her house.'

'I'll do anything I can to help.'

Page told Lenzer to call him any time, gave him his home number, then hung up. Lenzer had characterized Gordon as intense and Page had to agree. She was also dedicated. Ten years on the trail and still burning with that fire. Page had been like that once, but the years were getting to him. Tina's affair and the divorce had sucked him dry emotionally, but he had been losing ground even before her infidelity took over his life. Fighting for the office of District Attorney had been great. Every day was exciting. Then, he woke up one morning with the responsibilities of the job and the fear that he might not be able to fulfill them. He had mastered those fears through hard work, and he had mastered the job, but the thrill was gone. The days were all getting to be the same, and he was starting to think about what he would be doing ten years down the road.

The intercom buzzed and Page hit the com button.

'There's a man on line three with information about one of the women who was killed at the construction site,' his secretary said. 'I think you should talk to him.'

'Okay. What's his name?'

'Ramon Gutierrez. He's the clerk at the Hacienda Motel in Vancouver, Washington.'

Page hit the button for line three and talked to Ramon Gutierrez for five minutes. When he was done, he called Ross Barrow, then headed down the hall to Randy Highsmith's office. Fifteen minutes later, Barrow picked up Highsmith and Page on the corner and they headed for Vancouver.

2

'Can I watch TV?' Kathy asked.

'Did you have enough pizza?'

'I'm stuffed.'

Betsy felt guilty about dinner, but she had put in an exhausting day in court and didn't have the energy to cook.

'Is Daddy going to come home tonight?' Kathy asked, looking up at Betsy expectantly.

'No,' Betsy answered, hoping Kathy would not ask her any more about Rick. She had explained the separation to Kathy a number of times, but Kathy would not accept the fact that Rick was most probably never going to live with them again.

Kathy looked worried. 'Why won't Daddy stay with us?'

Betsy picked up Kathy and carried her to the living-room couch.

'Who's your best friend?'

'Melanie.'

'Remember the fight you two had last week?'

'Yeah.'

'Well, Daddy and I had an argument, too. It's a serious one. Just like the one you had with your best friend.'

Kathy looked confused. Betsy held Kathy on her lap and kissed the top of her head.

'Melanie and me made up. Are you and Daddy going to make up?'

'Maybe. I don't know right now. Meanwhile, Daddy is living someplace else.'

'Is Daddy mad at you because he had to pick me up at day care?'

'What made you ask that?'

'He was awful mad the other day and I heard you arguing about me.'

'No, honey,' Betsy said, hugging Kathy tight to her. 'This doesn't have anything to do with you. It's just us. We're mad at each other.'

'Why?' Kathy asked. Her jaw was quivering.

'Don't cry, honey.'

'I want Daddy,' she said, sobbing into Betsy's shoulder. 'I don't want him to go away.'

'He won't go away. He'll always be your Daddy, Kathy. He loves you.'

Suddenly, Kathy pushed away from Betsy and wriggled off her lap.

'It's your fault for working,' she yelled.

Betsy was shocked. 'Who told you that?'

'Daddy. You should stay home with me like Melanie's mom.'

'Daddy works,' Betsy said, trying to stay calm. 'He works more than I do.'

'Men are supposed to work. You're supposed to take care of me.'

Betsy wished Rick was here so she could smash him with her fists.

'Who stayed home with you when you had the flu?' Betsy asked.

Kathy thought for a moment. 'You, Mommy,' she answered, looking up at Betsy.

'And when you hurt your knee at school, who came to take you home?'

Kathy looked down at the floor.

'What do you want to be when you grow up?'

'An actress or a doctor.'

'That's work, honey. Doctors and actresses work just like lawyers. If you stayed home all day, you couldn't do that work.'

Kathy stopped crying. Betsy picked her up again.

'I work because it's fun. I also take care of you. That's more fun. I love you much more than I like my work. It's no contest. But I don't want to stay home all day doing nothing while you're at school. It would be boring, don't you think?'

Kathy thought about that.

'Will you make up with Daddy, like I did with Melanie?'

'I'm not sure, honey. But either way, you'll see plenty of Daddy. He still loves you very much and he'll always be your dad.

'Now, why don't you watch a little TV and I'll clean up, then I'll read you another chapter of *The Wizard of Oz*.'

'I don't feel like TV tonight.'

'Do you want to help me in the kitchen?'

Kathy shrugged.

'How about a hot chocolate? I could make one while we're cleaning the dishes.'

'Okay,' Kathy said without much enthusiasm. Betsy followed her daughter into the kitchen. She was too small to have to carry the heavy burden of her parents' problems, but she was going to anyway. That was the way it worked and there was nothing Betsy could do about it.

After they were finished in the kitchen, Betsy read Kathy two chapters of *The Wizard of Oz*, then put her to bed. It was almost nine o'clock. Betsy looked at the TV listings and was about to turn on the set when the phone rang.

She walked into the kitchen and picked up on the third ring.

'Betsy Tannenbaum?' a man asked.

'Speaking.'

'This is Martin Darius. The police are at my home with a search warrant. I want you over here immediately.'

A high brick wall surrounded the Darius estate. A policeman in a squad car was parked next to a black wrought-iron gate. As Betsy turned the Subaru into the driveway, the policeman got out of his car and walked over to her window.

'I'm afraid you can't go in, ma'am.'

'I'm Mr Darius's attorney,' Betsy said, holding her Bar card out the window. The officer examined the card for a second, then returned it to her.

'My orders are to keep everyone out.'

'I can assure you that doesn't include Mr Darius's attorney.'

'Ma'am, there's a search being conducted. You'd be in the way.'

'I'm here because of the search. A warrant to search doesn't give the police the right to bar people from the place being searched. You have a walkie-talkie in your car. Why don't you call the detective in charge and ask him if I can come in.'

The officer's patronizing smile was replaced by a Clint Eastwood stare, but he walked back to his car and used the walkie-talkie. He returned less than a minute later, and he did not look happy.

'Detective Barrow says you can go in.'

'Thank you,' Betsy answered politely. As she drove off, in the rear-view mirror she could see the cop glaring after her.

After seeing the old-fashioned brick wall and the ornate scroll work on the wrought-iron gate, Betsy assumed Darius would live in a sedate, colonial mansion, but she found herself staring at a collection of glass and steel fashioned into sharp angles and delicate curves that had nothing to do with the nineteenth century. She parked next to a squad car near the end of a curved driveway. A bridge covered by a blue awning connected the driveway with the front door. Betsy looked down through a glass roof as she walked along the bridge and saw several officers standing around the edge of an indoor pool.

A policeman was waiting for her at the front door. He guided her down a short set of stairs into a cavernous living-room. Darius was standing under a giant abstract painting in vivid reds and garish greens. Beside him was a slender woman in a black dress. Her shiny black hair cascaded over her shoulders and her tan spoke of a recent vacation in the tropics. She was stunningly beautiful.

The man standing next to Darius was not. He had a beer gut and a face that would be more at home in a sports bar than a condo in the Bahamas. He was dressed in an unpressed brown suit and white shirt. His tie was askew and his raincoat was draped unceremoniously over the back of a snow-white sofa.

Before Betsy could say anything Darius thrust a rolled-up paper at her.

'Is this a valid warrant? I'm not going to permit an invasion of my privacy until you've looked at the damn thing.'

'I'm Ross Barrow, Ms Tannenbaum,' said the man in the brown suit. 'This warrant's been signed by Judge Reese. The sooner you tell your client we can go through with this, the sooner we'll be out of here. I could have started already, but I waited for you to make certain Mr Darius had representation during the search.'

If Darius had been a black dope dealer instead of a prominent, white socialite and businessman, Betsy knew the house would have been a shambles by the time she arrived. Somebody had ordered Barrow to go very slowly with this case.

'The warrant seems okay, but I'd like to see the affidavit,' Betsy said, asking for the document the police prepare to convince a judge that there is probable cause for the issuance of a warrant to search someone's house. The affidavit would contain the factual basis for the suspicion that somewhere in the Darius mansion was evidence of a crime.

'Sorry, the affidavit's been sealed.'

'Can you at least tell me why you're searching. I mean, what are the charges?'

'There aren't any charges, yet.'

'Let's not play games, Detective. You don't roust someone like Martin Darius without a reason.'

'You're going to have to ask District Attorney Page about the case, Ms Tannenbaum. I've been told to refer all inquiries to him.'

'Where can I reach him?'

'I'm afraid I don't know that. He's probably home, but I'm not authorized to give out that number.'

'What kind of bullshit is this?' Darius asked angrily.

'Calm down, Mr Darius,' Betsy said. 'The warrant is legal

147

and he can search. There's nothing we can do now. If it turns out that the affidavit is faulty, we'll be able to suppress any evidence they find.'

'Evidence of what?' Darius demanded. 'They refuse to tell me what they're looking for.'

'Martin,' the woman in black said, laying a hand on his forearm. 'Let them search. Please. I want them out of here and they're not going to leave until they're through.'

Darius pulled his arm away. 'Search the damn house,' he told Barrow angrily, 'but you'd better get yourself a good lawyer, because I'm going to sue your ass all over this state.'

Detective Barrow walked away, the insults bouncing ineffectively off of his broad back. Just as he reached the steps leading out of the living-room, a gray-haired man in a windbreaker entered the house.

'The tread on the BMW matches and there's a black Ferrari in the garage,' Betsy heard him say. Barrow motioned to two uniforms who were standing in the entryway. They followed him back to Darius.

'Mr Darius, I'm placing you under arrest for the murders of Wendy Reiser, Laura Farrar and Victoria Miller.'

The color drained from Darius's face and the woman's hand flew to her mouth as if she was going to be sick.

'You have the right to remain silent . . .' Barrow said, reading from a laminated card he had taken from his wallet.

'What the fuck is this?' Darius exploded.

'What is he talking about?' the woman asked Betsy.

'I have to inform you of these rights, Mr Darius.'

'I think we're entitled to an explanation, Detective Barrow,' Betsy said.

'No, ma'am, you're not,' Barrow responded. Then he finished reading Darius his Miranda rights.

'Now, Mr Darius,' Barrow went on, 'I'm going to have to handcuff you. This is procedure. We do it with everyone we arrest.'

'You're not handcuffing anyone,' Darius said, taking a step back.

'Mr Darius, don't resist,' Betsy said. 'You can't do that, even if the arrest is illegal. Go with him. Just don't say a thing.'

'Detective Barrow, I want to accompany Mr Darius to the station.'

'That won't be possible. I assume you don't want him questioned, so we'll book him in as soon as we get downtown. I wouldn't go down to the jail until tomorrow morning. I can't guarantee when he'll finish the booking process.'

'What's my bail?' Darius demanded.

'There isn't any for murder, Mr Darius,' Barrow answered calmly. 'Ms Tannenbaum can ask for a bail hearing.'

'What's he saying?' the woman asked in disbelief.

'May I talk with Mr Darius for a moment in private?' Betsy asked.

Barrow nodded. 'You can go over there,' he said, pointing to a corner of the living-room away from the windows. Betsy led Darius to the corner. The woman tried to follow, but Barrow told her she could not join them.

'What's this about no bail? I'm not sitting in some jail with a bunch of drug dealers and pimps.'

'There's no automatic bail for murder or treason, Mr

Darius. It's in the Constitution. But there is a way to get a judge to set bail. I'll schedule a bail hearing as soon as possible and I'll see you first thing in the morning.'

'I don't believe this.'

'Believe it and listen to me. Anything you tell anyone will be used to convict you. I don't want you talking to a soul. Not the cops, not a cell-mate. No one. There are snitches at the jail who'll trade you to beat their case and every guard will repeat every word you say to the DA.'

'Goddamn it, Tannenbaum. You get me out of this fast. I paid you to protect me. I'm not going to rot in jail.'

Betsy saw Detective Barrow motion the two officers toward them.

'Remember, not a word,' she said as Barrow reached them.

'Hands behind you, please,' said one of the uniforms. Darius complied and the officer snapped on the cuffs. The woman watched in wide-eyed disbelief.

'I'll expect you first thing in the morning,' Darius said as they led him away.

'I'll be there.'

Betsy felt a hand on her arm.

'Ms Tannenbaum . . .?'

'It's Betsy.'

'I'm Martin's wife, Lisa. What's happening? Why are they taking Martin away?'

Lisa Darius looked bewildered, but Betsy did not see any tears. She seemed more like a hostess whose party has been a stunning flop than a wife whose husband had just been arrested for mass murder.

'You know as much as I do, Lisa. Did the police mention

anything about why they were at your home?'

'They said . . . I can't believe what they said. They asked us about the three women who were found at Martin's construction site.'

'That's right,' Betsy said, suddenly remembering why the names Barrow had spoken sounded so familiar.

'Martin couldn't have had anything to do with that. We know the Millers. They were out on our yacht this summer. This has to be a mistake.'

'Mrs Darius?'

Betsy and Lisa Darius looked toward the living-room stairs. A black detective dressed in jeans and a black and red Portland Trailblazer jacket was walking toward them.

'We're going to seize your BMW. May I have your key, please?' he asked politely, handing her a yellow carbon of a property receipt.

'Our car? Can they do this?' Lisa asked Betsy.

'The warrant mentioned cars.'

'Oh, God. Where will this end?'

'I'm afraid my men are going to have to search your house,' the detective told her apologetically. 'We'll try to be neat and put everything back that we don't take. If you like, you can come along with us.'

'I can't. Just be quick, please. I want you out of my house.'

The detective was embarrassed. He looked down at the carpet as he walked off. Barrow had taken his raincoat with him, but there was a damp spot on the sofa where it had lain. Lisa Darius looked at the spot with distaste and sat as far from it as she could. Betsy sat next to her.

'How long is Martin going to be in jail?'

'That depends. The State has the burden of convincing the court that it's got a damn good case, if it wants to hold Martin without bail. I'll ask for an immediate hearing. If the State can't meet its burden, he'll be out quickly. If they meet it, he won't get out at all, unless we get a not guilty verdict.'

'This is unbelievable.'

'Lisa,' Betsy asked cautiously, 'did you have any idea something like this might happen?'

'What do you mean?'

'It's been my experience that the police usually don't act unless they have a pretty good case. They make mistakes, of course, but that's rarer than you'd think from the way they're portrayed on television. And your husband's no street punk. I can't imagine Alan Page rousting someone of Martin's stature in the community without some pretty strong evidence. Especially on a charge like this.'

Lisa stared open-mouthed at Betsy for a moment.

'Are you suggesting . . . ? I thought you were Martin's lawyer. If you don't believe him, you have no business handling his case. I don't know why he hired you anyway. Daddy says Oscar Montoya and Matthew Reynolds are the best criminal lawyers in Oregon. He could have had either one of them.'

'A lawyer who only thinks what her client wants her to think isn't doing her job,' Betsy said calmly. 'If there's something you know about these charges, I have to know it, so I can defend Martin properly.'

'Well, there isn't,' Lisa answered, looking away from Betsy. 'The whole thing is outrageous.'

Betsy decided not to push. 'Do you have anyone who

can stay with you?' she asked.

'I'll be fine by myself.'

'This will get rough, Lisa. The press will be hounding you night and day and living in a spotlight is much worse than most people imagine. Do you have an answering machine you can use to screen your calls?'

Lisa nodded.

'Good. Put it on and don't take any calls from the media. Since we don't have any idea of the case against Martin, we don't know what can hurt him. For instance, where Martin was on a certain date might be crucial. If you tell the press he wasn't with you on that date, it could destroy an alibi. So don't say anything. If a reporter does get through to you, refer her to me. And never talk to the police or someone from the DA's Office. There's a privilege for husband-wife communications and you have a right to refuse to talk to anyone. Do you understand?'

'Yes. I'll be okay. And I'm sorry I said that. About how Martin could have gotten someone better. I'm just . . .'

'No need to apologize or explain. This must be very difficult for you.'

'You don't have to stay with me.'

'I'll stay until the search is finished. I want to see what they're taking. It might tell us why they think Martin's involved. I heard one officer tell Barrow they matched the tread on the BMW to something. That means they've placed Martin's car somewhere. Maybe the crime scene.'

'So what? He drives to his construction sites all the time. This whole thing is ridiculous.'

'We'll see soon enough,' Betsy said, but she was worried. Lisa Darius may have been shocked and surprised by her husband's arrest, but Betsy knew Martin Darius was not. No one gives a $58,000 retainer to a lawyer in anticipation of being arrested for shoplifting. That was the type of retainer a good lawyer received for representing someone on a murder charge.

Chapter Nine

'It's a pleasure to meet you, Ms Tannenbaum,' Alan Page said when Betsy was seated across his desk from him. 'Randy Highsmith was very impressed with the way you handled the Hammermill case. He had nothing but nice things to say about you. That's really high praise, because Randy hates to lose.'

'I think Randy might not have brought the charges if he knew how brutal Andrea's husband was.'

'That's being charitable. Let's face it. Randy thought he'd run over you. You taught him a good lesson. Losing Hammermill will make Randy a better prosecutor. But you're not here to talk about old business, are you? You're here to talk about Martin Darius.'

'Detective Barrow must have called you at home at the phone number he wouldn't give me.'

'Ross Barrow's a good cop who knows how to follow orders.'

'Do you want to tell me why you've arrested my client?'

'I think he murdered the four people we found buried at his construction site.'

'That's obvious, Mr Page . . .'

'Why don't you call me Al?'

'I'd be glad to. And you may call me Betsy. Now that we're on a first-name basis, how about telling me why you searched Martin's house and arrested him?'

Page smiled. ' 'Fraid I can't do that.'

'Won't, you mean.'

'Betsy, you know you're not entitled to discovery of our police reports until I've filed an indictment.'

'You're going to have to tell the judge what you've got at the bail hearing.'

'True. But that's not scheduled yet and there's no indictment, so I'm going to stick to the letter of the discovery statutes.'

Betsy leaned back in her chair and smiled sweetly.

'You must not have much confidence in your case, Al.'

Page laughed to cover his surprise that Betsy had seen through him so easily.

'I've got plenty of confidence in our case,' he lied. 'But I also have a healthy respect for your abilities. I won't make Randy's mistake of underestimating you. I must confess, though, that with your commitment to feminism I was surprised when Ross told me you were defending Darius.'

'What does feminism have to do with my representation of Martin Darius?'

'Hasn't he told you what he's done?'

'Martin Darius has no idea why you're holding him and neither do I.'

Page looked at her for a moment, then made a decision.

156

'I guess it's not fair leaving you completely in the dark, so I'll tell you that we plan to indict your client for the kidnapping, torture and murder of three women and one man.'

Page took a color photo of Wendy Reiser's body out of a manilla envelope and handed it to Betsy. She blanched. The picture had been taken right after the body had been dug up. The naked woman was sprawled in the mud. Betsy could see the incisions on her stomach and the cuts and burn marks on her legs. She could also see Wendy Reiser's face clearly. Even in death, she seemed to be suffering.

'That's what Martin Darius does to women, Betsy, and this may not be the first time he's done it. We have pretty solid information that ten years ago a man named Peter Lake murdered six women in Hunter's Point, New York in much the same way these victims were murdered. We also have conclusive proof that Peter Lake and Martin Darius are the same person. You might want to ask your client about that.

'One other thing. There's another missing woman. This is a one-time offer: if she's alive and Darius tells us where she is, we might be able to deal.'

The jail elevator opened on to a narrow concrete hallway painted in yellow and brown pastels. Across from the elevator were three solid doors. Betsy used the key the guard had given her when she checked in at the visitors' desk. The middle door opened into a tiny room. In front of her was a wall divided in half by a narrow ledge. Below the ledge was concrete, above a slab of bullet-proof glass. Betsy placed her legal pad on the ledge, sat down on an uncomfortable metal folding chair and picked up the receiver on the phone that was attached to the wall to her left.

On the other side of the glass, Martin Darius lifted his receiver. He was dressed in an orange jump-suit, but he still looked as imposing as he had in her office. His hair and beard were combed and he sat erect and at ease. Darius leaned forward until he was almost touching the glass. His eyes looked a little wild, but that was the only sign of discontent.

'When is the bail hearing scheduled?' Darius asked.

'It isn't.'

'I told you I wanted out of here. You should have scheduled the hearing first thing this morning.'

'This isn't going to work. I'm an attorney, not a gofer. If you want someone to order around I'll refer you to a maid service.'

Darius stared at Betsy for a moment, then flashed an icy smile of concession.

'Sorry. Twelve hours in this place doesn't help your disposition.'

'I met with Alan Page, the District Attorney, this morning. He had some interesting things to tell me. He also showed me the crime-scene photographs. The three women were tortured, Martin. I've seen a lot of cruelty, but nothing like this. The killer didn't just end their lives, he slaughtered them. Tore them open . . .'

Betsy stopped, as the memory of what she'd seen took her breath away. Darius watched her. She waited for him to say something. When he didn't, she asked, 'Does any of this sound familiar?'

'I didn't kill those women.'

'I didn't ask you if you killed them. I asked if anything about the crimes sounded familiar.'

Darius studied Betsy. She didn't like the way he made her feel like a lab specimen.

'Why are you interrogating me?' Darius asked. 'You work for me, not the DA.'

'Mr Darius, I decide who I work for and right now I'm not so sure I want to work for you.'

'Page said something, didn't he? He played with your head.'

'Who is Peter Lake?'

Betsy expected a reaction, but not the one she got. The look of icy calm deserted Darius. His lip trembled. He looked, suddenly, like a man on the verge of tears.

'So Page knows about Hunter's Point.'

'You haven't been honest with me, Mr Darius.'

'Is that what this is all about?' Darius asked, pointing at the bullet-proof glass. 'Is that why you didn't ask for a contact visit? Are you afraid to be locked in with me? Afraid I'll . . .'

Darius stopped. He put his head in his hands.

'I don't think I'm the right person to represent you,' Betsy told him.

'Why?' Darius asked, his voice filled with pain. 'Because Page claims I raped and murdered those women? Did you refuse to represent Andrea Hammermill when the district attorney said she murdered her husband?'

'Andrea Hammermill was the victim of a husband who beat her constantly during her marriage.'

'But she killed him, Betsy. I did *not* murder those women.

159

I swear it. I did *not* kill anyone in Hunter's Point. I was Peter Lake, but, do you know who Peter Lake was? Did Page tell you that? Does he even know?

'Peter Lake was married to the most wonderful woman in the world. He was the father of a perfect child. A little girl who never hurt anyone. And his wife and daughter were murdered by a madman named Henry Waters for an insane reason Peter could never fathom.

'Peter was a lawyer. He made money hand over fist. He lived in a magnificent house and drove a fancy car, but all that money and everything he owned couldn't make him forget the wife and daughter who'd been taken from him. So, he ran away. He assumed a new identity and started a new life, because his old life was impossible to bear.'

Darius stopped talking. There were tears in his eyes. Betsy did not know what to think. Moments ago, she was convinced Darius was a monster. Now, seeing his pain, she wasn't so sure.

'I'll make you a deal, Betsy,' Darius said, his voice barely above a whisper. 'If you reach the point where you don't believe I'm innocent, you can walk away from my case with my blessing, and you can keep your retainer.'

Betsy did not know what to say. Those pictures. She couldn't stop wondering how the women felt in those first, long moments of terror, knowing that the best that could ever happen to them in the rest of their lives was a death that would bring an end to their pain.

'It's all right,' Darius said, 'I know how you feel. You only saw the pictures. I saw the dead bodies of my wife and my child. And I still see them, Betsy.'

Betsy felt ill. She took a deep breath. She could not stay in

the narrow room any longer. She needed air. And she needed to find out a lot more about Peter Lake and what
happened in Hunter's Point.

'Are you okay?' Darius asked.

'No, I'm not. I'm very confused.'

'I know you are. Page laid a heavy trip on you. They said
I'd be arraigned tomorrow. You get a good night's sleep
and tell me what you've decided to do, then.'

Betsy nodded.

'Two things, though,' Darius said, looking directly at
Betsy.

'What's that?'

'If you decide to keep me as a client, you've got to fight
like hell for me.'

'And the other thing?'

'From now on, I want every visit to be a contact visit. No
more glass cage. I don't want my lawyer treating me like a
zoo animal.'

Chapter Ten

As soon as Rita Cohen opened the door wide enough, Kathy squeezed through and raced into the kitchen.

'You didn't buy that bubble-gum-flavored cereal again, did you, Mom?' Betsy asked.

'She's a little kid, Betsy. Who could stand that healthy stuff you feed her all the time? Let her live.'

'That's what I'm trying to do. If it was up to you, she'd be on an all-cholesterol diet.'

'When I was growing up, we didn't know from cholesterol. We ate what made us happy, not the same stuff you feed horses. And look at me. Seventy-four and still going strong.'

Betsy hugged her mother and gave her a kiss on the forehead. Rita was only five four, so Betsy had to bend down to do it. Betsy's dad never topped five nine. No one could figure where Betsy got her height.

'How come there's no school?' Rita asked.

'It's another teacher planning day. I forgot to read the flyer they sent home, so I didn't know until yesterday evening when Kathy mentioned it.'

'You have time for a cup of coffee?' Rita asked.

Betsy looked at her watch. It was only seven-twenty. They would not let her into the jail to see Darius until eight.

'Sure,' she said, dropping the backpack with Kathy's things on a chair and following her mother into the living-room. The television was already on, tuned to a morning talk show.

'Don't let her watch too much TV,' Betsy said, sitting down on the couch. 'I packed some books and games for her.'

'A little television isn't going to kill her any more than that cereal.'

Betsy laughed. 'One day with you undoes all the good habits I've instilled in a year. You're an absolute menace.'

'Nonsense,' Rita answered gruffly, pouring two cups of coffee from the pot she had prepared in expectation of Betsy's visit. 'So, what are you doing this morning that's so important you had to abandon that lovely angel to such an ogre?'

'You've heard of Martin Darius?'

'Certainly.'

'I'm representing him.'

'What did he do?'

'The DA thinks Darius raped and killed the three women they found at his construction site. He also thinks Darius tortured and killed six women in Hunter's Point, New York ten years ago.'

'Oh my God! Is he guilty?'

'I don't know. Darius swears he's innocent.'

'And you believe him?'

Betsy shook her head. 'It's too early to say.'

'He's a rich man, Betsy. The police wouldn't arrest some-one that important without proof.'

'If I took the State's word for everything, Andrea Hammermill and Grace Peterson would be in prison today.'

Rita looked concerned. 'Should you be representing a man who rapes and tortures women after all the work you've done for women's rights?'

'We don't know that he tortured anyone, Mom, and that feminist label is something the press stuck on me. I want to work for women's rights, but I'm not just a woman's lawyer. This case will help me be seen as more than one-dimensional. It could make my career. And, more important, Darius may be innocent. The DA won't tell me why he thinks Darius is guilty. That makes me very suspi-cious. If he had the goods on Darius he'd be confident enough to tell me what he's got.'

'I just don't want to see you get hurt.'

'I won't get hurt, Mom, because I'll do a good job. I learned something when I won Grace's case. I have a talent. I'm a very good trial attorney. I have a knack for talking to jurors. I'm damned good at cross-examination. If I win this case people across the country are going to know how good I am, and that's why I want this case so badly. But I'm going to need your help.'

'What do you mean?'

'The case is going to go on for at least a year. The trial could last for months. With the State asking for the death penalty I'm going to have to fight every step of the way and the case is extremely complicated. It's going to take all my time. We're talking about events that occurred ten years ago. I've got to find out everything there is to know about Hunter's Point, Darius's background. That means I'll be working long hours and weekends and I'm going to need help with Kathy. Someone has to pick her up from day care, if I'm tied up in court, make her dinner . . .'

'What about Rick?'

'I can't ask him. You know why.'

'No, I don't know why. He's Kathy's father. He's also your husband. He should be your biggest fan.'

'Well, he's not. He's never accepted the fact that I'm a real lawyer with a successful practice.'

'What did he think you'd be doing when you hung out your shingle?'

'I think he thought it was going to be a cute hobby like stamp collecting, something to keep me occupied when I wasn't cooking dinner or cleaning.'

'Well, he is the man of the house. Men like to feel they're in charge. And here you are, getting all the headlines and talking on the television.'

'Look, Mom, I don't want to discuss Rick. Do you mind? I just get angry.'

'All right, I won't discuss him and, of course, I'll help.'

'I don't know how I'd make it without you, Mom.'

Rita blushed and waved a hand at Betsy. 'That's what mothers are for.'

'Granny,' Kathy yelled from the kitchen, 'I can't find the chocolate syrup.'

'Why would she want chocolate syrup at seven-thirty in the morning?' Betsy asked menacingly.

'None of your business,' Rita answered imperiously. 'I'm coming, sweetheart. It's too high up. You can't reach it.'

'I've got to go,' Betsy said, with a resigned shake of the head. 'And please keep the TV to a minimum.'

'We're only reading Shakespeare and studying algebra this morning,' Rita answered as she disappeared into the kitchen.

Reggie Stewart was waiting for Betsy on a bench near the visitors' desk at the jail. Stewart had worked at several unsatisfying jobs before discovering a talent for investigation. He was a slender six-footer with shaggy brown hair and bright blue eyes, who was most comfortable in plaid flannel shirts, cowboy boots and jeans. Stewart had an odd way of looking at events and a sarcastic air that put off some people. Betsy appreciated the way he used his imagination and his knack for making people trust him. These attributes proved invaluable in the Hammermill and Peterson cases, where the best evidence of abuse came from the victims' relatives and would have remained buried under layers of hate and family pride if it was not for Reggie's persuasiveness and persistence.

'Ready, Chief?' Stewart asked, smiling as he unwound from the bench.

'Always,' Betsy answered with a smile.

Stewart had filled out visitor's forms for both of them. A guard sat behind a glass window in a control room. Betsy pushed the forms and their ID through a slot in the window and asked for a contact visit with Martin Darius. As soon as the guard told them it was set, she and Reggie emptied the metal objects from their pockets, took off their watches and jewelry and walked through the metal detector. The guard checked Betsy's briefcase, then called for the elevator. When it came, Betsy inserted the key for the seventh floor in a lock and turned it. The elevator rode up to seven and the doors opened on the same narrow hall Betsy had stepped into the day before. This time she walked to the far end and waited in front of a thick metal door with an equally thick piece of glass in the upper half. Through the glass she could see the two seventh-floor contact rooms. They were both empty.

'Darius is a going to be a demanding client,' Betsy told Stewart as they waited for the guard. 'He's used to being in charge, he's very bright and he's under tremendous pressure.'

'Gotcha.'

'Today, we listen. The arraignment isn't until nine, so we have an hour. I want to get his version of what happened in Hunter's Point. If we're not done by nine, you can finish up later.'

'What's he facing?'

Betsy pulled a copy of the indictment from her briefcase.

'This don't look good, Chief,' Stewart said after reading the charges. 'Who's "John Doe"?'

'The man. The police have no idea who he is. His face and fingertips were disfigured with acid and the killer even smashed his teeth with a hammer to try and prevent an ID from his dental records.'

Stewart grimaced. 'This is one set of crime-scene photos I'm not lookin' forward to seeing.'

'They're the worst, Reg. Look at them before breakfast. I almost lost mine.'

'How do you dope it out?'

'You mean, do I think Darius did it?' Betsy shook her

head. 'I'm not sure. Page is convinced, but either Darius put on a great performance for me yesterday, or he's not guilty.'

'So, we have a real whodunnit?'

'Maybe.'

Out of their sight, a heavy lock opened with a loud snap. Betsy craned her neck and saw Darius precede the guard into the narrow space in front of the two contact rooms. When her client was locked in one of them, the guard let Betsy and Stewart into the contact area, then secured the door to the hall where they had been waiting. After locking them in with Darius, the guard left the contact visiting area by the door through which he had entered.

The contact room was small. Most of the space in it was taken up by a large circular table and three plastic chairs. Darius was sitting in one of them. He did not stand up when Betsy entered.

'I see you brought a bodyguard,' Darius said, studying Stewart carefully.

'Martin Darius meet Reggie Stewart, my investigator.'

'You're only using one?' Darius asked, ignoring Reggie's outstretched hand. Stewart pulled his hand back slowly.

'Reggie is very good. I wouldn't have won Hammermill without him. If I think you need more investigators, you'll get them. Here's a copy of the indictment.'

Darius took the paper and read it.

'Page is charging you under several theories in the death of each person: personally killing a human being during the commission of the felony crime of kidnapping; torture killing; more than one victim. If he gets a conviction on any theory of Aggravated Murder, we go into a second, or penalty, phase of the trial. That's a second trial on the issue of punishment.

'In the penalty phase, the state has to convince the jurors that you committed the murder deliberately, that the victim's provocation, if any, did not mitigate the killing and that there's a probability you'll be dangerous in the future. If the jurors answer "yes" unanimously to these three questions, you'll be sentenced to death, unless there is some mitigating circumstance that convinces any juror that you should not get a death sentence.

'If any juror votes "no" on any question, the jurors then decide on whether you get life without parole or life with a thirty-year minimum sentence. Any questions so far?'

'Yes, Tannenbaum,' Darius said, looking at her with an amused smile. 'Why are you wasting your time on an explanation of penalty phase? I did not kidnap, torture or kill these women. I expect you to explain that to our jury.'

'What about Hunter's Point?' Betsy asked. 'That's going to play a huge part in your trial.'

'A man named Henry Waters was the killer. He was shot trying to escape arrest. They found the body of one of his victims disemboweled in his basement. Everyone knew Waters was guilty and the case was closed.'

'Then why is Page convinced you killed the Hunter's Point women?'

'I have no idea. I was a victim, for God's sake. I told you. Waters killed Sandy and Melody. I was part of the task-force that investigated the killings.'

'How did that happen?' Betsy asked, surprised.

'I volunteered. I was an excellent lawyer and I did a lot of criminal defense when I started out. I felt I could provide a unique insight into the criminal mind. The Mayor agreed.'

'Why didn't you set up a law practice in Oregon?'

Darius stopped smiling. 'Why is that important?'

'It looks like you're trying to hide. So does dying your hair black.'

'My wife and child were murdered, Tannenbaum. I found their bodies. Those deaths were part of my old life. When I moved here, it was my chance to start over. I didn't want to see my old face in the mirror because I would remember how Sandy and Melody looked beside me in old photographs. I didn't want to work at the same job, because there were too many associations between that job and my old life.'

Darius leaned forward. He rested his elbows on the table and supported his head on his lean fingers, massaging his forehead as if he was trying to wipe away painful memories.

'I'm sorry if that sounds crazy, but I was a little crazy for a while. I'd been so happy. Then that maniac . . .'

Darius closed his eyes. Stewart studied him carefully. Betsy was right. Either the guy was a great actor or he was innocent.

'We'll need the old files from Hunter's Point,' Betsy told Stewart. 'You'll probably have to go back there to talk to the detectives who worked the case. Page's theory falls apart if Martin didn't kill the Hunter's Point women.'

Stewart nodded, then he leaned toward Darius.

'Who are your enemies, Mr Darius? Who hates you enough to frame you for these murders?'

Darius shrugged. 'I've made lots of enemies. There are

those fools who are tying up the project where the bodies were found.'

'Mr Darius,' Stewart said patiently, 'with all due respect, you're not seriously suggesting a group dedicated to preserving historic buildings is responsible for framing you, are you?'

'They torched three of my condos.'

'You don't see a difference between setting fire to an inanimate object and torturing three women to death? We're looking for a monster here, Mr Darius. Who do you know who has no conscience, no compassion, who thinks people are no more valuable than bugs and hates your guts?'

Betsy did not expect Darius to put up with Stewart's insolence, but he surprised her. Instead of getting mad, he leaned back in his chair, his brow furrowing in frustration as he tried to think of an answer to Stewart's question.

'What I say doesn't leave here, right?'

'Reggie is our agent. The attorney-client privilege applies to anything you tell him.'

'Okay. One name comes to mind. There's a project in Southern Oregon I couldn't fund. The banks didn't trust my judgement. So I went to Manuel Ochoa. He's a man who doesn't do much, but has lots of money. I never asked where it came from, but I've heard rumors.'

'Are we talking Colombians, Mr Darius? Cocaine, tar heroin?' Reggie asked.

'I don't know and I didn't want to. I asked for the money, he gave me the money. There were terms I agreed to that I'll have trouble meeting if I stay in jail. If Darius Construction defaults, Ochoa will make a lot of money.'

'And druggies would snuff a woman or two without thinking twice,' Stewart added.

'Does Ochoa know about Hunter's Point?' Betsy asked suddenly. 'We're not just looking for a psychopath. We're looking for a psychopath with intimate knowledge of your secret past.'

'Good point,' Stewart said. 'Who knew about Hunter's Point besides you?'

Darius suddenly looked ill. He rested his elbows on the table again and let his head fall heavily into his open palms.

'That's the question I've been asking myself, Tannenbaum, ever since I realized I was being framed. But it's a question I can't answer. I've never told anyone in Portland about Hunter's Point. Never. But the person who's framing me knows all about it, and I just don't know how that's possible.'

'Coffee, black,' Betsy told her secretary as she flew through the front door, 'and get me a turkey and Swiss from the Heathman Pub.'

Betsy tossed her attaché case on her desk and took a brief look at the mail and messages Ann had stacked in the center of the blotter. Betsy tossed the junk mail in the waste basket, placed the important letters in her in-box and decided that none of the callers needed to be phoned immediately.

'The sandwich will be ready in fifteen minutes,' Ann said, as she put a cup of coffee on Betsy's desk.

'Great.'

'How did the arraignment go?'

172

'A zoo. The courthouse was swarming with reporters. It was worse than Hammermill.'

Ann left. Betsy sipped some coffee then punched out the phone number of Dr Raymond Keene, a former state medical examiner who was now in private practice. When a defense attorney needed someone to check the ME's results, they went to Dr Keene.

'What ya got for me, Betsy?'

'Hi, Ray. I've got the Darius case.'

'No kidding.'

'No kidding. Three women and one man. All brutally tortured. I want to know everything about how they died and what was done to them before they died.'

'Who did the autopsies?'

'Susan Gregg.'

'She's competent. Is there some special reason you want her findings checked?'

'It's not so much her findings. The DA thinks Darius did this before, ten years ago, in Hunter's Point, New York. Six women were murdered there, as far as I can tell. There was a suspect in that case who was killed resisting arrest. Page doesn't believe the suspect was the murderer. When we get the Hunter's Point autopsy reports, I want you to compare the cases to see if there is a similar MO.'

'Sounds interesting. Did Page clear it?'

'I asked him after the arraignment.'

'I'll call Sue and see if I can get over to the morgue this afternoon.'

'The quicker the better.'

'You want me to perform another autopsy or just review her report?'

'Do everything you can think of. At this point, I have no idea what might be important.'

'What lab tests has Sue done?'

'I don't know.'

'Probably not as many as she should. I'll check it out. The budget pressures don't encourage a lot of lab work.'

'We don't have to worry about a budget. Darius will go top dollar.'

'That's what I like to hear. I'll call as soon as I have something to tell you. Give 'em hell.'

'I will, Ray.'

Betsy hung up the phone.

'Are you ready for lunch?' Nora Sloane asked hesitantly from the office doorway. Betsy looked up, startled.

'Your receptionist wasn't in. I waited for a few minutes.'

'Oh, I'm sorry, Nora. We did have a lunch date, didn't we?'

'For noon.'

'I apologize. I forgot all about it. I just picked up a new case that's taking all my time.'

'Martin Darius. I know. It's the headline in the *Oregonian*.'

'I'm afraid today isn't good for lunch. I'm really swamped. Can we do it another day?'

'No problem. In fact, I was sure you'd want to cancel. I was going to call, but . . . Betsy,' Sloane said, excitedly, 'could I tag along on this case, sit in on conferences, talk to your investigator? It's a fantastic opportunity to see how you work on a high-profile case.'

'I don't know . . .'

'I wouldn't say anything, of course. I'd keep your

confidences. I only want to be a fly on the wall.'

Sloane seemed so excited, Betsy did not want to turn her down, but a leak about defense strategy could be devastating. The front door opened and Ann appeared in the doorway carrying a brown paper bag. Sloane looked over her shoulder.

'Sorry,' Ann said, backing away. Betsy motioned her to stop.

'I'll talk to Darius,' Betsy said. 'He'll have to give his okay. Then I'll think about it. I won't do anything that could endanger a client's case.'

'I understand perfectly,' Sloane said. 'I'll call in a few days to see what you decide.'

'Sorry about lunch.'

'Oh, no. That's okay. And thank you.'

There was a van with a CBS logo and another from ABC in Betsy's driveway when she pulled in.

'Who are they, Mom?' Kathy asked, as two beautifully dressed blondes with perfect features approached the car. The women held microphones and were followed by muscular men armed with portable television cameras.

'Monica Blake, CBS, Ms Tannenbaum,' the shorter woman said as Betsy pushed open the door. Blake stepped back awkwardly and the other woman took advantage of the break.

'How do you explain a woman who is known for her strong feminist views defending a man who is alleged to have kidnapped, raped, tortured and killed three women?'

Betsy flushed. She turned abruptly and glared at the reporter from ABC, ignoring the microphone thrust in her face.

'First, I don't have to explain anything. The State does. Second, I'm an attorney. One of the things I do is defend people – male or female – who have been accused of a crime. Sometimes these people are unjustly accused, because the State makes a mistake. Martin Darius is innocent and I am proud to be representing him against these false accusations.'

'What if they're not false?' asked the CBS reporter. 'How can you sleep nights, knowing what he did to these women?'

'I suggest you read the Constitution, Ms Blake. Mr Darius is presumed innocent. Now, I have dinner to make and a little girl to take care of. I won't answer any questions at my house. I consider this an invasion of my privacy. If you want to talk to me, call my office for an appointment. Please, don't come to my house again.'

Betsy walked around the car and opened Kathy's door. She jumped out, looking over her shoulder at the cameras as Betsy dragged her toward the house. The two reporters continued to shout questions at her back.

'Are we gonna be on TV?' Kathy asked, as Betsy slammed the door.

Chapter Eleven

1

Alan Page was trapped in a car, careening downhill through traffic at breakneck speed on a winding turnpike, brakes screeching, tires smoking, twisting the wheel furiously to avoid an inevitable collision. When he sat up in bed, he was inches from the burning headlights of a massive semi. Sweat glued his flannel pajamas to his damp skin and he could feel the thunderous pounding of his heart. Page gulped down lungfuls of air, still uncertain where he was and half expecting to die in a fireball of lacerated steel and shattered glass.

'Jesus,' he gasped, when he was oriented. The clock read four fifty-eight, an hour and a half before the alarm would go off, four and a half hours before the bail hearing. He fell back on to his pillow, anxious and sure sleep was impossible, haunted by the question that had hounded him since the arrest of Martin Darius. Had he moved too soon? Was there 'clear and convincing' evidence that

Martin Darius was a murderer?

Ross Barrow and Randy Highsmith had argued against searching Darius's house, even after hearing what Gutierrez had to say. They wanted to wait until Nancy Gordon was found and they had a stronger case, but he had overridden them and instructed Barrow to make an arrest if the tire tracks at the scene matched the treads on Darius's car. Now, he wondered if Barrow and Highsmith hadn't been right all along. He had counted on finding Nancy Gordon for the bail hearing, but even with three detectives working around the clock, they were still striking out.

If he could not sleep, he could rest. Page closed his eyes and saw Nancy Gordon. He had thought of the detective constantly since learning that her body was not in the pit. If she was alive, she would have gotten in touch with him as soon as she learned of Darius's arrest. If she was alive, she would have returned to the Lakeview. Was she dead, a look of unimaginable suffering on her face? Darius knew the answer to Page's questions, but the law forbade Alan to talk to him.

Page would need all of his energy in court, but the fear in his belly would not let him rest. He decided he would shower, shave, eat breakfast, then dress in his best suit and a crisp, starched shirt, fresh from the cleaner. A shower and a big breakfast would make him feel human. Then, he would drive to the courthouse and try to convince The Honorable Patrick Norwood, Judge of the Multnomah County Circuit Court, that Martin Darius was a serial killer.

2

Martin Darius slept peacefully and felt well rested when he awoke with the other inmates of the Multnomah County Jail. Betsy Tannenbaum had arranged to have his hair cut by his barber and the watch commander was permitting him an extra shower before court. Only a breakfast of sticky pancakes soaked in gluey, jailhouse syrup spoiled his mood. Darius used the acidic taste of the jail coffee to cut the sweetness and ate them anyway, because he knew it would be a long day in court.

Betsy had exchanged a full wardrobe for the clothes in which Darius was arrested. When Darius met her in the interview room before court, he was attired in a double-breasted, chalk-stripe, dark wool suit, a cotton broadcloth shirt and a navy blue, woven silk tie with white, pinpoint dots. Betsy wore a single-breasted jacket and matching skirt of black and white, windowpane plaid and a white silk blouse with a wide collar. When they walked down the courthouse corridor in the glare of the television lights, they would look like a couple you might see on *Life Styles of the Rich and Famous* rather than a suspected mass murderer and his mouthpiece.

'How are you feeling?' Darius asked.

'Fine.'

'Good. I want you at your best, today. Jail is interesting, if you treat it as an educational experience, but I'm ready to graduate.'

'I'm glad to see you're keeping your sense of humor.'

Darius shrugged. 'I have faith in you, Tannenbaum. That's why I hired you. You're the best. You won't let me down.'

The praise made Betsy feel good. She basked in it and believed what Darius told her. She was the best. That was why Darius chose her over Matthew Reynolds, Oscar Montoya and the other established criminal defense lawyers.

'Who's our judge?' Darius asked.

'Pat Norwood.'

'What's he like?'

'He's a crusty old codger who's nearing retirement. He looks like a troll and acts like an ogre in court. He's no legal scholar, either. But, he is completely impartial. Norwood's rude and impatient with the prosecution and the defense and he won't be buffaloed by Alan Page or the press. If Page doesn't meet his burden of proof on the bail issue, Norwood will do the right thing.'

'Do you think the state will meet its burden?' Darius asked.

'No, Martin, I don't think they will.'

Darius smiled. 'That's what I wanted to hear.' Then, the smile faded as he changed the subject. 'Is Lisa going to be in court?'

'Of course. I talked to her yesterday.'

'Looks like you're having more luck getting in touch with my wife than I am.'

'Lisa's staying with her father. She didn't feel comfortable alone in the house.'

'That's funny,' Darius said, flashing Betsy a chilly smile. 'I called His Honor last night and he told me she wasn't home.'

'She may have been out.'

'Right. The next time you talk to my wife, please ask her

180

to visit me, will you?'

'Sure. Oh, before I forget, there's a woman named Nora Sloane who's writing an article about women defense attorneys. She wants to follow me through your case. If I let her, there's a chance she might learn defense strategy or attorney-client confidences. I told her I had to ask your permission before I let her get involved. Do you have any objections to her tagging along?'

Darius considered the question for a moment, then shook his head.

'I don't mind. Besides,' he grinned, 'you'll have more incentive to do a great job for me if someone is writing about you.'

'I never thought of it that way.'

'That's why I'm a millionaire, Tannenbaum. I always figure the angles.'

3

There were several new courtrooms outfitted with state-of-the-art video equipment and computer technology that Patrick L. Norwood could have commandeered because of his senior status, but Judge Norwood preferred the courtroom where he had ruled with an iron fist for twenty years. It had high ceilings, grand marble columns and a hand-carved wooden dais. It was an old-fashioned courtroom, perfect for a man with the judicial temperament of a nineteenth-century hanging judge.

The courtroom was filled to capacity for the Martin Darius bail hearing. Those who were too late to find a seat stood in line in the hall. Spectators had to pass through a metal detector before entering the courtroom and there were extra security guards inside, because of death threats.

Harvey Cobb, an elderly black man, called the court to order. He had been Norwood's bailiff from the day the judge was appointed. Norwood came out of his chambers through a door behind the bench. Short and squat, he was ugly as sin, but his toad-like face was crowned by a full head of beautiful, snowy white hair.

'Be seated,' Cobb said. Betsy took her place beside Martin Darius and glanced briefly at Alan Page, who was sitting next to Randy Highsmith.

'Call your first witness, Mr Page,' Norwood ordered.

'The State calls Ross Barrow, Your Honor.'

Harvey Cobb had Detective Barrow raise his right hand and swear to tell the truth. Barrow sat in the witness box and Page established his credentials as a homicide investigator.

'Detective Barrow, sometime in mid-August did you become aware of a series of unusual disappearances?'

'Yes, I did. In August, a detective from our missing persons bureau told me that a woman named Laura Farrar was reported missing by her husband, Larry Farrar. Larry told the detective that . . .'

'Objection, hearsay,' Betsy said, standing.

'No,' Norwood ruled. 'This is a bail hearing. Not a trial. I'm going to permit the State some leeway. If you need to examine some of these witnesses, you can subpoena them. Let's move on, Mr Page.'

Page nodded at Barrow, who continued with his account of the investigation.

'Farrar told the detective that he had come home from work on August tenth, about eight o'clock. His house looked perfectly normal, but his wife was missing. None of her clothes were missing or her make-up. In fact, nothing was missing from the house, as far as he could tell. The only unusual circumstance was a rose and a note Mr Farrar found on his wife's pillow.'

'Was there anything odd about the rose?'

'Yes, sir. A lab report on the rose indicates that it had been dyed black.'

'What did the note say?'

' "Gone, But Not Forgotten".'

Page handed a document and a photograph to the judge's clerk.

'This is a photocopy of the Farrar note and a photograph of the rose, Your Honor. The originals are still at the lab. I talked about this with Ms Tannenbaum and she's willing to stipulate to the introduction of these and other copies, solely for purposes of this hearing.'

'Is that so?' Norwood asked Betsy. She nodded.

'The exhibits will be received.'

'Did the detective from missing persons tell you about a second disappearance in mid-September?'

'Yes, sir. Wendy Reiser, the wife of Thomas Reiser, was reported missing by her husband under identical circumstances.'

'Nothing disturbed in the house or missing?'

'Correct.'

'Did Mr Reiser find a black rose and a note on his wife's pillow?'

'He did.'

Page introduced a photocopy of the Reiser note and a photograph of the Reiser rose.

'What did the lab say about the second note and rose?'

'They are identical to the note and rose found at the Farrar house.'

'Finally, Detective, did you learn about a third, recent disappearance?'

'Yes, sir. Russell Miller reported his wife, Victoria, missing under circumstances that were identical to the other cases. Note and rose on the pillow. Nothing disturbed or missing in the house.'

'Several days ago, did you learn where the women were?'

Barrow nodded gravely. 'The three women, and an unidentified male, were found buried in a construction site owned by Darius Construction.'

'Who owns Darius Construction?'

'Martin Darius, the defendant.'

'Was the gate to the site locked?'

'Yes, sir.'

'Was a gaping hole located in the fence near the area where the bodies were found?'

'Yes, sir.'

'Were tire tracks located near that hole?'

'They were.'

'On the evening Mr Darius was arrested, did you execute a search warrant at his residence?'

'Yes, sir.'

'Did you locate any vehicles during the search?'

'We located a station wagon, a BMW and a black Ferrari.'

'Move to introduce exhibits ten to twenty-three, which

are photographs of the construction site, the hole in the fence, the tire tracks, the burial site and the bodies being removed from it, and the vehicles.'

'No objection,' Betsy said.

'Received.'

'Was a cast made of the tire tracks?'

'It was. The tracks at the site match the tread on the BMW we found at Darius's house.'

'Was the trunk of the BMW examined for trace evidence, such as hairs and fibers, that might have belonged to any of the victims?'

'Yes, sir. None were found.'

'Did the lab report explain why?'

'The trunk had been recently vacuumed and cleaned.'

'How old was the BMW?'

'A year old.'

'Not a brand-new car?'

'No, sir.'

'Detective Barrow, are you aware of any connections between the defendant and the murdered women?'

'I am. Yes. Mr Reiser works for the law firm that represents Darius Construction. He and his wife met the defendant at a party Mr Darius threw this summer to celebrate the opening of a new mall.'

'How soon before the disappearance of the first woman, Laura Farrar, was this party?'

'Approximately three weeks.'

'Were Mr and Mrs Farrar at that party?'

'They were. Mr Farrar works for the accounting firm that Mr Darius uses.'

'And Russell and Victoria Miller?'

'They were at the party, too, but they have closer ties with the defendant. Mr Miller was just put in charge of the Darius Construction account at Brand, Gates and Valcroft, the advertising agency. They also socialized with Mr and Mrs Darius.'

Page checked his notes, conferred with Randy Highsmith then said, 'Your witness, Ms Tannenbaum.'

Betsy looked at a legal pad on which she had listed several points she wanted to bring out through Barrow. She selected several police reports from the discovery she received from the district attorney.

'Good morning, Detective Barrow. Teams of criminalists from the Oregon State Crime Lab went through the houses of all three women, did they not?'

'That's true.'

'Isn't it also true that none of these fine scientists found a single piece of physical evidence connecting Martin Darius to the homes of Laura Farrar, Victoria Miller or Wendy Reiser?'

'The person who murdered these women is very clever. He knows how to clean up a crime scene.'

'Your Honor,' Betsy said calmly, 'will you please direct Detective Barrow to listen to the questions I ask him and respond to those questions. I'm sure Mr Page will try to explain the problems with his case during argument.'

Judge Norwood glared at Betsy. 'I don't need an editorial from you, Ms Tannenbaum. Just make your objections.' Then, Norwood swiveled toward the witness. 'And you've testified enough times to know you only answer what you're asked. Save the clever answers. They don't impress me.'

'So, Detective Barrow, what's your answer? Was a single shred of physical evidence linking my client to any victim found at any of the homes of the missing women?'

'No.'

'How about on the bodies?'

'We found the tire tracks.'

'Your Honor?' Betsy asked.

'Detective Barrow, were there tire tracks on the body of any of those women?' the judge asked sarcastically.

Barrow looked embarrassed. 'Sorry, Your Honor.'

'Are you catching on, Detective?' Judge Norwood asked.

'There was no physical evidence at the burial site connecting the defendant with any of the women.'

'A dead man was also found at the burial site?'

'Yes.'

'Who is he?'

'We don't know.'

'So, there's nothing connecting this man to Martin Darius?'

'We don't know that. Until we find out who he is, we can't investigate his possible connection with your client.'

Betsy was going to object, but decided to let the remark pass. If Barrow kept fencing, he'd keep pissing off the judge.

'You told the judge about the tire tracks you found near the fence. Don't you think you should tell him about the interview you had with Rudy Doschman?'

'I interviewed him. What about it?'

'Do you have your report of that interview?' Betsy asked, as she walked toward the witness stand.

'Not with me.'

'Why don't you take my copy and read this paragraph?' Betsy said, handing the detective a police report she had found in the discovery material. Barrow read the report and looked up.

'Mr Doschman is a foreman with Darius Construction who was working on the site where the bodies were found?' Betsy asked.

'Yes.'

'He told you Mr Darius visited the site on many occasions, did he not?'

'Yes.'

'In his BMW?'

'Yes.'

'He also explained that the hole in the fence was there for some time?'

'Yes.'

'In fact, it may have been the way the arsonists who burned down some of Mr Darius's townhouses entered the site, several weeks ago?'

'It could be.'

'There is no evidence connecting Mr Darius to the roses or the notes?'

Barrow looked like he was going to say something, but he choked it back and shook his head.

'And you stand by that statement, even though officers of the Portland Police Bureau made a thorough search, pursuant to a warrant, of Mr Darius's home?'

'We found nothing connecting him to the roses or the notes,' Barrow answered tersely.

'No murder weapons, either?'

'No.'

'Nothing in the trunk of the BMW connecting him to the crimes?'

'No.'

Betsy turned to Darius. 'Anything else you want me to ask?'

Darius smiled. 'You're doing just fine, Tannenbaum.'

'No further questions.'

Barrow hoisted himself out of the witness box and walked quickly to the back of the courtroom as Page called his next witness.

'Dr Susan Gregg,' Page said. An attractive woman in her early forties with salt-and-pepper hair, wearing a conservative gray suit, took the witness stand.

'Will counsel stipulate to Dr Gregg's qualifications for purposes of this hearing?' Page asked Betsy.

'We assume Dr Gregg is well known to the court,' Betsy said, 'so, for purposes of this hearing only, we stipulate that Dr Gregg is the State Medical Examiner and qualified to give opinions on cause of death.'

'Thank you,' Page said to Betsy. 'Dr Gregg, were you called to a construction site owned by Darius Construction earlier this week to examine the remains of four individuals who were found buried there?'

'I was.'

'And you conducted the autopsies of all four victims?'

'Yes.'

'What is an autopsy, Dr Gregg?'

'It's an examination of a body after death to determine, among other things, cause of death.'

'Will you explain what your autopsy involved?'

'Certainly. I examined the bodies carefully for serious

injuries, natural diseases and other natural causes of death.'

'Did any of the victims die a natural death?'

'No.'

'What injuries did you observe?'

'All four individuals had numerous burns and cutting injuries on various parts of their bodies. Three of the male's fingers had been severed. There was evidence of sharp cuts on the women's breasts. The nipples on the women had been mutilated, as had the genitalia of the man and the women. Do you want me to go into detail?'

'That won't be necessary for this hearing. How did the three women die?'

'Their abdomens had been deeply cut resulting in serious injuries to their bowel and abdominal viscera.'

'When a person is disemboweled, do they die quickly?'

'No. A person can stay alive for some time in this condition.'

'Can you give the court a rough estimate?'

Gregg shrugged. 'It's hard to say. Two to four hours. Eventually, they die from shock and loss of blood.'

'And that was the cause of death of these women?'

'Yes.'

'And the male?'

'He suffered a fatal gun-shot wound to the back of his head.'

'Did you order laboratory tests?'

'Yes. I had the blood tested for alcohol. The results were negative for all of the victims. I ordered a urine screen for drugs of abuse. This involves testing the urine for the presence of five drugs: cocaine, morphine, marijuana, amphetamine and PCP. Our results were all negative.'

Page studied his notes and conferred with Highsmith before turning the witness over to Betsy. She reread a portion of the autopsy report and frowned.

'Dr Gregg, I'm confused by some remarks you made on page four of your report. Were the women raped?'

'That's hard to say. I found bruises and tears around the genitalia and rectum. Tearing that would indicate invasion by a foreign object.'

'Did you test for semen?'

'I did not find any traces of seminal fluid.'

'So, you can't say conclusively that the women were raped?'

'I can only say there was penetration and violent injury. There was no evidence of male ejaculation.'

'Did you draw a conclusion concerning whether the women were murdered at the construction site?'

'I believe they were killed elsewhere.'

'Why?'

'There would have been a large amount of blood at the murder scene, because of their massive cutting injuries. There were also organs removed from two of the women.'

'Would the rain obscure traces of their blood?'

'No. They were buried. The rain would have washed away the blood on the surface, but we should have found larger quantities under the bodies in the graves.'

'So, you believe the women were killed some place else and transported to the site?'

'Yes.'

'If they were transported in the trunk of a BMW, could you erase all traces of blood from the trunk?'

'Objection,' Page said. 'Dr Gregg is not qualified to

answer that question. She is a medical doctor, not a forensic chemist.'

'I'll let her answer, if she can,' the judge ruled.

'I'm afraid that's outside my area of expertise,' the doctor answered.

'The male was not disemboweled?'

'No.'

'Nothing further.'

Alan Page stood. He looked a little unsure of himself.

'Your Honor, I'm going to call myself as a witness. Mr Highsmith will examine.'

'Objection, Your Honor. It's unethical for an attorney to testify as a witness in a case he's trying.'

'That might be true in a trial before a jury, Your Honor,' Page replied, 'but the court is not going to have any trouble deciding my credibility as a witness, if that comes into question, simply because I'm also arguing the State's position.'

Norwood looked troubled. 'This is unusual. Why do you have to testify?'

'What's he up to?' Darius whispered in Betsy's ear.

Betsy shook her head. She was studying Page. He looked ill-at-ease and grim. Something was troubling the District Attorney.

'Your Honor, I'm in possession of evidence you must hear if you are going to make a reasoned decision on the issue of bail. Unless I testify, you'll be without the most important evidence we have that Martin Darius is the man who killed Laura Farrar, Wendy Reiser and Victoria Miller.'

'I'm confused, Mr Page,' Norwood said, testily. 'How can you have this evidence? Were you an eye-witness?' Norwood shook his head. 'I don't get it.'

Page cleared his throat. 'Your Honor, there is a witness. Her name is Nancy Gordon.' Darius took a deep breath and leaned forward, intently. 'Ten years ago, an identical series of murders occurred in Hunter's Point, New York. The day before we found the bodies, Detective Gordon told me about those murders and why she believed Martin Darius committed them.'

'Then call Detective Gordon,' Norwood said.

'I can't. She's missing and she may be dead. She checked into a motel room after leaving me. I called her several times starting around eight, eight-thirty, the next morning. I think something happened to her shortly after she checked in. It looks like she was unpacking when something interrupted her. All of her possessions were in the room, but she hasn't come back for them. I have a team of detectives looking for her, but we've had no luck, so far.'

'Your Honor,' Betsy said, 'if Mr Page is going to testify about this woman's statements to prove my client murdered some women ten years ago, it will be pure hearsay. I know the court is giving Mr Page leeway, but Mr Darius has state and federal constitutional rights to confront the witnesses against him.'

'That's true, Mrs Tannenbaum. I'll tell you, Mr Page, this bothers me. Isn't there another witness from Hunter's Point you can call who can testify about these other crimes?'

'Not on such short notice. I know the names of the other detectives who worked on the case, but they don't work for the Hunter's Point police any more and I haven't traced them.'

Norwood leaned back and almost disappeared from view. Betsy was dying to know what the missing detective

193

had told Page, but she had to keep the testimony out, if it was the ammunition Page needed to keep Martin Darius in jail.

'It's eleven-fifteen, folks,' Norwood said. 'We'll adjourn until one-thirty. I'll hear legal argument then.'

Norwood stood up and walked out of the courtroom. Harvey Cobb rapped the gavel and everyone stood.

'Now I know why Page thinks I killed those women,' Darius whispered to Betsy. 'When can we talk?'

'I'll come up to the jail, right now.'

Betsy turned to one of the guards. 'Can you put Mr Darius in the interview room? I want to talk to him.'

'Sure, Ms Tannenbaum. We're gonna wait for the court to clear before taking him up. You can ride with us in the jail elevator, if you want.'

'Thanks, I will.'

The guard handcuffed Darius. Betsy glanced toward the back of the courtroom. Lisa Darius was standing near the door, talking to Nora Sloane. Lisa glanced toward Betsy. Betsy smiled. Lisa did not smile back, but she did nod toward her. Betsy raised a hand to let Lisa know she would be right with her. Lisa said something to Sloane. Sloane smiled and patted Lisa's shoulder, then left the courtroom.

'I'm going to talk to Lisa for a moment,' Betsy told Darius. Lisa was waiting just inside the door, looking nervously through the glass at the waiting reporters.

'That woman said she's working with you on an article for *Pacific West*,' Lisa said.

'That's right. She going to tag along while I try Martin's case to see how I work.'

'She said she'd like to talk to me. What should I do?'

'Nora seems responsible, but you make up your own mind. How are you holding up?'

'This is terrible. The reporters won't leave me alone. When I moved to Daddy's house I had to sneak out of the estate through the woods, so they wouldn't know where I was going.'

'I'm sorry, Lisa. This isn't going to get any easier for you.'

Lisa hesitated, then she asked, 'Will the judge let Martin out on bail?'

'There's a good chance he'll have to. The State's evidence has been pretty weak, so far.'

Lisa looked worried.

'Is something troubling you?'

'No,' Lisa answered too quickly.

'If you know anything about this case, please tell me. I don't want any surprises.'

'It's the reporters, they've really gotten to me,' Lisa said, but Betsy knew she was lying.

'We're ready,' the guard told Betsy.

'I've got to talk to Martin. He wants you to visit him.'

Lisa nodded, but her thoughts seemed far away.

'Who is Nancy Gordon?' Betsy asked Darius. They were sitting next to each other in the narrow confines of the courthouse jail visiting room.

'One of the detectives on the task-force. I met her the night Sandy and Melody died. She interviewed me at the house. Gordon was engaged to another cop, but he was killed a few weeks before the wedding. She was still grieving when I joined the task-force and she tried to help me deal with my grief.

'Nancy and I were thrown together on several occasions. I didn't realize it, but she took my friendliness as something else and, well . . .' Darius looked into Betsy's eyes. Their knees were almost touching. His head bent toward her. 'I was vulnerable. We both were. You can't understand what it feels like to lose someone you love like that, until it happens to you.

'I became convinced Waters was the rose killer and I did a stupid thing. Without telling anyone, I started following him. I even staked out his house, hoping I'd catch him in the act.' Darius smiled sheepishly. 'I made a mess of things and almost blew the investigation. I was so obvious, a neighbor called the police to complain about this strange man who was camped outside their house. The police came. I felt like an idiot. Nancy bailed me out. We met at a restaurant near the police station and she let me have it.

'By the time we'd finished eating, it was late. I offered to drive her home, because her car was in for repairs. We'd both had a few beers. I don't even remember who started it. The bottom line is, we ended up in bed.'

Darius looked down at his hands, as if he was ashamed. Then, he shook his head.

'It was a stupid thing to do. I should have known she would take it too seriously. I mean, it was good for us to have someone to spend the night with. We were both so lonely. But, she thought I loved her and I didn't. It was too soon after Sandy. When I didn't want to continue the relationship, she grew bitter. Fortunately, Waters was caught soon after that and my involvement with the task-force ended, so there was no reason for us to see each other. Only, Nancy couldn't let go. She called me at home and at the office. She wanted to meet and talk about us. I told her there was no us, but it was hard for her to accept.'

'Did she accept it?'

Darius nodded. 'She stopped calling, but I knew she was bitter. What I can't understand is how she could possibly think I killed Sandy and Melody.'

'If the judge lets Page testify,' Betsy said, 'we'll soon find out.'

Chapter Twelve

'Let me tell you how I see it, Ms Tannenbaum,' Judge Norwood said. 'I know what the constitution says about confronting the witnesses and I'm not saying you don't have a point, but this is a bail hearing and the issues are different at trial. What Mr Page is trying to do is convince me he's got so much evidence a guilty verdict at the trial is almost a sure thing. He thinks some of this trial evidence is going to come from this missing detective or from someone else in New York. I'm going to let him tell me what the evidence is, but I'm also going to take into account that he doesn't have his witness and may not be able to produce her, or these other detectives, at trial. So, I'll decide what weight to give to this testimony, but I'm going to let it in. If you don't like my ruling, I don't blame you. I might be wrong. That's why we have appeals courts. But, right now, Mr Page can testify.'

Betsy had already made her objections for the record, so she said nothing more when Alan Page was sworn in.

'Mr Page,' Randy Highsmith asked, 'the evening before

the bodies of Victoria Miller, Wendy Rieser, Laura Farrar and an unknown male were unearthed at a construction site owned by the defendant, did a woman visit you at your residence?'

'Yes.'

'Who was this woman?'

'Nancy Gordon, a detective with the Hunter's Point Police Department in New York.'

'At the time of Detective Gordon's visit were the details surrounding the disappearances of the three Portland women widely known?'

'To the contrary, Mr Highsmith. The police and the district attorney's office weren't certain of the status of the missing women, so we were treating them as missing persons cases. No one in the press knew of the links between the cases and the husbands were cooperating with us by not divulging details of the disappearances.'

'What were the links you spoke of?'

'The black roses and the notes that said "Gone, But Not Forgotten".'

'What did Detective Gordon say that led you to believe she had information that could be useful in solving the mystery surrounding these disappearances?'

'She knew about the notes and the roses.'

'Where did she say she had acquired this knowledge?'

'Ten years ago in Hunter's Point, when an almost identical series of disappearances occurred.'

'What was her connection with the Hunter's Point case?'

'She was a member of a task-force assigned to that case.'

'How did Detective Gordon learn about our disappearances and the similarities between the cases?'

'She told me she received an anonymous note that led her to believe that the person who was responsible for the Hunter's Point murders was living in Portland.'

'Who was this person?'

'She knew him as Peter Lake.'

'Did she give some background information on Peter Lake?'

'She did. He was a successful lawyer in Hunter's Point. He was married to Sandra Lake and they had a six-year-old daughter, Melody. The wife and child were murdered and a "Gone, But Not Forgotten" note and black rose were found on the floor near the mother's body. Lake had a lot of political clout and the Mayor of Hunter's Point ordered the Police Chief to put him on the task-force. Lake soon became the primary suspect, though he was not aware of that fact.'

'Have the prints of Peter Lake been compared to the fingerprints of Martin Darius?'

'Yes.'

'With what results?'

'Martin Darius and Peter Lake are the same person.'

Highsmith handed the clerk two fingerprint cards and a report from a fingerprint expert and introduced them into evidence.

'Mr Page, did Detective Gordon tell you why she believed the defendant murdered the Hunter's Point women?'

'She did.'

'Tell the court what she told you.'

'Peter Lake had a connection to each of the women who disappeared in Hunter's Point. Gloria Escalante sat on one of Lake's juries. Samantha Reardon belonged to the same country club as the Lakes. Anne Hazelton's husband was an attorney and the Lakes and Hazeltons had been to some of the same Bar Association functions. Patricia Cross and Sandra Lake, Peter's wife, were both in the Junior League.

'Detective Gordon met Lake the evening Sandra and Melody Lake were murdered. This was the first time a body was discovered. In all the other cases, when the women disappeared, the note and rose were found on the woman's pillow in her bedroom. None of these notes had fingerprints on them. The note found at Lake's house had Sandra Lake's prints on it. The detectives believed that Sandra Lake discovered the note and was killed by her husband so she would not connect him to the disappearances when the notes were made public. They also believed Melody saw her mother killed and was murdered because she was a witness.'

'Was there a problem with the time that Peter Lake reported the murders to the police?'

'Yes. Peter Lake told the police that he discovered the bodies right after he entered the house, that he sat down on the steps for a while, in shock, then called 911. The 911 call came in at eight-fifteen, but a neighbor, who lived near the Lakes, saw Peter Lake arrive home shortly after seven-twenty. The task-force members believed it took Lake fifty-five minutes to report the murders because the victims were alive when Lake got home.'

'Was there anything else that implicated Lake?'

'A man named Henry Waters worked for a florist. His truck was seen near the Escalante house on the day she disappeared. Waters had a sex-offender record as a peeping

Tom. The body of Patricia Cross was found in the basement of Waters' house. She was disemboweled, just like the three Portland women.

'Waters was never really a suspect, but Lake didn't know that. Waters was borderline retarded and had no history of violence. There wasn't any connection between him and any other victim. Without telling anyone, Lake staked out Waters' house and followed him for days before the body of Patricia Cross was discovered.'

'What led the police to Waters' house?'

'An anonymous male caller, who was never identified. The task-force members believed Lake brought Cross to Waters' house, murdered her in the basement, then made the phone call to the police.'

'Why wasn't Lake prosecuted in Hunter's Point?'

'Waters was killed during his arrest. The Police Chief and the Mayor made a public statement labeling Waters as the rose killer. There were no more murders and the cases were closed.'

'Why did Detective Gordon come to Portland?'

'When she learned about the Portland notes and roses, she knew the same person had to be responsible for the Hunter's Point and Portland crimes, because the color of the rose and the contents of the notes were never made public in Hunter's Point.'

'Where did Detective Gordon go after she left your residence?'

'The Lakeview Motel. The manager said she checked in about twenty minutes after leaving my place.'

'Have you seen or talked to Detective Gordon since she left your residence?'

'No. She's disappeared.'

'Have you searched her room at the motel?'

Page nodded. 'It looked like she was in the midst of unpacking when something happened. When she was at my place, she had an attaché case with a lot of material relating to the case. It was missing. We also found the address of the construction site where the bodies were found on a pad next to the phone.'

'What conclusion do you draw from that?'

'Someone called her with the address.'

'What do you believe happened then?'

'Well, she had no car. We've checked all of the taxi companies. None of them picked her up from the Lakeview. I believe the person who called her picked her up.'

'No further questions, Your Honor.'

Betsy smiled at Page, but he did not smile back. He looked grim and sat stiffly, back straight, with his hands folded in his lap.

'Mr Page, there was a lengthy investigation in Hunter's Point, wasn't there?'

'That's what Detective Gordon said.'

'I assume you've read the police reports from that investigation.'

'No I haven't,' Page answered, shifting uncomfortably

'Why is that?'

'I don't have them.'

'Have you ordered them from Hunter's Point?'

'No.'

Betsy's brow furrowed. 'If you're planning on having Detective Gordon testify, you'll have to produce her reports.'

'I know that.'

'Is there a reason you haven't ordered them?'

Page colored. 'They've been misplaced.'

'Excuse me?'

'The Hunter's Point police are looking for them. The reports were supposed to be in a storage area, but they aren't. We think Detective Gordon may know where they are, because she gave me some items, including Peter Lake's fingerprint card, we assume came from the file.'

Betsy decided to switch to another topic.

'On direct examination, you repeatedly said "the task-force members believed". Have you talked to these task-force members?'

'No, other than Detective Gordon.'

'Do you even know where they are?'

'I just learned that Frank Grimsbo is the Head of Security at Marlin Steel.'

'Where is his office located?'

'Albany, New York.'

Betsy made a note.

'You haven't talked to Grimsbo?'

'No.'

'What are the names of the other detectives?'

'Besides Gordon and Grimsbo, there was a criminalist named Glen Michaels and another detective named Wayne Turner.'

Betsy wrote down the names. When she looked up Page was stone-faced.

'Mr Page, isn't it true that you have no support for the story your mysterious visitor told you?'

'Other than what the detective said, no.'

'What detective?'

'Nancy Gordon.'

'This was the first time you saw this woman, correct?'

Page nodded.

'Have you ever seen a photograph of Nancy Gordon?'

'No.'

'So, you can't say that the person who introduced herself as Detective Nancy Gordon is really Nancy Gordon, can you?'

'A Nancy Gordon works for the Hunter's Point Police Department.'

'I don't doubt that. But we don't know that she is the person who visited you, do we?'

'No.'

'There's also no proof that this woman is dead or even a victim of foul play, is there?'

'She's missing.'

'Was there blood found in her room?'

'No.'

'Or signs of a struggle?'

'No,' Page answered grudgingly.

'Were there any witnesses to the murders of Melody and Sandra Lake?'

'Your client may have witnessed the killings,' Page answered defiantly.

'You have nothing but theories propounded by your mystery woman to support that position.'

'That's true.'

'Isn't it also true that the Chief of Police and the Mayor of Hunter's Point officially declared Henry Waters to be the murderer of all the women?'

'Yes.'

'That would include Sandra and Melody Lake?'

'Yes.'

'Which would make Mr Lake – Mr Darius – a victim, wouldn't it?'

Page did not answer and Betsy did not force him to.

'Mr Page, there were six victims in Hunter's Point, including a six-year-old girl. Can you think of any reason why a responsible public official would close a case like that and publicly declare an individual to be the killer if there was any possibility that the murderer was still at large?'

'Maybe the officials wanted to allay the fears of the community.'

'You mean the public announcement might be part of a ruse to make the killer lower his guard while the investigation continued?'

'Exactly.'

'But the investigation didn't continue, did it?'

'Not according to Detective Gordon.'

'And the murders stopped after Mr Waters was killed, didn't they?'

'Yes.'

Betsy paused and looked directly at Judge Norwood.

'No further questions, Your Honor.'

'Mr Highsmith?' Judge Norwood asked.

'I have nothing further of Mr Page.'

'You can step down, Mr Page.'

Page stood slowly. Betsy thought he looked tired and defeated. She took satisfaction in this. Betsy did not enjoy humiliating Page. He seemed a decent sort. But Page deserved any pain she inflicted. It was clear he had arrested Martin Darius on the flimsiest evidence, made him spend several days in jail and slandered him. A public defeat was a small price to pay for that kind of callous disregard of his public duty.

'Any other witnesses?' the judge asked.

'Yes, Your Honor. Two, both brief,' Highsmith answered.

'Proceed.'

'The State calls Ira White.'

A chubby man in an ill-fitting brown suit hurried forward from the back of the courtroom. He smiled nervously as he was sworn. Betsy guessed he was in his early thirties.

'Mr White, what do you do for a living?' Randy Highsmith asked.

'I'm a salesman for Finletter Tools.'

'Where is your home office?'

'Phoenix, Arizona, but my territory is Oregon, Montana, Washington, Idaho and parts of Northern California, near the Oregon border.'

'Where were you at two PM on October eleventh of this year?'

The date rang a bell. Betsy checked the police reports. Victoria Miller was reported missing that evening.

'In my room at the Hacienda Motel,' White said.

'Where is that motel located?'

'It's in Vancouver, Washington.'

'Why were you in your room?'

'I just checked in. I had a meeting scheduled for three and I wanted to unpack, take a shower and change out of my traveling clothes.'

'Do you remember your room number?'

'Well, you showed me a copy of the ledger, if that's what you mean.'

Highsmith nodded.

'It was 102.'

'Where is that located in relation to the manager's office?'

'Right next to it on the ground floor.'

'Mr. White, at approximately two PM did you hear anything in the room next to yours?'

'Yeah. There was a woman yelling and crying.'

'Tell the judge about that.'

'Okay,' White said, shifting so he could look up at Judge Norwood. 'I didn't hear anything until I got out of the shower. That's because the water was running. As soon as I turned it off, I heard a shriek, like someone was in pain. It startled me. The walls in that motel aren't thick. The woman was begging not to be hurt and she was crying, sobbing. It was hard to hear the words, but I'd catch a few. I could hear her crying, though.'

'How long did this go on?'

'Not long.'

'Did you ever see the man or the woman in the next room?'

'I saw the woman. I was thinking of calling the manager, but everything quieted down. Like I said, it didn't last long. Anyway, I dressed for my appointment and I left around two-thirty. She was coming out at the same time.'

'The woman in the next room?'

White nodded.

'Do you remember what she looked like?'

'Oh, yeah. Very attractive. Blonde. Good figure.'

Highsmith crossed over to the witness and showed him a photograph.

'Does this woman look familiar?'

White looked at the photograph. 'That's her.'

'How certain of that are you?'

'Absolutely positive.'

'Your Honor,' Highsmith said, 'I offer State's exhibit thirty-five, a photograph of Victoria Miller.'

'No objection,' Betsy said.

'No further questions,' Highsmith said.

'I don't have any questions for Mr White,' Betsy told the judge.

'You're excused, Mr White,' Judge Norwood told the witness.

'State calls Ramon Gutierrez.'

A neatly dressed, dark-skinned young man with a pencil-thin mustache took the stand.

'Where do you work, sir?' Randy Highsmith asked.

'The Hacienda Motel.'

'That's in Vancouver?'

'Yes.'

'What's your job there?'

'I'm the day clerk.'

'What are you doing in the evenings?'

'I'm in college at Portland State.'

'What's your field of study?'

'Pre-med.'

'So, you're working your way through?' Highsmith asked with a smile.

'Yes.'

'That sounds tough.'

'It isn't easy.'

'Mr Gutierrez, were you working at the Hacienda on

October eleventh of this year?'

'Yes.'

'Describe the layout of the motel.'

'It's two stories. There's a landing that goes around the building on the second floor. The office is at the north end on the ground floor, then we have the rooms.'

'How are the rooms numbered on the ground floor?'

'The room next to the office is 102. The one next to that is 103 and so on.'

'Have you brought the check-in sheet for October eleventh?'

'Yes,' Gutierrez said, handing the deputy district attorney a large, dull yellow ledger page.

'Who was checked in to Room 102 that afternoon?'

'Ira White from Phoenix, Arizona.'

Highsmith turned his back to the witness and looked at Martin Darius.

'Who was checked into Room 103?'

'An Elizabeth McGovern from Seattle.'

'Did you check in Ms McGovern?'

'Yes.'

'At what time?'

'A little after noon.'

'I am handing the witness State's exhibit thirty-five. Do you recognize that woman?'

'That's Ms McGovern.'

'You're certain?'

'Yeah. She was a looker,' Gutierrez said sadly. 'Then, I saw her picture in the *Oregonian*. I knew her right away.'

'To what picture are you referring?'

'The picture of the murdered women. Only it said her

name was Victoria Miller.'

'Did you call the District Attorney's Office as soon as you read the paper?'

'Right away. I talked with Mr Page.'

'Why did you call?'

'It said she disappeared that night, the eleventh, so I thought the police might want to know about the guy I saw.'

'What guy?'

'The one who was in the room with her.'

'You saw a man in the room with Mrs Miller?'

'Well, not in the room. But I saw him go in and come out. He'd been there before.'

'With Mrs Miller?'

'Yes. Like once or twice a week. She would register and he would come later.' Gutierrez shook his head. 'What I couldn't figure out is, if he wanted to sneak around, why did he drive that car.'

'What car?'

'This fantastic black Ferrari.'

Highsmith searched for a photograph among the exhibits on the clerk's desk, then handed it to the witness.

'I'm handing you State's exhibit nineteen, which is a photograph of Martin Darius's black Ferrari and I ask you if it looks like the car driven by the man who went into the room with Mrs Miller?'

'I know it's the car.'

'How do you know?'

Gutierrez pointed at the defense table. 'That's Martin Darius, right?'

'Yes, Mr Gutierrez.'

'He's the guy.'

'Why didn't you tell me about Victoria Miller?' Betsy asked Martin Darius as soon as they were alone in the visiting room.

'Calm down,' Darius said, patiently.

'Don't you tell me to calm down,' Betsy responded, infuriated by her client's icy composure. 'Damn it, Martin, I'm your lawyer. Don't you think I would find it interesting that you were screwing one of the victims, and beat her up, the day she disappeared?'

'I didn't beat up Vicky. I told her I didn't want to see her any more and she became hysterical. She attacked me and I had to control her. Besides, what does my fucking Vicky have to do with getting bail?'

Betsy shook her head. 'This could sink you, Martin. I know Norwood. He's strait-laced. Real old-fashioned. The guy's been married to the same woman for forty years and goes to church on Sunday. If you'd told me, I could have softened the impact.'

Darius shrugged. 'I'm sorry,' he said, without meaning it.

'Were you having sex with Laura Farrar or Wendy Reiser?'

'I hardly knew them.'

'What about this party for the mall?'

'There were hundreds of people there. I don't even remember talking to Farrar or Reiser.'

Betsy leaned back in her seat. She felt very uncomfortable alone with Darius in the narrow confines of the visiting room.

'Where did you go after you left the Hacienda Motel?'

Darius smiled sheepishly. 'To a meeting at Brand, Gates and Valcroft with Russ Miller and the other people working on the advertising for Darius Construction. I'd just seen to it that Russ was put in charge of the account. I guess that won't work any more.'

'You are one cold son-of-a-bitch, Martin. You screw Miller's wife, then throw him a bone. Now you're joking about her when she's been murdered. Dr Gregg said she could have been alive for hours, sliced open, in the most god-awful pain. Do you know how much she must have suffered before she died?'

'No, Tannenbaum, I don't know how much she suffered,' Darius said, the smile leaving his face, 'because I didn't kill her. So how about spreading a little of your sympathy in my direction? I'm the one who's being framed. I'm the one who wakes up every morning to this jail stench and has to eat the slop that passes for food.'

Betsy glared at Darius and stood up. 'Guard,' she shouted, pounding on the door. 'I've had enough of you for today, Martin.'

'Suit yourself.'

The guard bent down to put the key in the lock.

'The next time we talk, I want the truth about everything. And that includes Hunter's Point.'

The door opened. As Darius watched her walk away, the thinnest smile creased his lips.

Chapter Thirteen

1

International Exports was on the twenty-second floor of the First Interstate Bank Tower in a small suite of offices tucked away in a corner next to an insurance company. A middle-aged Hispanic woman looked up from her word processor when Reggie Stewart opened the door. She looked surprised, as if visitors were an uncommon sight.

Moments later, Stewart was seated across the desk from Manuel Ochoa, a well-dressed, heavy-set Mexican with a swarthy complexion and a bushy, salt-and-pepper mustache.

'This business with Martin is so terrible. Your district attorney must be insane to arrest someone so prominent. Certainly there is no evidence against him?' Ochoa said, as he offered Stewart a slender cigarillo.

Stewart raised his hand, declining the smoke.

'Frankly, we don't know what Alan Page has. He's playing his cards close to the vest. That's why I'm talking to people who know Mr Darius. We're trying to figure out what in the world Page is thinking.'

Ochoa shook his head sympathetically. 'I'll do anything I can to help, Mr Stewart.'

'Why don't you explain your relationship to Darius.'

'We are business partners. He wanted to build a shopping mall near Medford and the banks would not finance it, so he came to me.'

'How's the venture going?'

'Not well, I'm afraid. Martin has been having trouble lately. There is the unfortunate business with the site where the bodies were discovered. He has a lot of money tied up in the townhouse project. His debts are mounting. Our venture has also been stalled.'

'How serious is Darius's financial situation?'

Ochoa blew a stream of smoke at the ceiling. 'Serious. I am concerned for my investment, but, of course, I am protected.'

'If Mr Darius stays in jail or is convicted what will happen to his business?'

'I can't say. Martin is the genius behind his firm, but he does have competent men working for him.'

'How friendly are you with Mr Darius?'

Ochoa took a long drag on his cigarillo.

'Until recently, you could say we were friends, but not close friends. Business acquaintances would be more accurate. I have had Martin to my home, we socialized occasionally. However, business pressures have strained our relationship.'

Stewart laid photographs of the three women and a sheet of paper with the dates of their disappearances on the blotter.

'Were you with Mr Darius on any of these dates?'

'I don't believe so.'

'What about the photographs? Have you ever seen Mr Darius with any of these women?'

Ochoa studied the photos, then shook his head. 'No, but I have seen Martin with other women.' Stewart took out a pad. 'I have a large house and I live alone. I enjoy getting together with friends. Some of these friends are attractive, single women.'

'Do you want to spell this out for me, Mr Ochoa?'

Ochoa laughed. 'Martin likes young women, but he is always discreet. I have guest bedrooms for my friends.'

'Did Mr Darius use drugs?'

Ochoa eyed Stewart curiously. 'What does that have to do with your case, Mr Stewart?'

'I need to know everything I can about my client. You never know what's important.'

'I have no knowledge of drugs and,' Ochoa said, looking at his Rolex, 'I'm afraid I have another appointment.'

'Thanks for taking the time to see me.'

'It was my pleasure. If I can be of further help to Martin, let me know. And wish him the best for me.'

2

Nora Sloane was waiting for Betsy on a bench outside the courthouse elevator.

'Did you talk to Mr Darius?'

'Martin says you can tag along.'

'Great!'

'Let's meet after court and I'll set up some ground rules.'

'Okay. Do you know how Judge Norwood is going to rule?'

'No. His secretary just said to be here at two.'

Betsy turned the corner. Judge Norwood's court was at the far end of the hall. Most of the people in the corridor were congregating outside the courtroom door. Television crews were grouped around the entrance and a guard was checking people through the metal detector. Betsy flashed her Bar card at the guard. He stood aside. Betsy and Sloane cut behind him and went into the courtroom without having to go through the metal detector.

Martin Darius and Alan Page were in court. Betsy slid into the chair next to Darius and took her files and a pad out of her attaché case.

'Have you seen Lisa?' he asked.

Betsy scanned the packed courtroom. 'I told my secretary to call her, but she's not here yet.'

'What's he going to do, Tannenbaum?'

Darius was trying to sound casual, but there was an edge to his voice.

'We'll soon find out,' Betsy said as Harvey Cobb rapped the gavel.

Judge Norwood strode out of his chambers. He was clutching several sheets of yellow, lined paper. Norwood was a shoot-from-the-hip guy. If he'd taken the time to write out the reasons for his decision, he was expecting it to be appealed.

'This is a very troubling case,' the judge said without preliminaries. 'Someone brutally tortured and murdered four innocent people. That person should not be roaming our streets. On the other hand, we have a presumption in this country that a person is innocent until proven guilty. We also have a guarantee of bail in our Constitution, which can be denied a defendant in a murder case only on a showing by the State that there is clear and convincing evidence of guilt.

'Mr Page, you proved these people were murdered. You proved they were buried at a site owned, and visited by, Mr Darius. You proved Mr Darius knew the three women victims. You also proved he was having an affair with one of them and may have beaten her the day she disappeared. What you have not shown, by clear and convincing evidence, is a connection between the defendant and the murders.

'No one saw Mr Darius kill these people. There is no scientific evidence connecting him to any of the bodies or the homes from which they disappeared. You have matched the tires on the BMW to the tracks left at the murder site, but Mr Darius visited that site frequently. Granted, it is suspicious that the tracks led up to the hole in the fence, but that's not enough, especially when there is no evidence connecting the BMW with any victim.

'Now I know you'll tell me that Mr Darius destroyed the evidence by cleaning the trunk of his car, and that looks suspicious. But the standard I must use to deny bail is clear and convincing evidence and the absence of evidence, no matter how suspicious the circumstances, is not a substitute for evidence.

'Really, Mr Page, the crux of your case is the information

given to you by this Gordon woman. But she wasn't here to be cross-examined by Ms Tannenbaum. Why isn't she here? We don't know. Is it because of foul play or because she made up the story she told you and is smart enough to avoid committing perjury?

'Even if I accept what you say, Mr Darius is guilty of the Hunter's Point murders only if we accept Detective Gordon's theory. This Henry Waters fellow was named by the Hunter's Point police as the killer. If Waters is the killer, then Mr Darius was a victim of the man.'

Judge Norwood paused to take a sip of water. Betsy choked back a victory grin. She glanced to her left. Alan Page was sitting stiffly, eyes straight ahead.

'Bail will be set in the sum of one million dollars. Mr Darius may be released if he posts ten percent.'

'Your Honor,' Page exclaimed, leaping to his feet.

'This won't help you, Mr Page. I've made up my mind. Personally, I'm surprised to see you force this hearing with such a skimpy case.'

Judge Norwood turned his back on the prosecutor and walked off the bench.

'I knew I did the right thing hiring you, Tannenbaum,' Darius exclaimed. 'How long will it take to get me out of here?'

'As long as it takes you to post the bail and the jail to process you.'

'Then call Terry Stark, my accountant at Darius Construction. He's waiting to hear from you. Tell him the amount he has to post and tell him to get it down here immediately.'

*

Nora Sloane watched Betsy field questions from the press, then walked with her toward the elevators.

'You must feel great,' Sloane said.

Betsy was tempted to feed Sloane the same upbeat line she had given to the reporters, but she liked Nora and felt she could confide in her.

'Not really.'

'Why is that?'

'I admit, winning gives me a rush, but Norwood is right. Page's case was very skimpy. Anyone would have won this hearing. If this is the best Page can do, he won't get his case to a jury.

'Also, I don't know who Martin Darius is. If he's a husband and father who found his wife and child brutally murdered, then I did something good today. But what if he really murdered the women in the pit?'

'You think he's guilty?'

'I didn't say that. Martin insists he's innocent and I haven't seen anything to convince me otherwise. What I mean is, I still don't know for certain what happened here or in Hunter's Point.'

'If you knew for certain that Darius was the rose killer, would you still represent him?'

'We have a system in America. It's not perfect, but it's worked for two hundred years and it depends on giving a fair trial to every person who goes through the courts, no matter what they've done. Once you start discriminating, for any reason, the system breaks down. The real test of the system is when it deals with a Bundy or a Manson, someone everyone fears and despises. If you can try that person fairly, then you send a message that we are a nation of law.'

'Can you imagine a case you wouldn't take?' Sloane asked. 'A client you might find so repulsive that your conscience would not let you represent him?'

'That's the question you confront when you choose to practice criminal law. If you can't represent that client, you don't belong in the business.'

Betsy checked her watch. 'Look, Nora, that's going to have to be it for today. I've got to make certain Martin's bail is posted, and my mother's watching Kathy, so I've got to leave the office a little early.'

'Kathy is your daughter?'

Betsy smiled.

'I'd like to meet her.'

'I'll introduce you to Kathy soon. My Mom, too. You'll like them. Maybe I'll have you over for dinner.'

'Great,' Sloane said.

3

'Lisa Darius is waiting for you in your office,' Ann said, as soon as Betsy walked in. 'I hope you don't mind. She's very upset about something and she was afraid to sit in the waiting room.'

'That's okay. Does she know Martin's going to be released on bail?'

'Yes. I asked her how the judge ruled when she came in and she said you won.'

'I didn't see her in court.'

'I called her about the court appearance as soon as you told me to.'

'I'm sure you did. Look, call Terry Stark at Darius Construction,' Betsy said, writing down the name and phone number. 'I told him how to post the bail a few days ago. He'll need a cashier's check for one hundred thousand. If there are any problems, buzz me.'

Betsy did not recognize Lisa at first. She wore tight jeans, a blue turtle-neck and a multi-colored ski sweater. Her long hair was pulled back in a french braid, her emerald eyes were red from crying.

'Lisa, are you all right?'

'I never thought they'd let him out. I'm so scared.'

'Of Martin? Why?'

Lisa put her hands to her face. 'He's so cruel. No one knows how cruel. In public, he's charming. And, sometimes, he's just as charming with me when we're alone. He surprises me with flowers, jewelry. When he wants to, he treats me like a queen and I forget what he's really like inside. Oh God, Betsy, I think he killed those women.'

Betsy was stunned. Lisa started to cry.

'Do you want some water?' Betsy asked.

Lisa shook her head. 'Just give me a moment.'

They sat quietly while Lisa caught her breath. Outside, a winter sun was shining and the air was so crisp and brittle, it seemed you could crack it into a million pieces. When Lisa spoke, her words came in a rush.

'I understand what Andrea Hammermill went through. Taking it, because you don't want anyone to know how bad it is and because there are good times and . . . and you love him.'

Lisa sobbed. Her shoulders shook. Betsy wanted to comfort Lisa, but not as much as she wanted to learn what Darius had done to her to put her in this state, so she sat stiffly, waiting for Lisa to regain her composure.

'I do love him and I hate him and I'm scared of him,' Lisa said hopelessly. 'But this . . . If he . . .'

'Wife-beating is very common, Lisa. Serial murder isn't. Why do you think Martin may have killed these women?'

'It's more than beatings. There's a perverted side to . . . to what he does. His sexual needs . . . One time . . . This is very hard for me.'

'Take your time.'

'He wanted sex. We'd been to a party. I was tired. I told him. He insisted. We had an argument. No. That's not true. He never argues. He . . . he . . .'

Lisa closed her eyes. Her hands were clenched in her lap. Her body was rigid. When she spoke, she kept her eyes shut.

'He told me very calmly that I would have sex with him. I was getting angrier and angrier. The way he was speaking. It's the way you talk to a very small child or someone who's retarded. It enraged me. And the more I screamed, the calmer he became.

'Finally, he said "Take off your clothes", the way you'd command a dog to roll over. I told him to go to hell. The next thing I knew, I was on the floor. He hit me in the stomach. I lost my air. I was helpless.

'When I started to breathe, I looked up. Martin was smiling. He ordered me to take my clothes off again in that same voice. I shook my head. I couldn't talk, yet, but I was damned if I was going to give in. He knelt down, grabbed my nipple through my blouse and squeezed. I almost blacked out from the pain. I was crying now and thrashing around on the floor. He did it to my other nipple and I couldn't stand it. The horrible thing was how methodical he was. There was no passion in it. And he had the tiniest smile on his face, as if he was enjoying himself immensely, but didn't want anyone to know.

'I was on the verge of passing out when he stopped. I sprawled on the floor, exhausted. I knew I couldn't fight him any more. The next time he ordered me to, I took off my clothes.'

'Did he rape you?' Betsy asked. She felt queasy.

Lisa shook her head. 'That was the worst thing. He looked at me for a moment. There was a smile of satisfaction on his face I will never forget. Then, he told me that I must always submit to him when he wanted sex and that I would be punished any time I disobeyed him. He told me to get on all fours. I thought he was going to take me from behind. Instead, he made me crawl across the floor like a dog.

'We have a clothes closet in our bedroom. He opened the door and made me go in, naked. He said I would have to stay there without making a sound until he let me out. He told me I would be severely punished if I made any sound.'

Lisa started sobbing again.

'He kept me in the closet all weekend without food. He put in some toilet paper and a bucket to . . . to use if I . . . I was so hungry and so scared.

'He told me that he would open the door when he was ready and I would immediately have sex with him or I would go back. When he opened the door I just crawled out and . . . and did anything he wanted. When he was through with me, he led me into the bathroom and bathed me, as if I was a baby. There were clothes laid out on the bed. Evening clothes. And a bracelet. It must have cost a fortune. Diamonds, rubies, gold. It was my reward for obedience. When I was dressed, he took me to a restaurant for a lavish dinner. All evening he treated me like a queen.

'I was certain he would want me again when we got home. It's all I thought about at dinner. I had to force myself to eat, because I was nauseous thinking of what was coming but I was afraid he would do something to me if I didn't eat. Then when we got home he just went to sleep and he didn't touch me for a week.'

'Did he ever do anything like that to you again?'

'No,' Lisa said, hanging her head. 'He didn't have to. I learned my lesson. If he said he wanted sex, I did what he wanted. And I received my rewards. And no one knew, until now, what I've been going through.'

'Did you ever think of leaving him?' Betsy asked.

'He . . . he told me if I told anyone the things he did, or tried to run away, he would kill me. If you heard the way he said it, so calm, so detached . . . I knew he'd do it. I knew.'

Lisa took deep breaths until she was back in control.

'There's something else,' Lisa said. Betsy noticed a shopping bag lying next to Lisa's chair. Lisa leaned over and took a scrapbook out of it and placed it in her lap.

'I was certain Martin was having an affair. He never said anything and I never saw him with anyone, but I knew. One day, I decided to search his things while he was at work to see if I could find proof. Instead, I found this.'

Lisa tapped the cover of the scrapbook, then handed it across to Betsy. Betsy placed the book in the center of her blotter. The cover was a faded brown with a gold trim. Betsy opened the scrapbook. On the first page, under a plastic sheet, were clippings about the Hunter's Point case from the Hunter's Point paper, the *New York Times*, *Newsday* and other papers. Betsy flipped through some of the other pages without reading the articles. They were all about the Hunter's Point case.

'Did you ever ask Martin about this?' Betsy asked.

'No. I was too scared. I put it back. But, I did do something. I hired a private detective to follow Martin and to find out about Hunter's Point.'

'What's the detective's name?'

'Sam Oberhurst.'

'Do you have an address and phone number where I can reach him?'

'I've got a phone number.'

'No address?'

'I got his name from a friend who used him in her divorce. She gave me the number. It's an answering machine. We met at a restaurant.'

'Where did you send your checks?'

'I always paid him in cash.'

'Give me your friend's name and I'll have my investigator contact her, if it's necessary.'

'Her name is Peggy Fulton. Her divorce attorney was Gary Telford. He's the one who gave her the name. I'd rather you didn't go to her, unless you have to.'

'The lawyer's better,' Betsy said, as she pulled a sheet of

paper out of her drawer and filled in several blanks. 'This is a release of information form giving me or my investigator the right to see Oberhurst's files.'

While Lisa read the form, Betsy told Ann to have Reggie Stewart come to her office immediately. Lisa signed the release and handed it back to Betsy.

'What did Oberhurst tell you?'

'He was certain Martin was cheating, but he didn't have a name yet.'

'And Hunter's Point?'

'He told me he hadn't started working on that aspect of the investigation.'

Lisa's story had affected Betsy deeply. The thought of Darius treating his wife like an animal disgusted her and Lisa's description made Betsy physically ill. But it did not mean Darius was a murderer, and she was still his attorney.

'Why did you come to me, Lisa?'

'I don't know. I'm so confused by everything. You seemed so understanding at the house and I knew how hard you fought for Andrea Hammermill and the Patterson woman. I hoped you could tell me what to do.'

'Do you plan to tell the District Attorney what you've told me or to give him this book?'

Lisa looked startled. 'No. Why would I do that?'

'To hurt Martin.'

'No. I don't want to . . . I still love him. Or, I . . . Ms Tannenbaum, if Martin did those things . . . If he tortured and killed those women, I have to know.'

Betsy leaned forward and looked directly into Lisa's moist green eyes.

'I'm Martin's lawyer, Lisa. My professional loyalty lies with him, even if he is guilty.'

Lisa looked shocked. 'You'd continue to defend him, even if he did that?'

Betsy nodded. 'But he may not have, Lisa, and what you've told me could be very important. If Oberhurst was following Martin on a date when one of those women disappeared, he could provide Martin with an alibi. Page is going to argue that the same man killed all three women, and he probably did. All I have to do is show Martin didn't kill one of the victims and the DA's case disappears.'

'I hadn't thought of that.'

'When is the last time you talked to Oberhurst?'

'A few weeks ago. I left a few messages on his machine, but he didn't return my calls.'

'I'll have my investigator contact Oberhurst. Can I hold on to the scrapbook?'

Lisa nodded. Betsy walked around the desk and laid a hand on Lisa's shoulder.

'Thank you for confiding in me. I know how hard it must have been.'

'I had to tell someone,' Lisa whispered. 'I've kept it in so long.'

'I have a friend who might help you. Alice Knowland. She's very nice and very compassionate. I've sent other women with similar problems to her and she's helped some of them.'

'What is she, a doctor?'

'A psychiatrist. But don't let that scare you off. Psychiatrist is just a fancy title for a good listener with experience in helping troubled people. She might be good for you. You could go to her a few times, then stop if she isn't helping. Think it over and give me a call.'

'I will,' Lisa said, standing. 'And thank you for listening.'

'You're not alone, Lisa. Remember that.'

Betsy put her arms around Lisa and hugged her.

'Martin will be home late tonight. Will you stay with him?' Betsy asked.

'I can't. I'm living with my father until I decide what to do.'

'Okay.'

'Don't tell Martin I came, please.'

'I won't if I can help it. He is my client, but I don't want to hurt you.'

Lisa wiped her eyes and left. Betsy was drained. She pictured Lisa, hungry and terrified, cowering in the closet in the dark with the smell of her own urine and feces. Betsy's stomach rolled. She walked out of the office and down the hall to the rest-room and ran some cold water in the sink. She splashed her face, then cupped her hands and drank some water.

She remembered the questions Nora and the reporters had asked. How could she sleep if she saved Martin Darius, knowing what she knew about him? What would a man who treated his wife like a dog do to a woman he did not know, if she fell under his power? Would he do what the rose killer had done to his victims? Was Martin the killer?

Betsy remembered the scrapbook and dried her face, then returned to her office. She was half-way through the scrapbook when Reggie Stewart walked in.

'Congratulations on the bail hearing.'

'Pull a chair next to me. I've got something that might break Martin's case.'

'Excellent.'

'Lisa Darius was just here. She suspected Martin might be cheating on her, so she hired an investigator to tail him. Have you heard of a PI named Sam Oberhurst?'

Stewart thought for a moment, then shook his head.

'The name sounds vaguely familiar, but I'm sure we've never met.'

'Here's his phone number and a release from Lisa. Oberhurst has an answering machine. If you can't get through to him, try a divorce attorney named Gary Telford. Lisa got the name from one of his clients. Tell Gary you're working for me. We know each other. Find out if Oberhurst was tailing Darius on a date when any of the women disappeared. He could be Martin's alibi.'

'I'll get right on it.'

Betsy pointed to the scrapbook. 'Lisa found this in Martin's things when she was looking for evidence of the affair. It's filled with clippings from the Hunter's Point case.'

Stewart looked over Betsy's shoulder as Betsy turned the pages. Most of the stories concerned the disappearances. There were several stories about the murders of Sandra and Melody Lake. A section was devoted to the discovery of the disemboweled body of Patricia Cross in Henry Waters' basement and Waters' death. Betsy turned to the final section of the scrapbook and stopped cold.

'My God, there were survivors.'

'What? I thought all the women were murdered.'

'No. Look here. It says Gloria Escalante, Samantha

Reardon and Anne Hazelton were found alive in an old farmhouse.'

'Where?'

'It doesn't give any other information. Wait a minute. No, there's nothing else. According to the article, the women declined to be interviewed.'

'I don't get it. Didn't Darius tell you about this?'

'Not a word.'

'Page?'

'He always referred to them as if they were dead.'

'Maybe Page doesn't know,' Stewart said.

'How is that possible?'

'What if Gordon didn't tell him?'

'Why wouldn't she? And why wouldn't Martin tell me? Something's not right, Reg. None of this makes sense. Gordon and Martin don't mention the survivors, the Hunter's Point files have disappeared. I don't like it.'

'I know you love a mystery, Betsy, but I see this as our big break. The survivors will know who kidnapped and tortured them. If it wasn't Darius, we're home free.'

'Maybe Martin didn't mention the survivors because he knew they'd identify him.'

'There's only one way to find out,' Stewart said. 'Have Ann book me on an early flight to Hunter's Point.'

'I want you to go to Albany, New York, first. Frank Grimsbo, one of the other detectives on the task-force, is head of security at Marlin Steel. His office is in Albany.'

'You got it.'

Betsy buzzed Ann and told her what to do. When she got off the intercom, Stewart asked, 'What about the PI?'

'I'll run down Oberhurst. I want you on that flight, first

thing. There's something weird about this case, Reg, and I'm betting that the answers we need are in Hunter's Point.'

4

Alan Page left the courtroom in a daze. He barely heard the reporters' questions and answered them mechanically. Randy Highsmith told him not to take the loss personally, and assured him that it wasn't his fault that they couldn't find Nancy Gordon, but Highsmith and Barrow had warned him that he was making a mistake by rushing to arrest Darius. Even after they learned about the incident at the Hacienda Motel, the detective and the deputy district attorney wanted to move slowly. Page had overruled them. Now he was paying the price.

Page left work as soon as he could. There was an elevator in the rear of the District Attorney's Office that went to the basement. He took it and dodged across the street to the parking garage, hoping no one would see him and ask him about his public humiliation.

Page poured his first scotch as soon as he took off his raincoat. He drank it quickly, refilled his glass and carried it into the bedroom. Why was he screwing up like this? He hadn't been thinking straight since Tina left him. This was the first time his ragged thought processes had gotten him in trouble, but it had only been a matter of time. He wasn't sleeping, he wasn't eating right, he couldn't concentrate. Now, he was haunted by the ghost of a woman he had known for all of two hours.

Page settled down in front of his television in an alcoholic haze. The old movie he was watching was one he had seen many times before. He let the black-and-white images float across the screen without seeing them. Did he order the arrest of Martin Darius to protect Nancy Gordon? Did he think he could keep them apart and rescue her? What sense did that make? What sense did anything in his life make?

5

Martin Darius parked his Ferrari in front of his house. It was cold. The mist pressed against him when he stepped out of the car. After a week in jail, the chill, damp air felt good. Darius crossed over the bridge. The lights were out. He could barely see the placid pool-water through the glass roof. The rest of the house was also dark. He opened the front door and punched in the code that turned off the alarm.

Lisa was probably hiding from him at her father's house. He didn't care. After a week crowded in with unwashed, frightened men in the stale air of the county correctional facility, a night alone would be a pleasure. He would relish the quiet and bask in the luxury of soaping off the sour jail smell that had seeped into his pores.

There was a bar in the living-room, and Darius fixed himself a drink. He flipped on the outside lights and watched the rain fall on the lawn through the picture-window. He hated jail. He hated taking orders from fools and living with idiots. When he was practicing criminal law in Hunter's Point, he'd had only contempt for his clients. They were losers who were not equipped to succeed in the world, so they dealt with their problems through stealing or violence. A superior man controlled his environment and bent the will of others to him.

To Darius's way of thinking, there was only one reason to tolerate inferior minds. Someone had to do menial labor. Martin wondered what the world would be like if it was ruled by the strong with the menial work done by a slave class selected from docile, mentally inferior men and women. The men could do the heavy work. The inferior women could be bred for beauty.

It was cold in the house. Darius shivered. He thought about the women. Docile women, bred for beauty and subservience. They would make excellent pets. He imagined his female slaves instantly submitting to his commands. Of course, there would be disobedient slaves who would not do as they were told. Such women would have to be chastised.

Darius grew hard thinking about the women. It would have been easy to give in to the fantasy, to open his fly and relieve the delicious feeling of tension. But giving in would be a sign of weakness, so he opened his eyes and breathed deeply. The inferior man lived only in his fantasies, because he lacked will-power and imagination. The superior man made his fantasies a reality.

Darius took another sip, then placed the cool glass to his forehead. He had given his dilemma a lot of thought while he was locked up in jail. He was certain he knew what was coming next. He was free. The newspapers had printed Judge Norwood's opinion that the evidence was not strong enough to convict him. That meant someone else would have to die.

Darius looked at his watch. It was almost ten. Lisa would be up. Getting through to her was the problem. At the jail only collect calls were permitted. Justice Ryder had refused every one he made. Darius dialed the judge's number.

'Ryder residence,' a deep voice answered after three rings.

'Please put my wife on the phone, Judge.'

'She doesn't want to talk to you, Martin.'

'I want to hear that from her lips.'

'I'm afraid that's not possible.'

'I'm out now and I don't have to put up with your interference. Lisa is my wife. If she says she doesn't want to talk to me, I'll accept that, but I want to hear it from her.'

'Let me talk to him, Dad,' Lisa said in the background. The judge must have covered the receiver, because Darius could only hear a muffled argument. Then, Lisa was on the phone.

'I don't want you to call me, Martin.'

She sounded shaky. Darius imagined her trembling.

'Judge Norwood let me out because he didn't believe I was guilty, Lisa.'

'He . . . he doesn't know everything I know.'

'Lisa . . .'

'I don't want to see you.'

'Are you afraid?'

'Yes.'

'Good. Stay afraid. There's something going on here you know nothing about.' Darius heard an intake of breath and the judge asked Lisa if he was threatening her. 'I don't want you to come home. It's too dangerous for you. But I don't want you staying at your father's house, either. There isn't anywhere in Portland you'll be safe.'

'What are you talking about?'

'I want you to go away somewhere until I tell you to come back. If you're afraid of me, don't tell me where you go. I'll get in touch with you through your father.'

'I don't understand. Why should I be afraid?'

Darius closed his eyes. 'I can't tell you and you don't want to know. Believe me when I say you are in great danger.'

'What kind of danger?'

Lisa sounded panicky. Justice Ryder snatched the phone from her hand. 'That's it, Darius. Get off this phone or I'll call Judge Norwood personally and have you thrown back in jail.'

'I'm trying to save Lisa's life and you're endangering it. It's imperative that . . .'

Ryder slammed the phone down. Darius listened to the dial tone. Ryder had always been a pompous ass. Now his bullheadedness could cost Lisa her life. If Darius explained why, the judge would never believe him. Hell, he'd use what Darius said to put him on Death Row. Darius wished he could talk over his problem with Betsy Tannenbaum. She was very bright and she might come up with a solution, but he couldn't go to her either. She'd honor the attorney-client privilege, but she would drop him as a client and he needed her.

Darius had not seen the moon all the time he was in jail. He looked for it now, but it was obscured by clouds. He wondered what phase the moon was in. He hoped it was not full. That brought out the crazies. He should know. Martin shivered, but not from the cold. Right now, he was the only one who was not in danger, but that could change at any moment. Darius did not want to admit it, but he was afraid.

PART FOUR
THE DEVIL'S BARGAIN

Chapter Fourteen

1

Gary Telford had the smile and bright eyes of a young man, but his flabby body and receding hairline made him look middle-aged. He shared a suite of offices with six other lawyers in one of the thirty-story glass boxes that had sprung up in downtown Portland during the past twenty years. Telford's office had a view of the Willamette River. On clear days he could see several mountains in the Cascade range, including majestic Mount Hood and Mount St Helens, an active volcano that had erupted in the early eighties. Today, low-lying clouds owned the sky and it was hard to see the east side of the river in the fog.

'Thanks for seeing me,' Betsy said as they shook hands.

'It's been too long,' Gary said warmly. 'Besides, I'm dying to know how I'm connected with this Darius business.'

'When you represented Peggy Fulton in her divorce, did you use a PI named Sam Oberhurst?'

Telford stopped smiling. 'Why do you want to know?'

'Lisa Darius suspected her husband was having an affair. She asked your client for advice and Peggy gave her Oberhurst's name. He was tailing Darius. I was hoping Oberhurst was conducting surveillance when one of the women disappeared and can give Darius an alibi.'

'If Lisa Darius employed Oberhurst, why do you need to talk to me?'

'She doesn't have his address. Just a phone number. I've called it several times, but all I get is an answering machine. He hasn't returned my calls. I was hoping you'd have his office address.'

Telford considered this information for a moment. He looked uncomfortable. 'I don't think Oberhurst has an office.'

'What's he do, work out of his home?'

'I guess. We always met here.'

'What about bills. Where did you send his checks?'

'Cash. He wanted cash. Up front.'

'Sounds a little unusual.'

'Yeah. Well, he's a little unusual.' Telford paused. 'Look, I'll try to help you find Oberhurst, but there's something you need to know: some of the stuff he does isn't on the up and up. You follow me?'

'I'm not sure I do.'

Telford leaned forward conspiratorily. 'Say you want to find out what someone says when they think the conversation is private, you hire Oberhurst. See what I mean?'

'Electronics?'

Telford nodded. 'Phones, rooms. He hinted he's not above a little B & E. And the guy's got a record for it. I think he did penitentiary time down south somewhere for burglary.'

'Sounds pretty unsavory.'

'Yeah. I didn't like him, I only used him that one time and I'm sorry I did.'

'Why?'

Telford tapped his fingers on his desk. Betsy let him decide what he wanted to say.

'Can we keep this confidential?'

Betsy nodded.

'What Peg wanted . . . Well, she was a little hysterical. Didn't take the divorce well. Anyway, I was sort of like a middle man with this. She said she wanted someone to do something, a private investigator who wouldn't ask too many questions. I hooked them up and paid him his money. I never really used him to work on the case.

'Anyway, someone beat up Mark Fulton about a week or so after I introduced Oberhurst to Peg. It was pretty bad from what I hear. The police thought it was a robbery.'

'Why do you think different?'

'Oberhurst tried to shake me down. He came to my office a week after the beating. Showed me a newspaper article about it. He said he could keep me out of it for two thousand bucks.

'I told him to take a hike. I didn't know a goddamn thing about it. For all I knew, he could have been making the whole thing up. I mean, he reads the article, figures he can touch me for two grand and I won't squawk because the amount's not worth the risk.'

'Weren't you afraid?'

'Damn straight. He's a big guy. He even looks like a gangster. He has a broken nose, talks tough. The whole bit. Only, I figured he was testing me. If I'd given in, he would have kept coming back. Besides, I didn't do anything wrong. Like I said, I only hooked them up.'

'How do I get to Oberhurst?' Betsy asked.

'I got his name from Steve Wong at a party. Try him. Say I told you to call.'

Telford thumbed through a lawyers' directory and wrote Wong's number on the back of a business card.

'Thanks.'

'Glad I could help. And be careful with Oberhurst, he's bad news.'

2

Betsy ate lunch at Zen, then shopped at Saks Fifth Avenue for a suit. It was one-fifteen when she returned to her office. There were several phone messages in her slot and two dozen red roses on her desk. Her first thought was that they were from Rick and the idea made her heart pound. Rick sent her flowers when they were dating and on Valentine's Day. It was something he would do if he wanted to come home.

'Who are these from?' she asked Ann.

'I don't know. They were just delivered. There's a card.'

Betsy put down her phone messages. A small envelope

was taped to the vase. Her fingers trembled as she pried open the flap of the envelope and pulled out a small white card that said,

> For man's best friend, his lawyer. You did a
> bang-up job,
>
> A VERY GRATEFUL CLIENT
> Martin

Betsy put down the card. Her excitement turned sour.

'They're from Darius,' she told Ann, hoping her disappointment didn't show.

'How thoughtful.'

Betsy said nothing. She had wished so hard that the flowers were from Rick. Betsy debated with herself for a moment, then dialed his number.

'Mr Tannenbaum's office,' Rick's secretary said.

'Julie, this is Betsy. Is Rick in?'

'I'm sorry, Mrs Tannenbaum, he's out of the office all day. Should I tell him you called?'

'No, thanks. That's okay.'

The line went dead. Betsy held the receiver for a moment, then hung up. What would she have said if Rick had taken the call? Would she have risked humiliation and told him she wanted to get together? What would Rick have said? Betsy closed her eyes and took a few deep breaths to calm her heart. To distract herself, she looked through her phone messages. Most could be put off, but one was from Dr Keene. When Betsy was back in control, she dialed his number.

'Sue did a good job, Betsy,' the pathologist said when they finally got down to business, 'but I've got something for you.'

'Let me get a pad. Okay, shoot.'

'A medical examiner always collects urine samples from the body to screen for drugs. Most labs only do a DAU, which screens for five drugs of abuse to see if the victim used morphine, cocaine, amphetamines and so on. That's what Sue did. I had my lab do a urine screen for other substances. We came up with strong positive barbiturate readings for the women. I retested the blood. Every one of these ladies showed pentobarbital levels that were off scale.'

'What does that mean?'

'Pentobarbital is not a common drug of abuse, which is why the lab didn't find it. It's an anesthetic.'

'I don't follow.'

'It's used in hospitals to anesthetize patients. This is not a drug these women would take themselves. Someone gave it to them. Now, this is where it gets strange, Betsy. These women all had three to four milligrams percent of pentobarbital in their blood. That's a very high level. In fact, it's a fatal level.'

'What are you telling me?'

'I'm telling you that the three women died from an overdose of pentobarbital, not from their wounds.'

'But they were tortured.'

'They were mutilated, all right. I saw burn marks that were probably from cigarettes and electrical wires, they were cut with razor blades, the breasts were mutilated and there's evidence that objects had been inserted into their

246

anus. But, there's a chance the women were unconscious when these injuries were inflicted. Microscopic sections from around the wounds showed an early repair process. This tells me death occurred about twelve to twenty-four hours after the wounds were inflicted.'

Betsy was quiet for a moment. When she spoke she sounded confused. 'That doesn't make sense, Ray. What possible benefit is there in torturing someone who's unconscious?'

'Beats me. That's your problem. I'm just a saw-bones.'

'What about the man.

'Here, we have a different story. First, there's no pentobarbital. None. Second, there is evidence of repair around several wounds, indicating that he was tortured over a period of time. Death was some time later from a gunshot wound, just like Sue said.'

'How could Dr Gregg have been fooled about the cause of death of the women?'

'Easy. You see a person cut from crotch to chest, the heart torn out, the intestines hanging out, you assume that's what killed 'em. I would have thought the same, if I hadn't found pentobarbital.'

'You've given me a king-size headache, Ray.'

'Take two aspirin and call me in the morning.'

'Very funny.'

'I'm glad I could bring some joy into your life.'

They hung up, but Betsy kept staring at her notes. She doodled on the pad. The drawings made as much sense as what Dr Keene had just told her.

3

Reggie Stewart's cross-country flight arrived late at JFK, so he had to sprint through the terminal to catch the connecting, upstate flight. He felt ragged by the time the plane landed at Albany County Airport. After checking into a motel near the airport, Stewart ate a hot meal, took a shower, and exchanged his cowboy boots, jeans and a flannel shirt for a navy blue suit, a white shirt and a tie with narrow red and yellow stripes. He was feeling human again by the time he parked his rental car in the lot of Marlin Steel's corporate headquarters, fifteen minutes before his scheduled appointment with Frank Grimsbo.

'Thanks for seeing me on such short notice,' Stewart said, as soon as the secretary left him alone with the Chief of Security.

'Curiosity got the better of me,' Grimsbo answered with an easy smile. 'I couldn't figure out what a private investigator from Portland, Oregon would want with me.' Grimsbo gestured towards his wet bar. 'Can I get you a drink?'

'Bourbon, neat,' Stewart said, as he looked out the window at a breathtaking view of the Hudson River.

Grimsbo's office was furnished with an eight-foot rosewood desk and rosewood credenza. Old English hunting scenes hung from the walls. The couch and chairs were black leather. It was a far cry from the stuffy, converted storage area he had shared with the task-force members in Hunter's Point. Like his surroundings, Grimsbo had also changed. He drove a Mercedes instead of a beat-up Chevy and he'd long since lost his taste for polyester. His conservative, gray pinstripe suits were custom-tailored to conceal what was left of a beer belly that had been dramatically reduced by dieting and exercise. He had also lost most of his hair, but he had gained in every other way. If old acquaintances thought he missed his days as a homicide detective, they were mistaken.

'So, what brings you from Portland, Oregon to Albany?' Grimsbo asked as he handed Stewart his drink.

'I work for a lawyer named Betsy Tannenbaum. She's representing a prominent businessman who's been charged with murder.'

' So you told my secretary when you called. What's that have to do with me?'

'You used to work for the Hunter's Point Police Department, didn't you?'

'I haven't had anything to do with Hunter's Point PD for nine years.'

'I'm interested in discussing a case you worked on ten years ago. The rose killer.'

Grimsbo had been raising his glass to his lips, but he stopped abruptly.

'Why are you interested in the rose killer? He's ancient history.'

'Bear with me and I'll explain in a minute.'

Grimsbo shook his head. 'That's a hard case to forget.'

'Tell me about it.'

Grimsbo tilted his head back and closed his eyes, as if he was trying to picture the events. He sipped his scotch.

'We started getting reports of missing women. No signs of a struggle, nothing missing at the crime scenes, but there was always a rose and a note that said "Gone, But Not

Forgotten" left on the women's pillows. Then, a mother and her six-year-old daughter were murdered. The husband found the bodies. There was a rose and a note next to the woman.

'A neighbor had seen a florist truck at the house of one of the victims, or maybe it was near the house. It's been some time now, so I may not have my facts exactly right. Anyway, we figured out who the delivery man was. It was a guy named Henry Waters. He had a sex-offender record. Then, an anonymous caller said he was talking to Waters at a bar and Waters told him he had a woman in his basement. Sure enough, we found one of the missing women.'

Grimsbo shook his head. 'Man, that was a sight. You wouldn't believe what that bastard did to her. I wanted to kill him right there, and I would have, but fate took over and the son-of-a-bitch tried to escape. Another cop shot him and that was that.'

'Was Peter Lake the husband who found the two bodies? The mother and daughter?'

'Right. Lake.'

'Are you satisfied that the delivery man was the killer?'

'Definitely. Hell, they found some of the roses and a note. And, of course, there was the body. Yeah, we got the right man.'

'There was a task-force assigned to investigate the case, wasn't there?'

Grimsbo nodded.

'Was Nancy Gordon a member of the task-force?'

'Sure.'

'Mr Grimsbo . . .'

'Frank.'

'Frank. My client is Peter Lake. He moved to Portland about eight years ago and changed his name to Martin Darius. He's a very successful developer. Very respected. About three months ago, women started disappearing in Portland. Roses and notes identical to those left in the Hunter's Point case were found on the pillows of the missing women. About two weeks ago, the bodies of the missing women and a man were found buried at a construction site owned by Martin Darius. Nancy Gordon told our District Attorney that Darius – Lake – killed them.'

Grimsbo shook his head. 'Nancy always had a bee in her bonnet about Lake.'

'But you don't agree with her?'

'No. Like I said, Waters was the killer. I have no doubt about that. Now, we did think Lake might be the killer for a while. There was circumstantial evidence pointing that way, and I even had bad feelings about the guy. But it was only circumstantial evidence and the case against Waters was solid.'

'What about Lake leaving Hunter's Point?'

'Can't blame him. If my wife and kid were brutally murdered, I wouldn't want to be reminded of them every day. Leaving town, starting over – sounds like the smart thing to do.'

'Did the other investigators agree that Lake was innocent?'

'Everyone but Nancy.'

'Was there any evidence that cleared Lake?'

'Like what?'

'Did he have an alibi for the time of any of the disappearances.'

'I can't recall anything like that. Of course, it's been some time. Why don't you check the file. I'm sure Hunter's Point still has it.'

'The files are missing.'

'How did that happen?'

'We don't know.' Stewart paused. 'What kind of a person is Gordon?'

Grimsbo sipped his scotch and swiveled toward the window. It was comfortable in Grimsbo's office, but there was a thin coating of snow on the ground outside the picture-window and the leafless trees were swaying under the attack of a chill wind.

'Nancy is a driven woman. That case got to all of us, but it affected her the most. It came right after she lost her fiancé. Another cop. Killed in the line of duty shortly before her wedding. Really tragic. I think that unbalanced her for a while. Then the women started disappearing and she submerged herself in the case.

'Now I'm not saying she isn't a fine detective. She is. But she lost her objectivity in that one case.'

Stewart nodded and made some notes.

'How many women disappeared in Hunter's Point?'

'Four.'

'And one was found in Waters' basement?'

'Right.'

'What happened to the other women?'

'They were found in some old farmhouse out in the country, if I remember correctly. I wasn't involved with that. Got stuck back at the station writing reports.'

'How were they found?'

'Pardon?'

'Wasn't Waters shot almost as soon as the body was found in the basement?'

Grimsbo nodded.

'So who told you where the other women were?'

Grimsbo paused, thinking. Then he shook his head.

'You know, I honestly can't remember. It could have been his mother. Waters was living with his mother. Or he might have written something down. I just don't recall.'

'Did any of the survivors positively ID Waters as the killer?'

'They may have. Like I said, I didn't question any of them. They were pretty messed up, if I remember. Barely alive. Tortured. They went right to the hospital.'

'Can you think of any reason why Nancy Gordon wouldn't tell our DA there were survivors?'

'She didn't?'

'I don't think so.'

'Hell, I don't know. Why don't you ask her?'

'We can't. She's disappeared.'

'What?' Grimsbo looked alarmed.

'Gordon showed up at the home of Alan Page, our DA, late one night and told him about the Hunter's Point case. Then she checked into a motel. When Page called her the next morning, she was gone. Her clothing was still in the room, but she wasn't there.'

'Have they looked for her?' Grimsbo asked anxiously.

'Oh, yeah. She's Page's whole case. He lost the bail hearing when he couldn't produce her.'

'I don't know what to say. Did she return to Hunter's Point?'

'No. They thought she was on vacation. She never told anyone she was coming to Portland and they haven't heard from her.'

'Jesus, I hope nothing serious happened. Maybe she took off somewhere. Didn't you say Hunter's Point PD thought she was on vacation?'

'If she was going on vacation she wouldn't leave her clothes and make-up.'

'Yeah.' Grimsbo looked solemn. He shook his head. Stewart watched Grimsbo. The security chief was very upset.

'Is there anything else I can do for you, Mr Stewart?' Grimsbo asked. 'I'm afraid I have some work to do.'

'No, you've been a big help.' Stewart laid his and Betsy's business cards on Grimsbo's desk. 'If you remember anything about the case that might help our client, please call me.'

'I will.'

'Oh, there is one other thing. I want to talk with all the members of the Hunter's Point task-force. Do you know where I can find Glen Michaels and Wayne Turner?'

'I haven't heard from Michaels in years, but Wayne will be easy to find in about two weeks.'

'Oh?'

'All you gotta do is turn on your TV. He's Senator Colby's Administrative Assistant. He should be sitting right next to him during the confirmation hearings.'

Stewart scribbled this information into his notebook, thanked Grimsbo and left. As soon as the door closed behind Stewart, Grimsbo went back to his desk and dialed a Washington, D.C. phone number. Wayne Turner answered on the first ring.

Chapter Fifteen

1

Reggie Stewart eased himself into a seat across the desk from Dr Pedro Escalante. The cardiologist had put on weight over the past ten years. His curly black hair was mostly gray. He was still cheerful with patients, but his good humor was not second nature to him any more.

They were meeting in the cardiologist's office in the Wayside Clinic. A diploma from Brown University and another from Tufts Medical School hung on one wall. Beneath the diplomas was a child's crayon drawing of a stick-figure girl standing next to a yellow flower that was almost as tall as she was. A rainbow stretched from one side of the picture to the other.

'That your daughter?' Stewart asked. A photograph of Gloria Escalante holding a little girl on her lap stood on one corner of the doctor's desk. Stewart figured the child for the artist and asked about her as a way of easing into a conversation that was certain to evoke painful memories.

'Our adopted daughter,' Escalante replied sadly. 'Gloria lost the ability to conceive after her ordeal.'

Stewart nodded, because he could not think of a single thing to say.

'I'm afraid you've wasted your trip, if it was made solely to talk to my wife. We have tried our best to put the past behind us.'

'I appreciate why Mrs Escalante wouldn't want to talk to me, but this is literally a matter of life and death. We have the death penalty in Oregon and there's no doubt that my client will receive it, if he's convicted.'

Dr Escalante's features hardened. 'Mr Stewart, if your client treated those women the way my wife was treated, the death penalty would be insufficient punishment.'

'You knew my client as Peter Lake, Dr Escalante. His wife and daughter were killed by Henry Waters. He suffered the same anguish you suffered. We're talking about a frame-up of the worst kind and your wife may have information that can prove an innocent man is being prosecuted.'

Escalante looked down at his desk. 'Our position is firm, Mr Stewart. My wife will not discuss what happened to her with anyone. It has taken ten years to put the past behind her and we are going to keep it behind her. However, I may be of some help to you. There are answers to questions I may be able to give you.'

'Any help will be appreciated.'

'I don't want you to think her hard, Mr Stewart. We did consider your request for an interview most seriously, but it would be too much for Gloria. She is very strong. Very strong. Otherwise she would not have survived. But as strong as she is, it is only within the past few years that she has been anything like the woman she used to be. Since your call, the nightmares have returned.'

'Believe me, I would never subject your wife to . . .'

'No, no. I understand why you're here. I don't blame you. I just want you to understand why I can't permit her to relive what happened.'

'Dr Escalante, the main reason I wanted to talk to your wife was to find out if she saw the face of the man who kidnapped her.'

'If that's why you came, I'm afraid I must disappoint you. She was taken from behind. Chloroform was used. During her captivity, she was forced to wear a leather hood with no eyelets whenever . . . whenever her captor . . . When he came.'

'She never saw his face?'

'Never.'

'What about the other women? Did any of them see him?'

'I don't know.'

'Do you know where I can find Ann Hazelton or Samantha Reardon?'

'Ann Hazelton committed suicide six months after she was freed. Reardon was in a mental hospital for some time. She had a complete breakdown. Simon Reardon, Samantha's husband, divorced her,' Escalante said with obvious distaste. 'He moved away years ago. He's a neurosurgeon. You can probably locate him through the American Medical Association. He might know where Mrs Reardon is living.'

'That's very helpful,' Stewart said as he wrote the information in his notebook.

'You could ask the other investigator. He may have located her.'

'Pardon?'

'There was another investigator. I wouldn't let him speak to Gloria, either. He came during the summer.'

'The disappearances didn't start until August.'

'No, this would have been May, early June. Somewhere in there.'

'What did he look like?'

'He was a big man. I thought he might have played football or boxed, because he had a broken nose.'

'That doesn't sound like anyone from the DA's office. But they wouldn't have been involved that early. Do you remember his name or where he was from?'

'He was from Portland and I have his card.' The doctor opened the top drawer of his desk and pulled out a white business card. 'Samuel Oberhurst,' he said, handing the card to Stewart. The card had Oberhurst's name and a phone number, but no address. The number was the one Betsy had given him.

'Dr Escalante, what happened to your wife and the other women after they were kidnapped?'

Escalante took a deep breath. Stewart could see his pain even after all these years.

'My wife told me that there were three women with her. They were kept in an old farmhouse. She isn't clear where the house was situated, because she was unconscious when he brought her there and she was in shock when she left. Almost dead from starvation. It was a miracle.'

Escalante paused. He ran his tongue across his lips and breathed deeply again.

'The women were kept naked in stalls. They were chained at the ankles. Whenever he would come, he was masked and he would make them put on the hoods. Then, he . . . he would torture them.' Escalante closed his eyes and shook his head, as if trying to clear it of images too painful to behold. 'I have never asked her to tell me what he did, but I have seen my wife's medical records.'

Escalante paused again.

'I don't need that information, Doctor. It's not necessary.'

'Thank you.'

'The important thing is the identification. If your wife can remember anything about her captor that would help us to prove he was not Peter Lake.'

'I understand. I'll ask her, but I'm certain she won't be able to help you.'

Dr Escalante shook hands with Stewart and showed him out. Then he returned to his office and picked up the photograph of his wife and child.

2

Betsy had a trial scheduled to start Friday in a divorce case and she was putting the file in her attaché case to bring home when Ann told her Reggie Stewart was on the line.

'How was your trip?' Betsy asked.

'Just fine, but I'm not accomplishing much. There's something weird about this business and it's getting weirder by the minute.'

'Go on.'

'I can't put my finger on what's wrong, but I know I'm getting the run-around about the case when no one should have any reason to lie to me.'

'What are they lying about?'

'That's just it. I have no idea. But I know something's up.'

'Tell me what you've learned so far.' Betsy said, and Stewart recounted his conversations with Frank Grimsbo and Dr Escalante.

'After I left Escalante, I spent some time at the public library going over newspaper accounts of the case. I figured there would be interviews with the victims, the cops. Nothing. John O'Malley, the Chief of Police, was the Mayor's spokesman. He said Waters did it. Case closed. The surviving women were hospitalized immediately. Reardon was institutionalized. Escalante wouldn't talk to reporters. Ditto Hazelton. A few weeks of this and interest fades. On to other stories. But you read the news reports and you read O'Malley's statements and you still don't know what happened to those women.

'Then, I talked to Roy Lenzer, a detective with Hunter's Point PD. He's the guy who's trying to run down the case files for Page. He knows Gordon is missing. He searched her house for the files. No luck. Someone carted off all of the files in the case. I mean, we're talking a full shelf of case reports, photographs. But why? Why take a shelf-load of paper in a ten-year-old case? What was in those files?'

'Reg, did Oberhurst visit the police?'

'I asked Lenzer about that. Gave Grimsbo a call, too. As far as I can tell, Oberhurst never talked to anyone after he talked to Dr Escalante. Which doesn't make sense. If he was investigating the case for Lisa Darius, the police would be his first stop.'

'Not necessarily,' Betsy said. Then she told her investigator about her meeting with Gary Telford.

'I have a very bad feeling about this, Reg. Let me run something by you. Say you're an unscrupulous investigator. An ex-con, who works on the edge. Someone who's not averse to a little blackmail. The wife of a prominent businessman hires you, because she thinks her husband is having an affair. She also gives you a scrapbook containing clippings about an old murder case.'

'Let's suppose that this crooked PI flies to Hunter's Point and talks to Dr Escalante. He's no help, but he does tell the investigator enough information so he can track down Samantha Reardon, the only other surviving victim. What if Oberhurst found Reardon and she positively identified Peter Lake as the man who kidnapped and tortured her?'

'And Oberhurst returned to Portland and what?' Stewart said. 'Blackmailed a serial killer? You'd have to be nuts.'

'Who's the John Doe, Reg?'

The line was quiet for a moment, then Stewart said, 'Oh shit.'

'Exactly. We know Oberhurst lied to Lisa. He told her he hadn't started investigating the Hunter's Point case, but he was in Hunter's Point. And he's disappeared. I talked to every lawyer I could find who's employed him. No contact. He doesn't return calls. The John Doe is Oberhurst's size and build. What do you want to bet the corpse has a broken nose?'

'No bets. What are you going to do?'

'There's nothing we can do. Darius is our client. We're his agents. This is all confidential.'

'Even if he killed the guy?'

'Even if he killed the guy.'

Betsy heard a sharp intake of air, then Stewart said, 'You're the boss. What do you want me to do next?'

'Have you tried to set up a meeting with Wayne Turner?'

'No go. His secretary says he's too busy, because of the confirmation hearings.'

'Damn. Gordon, Turner, Grimsbo. They all know something. What about the Police Chief? What was his name?'

'O'Malley. Lenzer says he retired to Florida about nine years ago.'

'Okay,' Betsy said with a trace of desperation. 'Keep trying to find Samantha Reardon. She's our best bet.'

'I'll do it for you, Betsy. If it was someone else . . . I gotta tell you, I usually don't give a fuck, but I'm starting to. I don't like this case.'

'That makes two of us. I just don't know what to do about it. We're not even certain I'm right. I have to find that out, first.'

'If you are, what then?'

'I have no idea.'

3

Betsy put Kathy to sleep at nine and changed into a flannel night-gown. After brewing a pot of coffee, Betsy spread out the papers in Friday's divorce case on the dining-room table. The coffee was waking her up, but her mind wandered to the Darius case. Was Darius guilty? Betsy could not stop thinking about the question she had put to Alan Page during her cross-examination: with six victims, including a six-year-old girl, why would the Mayor and Chief of Police of Hunter's Point close the case if there was any possibility that Peter Lake, or anyone else, was really the murderer? It made no sense.

Betsy pushed aside the documents in the divorce and pulled a yellow pad in front of her. She listed what she knew about the Darius case. The list stretched for three pages. Betsy came to the information she had learned from Stewart that afternoon. A thought occurred to her. She frowned.

Betsy knew Samuel Oberhurst was not above blackmail. He'd tried it on Gary Telford. If Martin Darius was the rose killer, Darius would have no compunction about killing Oberhurst, if the investigator tried to blackmail him. But Betsy's assumption that John Doe was Samuel Oberhurst made sense only if Samantha Reardon identified Martin Darius as the rose killer. And that's where the difficulty lay. The police would have questioned Reardon when they rescued her. If the task-force suspected that Peter Lake, not Henry Waters, was the kidnapper, they would have shown Reardon a photograph of Lake. If she identified Lake as her kidnapper, why would the Mayor and the Police Chief announce that Waters was the killer? Why would the case be closed?

Dr Escalante said that Reardon was institutionalized. Maybe she couldn't be interviewed immediately. But she would have been interviewed at some point. Grimsbo told Reggie that Nancy Gordon was obsessed with the case and never believed Waters was the killer. So, Betsy thought, let's assume that Reardon did identify Lake as the killer at some point. Why wouldn't Gordon, or someone, have reopened the case?

Maybe Reardon wasn't asked until Oberhurst talked to her. But wouldn't she have read about Henry Waters and known the police had accused the wrong man? She could have been so traumatized that she wanted to forget everything that happened to her, even if it meant letting Lake go free. But, if that was true, why tell Oberhurst that Lake was her kidnapper?

Betsy sighed. She was missing something. She stood up and carried her coffee cup into the living-room. The Sunday *New York Times* was sitting in a wicker basket next to her favorite chair. She sat down and decided to look through it. Sometimes, the best way to figure out a problem was to forget about it for a while. She had read the *Book Review*, the *Magazine* and the *Arts* section, but she still hadn't read the *Week in Review*.

Betsy skimmed an article about the fighting in the Ukraine and another about the resumption of hostilities between North and South Korea. Death was everywhere.

Betsy turned the page and started reading a profile of Raymond Colby. Betsy knew Colby would be confirmed and it upset her. There was no more diversity of opinion on the Court. Wealthy, white males with identical backgrounds and identical thoughts dominated it. Men with no concept of what it was like to be poor or helpless, who had been nominated by Republican Presidents for no reason other than their willingness to put the interests of the wealthy and big government ahead of individual rights.

Colby was no different. Harvard Law, CEO of Marlin Steel, Governor of New York, then a member of the United States Senate for the last nine years. Betsy read a summary of Colby's accomplishments as a Governor and Senator and a prediction of the way he would vote on several cases that were before the Supreme Court, then skimmed another article about the economy. When she was finished with the paper, she went back to the dining-room.

The divorce case was a mess. Betsy's client and her husband didn't have children and they had agreed to split almost all of their property, but they were willing to go to the mats over a cheap landscape they had bought from a sidewalk artist in Paris on their honeymoon. Going to court over the silly painting was costing them both ten times its value, but they were adamant. Obviously, it was not the painting that was fueling their rage. It was a case like this that made Betsy want to enter a nunnery. But, she sighed to herself, it was also cases like this that paid her overhead. She started reading the divorce petition when she remembered something she had read in the article about Raymond Colby.

Betsy put the petition down. The idea had come so fast that it made her a little dizzy. She walked back to the living-room and reread Colby's biography. There it was. He had been a United States Senator for nine years. Hunter's Point Chief of Police John O'Malley retired to Florida nine years ago. Frank Grimsbo had been with Marlin Steel, Colby's old company, for nine years. And Wayne Turner was the Senator's Administrative Assistant.

The heat was on in the house, but Betsy felt like she was hugging a block of ice. She went back to the dining-room and reread her list of important facts in the Darius case. It was all there. You just had to look at the facts in a certain way and it made perfect sense. Martin Darius was the rose killer. The Hunter's Point police knew that when they announced that Henry Waters was the murderer and closed the case. Now, Betsy knew how Peter Lake could walk away from Hunter's Point with the blood of all those innocent people on his hands. What she could not imagine was why the Governor of New York State would conspire with the police force and Mayor of Hunter's Point to set free a mass murderer.

Chapter Sixteen

1

The sun was shining, but the temperature was a little below freezing. Betsy hung up her overcoat. Her cheeks hurt from the cold. She rubbed her hands together and asked Ann to bring her a cup of coffee. By the time Ann set a steaming mug on her coaster, Betsy was dialing Washington, D.C.

'Senator Colby's office.'

'I'd like to speak to Wayne Turner, please.'

'I'll connect you to his secretary.'

Betsy picked up the mug. Her hand was trembling. She wanted to sound confident, but she was scared to death.

'Can I help you?' a pleasant female voice asked.

'My name is Betsy Tannenbaum. I'm an attorney in Portland, Oregon. I'd like to speak to Mr Turner.'

'Mr Turner is very busy with the confirmation hearings. If you leave me your number, he'll call you when he gets the chance.'

Betsy knew Turner would never return her call. There

was only one way to force him to get on the phone. Betsy was convinced she knew what had happened in Hunter's Point and she would have to gamble she was right.

'This can't wait. Let Mr Turner know that Peter Lake's attorney is on the phone.' Then Betsy told the secretary to tell Turner something else. The secretary made her repeat the message. 'If Mr Turner won't talk to me, tell him I'm sure the press will.'

Turner's secretary put Betsy on hold. Betsy closed her eyes and tried a meditation technique she had learned in a YWCA yoga class. It didn't work, and she jumped when Turner came on the line.

'Who is this?' he barked.

'I told your secretary, Mr Turner. My name is Betsy Tannenbaum and I'm Martin Darius's attorney. You knew him as Peter Lake when he lived in Hunter's Point. I want to talk to Senator Colby immediately.'

'The Senator is extremely busy with the confirmation hearings, Ms Tannenbaum. Can't this wait until they're over?'

'I'm not going to wait until the Senator is safely on the Court, Mr Turner. If he won't speak to me, I'll be forced to go to the press.'

'Damn it, if you spread any irresponsible . . .'

'Calm down, Mr Turner. If you thought about this at all, you'd know it would hurt my client to go to the papers. I'll only do it as a last resort. But I won't be put off.'

'If you know about Lake, if you know about the Senator, why are you doing this?' Turner pleaded.

Betsy paused. Turner had asked a good question. Why was she keeping what she knew to herself? Why hadn't she confided in Reggie Stewart? Why was she willing to fly across the country for the answer to her questions?

'This is for me, Mr Turner. I have to know what kind of man I'm representing. I have to know the truth. I must meet with Senator Colby. I can fly to Washington tomorrow.'

Turner was silent for a few seconds. Betsy looked out the window. In the office across the street, two men in shirt sleeves were discussing a blueprint. On the floor above them, a group of secretaries were working away on word processors. Toward the top of the office building, Betsy could see the sky reflected in the glass wall. Green tinted clouds scudded across a green tinted sky.

'I'll talk to Senator Colby and call you back,' Turner said.

'I'm not a threat, Mr Turner. I'm not out to wreck the Senator's appointment. Tell him that.'

Turner hung up and Betsy exhaled. She was not used to threatening United States Senators or dealing with cases that could destroy the reputations of prominent public figures. Then she thought about the Hammermill and Peterson cases. Twice, she had shouldered the burden of saving a human life. There was no greater responsibility than that. Colby was just a man, even if he was a United States Senator, and he might be the reason Martin Darius was free to murder three innocent women in Portland.

'Nora Sloane is on one,' Ann said over the intercom.

Betsy's divorce client was supposed to meet her at the courthouse at eight forty-five and it was eight-ten. Betsy wanted to concentrate on the issues in the divorce, but she decided she could spare Sloane a minute.

'Sorry to bother you,' Sloane said apologetically. 'Remember I talked to you about interviewing your mother and Kathy? Do you suppose I could do that this weekend?'

'I might be out of town. My mom will probably watch Kathy, so you could talk to them together. Mom will get a kick out of being interviewed. I'll talk to her and get back to you. What's your number?'

'Why don't I call you? I'm going to be in and out.'

'Okay. I've got court in half an hour. I should be done by noon. Call me this afternoon.'

Betsy checked her watch. She had twenty minutes to prepare for court and no more time to spend thinking about Martin Darius.

2

Reggie Stewart found Ben Singer, the attorney who handled Samantha Reardon's divorce, by going through the court records. Singer had not heard from Reardon in years, but he did have an address near the campus.

Most of the houses around the University were older, single-family dwellings surrounded by well-kept lawns and shaded by oak and elm trees, but there was a pocket of apartments and boarding houses that catered to students located several blocks behind the campus near the freeway. Stewart turned into a parking lot that ran the length of a dull gray garden-apartment complex. It had snowed the night before. Stewart stepped over a drift on to the shoveled sidewalk in front of the manager's office. A woman in her early forties dressed in heavy slacks and a green wool sweater answered the door. She was holding a cigarette. Her face was flushed. There were curlers in her strawberry-red hair.

'My name is Reggie Stewart. I'm looking for the apartment manager.'

'We're full,' the woman answered brusquely.

Stewart handed the woman his card. She stuck her cigarette in her mouth and examined it.

'Are you the manager?' Stewart asked. The woman nodded.

'I'm trying to find Samantha Reardon. This was the last address I had for her.'

'What do you want with her?' the woman asked suspiciously.

'She may have information that could clear a client who used to live in Hunter's Point.'

'Then you're out of luck. She's not here.'

'Do you know when she'll be back?'

'Beats me. She's been gone since the summer.' The manager looked at the card again. 'The other investigator was from Portland, too. I remember, because you two are the only people I ever met from Oregon.'

'Was this guy big with a broken nose?'

'Right. You know him?'

'Not personally. When did he show up?'

'It was hot. That's all I remember. Reardon left the next day. Paid a month's rent in advance. She said she didn't know how long she'd be gone. Then, about a week later, she came back and moved out.'

'Did she store anything with you?'

'Nah. The apartment's furnished and she hardly had anything of her own.' The manager shook her head. 'I was up there once to fix a leak in the sink. Not a picture on the wall, not one knick-knack on a table. The place looked just like it did when she moved in. Spooky.'

'You ever talk to her?'

'Oh, sure. I'd see her from time to time. But it was mostly "good morning" or "how's it going" on my part and not much from her. She kept to herself.'

'Did she have a job?'

'Yeah. She worked somewhere. I think she was a secretary or receptionist. Something like that. Might have been for a doctor. Yeah, a doctor, and she was a bookkeeper. That was it. She looked like a bookkeeper too. Real mousy. She didn't take care of herself. She had a nice figure if you looked hard. Tall, athletic. But she always dressed like an old maid. It looked to me like she was trying to scare men off, if you know what I mean.'

'You wouldn't happen to have a picture of her?'

'Where would I get a picture? Like I said, I don't even think she had any pictures in her place. Weird. Everyone has pictures, knick-knacks, things to remind you of the good times.'

'Some people don't want to think about the past,' Stewart said.

The manager took a drag on her cigarette and nodded in agreement. 'She like that? Bad memories?'

'The worst,' Stewart said. 'The very worst.'

3

'Let me help you with the dishes,' Rita said. They had left them after dinner, so they could watch one of Kathy's favorite television shows with her before Betsy put her to bed.

'Before I forget,' Betsy said as she piled up the bread plates, 'a woman named Nora Sloane may call you. I gave her your number. She's the one who's writing the article for *Pacific West*.'

'Oh?'

'She wants to interview you and Kathy for background.'

'Interview me?' Rita preened.

'Yeah, Mom. It's your chance at immortality.'

'You're my immortality, honey, but I'm available if she calls,' Rita said. 'Who better to give her the inside story than your mother.'

'That's what I'm afraid of.'

Betsy rinsed the plates and cups and Rita put them in the dishwasher.

'Do you have some time before you go home? I want to ask you about something.'

'Sure.'

'You want coffee or tea?'

'Coffee will be fine.'

Betsy poured two cups and they carried them into the living-room .

'It's the Darius case,' Betsy said. 'I don't know what to do. I keep on thinking about those women, what they went through. What if he killed them, Mom?'

'Aren't you always telling me that your client's guilt or innocence doesn't matter? You're his lawyer.'

'I know. And that is what I always say. And I believe it. Plus I'm going to need the money I'm making on the case, if Rick and I . . . If we divorce. And the prestige. Even if I

274

lose, I'll still be known as Martin Darius's attorney. This case is putting me in the major leagues. If I dropped out, I'd get a reputation as someone who couldn't handle the pressure of a big case.'

'But, you're worried about getting him off?'

'That's it, Mom. I know I can get him off. Page doesn't have the goods. Judge Norwood told him as much at the bail hearing. But I know things Page doesn't and I . . .'

Betsy shook her head. She was visibly shaken.

'Someone is going to represent Martin Darius,' Rita said calmly. 'If you don't do it, another lawyer will. I listen to what you say about giving everyone, even killers and drug pushers, a fair trial. It's hard for me to accept. A man who would do that to a woman – to anyone. You want to spit on them. But you aren't defending that person. Isn't that what you tell me? You're preserving a good system.'

'That's the theory, but what if you feel sick inside? What if you can't sleep because you know you're going to free someone who . . . Mom, he did this same thing in Hunter's Point. I'm certain of it. And, if I get him off, who's next? I keep thinking about what those women went through. Alone, helpless, stripped of their dignity.'

Rita reached across the space between them and took her daughter's hand.

'I'm so proud of what you've done with your life. When I was a girl I never thought about being a lawyer. That's an important job. You're important. You do important things. Things other people don't have the courage to do. But, there's a price. Do you think the President sleeps well? And judges? Generals? So, you're finding out about the bad side of responsibility. With those battered women, it was easy.

You were on God's side. Now, God is against you. But you have to do your job even if you suffer. You have to stick with it and not take the easy way out.'

Suddenly, Betsy was crying. Rita moved over and threw her arms around her daughter.

'I'm a mess, Mom. I loved Rick so much. I gave him everything and he walked out on me. If he was here to help me . . . I can't do it alone.'

'Yes you can. You're strong. No one could do what you've done without being strong.'

'Why don't I see it that way. I feel empty, used up.'

'It's hard to see yourself the way others see you. You know you're not perfect, so you emphasize your weaknesses. But you've got plenty of strengths, believe me.'

Rita paused. She looked distant for a moment, then she looked at Betsy.

'I'm going to tell you something no other living soul knows. The night your father passed away, I almost took my own life.'

'Mom!'

'I sat in our bedroom, after you were asleep, and I took out pills from our bathroom cabinet. I must have looked at those pills for an hour, but I couldn't do it. You wouldn't let me. The thought of you. How I would miss seeing you grow up. How I would never know what you did with your life. Not taking those pills was the smartest thing I ever did, because I got to see you the way you are now. And I am so proud of you.'

'What if I'm not proud of myself? What if I'm only in this for the money or the reputation? What if I'm helping a man who is truly evil to escape punishment, so he can be

free to cause unbearable pain and suffering to other innocent people?'

'I don't know what to say to you,' Rita answered. 'I don't
know all the facts, so I can't put myself in your place. But I
trust you and I know you'll do the right thing.'

Betsy wiped at her eyes. 'I'm sorry I laid this on you, but
you're the only one I can let my hair down with now that
Rick's walked out.'

'I'm glad to know I'm good for something,' Rita smiled
back. Betsy hugged her. It had been good to cry, it had been
good to talk out what she had been holding inside, but
Betsy didn't feel she was any closer to an answer.

Chapter Seventeen

On Sunday afternoon, Raymond Colby stood in front of the fireplace in his den waiting for the lawyer from Portland to arrive. A servant had built a fire. Colby held his hands out to catch the heat and dispel a chill that had very little to do with the icy rain that was keeping his neighbors off the streets of Georgetown.

The front door opened and closed. That would be Wayne Turner with Betsy Tannenbaum. Colby straightened his suit coat. What did Tannenbaum want? That was really the question. Was she someone with whom he could reason? Did she have a price? Turner didn't think Lake's attorney knew everything, but she knew enough to ruin his chance of being confirmed. Perhaps she would come over to their side once she knew the facts. After all, going public would not only destroy Raymond Colby, it would destroy her client.

The door to the den opened and Wayne Turner stood aside. Colby sized up his visitor. Betsy Tannenbaum was attractive, but Colby could see she was not a woman who traded on her looks. She was dressed in a severe black suit with a cream-colored blouse. All business, a little nervous, he guessed, feeling somewhat out of her league, yet willing to confront a powerful man on his own turf. Colby smiled and held out his hand. Her handshake was firm. She was not afraid to look Colby in the eye or to look him over much the way he had scrutinized her.

'How was your flight?' Colby asked.

'Fine.' Betsy looked around the cozy room. There were three high-backed armchairs drawn up in front of the fire-place. Colby motioned toward them.

'Can I get you something to take off the chill?'

'A cup of coffee, please.'

'Nothing stronger?'

'No, thank you.'

Betsy took the chair closest to the window. Colby sat in the center chair. Wayne Turner poured coffee from a silver urn a servant had set up on an antique, walnut side-table. Betsy stared into the fire. She had barely noticed the weather on the ride from the airport. Now that she was inside, she shivered in a delayed reaction to the tension of the preceding hours. Wayne Turner handed Betsy a delicate china cup and saucer covered with finely drawn roses. The flowers were a pale pink and the stems a tracery of gold.

'How can I help you, Ms Tannenbaum?'

'I know what you did ten years ago in Hunter's Point, Senator. I want to know why.'

'And what did I do?'

'You corrupted the Hunter's Point task-force, you destroyed police files, and you engineered a cover-up to protect a monstrous serial killer who revels in torturing women.'

Colby nodded sadly. 'Part of what you say is true, but not all of it. No one on the task-force was corrupt.'

'I know about the pay-offs,' Betsy answered curtly.

'What do you think you know?'

Betsy flushed. She had been spurred on by the coincidences, the improbabilities, to the only possible solution, but she did not want to sound like she was bragging. On the other hand, letting Colby know how she figured it out would make him see that she could not be fooled.

'I know that a Senator's term is six years,' Betsy answered, 'and that you are in the middle of your second term. That means you've been a United States Senator for nine years. Nine years ago, Frank Grimsbo left a low-paying job on an obscure, small-city police force to assume a high-paying job at Marlin Steel, your old company. Nine years ago, John O'Malley, the Police Chief of that police force, retired to Florida. Wayne Turner, another member of the rose killer task-force, is your Administrative Assistant. I asked myself how three members of the same small-city police force could suddenly do so well, and why they would all do so well the year you decided to run for the United States Senate. The answer was obvious. They had been paid off to keep a secret and for destroying the files of the rose killer investigation.'

Colby nodded. 'Excellent deductions, but only partly correct. There were rewards, but no bribes. Frank Grimsbo earned his position as Head of Security after I helped him get a job on the security force. Chief O'Malley had a heart attack and was forced to retire. I'm a very wealthy man. Wayne told me John was having financial problems and I helped him out. And Wayne was working his way through law school when the kidnappings and murders occurred. He graduated two years later and I helped him get a job in Washington, but it was not on my staff. Wayne didn't come on board until a year before my first term ended. By then, he had established an excellent reputation on the Hill. When Larry Merrill, my AA, went back into law practice in Manhattan, I asked Wayne if he would take his place. So, you see, the explanations for these events are less sinister than you supposed.'

'But I'm right about the records.'

'Chief O'Malley took care of that.'

'And the pardon?'

Colby looked very old, all of a sudden.

'Everyone has something in their life they wish they could undo. I think about Hunter's Point all the time, but I can't see how it could have ended differently.'

'How could you have done it, Senator? The man's not human. You had to know he would do this again, some-where, sometime.'

Colby turned his face toward her, but he was not seeing Betsy. He looked completely lost, like a man who has just been told that he has an incurable illness.

'We knew, God forgive us. We knew, but we had no choice.'

PART FIVE

HUNTER'S POINT

Chapter Eighteen

1

Nancy Gordon heard a tinkle of glass when Peter Lake broke the lower left pane in the back door so he could reach between the jagged shards and open it from the inside. Nancy heard the rusty hinges squeak. She shifted under the covers and trained her eyes on the doorway, straining to see in the dark.

Two hours earlier, Nancy had been alone in the task-force office when Lake appeared to tell her he had heard about the shooting of Henry Waters on the late news. As planned, Nancy told Lake she had suspected him of being the rose killer because of the gap between the time he had been seen driving home and the call to 911 and his stake-out of Waters' home. Lake had been alarmed, but Nancy assured him that she was satisfied that Waters was the murderer and had kept her suspicions to herself. Then she had yawned and told Lake she was heading home. Since then Nancy had been in bed, waiting.

Black slacks, a black ski-mask and a black turtle-neck helped Lake blend into the darkness. There was an ugly, snub-nosed revolver in his hand. Nancy did not hear him cross the living-room. One second, her bedroom doorway was empty, then Lake filled it. When he snapped on the light Nancy sat up in bed, feigning surprise. Lake removed the ski-mask.

'You knew, didn't you, Nancy?' She gaped at him, as if the visit was unexpected. 'I really do like you, but I can't take the chance you'll reopen the case.'

Nancy looked at the revolver. 'You can't believe you'll get away with murdering a cop.'

'I don't have much choice. You're far too intelligent. Eventually, you would have realized Waters was innocent. Then you would have kept after me. You might even have dug up enough evidence to convince a jury.'

Lake walked around the side of the bed. 'Place your hands on top of the sheet and take it off slowly,' he said, gesturing with the gun. Nancy was sleeping under a single light sheet because of the heat. She pulled away the sheet slowly, careful to gather it up near her right hip so Lake would not see the outline of the gun that was hidden there. Nancy was wearing bikini panties and a tee-shirt. The tee-shirt had bunched up beneath her breasts revealing her rigid stomach muscles. Nancy heard a quiet intake of breath.

'Very nice,' Lake said. 'Remove the shirt.'

Nancy forced herself to look at him wide-eyed.

'I'm not going to rape you,' Lake assured her. 'It's not

that I don't want to. I've fantasized about playing with you quite a lot, Nancy. You're so different from the others. They're all so soft, cows really, and so easy to train. But you're hard. I'm certain you would resist. It would be very enjoyable. But I want the authorities to believe that Henry Waters is the rose killer, so you'll die during a burglary.'

Nancy looked at Lake with disgust. 'How could you kill your wife and daughter?'

'You can't think I planned that. I loved them, Nancy. But Sandy found a note and a rose I was planning to use the next day. I'm not proud of myself. I panicked. I couldn't think of a single explanation I could make to Sandy once the notes became public knowledge. She would have gone to the police and it would have been over for me.'

'What's your excuse for killing Melody? She was a baby.'

Lake shook his head. He looked genuinely distraught.

'Do you think that was easy?' Lake's jaw trembled. There was a tear in the corner of one eye. 'Sandy screamed. I got to her before she could do it again, but Melody heard her. She was standing on the stairs, looking through the bars on the banister. I held her and hugged her while I tried to think of some way to spare her, but there wasn't a way, so I made it painless. It was the hardest thing I've ever done.'

'Let me help you, Peter. They'll never find you guilty. I'll talk to the District Attorney. We'll work out an insanity plea.'

Lake smiled sadly. He shook his head with regret. 'It would never fly, Nancy. No one would ever let me off that easy. Think about what I did to Pat. Think about the others. Besides, I'm not crazy. If you knew why I did it, you'd understand.'

'Tell me. I want to understand.'

'Sorry. No time. Besides, it won't make any difference to you. You're going to die.'

'Please, Peter. I have to know. There has to be a reason for a plan this brilliant.'

Lake smiled condescendingly. 'Don't do this. It's not becoming. What's the purpose in stalling?'

'You can rape me first. Tie me up. You want to, don't you? I'd be helpless,' she begged, sliding her right hand under the sheet.

'Don't debase yourself, Nancy. I thought you had more class than the others.'

Lake saw Nancy's hand move. His face clouded. 'What's that?'

Nancy went for the gun. Lake brought the revolver down hard on her cheek. Bone cracked. She went blind for a second. Her closet door slammed open. Lake froze as Wayne Turner came out of the closet. Turner fired and hit Lake in the shoulder. Lake's gun dropped to the floor just as Frank Grimsbo hurtled through the bedroom door, tackling Lake into the wall.

'Stay down,' Turner yelled at Nancy. He scrambled across the bed, knocking the wind out of her. Lake was pinned to the wall and Grimsbo was smashing him in the face.

'Stop, Frank,' Turner yelled. He kept his gun trained on Lake with one hand and tried to restrain Grimsbo's arm with the other. Grimsbo delivered one more clubbing blow that bounced Lake's head off the wall. Lake's head lolled sideways. A damp patch spread across the black fabric that covered his right shoulder as blood seeped from his wound.

'Get his gun,' Turner said. 'It's next to the bed. And check on Nancy.'

Grimsbo stood up. He was shaking.

'I'm okay,' Nancy said. Her cheek was numb and she could barely see out of her left eye.

Grimsbo picked up Lake's gun. He stood over Lake and his breathing increased.

'Cuff him,' Turner ordered. Grimsbo stood there, the gun rising like something with a life of its own.

'Don't fuck around, Frank,' Turner said. 'Just put the cuffs on.'

'Why?' Grimsbo asked. 'He could have been shot twice when he attacked Nancy. You hit him in the shoulder when you came out of the closet and I fired the fatal shot when this piece of shit spun towards me, and, as fate would have it, caught him between the eyes.'

'It didn't happen that way, because I know it didn't,' Turner said evenly.

'And what? You'd turn me in and testify at my murder trial? You'd send me to Attica for the rest of my life, because I exterminated this scumbag?'

'No one would know, Wayne,' Nancy said quietly. 'I'd back Frank.'

Turner looked at Nancy. She was watching Lake with a look of pure hatred.

'I don't believe this. You're cops. What you want to do is murder.'

'Not in this case, Wayne,' Nancy said. 'You have to take the life of a human being to commit murder. Lake isn't human. I don't know what he is, but he's not human. A human being doesn't murder his own child. He doesn't strip a woman naked, then slice her open from groin to chest, pull out her intestines and let her die a slow death. I can't even imagine what he's done to the missing women.' Nancy shuddered. 'I don't want to guess.'

Lake was listening to the argument. He did not move his head, but his eyes focused on each speaker as his fate was debated. He saw Turner waiver. Nancy got off of the bed and stood next to Grimsbo.

'He'll get out someday, Wayne,' she said. 'He'll convince the parole board to release him or he'll convince a jury he was insane and the hospital will let him out when he is miraculously cured. Do you want to wake up some morning and read about a woman who was kidnapped in Salt Lake City or Minneapolis and the note that was left on her pillow telling her husband she was "Gone, But Not Forgotten"?'

Turner's arm fell to his side. His lips were dry. His gut was in a knot.

'It'll be me, Wayne,' Grimsbo said, pulling out his service revolver and handing Nancy Lake's weapon. 'You can leave the room, if you want. You can even remember it like it happened the way I said, because that's the way it will really have happened, if we all agree.'

'Jesus,' Turner said to himself. One hand was knotted into a fist and the one holding the gun was squeezed so tight the metal cut into his palm.

'You can't kill me,' Lake gasped, the pain from his wound making it hard for him to speak.

'Shut the fuck up,' Grimsbo said, 'or I'll do you now.'

'They're not dead,' Lake managed, squeezing his eyes shut as a wave of nausea swept over him. 'The other women are still alive. Kill me and they'll die. Kill me and you kill them all.'

2

Governor Raymond Colby ducked under the rotating helicopter blades and ran toward the waiting police car. Larry Merrill, the Governor's Administrative Assistant, leaped out after the Governor and followed him across the runway. A stocky, red-haired man and a slender black man were standing next to the police car. The red-head opened the back door for Colby.

'John O'Malley, Governor. I'm the Hunter's Point Police Chief. This is Detective Wayne Turner. He's going to brief you. We have a very bad situation here.'

Governor Colby sat in the rear seat of the police car and Turner slid in beside him. When Merrill was in the front, O'Malley started towards Nancy Gordon's house.

'I don't know how much you've been told, Governor.'

'Start from the beginning, Detective Turner. I want to make certain I don't miss anything.'

'Women have been disappearing in Hunter's Point. All married to professionals, childless. No sign of a struggle. With the first woman, we assumed we were dealing with a missing persons case. The only oddity was a note on the woman's pillow that said, "Gone, But Not Forgotten" pinned down by a rose that had been dyed black. We figured the wife left it. Then, the second woman disappeared and we found an identical rose and note.

'After the fourth disappearance, all with notes and black

roses, Sandra and Melody Lake were murdered. Sandra was the wife of Peter Lake, whom I believe you know. Melody was his daughter.'

'That was tragic,' Colby said. 'Pete's been a supporter of mine for some time. I appointed him to a Board, last fall.'

'He killed them, Governor. He murdered his wife and daughter in cold blood. Then he framed a man named Henry Waters by bringing one of the kidnapped women to Waters' house, disemboweling her in Waters' basement, planting some roses and one of the notes in Waters' house and calling the police anonymously.'

It was four AM and pitch black in the car, but Turner saw Colby blanch as the car passed under a street-light.

'Peter Lake killed Sandy and Melody?'

'Yes, sir.'

'I find that hard to believe.'

'What I'm going to tell you now is known only to Chief O'Malley, Detectives Frank Grimsbo and Nancy Gordon and me. The Chief created a task-force to deal with the disappearances. It consists of Gordon, Grimsbo and me, plus a forensic expert. We suspected Lake might be our killer, even after we found Patricia Cross's body at Waters' house, so we set him up. Gordon told Lake she suspected him, but had kept the incriminating evidence to herself. Lake panicked, as we'd hoped he would. He broke into Gordon's house to kill her. She tricked him into admitting the killings. We wired her house and we have his confession on tape. Grimsbo and I were hiding and heard it all. We arrested Lake.'

'Then, what's the problem?' Merrill asked.

'Three of the women are still alive. Barely. Lake's been

keeping them on a starvation diet – he only feeds them once a week. He won't tell us when he fed them last or where they are, unless the Governor gives him a full pardon.'

'What?' Merrill asked incredulously. 'The Governor's not going to pardon a mass murderer.'

'Can't you find them?' Colby asked. 'They must be in property Lake owns. Have you searched them all?'

'Lake's made a good deal of money over the years. He has vast real estate holdings. Most of them aren't in his name. We don't have the manpower or time to find and search them all before the women starve.'

'Then I'll promise to pardon Peter. After he tells us where he's holding the women, you can arrest him. A contract entered into under duress won't stand up.'

Merrill looked uncomfortable. 'I'm afraid it might, Ray. When I was with the US Attorney, we gave immunity to a contract killer for the mob in exchange for testimony against a higher-up. He said he was present when the hit was ordered, but he was in Las Vegas on the day the body was found. We checked out his story. He was registered at Caesar's Palace. Several honest witnesses saw him eating at the casino. We gave him his deal, he testified, the higher-up was convicted, he walked. Then, we found out he did the hit, but he did it at fifteen minutes before midnight, then flew to Vegas.

'We were furious. We rearrested him and indicted him for murder, but the judge threw out the indictment. He ruled that everything the defendant told us was true. We just didn't ask the right questions. I researched the hell out of the law on plea agreements trying to get the appellate court to rule for us. No luck. Contract principles apply, but so does Due Process. If both sides enter into the agreement in good faith and the defendant performs, the courts are going to enforce the agreement. If you go into this with your eyes open, Ray, I think the pardon will stick.'

'Then, I have no choice.'

'Yes, you do,' Merrill insisted. 'You tell him no deal. You can't pardon a serial killer and expect to be re-elected. It's political suicide.'

'Damn it, Larry,' Colby snapped, 'how do you think people would react if they found out I let three women die to win an election?'

Raymond Colby opened the door to Nancy Gordon's bedroom. Frank Grimsbo was seated next to the door, holding his weapon, his eyes on the prisoner. The shades were drawn and the bed was still unmade. Peter Lake was handcuffed to a chair. His back was to the window. No one had treated the cuts on Lake's face and the blood had dried, making him look like a badly defeated fighter. Lake should have been scared. Instead, he looked like he was in charge of the situation.

'Thanks for coming, Ray.'

'What's going on, Pete? This is crazy. I can't believe you murdered Sandy and Melody?'

'I had to, Ray. I explained that to the police. You know I wouldn't have killed them if I had a choice.'

'That sweet little girl. How can you live with yourself?'

Lake shrugged his shoulders. 'That's really besides the point, Ray. I'm not going to prison and you're going to see to that.'

'It's out of my hands, Pete. You killed three people.

You're morally responsible for Waters' death. I can't do anything for you.'

Lake smiled. 'Then why are you here?'

'To ask you to tell the police where you're keeping the other women.'

'No can do, Ray. My life depends on keeping the cops in the dark.'

'You'd let three innocent women die?'

Lake shrugged. 'Three dead, six dead. They can't punish me any more after the first life-sentence. I don't envy you, Ray. Believe me when I say that I wish I didn't have to put an old friend, whom I admire deeply, in this position. But, I won't tell you where the women are if I don't get my pardon. And, believe me, every minute counts. Those women are mighty hungry and mighty thirsty by now. I can't guarantee how much longer they'll last without food and water.'

Colby sat on the bed across from Lake. He bent forward, his forearms resting on his knees and his hands clasped in front of him.

'I do consider myself your friend, Pete. I still can't believe what I'm hearing. As a friend, I beg you to save those women. I promise I'll intercede on your behalf with the authorities. Maybe, a plea to manslaughter can be worked out.'

Lake shook his head. 'No prison. Not one day. I know what happens in jail to a man who's raped a woman. I wouldn't last a week.'

'You're expecting a miracle, Pete. How can I let you go free?'

'Look, Ray, I'll make this simple for you. I walk or the women die. There's no other alternative and you're using up valuable time jawing with me.'

Colby hunched his shoulders. He stared at the floor. Lake's smile widened.

'What are your terms?' Colby asked.

'I want a pardon for every crime I committed in New York State and immunity from prosecution for every conceivable crime the authorities can think up in the future. I want the pardon in writing and I want a videotape of you signing it. I want the original of the tape and the pardon given to a lawyer I'll choose.

'I want immunity from prosecution in Federal court . . .'

'I can't guarantee that. I have no authority to . . .'

'Call the US Attorney or the Attorney General. Call the President. This is non-negotiable. I'm not going to get hit with a federal charge for violation of civil rights.'

'I'll see what I can do.'

'That's all I ask. But, if you don't do what I want, the women die.

'There's one other thing. I want a guarantee that the State of New York will pay any civil judgments, if I get sued by the survivors or Cross's husband. I'm not going to lose any money over this. Attorney fees, too.'

Lake's last remark helped the Governor see Lake for what he was. The handsome, urbane young man with whom he had dined and played golf was the disguise worn by a monster. Colby felt rage replacing the numbness he'd experienced since learning Lake's true nature.

Colby stood. 'I have to know how much time those women have, so I can tell the Attorney General how quickly we must act.'

'I'm not going to tell you, Ray. You're not getting any

information from me until I have what I want. But,' Lake said with a smile, 'I will tell you to hurry.'

3

The police cars and ambulances bounced along the unpaved back-road, their sirens blaring in hopes that the captive women would hear them and take heart. There were three ambulances, each with a team of doctors and nurses. Governor Colby and Larry Merrill were riding with Chief O'Malley and Wayne Turner. Frank Grimsbo was driving another police car with Nancy Gordon riding shotgun. In the back of that car was Herb Carstairs, an attorney Lake had retained. A videotape of Governor Colby signing a pardon and a copy of the pardon with an addendum signed by the United States Attorney rested in Carstairs' safe. Next to Carstairs, in leg-irons and handcuffs, sat Peter Lake, who seemed indifferent to the high-speed ride.

The cavalcade rounded a curve in the country road and Nancy saw the farmhouse. It looked deserted. The front yard was overgrown and the paint was peeling. To the right of the house, across a dusty strip of yard, was a dilapidated barn.

Nancy was out and running as soon as the car stopped. She raced up the steps of the house and kicked in the front door. Medics and doctors raced after her. Lake had said the women were in the basement. Nancy found the basement door and threw it open. A stench of urine, excrement and unwashed bodies hit her and she gagged. Then, she took a deep breath and yelled 'Police, you're safe,' as she started down the stairs, two at a time, stopping her headlong rush the moment she saw what was in the basement.

Nancy felt like someone had punched a hole through her chest and torn out her heart. Later, it occurred to her that her reaction must have been similar to the reactions of the servicemen who liberated the Nazi concentration camps. The basement windows were painted black and the only light came from bare bulbs that hung from the ceiling. A section of the basement was divided by plywood walls into six small stalls. Three of the stalls were empty. All of the stalls were covered with straw and outfitted with dirty mattresses. A videotape camera sat on a tripod outside each of the three occupied stalls. In addition to the mattress, each stall contained a cheap clock, a plastic water bottle with a plastic straw, and a dog-food dish. The water bottles looked empty. Nancy could see the remains of some kind of gruel in the dishes.

Toward the rear of the basement was an open area. In it was a mattress covered with a sheet and a large table. Nancy could not make out all of the instruments on the table, but one of them was definitely a cattle prod.

Nancy stepped aside as the doctors rushed past her. She stared at the three survivors. The women were naked. Their feet were chained to the wall at the ankles. The chain extended just far enough to reach the water bottle and dog-food dish. The women in the first two stalls lay on their sides on their mattresses. Their eyes seemed to be floating in the sockets. Nancy could see their ribs. There were burn marks and bruises everywhere. The woman in the third stall was Samantha Reardon. She huddled against the wall, her face expressionless, staring blankly at her rescuers.

Nancy walked slowly to the bottom of the stairs. She recognized Ann Hazelton only from her red hair. Her legs were drawn up to her chest in a fetal position and she was whimpering pitifully. Ann's husband had furnished a photograph of her standing on the eighteenth hole of their country-club golf course, a smile on her face and a yellow ribbon holding back her long, red hair.

Gloria Escalante was in the second stall. There was no expression on her face, but Nancy saw tears in her eyes as a doctor bent next to her to check her vital signs and a policeman went to work on her shackles.

Nancy began to shake. Wayne Turner walked up behind her and put his hands on her arms.

'Come on,' he said gently, 'we're just in the way.'

Nancy let herself be led up the stairs into the light. Governor Colby had glanced into the basement for a moment, then backed out of the farmhouse into the fresh air. His skin was gray and he was sitting on one of the steps that led up to the porch, looking like he did not have the strength to stand.

Nancy looked across the yard. She spotted the car holding Lake. Frank Grimsbo was standing guard outside it. Lake's attorney had wandered off to smoke. Nancy walked past the Governor. He asked her if the women were all right, but she did not answer. Wayne Turner walked beside her. 'Let it be, Nancy,' he said. Nancy ignored him.

Frank Grimsbo looked up expectantly. 'They're all alive,' Turner said. Nancy bent down and looked at Lake. The back window was open a crack, so the prisoner could breathe in the stifling heat. Lake turned toward Nancy. He was rested and at peace, knowing he would soon be free.

Lake smirked, goading her with his eyes, but saying nothing. If he expected Nancy to rage at him, he was mistaken. Her face was blank, but her eyes bored into Lake. 'It's not over,' she said. Then she stood up and walked toward a stand of trees on the side of the house away from the barn. With her back to the farmhouse, all she could see was beauty. There was cool shade under the greenery. The smell of grass and wild flowers. A bird sang. The horror Nancy felt when she saw the captive women was gone. Her anger was gone. She knew the future and was not afraid of it. No woman would ever have to fear Peter Lake again, because Peter Lake was a dead man.

4

Nancy Gordon wore a black jogging outfit, her white Nikes were coated with black shoe polish, and her short hair was held back by a navy blue head-band, making her impossible to see in the dim light of the quarter moon that hung over The Meadows. Her car was parked on a quiet side street. Nancy locked it and loped through a backyard. She was strung tight and conscious of every sound. A dog barked, but the houses on either side stayed dark.

Until Peter Lake came into her life, Nancy Gordon had never hated another human being. She wasn't even certain she hated Lake. What she felt went beyond hate. From the moment she saw those women in the farmhouse basement, Nancy knew Lake had to be removed, the same way vermin were removed.

Nancy was a cop, sworn to uphold the law. She respected

the law. But this situation was so far outside normal human experience that she did not feel every-day laws applied. No one could do what Peter Lake had done to those women and walk away. She could not be expected to wait day after day for the newspaper that brought news of the next disappearance. She knew the minute Lake's body was found she would be a prime suspect. God knows, she did not want to spend the rest of her life in prison, but there was no alternative. If she was caught, so be it. If she killed Lake and walked away, it was God's will. She could live with the consequences of her act. She could not live with the consequences of letting Peter Lake go free.

Nancy circled behind Lake's two-story colonial by skirting the man-made lake. The houses on either side of Lake's were dark, but there were lights on in his living-room. Nancy glanced at her digital watch. It was 3:30 AM. Lake should be asleep. Nancy knew the security system in the house was equipped with automatic timers for the lights and decided to gamble that that was why the living-room was lit.

Nancy crouched down and ran across the backyard. When she reached the house, she pressed herself against the side wall. She was holding a .38 Ed had seized from a drug dealer, two years ago. Ed never reported the seizure and the gun could not be traced to her.

Nancy crept around to the front door. She had studied the crime-scene photographs earlier that evening. Mentally, she walked herself through Lake's house, remembering as much as she could about the layout from her only visit. She had learned Lake's alarm code during the murder investigation. The alarm panel was to the right of the door. She would have to disarm it quickly.

The street in front of Lake's house was deserted. Nancy had taken Sandra Lake's keys from an evidence locker at the police station. She turned the front-door key in the lock, then took out a pen light. Nancy grasped the door knob with her free hand, took a deep breath, and pushed it open. The alarm emitted a screeching sound. She trained the pen light on the keyboard and punched in the code. The sound stopped. Nancy swung around and held her gun out. Nothing. She exhaled, switched off the pen light and straightened.

A quick tour of the ground floor confirmed Nancy's guess about the lights in the living-room. After making certain no one was downstairs, Nancy edged up the stairs, her gun leading the way. The second floor was dark. The first room on the left was Lake's bedroom. When she came level with the landing, she saw his door was closed.

Nancy approached the door slowly, walking carefully even though the carpet muffled her footfalls. She paused next to the door and walked through the shooting in her head. Ease open the door, switch on the light, then shoot into Lake until the gun was empty. She breathed in and exhaled as she opened the door, an inch at a time.

Her eyes adjusted to the dark. She could see the outline of the king-size bed that dominated the room. Nancy cleared her mind of hate and all other feelings. She removed herself from the action. She was not killing a person. She was shooting into an object. Just like target practice. Nancy slipped into the room, hit the switch and aimed.

PART SIX
AVENGING ANGEL

Chapter Nineteen

'The bed was empty,' Wayne Turner told Betsy. 'Lake was gone. He started planning his disappearance the day after he murdered his wife and daughter. All but one of his bank accounts had been emptied the day after the murder and several of his real-estate holdings had been sold. His lawyer was handling the sale of his house. Carstairs said he didn't know where Lake was. No one could compel him to tell, anyway, because of the attorney-client privilege. We assumed that Carstairs had instructions to send the money he collected to accounts in Switzerland or the Grand Caymans.'

'Chief O'Malley called me immediately,' Senator Colby said. 'I was sick. Signing Lake's pardon was the most difficult thing I've ever done, but I couldn't think of anything else to do. I couldn't let those women die. When O'Malley told me Lake had disappeared all I could think of was the innocent victims he might claim because of me.'

'Why didn't you go public?' Betsy asked. 'You could

have let everyone know who Lake was and what he'd done.'

'Only a few people knew Lake was the rose killer and we were sworn to silence by the terms of the pardon.'

'Once the women were free, why didn't you say to hell with him and go public anyway?'

Colby looked into the fire. His voice sounded hollow when he answered.

'We discussed the possibility, but we were afraid. Lake said he would take revenge by killing someone if we breached our agreement with him.'

'Going public would have destroyed the Senator's career,' Wayne Turner added, 'and none of us wanted that. Only a handful of people knew about the pardon or Lake's guilt. O'Malley, Gordon, Grimsbo, me, the US Attorney, the Attorney General, Carstairs, Merrill and the Senator. We never even told the Mayor. We knew how courageous Ray had been to sign the pardon. We didn't want him to suffer for it. So, we took a vow to protect Ray and we've kept it.'

'And you just forgot about Lake?'

'We never forgot, Ms Tannenbaum,' Colby told her. 'I used contacts in the Albany Police and the FBI to hunt for Lake. Nancy Gordon dedicated her life to tracking him down. He was too clever for us.'

'Now that you know about the pardon, what are you planning to do?' Turner asked.

'I don't know.'

'If the pardon, and these new murders, become public knowledge, Senator Colby cannot be confirmed. He'd lose the support of the law-and-order conservatives on the Judiciary Committee and the liberals will crucify him. This would be the answer to their prayers.'

'I realize that.'

'Going public can't help your client, either.'

'Wayne,' Colby said, 'Ms Tannenbaum is going to have to make up her own mind about what to do with what she knows. We can't pressure her. God knows, she's under enough pressure as it is.

'But,' Colby said, turning to Betsy, 'I do have a question for you. I have the impression that you deduced the existence of the pardon.'

'That's right. I asked myself how Lake could have walked away from Hunter's Point. A pardon was the only answer and only the Governor of New York could issue a pardon. You could keep the existence of a pardon from the public, but the members of the task-force would have to know about it and they're the ones who were rewarded. It was the only answer that made sense.'

'Lake doesn't know you're here, does he?'

Betsy hesitated, then said, 'No.'

'And you haven't asked him to confirm your guess, have you?'

Betsy shook her head.

'Why?'

'Do you remember the conflicting emotions you felt when Lake asked you to pardon him? Imagine how I feel, Senator. I'm a very good attorney. I have the skills to free my client. He maintains his innocence, but my investigation turned up evidence that made me question his word. Until today, I didn't know for certain if Martin was lying. I didn't want to confront him until I knew the truth.'

'Now that you know, what will you do?'

'I haven't worked that out yet. If it was any other case, I wouldn't care. I'd do my job and defend my client. But, this isn't any case. This is . . .'

Betsy paused. What could she say that everyone in the room did not know first-hand?

'I don't envy you, Ms Tannenbaum,' the Senator said. 'I really believe I had no choice. That is the only reason I've been able to live with what I did, even though I regret what I did every time I think of the pardon. You can walk away from Lake.'

'Then I'd be walking away from my responsibilities, wouldn't I?'

'Responsibilities,' Colby repeated. 'Why do we take them on? Why do we burden ourselves with problems that tear us apart? Whenever I think of Lake I wish I hadn't gone into public life. Then I think of some of the good I've been able to do.'

The Senator paused. After a moment he stood up and held out his hand. 'It's been a pleasure meeting you, Ms Tannenbaum. I mean that.'

'Thank you for your candor, Senator.'

'Wayne can drive you back to your hotel.'

Wayne Turner followed Betsy out of the room. Colby sank back down into the armchair. He felt old and used up. He wanted to stay in front of the fire forever and forget the responsibilities about which he had just spoken. He thought about Betsy Tannenbaum's responsibility to her client and her responsibilities as a member of the human race. How would she live with herself if Lake was acquitted? He would haunt her for the rest of her life, the way Lake haunted him.

Colby wondered if the pardon would become public. If it did, he would be finished in public life. The President would withdraw his nomination and he would never be re-elected. Strangely, he was not concerned. He had no control over Betsy Tannenbaum. His fate rested with the decisions she made.

Chapter Twenty

1

'Dr Simon Reardon?'

'Yes.'

'My name is Reginald Stewart. I'm a private investigator. I work for Betsy Tannenbaum, an attorney in Portland, Oregon.'

'I don't know anyone in Portland.'

Dr Reardon sounded annoyed. Stewart thought he detected a slight British accent.

'This is about Hunter's Point and your ex-wife, Dr Reardon. That's where I'm calling from. I hope you'll give me a few minutes to explain.'

'I have no interest in discussing Samantha.'

'Please hear me out. Do you remember Peter Lake?'

'Mr Stewart, there is nothing about those days I can ever forget.'

'Three women were kidnapped in Portland, recently. A black rose and a note that said "Gone, But Not Forgotten" were left at each scene. The women's bodies were dug up recently on property belonging to Peter Lake. He's been charged with the homicides.'

'I thought the Hunter's Point police caught the murderer. Wasn't he some retarded delivery man? A sex offender?'

'The Multnomah County DA thinks the Hunter's Point police made a mistake. I'm trying to find the Hunter's Point survivors. Ann Hazelton is dead. Gloria Escalante won't talk to me. Mrs Reardon is my last hope.'

'It's not Mrs Reardon and hasn't been for some time,' the doctor said with distaste, 'and I have no idea how you can find Samantha. I moved to Minneapolis to get away from her. We haven't spoken in years. The last I heard, she was still living in Hunter's Point.'

'You're divorced?'

Reardon laughed harshly. 'Mr Stewart, this was more than a simple divorce. Samantha tried to kill me.'

'What?'

'She's a sick woman. I wouldn't waste my time on her. You can't trust anything she says.'

'Was this entirely a result of the kidnapping?'

'Undoubtedly her torture and captivity exacerbated the condition, but my wife was always unbalanced. Unfortunately, I was too much in love with her to notice until we were married. I kept rationalizing and excusing . . .' Reardon took a deep breath. 'I'm sorry. She does that to me. Even after all these years.'

'Dr Reardon, I don't want to make you uncomfortable, but Mr Lake is facing a death sentence and I need to know as much about Hunter's Point as I can.'

'Can't the police tell you what you want to know?'

'No, sir. The files are missing.'

'That's strange.'

'Yes, it is. Believe me, if I had those files I wouldn't be bothering you. I'm sure its painful having me dig up this period in your life, but this is literally a matter of life and death. Our DA has a bee in his bonnet about Mr Lake. Peter was a victim, just like you, and he needs your help.'

Reardon sighed. 'Go ahead. Ask your questions.'

'Thank you, sir. Can you tell me about Mrs Reardon, or whatever she calls herself now.'

'I have no idea what her name is. She still called herself Reardon when I left Hunter's Point.'

'When was that?'

'About eight years ago. As soon as the divorce was final.'

'What happened between you and your wife?'

'She was a surgical nurse at University Hospital. Very beautiful, very wanton. Sex was what she was best at,' Reardon said bitterly. 'I was so caught up in her body that I was oblivious to what was going on around me. The most obvious problem was the stealing. She was arrested for shoplifting, twice. Our lawyer kept the cases out of court and I paid off the stores. She was totally without remorse. Treated the incidents like jokes, once she was in the clear.

'Then, there was the spending. I was making good money, but we were in debt up to our ears. She drained my savings accounts, charged our credit cards to the limit. It took me four years after the divorce to get back on my feet. And you couldn't reason with her. I showed her the bills and drew up a budget. She'd get me in bed and I'd forget what I'd told her or she'd throw a tantrum or lock me out of the bedroom. They were the worst three years of my life.

'Then she was kidnapped and tortured and she got worse. Whatever slender string kept her tethered to reality snapped during the time she was a prisoner. I can't even describe what she was like after that. They kept her hospitalized for almost a year. She rarely spoke. She wouldn't let men near her.

'I should have known better, but I took her home after she was released. I felt guilty, because of what happened. I know I couldn't have protected her, I was at the hospital when she was kidnapped, but still, you can see how . . .'

'That's very common. That feeling.'

'Oh, I know. But knowing something intellectually and dealing with it emotionally are two different things. I wish I had been wiser.'

'What happened after she came home?'

'She wouldn't share a bedroom with me. When I was home, she would stay in her room. I have no idea what she did when I was at work. When she did speak, she was clearly irrational. She insisted that the man who kidnapped her was still at large. I showed her the newspaper articles about Waters' arrest and the shooting, but she said he wasn't the man. She wanted a gun for protection. Of course, I refused. She started accusing me of being in a conspiracy with the police. Then she tried to kill me. She stabbed me with a kitchen knife when I came home from the hospital. Fortunately, a colleague was with me. She stabbed him, too, but he hit Samantha and stunned her. We wrestled her to the floor. She was writhing and screeching about . . . She said I was trying to kill her . . . It was very hard for me. I had to commit her. Then, I decided to get out.'

'I don't blame you. It looks like you went above and beyond the call.'

'Yes, I did. But I still feel bad about deserting her, even though I know I had no choice.'

'You said you committed her. Which hospital was that?'

'St Jude's. It's a private psychiatric hospital near Hunter's Point. I moved and cut off contact with her completely. I know she was there for several years, but I believe she was released.'

'Did Samantha try to contact you after she was released?'

'No. I dreaded the possibility, but it never happened.'

'Would you happen to have a photo of Samantha? There weren't any in the newspaper accounts.'

'When I moved to Minnesota, I threw them away, along with everything else that might remind me of Samantha.'

'Thank you for your time, Doctor. I'll try St Jude's. Maybe they have a line on your ex-wife.'

'One other thing, Mr Stewart. If you find Samantha, please don't tell her you talked with me or tell her where I am.'

2

Randy Highsmith drove straight to the District Attorney's Office from the airport. He was feeling the effects of jet lag and wouldn't have minded going home, but he knew how badly Page wanted to hear what he had found out in Hunter's Point.

'It's not good, Al,' Highsmith said, as soon as they were sitting down. 'I was a day behind Darius's investigator, everywhere I went, so he knows what we know.'

'Which is?'

'Nancy Gordon wasn't straight with you. Frank Grimsbo and Wayne Turner told me only Gordon considered Lake a serious suspect. She was fixated on him and never accepted Waters as the rose killer, but everyone else did.

'There's something else she didn't tell us. Three of the Hunter's Point women didn't die. Hazelton, Escalante and Reardon were found alive in an old farmhouse. And, before you ask, Hazelton is dead, I haven't located Reardon and Escalante never saw the face of the man who abducted her.'

'Why did she let me think all the Hunter's Point women were murdered?'

'I have no idea. All I know is that our case against Martin Darius is turning to shit.'

'It doesn't make sense,' Page said, more to himself than to Highsmith. 'Waters is dead. If he was the rose killer, who murdered the women we found at the construction site? It had to be someone who knew details about the Hunter's Point case that only the police knew. That description only fits one person, Martin Darius.'

'There is one other person it fits, Al,' Highsmith said.

'Who?'

'Nancy Gordon.'

'Are you crazy? She's a cop.'

'What if she's crazy? What if she did it to frame Darius? Think about it. Would you have considered Darius a suspect if she didn't tell you he was Lake?'

'You're forgetting the anonymous letter that told her that the killer was in Portland.'

'How do we know she didn't write it herself?'

'I don't believe it.'

'Well, believe it or not, our case is disappearing. Oh, and there's a new wrinkle. A Portland private investigator named Sam Oberhurst was looking into the Hunter's Point murders about a month before the first Portland disappearance.'

'Who did he represent?'

'He didn't say and he didn't tell anyone why he was asking about the case, but I'm going to ask him. I have his phone number and I'll get the address through the phone company.'

'Have they had any luck with the files?'

'None at all.'

Page closed his eyes and rested his head against the back of his chair.

'I'm going to look like a fool, Randy. We'll have to dismiss. I should have listened to you and Ross. We never had a case. It was all in my head.'

'Don't fold yet, Al. This PI could know something.'

Page shook his head. He had aged since his divorce. His energy had deserted him. For a while, this case had recharged him, but Darius was slipping away and he would soon be a laughing stock in the legal community.

'We're going to lose this one, Randy. I can feel it. Gordon was all we had and now it looks like we never had her.'

3

'Hi, Mom,' Betsy said, putting down her suitcase and hugging Rita Cohen.

'How was your flight? Have you had anything to eat?'

'The flight was fine and I ate on the plane.'

'That's not food. You want me to fix you something?'

'Thanks, but I'm not hungry,' Betsy said as she hung up her coat. 'How was Kathy?'

'So-so. Rick took her to the movies on Saturday.'

'How is he?' Betsy asked, hoping she sounded disinterested.

'The louse wouldn't look me in the eye, the whole time he was here. He couldn't wait to escape.'

'You weren't rude to him?'

'I didn't give him the time of day,' Rita answered, pointing her nose in the air. Then, she shook her head.

'Poor kid. Kathy was all excited when she left with him, but she was down in the dumps as soon as he dropped her off. She moped around, picked at her food at dinner.'

'Did anything else happen while I was gone?' Betsy asked, hoping there had been some good news.

'Nora Sloane came by, Sunday evening,' Rita said, smiling mischievously. 'I told all.'

'What did she ask about?'

'Your childhood, your cases. She was very good with Kathy.'

'She seems like a nice woman. I hope her article sells. She's certainly working hard enough on it.'

'Oh, before I forget, when you go to school, talk to Mrs Kramer. Kathy was in a fight with another little girl and she's been disruptive in class.'

'I'll see her this afternoon,' Betsy said. She sounded defeated. Kathy was usually an angel at school. You didn't have to be Sigmund Freud to see what was happening.

317

'Cheer up,' Rita told her. 'She's a good kid. She's just going through a rough time. Look, you've got an hour before school lets out. Have some coffee cake. I'll make you a cup of decaf and you can tell me about your trip.'

Betsy glanced at her watch and decided to give in. Eating cake was a sure-fire way of dealing with depression.

'Okay. I am hungry, I guess. You fix everything. I want to change.'

'Now you're talking,' Rita said with a smile. 'And, for your information, Kathy won the fight. She told me.'

Chapter Twenty-one

When Betsy Tannenbaum was a very little girl, she would not go to sleep until her mother showed her that there were no monsters in her closet or under her bed. The stage passed quickly. Betsy stopped believing in monsters. Then, she met Martin Darius. What made Darius so terrifying was his dissimilarity to the slavering, fanged deformities that lurked in the shadows in her room. Give one hundred people the autopsy photographs and not one of them would believe that the elegantly dressed gentleman standing in the doorway to Betsy's office was capable of cutting off Wendy Reiser's nipples or using a cattle prod to torture Victoria Miller. Even knowing what she knew, Betsy had to force herself to make the connection. But Betsy did know, and the shining winter sun could not keep her from feeling as frightened as the very little girl who used to listen for monsters in the dark.

'Sit down, Mr Darius,' Betsy said.

'We're back to Mr Darius, are we? This must be serious.'

Betsy did not smile. Darius looked at her quizzically, but

took a seat without making any more remarks.

'I'm resigning as your attorney.'

'I thought we agreed that you'd only do that if you believed I was guilty of murdering Farrar, Reiser and Miller.'

'I firmly believe you killed them. I know everything about Hunter's Point.'

'What's everything?'

'I spent the weekend in Washington, D.C. talking to Senator Colby.'

Darius nodded appreciatively. 'I'm impressed. You unraveled the whole Hunter's Point affair in no time at all.'

'I don't give a damn for your flattery, Darius. You lied to me from day one. There are some lawyers who don't care who they represent as long as the fee is large enough. I'm not one of them. Have your new attorney call me so I can get rid of your file. I don't want anything in my office that reminds me of you.'

'My, aren't we self-righteous. You're sure you know everything, aren't you?'

'I know enough to distrust anything you tell me.'

'I'm a little disappointed, Tannenbaum. You worked your way through this puzzle part of the way, then shut down that brilliant mind of yours just as you came to the part that needs solving.'

'What are you talking about?'

'I'm talking about having faith in your client. I'm talking about not walking away from someone who desperately needs your help. I am *not* guilty of killing Reiser, Farrar and Miller. If you don't prove I'm innocent, the real killer is going to walk away, just the way I did in Hunter's Point.'

'You admit your guilty of those atrocities in Hunter's Point?'

Darius shrugged. 'How can I deny it, now that you've talked to Colby?'

'How could you do it? Animals don't treat other animals like that.'

Darius looked amused. 'Do I fascinate you, Tannenbaum?'

'No, Mr Darius, you disgust me.'

'Then why ask me about Hunter's Point?'

'I want to know why you thought you had the right to walk into someone else's life and turn the rest of their days on Earth into Hell. I want to understand how you could destroy the lives of those poor women so casually.'

Darius stopped smiling. 'There was nothing casual about what I did.'

'What I can't understand is how a mind like yours or Speck's or Bundy's works. What could possibly make you feel so badly about yourself that you can only keep going by dehumanizing women?'

'Don't compare me to Bundy or Speck. They were pathetic failures. Thoroughly inadequate personalities. I'm neither insane nor inadequate. I was a successful attorney in Hunter's Point and a successful businessman here.'

'Then why did you do it?'

Darius hesitated. He seemed to be in a debate with himself. 'Am I still covered by the attorney-client privilege?' Betsy nodded. 'Anything I tell you is between us?' Betsy nodded again. 'Because I'd like to tell you. You have a superior mind and a female viewpoint. Your reactions would be informative.'

Betsy knew she should throw Darius out of her office and her life, but her fascination with him paralyzed her intellect. When she remained silent, Darius settled back in his chair.

'I was conducting an experiment, Tannenbaum. I wanted to know what it felt like to be God. I don't remember the exact moment the idea for the experiment germinated. I do remember a trip Sandy and I took to Barbados. Lying on the beach, I thought about how perfect my life was. There was my job, which provided me with more money than I ever dreamed of, and there was Sandy, still sexy as all get out, even after bearing my lovely Melody. My Sandy, so willing to please, so mindless. I'd married her for her body, and never checked under the hood until it was too late.'

Darius shook his head wistfully.

'Perfect is boring, Tannenbaum. Sex with the same woman, day after day, no matter how beautiful and skilled she is, is boring. I've always had an intense fantasy life and I wondered what it would be like if my fantasy world was real. Would my life be different? Would I discover what I was searching for? I decided to find out what would happen if I brought my fantasy world to life.

'It took me months to find the farmhouse. I couldn't trust workmen, so I built the stalls myself. Then, I selected the women. I chose only worthless women. Women who lived off their husbands like parasites. Beautiful, spoiled women who used their looks to entice a man into marriage, then drained him of his wealth and self-respect. These women were born again in my little dungeon. Their stall became their world and I became their sun, moon, wind and rain.'

Betsy remembered Colby's description of the women he

had seen. Their hollow eyes, the protruding ribs. She remembered the vacant stares on the faces of the dead women in the photographs.

'I admit I was cruel to them, but I had to dehumanize them so they could be molded in the image I chose. When I appeared, I wore a mask and I made them wear leather masks with no eye-holes. Once a week, I doled out rations scientifically calculated to keep them on the brink of starvation. I limited the hours they could sleep.

'Did Colby mention the clocks and the videotape machines? Did you wonder what they were for? It was my crowning touch. I had a wife and child and a job, so I could only be with my subjects for short periods each week, but I wanted total control, omniscience, even when I was gone. So, I rigged the videotapes to run when I wasn't there and I gave the women commands to perform. They had to watch the clock. Every hour, at set times, they would bow to the camera and perform dog tricks, rolling over, squatting, masturbating. Whatever I commanded. I reviewed the tapes and I punished deviations firmly.'

Darius had an enraptured look on his face. His eyes were fixed on a scene no sane person could imagine. Betsy felt she would shatter if she moved.

'I changed them from demanding cows to obedient puppies. They were mine completely. I bathed them. They ate like dogs from a doggy bowl, they were forbidden to speak unless I told them to, and the only time I let them was to beg me for punishment and thank me for pain. In the end, they would do anything to escape the pain. They pleaded to drink my urine and kissed my foot when I let them.'

Darius's face was so tight Betsy thought his skin might

rip. A wave of nausea made her stomach roll.

'Some of the women resisted, but they soon learned that there can be no negotiations with a God. Others obeyed immediately. Cross, for instance. She was no challenge at all. A perfect cow. As docile and unimaginative as a lump of clay. That's why I chose her for my sacrifice.'

Before Darius started speaking, Betsy assumed there was nothing he could say that she would not be able to handle, but she did not want to hear any more.

'Did your experiment bring you peace?' Betsy asked to stop Darius from talking about the women. Her breathing was ragged and she felt light-headed. Darius snapped out of his trance.

'The experiment brought me the most exquisite pleasure, Tannenbaum. The moments I shared with those women were the finest moments in my life. But Sandy found the note and it had to end. There was too much danger of being caught. Then I was caught, and then I was free, and that freedom was exhilarating.'

'When was the next time you repeated the experiment, Martin?' Betsy asked coldly.

'Never. I wanted to, but I learn from experience. I had one lucky break and I was not going to risk life in prison or the death penalty.'

Betsy stared at Darius with contempt.

'I want you out of my office. I don't ever want to see you again.'

'You can't quit, Tannenbaum. I need you.'

'Hire Oscar Montoya or Matthew Reynolds.'

'Oscar Montoya and Matthew Reynolds are good lawyers, but they aren't women. I'm banking that no jury will believe that an ardent feminist would represent a man who treated a woman the way the murderer treated Reiser, Farrar and Miller. In a close case, you're my edge.'

'Then you just lost your edge, Darius. You're the most vile person I've ever known. I don't ever want to see you again, let alone defend you.'

'You're reneging on our deal. I told you, I did not murder Farrar, Reiser or Vicky Miller. Someone is framing me. If I'm convicted, this case will be closed and you'll be responsible for the killer's next victim and the one after that.'

'Do you think I'll believe anything you say after what you just told me, after all your lies?'

'Listen, Tannenbaum,' Darius said, leaning across the desk and pinning Betsy with an intense stare. 'I did not kill those women. I'm being set up by someone and I'm pretty certain I know who she is.'

'She?'

'Only Nancy Gordon knows enough about this case to frame me. Vicky, Reiser, those women would never have suspected her. She's female. She'd flash her badge. They'd let her in easy. That's why there were no signs of a struggle at the crime scenes. They probably went with her willingly and didn't know what was happening until it was too late.'

'No woman would do what was done to those women.'

'Don't be naive. She's been obsessed with me since Hunter's Point. She's probably insane.'

Betsy remembered what she had learned about Nancy Gordon. The woman had tried to murder Darius in Hunter's Point. She had dedicated her life to finding him. But, to frame him like this? From what she knew, it was more likely that Gordon would have walked up to Darius and shot him.

'I don't buy it.'

'You know Vicky left the Hacienda Motel at two-thirty. I was with Russell Miller and several other people at the advertising agency until almost five.'

'Who can alibi you after you left the ad agency?'

'Unfortunately, no one.'

'I'm not going to do it. You stand for everything in life I find repulsive. Even if you didn't kill the women in Portland, you did commit those inhuman crimes in Hunter's Point.'

'And you are going to be responsible for murdering the next victim in Portland. Think about it, Tannenbaum. There's no case against me now. That means another woman will have to die to supply the evidence the state can use to convict me.'

That evening, Kathy snuggled close to Betsy, her attention riveted on a cartoon special. Betsy kissed the top of her daughter's head and wondered how this peaceful scene could co-exist with a reality where women curled up in the dark waiting for a torturer to bring them unbearable pain? How could she meet with a man like Martin Darius at work and watch Disney with her daughter at home without losing her sanity? How could Peter Lake spend the morning as the horror god of a warped fantasy and the evening playing with his own little girl?

Betsy wished there was only one reality. The one where she and Rick sat watching Disney with Kathy squirreled between them. The one she thought was reality before Rick walked out on her and she met Martin Darius.

Betsy had always been able to separate herself from her work. Before Darius, her criminal clients were more pathetic than frightening. She represented shoplifters, drunk drivers, petty thieves and scared juveniles. She was still friendly with the two women she had saved from homicide charges. Even when she brought her work home with her, she saw it as something that was only temporarily in her house. Darius was in Betsy's soul. He had changed her. She no longer believed she was safe. And much worse, she knew Kathy was not safe either.

Chapter Twenty-two

1

St Jude's looked more like an exclusive private school than a mental hospital. A high, ivy-covered wall stretched back into deep woods. The administration building, once the home of millionaire Alvin Piercy, was red brick, with recessed windows and gothic arches. Piercy, a devout Catholic, died a bachelor in 1916 and left his fortune to the Church. In 1923, the mansion was converted into a retreat for priests in need of counseling. In 1953, a small, modern psychiatric hospital was constructed behind the house, which became the home of St Jude's administration. From the gate, Reggie Stewart could see the administration building through the graceful limbs of the snow-covered trees that were scattered across the grounds. In the fall, the lawn would be a carpet of green and the tree limbs would be graced with leaves of gold and red.

Dr Margaret Flint's office was at the end of a long corridor on the second floor. The window faced away from the hospital and toward the woods. Dr Flint was an angular, horse-faced woman with shoulder-length, gray hair.

'Thank you for seeing me,' Stewart said.

Dr Flint responded with an engaging smile that softened her homely features. She took Stewart's hand in a firm grip, then motioned him into one of two armchairs that were set up around a coffee table.

'I've often wondered what became of Samantha Reardon. She was such an unusual case. Unfortunately, there was no follow-up once she was released.'

'Why is that?'

'Her husband refused to pay after the divorce and it wasn't covered by insurance. In any event, I doubt Samantha would have permitted me to pry into her affairs after she gained her freedom. She hated everything associated with the hospital.'

'What can you tell me about Mrs Reardon?'

'Normally, I wouldn't tell you a thing, because of patient-doctor confidentiality rules, but your phone call raised the possibility that she may be a danger to others and that takes precedence over those rules in certain circumstances.'

'She may be involved in a series of murders in Portland.'

'So you said. Is there a connection between the murders and her captivity in Hunter's Point?' Dr Flint asked.

'Yes. How did you know?'

'I'll tell you in a moment. Please bear with me. I need to know the background of your request for information.'

'A man named Peter Lake was the husband of one of the Hunter's Point victims and the father of another. He moved to Portland eight years ago so he could start a new life. Someone is duplicating the Hunter's Point MO in Portland. Are you familiar with the way the Hunter's Point women were treated?'

'Of course. I was Samantha's treating psychiatrist. I had full access to the police reports.'

'Dr Flint, would Reardon be capable of subjecting other women to the torture she experienced in order to frame my client?'

'A good question. Not many women could go through torture then subject another woman to that same experience, but Samantha Reardon was in no way normal. We all have personalities that are thoroughly ingrained. Our personalities are usually very difficult, if not impossible, to change. People with personality disorders have maladaptive personalities. The signs they present vary with the disorder.

'Prior to her horrible victimization, Samantha Reardon had what we call a borderline personality, which lies between a neurosis and a psychosis. At times, she would exhibit psychotic behavior, but generally she would be seen as neurotic. She demonstrated perverse sexual interests, anti-social behavior, such as passing bad checks or shoplifting, anxiety, and strong self-centeredness. Her relationship with her ex-husband typifies this kind of behavior. There were periods of intense sexuality, frequent instability, and he found her impossible to reason with and totally self-centered. When she was caught stealing, she showed no interest in the charges, no remorse. She used sex to distract Dr Reardon and gain favors from him. She destroyed his finances without regard to the long-term consequences for both of them. When Samantha was kidnapped and tortured she became psychotic. She is probably still in that state.

'Samantha saw St Jude's as an extension of her captivity. I was the only doctor to whom she related, probably because I was the only female on the staff. Samantha Reardon hates and distrusts all men. She was convinced that the Hunter's Point Mayor, the Police Chief, the Governor, even, at times, the President of the United States – all men – were conspiring to protect the man who tortured her.'

'So,' Stewart interjected, 'it's possible she would act on these fantasies if she located the man she believed was responsible for her captivity?'

'Most certainly. When she was here, she spoke of nothing but revenge. She saw herself as an avenging angel arrayed against the forces of darkness. She hated her captor, but she is a danger to any man, because she sees them all as oppressors.'

'But the women? How could she bring herself to torture those women after what she went through?'

'Samantha would see any means that furthered her ends as acceptable means, Mr Stewart. If she had to sacrifice some women in the process of attaining her goal, in her eyes that would be a small price to pay for her revenge.'

2

Rick was sitting in the waiting room when Betsy arrived at work. He seemed subdued.

'I know I'm not expected, but I wanted to talk. Are you busy?'

'Come in,' Betsy told him. She was still angry with him for telling Kathy that her career was to blame for their separation.

'How's Kathy?' Rick asked as he followed her into her office.

'There's an easy way to find out.'

'Don't be like that. Actually, one of the reasons I stopped by is to ask if she can sleep over. I just moved into a new apartment and it has a guest room.'

Betsy wanted to say no, because it would hurt Rick, but she knew how much Kathy missed her father.

'Fine.'

'Thanks. I'll pick her up tomorrow, after work.'

'What else did you want to talk about?'

Rick was uncomfortable. He looked down at the desk top.

'I . . . Betsy, this is very hard for me. The partnership, my job . . .' Rick paused. 'I'm not doing this very well.' He took a deep breath. 'What I'm trying to say is that my life is in turmoil right now. I'm under so much pressure that I'm not thinking straight. This time by myself, it's given me some distance, some perspective. I guess what I'm saying is, don't give up on me. Don't close me out . . .'

'I never wanted to do that, Rick. You're the one who closed me out.'

'When I left, I said some things about how I felt about you that I didn't mean.'

'When you're certain how you feel, tell me, Rick. But I can't promise how I'm going to feel. You hurt me very badly.'

'I know,' he said quietly. 'Look, this merger I'm working

on, it's got me tied up night and day, but I think everything will be under control in a month. I've got some time off in December and Kathy has Christmas vacation, so she wouldn't miss school. I thought, maybe, the three of us could go somewhere where we could be by ourselves.'

Betsy's breath caught in her chest. She didn't know what to say.

Rick stood up. 'I know I sprang this on you without any warning. You don't have to answer me right away. We have time. Just promise me you'll think about it.'

'I will.'

'Good. And thanks for letting me see Kathy.'

'You're her father,' Betsy said.

Betsy opened the office door before Rick could say anything else. Nora Sloane was standing next to Ann's desk.

'Do you have a minute?' Sloane asked.

'Rick was just leaving,' Betsy answered.

Sloane stared at Rick for a second.

'Are you Mr Tannenbaum?'

'Yes.'

'This is Nora Sloane,' Betsy said. 'She's working on an article about women litigators for *Pacific West* magazine.'

'Your wife has been a wonderful help.'

Rick smiled politely. 'I'll pick up Kathy around six and take her to dinner,' he told Betsy. 'Don't forget to pack her school things. Nice meeting you, Ms Sloane.'

'Wait,' Betsy said. 'I don't have the address and phone number at your new place.'

Rick gave them to her and Betsy wrote them down. Then Rick left.

'The reason I dropped in is to see if we can schedule

some time to discuss the Hammermill case and your strategy in the Darius case,' Sloane said.

'I hope this won't upset your plans, Nora, but I'm getting off Martin's case.'

'Why?'

'Personal reasons I can't discuss with you.'

'I don't understand.'

'There's a conflict. Ethical problems are involved. I can't put it any other way without violating the attorney-client privilege.'

Nora rubbed her forehead. She looked distracted.

'I'm sorry if this affects the article,' Betsy said. 'There isn't anything I can do about what happened.'

'That's all right,' Nora replied, quickly regaining her composure. 'The Darius case isn't essential to the article.'

Betsy opened her appointment book. 'As soon as I'm officially off Martin's case, I'll have plenty of free time. Why don't we tentatively schedule a meeting for lunch next Wednesday?'

'That sounds fine. See you then.'

The door closed and Betsy looked at the work on her desk. They were cases she'd had to put off because of Martin Darius. Betsy pulled the top case off of a pile, but she did not open the file. She thought about Rick. He seemed different. Less self-assured. If he wanted to come back would she let him?

The buzzer rang. Reggie Stewart was calling from Hunter's Point.

'How's tricks?' Stewart asked.

'Not so good, Reg. I'm off the case.'

'Did Darius fire you?'

'No, it's the other way around.'

'Why?'

'I found out Darius did kill the women in Hunter's Point.'

'How?'

'I can't tell you.'

'Jesus, Betsy, you can trust me.'

'I know I can, but I'm not going to explain this so don't press me.'

'Well, I'm a little concerned. There's a possibility Darius is being framed. It turns out Samantha Reardon is a very weird lady. I talked to Simon Reardon, her ex. He's a neurosurgeon and she was one of his surgical nurses. He became infatuated with her and the next thing he knows, they're married and he's on the verge of bankruptcy. She's shoplifting like crazy, running up his credit cards and his lawyers are rushing around covering up the lady's indiscretions. Then Darius kidnaps and tortures her and she really goes over the edge. I met with Dr Flint, her shrink at St Jude's. That's where she was committed after she tried to kill Reardon.'

'What?'

'She knifed him and a friend he brought home. They subdued her and she spent the next few years in a padded cell insisting that the man who kidnapped her was still at large and she was the victim of a conspiracy.'

'She was, Reg. The authorities covered up for Darius. I can't fill you in on the details, but Samantha may not have been completely crazy.'

'She may have been right about the cover-up *and* insane. Dr Flint thought she was mad as a hatter. Reardon was an abused child. Her father ran away when she was two and her mother was a hopeless drunk. She learned morals from a street gang she ran with. She has a juvenile record for robbery and assault. That was a stabbing, too. She was smart enough to get through high school without doing any real work. Her IQ's been tested at 146, which is a hell of a lot higher than mine, but her school performance was lousy.

'There was an early marriage to Max Felix, a manager at a department store where she was working. I called him and he tells the same story Dr Reardon does. She must be a great lay. Her first husband says he couldn't see up from down while she was cleaning out his bank account and charging him into debt. The marriage only lasted a year.

'Next stop was a community college, then nursing school, then the good doctor. Dr Flint says Reardon had a personality disorder – borderline personality – to begin with, and the stress from the torture and captivity made her psychotic. She was obsessed with avenging herself on her captor.'

Betsy felt a queasy sensation in the pit of her stomach.

'Did you ask Dr Flint if she would be capable of subjecting other women to the kind of torture she endured just to frame Darius?'

'According to Dr Flint, it wouldn't bother her one bit to slice up those ladies, if that's what it took to accomplish her plan.'

'It's so hard to believe, Reg. A woman doing those things to other women.'

'It makes sense, though, Betsy. Think about it: Oberhurst interviews Reardon and shows her a photo of Darius;

Reardon recognizes Darius and follows Oberhurst to Portland; she reads about the hassle Darius is having at the construction site and figures it's the ideal place to bury Oberhurst after she kills him; later, she adds the other bodies.'

'I don't know, Reg. It still makes more sense for Darius to have killed them.'

'What do you want me to do?'

'Try to get a picture of her. There weren't any in the newspaper accounts.'

'I'm way ahead of you. I'm going to look at her college yearbook. She went to the State University in Hunter's Point, so that should be easy.'

Stewart hung up leaving Betsy very confused. Moments before, she was certain Darius had killed the Portland women. But if Reggie's suspicions were right, Darius was being framed, and everyone was being manipulated by a very intelligent and dangerous woman.

3

Randy Highsmith and Ross Barrow took I-84 down the Columbia River Gorge until they came to the turn-off for the scenic highway. Stark cliffs rose up on either side of the wide river. Waterfalls could occasionally be seen through breaks in the trees. The view was breathtaking, but Barrow was too busy trying to see through the slashing rain to enjoy it. The gusting winds that funnelled down the Gorge pushed the unmarked car sideways. Barrow fought the wheel and kept the car from skidding as he took the exit.

They were in country. National forest, farmland. The trees provided some protection from the rain, but Barrow still had to lean forward and squint to catch the occasional street signs.

'There,' Randy Highsmith shouted, pointing to a mailbox with the address stuck on in cheap, iridescent numerals. Barrow turned the car sharply and the back wheels slid sideways on the gravel. The house Samuel Oberhurst was renting was supposed to be a quarter mile up this unpaved road. The rental agent had described it as a bungalow, but it was only a step up from a shack. Except for the privacy the surrounding countryside provided, Highsmith could not see a thing to recommend it. The house was square with a peaked roof. It may once have been painted red, but the weather had turned it rust-colored. A beat-up Pontiac was parked out front. No one had cut the grass in weeks. Cinder blocks served as front steps. There were two empty beer cans next to the steps and an empty pack of cigarettes wedged into a crack between two of the blocks.

Barrow pulled the car as close to the front door as he could and Highsmith jumped out, ducking his head, as if that would somehow protect him from the rain. He pounded on the door, waited, then pounded again.

'I'm going around the side,' he yelled to Barrow. The detective cut the motor and followed him. The curtains on the front windows were closed. Highsmith and Barrow walked through the wet grass on the east side of the house and discovered that there were no windows on that side and the shades were down in the windows at the back. Barrow peered through a small window on the west side.

'Looks like a fucking sty in there,' he said.

'No one's home. That's for sure.'

'What about the car?'

Highsmith shrugged. 'Let's try the front door.'

Water dripped off Highsmith's face and he could barely see through his glasses. The front door was not locked. Barrow let them in. Highsmith took off his glasses and dried the lenses with his handkerchief. Barrow turned on a light.

'Jesus!'

Highsmith put on his glasses. A television stood on a low stand under the front window. Across from it was a second-hand sofa. The upholstery was torn in spots, stuffing was coming out and it sagged. A full suit of men's clothes had been thrown on the sofa. Highsmith saw a jacket, underwear, a pair of pants. Next to the TV, fitted into the corner, was an old gray stand-up filing cabinet. All the drawers were out and papers had been thrown around the room. Highsmith was suddenly distracted from the chaos in the front room. He sniffed the air.

'What's that smell?'

Barrow did not answer. He was concentrating on a heavy chair that lay on its side in the center of the room. As he edged around it, he could see blood stains on the chair and the ground around it. Scraps of heavy tape that could have been used to secure a man's legs stuck out from the sides of the chair legs. On a table a few feet from the chair was a kitchen knife encrusted with blood.

'How's your stomach?' Barrow asked. 'We've got a crime scene here and I don't want your breakfast all over it.'

'I've been in crime scenes before, Ross. I was at the pit, remember?'

'I guess you were. Well, take a gander at this.'

There was a plastic soup bowl next to the knife. Highsmith looked in it and turned green. The soup bowl contained three severed fingers.

'John Doe,' Barrow said softly.

Highsmith walked around the chair so he could see the seat. It was covered with blood. He felt queasy. In addition to the three fingers, Doe's genitals had been missing and Randy did not want to be the one who found them.

'I'm not certain who has jurisdiction here,' Barrow said as he walked around the chair. 'Call the state police.'

Highsmith nodded. He looked for a phone. There was none in the front room. There were two rooms in the back of the house. One was a bathroom. Highsmith opened the other slowly, afraid of what he might find. There was barely enough room in the bedroom for a single bed, a dresser and an end-table. The phone was on the end-table.

'Hey, Ross, look at this.'

Barrow came into the room. Highsmith pointed to an answering machine that was connected to the phone. A red light was flashing, indicating there were messages on the machine. Highsmith skimmed through a few messages before stopping at one.

'Mr Oberhurst, this is Betsy Tannenbaum. This is the third time I've called and I'd appreciate it if you would call me at my office. The number is 555-1763. It's urgent that you contact me. I have a release from Lisa Darius giving you permission to discuss her case. Please call any time. I have an answering service that can reach me at home if you call after hours or on a weekday.'

The machine beeped. Highsmith and Barrow looked at each other.

'Oberhurst is hired by Lisa Darius, then he's tortured and his body ends up in the pit at Darius's construction site,' Barrow said.

'Why did Lisa Darius hire him?'

Barrow looked through the door at the open filing cabinet.

'I wonder if that was what Darius was looking for. His wife's file.'

'Hold it, Ross. We don't know Darius did this.'

'Randy, say Darius found out what was in his wife's file and it was something that could hurt him. I mean, if he did this, tortured Oberhurst, cut off his fingers and dick, it was because that file had something in it that was dynamite. Maybe something that could prove Darius is the rose killer.'

'What are you getting . . . Oh, shit. Lisa Darius. He couldn't get at her before, because he's been in jail since we discovered the bodies.'

Barrow grabbed the phone and started dialing.

4

The Oregon Supreme Court sits in Salem, the state capitol, fifty miles south of Portland. The hour commute was the only thing Victor Ryder disliked about being a Supreme Court Justice. After all the years of seven-day work weeks and sixteen-hour days he had spent in private practice, the more leisurely pace of work at the Court was a relief.

Justice Ryder was a widower who lived alone behind a high evergreen hedge in a three-story, brown and white Tudor house in the Portland Heights section of the West

Hills. The view of Portland and Mount Hood from the brick patio in the rear of the house was spectacular.

Ryder unlocked the front door and called out for Lisa. The heat was on in the house. So were the lights. He heard voices coming from the living-room. He called out to Lisa again, but she did not answer. The voices he heard came from the television, but no one was watching it. Ryder switched off the set.

At the bottom of the stairs, Ryder called out again. There was still no answer. If Lisa had gone out, why was the set on? He headed down the hall to the kitchen. Lisa knew her father always snacked as soon as he got in the door, so she left notes on the refrigerator. The refrigerator door was covered with recipes and cartoons affixed to the smooth surface with magnets, but there was no note. There were two coffee cups on the kitchen table, and the remains of a piece of coffee cake on a cake dish.

'Must have gone off with a friend,' Ryder said to himself, but he was still bothered by the TV. He cut a piece of coffee cake and took a bite, then he walked to Lisa's room. There was nothing out of place, nothing that aroused his suspicion. Still, Justice Ryder felt very uneasy. He was about to go to his room to change when he heard the doorbell. Two men were huddled under an umbrella on the front steps.

'Justice Ryder? I'm Randy Highsmith with the Multnomah County District Attorney's Office. This is Detective Ross Barrow, Portland Police. Is your daughter in?'

'Is this about Martin?'

'Yes, sir.'

'Lisa's been staying with me, but she's not here now.'

'When did you see her last?'

'At breakfast. Why?'

'We have some questions we wanted to ask her. Do you know where she can be reached?'

'I'm afraid not. She didn't leave a note and I just got in.'

'Could she be with a friend?' Highsmith asked casually, so Ryder would not see his concern.

'I really don't know.'

Ryder remembered the TV and frowned.

'Is something wrong, sir?' Barrow asked, keeping his tone neutral.

'No. Not really. It's just that there were two coffee cups on the kitchen table, so I thought she was entertaining a friend. They'd been eating a piece of coffee cake, too. But the TV was on.'

'I don't understand,' Barrow said.

'It was on when I came home. I couldn't figure out why she'd leave it running if she was talking with a friend in the kitchen or leaving the house.'

'Is it normal for her to go out without leaving a note?' Barrow asked.

'She hasn't lived at home for some time and she's been staying in the house at night since Martin got out. But she knows I worry about her.'

'Is there something you're not telling us, sir?'

Justice Ryder hesitated.

'Lisa's been very frightened since Martin was released. She talked about leaving the state until he's back behind bars.'

'Wouldn't she have told you where she was going?'

'I assume so.' Ryder paused, as if he just remembered

something. 'Martin called Lisa the night he was released. He said there was nowhere in Portland she would be safe. Maybe he called again and she panicked.'

'Was he threatening her?' Barrow asked.

'I thought so, but Lisa wasn't certain. It was an odd conversation. I only heard Lisa's end of it and what she told me he said.'

Highsmith handed the judge his business card. 'Please ask Mrs Darius to give me a ring the minute you hear from her. It's important.'

'Certainly.'

Barrow and Highsmith shook hands with the judge and left.

'I don't like this,' Barrow said, as soon as the front door closed. 'It's too much like the other crime scenes. Especially the TV. She'd have turned that off if she was going out with a friend.'

'There was no note or rose.'

'Yeah, but Darius isn't stupid. If he's got his wife, he's not going to broadcast the fact. He could have changed his MO to put us off the track. Any suggestions?'

'None at all, unless you think we've got enough to pick up Darius.'

'We don't.'

'Then we wait, and hope Lisa Darius is out with a friend.'

PART SEVEN

GONE, BUT NOT FORGOTTEN

Chapter Twenty-three

1

Betsy heard a car pull into the car port and looked out the kitchen window.

'It's Daddy,' Kathy yelled. She had been waiting in the living-room all afternoon, giving only half-hearted attention to the television, since Betsy told her she was going to Rick's for the weekend.

'Get your things,' Betsy told Kathy as she opened the door.

'They're all here, Mom,' Kathy said, pointing to her backpack, book bag, small valise and Oliver, the stuffed skunk.

The door opened and Kathy jumped into Rick's arms.

'How you doin', Tiger?' Rick asked with a laugh.

'I packed myself,' Kathy said, pointing at her things.

'Did you pack your toothbrush?' Betsy asked suddenly.

'Uh oh,' Kathy said.

'I thought so. Run and get it right now, young lady.'

Rick put Kathy down and she raced down the hall for the bathroom.

'She's very excited,' Betsy told Rick. He looked uncomfortable.

'I thought I'd take her to the Spaghetti Factory.'

'She likes that.'

They stood without talking for a moment.

'You look good, Bets.'

'You should see how I look when I haven't had to spend the day in Judge Spencer's court,' Betsy joked self-consciously, sidestepping the compliment. Rick started to say something but Kathy was back with her toothbrush and the moment passed.

'See you Monday,' Betsy said, giving Kathy a big hug and kiss. Rick gathered up everything but Oliver. Betsy watched from the doorway until they drove away.

2

Alan Page looked up from his desk. Randy Highsmith and Ross Barrow were standing in the doorway. He glanced at his watch. It was six twenty-five.

'I just got off the phone with Justice Ryder. She's still missing,' Barrow said.

Page put down his pen.

'What can we do? There's not a shred of evidence pointing toward Darius,' Page said. He looked pale and sounded exhausted and defeated.

'We have a motive, Al,' Barrow said. 'Lisa Darius is the

only person who can connect Martin to Sam Oberhurst. He couldn't get to her when he was in jail. I say we have at least probable cause. No sooner is he out then she's missing.'

'And there was that phone call,' Highsmith added.

'Ryder can't be certain there was a threat. The call can even be interpreted as a warning to Lisa to be careful of someone else.' Page shook his head. 'I'm not making the same mistake twice. Unless I'm certain we have probable cause, I'm not asking for a search warrant.'

'Don't get gun shy, Al,' Highsmith warned. 'We're talking about a life here.'

'I know that,' Page answered angrily. 'But where do we search? His house? He's not going to be stupid enough to keep her there. Some property he owns? Which one? I'm as frustrated as you are, but we have to be patient.'

Highsmith was about to say something when the intercom buzzed.

'I know you didn't want to be disturbed,' his secretary said, 'but Nancy Gordon is on the line.'

Page felt cold. Highsmith and Barrow straightened. Page put the call on the speaker phone.

'Detective Gordon?'

'I'm sorry I disappeared on you, Mr Page,' a woman said. Page tried to remember what Gordon sounded like. He remembered a throaty quality to her voice, but their connection was bad and the woman's voice was distorted.

'Where are you?'

'I can't tell you that now,' Gordon said. Page thought she sounded sluggish and uncertain.

'Have you read the news? Do you know Darius is out because we didn't have your testimony at his bail hearing?'

'It couldn't be helped. You'll understand everything in a while.'

'I'd like to understand it now, Detective. We have a situation here. Darius's wife has disappeared.'

'I know. That's why I'm calling. I know where she is and you have to act quickly.'

3

Darius Construction was in trouble. When Darius was arrested, the company was on the verge of bringing in two lucrative projects. Both jobs were now with other construction companies and no new projects would appear while Darius was under indictment. Darius had been counting on the income the projects would generate to help him with the company's financial problems. Without the new income, bankruptcy was a real possibility.

Darius spent the day closeted with his accountant, his attorney and his vice presidents working on a plan to save the company, but he had trouble keeping his mind on business. He needed Betsy Tannenbaum and she had dropped him. At first, he'd wanted her to represent him simply because he thought a feminist attorney would give him an edge with the jury. Then Betsy won the bail hearing and convinced him that she had the skills to save him. Their recent meeting had increased his respect. Tannenbaum was tough. Most women would have been too frightened to confront him alone. They would have brought a man for protection. Darius believed Betsy would never break under the pressure of a trial and he knew she would fight to the end for a client in whom she believed.

When the meeting ended at six PM, Darius drove home. He punched in the alarm code for his gate and it swung open with a metallic creak. Darius glanced in the rear-view mirror. He saw the gleam of headlights as a car drove past the gate, then the driveway turned and he lost his angle.

Darius entered the house through the garage and deactivated the alarm. The house was cool and quiet. While Lisa was living with him, there was always an undercurrent of noise in the background. Darius was learning to live without the murmur of kitchen appliances, the muted chatter from the television and the sounds Lisa made passing from room to room.

The living-room looked sterile when he turned on the light. Darius took off his jacket and tie and poured himself a scotch. He wondered if there was a way to talk Betsy into coming back. Her anger was evident, but anger could cool. It was her fear that was keeping Betsy from him. He could not blame her for thinking him a monster after what she learned from Colby. Normally, a woman's fear would excite Darius, but Betsy's fear was driving her from him and he could not think of a way to allay it.

Darius draped his tie and jacket over his arm and walked upstairs to his bedroom. He had barely eaten all day and his stomach growled. He switched on the bedroom light and set his glass on his dresser. As he turned toward the closet, a flash of color caught his eye. There was a black rose on his pillow. Beneath the rose was a sheet of stationery. Darius stared at the note. His stomach turned. He spun toward the doorway, but there was no one there. He strained for the slightest noise, but heard only the normal house sounds.

Darius kept a gun in his dresser. He took it out. His heart was beating wildly. How could someone get into his house without setting off the alarm? Only he and Lisa knew the alarm code and . . . Darius froze. His mind made the logical jump and he headed for the basement, switching on the house lights as he went.

Darius paused at the top of the cellar stairs, knowing what he would see when he turned on the light. He heard the first siren when he was half-way down. He thought about going back, but he had to know. A police car skidded to a halt in front of the house as Darius reached the bottom of the stairs. He put his gun down, because he did not want to risk being shot. Besides, he would not need it. There was no one in the house with him. He knew that when he saw the way the body was arranged.

Lisa Darius lay on her back in the center of the basement. She was naked. Her stomach had been sliced open and her entrails poked through a gaping, blood-soaked hole. The body of Patricia Cross had been left in Henry Waters' basement in exactly this way.

4

As soon as Rick and Kathy drove away, Betsy went back to the kitchen and fixed herself something to eat. She had toyed with the idea of going out for dinner or calling a friend, but the idea of spending a quiet night alone was too appealing.

When she was finished with dinner, Betsy went into the living-room and glanced at the television listings. Nothing looked interesting, so she settled into an easy chair with an Updike novel. She was just starting to get into it when the phone rang. Betsy sighed and ran into the kitchen to answer it.

'Mrs Tannenbaum?'

'Yes.'

'This is Alan Page.' He sounded angry. 'I'm at Martin Darius's estate. We've re-arrested him.'

'On what grounds?'

'He just murdered his wife.'

'My God! What happened?'

'Your client gutted Lisa Darius in his basement.'

'Oh, no.'

'You did her a real favor when you convinced Norwood to release Darius on bail,' Page said bitterly. 'Your client wants to talk to you.'

'Do you believe me now, Tannenbaum?' Darius asked. 'Do you see what's going on?'

'Don't say anything. The police are listening, Martin. I'll see you in the morning.'

'Then, you're sticking with me?'

'I didn't say that.'

'You've got to. Ask yourself how the police found out about Lisa and you'll know I'm innocent.'

Was Darius really innocent? It didn't make sense that he would kill his wife and leave her body to decompose in his own basement. Betsy thought over what she knew about the Hunter's Point case. Betsy imagined Henry Waters answering the door, Nancy Gordon walking down the steps to Waters' basement, the shocked look on Waters' face when he saw Patricia Cross sprawled in her own blood, disemboweled. It was Patricia Cross, all over again. Darius had asked her to find out how the police knew Lisa Darius was in his basement. She tried to remember how the police had found out about Patricia Cross?

'Put Page back on,' she told Darius.

'I don't want anyone talking to Darius,' she told the District Attorney.

'I wouldn't think of it,' Page replied rudely.

'You're wasting your anger on me, Alan. I knew Lisa Darius better than you did. This hurts, believe me.'

Page was silent for a moment. He sounded subdued when he spoke.

'You're right. I had no business biting your head off. I'm as mad at myself for screwing up at the bail hearing as I am at you for doing such a good job. But he's staying in this time. Norwood won't make another mistake.'

'Alan, how did you know you'd find Lisa's body in the basement?'

Betsy held her breath while Page decided if he would answer.

'Ah, you'll find out anyway. It was a tip.'

'Who told you?'

'I can't tell you that now.'

A tip, just like the anonymous tip that led the Hunter's Point police to Henry Waters' basement. Betsy hung up the phone. Her doubts about Darius's guilt were starting to grow. Martin Darius had murdered the women in Hunter's Point, but was he innocent of the Portland murders?

Chapter Twenty-four

1

The door to the jail interview room opened and Darius walked in. He was dressed in the shirt and suit pants he had been wearing when he was arrested. His eyes were bloodshot and he seemed less self-assured than he looked during their other meetings.

'I knew you'd be here, Tannenbaum,' Darius said, trying to appear calm but sounding a little desperate.

'I don't want to be. I'm required to represent you until another attorney relieves me of my obligation.'

'You can't leave me in the lurch.'

'I haven't changed my mind, Martin. I meant everything I said the other day.'

'Even though you know I'm innocent?'

'I don't know that for certain. And even if you are innocent, it doesn't change what you did in Hunter's Point.'

Darius leaned forward slightly and locked his eyes on hers.

'You do know I'm innocent, unless you think I'm stupid enough to murder my wife in my basement, then call Alan Page and tell him where to find the corpse.'

Darius was right, of course. The case against him was too pat and the timing of this new killing too opportune. Doubts had kept Betsy up for most of the night, but they had not changed the way she felt about Darius.

'We'll be going up to court in a few minutes. Page will arraign you on a complaint charging you with Lisa's murder. He'll ask for a no-bail hold and ask Norwood to revoke your bail on the other charges. I can't see any way of convincing the judge to let you out on bail.'

'Tell the judge what we know about Gordon. Tell him I'm being framed.'

'We have no proof of that.'

'So, this is how it's going to be. I guess I figured you wrong, Tannenbaum. What happened to your high-blown sense of ethics? Your oath as an attorney? You're going to throw this one, aren't you, because you can't stand me?'

Betsy flushed with anger. 'I'm not throwing a goddamn thing. I shouldn't even be here. What I am doing is letting you know the facts of life. Judge Norwood took a big chance letting you out. When he sees the pictures of Lisa spread-eagled in your basement with her guts pulled through her abdominal wall, he is not going to feel like letting you out again.'

'The State calls Vincent Ryder, Your Honor,' Alan Page said, turning toward the rear of the room to watch the courtly Justice walk past the spectators and through the bar of the court. Ryder was six foot three with a full head of snow-white hair. He walked with a slight limp from a wound he had received in World War Two. Ryder kept his back rigid, scrupulously avoiding eye contact with Martin Darius, as if he was afraid of the rage that might overpower him if he set eyes on the man.

'For the record,' Page said as soon as Ryder was sworn, 'you are a Justice of the Oregon Supreme Court and the father of Lisa Darius?'

'Yes,' Ryder answered, his voice cracking slightly.

'Your daughter was married to the defendant, was she not?'

'Yes, sir.'

'When Mr Darius was arrested, did your daughter move in with you?'

'She did.'

'While Lisa was staying at your home, did her husband phone her?'

'Repeatedly, Mr Page. He phoned from jail several times each evening.'

'Is it true that inmates can only make collect calls?'

'Yes. All his calls were collect.'

'Did your daughter accept the calls?'

'She instructed me to refuse them.'

'To the best of your knowledge, did your daughter speak to the defendant while he was incarcerated?'

'She may have, once or twice immediately after his arrest. Once she moved in with me, she stopped.'

'What was your daughter's attitude toward her husband?'

'She was scared to death of him.'

'Did this fear increase or decrease when Mr Darius was released on bail?'

'It increased. She was terrified he would come for her.'

'Did the defendant phone Lisa Darius after his release on bail?'

'Yes, sir. The first evening.'

'Did you hear the conversation?'

'Snatches of it.'

'Did you hear the defendant make any threats?'

'I believe he told her she would not be safe in Portland.'

'When you say you believe he said this, what do you mean?'

'Lisa told me he said it. I was standing at Lisa's shoulder and could hear some of what he said.'

'Do you know if Mrs Darius believed the defendant meant this as a threat?'

'She was confused. She told me she wasn't certain what he meant. He seemed to be implying Lisa was in danger from someone else, but that didn't make sense. I took it that he was threatening her indirectly, so no blame could be placed on him.'

'Justice Ryder, when was the last time you saw your daughter alive?'

For a brief moment, the judge lost his composure. He sipped from a cup of water before answering.

'We had breakfast together between seven and seven-thirty AM. Then I drove to Salem.'

'When did you return home?'

'Around six in the evening.'

'Was your daughter home?'

'No.'

'Did you see anything in the house that alarmed you?'

'The television was on, but no one was home. The sound

358

was high enough so Lisa should have heard it and turned it off before she left.'

'Was there evidence that she'd had a visitor?'

'There were two coffee cups in the kitchen and some coffee cake was out, as if she'd been talking to someone.'

'Did your daughter leave a note telling where she was going?'

'No.'

'Nothing further.'

'Your witness, Mrs Tannenbaum,' Judge Norwood said.

'He's lying,' Darius whispered. 'I never threatened Lisa. I was warning her.'

'He's not lying, Martin. He's saying what he honestly believes happened. If I push him, he'll just harden his position.'

'Bullshit. I've seen you take witnesses apart. Ryder is a pompous asshole. You can make him look like a fool.'

Betsy took a deep breath, because she did not want to lose her temper. Then she leaned over to Darius and spoke quietly.

'Do you want me to push Justice Ryder until he breaks down, Martin? Do you really think it will help you get bail if I cause one of the most respected judges in the state, and the father of a young woman who has been brutally murdered, to crack up in open court in front of one of his colleagues?'

Darius started to say something, then shut up and turned away from Betsy.

'No questions, Your Honor,' Betsy said.

'Our next witness is Detective Richard Kassel,' Page told the judge.

Richard Kassel sauntered down the aisle. He was dressed in a brown tweed sports coat, tan slacks, a white shirt and a bright yellow print tie. His shoes were polished and his black hair was styled. He had the smug look of a person who took himself too seriously.

'Detective Kassel, how are you employed?'

'I'm a detective with the Portland Police Bureau.'

'Did you arrest the defendant yesterday evening?'

'Yes, sir.'

'Tell the judge how that came about.'

Kassel swiveled toward the judge.

'Detective Rittner and I received a call over the police radio. Based on that communication, I entered the grounds. The door to the defendant's house was locked. We identified ourselves as police and demanded that the defendant open the door. He complied. Detective Rittner and I secured the defendant and waited for the other cars to arrive, as we had been ordered to do.'

'Did other officers arrive soon after?'

Kassel nodded. 'About fifteen minutes after we arrived, you and Detective Barrow arrived followed by several others.'

Betsy's brow furrowed. She checked something she had written during Justice Ryder's testimony. Then she made some notes on her pad.

'Did you discover the body?' Page asked.

'No, sir. Our instructions were to stay with the defendant. The body was discovered by other officers.'

'Did you give Mr Darius his Miranda warnings?'

'Yes, sir.'

'Did Mr Darius make any statements?'

'Other than to ask to call his lawyer, no.'

'Your witness, Mrs Tannenbaum.'

Betsy looked unsure of herself. She asked the judge for a minute and pretended to look through a police report while she worked through her thoughts.

'Detective Kassel,' Betsy asked cautiously, 'who told you to enter the Darius estate and arrest Mr Darius?'

'Detective Barrow.'

'Did he say why you were to arrest Mr Darius?'

'Yes, ma'am. He said there was a tip that the defendant had killed his wife and her body was in his basement.'

'Did Detective Barrow tell you who gave him the tip?'

'I didn't ask.'

'How was Mr Darius dressed when he opened the door for you?'

'He was wearing a white shirt and pants.'

'Mr Darius, please stand up.'

Darius stood.

'Are these the pants?'

Detective Kassel took a second to look at Darius. 'Yeah. Those are the ones we arrested him in.'

'And this is the white shirt?'

'Yes.'

'It's in the same condition as when you arrested him?'

'Yes.'

'There's no blood on this shirt, is there?'

Kassel paused, then answered, 'No, ma'am.'

'Did you view the body of Lisa Darius at any point?'

'Yes.'

'When it was still in the basement?'

'Yes.'

'Mrs Darius was disemboweled, was she not?'

'Yes.'

'There was blood all over that basement, wasn't there?'

'Yes,' Kassel answered grudgingly.

'The gate to the Darius estate is locked. How did you get in?'

'Detective Barrow had the combination.'

'How is it that you arrived at the Darius estate so far ahead of Detective Barrow, Mr Page and the other officers?' Betsy asked with an easy smile that disguised the tension she was feeling. She would know if her suspicions were correct after a few more questions.

'We were parked outside it.'

'Was that by chance?'

'No, ma'am. We had the defendant under surveillance.'

'How long had you had him under surveillance?'

'We've been surveilling him for quite a while. Back before his first arrest.'

'Just you and Detective Rittner?'

'Oh, no. There were three teams. We switched off. You can't do that twenty-four hours.'

'Of course not. When did your shift start on the day you arrested Mr Darius?'

'Around three in the afternoon.'

'Where did you start?'

'Outside his office.'

'I assume you took over for another surveillance team?'

'Right. Detectives Padovici and Kristol.'

'When had they started?'

'Around five in the morning.'

'Where did they start?'

'The defendant's house.'

'Why did the other team start so early?'

'The defendant gets up around five-thirty and leaves for work around six-thirty. By getting there at five, we kept him covered when he left his place.'

'Is that what Kristol and Padovici did?'

'Yeah.'

'I suppose they followed Mr Darius to work?'

'That's what they said.'

'Anything unusual happen that day, according to the detectives?'

'No. He went right to work. I don't think he ever left his office. Detective Padovici said it looked like he sent out for sandwiches at lunch time. Around six, a bunch of guys in suits left. I think they were having a meeting.'

'When Mr Darius left, you followed him home?'

'Right.'

'Was he ever out of your sight?'

'No, ma'am.'

'How long after Mr Darius arrived home did you receive the instructions from Detective Barrow to enter the Darius estate and arrest Mr Darius?'

'Not long.'

'Give me your best guess.'

'Uh, about fifteen, twenty minutes.'

Betsy paused. She felt sick about asking the next series of questions, but her sense of duty, and the possibility that the answers could prove her client innocent, overcame her revulsion at the prospect of Martin Darius walking free.

'Did you ever see Mr Darius with Lisa Darius that day?'

'No, ma'am.'

'What about Padovici and Kristol? Did they say they saw Mr Darius with his wife?'

Kassel frowned, as if he suddenly realized where Betsy's questions were leading. Betsy looked to her left and saw Alan Page in an animated discussion with Randy Highsmith.

'I can't recall,' he answered hesitantly.

'I assume you wrote a daily surveillance log listing any unusual occurrences?'

'Yes.'

'And the other members of the surveillance team also kept logs?'

'Yes.'

'Where are the logs?'

'Detective Barrow has them.'

Betsy stood. 'Your Honor, I would like the logs produced and Detectives Kristol and Padovici made available for questioning. Justice Ryder testified that he last saw his daughter at seven-thirty AM. Detective Kassel says Padovici and Kristol reported that Mr Darius left his estate at six-thirty and went directly to work. If neither team saw Mr Darius with his wife during the day, when did he kill her? We can produce the people who were with Mr Darius yesterday. They'll say he was in his office from about seven AM until a little after six PM.'

Judge Norwood looked troubled. Alan Page leaped to his feet.

'This is nonsense, Judge. The surveillance was on Darius, not his wife. The body was in the basement. Mr Darius was with the body.'

'Your Honor,' Betsy said, 'Mr Darius could not have

killed his wife before he got home and he was only home for a short time when Detective Kassel arrived. The person who disemboweled Lisa Darius would have blood all over him. There was no blood on my client. Look at his white shirt and his pants.

'I suggest that Mr Darius is being set up. Someone was at Justice Ryder's house having coffee with Lisa Darius during the day. It wasn't the defendant. Lisa Darius left the house without turning off the television. That's because she was forced to leave. That person took her to the estate and murdered her in the basement, then phoned in the anonymous tip that led the police to the body.'

'That's absurd,' Page said. 'Who is this mysterious person? I suppose you'll suggest the mystery man also butchered the four people we found at your client's construction site.'

'Your Honor,' Betsy said, 'ask yourself who knew the body of Lisa Darius was in Mr Darius's basement. Only the killer or someone who saw the murder. Is Mr Page suggesting that Mr Darius found his wife alive in his home, butchered her in the fifteen minutes or so between the time Detective Kassel lost sight of him and the time Detective Kassel arrested him, got no blood on his white shirt while disemboweling her and was such a good citizen that he reported himself to the police so they could arrest him for murder?'

Judge Norwood looked troubled. Betsy and Alan Page watched him intently.

'Mrs Tannenbaum,' the judge said, 'your theory depends on Mr Darius leaving his estate at six-thirty and being in his office all day.'

'Yes, Your Honor.'

The judge turned to Alan Page. 'I'm keeping Mr Darius in jail over the weekend. I want you to give copies of the logs to Mrs Tannenbaum and I want the detectives here Monday morning. I'll tell you, Mr Page, this business has me seriously concerned. You better have a good explanation for me. Right now, I can't see how this man killed his wife.'

2

'Goddamn it, Ross, how did this slip by you?'

'I'm sorry, Al. I don't review the log entries every day.'

'If Darius didn't go near Justice Ryder's house, we have trouble, Al,' Randy Highsmith said.

'The surveillance teams must have screwed up,' Page insisted. 'She was there. She got into the basement somehow. Didn't you tell me there were paths through the woods? The surveillance teams weren't watching Lisa. She could have used the paths to sneak on to the estate while the teams were tailing Darius.'

'Why would she go to the estate if she was terrified of Darius?' Highsmith asked.

'He could have sweet-talked her over the phone,' Page said. 'They were man and wife.'

'Then why sneak in?' Highsmith asked. 'Why not drive through the front gate and up to the front door? It's her house. It makes no sense for her to sneak in if she was going back willingly.'

'Maybe the press had been hounding her and she wanted to avoid reporters.'

'I don't buy that.'

'There's got to be a logical explanation,' Page answered, frustrated by the seeming impossibility of the situation.

'There are a few other things that are nagging at me, Al,' Highsmith told his boss.

'Let's hear them,' Page said.

'How did Nancy Gordon know where to find the body? Tannenbaum's right. Darius couldn't have killed Lisa at night because she was alive in the morning. He couldn't have killed her off of the estate. We had him under surveillance every minute during the day. If Darius did it, he killed her in the house. There aren't windows in the basement. How would anyone else know what was going on? There are problems with the case, Al. We have to face them.'

3

'How was the meeting?'

'Don't ask,' Raymond Colby told his wife. 'My head's like putty. Help me with this tie. I'm all thumbs.'

'Here. Let me,' Ellen said, untying the Windsor knot.

'Can you fix me a drink? I'll be in the den. I want to watch the late news.'

Ellen pecked her husband on the cheek and walked toward the liquor cabinet. 'Why don't you just go to bed?'

'Bruce Smith made some dumb comment on the highway bill. Wayne insists I hear it. It should be on toward the top of the news. Besides, I'm too wound up to go right to sleep.'

Colby went into the den and turned on the news. Ellen came in and handed the Senator his drink.

'If this doesn't relax you, we'll think of something that will,' she said mischievously.

Colby smiled. 'What makes you think I have the energy for that kind of hanky-panky?'

'A man who can't rise to the occasion shouldn't be on the Supreme Court.'

Colby laughed. 'You've become a pervert in your old age.'

'And about time, too.'

They both laughed, then Colby suddenly sobered. He pointed the remote control at the screen and turned up the volume.

'. . . a startling new development in the case against millionaire builder Martin Darius, who is accused of the torture-murder of three women and one man in Portland, Oregon. A week ago, Darius was released on bail when trial judge Patrick Norwood ruled that there was insufficient evidence to hold him. Yesterday evening, Darius was re-arrested when police found the body of his wife, Lisa Darius, in the basement of the Darius mansion. A police spokesman said she had been tortured and killed in a manner similar to the other victims.

'Today, in a court hearing, Betsy Tannenbaum, Darius's attorney, argued that Darius was the victim of a frame-up after it was revealed that police surveillance teams followed Darius all day on the day his wife was murdered and never saw him with his wife. The hearing will resume Monday.

'On a less serious note, Mayor Clinton Vance is reported to have . . .'

Colby turned off the set and closed his eyes.

'What's wrong?' Ellen asked.

'How would you feel if I was not confirmed by the Senate?'

'That's not possible.'

Colby heard the uncertainty in his wife's voice. He was so tired. 'I have to make a decision. It concerns something I did when I was Governor of New York. A secret that I thought would stay buried forever.'

'What kind of secret?' Ellen asked hesitantly.

Colby opened his eyes. He saw his wife's concern and took her hand.

'Not a secret about us, love. It concerns something I did ten years ago. A decision I had to make. A decision I would make again.'

'I don't understand.'

'I'll explain everything, then you tell me what I should do.'

Chapter Twenty-five

1

Alan Page looked at the illuminated digital display on his alarm clock as he groped for the phone in the dark. It was four-fifteen.

'Is this Alan Page, the District Attorney for Multnomah County?' a man asked.

'It is, and I'll still be DA when the sun's up.'

'Sorry about that, but we have a three-hour time difference here and my flight leaves in thirty minutes.'

'Who is this?' Page asked, awake enough to be annoyed.

'My name is Wayne Turner. I'm Senator Raymond Colby's Administrative Assistant. I used to be a detective with the Hunter's Point Police Department. Nancy Gordon and I are good friends.'

Page swung his legs over the side of the bed and sat up.

'You've got my attention. What's this about?'

'I'll be at the Sheraton Airport Hotel by ten, your time. Senator Colby wants me to brief you.'

'This concerns Darius?'

'We knew him as Peter Lake. The Senator wants you fully informed about certain matters you may not know.'

'Such as?'

'Not over the phone, Mr Page.'

'Is this going to help my case against Darius?'

'My information will make a conviction certain.'

'Can you give me a clue about what you're going to say?'

'Not over the phone,' Turner repeated, 'and not to anyone but you.'

'Randy Highsmith is my chief criminal deputy. You talked to him. Can I bring him along?'

'Let me make myself clear, Mr Page. Senator Colby is going as far out on a limb for you as someone in public life can go. My job is to see that the limb doesn't get sawed off. When Mr Highsmith called, I gave him the run around. You're going to hear the things I did not want Mr Highsmith to know. This is not by my choosing. It's the Senator who insisted I fly to Portland. It's my job to do what he wants, but I'm going to protect him as much as I am able. So, there will be no witnesses, no notes and you can expect to be patted down for a wire. You can also be assured that what you hear will be worth any inconvenience you suffered by being awakened before dawn. Now, I've got to make my flight, if you still want me to.'

'Come on down, Mr Turner. I'll respect your wishes. See you at ten.'

Page hung up and sat in the dark, wide awake. What would Turner tell him? What possible connection was there between the President's nominee to the United States Supreme Court and Martin Darius? Whatever it was,

Turner thought it would guarantee Darius's conviction and that was what mattered. Darius would pay. Since the first bail hearing, the case seemed to be slipping away from him. Not even Lisa Darius's tragic death had given the prosecution substance. Maybe Turner's information would save him.

Wayne Turner opened the door and let Alan Page into his hotel room. Turner was impeccably dressed in a three-piece suit. Page's suit was wrinkled, his shoes unpolished. If anyone looked like he had just flown three thousand miles, it was Page.

'Let's get the strip-tease out of the way,' Turner said when the door was closed. Page took off his jacket. Turner patted him down expertly.

'Satisfied?' Page asked.

'Not one bit, Mr Page. If I had my druthers, I'd be back in D.C. You want some coffee?'

'Coffee would be nice.'

There was a thermos on a coffee table and the remains of a sandwich. Turner poured for both of them.

'Before I tell you a damn thing, we have to have some ground rules. There is an excellent chance that Senator Colby will not be confirmed if what I tell you is made public. I want your word that you will not call the Senator or me as a witness in any court proceeding or make what I tell you available to anyone else – even members of your staff – unless it is absolutely necessary to secure the conviction of Martin Darius.'

'Mr Turner, I respect the Senator. I want to see him on the Court. The fact that he's willing to risk his nomination to give me this information reinforces the feelings I've had about his worth to this country. Believe me, I will do nothing to jeopardize his chances if I can help it. But I want you to know, up front, this prosecution is in a lot of trouble. If I had to bet, I'd pick Martin Darius to walk, based on what I've got now.'

2

Kathy insisted on eating at the Spaghetti Factory again. There was the usual forty-five-minute wait and the service was slow. They were not back in Rick's apartment until after nine. Kathy was pooped, but she was so excited she did not want to go to bed. Rick spent half an hour reading to her. He was surprised how much he enjoyed reading to his daughter. That was something Betsy usually did. He enjoyed dinner, too. In fact, he had enjoyed all the time they spent together.

The doorbell rang. Rick checked his watch. Who would be calling at nine forty-five? Rick looked through the peephole. It took him a moment to remember the woman who was standing in the hall.

'Miss Sloane, isn't it?' Rick asked when the door was open.

'You have a good memory.'

'What can I do for you?'

Sloane looked embarrassed. 'I really shouldn't intrude like this, but I remembered your address. You told Betsy before you left the office. I was in the neighborhood. I know it's late, but I was going to arrange a meeting with you for background for my article anyway, so I thought I'd take a chance. If you're busy, I can come some other time.'

'Actually, that would be best. I've got Kathy with me and she just went to sleep. I don't want to disturb her and I'm pretty beat myself.'

'Say no more, Mr Tannenbaum. Could we meet later in the week?'

'Do you really want to talk to me? Betsy and I are separated, you know.'

'I do know, but I would like to talk to you about her. She's a remarkable woman and your view of her would be very informative.'

'I'm not sure I want to discuss our marriage for publication.'

'Will you think it over?'

Rick hesitated, then said, 'Sure. Call me at the office.'

'Thank you, Mr Tannenbaum. Do you have a card?'

Rick patted his pockets and remembered his wallet was in the bedroom.

'Step in for a minute. I'll get you one.'

Rick turned his back on Nora Sloane and started into the apartment. Nora was taller than Rick. She glided behind him and looped her left arm around his neck while she drew the knife out of her deep coat-pocket with her right hand. Rick felt himself jerked up on his toes when Sloane leaned back and tilted his chin up. He did not feel anything when the knife slashed across his throat because his body went into shock. There was a jolt when the knife slid into his back, then another jolt. Rick tried to struggle but he lost control of his body. Blood spurted from his neck. He viewed the red fountain like a tourist staring at a landmark.

The room wavered. Rick felt his energy drain out of him along with the blood that drenched the floor. Nora Sloane released her hold and Rick slid to the carpet. She closed the apartment door quietly and looked around. There was a living-room at the end of the hall. Sloane walked through it, down another hall and stopped at the first door. She pushed it open gently and stared at Kathy. The darling little girl was asleep. She looked lovely.

Chapter Twenty-six

Betsy was finishing breakfast when the doorbell rang. A light rain had been falling all morning and it was hard to see Nora Sloane through the streaked pane in the kitchen window. She was standing on the welcome-mat holding an umbrella in one hand and a large shopping bag in the other. Betsy carried her coffee cup to the front door. Nora smiled when it opened.

'Can I come in?' Sloane asked.

'Sure,' Betsy said, stepping aside. Sloane leaned her umbrella against the wall in the entryway and unbuttoned her raincoat. She was wearing tight-fitting jeans, a light blue work shirt and a dark blue sweater.

'Can we sit down?' Nora asked, gesturing toward the living-room. Betsy was confused by this morning visit, but she sat down on the couch. Nora sat in an armchair across from her and took a gun out of the shopping bag. The coffee cup slipped from Betsy's fingers and shattered when it struck the marble table top. A dark brown puddle formed around the shards.

'I'm sorry I frightened you,' Sloane said calmly.

Betsy stared at the gun.

'Don't let this bother you,' Sloane said. 'I wouldn't hurt you. I like you. I'm just not certain how you'll react when I explain why I'm here and I want to be certain you don't do anything foolish. You won't do anything rash, will you?'

'No.'

'Good. Now, listen carefully to me. Martin Darius must not be freed. On Monday, before the hearing starts, you will ask to use Judge Norwood's jury room to speak in private with your client. There's a door that opens into the corridor. When I knock on the door, you'll let me in.'

'Then what?'

'That's none of your concern.'

'Why should I do this for you?'

Nora reached into the shopping bag and pulled out Oliver. She handed the stuffed animal to Betsy.

'I have Kathy. She's a sweet child. She'll be fine, if you do what I tell you.'

'How . . . How did you get Kathy? Rick didn't call me.'

'Rick's dead.' Betsy gaped at Nora, not certain she had heard her correctly. 'He hurt you. Men are like that. Martin is the worst example. Making us act like dogs, forcing us to fuck each other, mounting us as if we were inanimate objects, cartoon women, so he could live out his fantasies. But other men do the same thing in different ways. Like Rick. He used you, then discarded you.'

'Oh, God,' Betsy wept, stunned and only half believing what Sloane said. 'He's not dead.'

'I did it for you, Betsy.'

'No, Nora. He didn't deserve this.'

Sloane's features hardened. 'They all deserve to die, Betsy. All of them.'

'You're Samantha Reardon, aren't you?'

Reardon nodded.

'I don't understand. After what you went through, how could you kill those women?'

'That was hard, Betsy. I made certain they didn't suffer. I only marked them when they were anesthetized. If there was another way, I would have chosen it.'

Of course, Betsy thought, if Reardon kidnapped the women to frame Martin Darius, it would be easier to deal with them if they were unconscious. A nurse who assisted in surgery would know all about anesthetics like pentobarbital.

Reardon smiled warmly, reversed the gun and held it out to Betsy.

'Don't be afraid. I said I wouldn't hurt you. Take it. I want you to see how much I trust you.'

Betsy half reached, then stopped.

'Go on,' Reardon urged her. 'Do as I say. I know you won't shoot me. I'm the only one who knows where Kathy is. If I was killed, no one would be able to find her. She'd starve to death. That's a cruel and horrible way to die. I know. I almost died from starvation.'

Betsy took the gun. It was cold to the touch and heavy. She had the power to kill Reardon, but she felt utterly helpless.

'If I do what you say, you'll give me Kathy unharmed?'

'Kathy is my insurance policy, just as I was Peter Lake's. Nancy Gordon told me all about the Governor's pardon. I've learned so much from Martin Darius. I can't wait to thank him in person.'

Reardon sat quietly for a while. She did not move. Betsy tried to stay just as still, but it was impossible. She shifted on the couch. The seconds passed. Reardon looked as if she was having trouble framing her thoughts. When she spoke, she looked into Betsy's eyes with an expression of deep concern and addressed Betsy the way a teacher addresses a prize pupil when she wants to make certain that the student understands a key point.

'You have to see Darius for what he is to understand what I'm doing. He is the Devil. Not just a bad person, but pure evil. Ordinary measures wouldn't have worked. Who would believe me? I've been committed twice. When I tried to tell people in Hunter's Point, no one would listen. Now I know why. I always suspected there were others working with Martin. Nancy Gordon confirmed that. She told me all about the conspiracy to free Martin and blame Henry Waters. Only the Devil would have so much power. Think of it. The Governor, the Mayor, policemen. Only Gordon resisted. And she was the only woman.'

Reardon watched Betsy intently. 'I'll bet you'll be tempted to call the police as soon as I leave. You mustn't do that. They might catch me. I'll never tell where Kathy is if I'm caught. You must be especially strong when the police tell you Rick is dead and Kathy has been kidnapped. Don't weaken and give me away.'

Reardon smiled coldly.

'You must not put your faith in the police. You must not believe that they can break me. I can assure you that nothing the police can do to me compares to what Martin did and Martin never broke me. Oh, he thought he did. He thought I was submitting, but only my body submitted.

My mind stayed strong and focused.

'At night, I could hear the others whimpering. I never whimpered. I folded my hate inside me and kept it safe and warm. Then, I waited. When they told me Waters was the one, I knew they were lying. I knew Martin had done something to them to make them lie. The Devil can do that. Twist people, change them around like clay figures, but he didn't change me.'

'Is Kathy warm?' Betsy asked. 'She can get sick if she's in a damp place.'

'Kathy is warm, Betsy. I'm not a monster like Darius. I'm not inhuman or insensitive. I need Kathy to be safe. I don't want to harm her.'

Betsy did not hate Reardon. Reardon was insane. It was Darius she hated. Darius knew exactly what he was doing in Hunter's Point when he created Reardon by stripping her of her humanity. Betsy handed the gun to Reardon.

'Take it. I don't want it.'

'Thank you, Betsy. I'm pleased to see you trust me as much as I trust you.'

'What you're doing is wrong. Kathy is a baby. She never did anything to you.'

'I know. I feel badly about taking her, but I couldn't think of any other way to force you to help me. You have such high principles. I was upset when you told me you were dropping Darius as a client. I counted on you to get me close to him. But I admired you for refusing to represent him. So many lawyers would have continued for the money. I helped you with your marital problems so you'd see how much I respect you.'

Reardon stood up. 'I've got to go. Please don't worry.

Kathy's safe and warm. Do what I told you and she'll be back with you soon.'

'Can you have Kathy call me? She'll be frightened. It would help her if she heard my voice.'

'I'm sure you're sincere, Betsy, but you might try to have my calls traced. I can't take that chance.'

'Then give this to her,' Betsy said, handing Oliver to Reardon. 'It will make her feel safe.'

Reardon took the stuffed animal. Tears streaked down Betsy's face.

'She's all I have. Please don't hurt her.'

Reardon closed the door without answering. Betsy ran into the kitchen and watched her walk up the driveway, back straight, unwavering. At that moment, Betsy suddenly knew how the husbands felt when they came home to find only notes that read 'Gone, But Not Forgotten'.

Betsy wandered back to the living-room. It was still dark, though a sliver of light was starting to show on the fringe of the hills. Betsy slumped on the couch, exhausted by the effort it took to keep her emotions at bay, unable to think and in shock. She wanted to mourn Rick, but all she could think about was Kathy. Until Kathy was safe, her heart would have no time to ache for Rick.

Betsy tried not to think of the women in the autopsy photographs, she tried to block her memory of the picture Darius had painted of his dehumanized prisoners, but she could not stop herself from seeing Kathy, her little girl, frantic and defenseless, curled up in the dark, terrified of every sound.

*

Time passed in a blur. The rain stopped and the sky changed from dark to light without her noticing. The pool of cold coffee had spread between the fragments of the broken cup and across the top of the coffee table. Betsy walked into the kitchen. There was a roll of paper towels under the sink. She tore some off of the roll, found a small paper bag and grabbed a large sponge. Doing something helped. Moving helped.

Betsy picked up the pieces of the cup and put them in the paper bag. She sponged off the table top and used the paper towels to wipe it down. As she worked, she thought about help. The police were out. She could not control them. Betsy believed Samantha Reardon. If Reardon thought Betsy betrayed her, she would kill Kathy. If the police arrested her, she would never tell where she was holding Kathy.

Betsy put the wet towels into the bag, carried the bag into the kitchen and put it in the garbage. Finding Kathy was the only thing she cared about. Reggie Stewart was an expert at finding people and she could control him, because Reggie worked for her. More important, he was sensitive. He would put finding Kathy ahead of arresting Samantha Reardon. Betsy would have to act quickly. It was only a matter of time before someone discovered Rick's body and the police investigation started.

Reggie Stewart's flight from Hunter's Point had landed in Portland after midnight and Betsy's call aroused him from a sound sleep. He wanted to go back to bed, but Betsy sounded upset and she had been so cryptic on the phone, he was concerned. Stewart smiled when Betsy opened the door, but his smile faded as soon as he saw Betsy's face.

'What's up, Chief?'

Betsy did not answer Stewart until they were seated in the living-room. She looked like she was barely under control.

'You were right. Samantha Reardon killed the people at the construction site.'

'How do you know that?'

'She told me, this morning. She . . .'

Betsy closed her eyes and took a deep breath. Her shoulders started to shake. She put a hand over her eyes. Betsy did not want to cry. Stewart knelt next to her. He touched her, gently.

'What's happening, Betsy? Tell me. I'm your friend. If I can help you, I will.'

'She killed Rick,' Betsy sobbed, collapsing into Reggie's arms.

Stewart held her close and let her cry.

'Have you told the police?'

'I can't, Reggie. She has Kathy hidden somewhere. The police don't know Rick is dead. If they arrest Samantha, she won't tell where she has Kathy hidden and she'll starve to death. That's why I need you. You have to find Kathy.'

'You don't want me, Betsy. You want the cops and the FBI. They're much better equipped to find Kathy than I am. They have computers, manpower . . .'

'I believe Samantha when she says Kathy will die if she learns I went to the police. Reardon has already murdered the four people at the site, Lisa Darius and Rick.'

'How do you know Reardon so well?'

'The day after Darius hired me, a woman calling herself Nora Sloane phoned me. She said she wanted to meet me

for lunch to discuss an article she was writing about women
defense attorneys. She wanted to use my cases as the centerpiece. I was flattered. When Darius was arrested, she was
already my friend. When she asked if she could tag along
while I worked up Martin's case, I agreed.'

'Reardon?'

'Yes.'

'Why did she kill Rick?'

'She said she killed Rick because he left me.'

'If she killed Rick because he hurt you, why hurt you
more by kidnapping Kathy?'

Betsy decided not to tell Stewart about Reardon's instructions. She trusted her investigator, but she was afraid
Stewart would warn the police if he learned of Reardon's
plan to get into the jury room with Darius.

'After I found out Martin killed the women in Hunter's
Point, I told him I wouldn't represent him and I told
Reardon I was dropping Martin as a client. She was very
upset. I think she wants to be able to control the case. With
Kathy as a prisoner, she can force me to do things that will
insure Martin's conviction. If you don't find Kathy, I'll have
to do what she says.'

Stewart walked back and forth, thinking. Betsy wiped
her eyes. Talking to someone helped.

'What do you know about Reardon?' Stewart asked.
'Have you seen her car, has she mentioned anything about
where she lives, when you met for lunch did she pay with
a credit card?'

'I've been trying to think about those things, but I really
don't know anything about her. I've never seen her drive,
but I'm certain she has a car. She had to transport the

bodies to the construction site, my house is out of the way and she's attended all of Darius's court appearances.'

'What about where she's living? Has she mentioned a long ride to town, how beautiful the view is in the country? Do you have her phone number?'

'She's never talked much about herself, now that I think about it. We've always talked about me or Darius or the battered women cases and never about her. I don't think I ever asked her where she lives. The one time I asked for her phone number, she said she would call me and I didn't press her. I do remember that she paid for the lunch with cash. I don't think I've ever seen a piece of ID.'

'Okay. Let's hit this from another angle. Darius chose an isolated farmhouse so no one would see him bringing the women there and to cut the chances that anyone would stumble on to the women while he was away. Sloane doesn't have the problem of a wife and job, she could stay with the women most of the time, but she came to court when Darius had appearances and she met with you a number of times. I'm betting she's living in a rural area that's near enough to Portland so she can come to town, then get back, easily. The house probably has a basement so she can keep her prisoners out of sight. She'd also have to have electricity . . .'

'I asked if she'd let Kathy phone me. She said she wouldn't, because she was worried I might trace her calls. She must have a phone,' Betsy said.

'Good. That's the way to think. Utilities, a phone, garbage service. And she's a single woman. I have contacts at Portland General Electric and the phone company who can check to see if a Nora Sloane or Samantha Reardon started phone service or electricity around the time Reardon came to Portland. I've got a buddy at the Motor Vehicle Division who can run her names to see if we can get her address off of a license application.

'She probably rented the house. I bet she set everything up the first time she was in Portland so it would be ready when she moved back, but she probably didn't start the services until she came here the second time.

'I'll call Reardon's landlady in Hunter's Point and try to get the exact date she followed Oberhurst and the date she returned to Portland. Then I'll check real-estate listings for rural houses with basements for rent in the tri-county area for the first time she was in Portland. I'll see how many were rented by a single woman . . .'

'Why not purchased? It would be safer. She wouldn't have to worry about the owner coming to the house to collect the rent or check on its condition.'

'Yeah. She'd think of that. But I had the impression she didn't have a lot of money. She was renting in Hunter's Point and she had a low-paying job. I'm guessing she's renting. I'll cross-check what we find about the utilities with the rentals.'

'How long will that take?'

The look of excitement on Stewart's face faded.

'That's the problem with using me instead of the police, Betsy. It's going to take a while. We can hire people to do some of the work, like checking the real-estate ads, then I can follow up, but this is all very time-consuming and we could miss her altogether. She may have said she was married and her husband was coming later. She may have found a house in the city that suited her purposes. She may have rented under one name and taken the phone and utilities under another. Fake ID is pretty easy to come by.

'Even if I've doped this out correctly, it's a weekend. I don't know how many of my contacts I can get through to and when they can get into their offices to do the work.'

Betsy looked defeated. 'We don't have a lot of time. I don't know how well she's taking care of Kathy or what she will do to her if she decides she doesn't need me.'

'Maybe you should reconsider. The police and the FBI can be discreet.'

'No,' Betsy said emphatically. 'She said Kathy would die if I told them. There would be too many people involved. There's no way I could be certain she wouldn't learn about the investigation. Besides, in her twisted way, I think Reardon likes me. As long as she doesn't see me as an enemy, there's always the hope she won't harm Kathy.'

The rest of the day was so bad Betsy had no idea how she would get through a second. It was hard to believe that only a few hours had passed since Samantha Reardon's visit. Betsy wandered into Kathy's room and sat on her bed. *The Wizard of Oz* lay on its side on Kathy's bookshelf. They had four more chapters to read. Was it possible that Kathy would never learn about Dorothy's safe return home? Betsy curled up on the bed, her cheek on Kathy's pillow, and hugged herself. She could smell Kathy's freshness on the pillow, she remembered the softness of her skin. Kathy, who was so precious, so good, was now in a place as distant as Oz where Betsy could not protect her.

The house was chilly. Betsy had forgotten to turn on the heat. Eventually, the cold made her uncomfortable. She sat up. She felt old and wasted, chilled to the bone by the icy air, as if her blood had been drained from her, leaving her too weak to cope with the horror that had invaded her life.

The thermostat was in the hall. Betsy adjusted it and listened to the rumble of the furnace starting up. She drifted aimlessly from room to room. The silence overwhelmed her. It was rare for her to be completely alone. Since Kathy's birth, she had always been surrounded by sound. Now, she could hear every raindrop fall, the creak of timbers, water dripping in the kitchen sink, the wind. So much silence, so many signs of loneliness.

Betsy saw the liquor cabinet, but rejected the idea of numbing herself. She had to think, even if each thought was painful. Liquor was a trap. There was going to be a lot of pain in her future and she had to get used to it.

Betsy brewed a cup of tea and turned on the television for company. She had no idea what show she was watching, but the sound of laughter and applause made her feel less alone. How was she going to get through the night if getting through the day was so unbearable?

Betsy thought about calling her mother, but rejected the idea. Rick's body would be discovered soon and Rita would learn that Kathy was missing. She decided to spare her mother suffering for as long as possible.

Stewart called at four to check on Betsy. He had talked to his contacts at the utility companies and the phone companies and had hired several investigators he trusted to scour the real-estate ads for the relevant time period. Stewart insisted on coming by with Chinese take-out. Betsy knew he was doing it so she would not be alone. She was too tired to tell him not to come and she appreciated the company when he arrived.

Stewart left at six-thirty. An hour later, Betsy heard a car pull into her car port. She hurried to the door, hoping, irrationally, that her visitor was Samantha Reardon bringing Kathy home. A police car was parked in one side of the car port. A uniformed officer was driving. Ross Barrow got out of the passenger side. He looked troubled. Betsy's heart beat wildly, certain he was here to tell her about Rick's murder.

'Hello, Detective,' she said, trying to sound nonchalant.

'Can we step inside, Ms Tannenbaum?' Barrow asked.

'Is this about Martin's case?'

Barrow sighed. He had been breaking the news of violent death to relatives for longer than he cared to remember. There was no easy way to do it.

'Why don't we go inside?'

Betsy led Barrow into the house. The other officer followed.

'This is Greg Saunders,' Barrow said. Saunders nodded.

'Do you want some coffee?'

'Not right now, thank you. Can we sit down?'

Betsy walked into the living-room. When they were seated, Barrow asked, 'Where were you last night and today?'

'Why do you want to know?'

'I have an important reason for asking.'

'I was home.'

'You didn't go out? No one visited you?'

'No,' Betsy answered, afraid to mention Reggie Stewart.

'You're married, aren't you?'

Betsy looked at Barrow for a moment, then looked down at her lap.

'My husband and I are separated. Kathy, our daughter, is

staying with him for a few days. I've been taking advantage of the peace and quiet to sleep late, catch up on some reading. What's this all about?'

'Where are Mr Tannenbaum and your daughter staying?' Barrow asked, ignoring her question.

'Rick just rented a new apartment. I have the address written down. But why are you asking?'

Betsy looked back and forth between Barrow and Saunders. Saunders would not meet her eye.

'Has something happened to Rick and Kathy?'

'Ms Tannenbaum, this isn't easy for me. Especially since I know you. The door to your husband's apartment was open. A neighbor found him.'

'Found Rick? How? What are you talking about?'

Barrow looked Betsy over carefully.

'Do you want some brandy or something? Are you gonna be okay?'

'Oh, God,' Betsy said, letting her head drop into her hands, so her face was covered.

'The neighbor has already identified Mr Tannenbaum, so you'll be spared that.'

'How did he . . .?'

'He was murdered. We need you to come to the apartment. There are some questions only you can answer. You don't have to worry, the body's been removed.'

Betsy suddenly jerked upright. 'Where's Kathy?'

'We don't know, Ms Tannenbaum. That's why we need you to come with us.'

Most of the lab technicians were gone by the time Betsy arrived at Rick's apartment. Two officers were smoking in the hall outside his door. Betsy heard them laughing when the elevator doors opened. They looked guilty when they saw her step out. One of them held his cigarette at his side as if he was trying to hide evidence.

The door to Rick's apartment opened into a narrow hall. At the end of the hall the apartment fanned out into a large living-room with high windows. The lights were on in the hall. Betsy saw the blood immediately. It had dried into a large brown stain. Rick had died there. She looked up quickly and followed Barrow as he stepped over the spot.

'In here,' he said, gesturing toward the guest room. Betsy walked into the room. She saw Kathy's book bag. Dirty jeans and a green, stripped long-sleeve shirt lay crumpled on the floor in a corner. On the ride over, Betsy wondered if she could fake crying when the time came. She need not have worried.

'They're Kathy's,' she managed. 'She was so proud because she packed everything herself.'

There was a commotion at the front door. Alan Page tore into the apartment and went directly to Betsy.

'I just heard. Are you okay?'

Betsy nodded. Gone was the self-confidence Page had seen in court. Betsy looked like she could break into a million pieces at any moment. He took her hands and gave them a gentle squeeze.

'We'll get your daughter back. I'm putting everything we've got into this. I'll call in the FBI. We'll find out who has her.'

'Thank you, Alan,' Betsy answered dully.

'Are you through with her, Ross?'

Barrow nodded.

Page led Betsy out of the room and into a small den. He made Betsy sit down and he sat opposite her.

'Can I do anything for you, Betsy?'

Page was concerned by Betsy's pallor. Betsy took a deep breath and shut her eyes. She was used to thinking of Alan Page as a stone-hard adversary. Page's show of concern disarmed her.

'I'm sorry,' Betsy said. 'I just can't seem to focus.'

'Don't apologize. You're not made of iron. Do you want to rest? We can talk about this later.'

'No. Go ahead.'

'Okay. Has anyone contacted you about Kathy?'

Betsy shook her head. Page looked troubled. It didn't make sense. Rick Tannenbaum had probably been killed the day before. If the person who took Kathy was after ransom he'd have called Betsy by now.

'This wasn't a robbery, Betsy. Rick's wallet was full of money. He had on a valuable watch. Can you think of anyone with a reason to hurt Rick?'

Betsy shook her head. It was hard lying to Alan, but she had to do it.

'He had no enemies?' Page asked. 'Personal, business, someone in his firm, someone he bested in court?'

'No one comes to mind. Rick didn't get into court. He does contracts, mergers. I never heard him say anything about personal problems with anyone in his firm.'

'I don't want to hurt you,' Page said, 'but Ross told me you and Rick were separated. What happened? Was he drinking, using drugs, was there another woman?'

'It was nothing like that, Alan. It was . . . He . . . he desperately wanted to be a partner at Donovan, Chastain and

Mills and it looked like they weren't going to let him. And . . . and he was terribly jealous of my success.' Tears welled up in Betsy's eyes. 'Making partner meant so much to him. He couldn't see that I didn't care. That I loved him.'

Betsy could not go on. Her shoulders shook with each sob. It all sounded so stupid. To break up a marriage over something like that. To leave your wife and daughter for a name on a letterhead.

'I'll be sending you home with an officer,' Page said quietly. 'I want to set up a command post in your house. Until we learn otherwise, we're treating Kathy's disappearance as a kidnapping. I want your permission to put a tap on your home and office phones, in case the person who has Kathy calls. We'll cut off any call from a client as soon as we know it's not the kidnapper. I'll have the office tapes erased.'

'Okay.'

'We haven't released Rick's identity yet and we aren't going to let the media know Kathy's missing until we have to, but we'll probably have to give out Rick's name in the morning. You're going to be hounded by the press.'

'I understand.'

'Do you want me to call someone to stay with you?'

There was no longer a reason to keep Kathy's disappearance from Rita. Betsy needed her more than ever.

'I'd like my mother to stay with me.'

'Of course. I can have an officer drive her to your house.'

'That won't be necessary. May I use the phone?'

Page nodded. 'One other thing. I'll explain what happened to Judge Norwood. He'll set over the Darius hearing.'

Betsy's heart leaped. She had forgotten about the hearing. How would Reardon react if it was set over? Reardon was holding Kathy because of the hearing. The longer it was put off, the greater was the danger that Reardon would harm Kathy.

'I'm going to work, Alan. I'll go crazy if I just sit at home.'

Page looked at her oddly. 'You won't want to tackle anything as complex as Darius's case now. You'll be too distracted to do a competent job. I want Darius more than I've ever wanted anyone, but I'd never take advantage of a situation like this. Believe me, Betsy. We'll talk about his case after the funeral.'

The funeral. Betsy hadn't even thought about a funeral. Her brother had taken care of her father's funeral. What did you do? Who did you contact?

Page saw how confused Betsy looked and took her hand. She had never noticed his eyes before. Everything else about the District Attorney, from his lean build to the angles that made up his face, were so hard, but his eyes were soft blue.

'You look like you're about to fold up,' Page said. 'I'm going to send you home. Try to get some sleep, even if you have to take something. You'll need all your strength. And don't give up hope. You have my word. I'll do everything in my power to get back your little girl.'

Chapter Twenty-seven

1

'Tannenbaum was killed Friday evening,' Ross Barrow said as he uncapped a Styrofoam cup filled with black coffee. Randy Highsmith pulled a jelly donut out of a bag Barrow had placed on Alan Page's desk. It was still dark. Through the window behind Page, a river of headlights flowed across the bridges spanning the Willamette River as the Monday morning commuters drove into downtown Portland.

'Three days without a call,' Page muttered to himself, fully aware of the implications. 'Anything last night at Betsy's house?' he asked Barrow.

'A lot of condolence calls, but no kidnapper.'

'How do you figure it?' Page asked Highsmith.

'First possibility, it's a kidnapping, but the kidnapper hasn't gotten in touch with Betsy for some reason known only to him.'

'The kid could be dead,' Barrow offered. 'He wants to

hold her for ransom, but fucks up and kills her.'

'Yeah,' Highsmith said. 'Or, possibility number two, he has Kathy and he's not interested in ransom.'

'That's the possibility I don't even want to consider,' Page said.

'Do we have anything new, Ross?' Highsmith asked.

Barrow shook his head. 'No one saw anyone leaving the apartment house with a little girl. The murder weapon is missing. We're still waiting on results from the lab.'

Page sighed. He'd had very little sleep in the past few days and he was exhausted.

'The only good thing to come out of this mess is the extra time it's bought with Darius,' Page said. 'What was in the surveillance logs?'

'Nothing that helps us,' Barrow answered. 'Padovici and Kristol were on Darius from the moment he left his estate at six forty-three AM. I talked to Justice Ryder again. He's positive he was eating breakfast with Lisa Darius at seven-thirty. The teams were on Darius constantly. Besides, Darius met with people all day, in his office. I've had every member of his staff and his visitors interviewed twice. If they're covering for him, they're doing a great job.'

'There has to be an answer,' Page said. 'Has the team we've got searching for Gordon turned up anything?'

'Nada, Al,' Barrow answered. 'No one's seen her since she checked into that motel.'

'We know she's alive,' Page said, his tone echoing his frustration. 'She made that damn call. Why won't she show herself?'

'We have to start facing the fact that Gordon may have lied to you,' Highsmith said. 'Darius may have been a victim in Hunter's Point. Waters may have been the killer.'

Page wished he could let Highsmith and Barrow know what Wayne Turner had told him. Then they would know Gordon was telling the truth.

'Remember I suggested Gordon might be our killer, Al,' Highsmith continued. 'I think we'd better start considering her very seriously. I can't see any way she could have known we would find Lisa Darius in the basement unless she put her there.

'What if she visited Lisa and convinced her to help her break into Martin's house to find evidence to convict him? They go through the woods. Lisa knows how to turn off the alarms. Martin Darius is at work all day and the house is deserted. She kills Lisa to frame Darius, waits until she sees him come home, then calls you. The only flaw in the plan is that Gordon doesn't know about the surveillance teams.'

'Nancy Gordon did not kill those women,' Page insisted. 'Darius killed them, and he's not beating this case.'

'I'm not saying Darius isn't guilty. I'm saying this case makes less and less sense every time I look at it.'

Alan Page checked his watch. It was ten-thirty in Washington, D.C.

'This is going nowhere. I want to attend Rick Tannenbaum's funeral, and, believe it or not, I have some work to do that has nothing to do with Martin Darius or Rick Tannenbaum's murder. Let me know about any developments immediately.'

'You want me to leave a donut?' Barrow asked.

'Sure. Why not? I should have at least one good thing happen to me today. Now, get out and let me work.'

Ross Barrow handed Alan a maple bar and followed

Highsmith into the hall. As soon as the office door closed, Page dialed Senator Colby's office and asked for Wayne Turner.

'Mr Page, what can I do for you?' Turner asked. Page could hear the tension in the Administrative Assistant's voice.

'I've been thinking about the Senator's information all weekend. My situation is desperate. Even my own staff is starting to doubt Darius's guilt. We know Darius killed three women in Hunter's Point, including his wife and daughter, but the judge is starting to see him as an innocent victim and me as his persecutor. If Darius is released, I have no doubt he'll kill again. I don't see I have any choice but to ask the Senator to testify about the pardon.'

The line was silent for a moment. When Wayne Turner spoke, he sounded resigned.

'I was expecting your call. I'd do the same thing in your shoes. Darius has to be stopped. But I think there might be a way to protect the Senator. Betsy Tannenbaum seems like a responsible person.'

'She is, but I wouldn't count on her staying on the Darius case. Someone murdered her husband on Friday and kidnapped her little girl.'

'My God! Is she okay?'

'She's trying to keep herself together. The husband's funeral is this afternoon.'

'That might complicate matters. I was hoping we could convince her to tell Judge Norwood about the pardon in camera. That way he could use the information to deny bail without the public finding out about it.'

'I don't know,' Page said hesitantly. 'You run into all

sorts of constitutional problems if you try to bar the press. Besides, Darius would have to give his okay. I can't imagine him not trying to pull down Senator Colby with him.'

'Take a shot at it, will you. The Senator and I have been talking this out. We might be able to weather the storm, but we don't want to if we don't have to.'

2

Storm clouds cast somber shadows over the mourners as the graveside service began. Then a light rain started to fall. Rick's father opened an umbrella over Betsy. Cold drops blew under it. Betsy did not feel them. She tried to pay attention to the eulogies, but her mind kept wandering to Kathy. She was grateful for the concern everyone had shown for her daughter, but every mention of Kathy drove a knife into her heart. When the rabbi closed his prayer book and the mourners began to drift away, Betsy stayed by the grave.

'Let her have some private time with him,' Betsy heard Rita tell Rick's parents. Rick's father pressed the umbrella into her hand.

The cemetery spread across low, rolling hills. The head-stones near Rick's grave were weathered, but well cared for. An oak tree would provide shade in the summer. Betsy stared at Rick's headstone. What was left of her husband's body was covered by the earth. His spirit had flown. The future they might have had together would be a mystery forever. The finality terrified her.

'Betsy.'

She looked up. Samantha Reardon was standing beside her. She wore a black raincoat and a wide-brimmed hat that left her face in shadow. Betsy looked around for help. Most of the mourners were walking quickly toward their cars to get out of the rain. Her brother was walking with the rabbi. Rita was talking to two of her friends. Rick's family was huddled together, looking away from the grave.

'The hearing was supposed to be today.'

'It's the funeral. I couldn't . . .'

'There will be no stalling, Betsy. I was counting on you and you let me down. I went to the courthouse and you weren't there.'

'It's Rick's funeral.'

'Your husband is dead, Betsy. Your daughter is still alive.'

Betsy saw it would be useless to try and reason with Reardon. Her face was void of compassion. Her eyes were dead.

'I can call the judge,' Betsy said. 'I'll do it.'

'You'd better, Betsy. I was so upset when I heard the hearing was delayed that I forgot to feed Kathy.'

'Oh, please,' Betsy pleaded.

'You've upset me, Betsy. When you upset me, I will punish Kathy. One meal a day is all she'll get until you've done as I say. There will be just enough water and just enough food so she can last. The same diet I received in Hunter's Point. Kathy will suffer, because you disobeyed me. Every tear she sheds will be shed because of you. I'll be checking with the court. I better hear that a date has been set for the hearing.'

Reardon walked away. Betsy took a few steps after her, then stopped.

'You forgot your umbrella,' Alan Page said.

Betsy turned and stared at him blankly. The umbrella had slipped from her hand while Reardon was talking to her. Page held it over them.

'How are you holding up?' Page asked.

Betsy shook her head, not trusting herself to talk.

'You'll get through this. You're tough, Betsy.'

'Thank you, Alan. I appreciate everything you've done for me.'

It was hard dealing with grief in a house full of strangers. The FBI agents and the police tried to be unobtrusive, but there was no way to be alone without hiding in her bedroom. Page had been wonderful. He had arrived with the first invasion on Saturday night and stayed until dawn. On Sunday, Page returned with sandwiches. The simple, humanitarian gesture made her cry.

'Why don't you go home. Get out of this rain,' Page suggested.

They turned away from the grave. Page covered them with the umbrella as they walked up the hill toward Rita Cohen.

'Alan,' Betsy said, stopping suddenly, 'can we hold the hearing for Darius tomorrow?'

Page looked surprised by the request. 'I don't know Judge Norwood's calendar, but why do you want to go to court tomorrow.'

Betsy scrambled for a rational explanation for her request.

'I can't stand sitting in the house. I don't think the kidnapper will call if he hasn't called by now. If . . . If this is a kidnapping for ransom, we have to give the kidnapper a chance to contact me. He may have guessed you'd tap the phones. If I'm at the courthouse, in a crowd, he might try to approach me.'

Page tried to think of a reason to dissuade Betsy, but she made sense. There had been no attempt to phone or write Betsy at her home or office. He was beginning to accept the possibility that Kathy was dead, but he did not want to tell Betsy. Going along with her would give Betsy some hope. Right now, that was all he could do for her.

'Okay. I'll set it up as soon as I can. Tomorrow, if the judge can do it.'

Betsy looked down at the grass. If Judge Norwood scheduled the hearing, Kathy might be home tomorrow. Page laid his hand on her shoulder. He handed the umbrella to Rita, who had walked down the hill to meet them.

'Let's go home,' Rita said. Rick's family closed around Betsy and her mother and followed them to the car. Page watched them walk away. The rain pelted down on him.

Chapter Twenty-eight

1

Reggie Stewart sat in his modest apartment staring at the lists spread across the kitchen table. Stewart did not feel good about what he was doing. He was an excellent investigator, but cross-checking hundreds of names on dozens of lists required manpower, and could be done a thousand times more efficiently by the FBI or the police.

Stewart was also concerned that he was obstructing justice. He knew the name of Kathy's kidnapper and he was concealing this information. If Kathy died, he would always wonder if the police could have saved her. Stewart liked and respected Betsy, but she was not thinking straight. He understood her concerns about the way the police and FBI might act, but he did not agree with her. He had half decided to go to Alan Page if he did not come up with something quickly.

Stewart took a sip of coffee and started through the lists again. They were from real-estate offices, utilities companies, phone companies. Some of them had cost him, but he had not considered the price. So far, there were no listings for a Samantha Reardon or a Nora Sloane, but Stewart knew it wouldn't be that easy.

On his second trip through a list of new Washington County phone subscribers Stewart stopped at Dr Samuel Felix. Samantha Reardon's first husband was named Max Felix. Stewart cross-checked the other lists and found that a Mrs Samuel Felix had rented a Washington County home the week Oberhurst returned to Portland from Hunter's Point. Stewart called Pangborn Realty as soon as their office opened. The saleswoman who handled the deal remembered Mrs Felix. She was a tall, athletic woman with short brown hair. A friendly lady who confided that she was not completely happy with moving from upstate New York, where her husband practiced neurosurgery.

Stewart called Betsy, but Ann told him she was on her way to court on the Darius case. Stewart realized the opportunity this presented. Reardon attended all the court hearings in the Darius case. She would probably attend this one and leave Kathy alone.

The house was at the end of a dirt road. It was white with a porch and a weather-vane, a happy house that was the least likely suspect to conceal suffering inside. Reggie Stewart circled around the house through the woods. He saw tire tracks in the front yard, but no car. The door to the small, unattached garage was open and the garage was empty. The curtains were closed on most of the windows, but were open on the front window. There were no lights on inside. Stewart spent twenty minutes watching for any movement in the front room and saw none. If Samantha Reardon lived in this house, she was not there now.

Stewart darted across the yard and ducked into a concrete well at the side of the house. Six steps led down to a basement door. The basement windows were blacked out with paint. If Reardon was duplicating Darius, Kathy would be in the basement. The painted windows reinforced that belief.

Stewart tried the basement door. It was locked. The lock did not look sturdy, and Stewart thought he could kick in the door. He backed up two steps and braced his arms against the sides of the concrete well, then reared back and snapped his foot against the door. The wood broke and the door gave a little. Stewart braced himself again and swung his leg against the damaged part of the door. It gave with a loud crack.

The basement was cloaked in darkness and Stewart could see inside only as far as the sunlight penetrated. He edged inside and was greeted by stale air and a foul odor. Stewart pulled a flashlight out of his coat pocket and played the beam around the room. Against the wall on his right were homemade shelves of unpainted wood holding a coil of hose, some cracked orange pots and miscellaneous gardening tools. A child's sled, some broken furniture and several lawn chairs were piled in the middle of the floor in front of the furnace. The odor seemed to emanate from the corner across from the door where the darkness was thickest. Stewart crossed the basement cautiously, maneuvering around objects, alert for any noise.

The flashlight beam found an open sleeping bag. Stewart knelt next to it. He saw encrusted blood where a head would lie and smelled a faint odor of urine and feces. Another open bag lay a few feet further into the darkness. Stewart was moving toward it when he saw the third bag and the body sprawled across it.

2

The night before the hearing, Betsy was so preoccupied with Kathy that she forgot about Martin Darius. Now, he was all she could think about. Samantha Reardon was forcing Betsy to chose between Kathy's life and the life of a man who did not deserve to live. The choice was simple, but it was not easy. As sick and twisted as he was, Darius was still a human being. When Betsy let Samantha Reardon into the jury room, she had no illusions about what would happen. If Martin Darius died, she would be an accomplice to murder.

Newspaper reporters surrounded Betsy as soon as she stepped off the elevator. She turned her head to avoid the glaring lights of the television cameras and the microphones as she hurried down the corridor toward Judge Norwood's courtroom. The reporters asked the same questions about Rick's murder and Kathy's disappearance over and over. Betsy answered none of them.

Betsy spotted Samantha Reardon as soon as she entered the packed courtroom. She walked past her quickly and hurried down the aisle to her seat. Darius was already at the counsel table. Two guards sat directly behind him and several others were spread through the courtroom.

Alan Page was just putting his file on the table when Betsy walked through the spectators. He caught Betsy as she entered the bar of the court.

'Are you certain you want to go through with this?'

Betsy nodded.

'Okay. Then there's something we have to discuss with Judge Norwood. I told him we would want to meet in his chambers before court started.'

Betsy looked puzzled. 'Should Darius be there?'

'No. This is between you, me and Norwood. I'm not letting Randy come in with us.'

'I don't understand.'

Page leaned close to Betsy and whispered, 'I know Senator Colby pardoned Darius. The Senator sent his AA to see me.'

'Wayne Turner?'

Page nodded. 'You know how the Senator's confirmation hearing will be affected if news of the pardon is made public. Will you meet with the judge in chambers or are you going to insist we do this in open court?'

Betsy considered the situation quickly. Darius was watching her.

'I'm going to have to tell Darius. I can't agree to anything unless he consents.'

'Can you wait until we meet with the judge?'

'All right.'

Page went back to his table and Betsy sat next to Darius.

'What was that about?'

'Page wants us to meet with the judge in chambers.'

'About what?'

'He's being mysterious.'

'I don't want anything going on behind my back.'

'Let me handle this, Martin.'

Darius looked like he was going to balk for a moment. Then he said, 'Okay. I trust you. You haven't let me down, so far.'

Betsy started to stand up. Darius put a hand on her forearm.

'I heard about your husband and daughter. I'm sorry.'

'Thank you, Martin,' Betsy answered coldly.

'I mean it. I know what you think of me, but I do have feelings and I respect you.'

Betsy did not know what to say. Before the hour was up, she would cause the death of the man who was trying to console her.

'Look, if the kidnapper wants money, I can help,' Darius said. 'Whatever he wants, I'll cover it.'

Betsy felt her heart contract. She managed to thank Darius, then pulled away.

Judge Norwood stood when Betsy walked into his chambers. He looked concerned.

'Sit down, Ms Tannenbaum. Can I get you anything?'

'I'm fine, Judge.'

'Do they have any news about Ms Tannenbaum's daughter, Al?'

'Nothing new, Judge.'

Norwood shook his head. 'I'm terribly sorry. Al, you tell your people to interrupt if they have to talk to you.'

'I will.'

The judge turned to Betsy.

'And, if you want to stop the hearing, if you aren't feeling well, anything at all, just tell me. I'll set over the hearing on my own motion, so your client won't be prejudiced.'

'Thank you, Judge. Everyone is being so kind. But I want to go through with the hearing. Mr Darius has been in jail for several days and he needs to know if he is going to be released.'

'Very well. Now, tell me why you wanted this meeting, Al.'

'Betsy and I are aware of information about the Hunter's Point incident that is known to very few people. One of those people is Senator Raymond Colby.'

'The President's nominee to the Court?' Norwood asked incredulously.

Page nodded. 'He was the Governor of New York when the murders occurred in Hunter's Point. His information could affect your decision on bail, but it would badly damage Senator Colby's chances of being nominated.'

'I'm confused. Are you saying Senator Colby is mixed up in the Hunter's Point murders?'

'Yes, sir,' Page answered.

'And you agree, Ms Tannenbaum?'

'Yes.'

'What is this information?'

'Before Mr Page tells you,' Betsy said, 'I want to object to you hearing any of this testimony. If this information is used against Mr Darius in any way, it will violate the Due Process guarantees of the United States Constitution and an agreement between Mr Darius, the State of New York and the federal government. I think we need to hash this out in much greater detail before you call your witness.'

'An agreement Darius made with those parties can't bind Oregon,' Page said.

'I think it would.'

'You two are getting way ahead of me. What type of agreement are we dealing with here?'

'A pardon, Judge,' Page said. 'Colby pardoned Darius when he was Governor of New York.'

'For what?'

'I'd prefer the contents of the pardon were not revealed until you decide the threshold question of admissibility,' Betsy said.

'This is getting extremely complicated,' Judge Norwood said. 'Ms Tannenbaum, why don't we have the guards take Mr Darius back to jail. It's obvious to me that this is going to take some time.'

Betsy's stomach churned. She felt like she might collapse.

'I'd like to confer with Mr Darius in private. Can I use your jury room?'

'Certainly.'

Betsy walked out of the judge's chambers. She felt light-headed as she told the guards that Judge Norwood was letting her confer with Darius in the jury room. One of the guards went into the judge's chambers to check with Norwood. He came out a minute later and the guards escorted Darius into the room. Betsy looked toward the rear of the courtroom, just as Reardon walked into the hall.

A guard stationed himself outside the door to the courtroom. Another guard was in front of the door that opened into the hall. Betsy shut the door to the jury room behind them and turned the lock. A table long enough to accommodate twelve chairs filled the center of the large room.

There was a narrow restroom in one corner and a sink, counter top and cabinet filled with plastic coffee cups and dishes against one wall. The other wall held a bulletin board covered with announcements and cartoons about judges and jurors.

Darius sat down at one end of the table. He was still dressed in the clothes he was wearing when he was arrested. The pants were rumpled and his shirt was wrinkled. He was not wearing a tie and he had jail-issue sandals on his feet.

Betsy stood at the edge of the table trying not to look at the door to the corridor.

'What's going on?' Darius asked.

'Page knows about the pardon. Colby told him.'

'That son-of-a-bitch.'

'Page wants to have the judge take Colby's testimony in secret, so the Senator's chances of being confirmed won't be affected.'

'Fuck him. If he tries to screw me, I'll take him down. They can't use that pardon, anyway, can they?'

'I don't know. It's a very complicated legal issue.'

There was a knock on the hall door. Darius noticed the way Betsy jerked her head around.

'Are you expecting someone?' he asked suspiciously.

Betsy opened the door without answering. Reardon was standing behind a guard. She was holding a black Gladstone bag.

'This lady says you're expecting her,' the guard said.

'That's true,' Betsy answered.

Darius stood up. He stared at Reardon. His eyes widened. Reardon looked into those eyes.

'Don't . . .' Darius started. Reardon shot the guard in the

411

temple. His head exploded, spraying flesh and bone over her raincoat. Betsy stared. The guard crumpled to the floor. Reardon pushed Betsy aside, dropped the bag and locked the hallway door.

'Sit down,' she commanded, pointing the gun at Darius. Darius backed away and sat in the chair at the end of the table. Reardon turned to Betsy.

'Take a chair on the other side from me, away from Darius, and fold your hands on the table. If you move, Kathy dies.'

Darius stared at Betsy. 'You planned this?'

'Shut up, Martin,' Reardon said. Her eyes were wide. She looked manic. 'Dogs don't talk. If you utter a sound without my asking, you'll suffer pain like you've never known.'

Darius kept his mouth shut and his eyes riveted on Reardon.

'You made me an expert on pain, Martin. Soon, you'll see how well I learned. My only regret is that I won't have those private moments with you that you shared with me. Those days alone together when you made me plead for pain. I remember each minute we shared. If we had time, I would make you relive every one of them.'

Reardon picked up the black bag and placed it on the table.

'I have a question for you, Martin. It's a simple question. One you should have no trouble answering. I give you permission to answer it, if you can. Considering the time we spent together, it should be a breeze. What's my name?'

Someone pounded on the hall door. 'Open up. Police.'

Reardon half turned toward the door, but kept her eyes on Darius.

'Get away or I'll kill everyone in here. I've got Betsy Tannenbaum and Martin Darius. If I hear anyone at the door, they die. You know I mean it.'

There was a scraping at the door to the courtroom. Reardon fired a shot through the top of the door. Betsy heard several screams.

'Get away from the doors or everyone dies,' Reardon yelled.

'We've backed off,' someone shouted from the hall.

Reardon pointed her gun at Betsy. 'Talk to them. Tell them about Kathy. Tell them she'll die if they try to come in here. Tell them you'll be safe if they do as I say.'

Betsy was shaking.

'Can I stand up?' she managed.

Reardon nodded. Betsy walked to the courtroom door.

'Alan,' she shouted, fighting to keep her voice from breaking.

'Are you okay?' Page shouted back.

'Please keep everyone away. The woman in here was one of the women Darius kidnapped in Hunter's Point. She's hidden Kathy and she's not feeding her. If you capture her, she won't tell me where she's holding Kathy and she'll starve to death. Please keep everyone away.'

'All right. Don't worry.'

'In the hall, too,' Reardon commanded.

'She wants everyone away from the hall door, too. Please. Do as she says. She won't hesitate to kill us.'

Reardon turned her attention back to Darius. 'You've had time to think. Answer the question, if you can. What's my name?'

Darius shook his head and Reardon smiled in a way

that made Betsy feel cold.

'I knew you wouldn't know, Martin. We were never people to you. We were meat, fantasy figures.'

Betsy could hear people moving around in the courtroom and the corridor. Reardon opened the bag. She took out a hypodermic. Betsy could see surgical implements lying on trays.

'My name is Samantha Reardon, Martin. You're going to remember it when I'm through. I want you to know something else about me. Before you kidnapped me and ruined my life, I was a surgical nurse. Surgical nurses learn how to mend broken bodies. They see parts of the body maimed and twisted and they see what a surgeon has to do to relieve the pain injuries cause. Can you see how that information might be useful to a person who wanted to cause pain?'

Darius knew better than to answer. Reardon smiled.

'Very good, Martin. You're a fast learner. You didn't speak. Of course, you invented this game. I remember what happened the first time you asked me a question after telling me that dogs don't speak and I was foolish enough to answer. I'm sorry I don't have a cattle prod handy, Martin. The pain is exquisite.'

Reardon laid a scalpel on the table top. Betsy felt sick. She sucked air. Reardon ignored her. She moved down the table closer to Darius.

'I have to get to work. I can't expect those fools to wait forever. After a while, they'll decide to try something stupid.

'You probably think I'm going to kill you. You're wrong. Death is a gift, Martin. It is an end to suffering. I want you to suffer as long as possible. I want you to suffer for the rest of your life.

'The first thing I'm going to do is shoot you in both kneecaps. The pain from this injury will be excruciating and it will cripple you sufficiently to prevent you from being a physical threat to me. I will then ease your pain by administering an anesthetic.'

Reardon held up the hypodermic.

'Once you're unconscious, I'm going to operate on you. I'm going to work on your spinal cord, the tendons and ligaments that enable you to move your arms and legs. When you wake up, you'll be totally paralyzed. But that won't be all, Martin. That won't be the worst part.'

A glow suffused Reardon's features. She looked enraptured.

'I'm also going to put out your eyes, so you won't be able to see. I'm going to cut out your tongue, so you won't be able to talk. I'm going to make you deaf. The only thing I'm going to leave intact will be your mind.

'Think about your future, Martin. You're relatively young. You're in good shape. A healthy specimen. With life support, you'll stay alive thirty, forty years, locked in the perpetual darkness of your mind.

'Do you know why they call prisons penitentiaries?'

Darius did not respond. Reardon chuckled.

'Can't fool you, can I. It's a place for penitence. A place for those who have wronged others to think about their sins. Your mind will become your penitentiary and you'll be locked in it, unable to escape, for the rest of your life.'

Reardon positioned herself in front of Darius and aimed at his right knee.

'You in there. This is William Tobias, the Police Chief. I'd like to talk to you.'

Reardon turned her head and Darius moved with uncanny speed. His left foot shot up, catching Reardon's wrist. The gun flew across the table. Betsy watched it skid toward her as Reardon staggered backwards.

Betsy's hand closed on the gun as Darius grabbed Reardon's wrist to shake loose the hypodermic. Reardon lashed out with her foot and kicked Darius in the shin. She jabbed the fingers of her free hand at his eyes. Darius moved his head and the blow caught him on the cheek. Reardon leaped forward and sank her teeth into Darius's throat. He screamed. They smashed against the wall. Darius held tight to the hand holding the needle. He grabbed Reardon's hair with his free hand and tried to pull her off. Betsy saw Darius turn white from pain. Reardon struggled to free the hypodermic. Darius let go of Reardon's hair and smashed his fist into her head several times. Reardon's grip loosened and Darius pulled away. The flesh around his throat was ragged and covered with blood. Darius grabbed Reardon's hair, held her head away from him and smashed his forehead against her nose, stunning her. Reardon's legs gave way. Darius snapped her wrist and the syringe fell to the floor. He moved behind Reardon, wrapping an arm around her neck.

'No!' Betsy screamed. 'Don't kill her. She's the only one who knows where Kathy is.'

Darius paused. Reardon was limp. He was holding her off the ground so only her toes were touching. His choke hold was cutting off her air.

'Please, Martin,' Betsy begged.

416

'Why should I help you?' Darius yelled. 'You set me up.'

'I had to. She would have killed Kathy.'

'Then Kathy's death will be a fitting punishment.'

'Please, Martin,' Betsy begged. 'She's my little girl.'

'You should have thought of that when you decided to fuck me over,' Darius said, tightening his hold.

Betsy raised the gun and aimed it at Darius.

'Martin, I will shoot you dead if you don't put her down. I swear it. I'll keep shooting you until the gun is empty.'

Darius looked across Reardon's shoulder. Betsy locked eyes with him. He calculated the odds, then he relaxed his grip and Reardon collapsed on the floor. Darius moved away from Reardon. Betsy reached behind her.

'I'm opening the door. Don't shoot. Everything is all right.'

Betsy opened the door to the courtroom. Darius sat down at the table with his hands in plain view. Two armed policemen entered first. She gave one of them the gun. The other officer handcuffed Reardon. Betsy collapsed on one of the chairs. Several policemen entered from the hall. The jury room was suddenly filled with people. Two officers lifted Reardon off of the floor and sat her in a chair opposite Betsy. She was still struggling for air. Alan Page sat next to Betsy.

'Are you all right?' he asked.

Betsy nodded mechanically. Her attention was riveted on Reardon.

'Samantha, where is Kathy?'

Reardon lifted her head slowly. 'Kathy is dead.'

Betsy turned pale. Her lips trembled as she tried to hold herself together. Reardon looked at Alan Page.

'Unless you do exactly what I say.'

'I'm listening.'

'I want what Peter Lake got. I want a pardon for everything. The cop in the hall, the women, the kidnappings. I want the United States Attorney to guarantee no federal prosecution. I want the Governor here personally. We'll videotape the signing. I'll walk. Just like Lake. Complete freedom.'

'If you get your pardon will you tell us where you're holding Kathy Tannenbaum?'

Reardon nodded. 'And Nancy Gordon.'

'She's alive?' Page asked.

'Of course. Nancy is the only one who continued to track Martin. She's the only one who believed me. I wouldn't kill her. And there's something else.'

'I'm listening.'

'I can give you the proof to convict Martin Darius of murder.'

Darius sat rigidly at the far end of the table.

'What proof is that?' Page asked.

Reardon turned toward Darius. She smiled.

'You think you've won, Martin. You think no one will believe me. A jury will believe a crazy woman if she has proof to back up her testimony. If she has photographs.'

Darius shifted a little in his seat.

'Photographs of what?' Page asked.

Reardon spoke to Page, but she stared at Darius.

'He wore a mask. A leather mask. He made us wear masks, too. Leather masks that covered our eyes. But there was one time, for a brief moment, when I saw his face. Just a moment, but long enough.

'Last summer, a private investigator named Samuel Oberhurst showed me pictures of Martin. As soon as I saw the pictures I knew he was the one. There was the beard, the dark hair, he was older, but I knew. I flew to Portland and I began to follow Martin. I was with him everywhere and I kept a photographic record of what I saw.

'The week I arrived, Martin threw a party to celebrate the opening of a new mall. I mixed with the guests and selected several women to use as evidence against Martin. One of the women was his mistress, Victoria Miller. I sent a picture of Martin leaving their room at the Hacienda Motel to Nancy Gordon to lure her to Portland.

'The evening after I gathered Victoria, I followed Martin. He drove into the country to Oberhurst's house. I watched for hours while Martin tortured Oberhurst. When Martin took his body to the construction site, I was there. I took pictures. Most of them did not come out, because it was night and there was a lot of rain, but there's one excellent photograph of Martin lifting the body out of the trunk of his car. The trunk light illuminated everything.'

Page looked across the table at Darius. Darius met Page's stare without blinking. Page turned back to Reardon.

'You'll get your pardon. We'll go to my office. It will take a while to firm up everything. Will Kathy and Nancy Gordon be all right?'

Sloane nodded. Then, she smiled at Betsy.

'You didn't have to worry. I lied about starving Kathy. I fed her before I came here, then I put her to sleep. I gave Kathy her stuffed animal, too, and made certain she was nice and warm. I like you, Betsy. You know I wouldn't hurt you if I didn't have to.'

419

Page was about to tell two of the officers to take Reardon to his office when Ross Barrow rushed into the room.

'We know where the girl is. She's all right. Tannenbaum's investigator found her in Washington County.'

3

The woman the medics carried out of the dark basement looked nothing like the athletic woman who told Alan Page about Hunter's Point. Nancy Gordon was emaciated, her cheeks sunken, her hair unkempt. Kathy, on the other hand, looked like an angel. When Stewart found her, she was in a drugged sleep, lying on a sleeping bag, hugging Oliver. The doctors let Betsy touch Kathy's forehead and kiss her cheek, then they rushed her to the hospital.

In the living-room, Ross Barrow took a statement from an excited Reggie Stewart while Randy Highsmith looked at photographs of Martin Darius that had been found during a search of the house. In one of the photos, the trunk light clearly showed Darius lifting the dead body of Samuel Oberhurst out of the trunk of Martin Darius's car.

Alan Page stepped out on to the porch. Betsy Tannenbaum was standing by the railing. It was cold. Page could see the mist formed by her breath.

'Are you feeling better, now that Kathy's safe?' Page asked.

'The doctors think Kathy will be fine physically, but I'm worried about psychological damage. She must have been terrified. And I'm frightened of what Reardon will do if she's ever released.'

'You don't have to worry about that. She's going to be locked up forever.'

'How can you be sure of that?'

'I'm having her civilly committed. I would have done that even if I was forced to give her a pardon. The pardon wouldn't have prevented me from committing her to a mental hospital if she's mentally ill and dangerous. Reardon has a documented history of mental illness and hospital commitments. I spoke to the people at the State Hospital. There will have to be a hearing, of course. She'll have a lawyer. I'm certain there will be some tricky legal issues. But the bottom line is that Samantha Reardon is insane and she will never see the light of day again.'

'And Darius?'

'I'm dismissing all of the counts except the one for killing John Doe. With the picture of Darius with Oberhurst's body and the evidence about the murders in Hunter's Point, I think I can get the death penalty.'

Betsy stared at the front yard. The ambulances were gone, but there were still several police cars. Betsy wrapped her arms around herself and shivered.

'A part of me doesn't believe you'll get Darius. Reardon swears he's the Devil. Maybe he is.'

'Even the Devil would need a great lawyer with the case we have.'

'Darius will get the best, Al. He's got enough money to hire anyone he wants.'

'Not anyone,' Page said, looking at her, 'and not the best.'

Betsy blushed.

'It's too cold to stand out here,' Page said. 'Do you want me to drive you to the hospital?'

Betsy followed Page off of the porch. Page held open the door of his car for her. She got in. He started the engine. Betsy looked back toward Kathy's prison. Such a charming place. To look at it, no one would ever guess what went on in the basement. No one would guess about Reardon, either. Or Darius. The real monsters did not look like monsters and they were out there, stalking.

Epilogue

At eleven-thirty AM on a sultry summer morning, Raymond Francis Colby placed his left hand on a Bible held by the Chief Deputy Clerk of the United States Supreme Court, raised his right hand and repeated this oath, after Associate Justice Laura Healy.

'I, Raymond Francis Colby, do solemnly swear that I will administer justice without respect to persons, and do equal right to the poor and to the rich, and that I will faithfully and impartially discharge and perform all the duties incumbent on me as Chief Justice of the Supreme Court of the United States according to the best of my abilities and understanding, agreeably to the Constitution and laws of the United States. So help me God.'

'Is she a judge, too, Mommy?' Kathy Tannenbaum asked.

'Yes,' Betsy whispered.

Kathy turned back to the ceremony. She was wearing a new blue dress Betsy bought for their trip to Washington. Her hair smelled of flowers and sunshine, as only the freshly shampooed hair of a little girl can smell. No one looking at Kathy would guess the ordeal she had undergone.

The invitation to Senator Colby's investiture arrived a week after the Senate confirmed his appointment to the Court. The Lake pardon had been the nation's hottest news story for weeks. Speculation ran rampant that Colby would not withstand the revelation that he had set free the rose killer. Then, Gloria Escalante publicly praised Colby for saving her life and Alan Page commended the Senator's bravery in making the pardon public while still unconfirmed. The final vote for confirmation had been wider than anticipated.

'I think he's going to make a good Justice,' Alan Page said, as they left the Court's chambers and headed toward the conference room, where the reception for the Justices and their guests was being held.

'I don't like Colby's politics,' Betsy answered, 'but I like the man.'

'What's wrong with his politics,' Page deadpanned. Betsy smiled.

A buffet had been set up at one end of the room. There was a courtyard with a fountain outside a set of french windows. Betsy filled a plate for Kathy and found a chair for her to sit in near the fountain, then Betsy went back inside for her own food.

'She looks great,' Page told her.

'Kathy's a trouper,' Betsy answered proudly. 'The investiture came at a good time, too. Kathy's therapist thought a change of scenery would be beneficial. And, we're going home by way of Disneyland. Ever since I told her, she's been on cloud nine.'

'Good. She's lucky. You too.'

Betsy stacked some cold cuts and fresh fruit on her plate

and followed Page back toward the courtyard.

'How are you doing with Darius?' Betsy asked.

'Don't worry. Oscar Montoya is making a lot of noise about the pardon, but we'll get it into evidence.'

'What's your theory?'

'We believe Oberhurst was blackmailing Darius about the Hunter's Point murders. The pardon is relevant to prove Darius committed them.'

'If you don't get the death penalty, you have to lock him up forever, Alan. You have no idea what Darius is like.'

'Oh, I think I do,' Alan answered smugly.

'No you don't. You only think you do. I know things about Darius – things he told me in confidence – that would change you forever. Take my word for it: Martin Darius must never leave prison. Never.'

'Okay, Betsy. Take it easy. I'm not underestimating him.'

Betsy had been so intense that she did not notice Justice Colby until he spoke. Wayne Turner was standing beside the new Chief Justice.

'I'm glad you came,' Colby told Betsy.

'I was flattered you invited me.'

'You're Alan Page,' Colby said.

'Yes , sir.'

'For you and Betsy, I will always be Ray. You have no idea how much your statement meant to my confirmation. I hope you can come to the party I'm throwing tonight at my home. It will give us a chance to talk. I'd like to get to know you two better.'

Colby and Turner walked off and Betsy led Page into the courtyard where they found Kathy talking to a woman with crutches.

'Nancy,' Alan Page said. 'I didn't know you'd be here.'

'I wouldn't have missed the Senator's swearing-in,' she said with a smile.

'Have you met Betsy Tannenbaum, Kathy's mother?'

'No,' Gordon said, extending her hand. 'It's a pleasure. This is one tough kid,' she added, ruffling Kathy's hair.

'I'm so pleased to meet you,' Betsy said. 'I tried to see you at the hospital, but the doctors wouldn't let me. Then you flew back to Hunter's Point. Did you get my note?'

'Yeah. I'm sorry I didn't write back. I've always been a lousy correspondent. Kathy tells me you're going to Disneyland after you leave Washington. I'm jealous.'

'You can come, too,' Kathy said.

Gordon laughed. 'I'd love to, but I have to work. Will you write me and tell me all about your trip?'

'Sure,' Kathy said earnestly. 'Mom, can I have more cake?'

'Certainly. Alan, will you show Kathy where the cake is?'

Alan and Kathy walked off and Betsy sat down beside Gordon.

'Kathy looks great,' Gordon said. 'How's she doing?'

'The doctors say she's fine physically and the psychiatrist she's seeing says she's going to be okay.'

'I'm glad to hear that. I was worried about how she'd come out of it. Reardon treated her pretty well most of the time, but there were some grim moments.'

'Kathy told me how you kept up her spirits. The psychiatrist thinks that having you there really helped.'

Gordon smiled. 'The truth is, she's the one who kept up my spirits. She's one brave little girl.'

'How are you feeling?'

'Better each day. I can't wait to get rid of these,' Gordon said, pointing at her crutches. Then, she stopped smiling. 'You're Martin Darius's attorney, aren't you?'

'Montoya is representing him now.'

'How did that happen?'

'After I spoke to Senator Colby and learned what he did to the Hunter's Point women I didn't want him as a client, and he didn't want me as his lawyer when he realized I helped Samantha Reardon get to him.'

'What's going to happen to Darius?'

'He tortured Oberhurst. I saw the autopsy photographs. They turned my stomach. Alan Page is certain he'll get the death penalty when the jury sees the photos and hears what happened in Hunter's Point.'

'What do you think will happen?'

Betsy recalled the smug look on Alan's face when he talked about how certain he was that he could convict Darius and she felt uneasy.

'I'm not as certain as Alan. He doesn't know Martin like we do.'

'Except for Gloria Escalante and Samantha Reardon, no one knows Darius like we do.'

Darius had told Betsy, 'The experiment brought me the most exquisite pleasure,' when he described his kingdom of darkness. There was no sign of remorse or compassion for the pain his victims had suffered. Betsy knew Darius would repeat his experiment if he thought he could get away with it and she wondered if Darius had any plans for her now that he knew she had betrayed him.

'You're worried he'll get out, aren't you?' Gordon asked.

'Yes.'

'Worried about what he might do to you and Kathy?'

Betsy nodded. Gordon looked directly into Betsy's eyes.

'Senator Colby has contacts at the FBI. They're monitoring the case and they'll keep a close watch on Darius. I'll be told if there's even a possibility that Darius will leave prison.'

'What would you do, if that happened?' Betsy asked.

When Gordon spoke, her voice was low and firm and Betsy knew she could trust anything Gordon promised.

'You don't have to worry about Martin Darius, Betsy. He'll never hurt you or Kathy. If Darius sets one foot out of prison, I'll make certain he never hurts anyone again.'

Kathy ran up with a plate piled high with cake.

'Alan said I could have as much as I wanted,' she told Betsy.

'Alan is as bad as Granny,' Betsy answered.

'Give the kid a break,' Page laughed, sitting next to Betsy. Then, he asked her, 'Do you ever day-dream about arguing here?'

'Every lawyer does.'

'What about you, Kathy?' Page asked. 'Would you like to come here as a lawyer and argue in front of the United States Supreme Court?'

Kathy looked over at Nancy Gordon, her features composed and very serious.

'I don't want to be a lawyer,' she said. 'I want to be a detective.'

AFTER DARK

PART ONE
THE PRICE
IS RIGHT

Chapter One

1

The Multnomah County Courthouse occupied the entire block opposite Lownsdale Park. When it was completed in 1914, it had been the largest courthouse on the West Coast, as well as Portland, Oregon's largest building. There were no Art Deco frills or spectacular walls of glass decorating its exterior. Those who were summoned to face their fate here entered a solemn, brutish building of riveted structural steel and forbidding gray concrete.

Tracy Cavanaugh was too excited to be intimidated by the somber exterior of the courthouse. Her job interview at the public defender's office had ended at two-thirty, leaving her with a free afternoon. It would have been tempting to wander around Portland enjoying the balmy May weather, but Abigail Griffen was prosecuting a murder case and Tracy simply could not pass up an opportunity to watch one of the best trial lawyers in the state in action.

Potential employers had trouble taking Tracy seriously when they saw her for the first time. Today, for instance, she was wearing a lightweight navy-blue business suit that should have made her look like a young executive, but the suit highlighted a deep tan that conspired with Tracy's lean, athletic figure, bright blue eyes and straight blond hair to make her look much more like a college cheerleader than a law clerk to an Oregon Supreme Court justice.

Tracy did not worry about those first impressions. It never took the interviewers long to conclude that they were dealing with a *very smart* cheerleader. Degrees with honors from Yale and Stanford Law, and the clerkship, made Tracy a prime candidate for any legal position and, at the conclusion of today's interview, she had been offered a job. Now Tracy faced the pleasant predicament of deciding which of several excellent offers to accept.

When Tracy got out of the elevator on the fifth floor, the spectators were drifting back into the courtroom, where a young woman named Marie Harwood was being tried for murder. The courtroom was majestic with a high ceiling, marble Corinthian columns and ornate molding. Tracy found a seat seconds before the bailiff smacked down his gavel. A door opened at the side of the dais. Everyone in the courtroom stood. Judge Francine Dial, a slender woman with thick tortoiseshell glasses, took the bench. Most of the court watchers focused on her, but Tracy studied the deputy district attorney.

Abigail Griffen's long legs, full figure and classic Mediterranean features made her stand out in the most elegant surroundings. In Judge Dial's drab courtroom, her beauty was almost startling. The prosecutor was dressed in a black linen designer suit with a long, softly draped jacket and a straight skirt that stopped just below her knees. When Griffen turned toward the judge, her long black hair swept across olive-colored skin and her high cheekbones.

'Any more witnesses, Mr. Knapp?' Judge Dial asked Marie Harwood's lawyer.

Carl Knapp uncoiled dramatically from his chair and cast a disdainful look at Griffen. Then he said, 'We call the defendant, Miss Marie Harwood.'

The slender waif seated beside Knapp at the defense table was barely over five feet tall. Her pale, freckled face and loose blond hair made her look childlike, and the ill-fitting dress made her look pathetic. She struck Tracy as being the type of person a jury would have a hard time convicting of murder. Harwood trembled when she took the witness stand, and Tracy could barely hear her name when Harwood stated it for the record. The judge urged the witness to use the microphone.

'Miss Harwood,' Knapp asked, 'how old are you?'

'Nineteen.'

'How much do you weigh?'

'Ninety-eight pounds, Mr. Knapp.'

'Now, the deceased, Vince Phillips, how much did he weigh?'

'Vince was big. Real big. I think around two-seventy.'

5

'Did he wrestle professionally at one time?'

'Yes, sir.'

'And how old was he?'

'Thirty-six.'

'Was Mr. Phillips a cocaine dealer?'

'When I was living with him, he always had a lot around.'

Harwood paused and looked down at her lap.

'Would you like some water, Miss Harwood?' Knapp asked with fawning concern.

'No, sir. I'm okay now. It's just . . . Well, it's hard for me to talk about cocaine.'

'Were you addicted to cocaine when you met Mr. Phillips?'

'No, sir.'

'Did you become addicted while you lived with Mr. Phillips?'

'Yeah. He hooked me.'

'How bad?'

'Real bad. Cocaine was all I thought about.'

'Did you enjoy being an addict?'

Harwood looked up at Knapp wide-eyed. 'Oh no, sir. I hated it. What it made me become and . . . and the things I had to do for Vince to get it.'

'What things?' Harwood shivered.

'Sex things,' she said quietly.

'Did you ever try to resist Mr. Phillips's sexual demands?'

'Yes, sir, I did. I didn't want to do those things.'

6

'What happened when you protested?'

'He . . .' She stopped, looked down again, then dabbed at her eyes with a handkerchief. This time, Harwood accepted a glass of water.

'Go ahead, Miss Harwood,' Knapp said.

'He beat me up.'

Harwood's head hung down, her shoulders hunched and she folded her hands in her lap.

'How badly?'

'He broke my ribs once, and he closed . . . closed my eye. Sometimes he beat me so hard I passed out.'

Harwood's voice was barely above a whisper.

'Did you go to the hospital after one of these beatings?' Knapp asked.

'Yes, sir. That's where I escaped.'

'You ran away from the hospital?'

'They wouldn't let him take me home. So I knew it was my only chance, 'cause he kept me a prisoner when I was with him.'

'Where did you go from the hospital?'

'Back to John John's.'

'Who is John John?'

'John LeVeque.'

'Now, Mr. LeVeque is also a drug dealer, is he not?'

'Yes, sir.'

'Why did you run to him?'

'Protection. He was who I was stayin' with before I took up with Vince. He don't . . . didn't like Vince, and Vince was scared of John John.'

7

'Did John John take you in?'

'Yes, sir.'

'Let's move to the day that you killed Mr. Phillips. Can you tell the jury what happened around four-thirty in the afternoon?'

'Yes, sir. I'd been at John John's for about two weeks and I guess I was starting to feel safe, so I went out for a walk. The next thing I knew, Vince's car screeched up beside me and he jumped out and yanked me in it by my hair.'

'Did you resist?' Harwood shook her head slowly. She looked ashamed.

'It happened too quick. One second I was on the street, then I was on the floor of the car. Every time I tried to get up he'd pull my hair or hit me. Finally, I just stayed still.'

'What happened when you got to his house?'

'He drug me into the bedroom.'

'Please describe Mr. Phillips's bedroom.'

'It's real big with this king-size water bed in the middle and mirrors on the ceiling. There's a stereo and big-screen TV. And it's weird. Vince painted it black and there are these black curtains around the bed.'

'What happened in the bedroom?'

'He . . . He ripped off all my clothes. Just ripped them.' Harwood started to cry. 'I fought, but I couldn't do nothin'. He was too big. After a while I just gave up. Then . . . then, he . . .'

'It's okay Marie,' Knapp said. 'Just take your time.'

Harwood took two deep breaths. Then, in a trembling voice, she said, 'Vince made me get down on my knees.

Then he put cocaine on his . . . his thing. I begged him. I didn't want to do it, but Vince just laughed. He grabbed me by the hair and made me. I . . . I had to suck it . . .'

Harwood broke down again. Her testimony was getting to Tracy and she wondered how the jurors were handling it. While the defendant regained her composure, Tracy glanced toward the jury box. The jurors were pale and tight-lipped. Tracy looked over at Abbie Griffen and was surprised to see the deputy district attorney sitting quietly, and apparently unconcerned, while Harwood stole her jury.

'What happened next?' Knapp asked when Harwood stopped crying.

'Vince raped me,' she answered quietly. 'He done it a couple of times. In between, he'd beat me. And . . . and all the time he was screamin' at me on how he was gonna kill me and cut me up.'

'Did he tell you what he would use?'

'Yes, sir. He had a straight razor and he brung it out and held it to my face. I squeezed my eyes tight, 'cause I didn't want to see it, but he slapped me in the face till I opened them.'

'After he raped you the last time, what happened?'

'Vince fell asleep.'

'How did you finally escape?'

'It was the razor,' Harwood said, shuddering. 'He left it on the bed and forgot. And . . . and I took it, and I . . .'

Harwood's eyes lost focus. She ran a hand along her cheek.

'I didn't mean to kill him. I just didn't want him to hurt me anymore.' She turned pleading eyes toward the jury. 'It was almost an accident. I didn't even know the razor was there until I touched it. When I picked it up off of the bed Vince's eyes opened and I was so scared, I just did it. Right under his chin is all I remember.'

Harwood started to gulp air.

'Do you need a break, Miss Harwood?' Judge Dial asked, afraid Harwood might faint or hyperventilate.

The witness shook her head. Tears coursed down her cheeks.

'Marie,' Knapp asked gently, 'you've seen the autopsy photos. Mr. Phillips was cut many times on his body. Do you remember doing that?'

'No, sir. I just remember the first one, then it's a blank. But . . . but I probably done that. I just can't picture it.'

'And why did you kill Mr. Phillips?'

'To get away. Just to get away, so he wouldn't hurt me no more. And . . . and the cocaine. I didn't want to be a slave to the cocaine no more. That's all. But I didn't mean to kill him.'

Harwood buried her head in her hands and sobbed. Knapp looked at Griffen with contempt. In a tone that suggested a dare, he said, 'Your witness, Counselor.'

Just before Griffen rose to begin her cross-examination, the courtroom door opened. Tracy looked over her shoulder and saw Matthew Reynolds slip into a vacant seat in the rear of the court next to a prim gray-haired woman. As he sat down, the woman glanced toward him, then flushed and snapped her head back toward the front of the courtroom.

Tracy could understand the woman's reaction, but it angered her. She supposed that Reynolds was used to those shocked first impressions and had conditioned himself to ignore them. Tracy's own reaction to seeing Reynolds was not one of shock or disgust, but of awe. If she could pick any job in the country, it would be as Matthew Reynolds's associate, but Reynolds had responded to her employment inquiry with a tersely worded letter that informed her that his firm was not hiring.

Reynolds was America's most famous criminal defense attorney and his specialty was defending against death penalty prosecutions. He was a strange-looking man who had been battling the grim reaper in courtrooms across America for so long that he was starting to resemble his adversary. Six-five and gaunt to the point of caricature, Reynolds seemed always on the verge of collapsing from the weight he bore on his frail shoulders. Though he was only forty-five, his hair was ash gray and had receded well back from his high forehead. His paper-thin skin stretched taut across sunken cheeks and a narrow, aquiline nose. The skin was as pale as bleached bone, except for an area that was covered by a broad hemangioma, a wine-red birthmark that started at the hairline above Reynolds's left eye, extended downward over his cheek and faded out above his upper lip. You would have thought that jurors would be put off by Reynolds's odd looks, but by trial's end they usually forgot them. His sincerity had been known to move jurors to tears. No one he represented had ever been executed.

Griffen started her cross-examination and Tracy turned back to the front of the courtroom.

'Do you feel up to continuing, Miss Harwood?' Griffen asked solicitously.

'I'm . . . I'm okay,' Harwood answered softly.

'Then let me start with some simple questions while you regain your composure. And anytime you want me to stop, just say so. Or if you don't understand a question, just tell me, because I don't want to trick you. Okay?'

Harwood nodded.

'When you were living with Mr. Phillips, it wasn't all bad times, was it?'

'I guess not. I mean, sometimes he could be sweet to me.'

'When he was being sweet, what did you do together?'

'Drugs. We did a lot of drugs. We partied.'

'Did you go out together?'

'Not a lot.'

'When you did, what did you do?'

'Vince liked movies. We'd see lots of movies.'

'What kind did Vince like?'

'Uh, karate movies. Action movies.'

'Did you like them?'

'No, ma'am. I like comedy movies and romantic ones.'

'You mentioned a stereo and a big-screen TV in the bedroom. Did you guys listen to music or watch TV?'

'Well, sure.'

'You didn't go to the police after you killed Mr. Phillips, did you?' Griffen asked, quickly shifting the subject.

'No, I was too scared.'

'Where did you go?'

'I went back to John John.'

'And that's the gentleman you were staying with when we arrested you, a week and a half after you killed Mr. Phillips?'

'Yes.'

'You were John John's girlfriend before you took up with Mr. Phillips, weren't you?'

'Yes, ma'am.'

'And he was a rival of Mr. Phillips in the drug trade?'

'Yes.'

'When did you take the money, Miss Harwood?' Griffen asked without missing a beat.

'What?'

'The thirty thousand dollars.'

'What are you talking about?'

'Do you know Roy Saylor?'

'Sure. He was Vince's friend.'

'His crime associate.'

'Whatever.'

'Roy's going to testify that Vince was planning to buy two kilos of cocaine from his connection that evening for fifteen a kilo.'

'He never mentioned that. He was too busy beating

13

and raping me to mention business,' Harwood answered bitterly.

'Roy will also testify that Vince went to the bank at four to take the money out of a safety-deposit box.'

'That could be, too. I just never seen it.'

'That's fair. But if you took it, we'd understand. You're terrified. He's dead. You know you might have to run, so you take the money with you.'

'Man, I wasn't thinking about money. I just wanted out of there. If I wanted money, I'd've stayed. Vince was always generous with money. It just wasn't worth it to me.'

'He really scared you?'

'You bet he did.'

'In fact, as I recall your testimony, Mr. Phillips abducted you, dragged you inside his house, stripped you right away and forced you to perform oral sex.'

'Yes, ma'am.'

'Then he raped and beat you repeatedly and fell asleep?'

Harwood nodded.

'This was one right after the other? He was either beating you or raping you?'

Harwood's eyes were on the rail in front of her. Her nod was barely perceptible.

In her trial practice classes in law school, Tracy had been taught that you never gave an opposing witness a chance to repeat her testimony during cross-examination because it reinforced the story in the jurors' minds. Tracy could not understand why Griffen had just repeated

Harwood's pathetic tale three times. She glanced over at Reynolds to catch his reaction. The defense attorney was leaning forward and his eyes were riveted on Griffen.

'There wasn't a moment when you weren't scared silly from the time he abducted you until you escaped, was there?' Griffen asked, giving Harwood yet another chance to tell her story.

'That's true.'

'Either he was raping you or beating you or sleeping. How long do you figure this went on?'

'I don't know. I wasn't watching a clock.'

'Well, there was a clock on the VCR on the big TV.'

'Yeah, but I didn't look at it.'

'That's a cable hookup Vince had, wasn't it?'

'I guess.'

'HBO, Pay-per-View, Showtime?'

Harwood looked uncomfortable. Tracy caught Reynolds out of the corner of her eye. He was frowning.

'You've watched that big TV with Vince, haven't you?' Griffen asked.

'I told you he was beating me up.'

'I'm sorry. I meant on other occasions.'

'Yeah. He had all those movie channels.'

'What's your favorite movie, Miss Harwood?'

'Your Honor,' Knapp said, playing to the jury, 'I fail to see the relevance of this question.'

'Miss Harwood does,' Griffen answered.

Tracy studied the witness. Harwood looked upset. When Tracy looked over at Reynolds, he was smiling, as if he had just figured out an in joke that only he and Griffen understood.

'This is cross-examination, Mr. Knapp,' Judge Dial said. 'I'm going to give Ms. Griffen some latitude.'

'Can you please answer the question?' Griffen asked the witness. 'What is your favorite movie?'

'I . . . I don't know.'

The prosecutor took a letter-size sheet of paper out of a file.

'How about *Honeymoon Beach*? Have you seen that one?'

'Yeah,' Harwood answered cautiously.

'Tell the jury what it's about.'

'Your Honor, this has gone too far,' Knapp shouted as his client shifted nervously in the witness box. 'This is not the Siskel and Ebert show.'

'I promise I will show relevance,' Griffen told the judge, her eyes never leaving Marie Harwood.

'Overruled. You may continue, Ms. Griffen.'

'Is *Honeymoon Beach* a comedy?' Griffen asked.

'Yeah.'

'About two honeymoon couples who swap mates at a resort?'

'Yeah.'

'Where did you see it, Miss Harwood?'

'In the movies.'

Griffen walked over to Harwood. 'Then you saw it twice,' she said, handing the paper she was holding to the witness.

'What's this?' Harwood asked.

'It's a billing record of all the movies ordered on Pay-per-View from Vince Phillips's phone. *Honeymoon Beach* showed from five-thirty to seven on the day you killed him. Someone ordered it at four-fifty using Mr. Phillips's phone. Did you watch the movie before or after you slit his throat?'

'I didn't watch any movie,' Harwood insisted.

Reynolds stood up quietly and slipped out of the courtroom just as Griffen said, 'Someone watched *Honeymoon Beach*, Ms. Harwood. According to your testimony, only you and Vince were in the house and the only Pay-per-View converter is in the bedroom. Did Vince order the movie while he was raping you or while he was beating you?'

'Never,' Harwood shouted. 'I told you we didn't watch that movie.'

'Or was it you who watched it while John John was torturing Mr. Phillips to find out where he hid the money?'

Harwood glared at Griffen.

'Did you arrange to meet Vince after John John found out about the money? Did you get him in bed and slash his throat while he was watching *Honeymoon Beach*?'

'That's a lie!' Harwood shouted, her face scarlet with rage. 'I never watched no movie.'

'Someone did, Marie, and someone ordered it by phone. Who do you think that was?'

2

The day after Marie Harwood's conviction, Abbie Griffen was looking through a stack of police reports when Multnomah County district attorney Jack Stamm stepped into her office. The weather had unexpectedly turned from mild to torrid in twenty-four hours and the court-house air conditioner was on the fritz. Stamm had taken off the jacket of his tan tropical-weight suit, pulled down his tie and rolled up his shirtsleeves, but he still looked damp and uncomfortable.

The district attorney was five feet eleven, rail thin and a bachelor, whose only passions were the law and dis-tance running. Stamm's wavy brown hair was starting to thin on the top, but his kind blue eyes and ready smile made him look younger than thirty-eight.

'Congratulations on nailing Harwood,' Stamm said. 'That was good work.'

'Why, thank you,' Abbie answered with a big smile.

'I hear Knapp is making noises about reporting you to the Bar.'

'Oh?'

'He says you didn't tell him about the Pay-per-View bill before trial.'

Abbie grinned at her boss. 'I sent that arrogant creep a copy of the bill in discovery. He was just too stupid to understand its significance, assuming he even read it. I don't know what I enjoyed more, convicting Knapp's client or humiliating him in public.'

'Well, you did both and you deserve to enjoy your triumph. That's why I'm sorry to be the bearer of sad tidings.'

'What's up?'

'I just got this.'

Stamm handed Abbie the Oregon Supreme Court's slip-sheet opinion in *State of Oregon* v. *Charles Darren Deems*. Almost two years ago, Abbie had convicted Deems, an especially violent psychopath, for the pipe-bomb murder of a witness and his nine-year-old daughter. The Supreme Court had taken the case on automatic review because Deems had been sentenced to death. The slip sheet was the copy of the opinion that was sent to the attorneys in the case as soon as the Supreme Court issued its ruling. Later, the opinion would be published in the bound volumes of the official reporter that were sent to law libraries.

Abbie looked down the cover sheet past the caption of the case and the names of the attorneys until she found the line she was looking for.

'Oh no!'

'It's worse than that,' Stamm said. 'They threw out his statements to Rice.'

'That was my whole case,' Abbie said incredulously. 'I won't be able to retry him.'

'You got it,' Stamm agreed grimly.

'Which judge wrote this piece of shit?' Abbie asked, her rage barely contained as she scanned the cover sheet to find the name of the justice who had authored the opinion. Stamm could not meet her eye.

'That son of a bitch,' she said, so softly that Stamm barely heard her. Abbie crumpled the opinion in her fist. 'I can't believe he would stoop this low. He did this to make me look bad.'

'I don't know, Abbie,' Stamm said halfheartedly. 'He had to convince three other judges to go along with him.'

Abbie stared at Stamm. Her rage, disappointment and frustration were so intense, he looked away. She dropped the opinion on the floor and walked out of her office. Stamm bent down to retrieve the document. When he smoothed it out, the name of the opinion's author could be seen clearly. It was the Honorable Robert Hunter Griffen, justice of the Oregon Supreme Court and Abbie's estranged husband.

Chapter Two

Bob Packard, attorney-at-law, was a large man going to seed. His belt cut into his waist, because he stubbornly insisted on keeping it a notch too tight. There were fat rolls on his neck and a puffiness in his cheeks. At the moment, Packard was not feeling well. His trust and general account ledgers were open on his desk. He had checked them twice and the totals had not changed. Packard unconsciously ran a hand across his dry lips. He was certain there was more money in both accounts. His billings were up, clients were paying. Where had the money gone? His office overhead had not changed and his household expenses had not increased. Of course, there was the money he was spending for cocaine. That seemed to be increasing recently.

Packard took a deep breath and tried to calm down. He

rotated his neck and shrugged his shoulders to work out the tension. If the white lady was the problem, he would just have to stop. It was that simple. Cocaine was not a necessity. He could take it or leave it and he would just have to leave it. Once his current supply ran out, there would be no more.

Packard felt better now that his problem was solved. He put away the ledgers and picked up a case he needed to read in order to prepare a pretrial motion that was due in two days. It was imperative that he win the motion. If his client went to trial he was doomed. This motion had to be an A number one, slam-bang winner.

Packard started to read the case, but it was hard to concentrate. He was still thinking about his money problems and still worried about that other problem. His supplier. The one who had been arrested two days ago, just before Packard was going to pick up a little something to augment his dwindling supply.

Of course, he was going to stop, so there was no problem. But what if, just for the sake of argument, he needed some coke and couldn't get any. It made him jittery just thinking about it and he needed to keep calm and focused so he could write the motion.

Packard thought about the Ziploc bag in his bottom drawer. If he took a hit, he could whiz through the research on the motion and get it written. And there would be that much less cocaine to worry about. After all, he was quitting, and getting rid of his stash was an important first step.

Packard was working on his final rationalization for doing a line when his receptionist buzzed him on the intercom.

'Mr. Packard, a Mr. Deems is here to see you.'

Packard suddenly felt an urgent need to go to the men's room.

'Mr. Packard?' the receptionist repeated.

'Uh, yes, Shannon. I'll be right there.'

Bob Packard had never felt comfortable in Charlie Deems's presence, even when the two men were separated by the bullet-proof glass through which they had been forced to communicate while the former drug dealer was on death row. The facts underlying Deems's conviction were enough to unsettle anyone. A man named Harold Shoe was trying to cut into Deems's territory. Two boys found Shoe's mutilated body in a Dumpster. According to the medical examiner, Shoe had died slowly over a long period of time. Packard had looked at the autopsy photos when he was reviewing the trial evidence and had not been able to eat for the rest of the day.

Larry Hollins, twenty-eight, married, a union man who worked the swing shift, just happened to be driving by the Dumpster when Deems was depositing his bloody package. Hollins thought he'd seen a body, then convinced himself he was imagining things, until he read about the discovery of Shoe's corpse.

Hollins could not make a positive ID from Deems's mug shot, but he was pretty sure he could identify the man he saw if he was in a lineup. Someone leaked

Hollins's identity to the press and Deems disappeared for a few days. On one of those days, Hollins decided to drive his nine-year-old daughter to school so he could talk to her teacher. A pipe bomb attached to the underside of the car killed both of them.

Packard looked longingly toward the bottom drawer, but decided it was better to face Deems with all his wits about him. Besides, Charlie would be in a good mood. Packard had just won his appeal for him. He was probably in the office to show his appreciation.

When Packard walked into the reception area, Deems was reading a copy of *Newsweek*.

'Charlie!' Packard said heartily, extending a hand. 'It's great to see you.'

Charlie Deems looked up from the magazine. He was a man of average height, but thick through the chest and shoulders. A handsome man with dark, curly hair who reminded Packard a little of Warren Beatty. Deems's most engaging feature was his toothy grin, which was a bit goofy and put you at ease. Unless, that is, you had read the psychological profile in Deems's presentence report.

'You're looking good, Bob,' Deems said enthusiastically when they were seated in Packard's office.

'Thanks, Charlie. You're looking pretty good yourself.'

'I should. There's plenty of time to work out in the joint. You can't imagine how many sit-ups and push-ups you can do when you're locked down for twenty-three hours a day.'

Deems was wearing a short-sleeve maroon shirt. He flexed his left biceps and winked.

'Lookin' good,' Packard agreed. 'So, what's up?'

'Nothing much. I just wanted to drop by to thank you for winning my case.'

Packard shrugged modestly. 'That's what you paid me for.'

'Well, you did great. I bet that cunt Griffen is pissed,' Deems said with a laugh. 'You seen her since the decision came down?'

'Once, over at the courthouse, but I didn't bring up the case. No sense gloating.'

'Ah, Bob, you're too bighearted. Me, I'd love to have seen her face, because I know this case was personal for her. I mean, she wanted me dead. Now she ain't got nothin'.'

'Oh, I don't think it was personal, Charlie.'

'You don't?' Deems asked with a look of boyish curiosity.

'No. I just think she was doing her job. Fortunately, I did mine better.'

'Yeah, well, you might be right, but I don't think so. I mulled this thing over while I was on the row. I had lots of time to think about her there. I'm convinced that bitch had it in for me, Bob.'

Deems had an odd look on his face that worried Packard.

'You should let it rest, Charlie. The cops are going to be on your butt, night and day. You don't want to do anything even slightly suspicious.'

'Oh, right. I agree with that,' Deems said reasonably. 'Water under the bridge. No, Bob, I just want to get on with my life. Which brings me to the other reason for my visit.'

'What's that?' Packard asked uneasily.

'I wanted to ask you for a little favor.'

'What favor?'

'Well, it seems to me that you won my appeal pretty easily. I mean, they're not even gonna retry me, so the judge must have really fucked up, right?'

'Well, he did make a mistake,' Packard answered cautiously, 'but it wasn't that easy to win the case.'

Deems shook his head. 'That's not the way I see it. And that's not just my opinion. There's a lot of guys in the joint that know their law. I asked 'em about the appeal. They all knew you'd win. Said it was a cakewalk. So, seeing how easy it was, I was thinking that I'd like a little refund on my fee.'

'That's not how it works, Charlie,' Packard said, trying to convince himself that this would be like any business discussion between two civilized and rational men. 'The fee is nonrefundable and it's not dependent on results. Remember we discussed that?'

'I remember,' Deems answered with a shake of his head. 'But you know, Bob, I'm thinking PR here. Your reputation is what brings in the clients. Am I right? And happy clients talk you up. That's free advertising. I'd be real happy if you refunded half the fee.'

Packard blanched. 'That's fifteen thousand dollars, Charlie. I can't do that.'

'Sure you can. And if I remember right, that was only the cash half. The kilo of cocaine I gave you was probably worth a lot more than fifteen after you resold it. Am I right? But I don't want any blow back. And I don't care what your profit was. You did a great job for me. I'd just really appreciate the cash back.'

A thin line of sweat formed on Packard's upper lip. He forced a smile.

'I know you've been inside and can use some dough, so why don't I loan you a grand? Will that help?'

'Sure, but fifteen grand would help even more,' Deems said. This time there was no smile.

'Not possible, Charlie,' Packard said stubbornly. 'A deal's a deal. You were convicted of murder and now you're a free man. I'd say I earned my fee.'

'Oh, you did. No question. And I don't want you to do anything you don't want to do. If you give me back the money, I want it to be of your own free will. A good deed you can be proud of.'

Deems stopped talking and leaned back in his chair. Packard's heart was beating overtime and he strongly regretted not taking that hit of cocaine.

'Hey, you look upset, Bob,' Deems said suddenly. 'Look, let's forget about this. Okay? I'm sorry I even brought it up. Let's talk about something else. Say, do you like TV game shows?'

'Game shows?' Packard repeated, puzzled by the transition, but relieved that Deems had let him off the hook so easily.

'Yeah, like *Jeopardy!* or *Let's Make a Deal*. You know.'

'I work during the day, so I rarely get a chance to watch them.'

'I didn't watch them either until they put me on the row. We had a set outside the bars. One of our few luxuries. The guards let us watch the game shows. I really got hooked on them. At first I thought they were kind of stupid, but the more I watched, the more I realized that you can learn as much from game shows as you can at school. For instance, have you ever seen *The Price Is Right*?'

'Isn't that the one where the contestants have to guess the price of a refrigerator or a set of dishes?'

'Right!' Deems said, snapping upright in his chair and grinning broadly. Then, in an imitation of a game-show host, he said, 'Bob Packard of Portland, Oregon, come on down! You can play *The Price Is Right*!! Then you run up from the audience. Have you seen it?'

'A few times.'

'Well, that's a great show,' Deems said animatedly, 'because it teaches you about the value of things. For instance, if I put two rocks on your desk and asked you to guess at their value, you'd say they weren't worth much, am I right? I mean, we're talking about two rocks. But what if one was a chunk of common granite and the other was a diamond? You see? Two rocks, both the same size, but your judgment of their value would be really different.'

Packard nodded automatically to avoid insulting Deems and cast a quick glance at his watch.

'That's interesting, Charlie, and I'd like to talk about it

some more, but I have a motion I need to write. It's due in two days and it's rather complicated.'

'I'm sure it is,' Deems said, 'but I think it's more important for you, in the long run, to discuss values.'

The fear Packard felt initially had faded as he grew annoyed and he missed the menace in Deems's tone.

'What are you getting at, Charlie? Come to the point.'

'Sure. You're a busy man. I don't want to waste your time. But I do think this little talk will help you put things in perspective. For instance, what's worth more, a good night's sleep or the shoddy legal services of a coked-up junkie lawyer.'

Packard flushed. 'That's not fair, Charlie. If it wasn't for me, you'd be dead.'

'Maybe, maybe not. As I said, more than one person I talked to was of the opinion that this was a pretty easy win. That would make the value of your services a lot less than thirty thousand dollars. See what I mean? But putting a price on abstractions, like the value of legal services, is a lot tougher than dealing with diamonds and granite, Bob. So why don't you start by guessing the price of a common, everyday item.'

'Look,' Packard said angrily, 'I just told you. I don't have time for this nonsense.'

Deems ignored Packard and pulled a pair of soiled woman's underpants from his pocket, then laid them on Packard's desk. Packard leaned forward and stared. The cotton panties looked familiar, but he could not remember where he had seen them.

'What's the value of these panties, Bob?'

'Where did you get those?' Packard asked.

'Let's see if you can guess. I'll give you a hint.'

Deems leaned forward and grinned in anticipation of Packard's reaction to his clue. He pitched his voice high and, in a falsetto, said, '"Get off of me, now! If you can't get it up at least let me get some sleep."'

Packard turned white. His wife, Dana, had said that to him last night after a failed attempt at sex with the same tone of disgust Deems had so adequately imitated.

'You know, Bob,' Deems said with an air of feigned concern, 'your technique leaves a lot to be desired. You completely ignored Dana's nipples. They're yummy. Fiddle with them a while tonight. They're like the knobs on a radio. If you twirl them the right way, you can find a mighty nice station.'

Packard suddenly recognized the panties as the ones Dana had taken off just before they got in bed. Dana had dropped them next to the bed before they started to have sex. That meant that Deems had been in their room while they were sleeping.

'You were in my house?'

'That's right, Bob.'

Packard bolted to his feet and shouted, 'Listen, you prick . . .'

'Prick?' Deems interrupted in a bemused tone. 'That's a fighting word. Now, a fight between the two of us might be interesting. Speed and youth against size and power. But I want to give you a word of advice, Bob. If you start

30

a fight with me, you better be prepared to kill me. If you leave me alive, I'll come for you when you least expect it and you'll die like Harold Shoe.'

Packard remembered Shoe's autopsy photographs. It was the medical examiner's opinion that Shoe's hands and feet had been removed with a chain saw while he was still alive. All the fight went out of Packard and he collapsed in his chair. He tried to compose himself. Deems watched patiently while Packard took several deep breaths.

'What do you want from me, Charlie?'

'I want you to play the game,' he said grimly. 'You don't really have a choice. Now, what is the value of these panties?'

'Three-fifty? Four dollars?' Packard guessed, on the verge of tears. 'I don't know.'

'You're too literal, Bob. Think about how I got these undies and you'll know their true value. I'd put it at about the same price as a lifetime of good sleep. Wouldn't that be worth fifteen thousand dollars? I'd say a lifetime of sound sleep is cheap at that price.'

Packard's jaw trembled. 'Charlie, you have to be reasonable,' he begged. 'I don't have fifteen thousand extra dollars. You paid that retainer over a year ago. It's gone now. How about something less? What about three? Three thousand? I might be able to manage that.'

'Well, Bob, to me three thousand sounds like a kiss-off.'

Packard knew he could not afford to pay the money.

His rent was due, there were car payments. Then he thought about the price he would pay if he could be assured that Charlie Deems would never slip into his room at night and spirit him away to a twisted world of torture and pain.

Packard took his checkbook out of his drawer. His hand was shaking so badly that his signature was barely legible. Packard gave the check for fifteen thousand dollars to Deems. Deems inspected it, thanked Packard and opened the door. Then he turned, winked and said, 'Sleep tight and don't let the bedbugs bite.'

PART TWO
LAURA

Chapter Three

1

Salem, Oregon's capital, was a sleepy little city surrounded by farmland and located about fifty miles south of Portland on the I-5 freeway. The Oregon Supreme Court had been in its present location on State Street since 1914. The square four-story building was faced with terracotta and surrounded on three sides by a narrow lawn. In the rear was a parking lot that separated the court from the back of another building that housed the Department of Justice and the offices of the Court of Appeals.

There were vans with network logos parked in front of the court when Tracy Cavanaugh arrived for work at 8 A.M. She glanced at them curiously as she strolled down the side street that divided the court from the grounds of the State Capitol. A radiant July sun made the gold statue of the pioneer on top of the Capitol building shine and gave the grass in the small park that bordered the Capitol the brilliance of a highly polished emerald. In keeping with the spirit of the day, Tracy wore a bright yellow dress and wraparound shades.

Tracy was at the tail end of a year serving as Oregon Supreme Court Justice Alice Sherzer's law clerk. Judicial clerkships were plums that fell to top law school graduates. Each justice had a clerk who researched complex legal issues, drafted memos about other justices' positions and checked opinion drafts to catch errors before the opinion was published. A judicial clerkship was a demanding but exciting job that lasted one to two years. Most clerks moved on to good positions with top law firms, which coveted these bright young men and women for their skills as well as their intimate knowledge of the way the justices thought.

Laura Rizzatti was as pale as Tracy was tan and possessed the delicate features and soft, rounded figure of a Botticelli model. When Laura was deep in thought, she played with her long black hair. She had several strands wrapped tightly around her left index finger when Tracy poked her head into Laura's closet-sized office.

'Why are the TV reporters waiting outside?'

Laura dropped the transcript she was reading and rose halfway out of her chair.

'Don't do that!'

'Sorry.' Tracy laughed, tilting her head sideways to see what had occupied Laura's attention so completely. She saw the title of the case and 'Vol. XI' before Laura turned the transcript over so Tracy could no longer read the cover.

'The *Deems* case?' Tracy said. 'I thought we reversed that a month ago.'

'We did. What did you just ask me?'

Tracy looked up from the transcript and noticed the dark circles under Laura's eyes. Laura's clothes were disheveled and she looked like she'd been up all night.

'The TV people. What are they doing here?'

'Matthew Reynolds is arguing *Franklin* v. *Pogue* at nine.'

'Reynolds! Let me know when you go up to court.'

'I'm not going.'

'How come?'

'Justice Griffen took himself off the case, so there's no reason to sit in on the argument.'

'Why'd he recuse himself?'

'His wife is arguing for the state.'

'No shit.' Tracy laughed.

'No shit,' Laura answered bitterly.

'She is one smart cookie.'

'She's a bitch. She could have asked another DA to argue the state's position.'

'Then Justice Griffen would have sat on the case. Now he can't sit because the state is represented by a member of his family. So she gets rid of the most liberal justice on the court and ups her chance of winning. I call that smart lawyering.'

'I think it's unethical.'

'Don't take this so personally.'

'I'm not,' Laura said angrily. 'But the judge is such a nice guy. The divorce is eating him up. Pulling a stunt like this is just pouring salt in his wounds.'

'Yeah, well, if she's as big a bitch as you say, he's better off without her. And you should see Reynolds argue anyway. He's amazing. Do you know he's been defending death penalty cases all over the United States for twenty years and he's never had a client executed?'

'Reynolds is just another hired gun.'

'That's where you're wrong, Laura. These cases are like a mission for him. And he's a genius. Did you read his brief in *State* v. *Aurelio*? His Fifth Amendment argument was absolutely brilliant.'

'He's smart, and he might be dedicated, but it's to the wrong cause.'

'Don't be so uptight. Listen to the argument. Reynolds is really worth seeing. I'll check with you before I go up.'

2

The most conspicuous feature of the Oregon Supreme Court is a stained-glass skylight in the courtroom ceiling that displays the state seal. The stained glass is protected by a second, clear skylight above it. On this sunny day, the light filtering through the two sets of glass cast a soft yellow glow over six justices of the seven-member court as they assembled to hear argument in *State ex rel. Franklin* v. *Pogue*.

Tracy found a seat on a couch against the rear wall of

the courtroom just after the justices took their places. The judges sat on an elevated dais that stretched across the courtroom in a gentle curve. Directly in front of Chief Justice Stuart Forbes was the wooden podium on which Abbie Griffen calmly arranged her papers. When the Chief Justice told her to commence her argument, Abbie said, 'If it please the court, my name is Abigail Griffen and I represent the Multnomah County district attorney's office and the interests of Denise Franklin. We are asking this court to order trial judge David Pogue to withdraw an order commanding Mrs. Franklin to open her home to forensic experts employed by the defense.'

'Judge Pogue was acting on a motion for discovery filed by the defendant, Jeffrey Coulter, wasn't he, Ms. Griffen?' asked Justice Mary Kelly, an attractive woman in her mid-forties who was appointed to the bench after a stellar career in corporate law.

'Yes, Your Honor.'

'What was the basis for the discovery motion?'

'According to the affidavit of Mr. Reynolds, the defendant's attorney, Denise Franklin's son, Roger, promised to sell Jeffrey Coulter stolen jewelry. Coulter went to Franklin's house, but Franklin had no jewelry and tried to rob Coulter. Mr. Coulter claims he shot Roger Franklin in self-defense after Franklin shot at him.'

'And the defense wants to examine Mrs. Franklin's house for evidence that will corroborate the defendant's story?'

'Yes, Your Honor.'

'That seems pretty reasonable to me. What's wrong with Judge Pogue's order?'

'Mrs. Franklin is in mourning, Your Honor. She doesn't want agents of the man who killed her son traipsing through her home.'

'We're sympathetic to Mrs. Franklin, Counselor, but it's not unusual for witnesses to also be relatives of a murder victim. They're inconvenienced all the time by police interviews, the press. Your people went through the house, didn't they?'

'With Mrs. Franklin's consent and while the house was a crime scene. It's no longer a crime scene. The state has returned the house to its owner, Mrs. Franklin, who is not a party to the criminal case between the state and Mr. Coulter. A judge doesn't have the power to order a nonparty to let the defense in her house.'

'Do you have legal authority for that contention, Counselor?'

Griffen smiled with the confidence of an attorney who has anticipated a question. While she told Justice Kelly about several Oregon cases that supported her position, Tracy looked across the courtroom at Griffen's opponent. The contrast between the two attorneys was stark. Abigail Griffen in her black tailored jacket, black pleated skirt, ivory silk blouse and pearls looked like a fashion model, while Matthew Reynolds in his plain, ill-fitting black suit, white shirt and narrow tie seemed more like a country preacher or an undertaker than America's premier criminal defense attorney.

A question by Justice Arnold Pope pulled Tracy's attention back to the legal argument.

'Mrs. Griffen, when Mr. Coulter was arrested did he claim he acted in self-defense?'

'No, Your Honor.'

'Did the police find the gun the defendant's counsel alleges was fired by the deceased?'

'No weapon was found at the scene.'

Pope, a barrel-chested ex-DA with a Marine crew cut, furrowed his brow, giving the impression that he was deep in thought. Justice Kelly rolled her eyes. Pope was a mental lightweight who tried to compensate for his lack of intelligence by being arrogant and opinionated. He was on the court because he had defeated a well-respected incumbent in one of the dirtiest judicial races in Oregon history.

'Could this self-defense business be hokum?' Pope asked.

'Yes, Your Honor. We believe Mr. Coulter manufactured the self-defense scenario.'

'Perhaps with the assistance of Mr. Reynolds?' Pope asked. Tracy was shocked by Pope's suggestion that Matthew Reynolds had sworn falsely in his affidavit. Reynolds was rigid, his face flushed.

'There is no evidence that Mr. Reynolds has been less than honorable in this case, Justice Pope,' Abbie answered firmly.

'Besides,' Justice Kelly interjected to shift the discussion from this unpleasant topic, 'that issue isn't before us, is it, Counselor?'

'No, Your Honor.'

'As I understand it,' Kelly continued, 'your position is that we must set aside the order of Judge Pogue, regardless of the truthfulness of the affidavit, because he had no power to order a nonparty to a criminal case to do anything.'

'Exactly.'

A tiny lightbulb at the front of the podium flashed red, indicating that Griffen's time was up.

'If the court has no further questions, I have nothing more to add.'

Chief Justice Forbes nodded to Griffen, then said, 'Mr. Reynolds?'

Matthew Reynolds uncoiled slowly, as if it took a great effort to stand, and walked to the podium. He was determined not to let his anger at Arnold Pope interfere with his duty to his client. Reynolds took his time arranging his papers and put the insult behind him. As soon as he looked up, Justice Frank Arriaga, a cherubic little man with an easy smile, asked, 'What about Mrs. Griffen's argument, Mr. Reynolds? I've read her cases and they seem to support the state's position.'

There was a hint of the Deep South when Reynolds spoke. His words rolled along softly and slowly, like small boats riding a gentle sea.

'Those cases should not control this court's decision, Justice Arriaga. The facts in the case at bar are substantially different. Mrs. Franklin is far more than a grieving mother. We believe she may be covering up her son's

42

criminal involvement in an attempted robbery. Every moment we are barred from the Franklin home presents another chance for Mrs. Franklin to destroy evidence.

'And that leads me to my main legal point. The Due Process Clause of the United States Constitution imposes a duty on a prosecutor to preserve evidence in her possession that is favorable to an accused on either the issue of guilt or the issue of punishment. When we filed our motion with Judge Pogue, the Franklin home was still sealed as an official crime scene. Our affidavit put the state on notice that we believed the Franklin home contained evidence that would clear Mr. Coulter and it also put the state on notice that we believed that Mrs. Franklin might destroy that evidence. Soon after we filed our motion, the police unsealed the crime scene and returned the home to Mrs. Franklin. We consider that a violation of the state's duty to preserve evidence favorable to an accused.'

'Can we approve an order issued by a judge who lacks the authority to make it?' Justice Arriaga asked.

'No, but we believe the court should address this issue as if the house was still under seal and an official crime scene. Otherwise, the state can frustrate legitimate motions of this sort by simply unsealing the scene before the court has the opportunity to act.

'The Due Process Clause codifies the concept of fundamental fairness into our law. It's a wonderful thing to have a jurisprudence based on fairness rather than power. You can see the tension between these two ideas in this case. The state symbolizes power. It used that power to take over the home of a private citizen so it could investigate a crime. Once the state was satisfied that it had identified the criminal, it used its power to arrest my client and deprive him of his liberty.

'These were proper uses of power, Your Honors. Fair uses. But the state's final use of its power was unfair. As soon as my client stood up to the state and requested an opportunity to examine the crime scene for evidence that would clear his name, the state exercised its power unjustly.

'Legal motions should be decided by unbiased judges, not unilaterally by zealous advocates. When the police released the crime scene to thwart our motion, they acted in violation of the concept of fundamental fairness that is the foundation of the Due Process Clause. All Mr. Coulter is asking for, Your Honors, is a chance to examine the crime scene. The same thing the state was able to do through the exercise of its power. All he is asking for is a fair shake. Judge Pogue understood that and we ask you to be fair and permit his order to stand.'

Court recessed when the argument ended. Matthew Reynolds watched Abigail Griffen collect her papers and close her attaché case. In a moment, she would be fighting her way through the reporters who were waiting for them outside the courtroom on the third-floor landing. If he was going to talk to her, Reynolds knew it had to be now. Abbie started toward the door.

'Mrs. Griffen.'

Abbie turned to find Reynolds following her. With his suit jacket flapping behind him like the wings of an ungainly crow, Reynolds looked like Ichabod Crane in flight from the headless horseman.

'Thank you for telling the court that you didn't believe I would falsify my affidavit,' Reynolds said with a tremor Abbie had not heard when he was arguing. 'My reputation means so much to me.'

'No need to thank me, Mr. Reynolds. But I'm curious. That was such an odd accusation to make. Is there bad blood between you and Justice Pope?'

Reynolds nodded sadly. 'I tried a murder case against Arnold Pope when he was the district attorney for Walker County. It was poorly investigated and an innocent man was arrested. Justice Pope had a penchant for trying his cases in the press when he was a prosecutor and he promised a swift conviction.'

'I take it he didn't deliver.'

'No. After the trial, he threatened to indict me for jury tampering.'

'What happened?'

'The judge told Pope he lost because he should have, and promised to dismiss any jury-tampering indictment Pope obtained. That was the end of it as far as I was concerned, but I guess he still harbors a grudge.'

'I'm sorry to hear that.'

'That's gracious of you, considering that Pope's animosity guarantees you his vote.'

'On the other hand, some of the judges will side with

you simply to be on the other side of Pope's position.'

'I hope you're right, Mrs. Griffen,' Reynolds answered solemnly, the joke going right by him.

'Why don't you call me Abbie. We're going to see too much of each other during this case to stay on formal terms.'

'Abbie, then.'

'See you in court, Matt.'

Reynolds hugged his briefcase to his chest like a shield and watched Abigail Griffen glide through the courtroom doors.

The reporters converged on Matthew Reynolds as soon as he walked into the hall, and Abbie was able to escape down the marble stairway and leave the courthouse through the rear door. Her car was parked around the block from the court because she'd expected the press. Reynolds could go nowhere without them. When she rounded the corner, she saw Robert Griffen sitting in the passenger seat of her car.

Justice Griffen looked like a golf pro in tan slacks, a navy-blue Izod shirt and loafers. His long brown hair fell casually across his forehead. When she opened the rear door and tossed her attaché case in the back seat, he smiled. Abbie saw the sparkle in his clear blue eyes and almost forgot why she had walked out on him.

'How'd the argument go?' Griffen asked.

'What are you doing in my car?' Abbie answered sharply as she slid behind the wheel.

His smile wavered.

'I missed you. I thought we could talk.'

'You thought wrong, Robert. Maybe one of the women you were fucking behind my back has time for a chat.'

Griffen flinched. 'Can't you spare a minute?'

'I have a meeting in Portland and I don't want to be late,' Abbie said as she turned on the engine. 'Besides, Robert, I know what you want and the bank is closed. I suggest you either find a rich mistress or change your lifestyle.'

'You don't know what you're saying. I was never interested in your money, and those other women . . . God, I don't know what got into me. But that's all behind me. I swear. It's you I love, Abbie.'

'Was reversing the *Deems* case a way of showing your love?'

Griffen paled. 'What are you talking about?'

'You reversed *Deems* to embarrass me.'

'That's nonsense. I decided that case on the law. So did the justices who joined the majority. Even Arnold Pope voted with me, for Christ's sake.'

'I'm not stupid, Robert. You adopted a rule that only three other states follow to reverse the conviction of a dangerous psychopath.'

'The rule made sense. We felt . . .' Griffen paused. 'This is ridiculous. I'm not going to sit here and justify my decision in *Deems*.'

'That's right, Robert. You're not going to sit here. You're going to get out of my car.'

'Abbie . . .'

Abigail Griffen turned in her seat and stared directly at her estranged husband. 'If you're not out of my car in ten seconds, I'm going to call the police.'

Griffen flushed with anger. He started to say something, then he just shook his head, opened the door and got out.

'I should have known I couldn't reason with you.'

'Please shut the door.'

Griffen slammed the car door and Abbie peeled out of the parking space. When Griffen walked back toward the court he was so angry that he did not notice Matthew Reynolds watching from the doorway of the Justice building.

3

In 1845, two Yankee settlers staked a claim to a spot on the Willamette River in the Oregon Territory and flipped a coin to decide if their proposed town would be called Portland or Boston. Portland was established in the most idyllic setting imaginable. Forest stood all around, backing up onto two high hills on the west side of the river. From the west bank you could look across the Willamette past the faraway foothills of the Cascade mountain range and see snow-covered Mount Hood, Mount Adams and Mount St. Helens pointing toward heaven.

The town had started on the water's edge at Front

Street and slowly moved away from the river as it became a city. Old buildings were torn down and replaced by steel and glass. But just below Washington Park, on the outskirts of downtown Portland, there were still beautiful Victorian mansions that now served as office space for architects, doctors and attorneys.

At 10 P.M. on the day he argued before the Oregon Supreme Court, the lights were off in the law offices and library on the first two floors of Matthew Reynolds's spacious Victorian home, but they still shone in the living quarters on the third floor. The argument had been hard on Reynolds. So much time had passed since the shooting that Reynolds's experts were no longer sure of the value of examining the Franklin home. No matter what the Supreme Court decided, Abigail Griffen's legal ploy might have cost his client the evidence that could win his case.

But that was not the only thing disturbing Reynolds. He was still shaken by his meeting with Abbie Griffen. Reynolds was captivated by Griffen's intellect. He considered her to be one of the few people who were his equal in the courtroom. But more than that, she was the most beautiful woman he had ever seen. Though he had spoken to her before in court as an adversary, it had taken all his nerve to approach Abbie in the Supreme Court chambers to thank her for standing up to Justice Pope, but her defense of his honor thrilled him and had given him the courage to speak.

Reynolds was dressed for bed, but he was not tired.

On his dresser were two photographs of his father and a framed newspaper article that showed his father outside a county courthouse in South Carolina. The article was old and the paper was starting to yellow. Matthew looked at the article briefly, then stared lovingly at the photographs.

Over the dresser was a mirror. Reynolds examined himself in it. There was no way of getting around the way he looked. *Time* had been charitable when the magazine described him as homely. As a boy, he had been the object of a million taunts. How many times had he returned home from school in tears? How many times had he hidden in his room because of the cruelty of the children in his neighborhood?

Matthew wondered what Abigail Griffen saw when she looked at him. Could she see past his looks? Did she have any idea how often he thought of her? Did she ever think of him? He shook his head at the temerity of this last idea. A man who looked like he did in the thoughts of someone like Abigail Griffen? The notion was ridiculous.

Matthew left his bedroom and walked across the hall. The law offices and his quarters were decorated with antiques. The rolltop desk in Matthew's study once belonged to a railroad lawyer who passed on in 1897. A nineteenth-century judge famous for handing down death sentences used to sit on Matthew's slat-back wooden chair. Reynolds took a perverse pleasure in crafting his arguments against death while ensconced in it.

Next to the rolltop was a chess table composed of green and white marble squares supported by a white marble base. Reynolds had no social life. Chess had been a refuge for Reynolds as a child and he continued to play it as an adult. He was involved in ten correspondence games with opponents in the United States and overseas. The pieces on the chessboard represented the position in his game with a Norwegian professor he had met when he spoke at an international symposium on the death penalty. The position was complicated and it was the only one of his games in which Reynolds did not have a superior position.

Reynolds bent over the board. His move could be crucial, but he was too on edge to concentrate. After a few minutes he turned off the ceiling light and seated himself at the rolltop desk. The only light in the study now came from a Tiffany lamp perched on a corner of the rolltop. Reynolds opened the bottom drawer of his desk and pulled out a large manila envelope. Not another soul knew it existed. Inside the envelope were several newspaper articles and many photographs. He took the articles and photographs out of the envelope and laid them on the desk.

The first article was a profile of Abigail Griffen that was featured in *The Oregonian* after her victory in *State* v. *Deems*. Reynolds had read the article so often, he knew it word for word. A black-and-white picture of Abbie took up a third of the first page of the profile. On the inside page, there was a picture of Abbie and Justice Griffen. The judge had his arm around her shoulder. Abbie, her silken hair held back by a headband, snuggled against her husband as if she did not have a care in the world.

The other articles were about other cases Abbie had won. They all contained pictures of the deputy district attorney. Reynolds pushed the articles aside and spread the photographs before him. He studied them. Then he reached forward and picked up one of his favorites, a black-and-white shot of Abbie in the park across from the courthouse, resting on a bench, her head back, face to the sun.

Chapter Four

1

When Alice Sherzer graduated from law school in 1958, she was one of three women in her class. Her job search in Portland consisted of interviews with one befuddled male after another, none of whom knew what to make of this lean, rawboned woman who insisted she wanted to be a trial lawyer. When one large firm offered her a position in its probate department, she politely declined. It was the courtroom or nothing. The partners explained that their clients would never accept a woman trial lawyer, not to mention the reactions they anticipated from judges and jurors.

Alice Sherzer would not bend. She wanted to try cases. If that meant going into practice for herself, so be it. Alice hung out her shingle. Four years later, a Greyhound bus totalled a decrepit Chevy driven by one of Alice's clients, a father of three who had lost his job in a sawmill. Now he was a quadriplegic. Alice sued Greyhound, which happened to be represented by the law firm that had offered her the position in probate.

Greyhound's lawyers would probably have advised the company to make a reasonable settlement offer if Alice's client was not represented by a woman, but the boys at the firm figured being represented by Alice was like not being represented at all. In court they ignored her, and when they spoke among themselves they made fun of her. The case was one big lark until the jury awarded four million dollars to the plaintiff, an award which stood up in the Supreme Court because the trial judge had ruled for his male buddies whenever he had the chance, leaving them nothing to appeal.

Money talks and four million dollars was a great deal of money in 1962. Alice was no longer a cute curiosity. Several firms, including the firm she had vanquished, made her offers. No, thank you, Alice answered politely. With her fee, which was a percentage of the verdict, and the new clients the verdict attracted, she did not need an associate's salary. She needed associates.

By 1975, Sherzer, Randolph and Picard was one of the top law firms in the state, Alice was married and the mother of two, and a seat opened on the Oregon Court of Appeals. In a private meeting, Alice told the governor that no woman had ever been appointed to an Oregon appellate court. When the governor explained the political problems inherent in making such an appointment, Alice reminded him of the large campaign contributions he had been willing to accept from a woman and the larger sums she had at her disposal for the campaign she would definitely run against any male he appointed. Seven years after her appointment to the Court of Appeals, Alice Sherzer became Oregon's first woman Supreme Court justice. She was now sixty-five. Every year brought new rumors of her retirement, but Alice Sherzer's mind was still in overdrive and she never gave a thought to leaving the bench.

Justice Sherzer had a corner office with a view of the Capitol and the red-brick buildings and rolling lawns of Willamette University. When Tracy knocked on her door-jamb on the day after Matthew Reynolds's argument at the court, the judge was sitting at a large desk that once belonged to Charles L. McNary, one of the first justices to sit in the Supreme Court building and the running mate of Wendell Willkie in the Republican's unsuccessful 1940 bid to unseat Franklin Delano Roosevelt. The antique desk contrasted sharply with the abstract sculpture and paintings Justice Sherzer used to decorate her chambers.

'Your clerkship is almost over, isn't it?' the judge asked when Tracy was seated in a chair across the desk from her.

'Yes.'

'Do you have a job lined up?'

'I have several offers, but I'm not certain which one I'm taking.'

'Justice Forbes asked me to find out if you're interested in something that's opened up.'

'What is it?'

'Matthew Reynolds is looking for an associate.'

'You're kidding!'

'One of his associates just went to the Parish firm and he needs someone right away.'

'I don't believe this. Working with Matthew Reynolds is my dream job.'

'It won't be easy, Tracy. Reynolds works his associates like dogs.'

'You know I don't mind hard work.'

'That's true, but with Reynolds we're talking slave labor. Most of his associates quit in less than two years.'

'Thanks for the warning, but nothing can stop me from giving it a try, if Reynolds takes me on.'

'I just want you to know what you're getting into. Reynolds lives at his law office. All he does is try cases and prepare for trial. He works fourteen-hour days, seven days a week. I know that sounds improbable, but I'm not exaggerating. Reynolds has no social life. He doesn't even understand the concept. He'll expect you to be at his beck and call and that can be at any hour of the night and weekends. I've been told Matt can exist on four hours' sleep and they say you can cruise by his office at almost any hour and see a light burning.'

'I'm still interested.'

'There's another thing. He's never had a woman associate. Quite frankly,' the judge said with a bemused grin, 'I'm not certain he knows what a woman is.'

'Pardon?'

'I don't know why, but he seems to shun women as if they were carrying the plague.'

'If he's never had a woman associate, why is he interested in me?'

The judge laughed. 'He's not. Reynolds has hired several clerks from our court because he went to school with Justice Forbes and trusts his recommendations. Reynolds called Stuart in a dither when he heard we wanted to send him a woman, but Stuart assured him you wouldn't bite. So he's willing to talk to you. This is his office number. His secretary will set up the interview.'

Tracy took the slip of paper. 'This is fantastic. I don't know how to thank you.'

'If it works out, you can thank me by doing such a good job that Reynolds will hire another woman.'

2

The library occupied most of the second floor of the Supreme Court building. The entrance was across from the marble staircase. A small glassed-in area with the checkout desk and an office for the librarians was directly in front of the doors. There were carrels on either side of the office. Behind the carrels, the stacks holding the law books stood two deep. A balcony overhung the stacks, casting shadows over the rows of bound volumes.

Laura Rizzatti was seated at a carrel surrounded by

law books and writing feverishly on a yellow pad. When Tracy touched her on the shoulder, Laura jumped.

'You up for a coffee break?' Tracy asked. 'I've got something fantastic to tell you.'

'I can't now,' Laura said, quickly turning over the pad so Tracy could not see what she was writing.

'Come on. A fifteen-minute break won't kill you.'

'I really can't. The judge needs this right away.'

'What are you working on?'

'Nothing exciting,' Laura answered, trying to appear casual, but sounding ill at ease. 'What did you want to tell me?'

'I've got an interview with Matthew Reynolds. He needs an associate and Justice Forbes recommended me.'

'That's great,' Laura said, but the enthusiasm seemed forced.

'I'd give my right arm to work with Reynolds. I just hope I make a good impression. Justice Sherzer says he's never had a woman associate and it sounds like he doesn't have much use for females.'

'He hasn't met you yet.' Laura smiled. 'I'm sure you'll knock him dead.'

'I hope so. If you change your mind about coffee, I'm going in about twenty minutes. I'll even buy.'

'I really can't. And congratulations.'

Tracy walked across the library and located the volume of the *New York University Law Review* she needed. She took it to her carrel and started making notes. Half an hour later, she walked over to Laura's carrel to try to convince her to go for coffee. She was really excited about the job interview and wanted to talk about it.

Laura wasn't at her desk. Tracy noticed the yellow pad on which Laura had been writing. There was a list of three criminal cases on it. Tracy studied the list, but could see nothing unusual about the cases. She wondered why Laura had turned over the pad to hide the list, then shrugged and went to look for her friend.

Tracy searched the long rows of books until she came to the section that held the Oregon Court of Appeals reporters. Laura was at the far end of the stacks near the wall and Tracy was surprised to see that she was talking with Justice Pope. She and Laura had discussed Pope on several occasions and Tracy knew that Laura despised him. Tracy's initial impulse was to walk up to her friend and the judge, but there was something about the attitude of their bodies that stopped her.

The space between the stacks was narrow and Laura and Pope were almost chest to chest. Laura looked upset. She moved her hands in an agitated manner when she spoke. Pope flushed and said something. Tracy could not hear what he said, because they were whispering, but the angry tone carried. Tracy saw Laura move away from the stocky judge until her back was against a bookshelf. Pope said something else. Laura shook her head. Then Pope reached up and touched Laura's shoulder. She tried to push his hand away, but the judge held her firmly. Tracy stepped into the aisle so Pope could see her.

'Ready for coffee?' Tracy asked loudly.

Pope looked startled and dropped his hand from Laura's shoulder.

'Laura and I have to discuss a case. I hope you don't mind, Judge,' Tracy said, in a tone that let Pope know she had seen everything. Pope flushed. His eyes darted to Laura, then back to Tracy.

'That's fine,' he said, stepping around Tracy.

'Are you okay?' Tracy asked, as soon as Pope was out of sight.

'What did you hear?' Laura asked anxiously.

'I didn't hear anything,' Tracy answered, confused by the question. 'It looked like Pope was coming on to you. Is he giving you a hard time?'

'No,' Laura said nervously. 'He was just trying to find out how Bob . . . Justice Griffen was going to vote on a case.'

'Are you being straight with me? Because you look pretty upset.'

'I'm okay, Tracy, really. Let's drop it.'

'Come on, Laura. I can help you, if you'll tell me what's bothering you.'

'How could you possibly help me?' Laura exploded. 'You have no idea what I'm going through.'

'Laura, I . . .'

'Please, I'm sorry, but you'd never understand,' Laura said. Then she edged away from Tracy and bolted out of the stacks. Tracy watched Laura go, stunned by her friend's reaction.

3

'Laura wants to see you, Judge,' Justice Griffen's secretary announced over the intercom.

'Send her in.'

The judge was preparing for the noon conference and hoped that Laura had finished her research in a tax case the justices would be discussing. The door opened as Griffen finished signing a letter. He looked up when the door closed and started to smile. But the smile disappeared when he saw his law clerk's face. She appeared to be on the verge of tears.

'We have to talk,' Laura said with a trembling voice.

Griffen stood up and walked around the desk. 'What's wrong?'

'Everything,' Laura answered. 'Everything.'

Then she started to cry.

The conference room of the Oregon Supreme Court was spacious, with few furnishings aside from a large conference table and some ancient glass-front bookshelves. Four former justices glowered down on their modern counterparts from portraits on the walls. Chief Justice Forbes sat at the head of the conference table with the sleeves of his white shirt rolled up and his tie loosened. Alice Sherzer put down her coffee cup and briefs at her place on Forbes's right. Vincent Lefcourt, snowy-haired and dignified, sat on Forbes's left.

Robert Griffen pushed through the door and almost ran

into Mary Kelly, who was working on her first cigarette of the conference.

'Sorry,' Griffen apologized.

Kelly was wearing a loose, sleeveless, forest-green dress. She brushed her honey-colored hair off her forehead and gave Griffen a casual smile.

'No damage done,' Kelly said. Then she noticed Griffen's face and her smile faded. Kelly touched Griffen lightly on his forearm. He stopped.

'What's wrong?' Kelly asked in a low voice.

Griffen shook his head. 'It's nothing.'

Kelly shifted so her back screened their conversation from the other justices.

'Tell me what happened,' she demanded.

Griffen looked away. Kelly's grip tightened. When Griffen looked at her, his face reflected his confusion. He was about to reply when Arnold Pope entered the room.

'Your wife looked terrific, Bob,' he said maliciously. 'Too bad you had to miss her argument.'

Griffen paled, and Kelly looked at Pope as if he was an insect she'd found in her salad. At that moment, Frank Arriaga rushed in. He held up a sack from the deli across the street.

'Sorry, guys. My clerk was late with my fuel. Did I miss anything?'

'Relax, Frank.' Forbes smiled. Arriaga sat next to Vincent Lefcourt, who looked on with amusement as Arriaga pulled a huge glazed jelly doughnut out of his brown paper bag.

'We're all here, so let's get started,' Justice Forbes said.

'We can talk later,' Mary Kelly assured Griffen.

Forbes squared the stack of briefs in front of him.

'I was going to begin with you, Frank, but you've got that monstrosity stuffed in your mouth, so how about it, Vincent? What's your take on the *State ex rel. Franklin*?'

4

Justice Sherzer needed a memo in the morning on a probate issue, but Tracy was so upset by what had happened in the library that she had trouble concentrating. At five o'clock, she decided to take a break and finish the memo after dinner.

Tracy's garden apartment was on the second floor of a two-story complex half a mile from the court. She had been a top student in college and law school, but she would have failed housekeeping. The front door opened into a living room that had not been cleaned in a week. Newspapers and mail were strewn across the sofa. Tracy rarely watched television, and her small black-and-white set was gathering dust in a corner. Tracy's rock-climbing equipment was well cared for, but it was piled high next to the television.

The apartment came furnished. The only marks Tracy had made on the personality of the place were several photographs detailing her athletic feats. One photo in the living room showed Tracy standing on a track in front of a grandstand with her hand gently touching the shoulder of a girl who was bent over from the waist. The two women were wearing Yale track uniforms. They had finished one-two in the 1,500 meters to clinch the Ivy League title and looked exhausted but triumphant.

Another photo showed Tracy climbing a snowcapped mountain. She was wearing a parka with the hood thrown back and was brandishing an ice ax over her head. A photo in the bedroom showed Tracy hanging upside down from a rockface on one of the more difficult ascents at Smith Rocks in eastern Oregon.

As soon as she arrived at her apartment, Tracy dumped her clothes on the bedroom floor and changed into her running gear. Then she set off along a seven-mile loop she had mapped out when she moved to Salem.

As Tracy ran, she thought about the incident in the library. She could not understand Laura's reaction. Laura disliked Justice Pope, so why would she protect him if he had made a pass at her? Maybe there was some other explanation for what she had seen, but Tracy could not think of one that made sense. Something was definitely going on in Laura's life. Tracy remembered how drawn and pale Laura looked when she surprised Laura reading the *Deems* transcript. Laura's angry outburst in the library was in keeping with the agitated state in which Tracy had observed her during the past few days, but what was causing Laura's anxiety?

After her run, Tracy showered, then ate a Caesar salad with baby shrimp and two slices of a thick-crusted sourdough bread. She threw the dirty dishes in the sink, then walked back to the courthouse across the Willamette University campus. In the daytime, the rolling lawns and old shade trees made Willamette a pleasant place to stroll. But at dusk, during summer break, the university was deserted. Streetlights illuminated the walking paths, and Tracy stayed on them when she could. The temperature had dropped and a cool breeze chilled her. Halfway across campus, Tracy thought she saw someone move in the shadow of a building. She froze and stared into the dying light. The wind rustled the leaves. Tracy waited a moment, then walked on, feeling silly for being so skittish.

The Supreme Court was deserted when Tracy let herself in at seven-thirty. It was eerie being alone in the empty building, but Tracy had worked at night before. The clerks' offices ran along the side of the Supreme Court building that faced the Capitol. An open area dominated by a conference table stood between their offices and the mail room. The top of the conference table was littered with staplers, plastic cups, paper plates and law books. No two chairs around the table were of the same type and none were in good repair. Behind the table was an alcove with a computer and the only printer. Scattered around the area were bookshelves, filing cabinets and a sagging couch. Tracy walked past the open area and down a short hall to her office. She found the notes she needed for the memo on the probate issue, turned off the lights in the clerks' area, and walked upstairs to the library.

A footnote in a law review article mentioned some

interesting cases. Tracy wandered around the stacks and found them. They led her to other cases and she became so absorbed in her work that she was surprised to discover it was almost ten o'clock when she was ready to write the memo. Tracy gathered up her notes and turned off the library lights. Her footsteps echoed on the marble staircase, creating the illusion that someone else was in the building. Tracy laughed at herself. She remembered how jittery she'd been earlier in the evening when she walked across the Willamette campus. What had gotten into her?

Tracy opened the door to the clerks' area and stopped. She was certain all the lights had been off when she went up to the library, but there was a light on in Laura Rizzatti's office. Someone must have come into the building while she was upstairs.

'Laura?' Tracy called out. There was no answer. Tracy strained to hear any sound that would tell her she was not alone. When she heard nothing, she looked in Laura's office. The drawers of Laura's filing cabinet were open and files were all over the floor. Transcripts were scattered around. Someone had ransacked the office while Tracy was upstairs in the library.

Tracy reached for the phone to call Laura. The door to the clerks' area closed. Tracy froze for a moment, then darted to the door and pulled it open. There was no one in the hallway. She ran to the back door and looked through the glass. No one was in the parking lot. Tracy tried to calm down. She thought about reporting what had happened to the police. But what *had* happened? Laura might have caused the mess in her office. That was not unreasonable, given the state Laura had been in recently. And she might have imagined hearing the door close. After all, she had not seen anyone in the building or the parking lot.

Tracy was too nervous to stay in the deserted courthouse. She decided to leave her notes and write the memo early in the morning. Tracy turned on the lights in the clerks' area and headed for her office. Out of the corner of her eye, she saw something under the conference table. Tracy stopped. A woman's leg stretched out into the light. The rest of the body was hidden in shadow. Tracy knelt down. The body was twisted as if the woman had tried to crawl away from her attacker. Blood ran through the curly black hair. The head was turned so that the dead eyes stared at Tracy. Tracy choked back a sob and lurched to her feet. She knew she should feel for a pulse, but she could not bring herself to touch Laura Rizzatti's slender wrist. She also knew instinctively that it would make no difference.

The first officers on the scene told Tracy to wait in her office. It was so narrow she could almost touch both walls if she stood sideways. Above her desk was a bulletin board with a chart of her cases. Next to the desk, on the window side, an old fan perched on top of a metal filing cabinet. Several briefs and some transcripts were stacked neatly on the desk next to a computer.

A slim woman in a powder-blue shirt, tan slacks and a light blue windbreaker walked into the office and held up a badge. She looked like she had been awakened from a deep sleep. Her blue eyes were bloodshot and her shaggy blond hair had an uncombed look.

'I'm Heidi Bricker, a detective with Salem PD.'

In Bricker's other hand was a container of hot coffee with a McDonald's logo. She offered it to Tracy.

'Can you use this?'

'Thanks,' Tracy answered wearily.

Bricker sat down beside Tracy. 'Was she a friend?'

Tracy nodded.

'It must have been some shock finding the body.'

Tracy sipped from the cardboard cup. The coffee was hot and burned the roof of her mouth, but she didn't care. The physical pain was a welcome distraction.

'What were you doing here so late?'

'I clerk for Justice Sherzer. She's working on a case with a complex probate issue and she needed a memo from me on a point of law, first thing in the morning.'

'What time did you start working?'

'Around seven-thirty.'

'Where were you working?'

'Upstairs in the library.'

'Did you hear or see anything out of the ordinary?'

'No. You can't hear anything that's said in the clerks' offices when you're upstairs in the library.'

Detective Bricker made some notes in a small spiral notebook, then asked, 'Was Laura a clerk?'

Tracy nodded. 'For Justice Griffen.'

'What did Laura do for Justice Griffen?'

'She researched legal issues being argued before the court, drafted opinions and read Petitions for Review filed by parties who've lost in the Court of Appeals.'

'Could she have been murdered because of something she was working on?'

'I can't imagine what. There isn't anything we know that isn't public record.'

'Why don't you explain that to me.'

'Okay. Let's say you were convicted of a crime or you lost a lawsuit and you didn't think you received a fair trial. Maybe you thought the judge let in evidence she shouldn't have or gave a jury instruction that didn't accurately explain the law. You can appeal. In an appeal, you ask the appellate court to decide if the trial judge screwed up. If the trial judge did make a mistake and it was serious enough to affect the verdict, the appellate court sends the case back for a new trial.

'A court reporter takes down everything that's said in the trial. If you appeal, the court reporter prepares a transcript of the trial that is a word-for-word record of everything that was said. An appeal must be from the record. If someone confesses to a crime after the trial, the confession can't be considered on appeal, because it's not in the record.'

'So there's nothing an appellate judge considers that's secret?' Bricker said.

'Well, sometimes there are sealed portions of the record, but that's rare. And no one is allowed to tell the public which justice is assigned to write the opinion in a case or what views the justices express in conference. But that wouldn't have anything to do with Laura.'

'Then why would someone ransack Laura's office?'

'I don't know. A burglar wouldn't be interested in legal briefs and transcripts. No one except the lawyers and judges involved in a particular case would be interested in them.'

'What about jewelry, cash?'

'Laura didn't have much money and I never saw her with any jewelry worth killing for.'

'Can you think of anyone who would want to hurt her? Did she have a boyfriend, an ex-husband with a grudge?'

'Laura was single. As far as I know, she didn't have a boyfriend. She kept to herself, so there might have been someone I didn't know about, but . . .'

Tracy paused.

'Yes?' Bricker asked.

'I feel odd about this.'

'About what?'

'Is what I tell you confidential?'

'Our reports have to be revealed to the defense in certain cases, if there's an arrest, but we try to keep confidences.'

'I don't know if I . . .'

'Tracy, your friend was murdered. If you know something that could help us catch the killer . . .'

Tracy told Detective Bricker how Laura had been acting and about the incident between Justice Pope and Laura in the library.

'It may have been nothing,' Tracy concluded. 'Laura never said Pope tried anything, but it was obvious to me he'd made a pass at her.'

'Okay. Thanks. If I talk to Justice Pope about this, I won't tell him my source. Can you think of anything else that might help?'

Tracy shook her head wearily.

'Okay. You've been a big help, but you look like you're at the end of your rope. I'm going to have someone drive you home. I may want to speak to you again,' Bricker said, handing Tracy her business card, 'and if anything else comes to you . . .'

'I'll definitely call, only I don't think I know anything I haven't told you. I can't imagine why anyone would want to kill Laura.'

5

Tracy waited on the landing while an officer checked her apartment. She was exhausted and had to lean against the railing to keep herself erect. It was hard to believe that Laura, to whom she'd spoken only hours before, was no longer alive.

'Everything's okay, miss,' the policeman said. Tracy hadn't heard him step out of the apartment and she jumped slightly. 'I checked the rooms, but you make certain you lock up tight. I'll cruise by every hour, just in case.'

Tracy thanked the policeman. She locked up, as he'd advised. Tracy wanted nothing more than to sleep, but she wondered if she could. The first thing she noticed when she entered her bedroom was the flashing light on her answering machine. Tracy collapsed on her bed and played back her only message. Laura's voice made her gasp.

'Tracy, I'm in trouble. I have to talk to you. It's nine-oh-five. Please call me as soon as you get in, no matter how late it is. I have to . . .'

Tracy heard a doorbell ringing in the background just before Laura stopped speaking. There was a pause, then Laura finished the message.

'Please call me. I don't know what to do. Please.'

Chapter Five

1

In the days following Laura's death, everyone at the court tiptoed around Tracy as if she had some rare disease, except for Justice Sherzer, who invited Tracy to move in with her. She declined, insisting on staying alone in her apartment and facing her fears.

Friday was oppressively humid. The portable fan barely stirred the air in Tracy's tiny office. The workmen's compensation case she was working on was as dry as dust and the heat made it hard to concentrate. Tracy was taking a sip from a diet Coke she had purchased more for the ice than the drink when Arnold Pope stormed in. His face was florid and he glowered at Tracy. With his bristly flattop and heavy jowls, he reminded her of a maddened bulldog.

'Did you talk to a woman named Bricker about me?' Pope demanded.

Tracy was frightened by the sudden verbal assault, but she refused to show it.

'I don't appreciate your yelling at me, Justice Pope,' she said firmly as she stood to confront the judge.

'And I don't appreciate a clerk talking about me behind my back, young lady.'

'What is this about?' Tracy asked, fighting to keep her tone even.

'I just had a visit from Detective Heidi Bricker of Salem PD. She said someone accused me of making a pass at Laura Rizzatti in the library. She wouldn't tell me who'd made the accusation, but only three of us were there. Did you think I wouldn't figure out who was slandering me?'

'I told Detective Bricker what I saw.'

'You never saw me make a pass at Laura Rizzatti, because that never happened. Now, I want you to call her and tell her you lied.'

'I'll do no such thing,' Tracy answered angrily.

'Listen, young lady, you're just starting your legal career. You don't want to make enemies. Either you call that detective or . . .'

'Is something wrong?' Justice Griffen asked from the doorway. He was wearing a short-sleeve white shirt. His top button was open and his red-and-yellow paisley-print tie was loosened. The heat had dampened his hair and it fell across his forehead. From a distance, he could have been mistaken for one of the clerks.

Pope whirled around. 'This is between Miss Cavanaugh and me,' he said.

'Oh? I thought I heard you threatening her.'

'I don't care what you think, Griffen. I'm not going to stand still while this girl makes false accusations about me behind my back.'

'Calm down, Arnold. Whatever happened between you and Ms. Cavanaugh, this is no way to deal with it. All the clerks can hear you yelling at her.'

Pope's shoulders hunched. He looked like he was going to say something to Griffen, then he changed his mind and turned back to Tracy.

'I expect you to make that call. Then I'll expect an apology.'

Pope pushed past Griffen and stormed down the hall and out of the clerks' area. As soon as the door slammed, Griffen asked, 'Are you okay?' Tracy nodded, afraid that the judge would see how frightened she was if she spoke.

'What was that about?'

Tracy hesitated.

'Please,' Griffen said. 'I want to help.'

'I told something to the police. Something about Justice Pope and Laura. That's why he was upset.'

'What happened between them?'

'I . . . I really shouldn't say. I don't have anything more than suspicions. Maybe I was wrong to tell the police in the first place.'

'Tracy, I feel terrible about what happened to Laura. If you know something, you have to tell me.'

Tracy hesitated, not certain if she should go on.

'What is it, Tracy?'

'I think Justice Pope was bothering Laura.'

'In what way?'

'Sexually. I . . . There was an incident in the library. I couldn't hear what Justice Pope said but it looked like he was making a pass at her. When I asked Laura what happened, she wouldn't come out and accuse him, but she was very upset. Laura was disturbed a lot recently. She looked like she wasn't sleeping and she was very jumpy.'

'And you think that was because Arnold was bothering her?'

'I don't know.'

Griffen considered what Tracy had told him. Then he closed the door to her office and sat down.

'I'm going to tell you something in confidence. You'll have to promise never to discuss this with anyone.'

'Of course.'

'We've had trouble with Arnold Pope since he came on the court. Justice Kamsky was highly respected. He was not only brilliant, he was very practical. I can't tell you how many times he was able to break a deadlock among the justices with his insights.

'When Pope beat Ted in the election we were crushed. Ted was not only the court's finest justice but a dear friend to us all. Still, we tried to treat Pope as a colleague. We bent over backward to be fair to him. But the man's been a disaster. And one of the worst problems we've had has been his relations with women.

'Stuart had a long talk with Pope about his conduct after we received complaints from a secretary and a woman clerk. We all hoped he learned his lesson, but it appears he hasn't.'

'What are you going to do?'

'I'll discuss what you've told me with Stuart, but I don't think there's anything we can do. You're our only witness and you can't say what really happened. But it helps us to know that there's still a problem.

'I hope you understand why you can't talk about this. The image of the court is very important. People have to believe that they are receiving justice when we decide matters. It's the public's acceptance of our decision-making authority that maintains the rule of law. Any scandal weakens the public's image of what we do.'

'I've already told the police.'

'Of course. You had to. And I appreciate your candor with me.'

Now it was Griffen's turn to pause. He looked uncomfortable.

'You were Laura's friend, weren't you?'

'I'd like to think that, but Laura was tough to get to know.'

'Oh?' Griffen said, surprised. 'I had the impression you two were close.'

'Not really. We were the only woman clerks, so we gravitated toward each other, but Laura didn't make friends easily. She came over to my apartment a few times for dinner and I was at her place once, but she never let her hair down with me.'

Tracy paused, remembering Laura's last message.

'I think she wanted to that night. I think she was desperate for a friend. I wish . . .'

Tracy let the thought trail off. Griffen leaned forward.

'Alice told me about the call. Don't blame yourself. There's nothing you could have done.'

'I know that, but it doesn't make me feel any better.'

'Laura was a tough person to befriend. I try to get to know my clerks. We go fishing or hiking a few times during the year. You know, do something that has nothing to do with law. Laura always had some excuse. I tried to draw her out, but our relationship stayed strictly professional. Still, recently I also had the feeling that something was troubling her. She seemed on the verge of confiding in me a few times, then she would back off. When I heard she'd been killed . . . I don't know . . . I guess I felt I'd failed her in some way. I was hoping she'd told you what was troubling her.'

'You should take your own advice. If I'm not allowed to blame myself, how can you feel guilty?'

Griffen smiled. He looked tired. 'It's always easier to give advice than to take it. I liked Laura. She seemed to be very decent. I wish she trusted me more. Maybe she would have told me what was bothering her and I could have helped.'

'She trusted you a lot, Judge. She was your biggest fan. She looked up to you.'

'That's nice to know.'

Justice Griffen stood up. Before he left, he said, 'You should know that your reputation among the justices is excellent. You aren't only the best clerk we've had this term but one of the finest lawyers I've worked with since I started on the court. I'm sure you'll make an excellent attorney.'

Tracy blushed.

'Thanks for talking to me,' Griffen continued. 'I know this has been hard for you. If there's ever anything I can do for you, I'd be pleased if you would consider me a friend.'

2

Raoul Otero was wearing a custom-tailored gray suit with a fine blue weave, a white silk shirt and a yellow-and-blue Hermès tie. In the subdued lighting of Casa Maria, he could easily be mistaken for a successful executive, but a brighter light would have revealed the pockmarked face and wary eyes of a child of Mexico City's most dangerous slum.

'You're looking good for a dead man, amigo,' Otero said as he threw his arms around Charlie Deems. Otero was putting on weight, but Deems could still feel muscle as the big man smothered him.

'I'm feeling good,' Deems said when Otero let him go.

'You know Bobby Cruz?' Otero asked. A thin man with a sallow complexion and a pencil-thin mustache was sitting quietly in the center of the booth. He had not risen when Otero greeted Deems, but his pale eyes never left Charlie.

'Sure. I know Bobby,' Deems said. Neither seemed pleased to see the other. Cruz was wearing an open-necked white shirt and a sports jacket. Deems knew Cruz was armed, but he was not concerned about Otero's bodyguard.

'So,' Otero said, sliding back into the booth, 'how does it feel to be out?'

'Better than being in,' Deems cracked. Otero laughed.

'That's what I like about you, amigo. You got a sense of humor. Most guys, they'd come off the row all bitter. You, you're making jokes.'

Deems shrugged.

'We already ate,' Otero said, gesturing apologetically at the remains of his meal. 'You want a beer, some coffee?'

'That's okay, Raoul. I'd rather get down to business. I've got fifteen and I want a key.'

Otero looked uncomfortable. 'That may be a problem, Charlie.'

'Oh? That's not the price?'

'The price is right, but I can't deal with you right now.'

'I know one key ain't much, Raoul, but this is just the beginning. I'm going to be into some big money soon and I just need the key to help me reestablish myself.'

'I can't do it.'

Deems cocked his head to one side and studied Otero.

'My money was always good before. What's the problem?'

'You're hot. You start dealing and the cops gonna be all over you and everyone you're seen with. There's plenty people still pretty mad about you takin' out that kid. It caused trouble. We couldn't push shit for three months. The operation was almost shut down. I wish you'd talked to me before you done it, amigo.'

'Hey,' Deems asked, 'what was I supposed to do? Stand in a lineup and hope Mr. Citizen didn't pick me? The fuck should have minded his own business.'

Otero shook his head. 'If you'd come to me, I could have worked it out. Taking out that little girl was bad for business, Charlie.'

Deems leaned across the table. Cruz tensed. Deems ignored Cruz and looked directly into Otero's eyes.

'Was it bad for business when I took care of Harold Shoe?' Deems asked. 'Was it bad for business when I didn't tell the cops the name of the person who thought it would be neato if someone performed unnecessary surgery on Mr. Shoe while he was wide awake?'

Otero held up a hand. 'I never said you wasn't a stand-up guy, Charlie. This is business. I bet the cops been following you since you got out. Any business we do is gonna be on videotape. Things are back to normal and I want to keep it that way.'

Charlie smiled coldly and shook his head.

'This is bullshit, Raoul. You owe me.'

Otero flushed. 'I'm tryin' to say this politely, Charlie, 'cause I don't want to hurt your feelings, okay? I ain't gonna do business with you. It's too risky. Maybe, in the future, when things quiet down, but not now. I can't make it any clearer.'

'It might be worse for business to fuck with me.'

'What's that supposed to mean?'

'You're a smart guy. Figure it out.' Charlie stood up. 'I'm gonna be in a position to move a lot more than a key pretty soon. When I'm ready, I'll be back to see you. That will give you time to think about how intelligent it is to stiff a guy who went to the row instead of trading your fat ass for a life sentence. A person like that isn't afraid of death, Raoul. Are you?'

Cruz started to bring his right hand out from under the table, but Otero clamped a hand on Cruz's forearm.

'I'll think about what you said, amigo.'

'It's always better to think than to act rashly, Raoul. See you soon.'

Deems walked out of the restaurant.

'Charlie Deems has been too long on this earth, Raoul,' Cruz told Otero in Spanish, still watching the front of the restaurant.

'Charlie's just upset,' Raoul answered in a tone that made it clear he was not certain about what he was saying. 'He's just being the man. When he calms down, he'll do what he told me to do. Think. Then he'll see things my way.'

'I don' know. Charlie, he ain't like other guys. He don' think like other guys. He's fucked up in the head. Better I take him out, Raoul. That way we don' take no chances.'

Otero looked troubled. Killing people was bad for business, but Bobby Cruz was right when he said Charlie

Deems didn't think like other people. Charlie Deems was different from any man Raoul Otero had ever met and he had met some bad hombres in his time.

Charlie Deems sat in his car behind the restaurant. Anger was flowing through him like a red tide. The anger was directed at Raoul, whom he'd gone to death row to protect and who now turned his back on him. It was also directed at Abigail Griffen, the bitch who was responsible for all his troubles. If she hadn't made prosecuting him a personal crusade, he would not have lost almost two years of his life.

Charlie let his imagination run wild. In his fantasy, Deems saw himself gut-shooting Raoul, then sitting in a chair with a beer as he watched him die slowly and in excruciating pain. His fantasy about Abigail Griffen was quite different.

3

Caruso's did not have the best Italian food in Portland or great atmosphere, but it did have subdued lighting, stiff drinks and the privacy Abigail Griffen needed to brood about her bastard husband, who was in her thoughts because she had just come from a two-hour conference with the attorney who was handling her divorce.

At thirty-three, Abbie felt she had lived long enough to have some idea of what life was supposed to be about, but she was still in a state of tortured confusion when the subject was love. Abbie's parents were killed in a car accident when she was three and she grew up believing that she was missing a special kind of love that all the children with mothers and fathers received.

Abbie was afraid to form relationships with men, because she was afraid that the love she shared would disappear like the love that had been snatched away when her parents were taken from her. It wasn't until her sophomore year at the University of Wisconsin that she fell in love for the first time.

Abbie sipped from her wineglass and thought about Larry Ross, a sure sign that she was courting severe depression. When she married Robert, Abbie had been so happy that she stopped thinking about Larry, but she found herself clinging to his memory with increasing urgency as her marriage soured.

The alcohol Abbie had consumed since entering Caruso's was beginning to make her woozy. She tried to remember what Larry looked like, but his image was blurred and insubstantial. What if Larry's memory slipped away forever?

Larry Ross was a quiet, considerate pre-med student who was a friend for a year before he became Abbie's first lover. When Larry started medical school at Columbia University, Abbie sent out applications to every law school within commuting distance of New York. They both felt that they would be together forever. She was accepted at New York University exactly one week before

Larry was fatally stabbed during a mugging. Abbie fled home to the aunt who had raised her.

After Larry's death, Abbie ran away from every man who tried to form a relationship with her, because she was certain she could never survive love's loss a third time. Then she met Robert Griffen, who made her love him and then betrayed her.

Abbie had downed several Jack Daniel's in rapid succession soon after sliding into a deep leather booth well away from the front door of the restaurant. She was through most of a bottle of Chianti and a dinner of linguine con vongole when Tony Rose blocked what little light there was in the booth.

Tony was a cop who had testified in a few of Abbie's cases when she was in the drug unit. He was handsome, well built, and had the testosterone level of a teenager. After two cases, Abbie stopped prepping him for his testimony unless someone else was present. Putting together a good direct examination while trying to fend off a horny cop was too exhausting.

'Hi,' Rose said, flashing a wide smile. 'I thought that was you.'

Alcohol had dulled Abbie's reactions and Rose was sitting across from her before she could tell him to buzz off.

'How you doin'?' Rose asked cheerily.

'Not so good, Tony.'

'What's the problem?' Rose asked with phony concern.

'My son-of-a-bitch husband, the Honorable Robert

Hunter Griffen,' Abbie answered with a candor she would never have offered if she was sober.

'Hey, that's right. I forgot. You're married to a Supreme Court justice, aren't you?'

'Not for long.'

'Oh?'

'I walked out on the bastard,' Abbie said, slurring her words. Rose noticed the half-empty Chianti bottle and the melting ice cubes in Abbie's last glass of Jack Daniel's. He was an old hand at bedding inebriated women and he guessed that Abbie's inhibitions were way out of town by now.

'Hey! Isn't Griffen the judge who let out Charlie Deems?'

'He certainly is. The next time Deems kills somebody, they can thank good old Robert. And I'll tell you something else. I think he reversed the case just to embarrass me. Maybe next time Deems will do us all a favor and blow my asshole soon-to-be-ex to kingdom come.'

Abbie reached for her wineglass and knocked it over. A river of ruby-red Chianti flowed over the edge of the table. Abbie tried to slide away from it, but she was too slow.

'Ah, shit,' she said, dabbing at her lap with a napkin.

'Are you okay?'

'No, Tony. I'm fucked up,' Abbie answered distractedly.

'Look, I was on the way out. Can you use a lift home?'

'I've got a car.'

'You've got to be kidding.' Rose laughed. 'If I saw you driving tonight, I'd have to bust you.'

Abbie slumped down on a dry section of the booth and put her head back.

'What a terrific way to end a rotten day.'

'Leave your car and take a taxi in the morning. Come on. I'll get the check and you can pay me back.'

Abbie was too tired to fight Rose and too drunk to care. She let him take her arm.

'What?' Abbie mumbled.

'I said, watch your head.'

Abbie opened her eyes. She was staring at Tony Rose's chest and she had no idea where she was. Then Rose shifted and she could see her house through the car door.

'Come on,' Rose said, easing her out of the car. Abbie stood unsteadily. Rose wrapped an arm around her waist. Abbie tried to stand up. Her head swam and her vision blurred. She leaned back against Rose's shoulder. He smiled.

'Take it easy. We're almost there. Where's your key?'

Abbie realized she was holding her purse. She fumbled with the clasp and finally got it open, but missed the keyhole on the first try.

'Here,' Rose said, taking the key from her.

Rose helped Abbie into the house and switched on the light. Abbie shut her eyes against the glare and leaned against the wall. She heard the door close and felt Rose near her. Then she felt Rose's lips. His breath smelled minty. His kiss was gentle. So was his touch when he slipped his arm around Abbie's waist. 'What are you doing?' she asked.

'What you want me to do,' Rose answered confidently.

'Don't,' Abbie said, pushing against Rose. The cop's muscular arm tightened around her and she was crushed against his chest. Abbie strained against Rose's grip, but he was very strong. She felt his hands on her buttocks. Fear suddenly coursed through her, cutting through her haze. She pulled her head away and Rose pressed his lips against her neck while his right hand groped under her skirt. Abbie shifted until she could get her teeth around Rose's ear, then she bit down hard.

'Hey,' Rose yelped, jumping back and holding a hand to his

Abbie slapped Rose as hard as she could. The policeman looked stunned.

'What's wrong with you?' he asked in a shocked tone.

'Get out, you son of a bitch,' Abbie yelled.

'What's going on here? I was just trying to help you out.'

'Was that what you were doing just now?'

'Look, I thought . . .'

'You thought I'd fall into bed with you because I'm smashed.'

'No. It's not like that. You looked like you needed a friend.'

'And that's what you were doing? Being my friend?'

'Hey,' Rose said angrily, 'when I kissed you, you didn't exactly faint.'

'You bastard. I'm drunk.'

'Man, you are one cold bitch.'

'Cut the shit, Tony. You wanted to get me into bed. Well, it didn't work out.'

Rose looked hurt, like a little boy.

'It could,' he said. 'I mean, we got off on the wrong foot here, but that's not my fault. You're the one who was giving off signals.'

'Tony, haven't you been listening . . . ?' Abbie started. Then she stopped herself. Whatever had happened had happened. She just wanted Rose out of her house.

'Look, Tony, this was a major mistake. Let's just forget it. Okay?'

Rose took his hand away from his ear. It was covered with blood.

'Jesus,' he said. 'You really hurt me.'

'I'm sorry,' Abbie answered, too exhausted to be angry anymore. 'Can you please leave? I want to go to bed.'

'I guess you are as frigid as everyone says,' he snapped, getting in the last word. Abbie let him save face. It was worth it to get him out of her house. He slammed the door and she locked it immediately. The engine of Rose's car started and she heard him drive away.

Abbie turned away from the door. She saw herself in the hall mirror. Her lipstick was smeared and her hair looked like it had been permed in a washing machine.

'Jesus,' Abbie muttered. She imagined herself in court looking like this. She started to laugh. That would be something. She laughed harder and could not stop.

What a fool she was. How had she let herself get into this situation?

Abbie slumped down on the carpet. When she stopped laughing, depression flooded over her. She leaned against the wall and started to cry. It was Robert's fault she was falling apart. She had loved him without reservation and he had deceived her. She hated him more than she ever thought possible.

Abbie closed her eyes. She was so tired. She started to fade out, then jerked herself awake and struggled to her feet. She was going to sleep, but not on the floor in the entryway.

Abbie's bedroom was at the end of a short hall. She staggered inside. The shades in the bedroom were open and the backyard looked like a black-on-black still life. The only light came from the window of the house next door. Abbie reached for the light switch. In the moment before the bedroom light went on, a shape erased the glow from the next-door window. Abbie stiffened. Someone was in the yard. She switched off the light so she could see outside, but she had been blinded momentarily when the bedroom light flashed on.

Abbie pressed her face against the windowpane, trying to see as much of the backyard as possible. There was no one there. She must have imagined the figure. She sagged down on the bed and closed her eyes. A doorknob rattled in the kitchen. Abbie's eyes flew open. She strained to hear, but her heart was beating loudly in her ears.

Abbie had received a number of threats over the years

from people she had prosecuted. She had taken a few of them seriously enough to learn how to shoot a semiautomatic 9mm Beretta that she kept in her end table. Abbie took out the gun. Then she kicked off her shoes and walked on stocking feet down the dark hall to the kitchen. Abbie heard the doorknob rattle again. Someone was trying to break in. Was it Rose? Had he parked his car and returned on foot?

Abbie crouched down and peered into the darkened kitchen. There was a man on the deck outside the kitchen bent over the lock on the back door. Abbie could not see his face because he was wearing a ski mask. Without thinking, she ran to the door and aimed her gun, screaming 'Freeze!' as she pressed the muzzle to the glass. The man did freeze for a second. Then he straightened up very slowly and raised his arms until they were stretched out from his sides like the wings of a giant bird. The man was clothed in black from head to foot and wore black gloves, but Abbie had the strange feeling that she knew him. Their eyes met through the glass. No one moved for a moment. The man took one backward step, then another. Then he turned slowly, loped across the yard, vaulted the fence and disappeared.

It never occurred to Abbie to pursue him. She was just glad he was gone. The adrenaline began to wear off and Abbie started to shake. She dropped onto one of her kitchen chairs and put the Beretta on the kitchen table. Suddenly she noticed that the safety was on. She felt sick for a moment, then felt relieved that she was safe.

Abbie contemplated reporting the attempted break-in, but decided against it. She was so tired that she only wanted to sleep, and she could not describe the man anyway. If she called the police, she would be up all night. Worse, she would have to tell the officers about Tony Rose, even though she was certain he wasn't the intruder, and there was no way she was going to do that.

Abbie rested for a few moments more, then dragged herself back to the bedroom after checking to make sure that all the doors and windows were locked. She put the Beretta on the end table and stripped off her clothes. She was certain she would drop off to sleep immediately because she was so exhausted, but every sound primed the pump of her overwrought imagination and she did not slip into sleep until an hour before dawn.

PART THREE

THE
SORCERER'S
APPRENTICE

Chapter Six

The intense leather, glass and stainless-steel decor of the big law firms was nowhere to be found in Matthew Reynolds's reception area. The hand-knit antimacassar draped over the back of the country sofa, the Tiffany lamps and the deep old armchairs had a calming effect that was equally appreciated by clients facing prison or a nervous young woman waiting for a job interview.

Masterful black-and-white photographs of jagged mountain peaks, pristine lakes and shadowy timberland trails graced the walls. One picture in particular caught Tracy's eye. A doe and her fawn were standing in a clearing nibbling on a bush, apparently oblivious to the presence of the photographer. A wide ray of sunlight shone down through the trees and bathed the bush in light. The picture had a quiet, almost religious feel to it that touched something in Tracy. She was admiring the photograph when the receptionist beckoned her down a corridor on whose walls hung more of the exceptional wilderness photography.

'Mr. Reynolds took those,' the receptionist proudly told Tracy as she stepped aside to admit her to Matthew Reynolds's office.

'They're terrific,' Tracy answered, genuinely impressed by the use of light and the unique perspectives. 'Has Mr. Reynolds ever shown them in a gallery?'

'Not that I know of,' the receptionist answered with a smile. 'Why don't you have a seat. Mr. Reynolds will be with you shortly.'

The receptionist left Tracy alone in the large corner room. Law books and legal papers were arranged in neat piles on the oak desk that dominated it. Two high-backed, dark leather client chairs stood before the desk. Through the windows Tracy could see sections of a flower garden and the cheerful green of a well-manicured lawn.

Tracy wandered over to the near wall, which was covered with memorabilia from Reynolds's cases. There were framed newspaper clippings and the originals of courtroom sketches that had appeared in newspapers around the country. Tracy stopped in front of a frame in which was displayed the cover of a brief that had been filed in the United States Supreme Court. Above the cover, in a narrow recess, was a white quill pen.

'Those pens are specially crafted for the Court,' Matthew Reynolds said from the doorway. 'If you ever argue there you'll find them at counsel table. You're expected to take one as evidence that you have appeared before the highest court in the land. I've argued seven cases in the United States Supreme Court, but that pen means the most to me.'

Reynolds paused and Tracy was transfixed, the way she imagined his juries were, as his homely features were transformed by his quiet passion.

'I won that case on an insignificant technicality. A procedural point. Saved Lloyd Garth's life, though. Took him off death row as surely as any great legal point would have.'

A gentle smile played on Reynolds's lips.

'Two weeks before the retrial, another man confessed to the murder. Lloyd always swore he was innocent, but few people believed him. Sit down, Ms. Cavanaugh. Sit down.'

Tracy had been caught up in Reynolds's tale and it took her a moment to respond. While she took her seat, Reynolds studied her résumé. Tracy was rarely at a disadvantage, but she felt that Reynolds had already begun to dominate the interview. To regain the initiative, Tracy asked, 'Are all the wilderness photographs yours?'

'Why, yes,' Reynolds responded with a proud smile.

'They're incredible. Have you had formal training?'

Reynolds's smile vanished. A look of sadness passed over him.

'No formal training with a camera, but my father was a hunter – a great hunter – and he taught me all about the woods. He could stay with an animal for days in the forest.

The sheriff asked him to track men on occasion. Lost hunters, once an escaped convict. He found a little boy alive after everyone else had given up hope.

'He taught me to hunt. I was good at it, too. Eventually, I lost heart in the killing, but I still loved the woods. Photography is my way of getting out of myself when life gets too ponderous.'

'I know what you mean. I rock-climb. When you're on a cliff face, and the difference between life and death is the strength in your hands, you pull into yourself. You forget everything else except the rock.'

Tracy realized how pretentious she sounded as soon as she spoke. Reynolds seemed to close off a little. When he addressed her, there was less warmth.

'You're from California?'

Tracy nodded.

'What do your parents do?'

'My father works in motion pictures. He's a producer.'

'Successful?'

Tracy smiled. 'Very.'

'And your mother?'

'She doesn't work, but she's involved with charities. She devotes a lot of her time to volunteer work.'

Tracy hoped this would sound good, but she was afraid her background would be anathema to someone like Reynolds.

'Yale,' Reynolds went on, his voice giving away nothing of how he felt about her or her background, 'math major, *Stanford Law Review*.'

Tracy shrugged, wondering if she'd already blown the interview.

'And you placed fifth in the NCAA cross-country championships. You appear to have been successful at everything you've tried.'

Tracy considered a modest answer, then decided against it. If she got this job, it would not be by being a phony.

'I've been lucky. I'm very smart and I'm a natural athlete,' Tracy said. 'But I also work my butt off.'

Reynolds nodded. Then he asked, 'Why did you choose the law as a profession?'

Tracy thought about the question, as she had many times before.

'When I was young, I couldn't understand the world. It made no sense that the earth and sun didn't collide. Why didn't we fly off into space? How could a chair be made of tiny, unconnected atoms, yet be solid enough to prevent me from putting my hand through it? Mathematics imposes order on the sciences. Its rules helped me to make sense out of insanity.

'Human beings like to think of themselves as rational and civilized, but I think we are constantly on the brink of chaos. Look at the madness in Africa or the carnage in Eastern Europe. I was attracted to the law for the same reason I was fascinated by mathematics. Law imposes order on society and keeps the barbarians in check. When the rule of law breaks down, civilization falls apart.

'America is a nation of laws. I've always marveled that

a country with so much power shows such restraint in the way it treats its citizens. Not that I think the country is perfect. Not by a long shot. We've condoned countless injustices. Slavery is the most obvious example. But that's because human beings are so fallible. Then I think of what the President could do if he wanted to. Especially with today's technology. Why don't we live in a dictatorship? Why did Nixon resign, instead of trying a coup d'état? I think it's because we are a nation of laws in the truest sense and lawyers are the guardians of the law. I really believe that.'

Tracy felt she was running on. She stopped talking and studied Matthew Reynolds, but his face revealed nothing and she could not tell if her speech had impressed him or made him think she was a fool.

'I understand that the young woman who was murdered at the court was a friend of yours.'

Reynolds's statement shook her and all Tracy could do was nod. An image of Laura, strands of curly black hair wrapped around her fingers as she worked through a legal problem, flashed into her mind. Then another image of Laura, dead, her curly black hair matted with blood, superimposed itself on the first image.

'What punishment should your friend's killer receive if he's caught?'

Tracy knew Reynolds would ask about her views on the death penalty, but she never expected him to come at her in this way. She had spent several hours reading articles about the death penalty, including some by

Reynolds, to prepare herself for the interview, but dealing with punishment in the abstract and asking her to decide the fate of Laura's murderer were two different things.

'That's not a fair question,' Tracy said.

'Why not?'

'She was my friend. I found the body.'

Reynolds nodded sympathetically.

'There's always a body. There's always a victim. There's always someone left alive to mourn. Don't you want revenge for your friend?'

It was a good question that forced Tracy to decide what she really thought about the death penalty. She looked across the desk at Matthew Reynolds. He was watching her closely.

'If I found the man who murdered Laura, I would want to kill him with my bare hands, but I would hope that the sober people around me would stop me. A civilized society should aspire to higher ideals. It should be above legalized killing for revenge.'

'Would you be in favor of the death penalty if it deterred crime?'

'Maybe, but it doesn't. I don't have to tell you that there's no statistical evidence that the penalty deters killing. Oregon had a record murder rate a few years after the penalty was reinstated.

'And then there's the mistake factor. I read recently that four hundred and sixteen innocent Americans were convicted of capital crimes between 1900 and 1991 and twenty-three were actually executed. Every other sentence can be corrected if the authorities realize they've made a mistake, except for a sentence of death.'

'Why do you want to work for me, Ms. Cavanaugh?'

'I want to work for you because you're the best and because everything in my life has been easy. I don't regret that, but I'd like to give something back to people who haven't been as fortunate.'

'That's very noble, but our clients are not the "less fortunate." They are sociopaths, misfits, psychotics. They are men who torture women and murder children. Not the type of people you associated with in Beverly Hills or at Yale.'

'I'm aware of that.'

'Are you also aware that we work very long hours? Evenings and weekends are the norm. How do you feel about that?'

'Justice Sherer warned me about your version of a workweek and I still called for this interview.'

'Tell me, Ms. Cavanaugh,' Reynolds asked in a neutral tone, 'have you ever been to Stark, Florida, to the prison, after dark?'

'No, sir,' Tracy answered, completely stumped by the question.

'And I suppose you have never been to Columbia, South Carolina, to visit after dark?'

Tracy shook her head. Reynolds watched her carefully, then continued.

'Several attorneys of my acquaintance have visited their clients in prison after dark. These attorneys have a number of things in common. They are brilliant, extremely skilled legal practitioners. They are what you would call the top of the bar in morality, ethics and commitment. They are people we can admire very much for what their lives are about and what their commitment to the criminal justice system is.

'These people have something else in common. They all visited these prisons after dark and left before sunrise with their clients dead.'

A chill ran up Tracy's spine.

'There is something else they have in common, Ms. Cavanaugh. They all left before dawn with their clients dead because of some act of another lawyer in not preserving an issue, in failing to investigate competently, in not seeing that that client was represented in the way that a co-defendant was. And the fact is that these co-defendants are on the street today, alive, just because of the quality of the words written or spoken in some court or some act by some lawyer.'

Reynolds paused. He leaned back in his chair and formed a steeple with his slender fingers.

'Ms. Cavanaugh, I've been a lawyer for more than twenty years and neither I nor any associate of mine has ever visited a prison in this country after dark. Not once. I take no pride in that fact, because pride has no place in the work we do. It is backbreaking, mind-numbing work. If you work for me, you won't sleep right, you won't eat right, and you certainly won't have time to climb or run. This work tears the soul out of you. It requires dedication to men and women who are pariahs in our society. It is work that will earn you no praise but will often earn you the hatred and ill will of decent citizens.'

Tracy's throat felt tight. There was a band around her heart. She knew she had never wanted anything more in life than to work for this man.

'Mr. Reynolds, if you give me this chance I won't let you down.'

Reynolds watched Tracy over his steepled fingers. Then he sat up in his chair.

'You know I've never worked with a woman?'

'Justice Sherzer told me.'

'What special gifts do you think you'll bring to this job as a woman?'

'None, Mr. Reynolds. But I'll bring several as a lawyer. I'll bring an exceptional ability to analyze legal issues and total dedication to my work. Justice Forbes knows my work. He wouldn't have told you to talk to me if he didn't think I could cut it. If you hire me, you won't have to worry about the quality of the words I write or speak.'

'We'll see,' Reynolds said. He sat up. 'When can you start?'

Chapter Seven

1

Tracy Cavanaugh was sitting on the floor in jeans and a faded Yale Athletic Department tee shirt taking law books out of a carton and putting them on bookshelves when she heard someone behind her. Standing in the doorway of her new office was a lean man with a dark complexion, curly black hair and a wide grin. To her surprise, Tracy felt an immediate attraction to him, and she hoped her deep tan was hiding the blush that warmed her cheeks.

'You must be the new associate. I'm Barry Frame, Matt's investigator.'

Frame was a little over six feet with wide shoulders and a tapered waist. He was wearing a blue work shirt and khaki slacks. The sleeves of his shirt were rolled back to the elbow, revealing hairy forearms that were corded with muscle. Tracy stood up and wiped her hand on her jeans before offering it to Frame. His grip was gentle.

'Getting settled in okay?' Frame asked, looking at the cardboard cartons.

'Oh, sure.'

'Can I help?'

'Thanks, but I don't have that much stuff.'

'Have you found a place to stay?'

'Yeah. I've got a nice apartment down by the river. I found it just before I moved up.'

'You were living in Salem, right?'

Tracy nodded. 'I was clerking for the Supreme Court.'

'Which justice?'

'Alice Sherzer.'

'I clerked for Justice Lefcourt five years ago.'

Tracy was confused. She was certain Frame had said he was an investigator. Frame laughed.

'You're wondering why I'm not practicing, right?'

'Well, I . . .' Tracy started, embarrassed that she was so transparent.

'It's okay. I'm used to getting that look from lawyers. And no, I didn't flunk the bar exam. After the clerkship with Justice Lefcourt, Matt hired me as an attorney, but I liked being a detective more than I liked practicing law. When his investigator quit, I asked for the job. I don't get paid as much, but I'm not stuck behind a desk and I don't have to wear a tie.'

'Does Mr. Reynolds have you do any legal work?'

'Not if I can help it, although I did fill in while we were

waiting for you to come on board. The last associate left precipitously.'

'Why did he go?'

'Burnout. Matt expects a lot from people and some of his requests are above and beyond the call of duty.'

'For instance . . . ?' Tracy asked, hoping Frame would give her examples of the horror stories others had hinted at when talking about the demands Reynolds put on his associates, so she could prepare herself for the worst.

'Well, Matt handles cases all over the country. Sometimes he'll expect an associate to become an expert on another state's law.'

'That doesn't sound unreasonable.'

'I've seen him give that type of assignment to some poor slob a week before trial.'

'You're kidding?'

'Absolutely not.'

'Boy, that would be tough,' Tracy answered, a bit worried. The work at the Supreme Court was demanding, but Justice Sherzer always emphasized that good scholarship was more important than speed. Tracy hoped she wasn't in over her head.

'Do you think you could do it?' Frame asked.

'I'm a quick study, but that's asking a lot. I guess I could in a pinch, if the area was narrow enough.'

'Good,' Frame said, grinning broadly, 'because you leave for Atlanta next Monday.'

'What!'

'Did I mention that Matt also uses me to bear grim

tidings? No? Well, I'm frequently the messenger that everyone wants to kill.'

'What am I supposed to do in Atlanta?' Tracy asked incredulously. 'I'm not even unpacked.'

'You'll be second-chairing the Livingstone case. The file is in the library. You'll want to get to it as soon as you get your stuff put away. It's pretty thick.'

'What kind of case is it?'

'A death penalty case. Matt rarely handles any other kind. The legal issues are tricky, but you can get up to speed if you work all week. There's a good place for Chinese takeout a few blocks from here. They stay open late.'

'Mr. Reynolds wants me to become an expert on Georgia law and learn everything I can about this case in five days?' Tracy asked with an expression that said she was certain this was some bizarre practical joke.

Frame threw his head back and laughed. 'There's nothing I enjoy more than that look. But cheer up. I hear Atlanta is lovely in August. A hundred twenty in the shade with one hundred percent humidity.'

Frame cracked up again. Tracy could hear him laughing long after he was out of sight. She sat back down on the floor and stared at the boxes that still had to be unpacked. She had planned on running after squaring away her office, but that was not possible now. It looked like the only exercise she would get in the near future would be from lifting law books.

2

'Thank you for seeing me on such short notice,' Matthew Reynolds said as Abigail Griffen ushered him into her office, three weeks after their argument at the Supreme Court.

'I don't have much choice,' Abbie answered, flicking her hand toward the slip-sheet opinion in the *State ex rel. Franklin* case. 'The court bought your due process argument. When can your people go into Mrs. Franklin's house?'

'I phoned California. The criminologist I'm working with can be here Tuesday. My Portland people are on call.'

'I'll tell Mrs. Franklin you'll be there sometime Tuesday. She doesn't want to see you. There'll be a policeman at the house with a key to let you in.'

'I'll be in Atlanta for a few weeks trying a case. Barry Frame, my investigator, will work with the forensic experts.'

'I'll be out of the office myself.'

'Oh?'

'Nothing as exotic as Atlanta. I'm taking a week of R. and R. at my cabin on the coast. Dennis Haggard can handle any problems while I'm away. I'll brief him.'

'Can we have a set of the crime-scene photographs and the diagrams your forensic people drew?'

'Of course.'

Abbie buzzed her trial assistant on the intercom and

asked her to bring what Reynolds had requested. While she talked, Reynolds took in the line of Abbie's chin and her smooth skin. She was wearing a black pantsuit and a yellow shirt that highlighted her tan. A narrow gold necklace circled her slender neck. A diamond in the center of the necklace matched her diamond earrings.

Abbie turned and caught Reynolds staring. He blushed and looked away.

'It's going to be a few minutes,' Abbie said, as if she had not noticed. 'Do you want some coffee?'

'Thank you.'

Abbie left, giving Matthew a chance to compose himself. He stood up and looked around her office. He had expected to see pictures of Abbie and her husband and was surprised to find the office devoid of personal items. Abbie's desk was covered with police reports and case files. One wall was decorated by her diplomas and several civic awards. Framed newspaper clippings of some of her cases hung on another. They were a testimonial to Abbie's trial skills and her tenacity. Death sentences in almost every case where she had asked for one. Lengthy sentences for Oregon's most wanted criminals. Abigail Griffen never gave the opposition an inch or a break.

Matthew noticed a blank spot on the wall. The framed article that had been hanging there lay facedown on top of a filing cabinet. Matthew turned it over. The headline read: BOMBER CONVICTED. There was a picture of Charlie Deems in handcuffs being led out of the courthouse by three burly guards.

'I forgot to ask if you take cream or sugar,' Abbie said as she reentered the office with two mugs of coffee.

Reynolds had not heard her come in. 'Black is fine,' he answered nervously, sounding like a small boy caught with his hand in the cookie jar. Abbie held out his coffee, then noticed what Reynolds was looking at.

'I'm sorry about Deems,' Reynolds told her.

'I never thought I'd hear Matthew Reynolds bemoaning the reversal of a death sentence.'

'I see nothing inconsistent in opposing the death penalty and being sorry that a man like Deems is not in prison.'

'You know him?'

'He tried to hire me, but I declined the case.'

'Why?'

'There was something about Deems I didn't like. Will you retry him?'

'I can't. The court suppressed statements Deems made to a police informant. Without the confession we don't have a case. He's already out of prison.'

'Are you concerned for your safety?'

'Why do you ask?'

'Deems struck me as someone who would hold a grudge.'

Abbie hesitated. She had forgotten about the man who tried to invade her home, assuming he was simply a burglar. Reynolds's question raised another possibility.

'Deems is probably so happy to be off death row that he's forgotten all about me,' Abbie answered, forcing a smile.

The trial assistant entered with a manila envelope. Abbie checked the contents then handed it to Matthew.

'I'd like to set a trial date,' she said. 'After your forensic people are through, you should have an idea of what you want to do. Get in touch with me.'

'Thank you for your cooperation,' Reynolds said, as if he was ending a business letter. 'I'll have the photos returned when my people are done.'

What a peculiar man, Griffen thought, after Reynolds was gone. So serious, so stiff. Not someone you'd go out with for a beer. And he was so awkward around her, blushing all the time, like one of those stiff-necked South Seas missionaries who didn't know how to deal with the naked Tahitian women. If she didn't know better, she'd guess he had a crush on her.

Abbie thought about that for a moment. It wouldn't hurt if Reynolds was a little bit in love with her. It might make him sloppy in trial. She could use any edge she could get. Reynolds might be an odd duck, but he was the best damn lawyer she'd ever gone up against.

Chapter Eight

1

Joel Livingstone was a handsome, broad-shouldered eighteen-year-old with soft blue eyes and wavy blond hair. On the most important day of his life, Joel wore a white shirt, a navy-blue blazer, gray slacks with a knife-sharp crease and his Wheatley Academy tie. This outfit was similar to the one he was wearing when he raped Mary Harding in the woods behind the elite private school before beating her to death with a jagged log.

Outside the office of Matthew Reynolds's Atlanta co-counsel, a torrid sun was shining down on Peachtree Street, but inside the office the mood was dark. Joel sprawled in a chair and regarded Reynolds with a smirk. An observer might have concluded that Joel was contemptuous of anything Matthew had to say, but the rapid tapping of Joel's right foot betrayed his fear. Reynolds imagined the tapping foot was asking the same question the boy had asked him over and over during the year they had spent as lawyer and client: 'Will I die? Will I die? Will I die?' It was a question Reynolds was uniquely qualified to answer.

'Are we going to the courthouse?'

'Not yet, Joel. There's been a development.'

'What kind of development?' the boy asked nervously.

'Last night, when I returned to my hotel, there was a message from the prosecutor, Mr. Folger.'

'What did he want?'

'He wanted to resolve your case without going to trial. We conferred in my hotel room until midnight.'

Matthew looked directly at his client. Joel fidgeted.

'Mary Harding was very popular, Joel. Her murder has outraged many people in Atlanta. On the other hand, your parents are prominent people in this community. They are well liked and respected. Many people are sympathetic to them. Some of these people are in positions of power. They don't want your mother and father to suffer the loss of their only son.'

Joel looked at Reynolds expectantly.

'Mr. Folger has made a plea offer. It must be accepted before the judge makes his ruling on our motions.'

'What's the offer?'

'A guilty plea to murder in exchange for his promise to not ask for a death sentence.'

'What . . . what would happen then?'

'You would be sentenced to life in prison with a ten-year minimum sentence.'

'Oh no. I'm not doing that. I'm not going to jail for life.'

'It's the best I can do for you.'

'My father paid you a quarter of a million dollars. You're supposed to get me off.'

Matthew shook his head wearily. 'I was hired to save your life, Joel. No one can get you off. You killed Mary and you confessed to the police. The evidence is overwhelming. It was never a question of getting you off. We talked about that a lot, remember?'

'But if we went to trial . . .'

'You would be convicted and you might very well die.'

Matthew held up a photograph of Mary Harding at her junior prom next to a full-face autopsy photograph of the girl.

'That's what the jury will see every minute of their deliberations. What do you think your sentence will be?'

Joel's lip quivered. His teenage bravado had disappeared. 'I'm only eighteen,' he pleaded. A tear trickled down his cheek. 'I don't want to spend my life in prison.' Joel slumped in his chair and buried his face in his hands.

Matthew leaned forward and placed a hand on Joel's shoulder. 'What, Joel?'

'I'm scared,' the boy sobbed.

'I know, Joel. Everyone I've ever represented has been scared when it was time to decide. Even the tough guys.'

Joel raised his tear-stained face toward Matthew. He was just a baby now and it was impossible to imagine what he must have looked like when he straddled Mary

Harding's naked body and slammed the log down over and over until he had smashed the life out of her.

'What will I do, Mr. Reynolds?'

'You'll do what you have to to make a life for yourself. You won't stay in prison forever. You'll be paroled. Your parents love you. They'll be there for you when you get out. And while you're in, you can take college courses, get a degree.'

Matthew went on, trying to sound upbeat, wanting Joel to have hope and knowing it was all a lie. Prison would be hell for Joel Livingstone. A hell he would survive, but one from which he would emerge a far different person from the boy he was today.

2

Matthew Reynolds and Tracy Cavanaugh had been in court for three solid days of pretrial motions when Joel Livingstone's late-afternoon guilty plea abruptly ended the case. As the judge took the plea, Tracy had glanced at Joel's parents, who were elegantly dressed, barely under control and totally at sea in the Fulton County Circuit Court.

Bradford Livingstone, a prominent investment banker, sat stiffly, hands folded in his lap, uncomfortable in the company of cops, court watchers and other types with whom he did not normally associate. On occasion, Tracy caught Bradford staring at his son in disbelief. Elaine

Livingstone pulled into herself, becoming more distant, pale and fragile every day. When the judge pronounced sentence, the couple seemed to age before Tracy's eyes.

After court, there was a tearful meeting between Joel and his parents, then an exhausting meeting between the parents and Matthew, which Matthew handled with great compassion.

It was almost seven when Tracy joined Reynolds in the hotel dining room for their final dinner in Atlanta. Tracy noticed that Reynolds was indifferent to food and every night had ordered steak, a green salad, a baked potato and iced tea. This evening, Tracy was as disinterested in food as her boss. She was toying with her pasta primavera and replaying the events of the day when Reynolds asked, 'What's bothering you?'

Tracy looked across the table. She knew Reynolds had said something, but she had no idea what it was.

'You've been distracted. I was wondering if something was wrong,' he said.

Tracy hesitated, then asked, 'Why did you convince Joel to take the deal?'

There was a piece of steak on Reynolds's fork. He put the fork on his plate and leaned back in his chair.

'You don't think I should have?'

Reynolds's tone gave no clue to what he was thinking. Tracy had a rush of insecurity. Reynolds had been trying cases for twenty years. She had never tried a case and she had worked for the man she was questioning for all of one week. Then again, Reynolds struck her as a man who

117

welcomed ideas and would not take offense if she had a sound basis for her views.

'I think Folger made the offer because he was afraid he might lose our motion to suppress the confession.'

'I'm sure you're right.'

'We could have won it.'

'And we could have lost.'

'The judge was leaning our way. Without the confession, we might have had a shot at manslaughter. There's no minimum sentence for manslaughter. Joel would have been eligible for parole anytime.'

'There's no minimum sentence with death either.'

Tracy started to say something, then stopped. Reynolds waited a moment, then asked, 'What was our objective in this case?'

'To win,' Tracy answered automatically.

Reynolds shook his head. 'Our objective was to save Joel Livingstone's life. That is the objective in every death case. Winning is one way of accomplishing that objective, but it must never be your main objective.

'When I started practicing, I thought my objective was always an acquittal.' Reynolds's lips creased into a tired smile. 'Unfortunately, I won my first three murder cases. It's difficult to avoid arrogance if you're young and undefeated. My next death case was in a small eastern Oregon county. Eddie Brace, the DA, was only a few years older than I and he had never tried a murder case. The rumor was that he'd run for DA because he wasn't making it in private practice. The first time we were in court, Brace stumbled around and spent half his time apologizing to the Judge.

'The night before we were to start motions, Mr. Brace came to my hotel, just like Folger did. We jawed for a while, then he told me flat out that he felt uncomfortable about asking a jury to take a man's life. He wanted to know if my client would take a straight murder if he'd give up the death penalty. Well, I had a winnable case and I'd gotten not-guilty verdicts in every murder case I'd tried, so I figured what you figured with Folger, that Brace was afraid to lose. I knew I was so good I'd run right over him.'

Reynolds looked down at his plate for a moment, then directly at his associate.

'The worst words a lawyer can hear is a verdict of death for his client. You don't ever want to hear those words, Tracy. I heard them for the first time in the case I tried against Eddie Brace.'

'What went wrong?'

'Only one thing. Brace stumbled along, I tried a brilliant case, but the jury was for hanging. They really wanted to see my client die. With hindsight I could see that it really didn't matter who tried the case, my man was going to die if a jury was deciding the matter. Brace knew that. He knew his people. That's why he tried so hard to convince me to take the deal. Not because he was afraid he would lose, but because he knew he couldn't lose.'

'But Joel's case . . . It's different. The judge might have . . .'

'No, Tracy. Not while there was any kind of argument on Folger's side. I know you don't believe that now, but you will after a while. What's important is that I know the judge would have found a way to keep the confession in and the jury would have no sympathy for a spoiled rich kid who took the life of that lovely girl.'

Reynolds looked at his watch.

'I'm going to take a walk then turn in. There'll be a limousine waiting to take us to the airport at seven. Get a good night's sleep. And don't let this case keep you up. We did a good job. We did what we had to do. We kept our client alive.'

3

Matthew Reynolds closed the door to his hotel room and stood in the dark. The sterile room was immaculately clean, the covers on his bed neatly tucked in at the corners, a chocolate mint centered on the freshly laundered pillowcase. It looked this way every night.

Reynolds stripped off his jacket and laid it over the back of a chair. The conditioned air dried the sweat that made his shirt stick to his narrow chest. Outside the hermetically sealed window, Atlanta sweltered in the sultry August heat. The lights of the city flickered all around. This was the last time Reynolds would see them. Tomorrow he would be home in Portland and away from the reporters, his client and this case.

Reynolds turned away from the window and saw the red message light blinking on the phone next to his bed. He retrieved the message and punched in Barry Frame's number, anxious to hear what he had uncovered in the Coulter case.

'Bingo!' Frame said.

'Tell me,' Reynolds asked anxiously.

'Mrs. Franklin hung a picture over the bullet hole. This horrific black velvet Elvis. The cops never thought to move it because they have no aesthetic taste. Fortunately for Jeffrey Coulter, I do.'

Frame paused dramatically.

'Stop patting yourself on the back and get to it.'

'You can relax, Matt. We don't have to worry about this case anymore. I guarantee Griffen will dismiss once she reads the criminologist's report. See, the picture was too high. No one would hang it like that. Not even some-one with Mrs. Franklin's awful taste. It bothered me in the crime-scene photos and it was worse when I walked into the hall.

'In Jeffrey's version of the shooting, he fell back when Franklin pulled out the gun. When he tripped, Franklin's shot missed him. Jeffrey is tall. If Franklin shot for the head, he'd be aiming high. We found a snapshot in the family album showing the hallway three months before the shooting with the Elvis on another wall. I moved the picture and there was a freshly puttied hole. We've got everything on videotape, as well as stills. We dug out the putty. The expert's pretty certain it's a bullet hole. The bullet's gone. Ma Franklin must have deep-sixed it.'

'When will we have the criminologist's report?'

'By the end of the week.'

'Let's step up the background investigation of Franklin. Put another man on it if necessary.'

'What for? The fact that Mrs. Franklin puttied over the bullet hole, then moved the picture to conceal it, proves she was covering up for her son. Griffen will have to drop the charges.'

'Never bank on the prosecution acting reasonably, Barry. Abigail Griffen is not the type to roll over. She may not draw the same conclusions from the evidence that we did. We go full-bore until the moment the indictment is dismissed.'

'You got it,' Barry said wearily. 'I'll put Ted French on the backgrounder. How are things in Atlanta?'

'Joel took the deal.'

'That's what you hoped, isn't it?'

'Yes.'

'How are his parents doing?'

'Not well.' Matthew paused for a moment and rubbed his eyes. 'I'm flying back tomorrow, Barry, but don't tell anyone. I want to take a few days off.'

'Are you okay? You don't sound so good.'

'I'm tired. I need some time to myself.'

'I've been telling you that for years. When do you land? I'll pick you up at the airport.'

'I'll be in at three-ten. And, Barry, that was good work at the Franklin house. *Very* good work.'

Matthew hung up. His eyes were glazed with fatigue and he was bone weary. He lay back on the bed in the dark and thought about Joel Livingstone and Jeffrey Coulter back in Portland and Alonso Nogueiras in Huntsville, Texas, and all the other people for whom he was the sole difference between life and death. It was too much for one man to do and he was beginning to think he just couldn't do it anymore.

Matthew thought about Tracy Cavanaugh's drive and desire. There had been a time when he moved from one cause to another with the energy of a zealot. Now the cases just seemed to grind him down, and it was taking all his strength to stand up after he was done with them. He needed time away from the clients and the ever present specter of death. He needed something . . . someone.

Matthew turned on his side and hugged a pillow to his cheek. The linen felt cool and comforting. He closed his eyes and remembered the way Abigail Griffen looked in one of the photographs he kept in the manila envelope in the lower right drawer of his desk. The photo was his favorite. In it, she stood relaxed and happy outside the French windows of her home, her arms at her side, her right knee slightly bent, looking toward the woods, as if she was listening to some faint sound that carried to her on the wind.

Chapter Nine

1

The morning had been cool and overcast, but the fog burned off by noon and the sun was shining. Abbie circled the cabin taking pictures from different angles with her Pentax camera. She tried to capture the cabin from every angle, because she needed a photographic record of the place that in all the world had come to be her favorite.

When she was finished photographing the cabin, Abbie followed a narrow dirt path through the woods to a bluff overlooking the Pacific. She took some shots from the bluff, then walked down a flight of wooden steps to the beach.

Abbie was wearing a navy-blue tee shirt, a bulky, hooded gray sweatshirt and jeans. She hung the camera around her neck and took off her sneakers and socks. There had been a storm the previous day and the Pacific was still in turmoil. Abbie pushed her toes through the sand until she reached the waterline. Gulls swooped overhead. She set up a shot, stepping sideways toward the bluff whenever the freezing water came too close. A wave rose skyward, spraying foam, then fell in a fury.

Abbie finished the roll of film and continued down the beach. She loved the ocean and she loved the cabin. The cabin was the place she came to escape. She would awake with the sun, but stay in bed reading. When she was hungry, Abbie would whip up marionberry, ginger or some other type of exotic pancakes and a *caffé latte*. She would nurse the *latte* while reading the escapist fiction she had no time for when she was in trial and which helped her to forget the grim work of prosecuting rapists and murderers. Then, for the rest of the day, she would continue to do absolutely nothing of importance and revel in her idleness.

Abbie hunched her shoulders against a sudden gust of wind. The sea air was bracing. The thought of losing the cabin was unbearable, but she was going to lose it. The cabin belonged to Robert and he had made it clear that she would never use it once the divorce was final, taunting her with the loss because he knew how dear the place was to her. It gave Abbie one more reason to hate him.

The sun began to set. Abbie reached a place where the beach narrowed at the base of a high bluff. She turned for home, leaning forward to fight the tug of the sand. By the time she arrived at the stairs that led back up to the cabin, she was feeling melancholy. She sat on the lowest step and tied her sneakers. She would be able to buy another cabin, but she doubted she would find one that suited her so perfectly.

Abbie rested her forearms on her thighs and lost herself in the rhythm of the waves. What would she do after the divorce? She would not mind being alone. She had lived alone before. She was living alone now. Living alone was better than living with someone who used you and lied to you. What she would miss was the special feeling of being in love she had experienced with Larry Ross and during the early days of her marriage to Robert. Abbie wondered if she would take the risk of falling in love again, knowing how easily love could be snatched away.

When the chill reminded her of the advent of night, Abbie hoisted herself to her feet and climbed the stairs. She walked slowly along the short path through the woods. Something moved deep in the forest and Abbie froze, hoping it was a deer. She had been on edge since the attempted break-in at her house. When Matthew Reynolds commented that Charlie Deems was the type of person who would seek revenge, Abbie remembered that the burglar's physique vaguely resembled Deems's. The thought that a man like Deems might be stalking her was profoundly unsettling.

Abbie waited nervously in the shadows cast by the pines, but the source of the sound remained a mystery. She returned to the cabin, showered, then ate dinner on the front porch. She sipped a chilled Chardonnay that went well with the trout amandine and saffron rice pilaf. Overhead, the stars were a river of diamonds so sharp they hurt her eyes. They never looked like this in the city.

Abbie loved to cook and usually felt upbeat after consuming one of her creations. Tonight, she was thinking about losing the cabin and she felt logy and maudlin. After dinner, she sipped a mug of coffee, but soon felt her eyelids drag. She emptied the coffee onto the packed earth below the porch rail and went inside.

Abbie sat up in bed, certain she had heard a noise but unable to tell what it was. Her heart was beating so loudly, she had to take deep breaths to calm herself. The moon was only a sliver and the room was pitch black. According to the clock on her nightstand, she had only been asleep for an hour and a half.

Abbie tried to identify the sound that had awakened her, but heard only the waves breaking on the beach. Just as she convinced herself that she was only having a bad dream, a stair creaked and her heart raced again. Abbie had taken to carrying her handgun since the attempted break-in, but as she reached for it, she remembered that her purse was downstairs.

She had been too exhausted to change her clothes when she went to bed, so Abbie was wearing her tee shirt and panties and had tossed her sneakers, socks and jeans onto the floor next to the bed. She rolled onto the floor and slipped on her jeans and sneakers.

There was a deck outside the bedroom window. Abbie grabbed the doorknob and tried to open the door quietly, but the salt air had warped the wood and the door stuck.

Abbie pulled a little harder, afraid that the intruder would hear her if she jerked open the door. It would not move.

Another step creaked and she panicked. The second she wrenched the door open footsteps pounded up the stairs toward her room. Abbie ran onto the deck. She slammed the deck door closed to slow the intruder, then she rolled over the low deck rail just as the door to her bedroom slammed open. For a brief moment, Abbie could see the silhouette of a man in her doorway. Then she was falling through the air and slamming against hard-packed earth.

The deck door crashed against the outside wall and Abbie was up and running. A dirt trail ran between the woods and the edge of the bluff for a mile until it reached the neighbors' property. There was no fence and the trail was narrow, but Abbie streaked along it, praying she would not be followed.

A hundred yards in was a footpath that led into the woods. Abbie's brain was racing as she weighed her choices and decided her chances of survival were better in the woods, where there were more places to hide. She veered to the left and shot down the trail, then moved off it and into the woods as silently as she could.

Abbie crouched behind a tree and strained to hear the man who was chasing her. A second later, footsteps pounded by on the path. Abbie gulped air and tried to calm herself. She decided to move deeper into the woods. She would hide until daylight and hope the man would give up before then. She had almost regained her composure when she heard a sound on her right.

Adrenaline coursed through her and she bolted into the underbrush, making no effort to be quiet. Her feet churned. She surged into the woods and away from the cliff, oblivious to the pain from branches that whipped across her face and ripped her shirt. Then she was airborne. She tried to cushion her fall but her face took the brunt of it. Blinding lights flashed behind her eyes. The air was momentarily crushed from her lungs. She hugged the earth, praying she would be invisible in the dark. Almost immediately, she heard the loud crack of branches breaking and the snap of bushes as they swung back after being pushed apart.

The sound was nearby and there was no way she could run. On her right was a massive, rotting tree trunk. Abbie burrowed under it, pressing herself into the earth, hoping that the mass of the log would shield her.

Something wet fell on Abbie's face. It started to move. Tiny legs scrambled across her lips and cheek. An insect! Then another and another. Abbie desperately wanted to scream, but she was afraid the insects would crawl into her mouth. She clamped her jaws shut and took in air through her nose. Every part of her wanted to bolt, but she was sure she would die if she did.

The woods were silent. The man had stopped to reconnoiter. Abbie brought a hand to her face and brushed off the bugs. She expelled air slowly. Her heart was beating wildly in her ears and she calmed herself so she could hear.

There was cool earth against her cheek and the silhouettes of tall evergreens against the night sky. Suddenly the space between two large trees was filled by the outline of a man. His back was to her, but she was certain he would see her if he turned and looked down. Abbie pressed herself closer to the log, praying that the man would not turn. He did. Slowly. A few inches more and he would see her. Abbie felt for a rock or a thick tree limb she could use as a weapon, but her hand closed on nothing of substance. Now the man was facing the log. He started to look directly at Abbie. Then the sky lit up.

2

The ringing of the phone wrenched Jack Stamm out of a deep sleep. He groped for the receiver. When he knocked it off the cradle, the ringing mercifully ceased.

'District Attorney Stamm?'

Stamm squinted at the bright red numerals on his digital alarm clock. It was 4:47 A.M.

'Who's this?'

'Seth Dillard. I'm the sheriff in Seneca County. We met at a law-enforcement conference in Boise two years ago.'

'Right,' Stamm said, trying to picture the sheriff and coming up blank. 'What couldn't wait until morning?'

'We have one of your people here. Abigail Griffen.'

'Is she all right?' Stamm asked, suddenly wide awake.

'Yes, sir, but she's mighty shaken up.'

'Why? What happened?'

'She says someone tried to kill her.'

*

Seneca County was two hours west of Portland and it was almost seven-thirty when Jack Stamm stopped beside one of the two county police cars that were parked in front of an A-frame that belonged to Evelyn Wallace, Abbie's neighbor. When Stamm stepped out of his car, he could see the sun through breaks in the trees and heard the dull *shoosh* of the surf through the woods behind the house.

A Seneca County sheriff's deputy opened the front door and Stamm showed his ID. The A-frame was small. A kitchen and the living room took up the ground floor. Abbie was huddled on the living-room couch wrapped in a blanket and sipping a cup of coffee. Evelyn Wallace, a slender woman in her mid-sixties, sat beside her.

Stamm was shocked by the way Abbie looked. Her hair was uncombed, there were streaks of dirt on her cheeks and her eyes were bloodshot. Stamm also noticed a number of cuts and bruises on her face.

'My God, Abbie. Are you all right?' Stamm asked.

Abbie looked up at the sound of Stamm's voice. At first she did not seem to recognize her boss. Then she mustered the energy for a tired smile.

'I'm exhausted but I'm okay. Thanks for coming.'

'Don't be ridiculous. Do you think I'd let you drive yourself to Portland after what the sheriff said?'

Before Abbie could answer, the door opened and a tall man with leathery skin and a salt-and-pepper mustache entered. He wore a Stetson and the uniform of the Seneca County sheriff's office.

'Mr. Stamm?' asked the uniformed man.

'Sheriff Dillard?'

'Yes, sir. Thanks for comin'.'

The sheriff turned his attention to Abbie.

'Do you think you're up to going back to the cabin? My men are almost through and I'd appreciate it if you could walk me through what happened.'

Abbie stood up. The blanket slipped down. She was wearing a tee shirt without a bra, jeans and sneakers without socks, and she was covered with caked brown-gray mud from head to toe.

'You're sure you're up to it, dear?' Mrs. Wallace asked.

'I'm fine. Thank you so much, Mrs. Wallace. You've been wonderful.'

When Abbie was ready, she got in the sheriff's car. Stamm followed along a short driveway until they reached the highway. The sheriff turned left and drove for a little over a mile, then turned down the narrow dirt road that led to the Griffen cabin. Abbie and the sheriff were going inside by the time Stamm parked and climbed the steps to the front porch.

The front door of the Griffen cabin opened into a large living room with a stone fireplace. There were two bedrooms and a kitchen on the first floor and two more bedrooms, plus the deck, upstairs.

'Forensic people through?' Sheriff Dillard asked a lanky deputy who was waiting in the living room holding a Styrofoam cup filled with lukewarm coffee.

'Left a few minutes ago.'

'Before you tell us what happened,' the sheriff asked

Abbie, 'can you check to see if anything was stolen?'

Abbie went through the downstairs as quickly as possible, then led everyone upstairs to the bedroom. Her terrifying ordeal had drained her physically and emotionally, and she climbed the stairs slowly. When she reached the bedroom doorway, she paused, as if expecting to find the intruder inside. Then she took a deep breath and entered.

The shades on the big picture window were open and pale morning light filled the room. Only a lamp that lay with its shade askew on the floor next to an oak chest of drawers suggested an intruder, but Abbie could feel a presence in the bedroom that made her skin crawl. She hugged herself and shivered slightly. She had been scared after the burglary attempt, but the fear passed quickly because she convinced herself that the attempted burglary was a random incident. Now she knew it wasn't.

'Are you all right, Mrs. Griffen?' Sheriff Dillard asked.

'I'm fine, just tired and a little scared.'

'It wouldn't be normal if you weren't.'

Abbie checked the chest of drawers and her end table. She went through her wallet carefully. Then she looked in the closets.

'As far as I can see, nothing's missing.'

'Why don't you come on out to the deck so you can sit down and get some fresh air,' the sheriff said solicitously.

Abbie walked out of the room into the bracing salt air and sat on one of the deck chairs. She looked out past the rail and saw the wide blue plain that was the sea.

'Do you think you're up to telling us what happened?' the sheriff asked.

Abbie nodded. She started with the sound she had heard in the woods before dinner and walked Stamm and Sheriff Dillard through the events of the night, stopping occasionally to give them specific details she hoped would prove helpful to the investigation. Remembering what happened was almost more terrifying than experiencing it, because now she had time to think about what would have happened if she hadn't escaped. To her surprise, Abbie found she had to pause on occasion to fight back tears.

When Abbie told the sheriff about seeing the intruder in the doorway, Sheriff Dillard asked her if she could describe the man.

'No,' Abbie replied. 'I only saw him for a second before I dropped off the deck. I just had an impression of someone dressed in black. I'm certain he wore a ski mask or a stocking over his face, but I saw him for such a short time and it was just before I jumped. I was mostly concentrating on the ground.'

'Go on.'

'When I hit I rolled and took off. There's a dirt trail along the bluff. I heard the deck door slam. He must have pushed it hard. Then I was running in the dark. I could hear the ocean and see the whitecaps, but that was it. I was scared I'd go off the trail and fall from the bluff.

'About a hundred yards along the cliff, the trail branches into the woods. I saw a gap in the woods and took the offshoot, hoping the man would go straight. I tried to be quiet. He passed on the trail. I could hear his footsteps and his breathing. I was starting to feel like I'd gotten away when I heard something off to my right.'

'What kind of thing?'

'I don't know. Just . . .' Abbie shook her head. 'Just something. It spooked me.'

'Could there have been a second person?'

'That's what I thought. When I heard the sound, I jumped off the trail and dodged through the under-growth. I was really scared and not making any effort to be quiet. Just plunging away from the bluff and the place where I'd heard the sound.'

Abbie told Stamm and the sheriff about her hiding place under the log. She remembered the insects and shivered involuntarily.

'For a while it was quiet,' she continued. 'I hoped the man had gone off. Then a shadow moved between two large trees a short distance from me. I think it was the man I'd seen in the doorway.'

'Couldn't you be sure?' the sheriff asked.

'No. He seemed to be the same size and shape, but it was so dark and I only saw the man in my room for a second.'

'Go on.'

'I knew if he turned and looked down he'd see me. I was certain he could hear me breathing. Suddenly, he did turn and I was sure I'd been discovered. Then the woods lit up.'

'Lit up?' Sheriff Dillard repeated.

'There was a brief, but intense flash. It came from the other side of the log.'

'Do you know what caused the flash?' the sheriff asked.

'No. I was under the log. I could just see a change in the light.'

'Did you recognize the man?' the sheriff asked.

Abbie hesitated. 'Two weeks ago, a man tried to break into my house in Portland. I scared him away, but I got a good look at him while he was on my back porch. He was dressed like the man who broke into the cabin tonight. I'm certain it was the same person. I could never identify him in a lineup. He was wearing something over his face both times, but something about him reminded me of Charlie Deems.'

Stamm looked startled.

'Who is Charlie Deems?' the sheriff asked.

'A man I convicted on a murder charge more than a year ago. He was sentenced to death, but the Supreme Court reversed his sentence recently and he's out of prison.'

'Right. I knew the name sounded familiar. But why do you think it was Deems?'

'The size, his build. I could never swear it was Deems. It was just a feeling.'

'Did you report the attempted break-in in Portland?' the sheriff asked.

'No. I didn't see any purpose in reporting it. I couldn't identify the man and nothing was taken. He wore gloves, so there wouldn't be any prints. And at the time I thought he reminded me of someone, but I didn't make the connection with Deems then.'

The sheriff nodded and said, 'Okay. Why don't you finish telling us what happened tonight, so you can go home.'

'After the flash, the man froze for a second, then took off in the direction of the light. I heard him crashing through the underbrush away from me. After a while, I couldn't hear him anymore. I decided to stay still for a long time. I wanted to be sure he wasn't waiting for me to move. I didn't have a watch, so I don't know how long I stayed put, but it seemed forever. When I thought I was safe I made my way to the Wallace cabin and Mrs. Wallace called you.'

'When the man ran off, did you hear anything else?'

'No, but there had to be someone else out there. The flash, those sounds.'

'Okay. I guess you'd like to shower and change. Why don't I take Mr. Stamm downstairs. We'll be in the living room when you're ready to go.'

'Tell me some more about Charlie Deems,' Sheriff Dillard said when they were downstairs.

'If Deems is after Abbie, she's in serious trouble,' Stamm said. 'He's a stone killer. As cold as they come. He tortured a rival drug dealer to death, then he killed a little girl and her father to keep the father from testifying. I sat in on Deems's interrogation. He never blinked. Smiled the whole time. Super polite. He treated the whole thing as if it was a joke. I watched his face when the jury came in with the death sentence. I'll bet his heart rate didn't go up a beat.'

'Would he try to kill Mrs. Griffen?'

'If he wanted to, he would. Charlie Deems is basically a man without restraints. I just don't know why he'd go to the trouble, now that he's out. Then again, rational thought is not one of Deems's biggest assets.'

Sheriff Dillard looked distracted and troubled.

'I'll tell you what concerns me, Mr. Stamm. Nothing was stolen. That could mean that the intruder was a thief who panicked. But I don't think so. If he was a thief, why follow Mrs. Griffen into the woods? Why hunt for her? No, I think the intruder was here to do your deputy harm.'

Chapter Ten

1

The Griffens' yellow three-story colonial stood at the end of a winding gravel drive on five acres of wooded land. A sawhorse blocked entry to the driveway. Despite the late hour, curious neighbors milled around in front of the barrier straining for a glimpse of the house and debating the cause of the explosion that had shattered the silence of their exclusive Portland residential neighborhood.

Nick Paladino drove through the crowd slowly, pausing in front of the sawhorse. A uniformed officer ducked his head down and looked through the driver's window. Paladino had the face of a gym-scarred boxer. The officer studied him suspiciously until the homicide detective flashed his badge, then he quickly moved the barrier aside.

Jack Stamm stared morosely out of the passenger window as the unmarked police car rolled slowly up the drive. The news of the explosion had stunned Stamm, who spent the ride to the crime scene blaming himself for not doing 'something' in the week following the attack on Abigail Griffen.

Paladino parked near a Fire Rescue Unit. The men from Fire Rescue were watching the bomb squad work. There was nothing else for them to do. There was no fire, just the shattered remains of a new Mercedes-Benz. There was definitely no one to rescue. The driver of the Mercedes was unquestionably dead.

Paul Torino, the Team Leader of the Explosive Disposal Unit, intercepted the district attorney and the detective before they crossed the barriers the squad had erected around the blast site. Torino was balding, five-eleven, thick through the neck and shoulders and bowlegged. He was wearing the unit's black combat fatigues under a Tyvex paper throwaway chemical suit, which protected against blood-borne pathogens.

'Put these on and I'll give you the grand tour,' Torino said, handing Stamm and Paladino Tyvex suits. Stamm slipped into his easily, but Paladino struggled to pull the paper suit over his beer gut.

'When did the bomb explode?' Stamm asked.

'The 911 came in at 10:35 P.M.,' Torino answered as he led them through the police barrier. Portable lighting had been set up to illuminate the front yard and someone had turned on all the lights in the house. The bomb squad members were searching the crime scene for parts of the bomb so they could discover how it had been made. One officer had been designated evidence custodian. Another sketched the area to show where each piece of evidence was found.

Stamm noticed a man photographing a jagged hole in the garage door. The ruined Mercedes was just outside the garage, facing the door. Stamm guessed that the car had been parked in the driveway and was backing out when the bomb exploded. He circled the Mercedes before looking inside. An acrid smell that had not been dispersed by the evening breeze hung in the air. The safety glass in the windshield was shattered but intact, but the side and rear windows had been blown out by the blast. There were shards of glass and chunks of bent and twisted metal scattered across the driveway and the front lawn. The roof on the driver's side was puffed out from the inside as if a giant fist had struck upward with tremendous force. Torino pointed out two one-inch holes in the roof and explained that they'd been made by pipe fragments. Then he motioned the two men toward the driver's window.

'When we get the chance to examine the underside,' Torino said, 'we're gonna find a large hole in the floor-board under the driver's seat. That's where the bomb was attached. Notice the seat belt.' It had been sheared in two. 'The victim was blown up into the roof, breaking the restraint. Then the body settled back in the bucket seat.'

Stamm took a deep breath and looked inside. Viewing a murder victim was never easy. It was infinitely harder if the victim was someone you knew. What helped here was the impression that the victim, slumped to the right, eyes closed, seemed merely asleep. The upper torso and head were intact, as was the body from the knees down, but there were massive injuries to the body between the knees and the torso. The pieces of flesh Stamm discerned were confined to the roof and the inside of the windshield on the driver's side and there was not as much blood as Stamm expected because death was the result of internal injuries. Stamm gathered himself and focused on the face once more, remembering it in life. He felt light-headed and turned away.

'Paul,' someone shouted from the garage. 'Look at this.'

The garage door was up now. Inside, a member of the bomb squad squatted in front of a white refrigerator that stood against the back wall. Torino bent over him and Paladino and Stamm looked in from the side. Embedded in the refrigerator door was a rounded piece of metal.

'Did it come through the hole in the garage door?' Torino asked the man who had summoned them into the garage.

'Yeah. We measured the trajectory. I'm glad I wasn't looking in here for a beer. I'd have me two assholes.'

'Have Peterson photograph this,' Torino said. 'Don't pry it out until he gets here.'

Stamm bent closer and noticed two short pieces of copper wire and something he could not identify embedded in the piece of metal.

'That's one of the end caps from the bomb,' Torino explained, 'and that's the remains of a lightbulb that was used as the bomb's initiator. When the bomb exploded, the end caps flew off like bullets in the direction they were pointing. This one penetrated the garage door and wedged itself in the refrigerator door.'

The squad member returned with the sketch artist and the evidence custodian.

'It's getting crowded in here,' Torino said. He led Stamm and Paladino outside.

'Paul,' Stamm asked the captain, 'you worked the Hollins bombing, didn't you?'

'The *Deems* case?'

Stamm nodded.

'I'm not surprised you asked,' Torino said, 'because I started getting a dose of déjà vu as soon as I saw that end cap. I just didn't want to say anything until the investigation was complete. I'll know for sure when we get all the pieces of the bomb, but I'd bet a year's salary that this bomb is identical to the bomb that killed Hollins and his little girl.'

2

Shortly before midnight, Jack Stamm followed Harvest Lane through Meadowbrook, a development consisting of twenty small but attractive homes scattered over three winding streets on the outskirts of Portland, a twenty-minute drive from the site of the explosion. Stamm parked in the driveway of a modern, one-story gray house with an attached garage. By the time a marked police car was parked at the curb, Stamm was ringing the bell and pounding on the front door. The small house was only a few years old. The development was so new that the trees provided no shade. The house was loaded with glass to catch the sun in the daytime. Stamm peered into the dark interior of the living room through the front window, then he turned to the uniformed officers whom he had ordered to follow him.

'Check the rear. See if there's any sign that someone's broken in.'

The officers separated and circled the house. Stamm was worried. Why was the house deserted? Just then headlights appeared at the end of the street. A car started to turn into the driveway, then braked. The driver's door opened and Abbie got out. She was dressed in jeans, a dark long-sleeved cotton shirt and a navy-blue windbreaker. Her hair was tied back in a ponytail.

Abbie looked at the marked patrol car just as the police officers came around the side of the house. Abbie looked from the officers to Stamm.

'What's wrong, Jack?' Abbie asked anxiously.

'Where were you?' Stamm said, avoiding her question.

'On a wild-goose chase. What's going on?'

Stamm hesitated. Abbie gripped his arm.

'Tell me,' she said.

Stamm put his hands firmly on Abbie's shoulders. 'I've got bad news,' Stamm said. An array of emotions flashed across Abbie's face. 'It's Robert. He's dead.'

'How?' was all she managed.

'He was murdered.'

'Oh my God.'

'It was a car bomb, Abbie. Just like the one Charlie Deems used to kill Larry Hollins and his little girl.'

Abbie's legs gave way and Stamm helped her to the front stoop, where he eased her down.

'I want you to listen carefully,' Stamm told Abbie. 'There's no evidence Deems did this, but the bombs are very similar. So I'm not taking chances. These officers are going to stay with you tonight and I'm going to arrange twenty-four-hour police protection.'

'But why Robert?' Abbie asked in apparent disbelief. 'He's responsible for taking Deems off of death row.'

'Deems is a sadist. Maybe he wants to kill you, but only after he's made you suffer by killing someone close to you.'

Abbie looked dazed. 'First the attempted break-in, then the attack on the coast. Now Robert is dead. I don't believe this is happening.'

'You're going to be all right, Abbie. We'll protect you and we'll find the person who killed Robert. But you have to be careful. You have to take this very seriously.'

Abbie nodded slowly. 'You're right. I can't believe I went off by myself tonight.'

'What were you doing out so late?'

'I got a call about a case. This man wanted me to meet him, but he didn't show up.'

'What time was this?'

'Around nine.'

Abbie paused, suddenly realizing why Stamm was asking about the call.

'You don't think the call and the bombing are connected, do you?' Abbie asked, but Stamm was not listening. He turned to one of the officers.

'Move your car away from the house, fast. Then get on the radio to Paul Torino. He's still at Justice Griffen's house. Tell him I need the bomb squad over here, right away.'

Stamm pulled Abbie to her feet and started dragging her toward his car.

'What are you doing?' Abbie asked, still too dazed to realize what was frightening the district attorney.

'I'm getting you away from the house until the bomb squad's checked it thoroughly. If you've been out since nine, the person who set the bomb in your husband's car would have had plenty of time to rig something here.'

Chapter Eleven

1

The small windowless room in the basement garage of the Portland Police Bureau looked more like a storeroom than the office of the bomb squad. Its walls were unpainted concrete and the floor was littered with cardboard cartons filled with scraps of metal, copper wire and pieces of pipe. A gray gunmetal desk next to the door was the only hint that the room was used for something other than storing junk, but the desk was covered with an unorganized collection of miscellaneous clutter and could have been mistaken for abandoned furniture.

Paul Torino opened the door and let Nick Paladino into his workroom. Paladino had taken the elevator from the Homicide Bureau to the basement after Torino called.

'What's up, Paul?'

'I want to show you something.'

Torino sat at the desk and gestured Paladino into a chair beside him. Then Torino cleared the top of the desk by shoving everything into a big pile on one of the edges. There was a torn cardboard carton next to one of the desk legs. Torino pulled several items out of it and placed them on the desk in a line. Then he drew a side view of a piece of pipe on a yellow writing tablet.

'This is a rough drawing of the pipe bomb that killed Justice Griffen. The bomber has to attach the bomb to the underside of the car and there is a simple way to do that.'

Torino bent over the yellow sheet again and drew a rectangle. Then he drew a horseshoe on the left end of the rectangle and another on the right end and placed a black dot in the center of the curve of each horseshoe.

'This is a strip of metal,' Torino said pointing to the rectangle. 'These are magnets,' he continued, pointing to the horseshoes. 'You drill holes in the strip and affix the magnets to the plate with nuts and bolts, then you tape the magnetic strip to the pipe bomb. When you're ready to use the bomb, you just have to stick it to the underside of the car.'

'Okay.'

Torino picked up a charred and twisted strip of flat metal approximately six inches in length, one and a half inches wide and one quarter of an inch thick.

'What do you think this is?' Torino asked Nick Paladino.

Paladino studied the object and the drawing. 'The metal strip that the magnets are attached to?' he guessed.

'Right. I took this from the evidence room this morning. It was part of the pipe bomb that killed Larry and Jessica Hollins. Do you notice anything unusual about it?'

Paladino took the metal strip from Torino and examined it closely. It was heavy. One end of the rectangle was flat and looked like it had been shaped by a machine. The other end was uneven and there was a notch in the metal that formed a jagged vee.

'The ends are different,' Paladino said.

'Right. This steel strip came from a longer strip. Someone put it in a vise and used a hacksaw to cut it so it would fit the top of the pipe.'

Torino pointed to the uneven end. 'Notice how this notch overlaps. That's because the person who cut it cut from two directions.'

Torino picked up a clear-plastic bag with another twisted and charred metal strip.

'When the bomb exploded yesterday, Justice Griffen was seated directly over it. This strip was blown through the bottom of the car into the judge. It's what killed him. The medical examiner found it during the autopsy. Take a look at the right edge.'

The similarities between the notch on the metal strip that had killed Robert Griffen and the notch on the end of the strip from the Hollins bomb were obvious.

'So you think the same person cut both strips?' Paladino asked.

'There's no way I could say that for sure, but I *can* say that I've only seen a bomb constructed like this once before. This is the bomber's signature. It's unique like a fingerprint.'

'So Deems is probably our man?'

Torino did not answer. Instead, he picked up the last item on the desk. It was also in a clear-plastic bag along with some metal shavings. Paladino examined it. It was a clean steel rectangle with one machine-cut end and one end that had been cut by hand.

'What's this?' Paladino asked, certain he knew the answer.

2

'Detective Bricker,' Tracy Cavanaugh said when the receptionist connected her to the Salem Police Department's Homicide Bureau, 'I don't know if you remember me . . .'

'Sure I do. You're Justice Sherzer's clerk.'

'Well, I used to be. I'm working in Portland now. I've got a new job.'

'I hope you didn't leave because of what happened to your friend.'

'No, no. The clerkship was only for a year.'

'How are you doing? Emotionally, I mean.'

'I think about Laura a lot, but I'm okay. The new job helps. I'm pretty busy.'

'That's good. What's up?'

'I wanted to know how you're doing with the investigation. Are there any suspects?'

'No. We believe Ms. Rizzatti was the intended victim rather than someone a burglar chanced upon, because someone ransacked Ms. Rizzatti's cottage. It may have been the person who rang the doorbell while she was leaving the message on your answering machine. But we have no idea who killed her, yet.'

'Oh.'

There was dead air for a moment. Then Detective Bricker asked, 'Did you have another reason for calling?'

'Yes, actually. It's . . . Did you hear about Justice Griffen?'

'Yes,' Bricker answered. Tracy thought she heard a little caution in the detective's tone.

'When I heard he was murdered, I couldn't help thinking . . . Have you considered the possibility that the two murders might be connected? Doesn't it seem like too big a coincidence? First Justice Griffen's clerk, and now the judge.'

'I contacted Portland PB as soon as I heard Justice Griffen was killed. Both agencies are looking into the possibility that there's a connection between the two murders, but right now we don't have any evidence to support that theory. Do you know anything that suggests the cases are related?'

'No. I just . . . I didn't know if you'd thought about it. I wanted to help.'

'I appreciate your interest.'

'Okay. That's all, I guess. Thanks for talking to me.'

'Anytime.'

3

When Nick Paladino finished explaining what he had learned from Paul Torino, Jack Stamm stood up and walked over to his window. Summer in Oregon was a dream. Snowcapped mountains loomed over miles of bright green forest. Pleasure boats cruised the Willamette, their sails a riot of color. Crime and despair should not exist in such a place, but the real world kept intruding on paradise.

'What about Deems? Do you know where he is?'

'He's vanished.'

'That's the same thing he did before he killed Hollins. And what about the similarity between the two bombs?'

'Torino described how to make that bomb at Deems's trial.'

Stamm turned away from the view. Paladino waited patiently for the district attorney.

'Is Paul certain about the metal strips?'

'I know you don't want to hear this, Jack. You don't need Torino's opinion. You can see the fit.'

'That's not what I asked, damn it.'

The detective looked down, embarrassed. 'Paul will swear they fit.'

Stamm picked up a paper clip from his desk and began to unbend it absentmindedly as he paced around the room. Paladino watched him. He knew exactly what Stamm was thinking, since he had been going through the same mental anguish since his meeting with Torino.

'Jesus,' Stamm said finally.

'I know how you feel, Jack. It's ridiculous. I don't believe it for a minute. But we have to deal with the possibility. Abbie has a motive, she has no alibi for the time the bomb was attached to Griffen's car, she knows how to make the bomb. Paul says he walked her through it step by step when they prepared his direct examination at Deems's trial.'

'This is total bullshit,' Stamm said angrily. He threw the mangled paper clip into his wastepaper basket. 'Nick, you know Abbie. Can you see her killing anyone?'

'No. And that's the biggest reason why I'm not gonna continue on this investigation. I know Abbie too well to be objective. You have to get out, too.'

Stamm walked back to his desk and slumped in his chair.

'You're right. I might even be a witness. I'll have to get a special prosecutor from the Attorney General's office. Shit. This is impossible.'

'I think you should call the AG right now and set up a meeting.'

Stamm was furious. He knew Abbie did not murder her husband. If anyone did, it was Charlie Deems. But even the possibility that one of his deputies was guilty made it imperative that his office turn over the investigation and prosecution to another agency.

The intercom buzzed. 'Mr. Stamm,' Jack's secretary said, 'I know you don't want to be disturbed, but Charlie Deems is here. He says he wants to see you.'

'Charlie Deems?'

'At the front counter. He said it was important.'

'Okay. Tell him I'll be right out.'

Stamm looked across the desk at Nick Paladino. The detective seemed as surprised as the district attorney.

'What the fuck is going on, Nick?'

'I don't have a clue, Jack.'

'You don't think he's turning himself in?'

'Charlie Deems? Not a chance.'

Stamm put on his jacket and straightened his tie. His office was only a few steps from the reception area. When he stepped into the narrow hall that led to it, he saw Deems sitting in one of the molded plastic chairs reading *Sports Illustrated*.

'Mr. Deems, I'm Jack Stamm.'

Deems looked up from the magazine, grinned and walked over to the low gate that separated the reception area from the rest of the office.

'I hear you've been looking for me,' Deems said.

'Yes, sir. We have.'

' Here I am.'

'Would you like to step into my office?'

'Okay,' Deems answered agreeably.

Stamm led Deems past his secretary and into his office.

'You know Nick Paladino.'

'Sure. He arrested me, but I don't have any hard feelings. Especially since we'll be working together.'

'Oh?' Stamm said.

'Yeah. I'm turning over a new leaf. I want to work for the forces of justice.'

'What brought about this miraculous conversion, Charlie?' Paladino asked sarcastically.

'While you're sitting on death row you have plenty of time to think about life. You know, life, what does it all mean. I don't want to waste mine anymore. I'm a new man.'

'That's very nice, Charlie. Is that why you came here? To tell us about your change of heart?' Paladino asked.

'Hey, I know how busy you guys are. If all I wanted to do was to tell you I turned over a new leaf, I'd have dropped you a letter. No, I'm here to help you catch criminals.'

'Anyone in particular?' Stamm asked.

'Oh, yeah. Some people I'm gonna enjoy sending to prison for a long, long time.'

'And who might they be?'

'How about Raoul Otero? I know everything about his operation: how he brings the stuff into the country, where they cut it and who's working for him. Interested?'

'I might be.'

'"Might be,"' he repeated. Then Deems chuckled. 'Mr. Stamm, right now you're creaming in your pants, but it's okay to play it cool. I respect you for that. Hell, if you acted real excited it would just encourage me to boost the price I'm gonna ask for the information.'

'And what is your price?' Paladino asked.

Deems turned slowly toward the detective. 'I'm glad you asked. First, I'm gonna need protection. Raoul isn't the forgive-and-forget type.'

'Get to the good part, Charlie,' Paladino said.

'Naturally, I'd appreciate some remuneration.'

'Why doesn't that surprise me?'

'Hey, if I'm working for you I can't be working for me. Let's not quibble over money. I'm risking my life here.'

'I'll check to see about the money. But you're going to have to prove you can deliver.'

'That's fair. Oh, and there's something else to sweeten the pot.'

'What's that?' Jack Stamm asked. 'Not what, who.'

'Who, then?'

Deems grinned broadly. He paused to savor the moment. Then he asked Stamm and Paladino, 'How would you like to know who iced Supreme Court Justice Robert Griffen?'

4

'All work and no play makes Tracy a dull girl,' Barry Frame said from the doorway of the office law library.

'Don't I know it,' Tracy said, looking up from the case she was reading. Barry sat down next to Tracy at the long polished oak conference table that took up the center of the room. Around them were floor-to-ceiling bookshelves filled with Oregon and federal statutes and cases.

'It's after eight, you know.'

Tracy looked at her watch.

'And I bet you haven't eaten dinner.'

'You win.'

'How about some Thai food?'

'I don't know . . .' Tracy stared at the stack of law books in front of her.

Frame smiled and shook his head. 'He's really got you going, doesn't he?'

'No, it's just . . .'

'I bet he gave you his "If you work for me, you won't sleep right, you won't eat right" speech.'

Tracy's mouth opened in astonishment, then she grinned sheepishly.

'He gives that speech to all the new associates and everybody falls for it. He even had me going for a while, but I wised up. Just because Matt practices what he preaches, that doesn't mean you have to become a machine. Whatever you're working on can wait until tomorrow. You won't be able to write your memo if you die of malnutrition.'

'I guess I am a little hungry.'

'So?'

'So take me to this Thai place. But we go Dutch.'

'I wouldn't have it any other way.'

Outside, the night air was warm, but not oppressive. Tracy stretched and looked up at the sky. There was a quarter moon and a sprinkling of stars. In the hills that towered over downtown Portland, the house lights looked like giant fireflies.

'Is the restaurant close enough to walk? I need the exercise.'

'It's about seven blocks. No sweat for someone who placed in the NCAA cross-country championships.'

'How did you know that?'

'Matt has me read the résumés he receives.'

'Oh. Did you read the one I sent about six months ago?'

'Yup.'

'Why didn't I get an interview?'

'You're a broad,' Frame joked. 'For what it's worth, I told him he was a jerk for ignoring you, but the Sorcerer's got no use for women. I couldn't believe it when he hired you. Justice Forbes must have made some pitch.'

'Why did you call Mr. Reynolds the Sorcerer?'

'Three years ago, Matt won that acquittal at Marcus Herrera's retrial. *Time* did a cover story and called him the Sorcerer because everyone was saying that only a magician could save Herrera. He hated it.'

'I think it's romantic.'

'It's also accurate. There are a lot of people who owe their lives to Matt's magic.'

'Why do you think he's so successful?'

'It's simple. Matthew Reynolds is smarter than anyone he's ever faced.'

Tracy thought about that for a moment. Matthew Reynolds was smart, but there were a lot of smart lawyers. If someone had asked her the question she had just posed to Barry, Tracy would have emphasized the hours Reynolds devoted to his cases. She had never met anyone who worked harder at any job.

'What drives him, Barry? What makes him push himself the way he does?'

'Do you know about his father?' Barry asked.

'Mr. Reynolds mentioned him during my interview. It sounds like he loves him very much.'

'Loved. Oscar Reynolds was executed at the state penitentiary in Columbia, South Carolina, when Matt was eight years old. He was sentenced to death after being convicted of rape and murder.'

'My God!'

'Two years later, another man confessed to the crime.

'Matt doesn't talk about it, for obvious reasons. His mother had a nervous breakdown when Matt's dad was sentenced to prison. She committed suicide a week after the execution. Matt stayed in a series of foster homes until a distant relative took him in. He never talks about what happened there, but I think it was pretty bad.'

Tracy felt she should say something, but she could not think of anything even remotely appropriate. What Barry had just told her was too enormous. And it certainly explained all of the questions she had about Reynolds's fanatic devotion to his cause.

Tracy tried to imagine what life must have been like for eight-year-old Matthew Reynolds, growing up with a mother who committed suicide, a father who was executed for a sex crime and murder and a disfiguring birthmark that would be an easy target for the cruelty of children.

'He must have been so alone,' Tracy said.

'He's still alone. I'm probably the closest thing he has to a friend.'

Barry paused. They walked together in silence, because Barry was obviously struggling with what he wanted to say and Tracy sensed it was important enough to wait to hear.

'There's another reason Matt's so successful,' Barry said finally. 'Other lawyers have a life outside the law. Matt's life is the law. And I'm not exaggerating. He literally has no interests outside of his job, except maybe his correspondence chess. I think the real world has been so unbearably cruel to him that he uses the law as a place to hide, a place where he can feel safe.

'Think about it. It's like his chess. There are rules of law, and he knows every damn one of them. In the courtroom, the rules protect him from harm. He can bury himself in his cases and pretend that nothing but his cases exist.

'And as a lawyer, he's needed. Hell, he's the only friend some of his clients have ever had.'

Barry looked down and they walked in silence again. Tracy waited for him to talk about his boss some more, so she could better understand him. Instead, Barry suddenly asked, 'Do you still run?'

'What?'

'I asked if you still run.'

'I've been getting in a workout on the weekends,' Tracy answered distractedly, finding it hard to switch to this innocuous topic after what she had just learned. 'I'm lucky if I get out at all during the week.'

'How far do you go?'

'Seven, eight miles. Just enough to keep the old heart and lungs going.'

'What's your pace?'

'I'm doing six-and-a-half-minute miles.'

'Mind if I join you sometime?'

Tracy hesitated. She wasn't sure if Frame wanted a workout partner or a date. Then she decided it didn't matter. It was more fun running with someone than running alone. Frame was a good-looking guy and she wasn't seeing anyone. She would go with the flow.

'I used to run after work on weekdays back in the good old days. But now I run before work, which means before dawn, when I can, and on the weekends.'

'Tell you what,' Frame said. 'Why don't we run about nine on Sunday, then eat brunch at Papa Haydn's.'

'You're on,' Tracy said, smiling, as she started to detect the direction the river was running.

Chapter Twelve

Assistant Attorney General Chuck Geddes reluctantly agreed to wait until the day after the funeral to interview Abigail Griffen, but only after Jack Stamm suggested that confronting a widow on the day her husband was buried might be seen as insensitive and in bad taste. It was the 'bad taste' part that swayed Geddes, who prided himself on his impeccable judgment in all things.

Geddes had the rugged good looks of the men who modeled in cigarette commercials, and he walked like a man with a steel rod for a spine. He had developed this marching style while in the Judge Advocate's office during his military service. His views were as unbending as his posture. When he lost a trial, it was always due to the judge's intellectual deficits, the underhanded tactics of an unscrupulous opponent or the stupidity of the jurors.

To give him his due, Geddes did win his share of tough cases. He had been appointed attorney-in-charge of the District Attorney Assistance Program at the Department of Justice because he was the most successful trial attorney in the section. Geddes was relentless, possessed of animal cunning and quite able to charm a jury.

The policeman guarding Abbie's house relaxed when he recognized Jack Stamm. As soon as Stamm parked, Geddes got out of the front passenger seat and straightened the jacket of his tan lightweight Brioni suit. Neil Christenson, his investigator, got out of the back seat while Geddes was adjusting his French cuffs. Christenson was third-generation law enforcement and a former state trooper who had been with the Department of Justice for nine years. He had the type of heavy build you would expect from an ex-Oregon State lineman who was too busy to keep in top shape but still managed to jog a little and pump iron on occasion. Christenson wore his hair in a crew cut, but his friendly blue eyes and easy smile made him less intimidating than normal for a man his size. While Geddes dressed to kill, Christenson wore a worn tweed sports jacket that was too heavy for summer, lightweight tan slacks, a blue oxford dress shirt with a frayed collar and no tie.

Abbie looked exhausted when she opened the door. She wasn't wearing makeup, her hair had only received a perfunctory brushing and there were dark circles under her eyes. She had made only the briefest attempt to clean up after the mourners who had followed her home from the cemetery. Overflowing ashtrays, dirty plates and partially filled cups of coffee littered the living room.

'How are you feeling?' Stamm asked.

'I'm doing okay.'

Abbie looked past Stamm to the two men who were standing behind him.

'This is Chuck Geddes. He's with the District Attorney Assistance Program at the Department of Justice, and this is his investigator, Neil Christenson.'

'My condolences. Justice Griffen's death was a terrible tragedy,' Geddes said, stepping around Stamm and offering his hand.

Abbie looked confused and a little wary. 'What's going on, Jack?'

'Can we come in?' Stamm asked. Abbie stepped aside. She looked at the mess in the living room and led everyone into the kitchen, where there had been some damage control.

'I've got coffee if anyone's interested.'

'Is it decaf?' Geddes asked.

'Not this morning,' Abbie answered.

Stamm and Christenson asked for theirs black, but Geddes demurred.

The kitchen window looked out at a small deck and beyond to a fenced backyard. A flower garden separated the fence from the lawn. Scarlet fuchsias, yellow gladioli and pink tea roses created a bouquet of bright colors that contrasted with the gloom in the kitchen.

'What brings you here?' Abbie asked when everyone

was seated around the kitchen table. Stamm looked at Abbie briefly, then looked down at his cup.

'I'm in a very unpleasant position. One that makes it impossible for me to continue the investigation of Justice Griffen's murder. The Portland police are also stepping aside. Chuck has been appointed as a special deputy district attorney for Multnomah County. It's his case now.'

Abbie looked perplexed. 'Why do you have to bow out? What happened?'

'There's no easy way to put this, Abbie. You've become a suspect in Robert's murder.'

Abbie stared at Stamm. 'Are you serious?' she asked with a confused smile.

'I'm very serious,' Stamm answered quietly.

Abbie looked back and forth between the three men. Then her features clouded. 'This is utter nonsense.'

Geddes had been sitting back, legs crossed, observing Abbie's reaction. 'We have a witness who claims you solicited him to kill Justice Griffen and evidence to support his story.'

'That's ridiculous. What witness? What evidence?' Abbie challenged.

'I'm not at liberty to say at the moment, but you can assist us in clearing up this matter by answering a few questions. Of course, I do have to warn you that you have a right to remain silent and that anything you say can be used to convict you in a court of law. You also have a right to consult with an attorney and, if you cannot afford an attorney, the court will appoint one to assist you, free of charge. Do you understand these rights?'

Abbie stared at Chuck Geddes in disbelief. 'Are you being intentionally insulting?'

'I'm being a professional,' Geddes answered with unruffled calm.

Abbie turned to Stamm. 'Is this for real, Jack? Am I a suspect?'

'I'm afraid so. And you should think seriously about talking to Chuck without counsel.'

Geddes glared angrily at Stamm for a second, then regained his composure.

'I don't need a lawyer, Jack. I didn't kill Robert. Ask me anything you want to.'

'Abbie . . .' Stamm started.

'She says she's willing to talk to us, Jack,' Geddes interjected forcefully. 'Maybe she can clear up the confusion. If we're on a wild-goose chase, let's straighten this out, so I can go back to Salem.'

Stamm did not regret warning Abbie, but he backed off. This was Geddes's case now.

'Mrs. Griffen, why don't you tell us where you were from nine to midnight on the evening Justice Griffen was killed?'

'I already explained that to Jack.'

'I know, but Neil and I would like to hear what you have to say firsthand.'

'I'm prosecuting a murder case involving a defendant named Jeffrey Coulter, who is represented by Matthew Reynolds.' At the mention of Reynolds's name Geddes leaned forward slightly. 'Reynolds's forensic experts conducted experiments in the Franklin home recently. The results were favorable to Coulter. The night my husband was killed, a man called around nine o'clock and told me that Reynolds's experts manufactured evidence at the Franklin home. He wanted to meet me immediately at the rose garden at Lewis and Clark College.'

'The rose garden is in an isolated area of the campus, isn't it?' Geddes asked.

'That's right. It's on the edge of the campus behind the outdoor pool.'

'Jack told me about your close call at the coast. Weren't you afraid of meeting someone in such a deserted spot so soon after being attacked?'

'I couldn't pass up the chance to nail Coulter. And I went armed. I was almost hoping it was the bastard who broke into my cabin.'

'Did you think about bringing backup with you?'

'The caller told me to come alone or he wouldn't talk to me. I didn't want to scare him off. It didn't matter anyway, because no one showed.'

'Can someone substantiate your story?'

'No. The parking lot was deserted by the time I got there and I didn't meet anyone.'

'Mrs. Griffen, was your divorce acrimonious?'

'I don't want to discuss my private life.'

'That's going to be a difficult subject to avoid.'

'I'm sorry. Robert is dead. What went on between us is over.'

'I can appreciate your reluctance, but this is a murder investigation. How many times have you asked that question of a suspect or a witness?'

'Many times, but I won't talk about my personal relations with Robert.'

'Okay. I can accept that, for now. What about your financial relationship?'

'What do you mean?'

'Is it fair to say that a divorce would have hurt you financially.'

'Yes, but I knew that when I filed.'

'Can you tell us about your relative financial positions?'

Abbie looked from Geddes to Christenson. Their faces showed no emotion. Then she turned to Jack Stamm. Stamm was hunched forward slightly and he looked like he wanted to be anywhere but where he was.

'I don't like the tone of this conversation, Mr. Geddes, or where it's going, so I'm going to end it. Jack is right. I should consult an attorney.'

'As you wish.'

'What is my status, Jack?' Abbie asked.

'Status?'

'Can I work? Am I suspended, fired?'

Stamm could not look Abbie in the eye.

'I think it's best if you take some time off with pay. You would have anyway, because of the funeral. I'll assign your cases to the other assistants.'

'And if I don't want to take time off?'

Stamm looked up. He was in obvious distress. 'You can't be at the office. You're under investigation.'

'I see,' Abbie said slowly.

'This isn't what I want personally, Abbie. For what it's worth, I'm sure you're innocent. That's part of the reason I stepped aside and turned over the investigation to the Attorney General. It's what I have to do as an officer of the law.'

Abbie stood up. 'I'm sorry if I was rude, Mr. Geddes. I'm very tired. I'll contact you after I've spoken to my attorney.'

'I understand,' Geddes said with a condescending smile. 'This is very unpleasant for me as well, Mrs. Griffen, but there is one more thing.'

'Yes?'

Geddes held out his hand. Christenson was carrying an attaché case. He opened it and handed a legal document to Geddes. Geddes gave it to Abbie.

'This is a warrant to search your home.'

'What!'

'I obtained it from Judge Morosco this morning.'

Abbie turned on Jack Stamm. 'You bastard. I thought you were my friend. I can't believe you'd do this.'

Stamm's face flushed in anger. 'I didn't know anything about the warrant, Abbie.'

'That's true, Mrs. Griffen. I didn't inform Jack. Neil, please signal the troopers.'

Christenson walked out the front door and waved a hand toward the far end of the block. Several car engines came to life and, moments later, three Oregon State Police cars pulled up in front of the house.

'I'd like you to confine yourself to one place in the house, Mrs. Griffen,' Geddes said. 'Or if you prefer, you can visit someone. We're going to search your car, so I can offer you a ride.'

Everything was happening so fast that Abbie had to fight to keep from being overwhelmed, but her anger gave her strength. She looked directly at Geddes.

'I'm staying right here,' she said, 'and I'm going to watch every move you make.'

PART FOUR

THE
PRISONER

Chapter Thirteen

1

'Mrs. Griffen,' Matthew Reynolds said as he walked across his reception area, 'there was no need to meet with me so soon after your husband's funeral. Mr. Coulter's case could have waited a few more days.'

'I'm not here about the Coulter case. Can we go to your office?'

A look of curiosity and concern crossed Reynolds's face as he guided Abbie down the hall. As soon as they were seated, Abbie asked, 'What can you tell me about Chuck Geddes?'

Reynolds didn't ask why Abbie wanted this information. Instead, he studied her while he gathered his thoughts. She was beautiful in black with a single strand of pearls, but she looked exhausted and sat stiffly, her hands folded, her face tight, as if she was afraid that she might break apart if she moved.

'Chuck Geddes is intelligent and single-minded, but he is rigid. As long as a trial goes as he's foreseen, he does a good, workmanlike job, but let the slightest thing go wrong and he can't bend with it.

'About four years ago, the La Grande district attorney called in the Attorney General's office to help in the prosecution of a complex murder case I was defending. Mr. Geddes was condescending to me at first. Then, as his case began to get away from him, he became strident, demanding and rude. I had the feeling he thought my legal motions were part of some conspiracy aimed at him.

'Two years later, we tried a case in John Day. He was offensive from the start. Paranoid about every detail. I prevailed on a motion to suppress the state's key evidence, so the case never came to trial. Later, I learned that he violated the discovery rules by failing to notify me about a witness whose testimony would have been damning. I have the impression that when he's under pressure he'll do anything to win.'

'Is Geddes ambitious?'

'Very. And now, if I may,' Reynolds asked, sighting Abbie over his tented fingers, 'why this sudden interest in Mr. Geddes?'

An array of emotions crossed Abbie's face. She looked down and gathered herself. When she raised her head, her features showed the strain of maintaining her composure.

'I need a lawyer to represent me.'

'In what type of case?'

'Yesterday, Geddes came to my home to question me about Robert's death. I'm a suspect.' Reynolds sat up. 'He had a warrant to search my house. They have a witness who says I'm involved and evidence that supposedly supports the accusation.'

'Who is the witness?'

'They won't tell me. Geddes treated me like a criminal.' Abbie's heart was beating furiously and she had to breathe deeply before she could say the next sentence. 'I have the feeling that it's only a matter of time before I'm . . . before they arrest me.'

'This is preposterous. Have you talked with Jack Stamm?'

'Jack is off the case. Geddes has been appointed a special deputy district attorney. He'll run the investigation and he'll prosecute.'

'I can give you the names of several excellent defense attorneys.'

'No. I want you to represent me.'

Reynolds looked at Abbie and she sensed that he was torn by conflicting emotions.

'I'm flattered, Mrs. Griffen, but I don't see how I can do that when you're prosecuting Jeffrey Coulter.'

'I'm not. I'm suspended. Dennis Haggard has the Coulter case.'

'Jack Stamm suspended you?'

'I was angry at first. I'm still angry. I'm furious. But Jack had no choice. I'm a suspect in a murder case his office is investigating. In any event, there is no conflict.'

'Why me?' Matthew asked.

Abbie's expression was grim. 'You're the best, Matthew. If I'm charged I'll need the best. They wouldn't have gone this far if they didn't think they had a case. Searching the home of a deputy district attorney . . .' Abbie shook her head. 'There's no way Geddes would have done that unless there was strong evidence of guilt.'

'Are you guilty?'

Abbie looked directly at Matthew. 'I did not kill my husband,' she said firmly.

Matthew studied her, then said, 'You have yourself a lawyer.'

The uncertainty that clouded Abbie's features vanished like mist evaporating in sunlight. Her shoulders relaxed and she slumped down, visibly relieved. 'I was afraid you wouldn't help me.'

'Why?'

'Because . . . I don't know. Coulter. The fact that I'm a prosecutor.'

'You're a human being in trouble and I'm going to do everything I can to protect you.'

'Thank you, Matthew. You don't know what that means to me.'

'It means our relationship has changed. First, we're no longer adversaries. We work together from now on. Second, I'm still an attorney, but in this relationship you're not. You're my client. That's going to feel strange to you. Especially since you're used to being in charge. From now on, I'm in charge. Can you accept that?'

'Of course. But I can help. I want to participate in my defense.'

'Of course you'll participate, but not as an attorney. It wouldn't work. You've seen what happens when a defendant represents himself. You're too emotionally involved to be objective.'

'I know, but . . .'

'If we're going to work together you've got to trust my judgment. Can you do that?'

'I . . . I don't know. I'm not used to being helpless.'

'I'm not asking you to be helpless. I'm asking you to trust me. As of this moment, your case is the single most important matter in this office. Do you believe that?'

Matthew's bright blue eyes blazed with a passionate intensity that transformed his plain features. Abbie had seen Reynolds like this before, in the Supreme Court, when he challenged the justices to be fair to Jeffrey Coulter. A calm feeling flooded over her.

'Yes, I believe you.'

'Good. Then we can begin. And the first thing I want to do is explain the attorney-client relationship to you.'

'I'm aware of . . .' Abbie started, but Matthew held up his hand.

'Do you believe that I respect your intelligence and your abilities as an attorney?'

'I . . . Yes.'

'I am not trying to insult you. I am trying to help you.

This is not a position you've been in before. You're a client and a suspect in a murder. I'm going to give you every piece of advice I give to every other client. I'm going to assume nothing, because I don't want to make the mistake of skipping a step because of the respect I have for your abilities.'

'Okay.'

'Abbie, everything you tell me is confidential. I will guard your disclosures completely. I am the only person on earth in whom you can confide with the certainty that what you say will not be repeated to the people investigating you.

'I don't want you to be upset by what I say next. I am a criminal defense attorney. Many of the people I represent are criminals and many of these people lie to me at some point during my representation. I am never upset when they lie. I know that people under pressure do things that they would never do under normal circumstances. So if you intend to lie to me, I won't be upset, but you could cause me to go off and do something that would put you in a worse position than you would be in if you told me the truth.'

Abbie sat up straight in her seat and looked into Matthew's eyes. 'I will never lie to you, Matthew,' she said with great intensity. 'I promise you that.'

'Good. Then tell me why Chuck Geddes thinks you murdered your husband. Let's start with motive.'

'We were separated, if that's what you mean,' Abbie said, coloring slightly.

'Was the separation amicable?'

'No.'

'Whose idea was it to separate?'

'Mine,' Abbie said firmly.

'Justice Griffen wanted to stay married?'

'Robert liked to live well,' Abbie answered, unable to hide her bitterness, 'but he couldn't do a lot of that on a judge's salary.'

'Surely he had his own money? I thought Justice Griffen had a successful law practice before he went on the bench.'

'Robert was intelligent, and he was certainly charming, but he was not a good attorney. He was lazy and he didn't care about his clients. He used to talk about what idiots they were. How much he was overcharging them. After a while, the clients caught on and complained to the other partners. Robert was losing clients. He was making good money at one time, but he spent what he earned and more. As I said, Robert really enjoyed the good life. He put his name in for the bench because his partners were carrying him and he knew his time at the firm was limited.'

'Why did the governor appoint Justice Griffen if his reputation was so bad?'

'It wasn't. Most people saw Robert's corner office with a view of the Willamette, read his name on the door of one of Portland's most prestigious firms and met him in social settings, where he shined.

'Then there were the markers. The firm contributed a great deal of money to the governor's campaign and they wanted Robert out. In all honesty, he wasn't a bad judge. He was always smart. And for a while he tried hard to do a good job. Robert wasn't evil so much as he was self-absorbed.'

Matthew made some notes, then asked, 'Who stood to gain if the divorce became final?'

'Robert. My attorney said he wanted a two-million-dollar settlement.'

Reynolds was surprised by the amount. He had never thought of Abbie as a wealthy woman, always assuming that Robert Griffen was the one with the money because he had been a partner in a prestigious law firm while Abbie worked in the district attorney's office.

'Could you afford that?' Reynolds asked.

'Yes. It would have been worth it to get him out of my life.'

'Two million dollars is a very good motive for murder.'

'He would have settled for less and I could have survived nicely, even if it cost me that much to get rid of him.'

'Most jurors would find it hard to believe that you could give away two million dollars and not care.'

'It's the truth.'

'I didn't say it wasn't. We're talking about human nature, Abbie. What the average person will think about a sum that large.'

Abbie thought about that for a moment.

'Where did your money come from?' Reynolds asked.

'My parents were both killed in an auto accident when

I was very young. There was a big insurance policy. My Aunt Sarah took me in. She made certain the money was invested wisely.'

'Tell me about your aunt.'

'Aunt Sarah never married and I was her only family. A few years before I came to live with her, she started Chapman Accessories in her house to supplement her income. It kept growing. She sold out to a national chain when she was fifty for several million dollars. I was seventeen and I'd just graduated from high school. We went around the world together for a year. It was the best year of my life. Aunt Sarah died five years ago. Between the money she invested for me and the money she left me, I'm quite wealthy.'

'I take it that you were very close to your aunt.'

'I loved her very much. As much as if she was my real mother. She made me strong and self-sufficient. She convinced me that I didn't have to be afraid of being alone.'

Abbie paused, momentarily overcome by emotion. Then she said, 'I wish she was here for me now.'

Reynolds looked down at his desk, embarrassed by Abbie's sudden display of emotion. When Reynolds looked up, he looked grim.

'You must never think you're alone, Mrs. Griffen. I am here for you, and so are the people who work for me. We are very good at what we do. You must believe that. And we will do everything in our power to see that you are cleared of this terrible accusation.'

2

Jack Stamm had assigned Chuck Geddes a room in the Multnomah County district attorney's office that overlooked the Fifth Avenue transit mall. With the window open, Geddes could hear the low hum of the city. The white noise was lulling him into a state of somnolence when he was suddenly struck by an idea.

Geddes sat up and grabbed his legal pad. If Neil Christenson could find evidence to support his new theory, that evidence would not just put a nail in Abigail Griffen's coffin, it would seal it hermetically.

When Geddes was through with his notes he made a call to the Supreme Court in Salem. Then he buzzed Neil Christenson and told him to come to his office immediately. While he waited, Geddes marveled at his ability to make this type of intuitive leap. There were lots of good prosecutors, Geddes thought with a smile of smug satisfaction, but the truly great lawyers were few and far between.

Geddes was so lost in thoughts of self-congratulation that the ringing phone startled him.

'Geddes,' he barked into the receiver, angered by the inopportune interruption.

'Mr. Geddes, this is Matthew Reynolds.'

Geddes stiffened. He genuinely hated Reynolds because of the way the defense attorney had humiliated him in court both times they had faced each other, but he would never give Matthew the satisfaction of knowing how he felt.

'What can I do for you, Matt,' Geddes asked in a tone of false camaraderie.

'Nothing right now. I'm calling because I understand you are in charge of the investigation into Justice Griffen's murder.'

'That's right.'

'I have just been retained to represent Abigail Griffen and I would appreciate it if neither you nor any other government agent contacts her in connection with this case. If you need to speak to her, please call me and I'll try to assist you, if I can. I already mailed you a letter that sets out this request. Please put it in your file.'

Listening to Reynolds give him orders as if he was some secretary set Geddes's teeth on edge, but you could never tell that from the way he calmly responded to Abbie's attorney.

'I'll do that, Matt, and I appreciate the call, but I don't know why Mrs. Griffen is so bent out of shape. You both know that the wife is always a natural suspect. I was sorry to have to upset her so soon after her husband's funeral, but we're not looking at her any more than anyone else.'

'Then you have other suspects?'

'Now, you know better than that. I can't discuss an ongoing investigation.'

'I understand,' Reynolds said abruptly, to let Geddes know that he was in no mood to play games. 'I won't keep you any longer.'

'Nice talking to you,' Geddes said, just as Neil Christenson walked in.

'Well, well,' Geddes mused, breaking into a grin. 'If we needed any more proof that Abigail Griffen is guilty, we just got it.'

'What proof is that?'

'She's hired Matthew Reynolds as her attorney.'

Christenson wasn't smiling.

'What's bothering you?' Geddes asked, annoyed that Christenson did not react to his joke.

'I think we should move slowly with this investigation. Something just doesn't feel right to me.'

Geddes frowned. 'For instance?'

'There's Deems for one thing. He's the worst possible person we could have for a key witness, especially now with Reynolds defending. Can you imagine what a lawyer like Reynolds will do to Deems on cross? He has a terrific motive to lie. Griffen put him on death row, for God's sake. And don't forget, Deems was the prime suspect before he waltzed into Stamm's office with his story.'

'Good points, Neil. But think about this. You'll admit Deems is intelligent?'

'Oh, that's for sure. Most psychopaths are.'

'Then why would he kill Justice Griffen with a bomb that is identical to the bomb he used to kill Hollins? Does that make sense? Or does it make more sense that someone who knew how Deems made the Hollins bomb, and who knew that the bomb squad would immediately connect the Griffen bomb to Deems, would use the bomb to frame Deems?'

'The point's well taken, Chuck, but I don't trust him.

Why is he here? Why would someone like Deems want to help the police?'

'That's simple. He hates Griffen for putting him on death row. Revenge is one of man's oldest motives.

'And don't forget the metal strip and her alibi, or lack of one. You don't buy that fairy story about the meeting in the rose garden, do you? Talk about leading someone down the garden path.'

Geddes laughed at his own joke, but Christenson looked grim. 'There's still the attack on the coast. Griffen said the man could have been Deems.'

'If there was an attack. Remember what Sheriff Dillard told you when you talked to him yesterday. But let's assume the attack did take place. Does it make sense that Griffen would go off in the middle of the night alone, and meet someone in an isolated place, a week after someone tried to rape or murder her? No, Neil, this little lady is weaving a web of bullshit and a jury won't buy it any more than I do.'

Christenson frowned. 'What you say makes sense, but I still . . .'

Geddes looked annoyed. 'Neil, I have no doubts about Griffen. She's guilty and I'm going to get her. I need an investigator on this case who's going to nail Griffen to the wall. If you feel uncomfortable working on this, say so. I can get someone else.'

'It's not that . . .'

'Good, because I respect your work.'

Geddes turned his chair sideways. He looked out the

window. 'You know, Neil, I'm not staying in this job for-ever.' Geddes paused. 'Gary Graham is not going to run for Attorney General after his term is up.'

'I didn't know that.'

'It's not public knowledge, so let's keep it between us, okay?' Geddes swiveled back toward Christenson. He put his forearms on the desk and leaned forward. 'If I put a top prosecutor away for the murder of a Supreme Court justice, with Matthew Reynolds defending, I can write my own ticket, Neil.'

Geddes let that hang in the air for a moment, then he said, 'When I make my move, I'm going to need good men with me. Men I can count on. Do you catch my drift?'

'Yeah, Chuck. I hear you.'

'It's not enough to hear me, Neil. I need your undi-vided loyalty. Do I have it? Are you going to give me one hundred percent on this?'

'I always give one hundred percent, Chuck.'

Geddes smiled. 'That's good, because I've just figured out how to bust this case wide open. Have a chair and hear me out.'

Christenson sat down. Geddes leaned back and folded his hands behind his neck.

'I've always believed that you solve a crime by figuring out the motive behind it,' Geddes pontificated. 'Now, what was Abbie Griffen's motive? We know the divorce would have cost her money, but she has a lot of money. So I asked myself, what other motive could she have had? Then I thought about *the way* Justice Griffen was killed.' Geddes shook his head. 'That type of carnage tells me that this was a crime of passion. The person who killed Justice Griffen hated him so much that she wanted to destroy him totally.

'Now, what breeds that kind of hate? Sex, Neil. Lust, jealousy. So I thought about the Griffens' divorce. Why were they splitting up? It had to be sex. Either she was cheating on him or he was cheating on her. That's when I got my idea.'

Geddes paused dramatically. Christenson was used to his boss's theatrics and he endured them stoically.

'Laura Rizzatti, Neil. Laura Rizzatti. It was under our noses all the time.'

Now Geddes had his investigator's attention.

'Did you ever see her, Neil? I have. The Supreme Court clerks use the cafeteria in the basement of the Justice building all the time. I once had lunch with her and Justice Griffen. That's what gave me the idea. Seeing them together.

'She was attractive. *Very* attractive. One of those full-bodied Italian girls with pale skin and beautiful eyes. I think the judge noticed just how good-looking she was.' Geddes paused. 'I think the good judge was fucking her.'

'Now, wait a minute . . .' Neil started.

Geddes held up a hand. 'Hear me out. It's just a theory, but it makes sense. Abbie Griffen's a good-looking woman, but she might be as cold in bed as she is in the courtroom. Suppose the judge got frustrated and started hitting on his clerk. The next thing you know, they're in the sack together.'

'We don't know that.'

'Don't we?' Geddes answered smugly. 'I've already done a little investigating on my own. Before I buzzed you, I talked to Ruth McKenzie at the Supreme Court. She was Justice Griffen's secretary. I asked her if she was aware of any unusual occurrences involving Rizzatti and the judge around the time Laura was killed. Do you know what she told me? On the very day she was murdered, Laura came to the judge's office in a highly emotional state. Mrs. McKenzie couldn't hear what they talked about, but Laura looked like she had been crying and the judge was very upset.

Christenson thought about Geddes's theory and had to admit that there might be something to it.

'First Griffen's clerk is murdered, then Griffen,' Geddes said. 'It's too big a coincidence, Neil. I think Abbie Griffen found out that her husband and Laura Rizzatti were having an affair and killed them both.'

3

As soon as Matthew Reynolds hung up on Chuck Geddes he told his secretary to hold his calls, then he went upstairs to his living quarters. Dreams come true, he thought as he climbed the stairs to the third floor. Sometimes we do have our greatest wish fulfilled.

Matthew entered his study without even glancing at his chessboard and locked the door. The bright midday light illuminated the room. Motes of dust floated on the sunbeams. He took the manila envelope from the bottom drawer and spread the photographs of Abigail Griffen across his desk. The photos did not capture her essence. How much more beautiful she was in person. How perfect. And she was his now.

Chapter Fourteen

'You're awfully quiet,' Barry Frame said as Tracy Cavanaugh turned off Macadam Boulevard onto the side street that led to the house where Robert Griffen died. It was a beautiful day and the top was down on Tracy's convertible, but Tracy was off in a world of her own.

'I knew him, Barry, and I liked him. He went out of his way to be nice to me after Laura was killed.'

'And it bothers you to work for a woman who might have murdered him.'

Tracy didn't answer.

'What if Mrs. Griffen is innocent? Matthew believes in her. If she's innocent and she goes to prison that's worse than dying. When you're dead, you don't feel anything. If you're alive and living in a cage for a crime you didn't commit, you suffer every second of every interminable day.'

'What are we supposed to be doing?' Tracy asked, intentionally changing the subject. Barry was tempted to push her, but decided against it.

'Now that the police have released the crime scene, Matt wants us to go through the house to see if we can find anything that might help Mrs. Griffen.'

'Didn't the police search the house after the explosion?'

'Sure, but they might have missed something.'

'It sounds like a waste of time.'

Barry turned toward Tracy.

'Matt doesn't consider any time spent on a case a waste of time. If we don't turn up anything, we can move on to something else. But Matt always asks, "What if we didn't search and there was something?" I've seen some good results in situations where I didn't think a job was worth the effort and Matt made me do it anyway.'

Tracy turned into the driveway. Matthew's car was parked in front of the house. He was sitting on the ground, his back against an old shade tree, his knees bent and almost touching his chin, looking impossibly out of place on the wide green lawn in his black suit, thin tie and white shirt.

Abigail Griffen drove up as Tracy was parking. Tracy studied their new client as Griffen got out of her car. She was dressed in a blue sleeveless blouse and a tan skirt, looking regal and self-assured in spite of the strain Tracy knew she had to be under. A woman who could take care of herself in any situation, a woman who was always in control. Tracy wondered how far this woman would go if she was threatened. Would Abigail Griffen kill if that was the only way to end the threat?

Griffen ignored Tracy and Barry Frame and walked over to Reynolds.

'Have you been waiting long, Matt?'

'I've been enjoying the solitude,' Reynolds said as he stood up awkwardly while brushing dirt and blades of grass from his pants. 'I'd like you to meet Tracy Cavanaugh, my associate. She'll be working with us. And this is Barry Frame, my investigator.'

Abbie acknowledged them with a nod, but didn't offer to shake hands.

'Let's go in,' she said.

The Griffen house had the musty smell of a summer home on the first day of the season. The doors and windows had been closed since the murder, trapping the stifling summer heat. Tracy felt queasy, as if there was insufficient air.

All the curtains were drawn and only a hint of sunlight filtered through them, giving the living room a pale yellow cast. Abbie went from window to window pulling back the curtains to let in the light. Tracy stood to one side near the entrance and watched Abbie move around her domain. The living room was spacious with a high ceiling. A white couch and several highbacked armchairs faced a stone fireplace. To one side of the grate, a set of wrought-iron fireplace tools hung on a long, twisted black metal hook. As Abbie opened the last curtain, a ray of sunlight illuminated the rich greens and browns of a forest scene portrayed in an oil painting that hung above an oak side-board. Then Abbie threw open a set of French windows. A fresh breeze rushed into the room. Just outside the doors were a patio and a circular metal table shaded by an umbrella. Beyond the patio was a rambling lawn with several large trees and a pool. The lawn ended where woods began.

'That's better,' Abbie said. She turned slowly, taking in the room.

'Where would Justice Griffen have kept his personal papers?' Matthew asked.

'In here.'

Abbie entered the den through a door at the far end of the living room and the others followed her. The room was windowless with dark wood paneling and floor-to-ceiling bookshelves filled with a combination of classics, popular fiction, history books, law books and legal periodicals. There was a Persian rug on the hardwood floor and a desk against one wall. A computer took up one side of the desk.

Abbie opened the desk drawers, but they were empty.

'It looks like the police were already here,' Abbie said.

'I assumed they had been,' Matthew answered as he looked around. 'Do you have a safe? Something the police wouldn't have been able to get into, where Justice Griffen might have put something he didn't want anyone to see?'

Abbie walked over to a small portrait that hung in a space between two bookshelves and lifted it off, revealing a wall safe. Abbie spun the dial and it opened. Matthew and Barry Frame crowded around Abbie as she reached in to bring out the contents. Tracy walked around the edge of the desk to try to see what Abbie had pulled out.

'Stock certificates, tax records,' Abbie said. 'I don't see anything unusual, Matt.'

The front door opened. Abbie turned her head. Barry left the den and stepped into the living room.

'District attorney's office,' someone said. 'Please identify yourself.'

'I'm Barry Frame, an investigator for Matthew Reynolds. We represent Abigail Griffen. This is her house and she let us in. We're in the den.'

A moment later, Barry reentered the room followed by Chuck Geddes, Neil Christenson and two uniformed officers.

'Hello, Matt,' Geddes said.

'Good afternoon, Mr. Geddes.'

'Mind telling me what you're doing here?'

'I'm Mrs. Griffen's attorney. This is Mrs. Griffen's home. We're here at Mrs. Griffen's invitation.'

'How did you get in and what are you doing in my house?' Abbie demanded. Matthew put a restraining hand on his client's arm and stepped between Abbie and Geddes.

'I was about to ask the same questions,' Reynolds said.

Geddes flashed a condescending smile at Reynolds. 'I'll be glad to answer them. I opened your front door with a key that the medical examiner found in your husband's pocket, Mrs. Griffen, and I'm here to place you under arrest for Justice Griffen's murder.'

Reynolds turned to Abbie. 'Not another word,' he said sternly. Then he turned back to Geddes. 'May I see your warrant?'

'Sure,' Geddes answered with a smirk. Christenson handed the warrant to Matthew, who read it carefully. Tracy was impressed with Reynolds's calm demeanor.

'I assume you'll agree to release Mrs. Griffen pending arraignment, after she's been booked and printed,' Matthew said when he was done.

'No, sir,' Geddes answered. 'Your client is charged with the murder of a Supreme Court justice. She's wealthy enough to be a serious flight risk. We're holding Mrs. Griffen in jail pending arraignment. You can ask for a bail hearing.'

'You're not serious. Mrs. Griffen is a deputy district attorney with an excellent reputation.'

'Save the passionate oratory for the judge. You got lucky the last time we were in front of one. Maybe you'll get lucky again.'

'This isn't about us, Mr. Geddes. Mrs. Griffen is a human being. There's no need to strip her of her dignity by making her spend several days in jail.'

'Mrs. Griffen is accused of premeditated murder,' Geddes shot back. 'She's the worst kind of criminal – a prosecutor who's broken the law. She's going to be convicted for the murder of her husband and I'm going to see that she gets a death sentence.'

Abbie paled. Tracy felt a shock go through her and she was suddenly very frightened for their client.

Reynolds stared at Geddes with contempt. 'You are a little man,' he said quietly. 'A tiny little man. I'm going to enjoy destroying you in front of everyone.'

Geddes flushed with anger. He turned to one of the policemen. 'Cuff her and take her downtown.'

Abbie turned to Reynolds. She looked scared.

'Go with them,' Matthew said. 'You know you have to. And don't say anything to anyone about the case. Not the police, not a cellmate, not a soul.'

'Matt I can't go to jail.'

Reynolds placed his hands on Abbie's shoulders.

'You have to be strong. Don't let them demean you. And trust me. I'll have you out as soon as possible.'

The policeman with the handcuffs looked embarrassed. He waited until Reynolds stepped aside, then politely asked Abbie to put her hands behind her back. When he'd secured the cuffs, he asked if they were hurting her. Abbie shook her head.

'Let's go,' Geddes said, executing a military turn and striding out of the den. Tracy followed Matthew outside and watched the officer help Abbie into the back seat of a police car.

'Do you think it was smart to insult Geddes that way?' Barry asked Matthew as soon as the police were gone.

'Mr. Geddes is no concern of mine,' Matthew said.

'Geddes has a thin skin. He's going to make everything extra hard now.'

Reynolds turned to Frame. Tracy saw an almost frightening determination on his face and in the way he held himself. She imagined his body as pure energy, and for the first time realized what a formidable adversary he would be.

'Leave Chuck Geddes to me, Barry. I have other work for you. If Geddes has an indictment, he'll have to make discovery available to us immediately. We'll soon know the identity of this mystery witness and their evidence. You're going to be very busy.'

Chapter Fifteen

1

The fourth floor of the Justice Center jail was reserved for security risks, prisoners with psychiatric problems and prisoners who had to be isolated. The jail commander had known Abbie for years and liked her. When she appeared at the jail on the preceding day, he booked her in personally, then made sure she was held in her own cell on the fourth floor, because he knew what would happen if he put a deputy district attorney in with the other inmates.

The jail elevator opened onto a narrow hall of concrete blocks painted in yellow and brown pastels. The fourth-floor contact visiting room was across from the elevator. It was small with a circular wooden table and two plastic chairs. Matthew stood when the guard brought Abbie into the room through a heavy metal door that opened into the jail.

Abbie's hair was combed, but she wore no makeup. There were dark circles under her eyes. The guard took off Abbie's handcuffs. She sat down and rubbed her wrists. Her face stayed expressionless while the guard was in the room. As soon as he left, she spread her arms to show Reynolds the blue cotton pants and short-sleeved blue pullover shirt that all the women prisoners wore. Then she flashed him a tired smile.

'Not exactly high fashion, huh?'

'I'm glad to see you haven't lost your sense of humor.'

'I know exactly what Geddes is trying to do. Do you think I'd let that asshole spook me?' Abbie paused. Her smile disappeared and she was suddenly subdued. 'It ain't been easy, though. I barely slept. It's so noisy. The woman next to me cried all night.

'There was one time, last night, when I was so tired I let my defenses down and started thinking about what it would be like to spend the rest of my life in a place like this. That's when I understood why the woman in the next cell was crying.'

Abbie caught herself. 'Sorry. I'm getting maudlin and I promised myself I wouldn't do that.'

'It's okay. That's what I'm here for. To listen. To help relieve some of the pressure.'

Abbie smiled again. 'I appreciate that. When's the arraignment?'

'Late this afternoon. They couldn't hold the hearing

sooner because they had to bring in a judge from another county. All the Multnomah County judges have a conflict, because they know you.'

'Who's the judge?'

'Jack Baldwin. He's from Hood River. Don't worry. I've appeared in front of him and he's all right.'

'Can you get me out of here?' Abbie asked, trying not to sound desperate.

'I don't know. Geddes won't give an inch. He'll want you held without bail and, as you well know, there's no automatic bail in murder cases.'

'What are you going to do?'

'I'm going to try an end run. Meanwhile, I've sent Tracy to your house to pick out an outfit for court.'

'Thank God. I don't know if I'm more afraid of the death penalty or having to appear in public in these awful rags.'

Matthew couldn't help smiling. 'You'll have to run a media gauntlet and I don't want you looking like Squeaky Fromme.'

Abbie smiled. Then her eyes lost focus and she looked tired and dispirited.

'What's wrong?' Matthew asked.

Abbie took a deep breath. 'I'm afraid I'll lose everything, Matt. My reputation, my career.'

'You haven't lost a thing and you're not going to. Geddes can't rob you of your pride unless you let him. You know you're innocent. It doesn't matter what the papers say or what the public thinks, if you can look at yourself in the mirror and know you're right.'

Abbie laughed. 'They don't let me have a mirror. Broken glass. It's a suicide precaution.'

Matthew smiled back. It was a perfect moment. The shared fears the shared intimacy, the trust she showed in him. He didn't want the visit to end.

'I have to go,' Matthew said reluctantly. 'I have an appointment with Jack Stamm in a few minutes.'

'Your end run?'

'If we're lucky.'

2

'It's been a while, Matt,' Jack Stamm said after they shook hands and Reynolds was seated across from him in the district attorney's office.

'Thank you for seeing me.'

'I'm not sure I should be,' Stamm said, unconsciously picking up a paper clip that lay on top of a stack of legal documents.

'You know what Geddes has done, don't you?'

Stamm nodded noncommittally.

'Do you think it's right?'

Stamm looked uncomfortable. He unbent one end of the paper clip.

'Abbie is a friend of mine,' he said evenly. 'I have a conflict. That's why I called in the Attorney General. I can't get involved in this case.'

'You're the district attorney of this county. As long as

Geddes is a special deputy district attorney, he's your employee.'

'That's true in theory, but you know very well that I can't interfere with Geddes.'

'Geddes is using this case to settle a score with me and for self-aggrandizement. You saw his press conference after the arrest.'

'We shouldn't even be having this conversation. I have to let him try his case.'

'I'm not asking you to interfere with the way he tries this case. I'm asking you to talk to him about his position on bail. You can't believe it's right for Abbie to stay in jail for months while we get ready for trial. I just came from visiting her. She looks terrible. She's trying to hold herself together, but you can see the toll the effort is taking.'

'Abbie is wealthy. She can afford to go to a country that doesn't have an extradition treaty with the United States. Geddes is afraid she'll rabbit.'

'Only if she's guilty. You know her far better than I, Jack. Do you think Abbie killed Robert Griffen?'

Stamm straightened the paper clip, then bent it in two. After a moment, he said, 'No. I don't think she's guilty.'

'Then how can you let Geddes keep her in a cage?'

'Look, Matt, you've tried cases against Geddes. You know how he gets. I've spoken to him, and he knows I think he's wrong. But he won't budge. What more can I do?'

'You can call the Attorney General. Tell Gary Graham what Geddes is doing. Tell him it's not right.'

'I don't know . . .'

'When you talk to Graham, tell him I assured you that Abbie will surrender her passport and she'll submit to ESP, the electronic surveillance program. I've already checked with the people who run the program and they'll supervise Abbie. She won't be able to leave her house without Geddes knowing immediately and she won't have to endure the jail.'

Stamm worried the paper clip while he thought over Reynolds's proposal. Then he said, 'I don't know if Geddes will agree but I think I can convince Gary to order him to go along.'

'Then please call Graham.'

Stamm hesitated. 'If I call Gary, there's something you'll have to do.'

'Name it.'

'Geddes is going to be furious because I went behind his back. And he'll be right. If I do this for Abbie, you've got to let Geddes save face. I want you to let him make the house arrest suggestion in open court and praise him for his thoughtfulness.'

Reynolds's lips quivered for a moment as he held back a smile. Then, without any emotion, he said, 'I have nothing personal against Mr. Geddes. I only want what's best for my client.'

'I'm glad to hear that. Now I want you to listen carefully.' Stamm put down the paper clip and leaned toward Reynolds. 'I'm going way out on a limb with this. I'm probably violating the Canon of Ethics to help a friend. Once it's done, I won't do anything more. Do you understand?'

'Yes.'

Stamm stood. He held out his hand. 'Do everything you can for Abbie. Good luck.'

3

The sun was fading by the time the technician from the electronic surveillance program finished hooking up an oblong foot-long box to Abbie's phone. Abbie was now wearing a bracelet with a tapered piece of metal attached to it. A computer at a monitoring center was programmed to call her at her home phone at random intervals. When the calls came, she had to answer the phone and state her name and the time, then insert the metal piece into a slot in the box. People at the monitoring center would be trained to identify Abbie's voice and the insertion of the metal strip confirmed her presence in the house. A unit in the bracelet also broadcast a radio frequency. If Abbie went more than one hundred and fifty feet from the box, a signal would go off in the monitoring center and trigger a pager that would alert the staff.

Matthew accompanied the technician to the door, then returned to the living room. The French windows were open and Abbie was standing on the patio, her arms wrapped around herself, looking at the sunset. Matthew paused to watch her. Abbie closed her eyes and tilted her head back, savoring the warm and comforting breeze.

The scene was something Matthew had dreamed about. He and Abbie alone at dusk at the end of a perfect summer day. Already there were long shadows creeping across the wide expanse of lawn, changing green into black where the silhouettes of the oaks and evergreens fell. On the horizon, the scarlet sun shimmered above the trees, its dying rays reflecting in the cobalt blue of the pool.

Abbie sensed Matthew's presence. She opened her eyes and turned slightly. He started, afraid she could read his mind, and frightened of what she would think of him if she knew his deepest thoughts. But Abbie just smiled and Matthew walked toward her.

'The police are gone,' he said.

'It's so nice just being alone.'

'I can go, if you'd like.'

'No, stay. I didn't mean you.'

Matthew stopped beside Abbie. It was part of the fantasy. Abbie at his side.

'I bought this house because I fell in love with it,' Abbie said wistfully, 'but I just couldn't stay with Robert after I found out he'd betrayed me. When I was living in Meadowbrook, I missed not being here. Still, I don't think I ever really appreciated how beautiful it is until tonight. Maybe everyone should spend a few days in jail.'

Matthew didn't answer right away, wanting the

moment to last as long as possible. Finally he said, 'It is beautiful.'

They stood quietly for a moment more. Then Abbie looked up at Matthew. 'Are you hungry?' she asked.

'A little.'

'The jail chow lived up to its reputation and I'm famished for real food. Will you join me?'

'I had Barry stock the refrigerator.'

'I know. You've thought of everything.'

Matthew blushed. Abbie laughed.

'When are you going to stop doing that? We're going to be spending a lot of time together and I can't always walk on eggshells so as not to embarrass you.'

'I'm sorry.'

'Don't be. So will you stay for dinner?'

'If you'd like.'

'Good, but you'll have to wait until I shower. I've got to get this jail smell off of me. Then I'll fix us bacon and eggs. Lots of eggs. Soft scrambled. And stacks of toast. Will that be okay? For some reason, bacon and eggs sounds so good to me.'

'That's fine.'

'There's coffee in the cupboard over the refrigerator. Why don't you make a pot while I'm upstairs.'

Matthew wandered into the kitchen, taking his time, savoring each moment. He lingered in the hall and ran his hand over the molding and along the wall. Somewhere on the second floor the shower started. Matthew strained to hear, imagining Abbie with the water cascading down her body. He was suddenly terrified by the possibility, no matter how fanciful, no matter how remote, of intimacy with a woman like Abigail Griffen.

After starting the coffee, Matthew sat at the kitchen table waiting for Abbie to come downstairs. She had asked him to stay with her. Would she have asked *anyone* to stay with her, just to have someone with her after her ordeal in the county jail? Was he special to Abbie in any way or was he simply an object she was using to ward off loneliness, like a television kept on through the night for the comfort of the sound?

The shower stopped. The silence was like an alarm. Matthew was as nervous as a schoolboy. He stood up and rummaged through the kitchen drawers and cupboards for silverware, cups and plates. When he was almost done setting the table, he heard Abbie in the doorway of the kitchen. Matthew turned. Her hair was still damp, falling straight to her shoulders. Her face was fresh-scrubbed. She wore no makeup, but she looked like a different person from the woman he had visited in the jail. There was no sign of despair or exhaustion. She glowed with hope.

The phone rang. They froze. Abbie looked at the bracelet on her wrist and the glow vanished. The phone rang a second time and she crossed to it slowly, her arm hanging down as if the bracelet was a great weight.

Abbie raised the receiver on the third ring. She listened for a moment, then in a lifeless voice said, 'This is Abigail Griffen. The time is eight forty-five.'

She put down the receiver and inserted the tapered metal strip that was attached to the bracelet into the slot in the box. The effort to answer the phone and complete this simple task exhausted her. When she turned around, the face Matthew saw was the face he had seen in the visiting room. He felt helpless in the presence of such grief.

Chapter Sixteen

1

'You are not going to believe who the mystery witness is,' Barry Frame said as he dropped the police reports in Abbie's case on Matthew Reynolds's desk.

'Tell me,' Matthew said, looking at Frame expectantly.

'I should make you guess, but you'd never get it.' Frame flopped into a chair. 'So I'll give you three choices: Darth Vader, Son of Sam or Charlie Deems.'

Matthew's mouth gaped open. Frame couldn't hold back a grin.

'Is this good news or what?' he asked Reynolds. 'Geddes is basing his case on the word of a drug-dealing psychopath who murders nine-year-old girls.'

Matthew did not look happy.

'What's the matter, boss?'

'Have you read all the discovery?' Reynolds asked,

pointing toward the thick stack of police reports.

'I barely had time to pick it up from the DA's office and make your copy. But I did read the report of Jack Stamm's interview with Deems. That was also a piece of luck. If Geddes had been the first one at him, he'd never have written a report.'

'Something is wrong, Barry. Geddes would never base a case on the testimony of Charlie Deems unless he could corroborate it. I want you and Tracy to go over the reports. I'll do the same.'

'Tonight?' Barry asked, knowing that his plans for the evening had just set with the sun. Reynolds ignored him.

'I want a list of our problem areas and areas where the prosecution is soft. I want your ideas on what we should do. It scares me to death that Geddes is confident enough to base his case on the testimony of Charlie Deems.'

2

Abbie was wearing tan shorts and a navy-blue tee shirt when she answered the door. Her hair was pulled back into a ponytail. Her legs and arms were tanned and she looked rested. When she saw Matthew her face lit up and he could not help smiling back.

Matthew was wearing his undertaker's uniform and Tracy looked businesslike in a gray linen dress, but Barry Frame was casually dressed in a denim work shirt and a pair of chinos.

Abbie ignored Barry and Tracy and took Matthew's arm.

'Let's sit outside,' she said, leading Reynolds onto the patio. A tall pitcher of iced tea and a bowl of fruit were standing on a low glass table next to Abbie's copies of the police reports. Matthew waited until Tracy and Abbie were seated, then he took a chair and placed his copies of the discovery on his lap. Barry took out a pad and pen. Tracy leaned back and listened.

'You've read everything?' Matthew asked.

Abbie nodded.

'What do you think?'

'The whole case is preposterous. The things Deems says, they're simply not true.'

'Okay, let's start with Deems's story. What's not true?'

'All of it. He says I asked him to come to the beach house the day of the attack and offered to pay him to kill Robert. That never happened. I haven't seen Deems since his trial and I've never spoken to him, except in court.'

'What about the dynamite?'

Abbie looked concerned. 'Robert did buy dynamite to clear some stumps on the property.'

'How would Deems know about the dynamite if you didn't tell him?' Barry asked.

'Robert kept the dynamite in a toolshed. Maybe Deems cased the cabin when he was planning the attack and saw the dynamite in the shed.'

'Was there dynamite in the shed on the day of the attack?' Matthew asked. 'Is it possible that Justice Griffen used all of it when he blew up the stumps?'

'I don't know. Robert told me he cleared the stumps, but he didn't say if he used all the dynamite.'

'Do you remember looking in the shed, the day of the attack?' Matthew asked.

'No. The shed's in back of the cabin. I wasn't in the back that much. Mostly I was on the beach or the front porch or in the house.'

'Have you gone to the coast since the attack?' Barry asked.

'No. I don't think Robert was there either. The court heard arguments in Salem that week.'

'Barry, make a note to go out to the cabin. We can check the shed,' Matthew said. Then he asked Abbie, 'Can you think of a way we can show Deems is lying?'

'No. It's just his word against mine, but his word shouldn't carry much weight. My God, he's the worst scum. I can't imagine why even someone like Geddes would give credit to anything he said.'

'But he did,' Matthew said. 'And Jack Stamm thought there was enough to it to call in the AG's office. Why, Abbie? What evidence do they have that corroborates Deems's story?'

Abbie shook her head. 'I've been over and over the reports. I don't get it.'

Tracy felt nervous about interrupting, but an idea occurred to her.

'Excuse me, Mr. Reynolds,' she said, 'but I know where we might be able to get evidence to show that Charlie Deems is a liar. Deems received a death sentence when

Mrs. Griffen prosecuted him. To get a death sentence from the jury, she had to prove he would be dangerous in the future . . .'

'Of course,' Abbie said to Reynolds. 'How stupid of me.'

Matthew beamed. 'Good thinking, Tracy.'

Abbie studied Tracy, as if noticing her for the first time.

'Who handled Deems's appeal?' Reynolds asked Abbie.

'Bob Packard.'

'Tracy,' Reynolds said, 'call Packard. He may have the transcripts of Deems's trial. It could be a gold mine of information about Deems's background.'

It was warm on the patio. While Tracy made a note to contact Packard, Matthew took a sip of iced tea. When Tracy looked up, she noticed the interplay between her boss and his client. From the moment he entered the house, Matthew rarely took his eyes off Griffen, and Abbie's attention was totally focused on him. Even when Tracy or Barry was asking a question, Abbie directed her answers to Matthew.

'How did you meet Justice Griffen?' Reynolds asked.

'I was prosecuting a sex-abuse case involving a minor victim. The defendant was from a wealthy family and they talked the victim's family into settling the case out of court for a lot of money. Robert represented the victim in the civil matter. We consulted about the case. He asked me out. The relationship became serious about the time the governor appointed Robert to the Supreme Court.'

'That's about five years ago?'

'Yes.'

213

'Was it a bad marriage from the start?'

'No,' she answered quietly, shifting uneasily in her chair and casting a brief look at Tracy. Tracy could see that the question made Abbie uncomfortable and she wondered if their client would have felt less self-conscious if there were no other woman present.

'At first the marriage was good,' Abbie continued. 'At least I thought it was. With hindsight, I can't really be sure.'

'What went wrong?'

'I guess you could say that our relationship was like the relationship Robert had with his clients,' Abbie said bitterly. 'He romanced me. Robert knew the right things to say, he could choose wines and discuss Monet and Mozart. He was also a wonderful lover.' Matthew colored. 'By the time I realized it was all bullshit, it was too late. I'm certain he talked about me to his other women, the way he talked about his clients to me.'

'Justice Griffen was cheating on you?' Barry asked.

Abbie laughed harshly. 'You could say that. I don't know their names, but I'm pretty sure there were more than one.'

'How do you know he was cheating?'

'He slipped up. One time I overheard the end of a conversation on an extension and confronted him. He denied everything, of course, but I knew he was lying. Another time, a friend said she'd seen Robert with a woman at a hotel in Portland on a day he was supposed to be in Salem. That time, he admitted he'd been with someone, but he wouldn't tell me who. He promised he would stop.

I told him I would leave him if it ever happened again.'

'And it did?'

'Yes. On May third. A woman called me at work and told me Robert was meeting someone at the Overlook Motel. It's a dive about twenty-three miles south on I-5, roughly halfway between Salem and Portland. The caller didn't identify herself and I never learned who she was. I drove down immediately hoping to catch Robert in the act, but the woman was gone by the time I got there. Robert was getting dressed. It wasn't a pleasant scene. I moved out the next day.'

'Check out the Overlook,' Matthew told Barry. 'Get their register and see if you can find out the identity of the woman.'

Frame made a note on his pad.

'Abbie,' Matthew asked, 'who do you think killed Justice Griffen?'

'Charlie Deems. It has to be. This is his revenge on me for sending him to prison. I'm more certain than ever that he's the man who tried to kill me at the cabin. And he may have tried to break into my house in Portland.'

'Tell us about that,' Barry said.

Abbie told them about the man she had frightened away on the evening Tony Rose accosted her.

'Did you report the burglary attempt?' Frame asked.

'No. I thought it would be a waste of time. He didn't take anything and I couldn't identify the man.'

'Barry,' Reynolds said, 'we have to find Deems.'

'There's no address for him in the discovery, Matt.'

Reynolds's brow furrowed. 'The discovery statutes require the state to give us the address of all witnesses they're going to call.'

'I know, but it's not there.'

Reynolds thought for a moment. Then he said, 'Don't ask Geddes for it. Get it from Neil Christenson. He's working out of the Multnomah County DA's office.'

'Gotcha,' Barry said, writing himself another note.

Matthew turned his attention back to Abbie.

'If Deems *didn't* kill Justice Griffen, who did? Do you have any other ideas?'

'No. Unless it was a woman. Someone he seduced then threw over. But I'm just guessing. If it's not Deems, I don't know who it could be.'

Matthew reviewed his notes, then said, 'There doesn't seem much more to discuss about the discovery material. Do you have any more questions, Barry? Tracy?'

They shook their heads.

'Why don't you take Tracy back to the office,' Matthew told Barry. 'Set up an appointment to view the physical evidence and get Deems's address. I have a few more things I want to discuss with Mrs. Griffen.'

'Okay,' Barry said. 'We'll find our way out.'

'Thanks for the iced tea,' Tracy said. Abbie flashed her a perfunctory smile.

'What did you want to ask me?' Abbie said when Barry and Tracy were out of earshot.

'Nothing about the case. Are the security guards working out?'

'I guess so. One reporter made it through the woods, but they got him before he could get to me.'

'Good. How are you holding up?'

'I'm doing okay, but I get depressed if I drop my guard. When I get blue, I remind myself how much nicer this place is than my cell at the Justice Center.' Abbie held up her wrist, so Matthew could see the bracelet. 'I'm even getting used to this.'

'Do you have friends who can visit?'

'I'm not the kind of woman who makes friends, Matt. I've always been a loner. I guess the closest I've come to a friendship is with some of the other prosecutors, like Jack or Dennis Haggard, but they can't visit me now that I'm under indictment.'

'But you must have friends outside of work?'

'I met a lot of people when I was married but they were Robert's friends.'

Abbie made a halfhearted attempt to smile and shrugged.

'My work was my life until I met Robert. Now I'm pretty much on my own.'

'Abbie, I understand how it is to be alone. All of my clients know they can call me at any time. I'm here for them and I'm here for you.

'I know, Matt,' Abbie said softly, 'and I appreciate that.'

'Please, don't give up hope. Promise me you'll call anytime you feel all this getting the best of you. Anytime you need someone to talk to.'

'I will. I promise.'

*

Barry turned his Jeep Cherokee onto Macadam Boulevard and headed toward downtown Portland. The road ran along the river and they had occasional glimpses of pleasure boats cruising the Willamette. Barry envied the weekday sailors and watched them longingly, but Tracy seemed oblivious to the scenery.

'What's bothering you?' Barry asked.

'What?'

'What's bothering you? You haven't said a word since we left the house.'

Tracy shook her head.

'Come on, we're a team. What's on your mind?'

'It's our client,' Tracy said.

'What about her?'

'I don't trust her.'

'Matt sure does.'

'You've noticed, have you?'

'I didn't have to be much of a detective to pick up on that,' Barry said.

'I mean, it's like a mutual admiration society,' Tracy went on. 'I don't think she gave either of us more than a glance the whole time we were at the house.'

'So?'

'Barry, Matthew Reynolds is a brilliant attorney and a nice man, but he is not the type of guy a woman like Abigail Griffen makes goo-goo eyes at.'

'Hey, don't put down the boss.'

'I'm not. I really like him. I just don't want to see Abigail Griffen take advantage of him.'

'How would she do that?'

'By using her obvious attractions to convince a vulnerable man she's innocent when she's not.'

'You think she did it?'

'I think it's possible.'

'Based on the statement of a scumbag like Deems?'

'Based on what I know about Justice Griffen. This business about his affairs . . . I don't buy it. If he was seeing other women, I'll bet she drove him to it.'

'Why does Mrs. Griffen have to be the bad guy?'

'Laura respected the judge.'

'Laura is . . . ?'

'I'm sorry. Laura Rizzatti. She was his clerk. She was murdered just before I left the court.'

'That's right. You found the body. Sorry, I didn't recognize the name.'

'That's okay. I don't talk about it.'

'Do the police know who killed her?'

'No. I call the detective in charge of the case occasionally, but she says they don't have any leads.'

'Let's get back to our client. Talk it out. If you've got something, we need to know. You were saying that Laura respected Justice Griffen.'

'She did. I don't think she'd feel that way if she knew he was a womanizer.'

'Maybe she didn't know. She only saw him at work. He might have been very different around his law clerk.'

Tracy stared out the window without speaking for a while. They rounded a curve and the Portland skyline appeared, tall buildings of glass and steel dwarfed by the green hills that loomed behind them.

'You're right, I guess I really didn't know Justice Griffen. I only saw him at work, too. It's just . . . Barry, he was a really nice guy. He was so concerned about Laura. I just don't see how he could be the way Mrs. Griffen portrays him.'

'What I'm getting from this is that you don't know the truth about Justice Griffen, but you don't like Abigail Griffen, so you don't want to believe what our client is saying. That ain't the way it works, Tracy. Nothing you've told me disproves anything Mrs. Griffen told us. We represent Abigail Griffen and our job is to save her butt. So until we learn otherwise, we've got to assume the worst about the deceased and the best about our client. If evidence turns up that convinces us otherwise, we'll deal with it. But for now let's operate on the theory that Justice Griffen was a cheat and a slimeball and see where that leads us.'

Chapter Seventeen

1

'I've got good news and bad news,' Barry Frame told his boss as soon as Reynolds walked through the front door. 'Which do you want first?'

'The good news,' Reynolds said as he headed for his office with Barry in tow.

'Christenson set up a time for us to view the physical evidence. He's bringing it to a conference room at the DA's office on Friday at ten.'

'Good. What's the bad news?'

'Geddes talked Judge Baldwin into issuing a protective order for Deems. They don't have to give us his address.'

Reynolds looked furious. 'That's preposterous.'

'Yeah, but Geddes convinced the judge to do it. The affidavit in support of the order is sealed, so I've got no idea what story Geddes cooked up to convince Baldwin to issue the order. The bottom line is I'm going to have to find another way to get the address.'

'Do it, then. Whatever it takes. We have to talk to Deems. He's the key to their case. I'm certain Deems is framing Abbie.'

'Why would he do that?'

'For revenge, of course. She put him in prison.'

'I know that's Mrs. Griffen's theory, but it doesn't make sense. Now that he's off death row, why risk going back to prison for perjury or worse, if he killed Justice Griffen?'

Matthew thought about that. 'Could someone have paid Deems to kill Griffen and frame Abbie?' he asked Barry.

'Sure, but why?'

Matthew shook his head. 'I don't know. We have to look deeper into Justice Griffen's background.'

Reynolds paused. Barry waited patiently.

'Barry, see if Deems has a bank account. If someone paid him to kill Griffen, it would have been a substantial amount. He may have put the money in an account.'

Barry laughed. 'You're kidding. A guy like Deems doesn't deal with banks, unless he's robbing them.'

Reynolds flashed Barry a patient smile. 'Humor me.'

'Sure thing. Oh, before I forget. Neil Christenson and I engaged in a little small talk. He let it slip that Geddes is really pissed at you.'

'Oh?'

'You did insult him when he arrested Mrs. Griffen.

Then there's the business with Mrs. Griffen's release. Geddes blames you for getting the Attorney General involved. We won't be getting any breaks from him. He's determined to get a death sentence in the case and he's going to fight us every step of the way.'

'Is that so?' The tiniest of smiles creased Reynolds's lips, as if he was enjoying a private joke. 'Well, back to work.'

Reynolds turned abruptly and walked away. Frame was about to go to his office when a thought occurred to him. When Deems was arrested for the Hollins murders, he tried to hire Reynolds to represent him. Barry was certain Matthew had talked to Deems two or three times before declining the defense, and he wondered if there was a file on the case with phone numbers and addresses for Deems and his acquaintances. Barry walked toward the back of the house where a rickety flight of stairs led down to the damp concrete basement where the old files were stored.

Tracy's office was near the basement door. She was at her desk, working at her word processor.

'Hi,' Barry said.

Tracy didn't move. Her thoughts were focused on the words that were scrolled across her monitor.

'Earth to Tracy.'

This time she turned.

'The Griffen case?' Barry asked, pointing at the computer screen.

'No. It's the Texas case. One of the issues in the brief.

The Supreme Court just handed down an opinion that had some useful language and Matt wanted me to expand our assignment of error to include a new argument.'

'Are you going to be working all weekend?'

'I'll be here Saturday, but I don't have any plans for the Sabbath.'

'I'm going to take some pictures at Griffen's cabin on Sunday. Want to come out to the coast with me?'

'I don't know. I should stay in town in case Matt needs me.'

'Matt will survive without you for one day. Come on. There's a beautiful spot I want to show you a few miles from the cabin.'

Barry held his hands out in front of him like a film director framing a shot.

'Picture this. We hike a mile or so through verdant woods and a field covered with wildflowers that create a riot of colors worthy of an artist's palette. Finally, weary, but at peace, we arrive at a rugged cliff overlooking a boiling ocean.'

Tracy laughed. 'And then what?'

'We have a picnic lunch. I've got a terrific Merlot I've been saving for a special occasion. Whaddaya say?'

Tracy looked at the pile of work on her desk. Then she made some quick mental calculations.

'Okay, but I want to clear it with the boss.'

'Tell him you're helping me investigate,' Barry said. Then he was gone. Tracy watched Barry walk away and smiled. He sure had a cute butt. They'd run together a few times and it had been fun. So far Barry had been a perfect gentleman, which was fine, but Tracy had decided she liked him enough to take matters a little further herself, if he didn't make a move. A romantic picnic in a beautiful setting seemed an ideal time to get started.

Tracy knew she was going to enjoy the coast, no matter what happened between her and Barry. She tried to remember what fresh air and sunshine were like. She had not seen much of either since she started as Reynolds's associate. Not that she was complaining. Working for Matthew Reynolds was everything she thought it would be. Still, the coast would be a great change of scenery after being cooped up with law books all week.

2

There were two addresses listed in the file Reynolds had opened for Charlie Deems. The first was for the apartment where Deems lived when he was arrested for the Hollins murders. Deems never returned to it. He had been in the county jail or on death row until his conviction was reversed. The apartment was rented to someone else now and the landlord had no idea how to reach Deems.

The second address was in a run-down section of north Portland. Barry Frame peered out the passenger window into the fading daylight and tried to read the numbers on a bungalow that stood back from the street. A chain-link fence surrounded the bungalow. Its gray paint was peeling. The yard had not been mown in weeks. One of the metal numbers on the front door was missing, but the other three numbers were right.

Barry opened the gate and walked up a slate path. Loud music blasted through the front door. Barry recognized grating guitars, rowdy drums and a sound that was closer to screaming than singing and quickly identified the group as another Pearl Jam knockoff. He rang the doorbell twice, then tried heavy pounding. Someone turned down the volume and Barry knocked again.

'Stop that racket. I'm coming,' a woman shouted.

The living-room curtains moved. Barry stepped away from the door and tried his best to look nonthreatening. A moment later, the front door was opened by a slender, barefoot blonde who was dressed in cutoffs and a bikini top. The shadows cast by the setting sun smoothed the lines hardship had etched into her features and for a moment Barry was fooled into thinking she was a teenager.

'Who are you?' the woman asked belligerently.

Barry held out his identification. 'My name's Barry Frame. I'm an investigator working with Matthew Reynolds. He's an attorney.'

'So?'

'Are you Angela Quinn?'

'What's this about?' she asked, cocking her hip and leaning against the doorjamb. The pose was intended to distract him and it worked. Barry could not help noticing her long, smooth legs and the impression her nipples made on the fabric of the bikini top.

'We're trying to get in touch with Charlie Deems. Mr. Deems consulted with Mr. Reynolds a few years ago and he gave him this address and phone number for messages. Are you Angela?'

Barry saw fear flicker in Angela Quinn's blue eyes.

'I don't know where Charlie is,' Angela said as she started to close the door.

'Wait. You were his girlfriend, right?'

'Look, mister, I'll make this simple. I dance at Jiggle's. Charlie used to hang out there and we were friends for a while. Then he killed that kid.'

Angela shook her head, as if she still couldn't believe it.

'Charlie wrote me from death row. I'm a sucker. I wrote him back, once or twice, because the guy doesn't have anyone else and I never figured I'd see him again. My mistake. The first place he goes after they let him out is my house. I let him stay. But he's gone now, and I don't know where he is.'

'If you dislike Deems so much, how come you let him stay?'

Angela laughed, but there was no humor in it.

'Mister, you must not know Charlie very well. You just don't say no to him.' Angela shuddered. 'The bastard stayed more than a month and that was a month too long. I hope I never see him again.'

'Can you remember when Charlie left?'

'It was about two weeks ago.'

'Do you remember hearing about a Supreme Court justice who was killed by a car bomb?'

Barry saw the fear again. 'Why do you want to know?' Angela asked, suddenly suspicious.

'Mr. Reynolds, my boss, is representing the woman who's charged with killing the judge. Charlie is going to be a witness in the case and we want to talk to him about his testimony.'

'I told you I don't know where he is.'

'Did Charlie ever say anything about the judge's murder to you?'

Angela looked like she was debating whether to talk to Barry.

'This is just between us,' he said, giving her his most reassuring smile.

'Why should I believe that?'

Barry stopped smiling. 'Look, Angela, I know how dangerous Deems is and I'm not going to put you in danger. I just want this as background. Did Charlie discuss Justice Griffen's murder with you?'

'No, he didn't say nothin' to me, but he was watching a story about it on the news when I was getting ready for work one night, and he seemed real interested. He even asked me if I had the paper, because he wanted to read about the killing. Now that I think about it, Charlie left right after that.'

'And there hasn't been any contact since he left? He's never called? You didn't have to send him any clothes? Stuff he left behind?'

'Nope. I have no idea where he is.'

'Well, thanks. You've been a real help. Here's my card.

If he does contact you, I'd appreciate it if you'd let me know where I can find him.'

'Yeah, sure,' Angela said. The door closed and Barry wondered how long it would take for his business card to find its way into the trash.

3

Charlie Deems sat on the back porch of a farmhouse in Clackamas County smoking a cigarette and watching the grass sway back and forth. It was the most exciting thing that happened at the farm, but that was okay with Charlie. Two years of living in a cell the size of a broom closet, locked down twenty-three out of every twenty-four hours, had taught him how to deal with idle time.

Out past the high grass was a stand of cottonwoods. Past the cottonwoods were low rolling hills behind which the sun was starting to set. Charlie felt content. His plans were moving forward slowly, but steadily. He was living rent-free and, except for a steady diet of pizza and Big Macs, he didn't have much to complain about.

As soon as Charlie was released from the Oregon State Penitentiary, but before he contacted Raoul, he reestablished contact with people who worked for Otero. Raoul had changed some of his ways of doing business, but for the most part the cocaine flowed along the same river it was travelling when Deems was working the waterways. For instance, there was a certain rest stop on the interstate where trucks from Mexico stopped on their way to Seattle. While the drivers relieved themselves, shadowy figures relieved the drivers of a part of their cargo that never showed on the manifest, then faded into the night. This evening, one of his babysitters had told him that several arrests had been made at that rest stop and a large amount of cocaine had been confiscated. Charlie's steak dinner reflected the DA's appreciation.

Charlie took another drag on his cigarette. He smiled as he pictured the confusion Raoul would experience as each piece of his organization crumbled. Soon the cops would catch the fish who was more afraid of prison than Raoul. Someone would wear a wire and Raoul's own words would weave themselves into the rope that would hang him. Then the grand jury would start to meet. It would take a while, but Charlie could wait.

What he could not wait for was the day he would testify against Abigail Griffen. He wanted to look her in the eye as his testimony brought her down. For two years, the bitch had been at the center of every one of his sexual fantasies. If he had a dollar for every time he had raped or tortured her in his dreams, he would be living in a villa on the French Riviera. And while he would certainly enjoy a chance to visit with Ms. Griffen personally, he felt greater satisfaction at the thought of Abbie pacing back and forth in the same concrete cell where he had spent interminable hours that crept by so slowly that sometimes he felt he could actually see the progress of each second.

Maybe Charlie would write to Abbie. He would send

her postcards from faraway places to let her know that he was thinking of her always. He imagined Abbie's beauty fading, her dark skin turning pale from lack of sunlight, her body withering. But even more satisfying would be the destruction of the bitch's spirit. She, who was so proud, would weep interminably or stare with dead eyes at the never-changing scene outside her cell. The thought brought a smile to Charlie's lips.

He glanced at his watch and stood up. It was almost 7 P.M., time for *Jeopardy!*, his favorite game show. He ground out his butt on the porch railing and flicked it into the grass. Free pizza, peace and quiet and all the game shows he could watch. Life was good.

Chapter Eighteen

1

Tracy parked her car in front of the Griffen cabin shortly after ten on Sunday morning. She got out while Barry reached into the back seat to retrieve his camera. It was cool for early September and Tracy was glad she'd brought a sweatshirt.

'I'm going to have a look around,' Barry said. 'I've gone over the crime-scene photos the Seneca County deputies shot and I've read the police reports. I thought I'd retrace Mrs. Griffen's steps. I doubt I'll find anything this long after the incident, but you never know.'

'Go ahead. I'm going down to the beach.'

Tracy saw the shed as soon as she rounded the corner of the cabin. It was tall and square and constructed from graying timber. The door was partly open. From where Tracy was standing, she could see a rake and a volleyball resting on a volleyball net, but no dynamite. She walked over and opened the door the whole way. There was an empty space that would have been big enough for a box of dynamite, but there was no box. She saw some rusted gardening tools and a barbecue grill. Tracy repositioned the door as it had been. She put her hands in her pockets, hunched her shoulders against the bracing sea air and walked down the path.

A flight of wooden steps led from the top of the bluff to the beach. Tracy sat down on the top step and let the wind play havoc with her long blond hair. High waves curled onto the beach, crashing against the sand with a sound that shut out the world. Tracy scanned the beach slowly, focusing on the low dunes and the gulls cruising the blue-green water, and thought about Barry Frame.

It had been a while since she'd had anything that could be classified as a relationship, but it wasn't anything she regretted. Tracy had decided long ago that being alone was preferable to being with someone she did not really care about. She missed sex sometimes, but having sex just to have sex never appealed to her. Tracy wanted love, or at least affection, from a partner. What she really missed was intimacy. Of course, sex with the right guy could be pretty good, too.

Tracy liked Barry's openness, his casual independence and his easy humor. And she thought he enjoyed her company as much as she enjoyed his. She also thought he was damn good-looking. Tracy had imagined what he would look like naked on more than one occasion. She also wondered what he would be like in bed and had a feeling she would enjoy finding out.

'Look what I've got.'

Tracy turned around. Barry was smiling and lipping the volleyball Tracy had seen in the shed from hand to hand.

'Are you finished?' she asked.

'All done.'

'Find anything?'

'Except for a vial of exotic poison, a Chinese dagger and a series of hieroglyphics written in blood, I struck out. Let's go down to the beach.'

Tracy stood up and they walked down the steps. When they reached the bottom, she ran ahead and Barry heaved the ball as if it was a football. Tracy caught it easily and returned it with a fancy overhand spin serve.

'Whoa!' Barry said. 'Very impressive. All you need are those weird shades and you're ready for ESPN.'

'You can't grow up in California and not play beach volleyball.'

'I love it here,' Barry said, tossing the ball back to Tracy underhand. 'When I retire, I'm gonna get a house at the beach.'

'If I had a beach house,' Tracy said as she served the ball back to Barry, 'I'd want it to be just like this place, so I could see the ocean. I'd have a huge picture window.'

Barry tried an overhand serve but the ball sailed over Tracy's head and bounced toward the water. They both raced toward it.

'You know the best thing?' Barry asked as they met over the ball at the water's edge. Tracy shook her head.

'Storms.' Barry bent down and picked up the volleyball. 'Have you ever watched a storm when the waves are monstrous and the rain comes down in sheets? It's incredible. When it's dark, you build yourself a fire and drink some wine and watch the whitecaps through the rain.'

'I had no idea you were such a romantic,' Tracy kidded.

Barry stopped smiling. 'I can be under the right circumstances,' he said softly.

Tracy looked at him, shielding her eyes because the sun was perched on his shoulder. Barry dropped the ball. Tracy was surprised, but pleased, when Barry took her in his arms and kissed her. His lips tasted salty and it felt good being held. She rested her head on his shoulder and he stroked her hair.

'Not a bad kiss for a lawyer,' he murmured. 'Of course, it could be beginner's luck.'

'What makes you think I'm a beginner?' Tracy asked with a smile. Then she grabbed a handful of his hair, pulled Barry's head back, planted a wet kiss on his forehead and dumped him in the sand.

'That was just like a lawyer.' Barry laughed as he pulled himself to his feet.

'Don't forget the volleyball.'

Barry held it in one hand and draped his arm around Tracy's shoulder.

'You ready to visit one of the most beautiful spots on the planet?' he asked.

'Yup.'

'Then let's go have our picnic. We'll hit the Overlook on the way back to Portland.'

They climbed the stairs. Tracy liked the feel of his hip bumping against hers and the pressure of his arm across her shoulder. Barry tossed the volleyball into the shed. Tracy saw it roll to a stop in the empty space as they headed for the car.

2

Barry's special place was everything he had promised and they had lazed around enjoying Barry's Merlot and each other's company until the setting sun reminded them that they still had work to do. Tracy drove fast along the winding mountain roads that traversed the Coast Range and they hit I-5 a little before six o'clock and started looking for the Overlook Motel.

'There it is,' Barry said finally, pointing past the freeway exit. Tracy took the off-ramp and drove down an access road for two hundred feet, then turned into the parking lot of the Overlook Motel. Sunset would save the Overlook's dignity by cloaking its shabby exterior in shadow, but by daylight it was a tired, fading, horseshoe-shaped failure with an empty pool and a courtyard of chipped concrete and peeling paint.

Tracy pulled up in front of the office. She took a close look at three bikers who were parking their Harleys in front of one of the rooms and locked her car. A heavyset woman in a flower-print muumuu was sitting behind the registration desk eating potato chips and watching a soap opera. She put down the chips and struggled to her feet when the office door opened.

'Hi,' Tracy said as she took her business card out of her wallet and handed it across the counter. 'I'm Tracy Cavanaugh. I'm an attorney. This is Barry Frame, my investigator.'

The woman read the card carefully, then studied Tracy through her thick-lensed glasses, as if she didn't believe Tracy could possibly be a lawyer. Tracy didn't blame her. She was wearing shades, her hair was pulled back in a ponytail and she was still dressed in the cutoffs and navy-blue tank top she had worn all day.

'We're working on a murder case and we'd like your help.'

'What murder case?' the woman asked suspiciously.

'You may have seen it on TV, Mrs . . . ?' Barry said.

'Hardesty. Annie Hardesty.'

'. . . Mrs. Hardesty. It's the case where the judge was blown up in his car. We represent Abigail Griffen, his wife.'

The woman's mouth opened. 'You're kidding.'

'No, ma'am.'

'I've been following that case and I don't think she did it. A bomb isn't a woman's weapon.'

'I wish you were on our jury,' Tracy said with a smile.

'I was on jury duty once. The lawyers wouldn't let me sit on any of the cases, though.'

Barry nodded sympathetically. 'Isn't that the way it always goes. Mrs. Hardesty, can you spare a few minutes to talk to us?'

'Sure.'

'You're not too busy?' Tracy asked.

'No, it's slow on Sundays. What can I do for you, honey?'

'We'd like to see your guest register for May third of this year.'

'I don't know if Mr. Boyle would like that.'

'Well, we could subpoena it, but then Mr. Boyle would be the witness.'

'You mean I might have to testify in court?' Mrs. Hardesty asked excitedly.

'If you're the one who shows us the register.'

Mrs. Hardesty thought for a moment, then bent down behind the desk and came up with the register. Tracy opened the ledger to May and scanned the entries for May 3, the day Abigail Griffen said she had confronted Justice Griffen at the motel. Seven people had checked into the motel that day. She took out a pen and copied the names. Craig McGowan, Roberto Sanchez, Arthur Knowland, Henrietta Rainey, Louis Glass, Chester Walton and Mary Jane Simmons.

'If Justice Griffen checked into the Overlook, he didn't do it under his own name,' she said.

'I wasn't expecting him to,' Barry said, laying a brochure about the Supreme Court on the counter. There were pictures of all the justices in it.

'Does anyone look familiar to you, Mrs. Hardesty?'
Barry asked. The woman studied the pictures intently.
Then she put her finger on Justice Griffen's picture. 'I've
seen him a few times, but I can't say when. Is that the
judge who was killed?'

'Yes, ma'am,' Barry said as he started to pick up the
brochure. Mrs. Hardesty stopped him. Then she put her
finger on the picture of Mary Kelly.

'Is that the wife?'

'No. Why?'

'She was with him one of the times he came here.'

3

'Tracy,' Mary Kelly said with surprise when she opened
the door to her condominium. Even wearing reading
glasses and without makeup, the judge was an
impressive-looking woman, and Tracy could see why
Justice Griffen would have been interested in her.

'I'm sorry to bother you so late, Justice Kelly. This is
Barry Frame. He's Matthew Reynolds's investigator.'

The judge studied Barry for a moment, then invited the
couple in. The condominium had a high ceiling and a
view of the Willamette. Her taste was modern and there
was a lot of glass and designer furniture in the living
room. A cigarette was smoking in an ashtray that balanced on the arm of a deep alabaster armchair. A
biography of Louis Brandeis was open on the seat where

Justice Kelly had left it when she answered the door.

'How's your new job?' Kelly asked. Tracy had the impression that the judge was asking the question to forestall her own.

'It's a lot of work, but it's exciting, most of the time. Sometimes, though, it's not so much fun.'

Tracy paused. During her year at the court, she had come to respect Justice Kelly and she felt very uncomfortable about questioning her, especially about her private life.

'I've been following Abigail Griffen's case in the papers,' Kelly said. 'How is it going?'

'We've just come from the Overlook Motel,' Tracy answered, her voice catching slightly.

'I see,' Kelly said, growing suddenly thoughtful.

'The desk clerk identified your picture and Justice Griffen's.'

Justice Kelly took a moment to think about that. Then she said, 'You two look too healthy to smoke. Do you want a drink?'

'No, thanks,' they answered.

'Sit down.' She placed the book on the floor, sat in the armchair and took a drag on her cigarette. 'I was hoping to avoid talking about Robert and me, but it looks like the cat's out of the bag. What do you want to know, Tracy?'

'Were you having an affair with Justice Griffen?'

Kelly laughed self-consciously. 'An affair sounds a little too formal for what we were doing.'

Kelly suddenly sobered. She looked very tired.

'Poor Robert.' She shook her head. 'I just can't imagine him dying like that.'

Kelly took a long drag on her cigarette and stared out the window. Tracy waited respectfully for the judge to continue. After a moment, Kelly looked up. Then she stubbed out her cigarette.

'Look, I'll make this simple,' she told Tracy quietly. 'My husband and I are separated. The whole thing is very amicable. I'm going to file for divorce as soon as I'm certain I have no opposition in next year's election. If my relationship with Robert makes the papers, the bad publicity could give someone the courage to run against me. If possible, I would appreciate it if you didn't go public about us. I doubt it has anything to do with Robert's murder anyway.'

'We have no interest in hurting you,' Tracy said, 'but I'll have to tell Mr. Reynolds. It's his decision.'

'I guess I'll have to live with that.'

'How did you two get together?' Barry asked.

'My problems at home were fairly obvious to an astute observer of human nature, like Robert. He was having his own problems with the ice princess. Since we had a problem in common, it was natural for us to talk. One thing led to another. Both of us were consenting adults. Neither one of us took the sex that seriously.'

'How long did it go on?'

'Two years, off and on. It wasn't a regular thing.'

'Why the Overlook?' Barry asked.

Kelly chuckled. 'Good question.' She lit another cigarette. 'It certainly wasn't the ambience.'

Justice Kelly laughed nervously again, then took a drag.

'Robert and I are public figures. We needed an out-of-the-way place where we wouldn't be seen by anyone we knew. None of our friends would be caught dead at the Overlook.'

'Did you meet Justice Griffen there on May third?'

'Yes.'

'Someone called Mrs. Griffen anonymously and told her Justice Griffen would be at the Overlook that day.'

'Robert told me about that. I gather Little Miss Perfect was pissed. She must have missed me by a minute or so. Robert, always the gentleman, assured me he didn't tell the little woman who I was.'

'You don't seem to like Mrs. Griffen,' Barry said.

Kelly drew in some smoke. She looked thoughtful.

'I guess I'm not being fair, since I only met Abbie a few times. I'm really echoing what Robert told me. Though Abbie did live up to her advance billing on the occasions we met.'

'How so?'

'Have you ever tried talking to her? To say she was a bit chilly would be generous.' Kelly laughed again. 'I guess I shouldn't throw stones. I've heard that I had a nasty reputation when I was practicing with my firm. It was just tough to get the time of day from her.'

'Maybe she suspected you were sleeping with her husband,' Tracy said, shifting uncomfortably when she realized that the statement, which she had not intended to be a reproach, could be interpreted as one.

Kelly stared at her for a second.

'That would explain it,' she answered bluntly.

'What did Justice Griffen say about his relationship with Mrs. Griffen?' Barry asked.

'He told me his wife was all work and no play, and barely tolerated sex. That would be tough for someone like Robert.'

'Who do you think tipped off Mrs. Griffen to your meeting at the Overlook on May third?' Barry asked.

'Probably someone he was sleeping with who was jealous.'

'Was there someone else?'

'I always assumed so. Robert was a rabbit where women are concerned.'

The statement shocked Tracy, but she concealed her surprise. She found it hard to reconcile her image of Justice Griffen with the blatant womanizer Justice Kelly and Abbie Griffen believed him to be.

'Do you have any idea who the other woman is?' Barry asked.

'No.'

'Do you have any idea who killed him?' Tracy asked.

Kelly crushed out her cigarette. Tracy thought she was debating whether to give her opinion. Then Kelly shrugged her shoulders and said, 'Abbie, of course. She's the first person I thought of when I heard Robert had been murdered.'

243

Chapter Nineteen

1

Bob Packard did not look well. He seemed jittery. His complexion was pasty and his skin was slack, as if he'd lost weight rapidly. Tracy wondered if Charlie Deems's lawyer had been ill recently.

'Thanks for seeing me,' she said as she took a seat in his office.

'No problem. What can I do for you?'

'I'm an associate of Matthew Reynolds. Mr. Reynolds is representing Abigail Griffen, who has been accused of killing Oregon Supreme Court Justice Robert Griffen.'

'Of course. I read about that in the paper. Boy, that was awful. You know, I won a case in the Supreme Court a few months ago and he wrote the opinion.'

'That's why I wanted to see you. Mr. Reynolds would like to borrow the transcript in the *Deems* case.'

Packard looked uncomfortable. He shifted nervously in his chair.

'If you don't mind my asking, why do you need the transcript?'

'Charlie Deems is the key witness against Abigail Griffen.'

Packard's jaw dropped and he looked at Tracy as if he was waiting for a punch line. When none came, Packard said, 'This is a joke, right?'

'Mr. Deems claims Mrs. Griffen hired him to murder her husband.'

Packard remembered worrying that Deems might try to harm Abigail Griffen. He'd been thinking about violence, but framing Griffen for murder was diabolical.

'The DA is buying Charlie's story?' Packard asked incredulously.

'He seems to be.'

'Well, if it was me, I'd be looking at Charlie long before I'd peg Abbie Griffen as a suspect.'

'Do you have any specific reason for suspecting Deems?'

'Are you kidding? Blowing people up is Charlie's thing, and he has plenty of reason to frame Griffen. She made putting Charlie on death row a personal crusade.'

'Mr. Reynolds thinks Deems is framing Mrs. Griffen, too. We're going after Deems and he thought there might be something useful in the transcript. Especially the penalty-phase testimony.'

'I'd be careful about going after Charlie if I were you.'

'Why's that?'

Packard remembered playing *The Price Is Right* and his stomach turned. He had been off cocaine, cold turkey, since Deems's visit, but he wished he had some snow right now.

Packard was quiet for so long, Tracy wondered if he had heard the question. Finally he said, 'If I tell you something, will you swear not to say where you heard it?'

'That depends. Our first loyalty is to our client.'

'Yeah, well, I have to think of myself. I don't want it getting back to Charlie that I talked to anyone about this. I've got him out of my life now, and I don't want him back in.'

Packard was fidgeting in his chair and Tracy noticed beads of sweat on his upper lip. She was surprised at how nervous he was.

'It isn't anything concrete anyway,' Packard went on. 'Not like a confession. It's just something you should know about Deems. I don't want to see anyone get hurt.'

'Okay. Go ahead,' Tracy said, curious to find out what Deems had done to scare Packard so much.

'Charlie Deems is crazy. I mean really crazy. He thinks he can do anything and nothing will happen to him. And the funny thing is, he's right. I mean, look at what happened with the case I handled. He tortures this guy Shoe, then he kills Hollins and his kid. The jury says death, but he walks away.'

'Most criminals don't think they'll get caught.'

'You don't understand. How do I say this?'

Tracy waited patiently while Packard searched for the words to explain why Charlie Deems terrified him.

'Charlie not only believes he can break the law with impunity, he believes he's impervious to any kind of harm.'

'I'm not following you.'

'He doesn't think he can be killed. He thinks he's immortal.'

Tracy's mouth opened. Then she laughed out loud.

'It's not funny,' Packard said.

'I'm sorry, but I'm not sure I understand you. Are you saying that Deems thinks nothing would happen if I shot him?'

'That's exactly what I mean.'

'Oh, come on.'

'I visited Charlie at the penitentiary when I was handling his appeal. At some point, we got to talking about what steps he should take if he lost in the Oregon Supreme Court. I noticed he wasn't paying attention, so I tried to shock him into listening by talking about his death sentence. Charlie just smiled. He told me he wasn't worried about dying because he has an angel who protects him.'

'An angel?' Tracy asked, thinking she had not heard Packard correctly.

'That's right. An angel. At first I thought he was kidding. I told him that with the stuff he'd done, the last thing he had was an angel. But he was dead serious. He said his angel is a dark angel. Then he told me this story.

'When Deems was in his late teens there was this woman he was screwing. An older woman. Maybe thirty-five. She was the wife of Ray Weiss, who was doing time for murder. Weiss was paroled. When he got home he beat up his wife because he heard she was cheating on him. She named Charlie as the guy.

'The wife had kept Weiss's handgun and ammunition in the house all those years. As soon as Weiss got the name, he loaded the gun and went looking for Charlie. He found him sitting on his front stoop. Weiss pulled the gun and accused Charlie of fucking his wife. Charlie denied everything. Weiss called Charlie a liar. Then he shot him. Charlie told me he was sure he was a dead man. The bullet hit him right in the chest. But the thing is, it bounced off.'

'It what?'

'The bullet bounced off Charlie's chest, just like in the Superman comics.'

'But how . . . ?'

'I asked a ballistics expert about the story. He said it was possible. The bullets had been sitting around all that time. Ten years. The powder could have gotten damp or oil might have seeped into it. Whatever the reason, Weiss was in shock. He fired again and the same thing happened. Charlie said Weiss's eyes bugged out of his head. Then he threw the gun at Charlie and took off running.

'Now, here's the scary part. Charlie told me that when the first bullet hit him, he saw the dark angel. She was dressed in a black gown that went from her neck to her feet. She was wearing sandals. He remembered that. And she had wings. Beautiful wings, like the wings of a dove, only huge and black. The angel loomed over Charlie with her wings spread out. When the bullet struck him, he saw a flash of light and the angel said, "I'll protect you, Charlie."

'From that minute on, Charlie Deems has believed that he can do anything he wants and nothing can hurt him. That means he can't be scared off and he can't be stopped, once he sets his mind to something.'

The story was so bizarre that Tracy didn't know what to say. How did you deal with someone who thought he was immortal?

'Tell Reynolds to tread very carefully where Charlie Deems is concerned,' Packard warned her.

'I will.'

'Good. Now, I'll get you those transcripts.'

'Thanks.'

'Don't thank me. I'm all too glad to get rid of anything that reminds me of Charlie Deems.'

2

Matthew Reynolds watched the light blinking on his personal phone line. All calls to the office were handled by an answering service after the receptionist left, but the personal line bypassed the service. Few people knew his private number, but he had given it to Abbie.

Matthew picked up the receiver, hoping it was Abbie. He had not seen her for two days, but she had never left his thoughts.

'Matt?'

'Yes.'

Matthew's heart raced.

'I remembered something. I don't know if it will help.'

'Tell me.'

'I shot a roll of film the day I was attacked at the coast. I forgot all about it in the excitement. When Jack drove me back to Portland, he packed up the car. He must have put my camera in the trunk. Then he brought my things in when we got to the rental house in Meadowbrook. Your investigator must have brought the camera when he moved my belongings here. I just found it. The film is in the camera. I think I took some shots behind the cabin. There might be a shot of the shed where the dynamite was stored.'

'Barry was at the cabin on Sunday. He looked in the shed and there was no dynamite. If we had an earlier picture of the shed . . .'

Matthew thought for a moment. 'What make is the camera?'

'It's a Pentax 105-R.'

'That could be a break. The Pentax date-stamps the negatives. That will prove the date the pictures were taken. If there is something useful on the film, Geddes won't be able to argue that the pictures were taken at a later date.'

'What should I do?'

'Don't do anything. Leave the film in the camera. I'm going to send Tracy Cavanaugh to pick it up. I'll want the camera, too.'

'Couldn't you come?' Abbie asked.

'I can't tonight.'

'Oh.'

Matthew could hear the disappointment in her voice and could not help smiling.

'I'm sorry. I'm handling an appeal in Texas. The man is on death row. The brief is due in two days.'

'You don't have to explain, Matt. I know you have other people who depend on you. It's just that . . .'

'Yes.'

'Oh, I was feeling sorry for myself. You cheer me up, that's all.'

'Good. That's the part of my job I like the best.'

Abbie laughed. 'Will I see you soon? I'm getting a little stir crazy.'

'I promise. As soon as this brief is done.'

Tracy brought the transcripts and a takeout order of kung pao chicken to the office as soon as she left Bob Packard. Deems's trial had lasted several weeks, so the transcript was twenty-nine volumes long. She was reading Volume III when Matthew Reynolds said, 'I'm glad you're still here.'

Tracy looked up from the transcript and saw Reynolds and the time simultaneously. It was 8:15. How had that happened? She was certain she had started reading at 5:30. Where had the hours gone?

'Mrs. Griffen just phoned me. We could be in luck. She shot a roll of film at the coast the day she was attacked. In the excitement, she forgot about it. I want you to drive to her home and get the camera and the film. Bring the film to a commercial developer first thing in the morning. I want a receipt showing the date the film was delivered for processing. Then bring me the camera.'

'I'll go right now.'

Reynolds turned to leave.

'Mr. Reynolds.'

Matthew paused.

'These are the transcripts from Deems's trial.'

'Ah. Good. I want a synopsis of everything you think will be of use. Make certain you give me cites to the pages in the transcript, so I can find the information quickly.'

'I'm working on it now,' Tracy said, holding up a yellow pad to show Reynolds her notes. 'Oh, and there's something Bob Packard thought you should know.'

Tracy told Reynolds about Charlie Deems's dark angel. As she talked, she watched Reynolds's face show surprise, disbelief and, finally, a look of amused satisfaction. She expected him to ask her questions about Packard or Deems when she was done, but all he said was 'That's very interesting, Tracy. Excellent work.'

When Reynolds was gone, Tracy shook her head. She could never tell what her boss was thinking and he rarely expressed his thoughts. He acted like an all-wise and all-knowing Buddha who silently weighed the worth of what he heard but never let on what he was thinking until it was absolutely necessary.

During the pretrial motion to suppress evidence in the Livingstone case in Atlanta, Tracy was unaware of the direction his cross-examination was taking until the moment before Reynolds sprang his trap. Tracy had been very impressed by Reynolds's technique, but she had also been a little upset that he had not confided to her what he was planning.

When Tracy clerked for Justice Sherzer there were never any secrets between them and she felt as if she was part of a team. Reynolds worked alone and at times made her feel like a piece of office equipment. Still, the opportunity to work with a genius like Reynolds was adequate compensation for her bruised feelings.

As she drove along the dark highway toward the Griffen place, Tracy realized that her feelings about Abigail and Robert Griffen had changed since her talk with Justice Kelly. The judge had cheated on his wife and to Tracy that was indefensible. She was also upset with herself for being so quick to conclude that Abigail was lying about her husband simply because she liked the judge.

On the other hand, Tracy had been around Mrs. Griffen enough to concur in Mary Kelly's opinion that Griffen was a cold, calculating woman who could easily have been frigid enough to drive Justice Griffen into the arms of other women. And the fact that the judge had been cheating gave Abigail Griffen a powerful motive for murder.

The Griffens' driveway had been resurfaced as soon as the police removed the crime-scene tapes, but here and there, on the edges, Tracy's headlight beams picked out burn marks and scarred asphalt. When she parked, Tracy saw Abigail Griffen standing in the doorway. Abbie was smiling, but the smile looked forced. Tracy wondered how long Mrs. Griffen had been waiting for her near the front door.

'It's Tracy, right?'

Tracy nodded. 'Mr. Reynolds sent me for the film and the camera.'

Tracy expected Abbie to be holding them, but her hands were empty. She did not see the camera on the hall table.

'Come in,' Abbie said. 'They're upstairs. Would you like a cup of coffee?'

'No, thanks. It's a little late.'

The smile left Abbie's lips for a moment. 'Oh, come on. I was going to pour myself a cup when you drove up.'

Tracy was going to decline again, but Mrs. Griffen sounded a little desperate.

'Okay. Sure.'

There were two settings on the kitchen table. Tracy realized that Abbie had been counting on her to stay. Tracy sat down. She felt uncomfortable. Abbie carried over the coffeepot.

'Do you take milk or sugar?'

'Black is fine.'

Abbie filled Tracy's cup. 'How long have you worked for Matt?' she asked nervously, like a blind date fishing for a way to start a conversation. Tracy got the feeling that making small talk was not one of Abbie's strengths.

'Not long,' Tracy answered tersely, unwilling to have their relationship be anything more than a professional one while she still harbored doubts about Abbie.

'You clerked for Alice Sherzer, didn't you?'

'Yes. How did you know?'

Abbie smiled. 'You looked familiar. I visited Robert at the court occasionally. He may have pointed you out. Did you enjoy your clerkship?'

'Yes. Justice Sherzer is a remarkable woman.'

Abbie sipped at her coffee. Tracy sipped at hers. The silence grew. Tracy shifted in her seat.

'Are you working with Matt on my case?'

'I'm reviewing the evidence to see if we've got any good legal motions.'

'And what have you concluded?'

Tracy hesitated. She wasn't sure that Reynolds would want her to answer the question, but Abigail Griffen was no ordinary client. She was also a brilliant attorney. And Tracy was relieved to be freed from making small talk.

'I haven't reached a final decision, but I don't think we're going to win this case on a legal technicality. Do you have any ideas for a pretrial motion?'

Abbie shook her head. 'I've thought about it, but I don't see anything either. What's it like working for Matt?'

'I like it,' Tracy answered guardedly, not willing to discuss her boss with Griffen.

'He seems like such a strange man,' Abbie said. When Tracy didn't respond, she asked, 'Is he as passionate about all his cases as he is about mine?'

'He's very dedicated to his clients,' Tracy answered in a neutral tone.

Abbie's eyes lost focus for a moment. Tracy waited uncomfortably for the conversation to resume. 'He used to watch my trials. Did you know that?'

There was no rhythm to their discussion and the statement fell into the conversation like a heavy object. Tracy remembered seeing Reynolds at the Marie Harwood trial, but she wasn't certain where Mrs. Griffen was going, so she didn't respond. Abbie went on as if she had not expected a response.

'I saw him more than once in the back of the courtroom, watching me. He would sit for a while, then leave. I don't think he realized that I'd seen him.'

Abbie looked directly at Tracy when she said this. Tracy felt compelled to say something.

'What do you think he was doing there?'

Abbie warmed her hands on her cup. Instead of answering Tracy's question, she changed the subject.

'Does Matt like me?'

'What?'

The question made Tracy very uncomfortable.

'Has he said anything . . . ?' She paused and looked across the table at Tracy. 'Do you think he likes me?'

All of a sudden, Abigail Griffen seemed terribly vulnerable to Tracy.

'I think he believes you,' she replied, warming to Abbie a little.

'Yes. He does,' Abbie said, more to herself than to Tracy.

Tracy was surprised to find herself feeling sorry for Abbie. She had thought a lot about her as a defendant, but she suddenly saw her as a person and she wondered what it must be like to be confined, even if the prison was as luxurious as the Griffen house. Mary Kelly had portrayed Abbie as an ice princess, but she did not seem very tough now.

Tracy suddenly realized how sad it was that Mrs. Griffen had looked forward to her visit and she reevaluated her earlier opinion that Abbie was coming on to Reynolds to blind him to her possible guilt. Abbie was totally alone and Matthew was one of her few links to the outside world. Tracy had read about hostages in the Middle East and kidnap victims, like Patty Hearst, who became dependent on their kidnappers and developed a bond with them. The condition even had a name, the Stockholm syndrome. Maybe Abbie's enforced isolation was making her dependent on Reynolds and that was why she appeared to be playing up to him.

'Are you getting along okay?' Tracy asked.

'I'm lonely. I'm also bored to death. I tried to convince myself that this would be like a vacation, but it's not. I read a lot, but you can't read all day. I even tried daytime television.' Abbie laughed. 'I'll know I'm completely desperate when I start following the soaps.'

'The trial will start soon. Mr. Reynolds will win and your life will go back to normal.'

'I'd like to think that, but I doubt my life will ever be normal again, even if Matt wins.' Abbie stood up. 'I'll get you the camera.'

When Abbie went upstairs, Tracy waited in the entryway. Abbie returned with a camera case. She handed it to Tracy.

'Thank you for having the cup of coffee. I know you didn't want to.'

'No, I . . .'

'It's okay. I was hungry for company. Thanks for putting up with me.'

They shook hands and Tracy took the camera. As she pulled out of the driveway, she glanced back at the house. Mrs. Griffen was watching her from the front door.

3

2313 Lee Terrace was a single-story brown ranch-style house with a well-tended yard in a pleasant middle-class neighborhood. A nondescript light blue Chevy and an equally nondescript maroon Ford were parked in the driveway. As the officers assigned to raid the house drew closer to it, they could hear the muted sounds of music.

Inside the living room of the house, three young

women sat in front of a low coffee table talking and laughing while they worked. In the center of the table was a large plate piled high with cocaine. The woman on the end of the couch closest to the front door picked up a small plastic bag from a pile and filled the bag with cocaine. The next woman folded over the Baggie, then used a Bic lighter to seal it. The third put the sealed Baggie in a cooking pot that was close to overflowing with packaged dreams.

Two men in sleeveless tee shirts lounged in chairs, smoking and watching MTV. One man cradled an Uzi. A MAC-10 submachine gun was lying next to the second man's chair within easy reach. Two other men with automatic weapons were in the kitchen playing cards and guarding the back of the house.

Bobby Cruz watched the women work. He was doing his job, which was to protect Raoul Otero's product. From his position he would see if one of the women tried to slip a Baggie down her blouse or up her skirt. Cruz knew that the women were too frightened of him to steal, but he hoped they would anyway, because Raoul permitted him to personally punish the offender.

'Julio,' Cruz said. One of the men watching TV turned around. 'I'm going to pee.'

Julio picked up the MAC-10 and took Cruz's post against the wall. Cruz knew that Julio would not be tempted to look the other way by a glimpse of breast or thigh and a promise of future delights. Once upon a time, Cruz had forced Julio to assist him while he interrogated

a street dealer Raoul suspected of being a police informant. Ever since, Julio had been as frightened of Cruz as the
women were.

As Cruz walked down the hall toward the bathroom,
the front and back doors exploded.

'Police! Freeze!' echoed through the house. Cruz heard
the women scream. One of them burst down the hall
behind him as he ducked into the bedroom. There were
more screams in the front room and shots from the
kitchen. Someone was shrieking in Spanish. An Anglo
was bellowing that he'd been hit. Cruz calmly ran through
his possible courses of action.

'Put 'em down,' someone yelled in the living room.
Cruz opened the clothes closet and moved behind the
clothes hangers. The closet was crowded with dresses
because two of the women who were packaging the
cocaine lived here. Cruz pressed himself into a corner of
the closet and waited. The odds were that someone would
search the closet. If it was his fate to be arrested, he would
go peacefully and let Raoul fix things later. But he would
try to cheat fate if that was at all possible.

There were heavy footfalls in the bedroom. He heard
the voices of two men. The closet door opened. Cruz could
see a man in a baseball cap and a blue jacket through a
break in the dresses. He knew these jackets. They were
worn on raids, and POLICE was stenciled on the back in
bold yellow letters.

'Sanchez, get in here,' someone called from the hall.
'This asshole claims he doesn't *habla inglés*.'

The man at the closet door turned his head to watch Sanchez leave. When he turned back, Bobby Cruz stepped through the curtain of dresses and calmly stuck his knife through the officer's voice box. The policeman's eyes widened in shock. His hands flew to his throat. He tried to speak, but he could only gurgle as blood and spittle dripped out of his mouth. Cruz pulled the policeman through the dresses and laid his body on the floor. He was still twitching when Cruz worked off his jacket, but he was dead by the time Cruz adjusted the baseball cap and slipped out of the bedroom into the hall.

A policeman rushed by Cruz without seeing him. Cruz followed the man into the kitchen. Two men lay on the floor, their hands cuffed behind them. They were surrounded by police. A wounded officer was moaning near the sink and several men huddled around him. A medic rushed through the back door into the kitchen. Cruz stepped aside to let him in, then drifted into the backyard and faded into the night.

Two houses down, Cruz cut through the backyard, dropping the police jacket and cap. Then he headed toward a bar that he knew had a phone. In the three years Raoul had been using 2313 Lee Terrace they had never had any problems. The people at the house were all family or trusted employees and they were all extremely well paid. They might cop some cocaine, but they would never go to the police. But someone had, and whoever it was knew a lot about Raoul's operation if he knew about Lee Terrace.

PART FIVE
THE MAGIC
SHOW

Chapter Twenty

1

Matthew Reynolds chose five o'clock on the Friday before the trial to review the questions he would ask during jury selection. Tracy knew better than to complain. With the trial so close, all hours were working hours.

Reynolds was explaining his system for questioning jurors about their views on the death penalty when his secretary buzzed to tell him that Dennis Haggard was in the reception area.

'Do you want me to leave?' Tracy asked.

'No. I definitely want you to stay. This could be very interesting.'

Dennis Haggard was balding, overweight and unintimidating. He was also Jack Stamm's chief criminal deputy and an excellent trial attorney. Reynolds walked over to Haggard as soon as the secretary showed him in.

'Don't you ever quit?' Haggard asked as he looked at the files, charts and police reports strewn around Matthew's office.

Matthew smiled and pointed to his associate. 'Do you know Tracy Cavanaugh?'

'I don't think we've met.'

'She just started with me. Before that, she clerked for Justice Sherzer.'

As Haggard and Tracy shook hands, Haggard said, 'The Department of Labor takes complaints. If he works you more than seventy-six hours straight, there's a grievance procedure.'

Tracy laughed. 'I'm afraid we're way past seventy-six hours, Mr. Haggard.'

Reynolds seated himself behind his desk. Tracy took a stack of files off the other client chair so Haggard could sit on it.

'What brings you here, Dennis?' Reynolds asked.

'I've come because Chuck Geddes wouldn't.'

'Oh?'

'He's still mad about the bail decision and this put him through the roof.'

'And "this" is?'

'A plea offer, Matt. Geddes wouldn't consider it, but the AG insisted. Then Geddes said he'd quit rather than make the offer, so everyone agreed I would carry it over.'

'I see. And what is the offer?'

'We drop the aggravated-murder charge. There's no death penalty and no thirty-year minimum. Abbie pleads to regular murder with a ten-year minimum sentence. It's the best we can do, Matt. No one wants to see Abbie on death row or in prison for life. Christ, I can't even believe we're having this conversation. But we wanted to give her the chance. If she's guilty, it's a very good offer.'

Reynolds leaned back and clasped his hands under his chin. 'Yes, it is. If Mrs. Griffen is guilty. But she's not, Dennis.'

'Can I take it that you're rejecting the offer?'

'You know I can't do that without talking to Mrs. Griffen.'

Haggard handed Matthew a business card. 'My home number is on the back. Call me as soon as you talk to Abbie. The offer is only good for forty-eight hours. If we don't hear by Sunday, Geddes takes the case to trial.'

Haggard let himself out. Reynolds turned back to his notes on jury selection. When he looked up, Tracy was staring at him.

'What's wrong?'

Tracy shook her head.

'If you're concerned about something, I want to know.'

'You're going to advise Mrs. Griffen to reject the offer, aren't you?'

'Of course.'

Tracy frowned.

'Say what's on your mind, Tracy.'

'I'm just . . . That was a good offer.'

Reynolds cocked his head to one side and studied his associate like a professor conducting an oral examination.

'You think I should advise Mrs. Griffen to accept it?'

'I don't think you should reject it out of hand. I can't help remembering what you told me in Atlanta.'

'And what was that?'

'When I asked you why you accepted the plea bargain for Joel Livingstone, you said that the objective in every death penalty case was to save our client's life, not to get a not-guilty verdict.'

Reynolds smiled. 'I'm pleased to see you've learned that lesson.'

'Then why won't you advise Mrs. Griffen to take this offer?'

'That's simple. Joel Livingstone murdered Mary Harding. There was no question of his guilt. Abigail Griffen is innocent of the murder of Robert Griffen. I have never advised an innocent person to plead guilty.'

'How can you know she's innocent?'

'She's told me she's innocent and until she tells me otherwise, I will continue to believe in her innocence.'

Tracy took a deep breath. She was afraid to ask the next question and afraid not to.

'Mr. Reynolds, please don't take offense at what I'm going to say. I respect your opinion and I respect you very much, but I'm concerned that we're making a mistake in not recommending this plea.'

Tracy paused. Reynolds watched her with icy detachment.

'Go ahead,' Reynolds said, and Tracy noticed all the warmth was gone from his voice.

'I can't think of another way to put this. Do you think it's possible that you're being influenced by your personal feelings toward Mrs. Griffen?'

Reynolds colored angrily. Tracy wondered if she had overstepped her bounds. Then Reynolds regained his composure and looked down at the jury selection questions.

'No, Tracy,' he said, his calm restored. 'I am not being influenced by personal feelings. And while I appreciate your concern, I think we've spent too much time on this matter. Let's get back to work.'

2

The days and nights were endless. Minutes seemed like hours. Abbie never expected it to be this way. She prided herself on being able to live alone. When she lost her parents, she built a shell around herself to keep out the horror of loneliness. Then she survived the death of her lover, Larry Ross. When her aunt passed on, she pulled inside the shell once more and she had been able to walk out on Robert Griffen without a backward glance, because she needed no one but herself. But now, trapped in the house, virtually helpless and almost totally deprived of human contact, her shell was cracking.

Even the weather was conspiring against her. The sunny days of summer had given way to the chill of fall and it was often too cool to sit outdoors. She would have given anything to take a walk, but the bracelet on her wrist was a constant reminder that even such simple pleasures were forbidden to her.

On Friday night, the weather was balmy. A last-gasp attempt by nature to fight off the cruel and depressing rains that were sure to come. Abbie sat on the patio, close to her invisible electronic wall, and watched the sunset. A large glass of scotch rested on the table at her elbow. She was drinking more than she wanted to, but liquor helped her sleep without dreams.

A flock of birds broke free from the trees at the edge of her property and soared into the dying light in a black and noisy cloud. Abbie envied them. Her spirit was weighted down by the gravity of her situation and confined to a narrow, airless place in her breast. Even Matthew's boundless confidence could not give it wings.

The sound of tires on gravel made Abbie's heart race, as it did whenever there was any break in the monotony of her routine. She left the glass of scotch on the table and hurried to the front door. She smiled when she saw that it was Matthew. He had been so good to her, visiting almost every day on the pretext that he was working on her case, when she knew that most of what they discussed could have been covered in a short phone call.

'How are you?' Matthew asked, as he always did.

'I was on the patio, enjoying the weather.'

'May I join you?'

'Of course. A drink?'

'No, thanks.'

They walked through the living room in silence, then

stood side by side on the patio for a moment without speaking.

'Are you ready for trial?' Matthew asked.

'I should be asking you that.'

Matthew smiled. Abbie was pleased to see that he was not as stiff around her as he had been when they first met.

'Actually,' she said, 'I can't wait. I would endure anything to get out of here.'

'I can't imagine how hard it's been for you.'

Abbie turned toward Matthew. She felt she could say anything to him.

'It hasn't been hard, Matt, it's been hell. Do you know what the worst part is? The absence of phone calls. Except for you and the electronic surveillance monitors, my phone never rings. Before the indictment, I had my work to occupy me. I guess it kept me from realizing how alone I've been. I think you may be the last person left who cares about me.'

'The people who have deserted you aren't worthy of your friendship,' Matthew said. 'Don't waste your time worrying about them.'

Abbie took his hand. 'You've been more than my attorney, Matt. You've been my friend and I'll never forget that.'

Matthew needed all of his courtroom skills to keep from showing how happy her simple words had made him.

'I'm glad you think of me that way,' he said as calmly as he could.

Abbie squeezed his hand, then let it go. 'Why did you come out?'

'Business. Dennis Haggard visited me. He made a plea offer . . .'

'No,' Abbie said firmly.

'I have an ethical obligation to communicate the offer. They'll take a plea to murder. Life with a ten-year minimum sentence. There would be no possibility of a death sentence.'

'I'm innocent. I will not plead guilty to a crime I did not commit.'

Matthew smiled. 'Good. That's what I hoped you'd say.'

'You're that certain you'll win?'

'I'm positive.'

'I'm scared, Matt. I keep thinking about what will happen if we lose. I used to think I could take anything, but I can't. If I have to go to jail . . .'

Abbie looked as frightened and vulnerable as a child. Matthew hesitated for a second, then put his arms around her. Abbie collapsed into him, letting go completely. Matthew wished he could make time stop, so he would never have to let her go.

Chapter Twenty-one

1

Matthew Reynolds was right. While working on *State of Oregon* v. *Abigail Griffen*, Tracy did not have time to run or rock-climb or eat right, and she sure wasn't sleeping right. But she didn't care. Trying a death penalty case was more exhilarating than anything she had ever done.

All her life Tracy had been fiercely competitive. That was why she had turned down jobs at several corporate law firms, which offered more money, to work for Matthew Reynolds. Criminal law provided the biggest challenge. There were no higher stakes than life or death. She played for those stakes occasionally when she climbed, but the life that was at risk was her own. It surprised her how much more difficult it was when the life in the balance was someone else's and that person was totally helpless and dependent on her skills.

When Reynolds spoke about the lawyers who visited

their clients after dark during her interview, Tracy felt an electric current passing through her. Reynolds had never faced the ultimate failure of watching a client die, and she vowed that it would never happen to her.

Matthew had put her in charge of the legal research so he could concentrate on the facts of the case. This was tremendously flattering because Reynolds was known nationally for his innovative legal thinking. But it also meant working in the library from morning to night, learning everything there was to know about the specialized area of death penalty law, as well as the legal issues that were specific to Abbie's case. Tracy's head was so crammed with information that she was waking up at odd hours with ideas that had to be jotted down. When the alarm startled her out of bed each morning, she was groggy, but an adrenaline high kicked in and carried her through days that passed in a flash.

Once the trial started, Tracy set her alarm even earlier so she could meet Reynolds at the office at six-thirty for the day's pretrial briefing. At eight-thirty, Barry Frame would arrive with Abigail Griffen and they would drive to the Multnomah County Courthouse, where they would fight their way through the crowd of reporters and spectators who mobbed the fifth-floor corridor outside the courtroom.

Their judge, the Honorable Jack Baldwin, was a gaunt, diminutive man with curly gray hair and a pencil-thin mustache. His complexion was unnaturally pale. When they were introduced, Tracy noticed liver spots on the back of the judge's hand and felt a slight tremor when they shook. Lines on his face showed Baldwin's seventy-four years. The Oregon constitution made it mandatory that judges retire at seventy-five.

Although Baldwin was dwarfed by Geddes and Reynolds, he carried himself with an easy authority that commanded respect and made him seem equal in stature to the attorneys. Baldwin had a reputation for being fair and his intelligence was unquestioned. The judge let the parties know that his last major trial was going to be a model for death penalty litigation.

The first week and a half in court was taken up with jury selection and opening statements. On Thursday of the second week, Geddes called his first witness, the attorney who represented Justice Griffen in his divorce. When he was through testifying on direct examination, the jury was fully aware that Abigail Griffen stood to lose a lot of money if the divorce became final. Tracy was worried about the damage the testimony had caused, but Matthew's cross-examination left everyone in the courtroom convinced that two million dollars was chump change for a woman like Abbie Griffen.

Next Geddes called Jack Stamm, who reluctantly told the jury about Abbie's angry reaction when she learned that Justice Griffen had authored the opinion that reversed the conviction of Charlie Deems. Stamm's testimony was no surprise to the defense. He believed in Abbie's innocence and had spoken freely with Matthew and Barry Frame before the trial.

'Mr. Stamm,' Matthew asked the district attorney when

it was his turn to cross-examine, 'are your deputies usually overjoyed when the case of a convicted criminal is overturned on appeal?'

'No, sir.'

'Have you heard deputy district attorneys other than Mrs. Griffen curse a particular judge because that judge wrote an opinion reversing a conviction?'

'Yes.'

'So Mrs. Griffen's reaction was not unusual?'

'No, Mr. Reynolds. She reacted the way a lot of my deputies react when a case is reversed.'

Reynolds smiled at Stamm. 'I suspect even you have taken the name of a few appellate judges in vain?'

'Can I take the Fifth on that?' Stamm answered with a grin. Everyone in the courtroom laughed, except Chuck Geddes.

'I'm going to let him exercise his rights here, Mr. Reynolds,' Judge Baldwin said with a smile.

'Very well, Your Honor. I'll withdraw the question. But I do have another for you, Mr. Stamm. How seriously does Mrs. Griffen take her cases?'

Stamm turned to the jury.

'Abigail Griffen is one of the most dedicated prosecutors I have ever met. She is brilliant, thorough and scrupulously fair.'

'Thank you, sir. No further questions.'

'Mr. Geddes?' Judge Baldwin asked. Geddes thought about going after Stamm, but he knew Stamm would try to help Griffen if given the chance.

'No further questions, Your Honor. The state calls Anthony Rose.'

Tony Rose entered the courtroom looking impressive in his police uniform. He would not look at Abbie. When he took the witness stand, he sat with his shoulders hunched and shifted uncomfortably in his seat. Geddes established that Rose was a police officer who had testified in several cases which Abigail Griffen had prosecuted. Then he stood up and walked over to the end of the jury box farthest from the witness.

'Officer Rose, when did you learn that the Supreme Court had reversed the conviction of Charlie Deems?'

'The day it happened. It was all over the station house.'

'At some point after you learned of the reversal, did you have an opportunity to talk about it with the defendant?'

'Yes, sir.'

'Tell the jury about that conversation.'

'There's an Italian place, Caruso's. It's downtown on Second and Pine. I eat there every once in a while. One night I saw Mrs. Griffen, the defendant, as I was leaving. She was by herself, so I went over to say hello. While we were talking, I told her I was sorry the case was reversed.'

'What was her reaction?'

'She was furious.'

'Did she mention her husband, Justice Griffen?'

'Yeah, and, uh, she wasn't too complimentary.'

'What did she say about him?'

'She called him a son of a bitch and she said he reversed the case to get her. I guess she was going through a divorce and figured he was trying to make her look bad.'

Geddes paused long enough to get the jurors' attention. Then he asked, 'Officer Rose, did Mrs. Griffen tell you about something she wished Charlie Deems would do to Justice Griffen?'

'Yes, sir. She did.'

'Tell the jury what she said.'

'Right after she said she thought the judge had reversed the case to make her look bad, she said she hoped Deems would blow Justice Griffen to kingdom come.'

Geddes nodded. 'Blow him to kingdom come. Those were her words?'

'Yes, sir. They were.'

Geddes turned toward Matthew Reynolds. 'Your witness, Counselor.'

Rose turned toward the defense counsel table, but he still refused to look Abigail Griffen in the eye. Matthew Reynolds stood and walked slowly toward the witness stand.

'You don't like Mrs. Griffen, do you?' Matthew asked, after taking a position that would not block the jurors' view of the witness.

Rose shrugged nervously. 'I've got nothing against her.'

'Do you respect her, Officer Rose?'

'What do you mean?'

'Is she a woman you treat with respect?'

'Well . . . Yeah. Sure. I respect her.'

'Did you treat her with respect on the evening you have spoken about?'

Rose shifted nervously in his seat.

'Your Honor, will you instruct Officer Rose to answer.'

'You must answer the question,' Judge Baldwin said.

'Look, that was a misunderstanding.'

'I don't believe we were discussing a misunderstanding, Officer. We were discussing the concept of respect in the context of the respect a gentleman should have for a lady. Did you treat Mrs. Griffen with respect that evening?'

'I thought she was sending signals. I was wrong.'

'Signals that indicated she wished to be raped?'

'Objection,' Geddes shouted.

'This goes to bias, Your Honor.'

'Overruled,' Judge Baldwin said. 'Answer the question, Officer.'

'I didn't try to rape the defendant.'

'Then why did she have to slap you to make you leave her house?'

'She . . . Like I said, there was a misunderstanding.'

'That reached the point where she had to use physical force to make you leave her home?'

'That wasn't necessary. If she'd asked I would have left.'

'At the time Mrs. Griffen slapped you, was she pinned to the wall?'

'I . . . I'm not certain.'

'Was your hand up her dress?'

'Look, everything happened very fast. I already said it was a mistake.'

'This was not the first time Mrs. Griffen had rebuffed you, was it?'

'What do you mean?'

'On two occasions, when she was trying to prepare your testimony for trial, did you make sexual advances to her?'

'It wasn't like that.'

'How was it, Officer Rose?'

'She's a good-looking woman.'

'So you suggested a date?'

'I'm only human.'

'And she was married. You knew that when you propositioned her, did you not?'

Rose looked toward Chuck Geddes for help, but the prosecutor was stone-faced.

'Did you know she was married when you propositioned her the first time?'

'Yes.'

'And the second time? You were still aware that she was a married woman?'

'Yes.'

'Nothing further, Officer Rose.'

2

'You were fantastic,' Abbie said as soon as her front door closed. 'You crucified Rose.'

'Yes, but the jury heard that you wished Deems would blow up Justice Griffen.'

'It doesn't matter. Rose's credibility was destroyed. You weren't watching the jurors. You should have seen the way they were looking at him. They were disgusted. If that statement's all they've got . . .'

'But we know it isn't. There has to be something more.'

'Well, I don't want to think about it now. I want to relax. Can I get you a drink?'

'I have to work tonight. Geddes is calling several important witnesses tomorrow.'

'Oh,' Abbie said, disappointed.

'You know I want to stay.'

'No, you're right. It's just . . . I don't know. I'm so happy. Things went well for once. I want to celebrate.'

'We'll celebrate when you're acquitted.'

'You believe I will be, don't you?'

'I know you'll never go to prison.'

Abbie was standing inches from Matthew. She reached out and took his hand. The touch paralyzed him. Abbie moved into his arms and pressed her head against his chest. She could hear his heart beating like a trip-hammer. Then she looked up and kissed him. Matthew had imagined this moment a thousand times, but never believed it would really happen. He felt Abbie's breasts press against his chest. He let his body fit into hers. Abbie's head sank against his chest.

'When this is over, we'll get away from here,' Abbie said. 'We'll go to a quiet place where no one knows us.'

'Abbie . . .'

She placed her fingertips against Matthew's lips.

'No. This is enough for now. Knowing you care for me.'

'I do care,' Matthew said, very quietly. 'You know I care.'

'Yes,' Abbie said. 'And I know you'll win. I know you'll make me free.'

Chapter Twenty-two

1

'The state calls Seth Dillard,' Chuck Geddes said. Tracy checked off Dillard's name on the defense witness list. Dillard followed Mrs. Wallace, who told the jury about Abbie's hysterical appearance at her door on the evening of the attack at the coast.

'What is your profession?' Geddes asked.

'I'm the sheriff of Seneca County, Oregon.'

'Sheriff, if I wanted to buy some dynamite to clear stumps on property in Seneca County, what would I have to do?'

'You'd have to come to my office and fill out an application for a permit to purchase explosives. There's a fifteen-dollar fee. We'd take a mug shot and print you to make certain you weren't a felon. If everything checked out, you'd go to the fire marshal, who'd issue you a permit.

Once you had the permit, you'd take it to someone who sells explosives.'

'Did Justice Griffen secure a permit from your office for dynamite to clear stumps on his property?'

'Yes.'

'When did he do that?'

'Middle of the summer. July third.'

'Now, Sheriff, a week or so before Justice Griffen was killed did you investigate a complaint by the defendant that she had been attacked by an intruder in her cabin?'

'I did.'

'Can you tell the jury what the defendant told you about the alleged attack?'

'Early Saturday morning, August thirteenth, I interviewed Mrs. Griffen at a neighbor's house. She claimed that a man broke into her cabin close to midnight on the twelfth and she escaped by jumping from her second-story deck. According to Mrs. Griffen, the man chased her and she hid in the woods until she thought he was gone. About three-thirty A.M., she woke up the neighbor, Mrs. Wallace, by pounding on the door.'

'Did the defendant see the face of this alleged intruder?'

'Mrs. Griffen said the man wore something over his face.'

'I see. Now, Sheriff, did the defendant tell you about another alleged attack that occurred two weeks before this alleged attack at the coast?'

'Yes, sir. She said she thought the same person tried to break into her house in Portland.'

'Did she report this alleged break-in to the police?'

'Mrs. Griffen said she didn't.'

'Did she see who attempted this alleged break-in in Portland?'

'She told me that the man also wore a mask in Portland, so she didn't see his face.'

'Now, Sheriff, despite the fact that Mrs. Griffen never saw this person's face, did she suggest a person for investigation?'

'Yes. She said she thought her attacker might be a man she put on death row a year or so ago, who just got out of prison.'

'Charlie Deems?'

'Right, but it wasn't much of an ID. More like a guess.'

'She was the one who brought up the name?'

'Yes.'

'Sheriff Dillard, did you find anything at the crime scene linking Charlie Deems to the alleged attack?'

'No.'

'What did your investigation turn up?'

Dillard weighed his answer carefully. Then he told the jurors, 'Truthfully, we haven't found much of anything.'

'I don't follow you.'

'We don't have any evidence that anyone besides Mrs. Griffen was there. We did not find Mr. Deems's prints in the cabin. There was no sign of forced entry and nothing was taken. Mrs. Griffen says that she and the intruder jumped from the deck. Well, someone did jump from the deck, but the ground was so churned up we can't say if it was one person or two. When it got light I walked the trail along the bluff where she said she was chased by this fella and I searched the woods. I didn't find anything to support her story. Neither did my men.'

'Thank you, Sheriff. No further questions.'

Matthew Reynolds reviewed his notes. The jurors shifted in their seats. A spectator coughed. Reynolds looked up at the sheriff.

'How did Mrs. Griffen seem to you when you questioned her?' Matthew asked.

'She was shaken up.'

'Would you say her behavior was similar to other assault victims you've interviewed?'

'Oh, yeah. She definitely acted like someone who'd been through an ordeal. Of course, I wasn't looking for deception. After all, she's a district attorney. I naturally assumed she'd be telling the truth and she didn't do anything that raised my antennas.'

'You've testified that you haven't found any evidence to corroborate Mrs. Griffen's story. If the intruder wore gloves, you wouldn't find fingerprints, would you?'

'That's right. And I don't want to be misunderstood here. I'm not saying Mrs. Griffen wasn't attacked. I'm just saying we haven't found any evidence that there was an intruder. There could have been. She sure seemed like someone who'd been attacked. I just can't prove it.'

'One thing further, Sheriff. About a week or so after Justice Griffen was killed, did you receive a call from Mr. Geddes's investigator, Neil Christenson?'

'Yes, sir.'

'Did he ask you to go to the Griffen cabin and check in a shed behind it to see if there was a box of dynamite in the shed?'

'Yes, sir.'

'Did you find any dynamite?'

'Well, there was a cleared space on the floor of the shed big enough for the kind of box that holds it, but there wasn't any dynamite there.'

'Nothing further.'

'I have a few questions on redirect, Your Honor.'

'Go ahead, Mr. Geddes,' Judge Baldwin said.

'Did you or your men look in the shed on the day Mrs. Griffen reported the attack?'

'No, sir. There wasn't any reason to.'

'Did you post a guard at the Griffen cabin?'

'No reason to do that either.'

'So there was plenty of time and plenty of opportunity between the day of the alleged attack and the day you searched the shed for someone to remove the dynamite, if there was some in the shed on the day of the attack?'

'Yes, sir.'

Barry Frame was waiting in the courtroom when Matthew Reynolds returned from lunch. As soon as Reynolds walked through the door, Frame broke into a grin.

'Bingo,' he said, handing Reynolds a thick manila envelope.

'What's this?'

'Charlie Deems's bank records.'

'You found an account?' Reynolds asked excitedly.

'Washington Mutual. The branch across from Pioneer Square.'

'Have you reviewed the records?'

'You bet.'

'And?'

'See for yourself.'

Geddes's next witness was the neighbor who called 911 to report the explosion that killed Justice Griffen. He was followed by the first officers at the crime scene. Then Geddes called Paul Torino to the stand.

'Officer Torino, how long have you been a Portland police officer?'

'Twenty years.'

'Do you have a special job on the force?'

'Yes, sir. I'm assigned to the bomb squad.'

'What is your official title?'

'Explosive Disposal Unit Team Leader.'

'Officer Torino, will you tell the jury about your background and training in police work with an emphasis on your training in dealing with explosive devices?'

'Yes,' Torino said, turning toward the jury. 'I enlisted in the Army immediately after high school and was assigned to an Explosive Ordnance Disposal Unit. I received training in dealing with explosive devices at the United States Navy Explosive Ordnance Disposal training center at Indian Head, Maryland. Then,' Torino said with a grin, 'I served four years in Vietnam and received more practical experience in dealing with explosive devices than I really wanted.'

Two male jurors chuckled. Tracy noted that they were both veterans.

'What did you do after the Army?'

'I went to college and received an AA from Portland Community College in police science. Then I joined the force. After three years, which is the minimum experience you need, I qualified for the month-long course run by the FBI at the Hazardous Device Division of Redstone Arsenal in Huntsville, Alabama.'

'Did you graduate from that course?'

'Yes, sir.'

'Do you have any more formal training in dealing with explosive devices?'

'I'm a graduate of a two-week post-blast investigative school run by the Bureau of Alcohol, Tobacco and Firearms. I'd estimate that I have a total of more than four-teen hundred hours of formal education in bomb disposal through the military and the government.'

'How long have you been doing post-blast investiga-tion for the Portland police?'

'Around twelve years.'

'Did you go to the home of Oregon Supreme Court Justice Robert Griffen in your capacity as Team Leader of the Explosive Disposal Unit?'

'Yes.'

'Were you the first unit to arrive at the scene?'

'No, sir. A Fire Rescue Unit and uniformed officers were the first to respond. As soon as it was determined that an explosive device had been detonated, they secured the scene, notified us, the medical examiner and the homicide detectives, then backed off until we checked the scene to make certain there were no more unexploded bombs.

'We made a determination that it was safe to proceed with the investigation. Before the victim was removed from the car, my people photographed the area to make a record of the scene.'

'What did you do then?'

'A bomb breaks up when it explodes and parts of the bomb are propelled to different areas of the crime scene. My people have a routine we follow. We roped off the area around the car and divided it into search areas. I had two men working at the seat of the blast, the place where the bomb was located. They examined the radius around the car to pick up pieces of the car and the bomb that were thrown off by the blast. I had other men working in other sections of the roped-off area. Whenever a piece of the bomb, or other relevant evidence, was found, an officer recorded where on the grid it was located and another officer took possession of the item and logged it in.'

'Officer Torino, can you tell the jury a little about how this bomb was constructed?'

'Certainly. All bombs have four things in common: explosives, an initiator, a power source and a switch or delay. When you look for a bomb, you see if you can find these components. This bomb consisted of a piece of pipe two inches in diameter and ten inches long that was filled with smokeless powder. A nine-volt battery was the power source. End caps sealed in the powder. These end caps flew off like they'd been shot from a rifle when the bomb exploded. The back end cap was found in the trunk, lodged in the frame of the car. The front end cap went through the garage door and was found embedded in the door of a refrigerator that was in the garage.

'The metal tube that made up the body of the bomb shattered into three pieces. One large part was found in the interior of the car lodged in the rear seat. Two other parts went through the roof of the car and were found on the lawn.'

'What set the bomb off?'

'A flashlight bulb was placed inside the body of the bomb in contact with the powder. The glass of the bulb was shattered. Wires from the bulb were threaded through one of the end caps and attached to a nine-volt battery. The wires were peeled back and the copper ends were wrapped around the teeth of a clothespin. Then a strip of plastic from a Clorox bottle was placed between the teeth of the clothespin, preventing the teeth from closing. The bomber attached a lead sinker to the strip of plastic. When Justice Griffen moved the car, the sinker held down the plastic strip and the strip was pulled out from between the teeth of the clothespin. That permitted the copper wires to touch, completing the circuit. A spark from the exposed wires in the lightbulb ignited the powder and caused the explosion.'

'How do you know all this about the bomb?'

'We located two short pieces of copper wire and the remains of the lightbulb embedded in the end cap we removed from the refrigerator door in the garage. A wooden clothespin was found in the front yard on the south side of the car. The plastic strip, monofilament fishing line and a lead sinker were found on the ground near the right front wheel. We also found a shattered battery, mostly intact.'

'Officer Torino, how was the bomb attached to the car?'

'We found chunks of magnets and nuts and bolts that had been bent and twisted from the blast. These did not match anything in the car, but I was familiar with them already, so I knew they were part of the bomb.'

'We'll get to that in a moment. Would you explain to the jury how the magnets were used?'

'Yes. A strip of metal eight inches long and two inches wide and a quarter inch thick was used. Holes were drilled in it and four magnets were affixed to the strip with nuts and bolts. Black electrical tape was then used to tape the strip to the bomb. When the bomb was ready to be used, it was pressed against the undercarriage of the car and the magnets held it in place.'

'Officer Torino, you mentioned that you were familiar with this bomb. Explain that statement to the jury.'

'A bomb of almost identical construction was the murder weapon in a case tried approximately two years ago.'

'Who was the defendant in that case?'

'Charles Deems.'

Geddes paused for effect, then faced the jury.

'Who was the prosecutor?'

'Abigail Griffen.'

'The defendant in this case?'

'Yes, sir.'

'Did the defendant know how to construct the bomb that killed her husband?'

'Yes.'

'How do you know that?'

'I showed her how to make one. We went into great detail so she could examine me about the construction of the bomb on direct examination. Then I told the jury the same information in court. It's in the record of the case.'

Geddes walked back to his table and picked up several plastic evidence bags. He returned to the witness stand and handed one of the plastic bags to Torino.

'This has been marked as State's Exhibit 35. Can you tell the jury what it is?'

Torino opened the plastic bag and took out a charred and twisted strip of metal approximately six inches long, one and a half inches wide and a quarter inch thick.

'Yes, sir. I personally took this from the Portland Police Bureau evidence room. This is the strip to which the magnets were attached by the bomber in the case Mrs. Griffen prosecuted against Mr. Deems.'

'Is there anything unusual about it?'

Torino held out one end of the strip to the jury. 'You can see that this end is flat and looks like it was shaped by a machine.' Torino turned the other end toward the jury.

'But this end is uneven and there is a notch that forms a jagged vee in the middle. That's because this strip came from a longer strip. Someone sawed it off of the large strip to shorten it so it would fit onto the top of the pipe bomb.'

'Is it unusual to find a notch like this in the strip that secures the magnets?'

'Yes, sir. With one exception, I've never seen a notch like this on another pipe bomb.'

'Was the defendant aware of the unique nature of the notch?'

'Oh yes. I told her that several times. She knew it was like a fingerprint.'

'So,' Geddes asked with heavy emphasis after turning toward the jury, 'the defendant was also aware that a Portland police explosives expert who found a strip of metal like this one with such a notch at the site of a bombing would immediately think that Mr. Deems was responsible for making the bomb?'

'Yes, sir.'

'Thank you. I now hand you State's Exhibit 36. What is it?'

Torino held up another strip of charred and twisted metal that was eight inches long, two inches wide and a quarter inch thick and very similar in appearance to State's Exhibit 35.

'This is the strip of metal to which the magnets were attached in the bomb that killed Justice Griffen. When the bomb exploded, it was blown through the bottom of the car into the judge. The medical examiner found it during the autopsy.'

'Is it similar to the strip used by the killer in the case which the defendant prosecuted against Mr. Deems?'

'Yes. One end is flat and the other has an almost identical notch.'

'How was that notch formed?'

'By putting the strip in a vise and using a hacksaw to cut it from the larger strip. The person who used the hacksaw cut from two directions and that's why the notch overlaps here,' Torino said, pointing to the center of the vee.

'And you say you've only seen one other magnet strip with a similar notch?'

'Yes, sir. The only other time I've seen one like it was in the case Mrs. Griffen prosecuted against Mr. Deems.'

'As an expert in the area of explosive devices, what conclusion do you draw from the similarity in appearance of these two strips?'

'Either the same person cut them or someone intentionally tried to make the second strip look like the first.'

'Why would someone intentionally do that?'

'One reason would be to frame Mr. Deems.'

'Objection,' Reynolds said, standing. 'That is pure speculation.'

'Sustained,' Judge Baldwin said, turning toward the jury. 'You jurors will disregard that last remark.'

'Officer Torino, you did say that the defendant knew about the unusual notch in the end of Exhibit 35?'

'Yes, sir. I pointed it out to her during the investigation of the Hollins murders.'

'Thank you. Now, Officer Torino, on the evening that Justice Griffen was killed, were you called to another location to search for explosive devices?'

'I was.'

'Where did you go?'

'To a home the defendant was renting. District Attorney Stamm was concerned that the same person who killed the judge might have rigged a bomb at Mrs. Griffen's house.'

'In the course of your search did you look in Mrs. Griffen's garage?'

'Yes, sir.'

'Describe it.'

'It was a typical two-car garage with a work area in one corner. The work area consisted of a workbench and table with a vise. Tools were hanging from hooks on the wall.'

Geddes handed Torino a photograph. 'Can you identify State's Exhibit 52 for the jury?'

'That's a shot of the garage.' Torino held up the photograph so the jury could see it and pointed to the left side of the picture. 'You can see the workbench over here.'

Geddes took the photograph and handed Torino the last plastic bag. It contained a clean strip of metal. It was not charred or twisted. One end was flat and obviously shaped by a machine. The other end came to a point. The point was jagged and appeared to have been cut by hand.

'This is State's Exhibit 37. Can you tell the jury what it is?'

Torino took Exhibit 36 in one hand and Exhibit 37 in the other and fit the jagged point from Exhibit 37 into the notch at the end of Exhibit 36.

'Exhibit 37 appears to be the other part of the longer strip from which Exhibit 36 was cut. They don't fit exactly because Exhibit 36 was mangled in the explosion.'

Geddes paused and turned toward Abigail Griffen.

'Did you find Exhibit 37, Officer Torino?'

'Yes, sir.'

'Where did you find it?'

'Under the workbench in Abigail Griffen's garage. You can see the strip in the bottom right corner of Exhibit 52. We also have a close-up in another photo.'

Tracy suddenly felt sick. Torino's testimony was devastating. She glanced quickly at the jurors. Every one of them was leaning forward and several were writing furiously on their notepads. Then she looked at Matthew. If he was feeling any stress as a result of Torino's testimony, Tracy could not see it.

'Officer Torino, there are what appear to be metal shavings in the plastic bag that we've been using to hold Exhibit 37. Where did they come from?'

'They were found on the floor under the vise.'

Geddes went back to counsel table and pulled a plastic Clorox bottle from a shopping bag.

'Can you tell the jury where State's Exhibit 42 was found?'

'It was also found in Mrs. Griffen's garage.'

Tracy glanced at Reynolds. He still appeared to be unconcerned.

'Your Honor, at this time I move to introduce State's Exhibits 35, 36, 37, 42 and 52,' Geddes said.

'Any objection, Mr. Reynolds?'

'May I see 42, please,' Reynolds said calmly as he climbed to his feet. Tracy could not believe how well he concealed the shock he had to be experiencing. Geddes handed Reynolds the Clorox bottle.

'May I ask a question in aid of objection, Your Honor?'

'Go ahead.'

'Officer Torino, this Clorox bottle is in one piece, is it not?'

'Yes.'

'Then it could not be the bottle from which was cut the plastic strip used in the detonating device?'

'That's true.'

Matthew turned toward the bench. 'I object to the admission of State's Exhibit 42. It has no relevance.'

'Mr. Geddes?' the judge said.

'It is relevant,' Geddes answered. 'This is obviously not the bottle from which the strip was cut, but it proves that the defendant uses the brand.'

'I'll let it in. It has limited relevance, but as long as it has some, it meets the evidentiary threshold for admissibility.'

'I have no further questions of this witness, Your Honor. Mr. Reynolds may examine.'

'Mr. Reynolds?' Judge Baldwin asked.

'May I have a moment, Your Honor?'

Baldwin nodded. Matthew turned to Abbie. His features were composed, but Tracy could tell that he was very upset.

'What was that metal strip doing in your garage?' he asked in a tone low enough to keep the jurors or Geddes from hearing what was said.

'I swear, I don't know,' Abbie answered in a whisper. 'My God, Matthew, if I made that bomb in the garage, don't you think I'd have the brains to get rid of anything that could connect me to it?'

'Yes, I do. But we're stuck with the fact that the strip was found in the garage of the house you were renting together with metal shavings that would be created when it was sawed off the rest of the strip. When was the last time you remember being around the worktable?'

'I put the car in the garage every evening. The people I'm renting from own the workshop furniture and the tools. I've never used them. Deems planted the strip and the shavings. Don't you see that? I'm being framed.'

'This is very bad,' Matthew said. 'Now I understand why Stamm felt he had to get off the case.'

Reynolds turned to Tracy. 'Do you remember seeing the three strips when we examined the physical evidence?'

'Of course, but I didn't think anything about them. They weren't together, I'm sure of that. If I recall, they were scattered among the other pieces of metal from the bomb and there were a lot of metal chunks on the table.'

'Geddes did that on purpose,' Matthew muttered. 'He set us up.'

'What are we going to do?'

Reynolds thought for a moment, then addressed the judge.

'Before I cross-examine, I have a matter I would like to take up with the court.'

Judge Baldwin looked up at the clock. Then he turned to the jurors. 'Ladies and gentlemen, this is a good time to take our morning recess. Let's reconvene at ten forty-five.'

As the jurors filed out, Barry came through the bar of the court and stood next to Tracy.

'As soon as we break for the day,' Reynolds told them, 'I want you two to look at all of the physical evidence again, to make certain there aren't any more surprises.'

The door to the jury room closed and Judge Baldwin said, 'Mr. Reynolds?'

'Your Honor, I would like to reserve my cross-examination of Officer Torino. His testimony, and this exhibit, are a complete surprise to the defense.'

'Will you explain that to me? Didn't Mr. Geddes let you know that he was introducing it?'

'There are no written reports about the metal strips that were used in the bombs and the strip found in Mrs. Griffen's garage . . .'

Chuck Geddes leaped to his feet. He was fighting hard to suppress a smile of satisfaction.

'Exhibits 35, 36 and 37 were listed on evidence reports supplied to the defense, Your Honor. We also made all of the physical evidence available to the defense for viewing.'

'Is that so, Mr. Reynolds?'

Matthew cast a withering glance at Geddes, whose lips twisted into a smirk.

'Mr. Geddes may have listed the exhibits, Your Honor, but no report furnished to the defense explained the significance of the items. If I remember correctly, the strips were noted on the evidence list simply as pieces of metal and the three metal strips were scattered among the remnants of the bomb that killed Justice Griffen, giving the impression that all three strips were unconnected and found at the crime scene.'

'What do you have to say about that, Mr. Geddes?'

'The discovery rules require me to list all the witnesses and exhibits I intend to introduce at trial. They do not require me to explain what I intend to do with the exhibits or what my witnesses have to say about them. I did what was required by law. If Mr. Reynolds was unable to understand the significance of the exhibits, that's his problem.'

'Your Honor, there is no way any reasonable person could have understood the significance of this evidence,' Matthew answered angrily. 'Mr. Geddes made certain of that by scattering them among the other exhibits. Ask him why he did that and ask him why he didn't have Officer Torino write a report about them.'

'If you're implying that I did anything unethical . . .' Geddes started.

'Gentlemen,' Judge Baldwin interrupted, 'let's keep this civilized. Mr. Reynolds, if Mr. Geddes gave you notice that Officer Torino was testifying and he listed the strips as exhibits, he complied with the law. However, I want you to have a fair opportunity to cross-examine on this matter, which is of obvious importance. What do you suggest we do?'

'Your Honor, I would like to have custody of the three strips so I can have them examined by a defense expert. I have someone in mind.'

'How long will you need the evidence, Mr. Reynolds?'

'I won't know until I talk to my expert. He may be able to accomplish what I want this weekend.'

'I object, Your Honor,' Geddes said. 'We're in the middle of trial. Mr. Reynolds had ample opportunity to examine and test the evidence.'

'And I'm sure he would have if you'd given him some notice of the use to which you were putting it,' Judge Baldwin said sternly. 'Quite frankly, Mr. Geddes, while you're within the letter of the law on this, I don't think you're within its spirit.'

'Your Honor . . .' Geddes began, but Judge Baldwin held up his hand.

'Mr. Geddes this could have been avoided if you had informed Mr. Reynolds about Officer Torino's testimony in advance of trial. I'm going to let Mr. Reynolds have the metal strips, if he can find an expert to examine them.'

2

The rest of the afternoon was taken up with the testimony of several bomb squad members, who identified evidence taken from the crime scene and explained where each item was found. Outside, a gentle rain was falling, but the heat was on in the courthouse and the drone of the witnesses was putting Tracy to sleep. She sighed with relief when the judge called the weekend recess.

As soon as court was out, Matthew took custody of the three metal strips and left with Abigail Griffen. Tracy and Barry Frame looked over all of the evidence that was in the courtroom. When they were through, Neil Christenson escorted them to a conference room in the district attorney's office that was being used to store the physical evidence that had not been introduced. Some of the evidence was spread over the top of a long conference table. Other evidence was in cardboard boxes on the floor of the conference room. Christenson parked himself in a chair at the far end of the room.

'How about some privacy?' Barry asked.

'Sorry,' Christenson replied. 'If it was up to me, I'd be home with a cold beer, but Chuck told me to keep an eye on you.'

'Suit yourself.'

Tracy started with the items on the table, conferring with Barry in whispers if she saw anything that might be significant and making notes on a legal pad. When they were done with the items on top of the table, Barry cleared a space at one end and emptied the contents of the first cardboard carton, which contained items taken from Abbie's rented house.

Tracy's stomach was starting to growl by the time they finished with the evidence from the rented house and Barry emptied the first box of items from Justice Griffen's den. The box contained personal papers, household receipts, bills and other documents of this type. Tracy emptied a second box that contained papers found in the bottom right drawer of Justice Griffen's desk. At first glance, the papers looked like they would be similar to the papers in the other box. Then Tracy spotted something that was out of place. At the bottom of the pile was a volume from a trial transcript. A sheet from a yellow legal pad was jutting out from between two of the transcript pages. Tracy thought that Barry must have gone through this box when they looked through the evidence the first time, because she did not remember seeing the transcript before.

When Tracy saw the cover page of the transcript, she concealed her surprise. She was looking at Volume XI of *State of Oregon, Plaintiff-Respondent* v. *Charles Darren Deems, Defendant-Appellant*, the transcript Laura Rizzatti had been reading the day Matthew Reynolds and Abigail Griffen argued at the Supreme Court. Tracy remembered how nervous Laura had seemed when she found her reading it.

Tracy glanced over at Christenson. He was reading the sports section of *The Oregonian* and looked bored stiff.

Tracy shifted her body to block Christenson's view, then opened the transcript enough to see what was written on the sheet from the legal pad. The sheet was wedged between pages 1289 and 1290 of the transcript. It was a sheet from the legal pad on which Laura was writing in the library on the day Justice Pope accosted her. The names of three criminal cases were written on the page. Tracy remembered how quickly Laura had turned over the yellow pad to prevent Tracy from seeing what was on it. Tracy wrote down the names of the cases and the volume numbers of the Oregon reports in which they were published.

What was so special about the transcript and these cases, and what were this transcript and Laura's notes doing in Justice Griffen's den? The transcript was part of the official record of the *Deems* case and should be with the rest of the transcripts in the case in the file room of the Supreme Court.

Twenty minutes later, Barry stretched and announced, 'That's the lot.'

Christenson showed them out, then returned to the conference room. Barry pressed the down button on the elevator. As they waited for it to arrive, he asked, 'Any brilliant insights?'

Tracy was tempted to tell him about the transcript, but there was nothing to tell. She had no idea what was in Volume XI. Whatever was there wouldn't have anything to do with Abbie's case anyway.

'I didn't see anything I didn't spot the first time we

went through this stuff. If there are any more surprises, Geddes slipped them past me.'

'I agree. Are you up for dinner?'

Tracy wanted to get to the office so she could read Volume XI in the set of transcripts she'd taken from Bob Packard.

'I'll pass. I'm going to grab some takeout and head for the office. There are a few things I have to go over tonight.'

'Hey, it's the weekend. *Casablanca* is on. I thought we'd whip up some gourmet popcorn, crack open a bottle of wine and watch Bogie. You don't want to pass that up, do you?'

Barry sounded disappointed. The elevator doors opened. They stepped into the empty car. Tracy touched him on the arm.

'I'll tell you what. I'm big on Bogie myself. When's the movie start?'

'Nine.'

'Save me a seat. I should be able to finish by then.'

Barry grinned. 'I'll be waiting. Do you like red or white wine with your popcorn?'

'Beer, actually.'

'A woman after my own heart. I'll even spring for imported.'

Neil Christenson showed Barry Frame and Tracy Cavanaugh out of the district attorney's office, then he returned to the conference room and emptied the box with the evidence that had been found in the bottom right drawer of Justice Griffen's desk onto the conference table. Christenson had only been pretending to read the paper while Barry and Tracy went through the evidence and he noticed that Tracy was intentionally blocking his view when she went through this box. Christenson was determined to discover the piece of evidence that had created so much interest.

The transcript and yellow paper attracted his attention immediately because they were out of place. Christenson frowned when he saw that the transcript was from the *Deems* case. Then he remembered that Justice Griffen had written the opinion that reversed Deems's conviction. How ironic, he thought, that the person Justice Griffen had freed from prison was going to help convict the judge's killer.

Christenson flipped through the transcript, but found nothing that looked important. He put it down on the table and started on the other documents. There were miscellaneous papers, a file filled with correspondence between Justice Griffen and his stockbroker, another file with paperwork about his beach property and an envelope stuffed with credit card receipts. Christenson went through the receipts. Several were from a restaurant in Salem that was close to the court, a few were from stores in Salem and Portland, three were from a motel called the Overlook and a number of receipts were from gas stations. Nothing relevant to the case.

Christenson went through the contents of the box once

more, then gave up. It was late and he was tired. If Tracy Cavanaugh had spotted something important, it had gone right by him. Christenson yawned, closed the door to the conference room and headed home.

3

As soon as she was alone in the office, Tracy found Volume XI. To her great disappointment, it was incredibly dull. It contained the testimony of the police officers who searched Charlie Deems's apartment after his arrest. They told about items they had discovered during the search. Tracy could not imagine why Laura Rizzatti would have been interested in anything she read.

The sheet from Laura's yellow legal pad had been stuck between pages 1289 and 1290. Tracy wondered if that meant those pages contained something important or if the yellow sheet with the list of cases had ended up there by chance. When she reached pages 1289 and 1290, she found nothing that helped clear up the mystery.

Portland police detective Mark Simon's testimony started on page 1267 and continued past the two pages. He was the detective in charge of the search of Deems's apartment. In the early part of his testimony, he outlined the assignments of the officers who searched the apartment. Then he talked about various items found during the search and their significance to the homicide investigation. Deems had been arrested at a nightclub. Several people had phoned him while he was out. The direct examination by Abigail Griffen on pages 1289 and 1290 concerned messages found on Deems's answering machine.

'GRIFFEN: So these were messages that were waiting for the defendant, which he was unable to return because he was arrested?'

'SIMON: Yes, ma'am.

'Q: The jury has heard the message tape. I'd like to go through the messages with you and ask you to comment on their significance, if you can.'

'A: All right.

'Q: The first message is from "Jack." He leaves a number. What significance do you attach to that call?'

'A: I don't have enough information to comment on that call. The number was for a pay phone. We did send someone to the phone, but there was no one there when the officers arrived.'

'Q: Okay. Message number two was from Raoul. He leaves a pager number and asks the defendant to call him when he gets in. What is the significance of that call?'

'A: Okay. Well, with this one, I can comment. Subsequent investigation revealed that the pager was rented from Continental Communications by Ramón Pérez, a known associate of Raoul Otero. Mr. Otero is reputed to be one of the major players in an organization that distributes cocaine in Oregon, Washington, Texas and Louisiana. I believe this call indicates a connection between the defendant and this organization.'

'Q: Thank you. Now, the next call was from Arthur Knowland. He did not leave a phone number. He did say that he needed some "shirts" and wanted the defendant to call him as soon as possible.'

'A: Okay. I believe this call is from someone who wants to buy drugs from the defendant. We see this all the time when we have electronic surveillance on individuals who are talking about drug deals. They rarely use the names of narcotics in their discussions. They will call heroin or cocaine "tires" or "shirts" or whatever they have agreed on in the belief that this will somehow protect them if the person they are dealing with is an undercover officer or a recording is being made of their conversation.'

'Q: The last message is from Alice. She leaves a message and a phone number.'

'A: We contacted the person who subscribes to the phone number. Her name was Alice Trapp. She admitted that her call was an attempt to purchase cocaine.'

The examination continued on the next page, but it changed to a discussion of the contents of a notebook that had been found in Deems's bedroom. Tracy reread the two pages, but had no idea why they might be significant. Then she glanced at her watch. It was eight-thirty. Tracy put Volume XI back with the other transcripts and turned out the lights.

The idea of watching *Casablanca* with Barry Frame seemed like heaven compared to reading another page of boring transcript. In fact, spending the evening with Barry was preferable to anything else she could imagine.

The trial was leaving Tracy so exhausted that sex had been completely banished from her thoughts. Until now. She and Barry had not made love yet, but the way they felt about each other meant it was only a matter of time and the right setting.

Chapter Twenty-three

1

'You know the drill. Keep your head up, keep moving and let me do the talking,' Matthew told Abbie when Barry Frame stopped his car in front of the Multnomah County Courthouse on Monday morning. A torrential rain cascaded off the car as Matthew opened the back door on the driver's side. Huge drops bounced off of the hood and windshield. Matthew held up a large black umbrella to shield Abbie from the downpour. Tracy grabbed the huge leather sample case with the trial files, smiled quickly and shyly at Barry, then ran around the car to help screen Abbie from the crowd that blocked the courthouse entrance. She was soaking wet by the time they fought their way through the reporters and into the elevator.

The court guards recognized the defense team and

waved them around the metal detector that stood between the courtroom door and the long line of spectators. Matthew led the way through the low gate that separated the spectators from the court. He set his briefcase next to the counsel table and shook the water off the umbrella. When he turned around, Abbie was staring at Charlie Deems, who was lounging on a bench behind Chuck Geddes inside the bar of the court. Deems looked surprisingly handsome in a blue pinstripe suit, freshly pressed white shirt and wine-red tie that Geddes had purchased for his court appearance. His shoes were polished and his hair had been cut.

'Howdy, Mrs. Prosecutor,' Deems said, flashing his toothy grin. 'You learnin' what it feels like to be in the frying pan?'

Before Abbie could respond, Matthew stepped in front of her. He stared down at Deems. Deems stopped grinning. Reynolds held him with his eyes a moment more. Then he spoke in a voice so low that only Charlie Deems heard him.

'You are a hollow man, Mr. Deems. There is no goodness in you. If you tell lies about Mrs. Griffen in this courtroom, not even a dark angel will protect you.'

Charlie Deems turned pale. Reynolds turned his back to Deems. Deems leaped to his feet.

'Hey,' Deems shouted, 'look at me, you freak.'

Reynolds sat down and opened his briefcase. Deems took a step toward Matthew, his face tight with rage.

'What did you just say?' Geddes demanded of Reynolds

313

as he and Christenson restrained Deems. Matthew ignored Geddes and calmly arranged his notes while the prosecutor tried to calm his star witness.

'Mr. Deems,' Chuck Geddes asked, 'are you acquainted with the defendant?'

'In a manner of speaking.'

'Please explain how you two first met.'

'She prosecuted me for murder.'

'Had you ever met the defendant before she prosecuted you?'

'No, sir.'

'What was the result of your case?'

'I was convicted and sentenced to death.'

'Where did you spend the next two years?'

'On death row at the Oregon State Penitentiary.'

'Why aren't you still on death row?'

'The Oregon Supreme Court threw out my case.'

'It reversed your conviction?'

'Right.'

'And the Multnomah County district attorney's office elected not to retry you?'

'Yes.'

'Shortly after your release from prison, did the defendant contact you?' Geddes asked.

'Yes, sir. She sure did.'

'Did that surprise you?'

Deems laughed and shook his head in wonder. 'I would have been less surprised if it was the President.'

The jury laughed.

'Why were you surprised?' Geddes asked.

'When a woman spends a year of her life trying to get you executed, you start to think she might not like you.'

Deems smiled at the jury and a few jurors smiled back.

'Tell the jury about the conversation.'

'Okay. As I recollect, she asked me how it felt to be off death row. I said it felt just fine. Then she asked how I was fixed for money. I asked her why she wanted to know. That's when she said she had a business proposition for me.'

'What did you think she had in mind?'

'I knew she didn't want me to mow her lawn.'

The jurors and spectators laughed again. Tracy could see them warming to Charlie Deems and it worried her. She glanced at Reynolds, but he seemed completely unperturbed by Deems's testimony. Tracy marveled at the way he kept his cool.

'Did you ask the defendant what she wanted?' Geddes continued.

'I did, but she said she didn't want to discuss it over the phone.'

'Did you agree to meet the defendant?'

'Yes, sir.'

'Why?'

'Curiosity. And, of course, money. I was dead broke when I got off the row and she implied there was a lot of money to be made.'

'Where did you meet?'

'She wanted me to come to a cabin on the coast. She gave me directions.'

'Do you remember the date?'

'I believe it was Friday, August twelfth.'

Abbie leaned toward Reynolds. She was upset and Tracy heard her whisper, 'These are all lies. I never called him and we never met at the cabin.'

'Don't worry,' Tracy heard Reynolds say. 'Let him hang himself.'

'What happened when you arrived at the cabin?' Geddes asked.

'Mrs. Griffen was waiting for me. There were some chairs on the porch, but she wanted to sit inside, so no one would see us.

'At first she just made small talk. How was I getting by, did I have any jobs lined up? She seemed real nervous, so I just went along with her, even though it didn't make any sense.'

'What do you mean?'

'I knew damn well she wasn't concerned about my welfare. Hell, the woman tried to get me lethally injected. But I figured she'd get to it soon enough.'

'And did she?'

'Yes, sir. After we'd been talking a while, Mrs. Griffen told me she was real unhappy with her husband and wanted a divorce. But there was a problem. She was very rich. Justice Griffen's divorce lawyer was asking for a lot of money and she was afraid the court would give it to him. I asked her what that had to do with me. That's when she led me out back of the cabin and showed me the dynamite.'

'Where was this dynamite?'

'In a toolshed behind the house.'

'Describe the shed and its contents.'

'It's been a while and I only looked in a minute, but it seems like the shed was made out of weathered gray timber. The dynamite was in a box on the floor. I know there were some gardening tools in the shed, but I can't remember what kind.'

'What did Mrs. Griffen say to you when she showed you the dynamite?'

'She said she knew I was good with explosives and wanted to know if I could use the dynamite to kill her husband. She told me she had a workshop in her garage and I could make the bomb there. She also said no one would suspect us of working together since she was the one who prosecuted me.'

'What did you tell her?'

'I told her she'd made a big mistake. I said I didn't know anything about making bombs and that I hadn't killed any of the people she thought I'd killed. But even if I had, I wasn't going to kill the guy who was responsible for taking me off death row. Especially when that guy was a justice of the Oregon Supreme Court. You'd have to be an idiot. I mean, every cop in the state would be hunting you down if you killed someone important like that and they'd never give up.'

'What did the defendant say to that?'

'She offered me fifty thousand dollars. She told me I was smart and could figure out how to do it without being caught.'

'How did you respond?'

'I said I wasn't going to do it.'

'What did the defendant say then?'

'She got real quiet. I'd seen her in court like that. It made me a little nervous. Then she said she was sorry she'd troubled me. I didn't want to hang around any more than I had to, so I took off.'

'Did you go to the police after you left?'

'Are you kidding? She warned me about that. She said no one would believe me if I accused her, because the cops still thought I killed that kid and her father. She also said she'd have dope planted on me and send me away forever if she even heard I was in spitting distance of a police station or the DA's office.'

'Was that the last time you had any contact with Mrs. Griffen?'

'Yes, sir.'

'Despite her warning, you did come to the district attorney and explain what happened.'

'Yes, sir.'

'Why did you come forward?'

'Self-preservation. As soon as the judge was blown up, I knew she was trying to frame me. Hell, she did it once with that phony confession, and the newspapers said the bomb was similar to the one that killed Hollins and his kid. Then I heard the cops were looking for me. I figured my only chance was to go to the DA and hope he'd believe me.'

Geddes reviewed his notes, then said, 'No further questions.'

Deems had stared at Reynolds frequently during his testimony, growing frustrated when Matthew refused to pay any attention to him. The slight had been intentional. Matthew wanted Deems angry and combative.

'Did you know a man named Harold Shoe, Mr. Deems?' Matthew asked.

'Yeah, I knew Shoe.'

'Was he a drug dealer?'

'So they said.'

'Did "they" also say he was a rival of yours in the drug trade?'

'I don't know everything people said about Shoe.'

'Did you know that Mr. Shoe was tortured to death?'

'I heard that.'

'Did you also hear that Larry Hollins was prepared to identify you as the man he saw putting Mr. Shoe's body in a Dumpster?'

'My lawyer told me that after Hollins was killed. That's the first I knew of it.'

'While you were awaiting trial for the murder of Larry Hollins and Jessica Hollins, his nine-year-old daughter, did you have a cellmate named Benjamin Rice?'

'Yeah. The cops planted him in my cell.'

'Did you tell Benjamin Rice that Shoe was "a worthless piece of shit who couldn't even die like a man"?'

'I never said that. Rice made that up.'

'Did you tell Mr. Rice that it was "tough that the kid had to die, but that's the risk a snitch takes"?'

'I never said that either.'

Tracy cast a quick look at the jurors. They no longer looked amused by Charlie Deems.

'What time of day did you meet with Mrs. Griffen at the coast?'

'Late afternoon.'

'Can you be more specific?'

'She said to come out around four.'

'The sun was still shining?'

'Right.'

'And this meeting was arranged during the phone call you received from Mrs. Griffen?'

'Right.'

'Where were you when you received the call?'

'A friend's.'

'What friend?'

'Her name is Angela Quinn.'

'Did you go to Ms. Quinn's as soon as you were released from prison?'

'Yeah.'

'And you were in prison for two years?'

'Two years, two months and eight days.'

'And before that, you were in jail, awaiting trial?'

'Yes.'

'And before that, you lived in an apartment?'

'Right.'

'Not with Ms. Quinn?'

'No.'

'How did Mrs. Griffen know where to call you?'

'What?'

'You testified that you were living in an apartment when you were arrested, then jail, then prison. You've also testified that the first conversation you ever had with Mrs. Griffen was the phone call you received at Angela Quinn's residence. How would Mrs. Griffen know where to contact you? How would she know Angela Quinn's phone number?'

Deems looked confused and glanced at Chuck Geddes for help.

'While you're trying to think up an answer to that question, why don't you tell the jury what Mrs. Griffen was wearing when you met at the cabin.'

'Uh, let's see. Jeans, I think, and a tee shirt.'

'What color tee shirt?'

'Uh, blue, I think.'

'How long were you with Mrs. Griffen?'

'Forty-five minutes. An hour.'

'Face to face?'

'Yeah.'

'And you can't recall what she was wearing?'

'I wasn't paying attention,' Deems snapped angrily. 'I'm not a fashion expert.'

Deems sounded flustered and Geddes leaned over to confer with Neil Christenson.

'You talked inside the cabin, did you not?'

'Right.'

'Maybe you'll have better luck describing the furnishings of the cabin to the jury.'

'What do you mean?'

'Tell the jury what the inside of the cabin looked like. You should have no trouble if you were inside it for forty-five minutes to an hour.'

Several of the jurors leaned forward.

'Uh, there's a kitchen and a living room.'

'When you spoke with Mrs. Griffen, where did you sit?'

'In the living room.'

'Where in the living room?'

'Uh, on the couch.'

'What color is the couch?'

Deems paused for a moment. Then he shook his head. 'I don't really remember. Look, I told you, the woman wanted me to murder her husband. I wasn't paying attention to the furniture.'

'How about the living-room rug, Mr. Deems?' Reynolds asked, ignoring Deems's discomfort.

'I don't remember. Brown. Maybe, it was brown.'

'Can you tell the jury the color of anything in the Griffen cabin?'

Deems was upset. He shifted in his seat.

'Do you want to know why you can't recall the colors, Mr. Deems?' Deems just stared at Reynolds. 'It's because you were in the Griffen cabin but not when you claim you were there. You entered the cabin at night, after sunset, when you tried to kill Mrs. Griffen. In the absence of light, the human eye cannot distinguish colors.'

Deems flushed. He shook his head and glared at Reynolds.

'That's not it. I wasn't paying attention to colors. I was nervous. I mean, this woman prosecuted me for a murder I didn't commit. Then she turns around and asks me to kill her husband. Colors were the last thing on my mind.'

Reynolds picked up a stack of photographs and crossed the courtroom to the witness box. Then he smiled at Deems, but there was no warmth in it.

'By the way,' Matthew said, handing Deems one of the pictures, 'there is no rug in the living room. It's hardwood.'

'What are those photographs?' Geddes asked as he leaped to his feet.

'They are pictures of the cabin taken on August twelfth, the day Mr. Deems claims he visited Mrs. Griffen. The pictures were mentioned in discovery.'

'Objection,' Geddes said desperately. 'There's no foundation for them.'

'All of these photographs were taken by Mrs. Griffen. The camera she used date-stamped the negatives. I'll lay the foundation later,' Reynolds said.

'With that assurance, I'll permit you to use them,' Judge Baldwin ruled.

Deems examined the picture quickly. While the attorneys argued, he looked over at Abigail Griffen. She was smiling a hard, cold smile at him. Deems flushed with rage. He wanted Abbie to suffer, but she looked triumphant.

'Well?' Matthew asked. 'Is there a rug?'

'No,' Deems answered grudgingly. 'At least not in these pictures.'

'Do you have other photographs showing a rug in the Griffen cabin, Mr. Deems?' Reynolds snapped.

Suddenly, it appeared to Tracy that Charlie Deems had thrown a switch and cut off all of his emotions. The anger disappeared to be replaced by a deadly calm. The witness relaxed visibly and leaned back in his chair. Then he grinned at Matthew and answered, 'No, sir. These are the only photos I know about.'

Tracy was suddenly frightened for Matthew and glad that he was not alone with Charlie Deems.

'Thank you, Mr. Deems. Now, you've explained that Mrs. Griffen wanted you to use dynamite that was in a shed behind the house?'

'Right,' Deems replied evenly.

'You remember the dynamite because she showed it to you?'

'Definitely.'

Matthew Reynolds handed another picture to Deems. 'I remind you that the negative of this picture of the shed is date-stamped. Where is the dynamite?'

In the photograph, the shed door was ajar enough to show the interior. Deems saw gardening tools, a volleyball net and an empty space with a volleyball resting dead center. What he did not see was a box of dynamite.

'I don't know,' Deems said with a marked lack of interest. 'Maybe she moved it.'

Reynolds left the pictures and returned to the defense table. He picked up a manila envelope and walked back to Deems.

'I believe you said that you were tempted by Mrs. Griffen's offer of fifty thousand dollars because you could use the money?'

'Yes.'

'I assume you were broke when you left prison?'

'You assume right.'

'Have you gotten a job yet?'

'No.'

'Any savings?'

'No.'

'Did someone hire you to blow up Justice Griffen and frame Mrs. Griffen for the murder?'

Deems laughed. 'That's nonsense.'

'Then how do you explain this?' Reynolds said as he withdrew a sheaf of papers from the envelope and handed them to Charlie Deems. Deems completely lost his cool and his mouth gaped open. He looked at the bank records, then at Reynolds.

'What the hell is this?'

'A bank account at Washington Mutual in your name with a hundred thousand dollars in it.'

'I don't know anything about this,' Deems shouted.

'I see. Then I have no further questions.'

'Any redirect, Mr. Geddes?' Judge Baldwin asked.

'May I have a moment, Your Honor?'

Baldwin nodded and Geddes continued the intense

conversation he had been having with Neil Christenson since Matthew Reynolds announced the contents of the manila envelope. After a moment, Geddes stood. He had learned how to look composed in the worst situations from years of courtroom combat and he appeared to be unconcerned about the destruction of his key witness.

'Nothing further,' Geddes said. 'And the state rests.'

'I imagine you have some motions, Mr. Reynolds?' Judge Baldwin said.

'Yes, sir.'

'How many witnesses do you have?' the judge asked Matthew.

'Twenty-seven.'

'Can you put any of them on this afternoon?'

'I'd prefer to start tomorrow.'

'Why don't we take our morning recess now. I'll send the jury home. We can take up your motions after the recess, then take witnesses in the morning.'

The jurors filed out. As soon as the judge left the bench, Charlie Deems left the witness box. Chuck Geddes and Neil Christenson hustled Deems out of the courtroom and up the stairs to the sixth floor.

'Where did you get that money?' Geddes demanded as soon as they were in his office.

'That's not my account,' Deems said.

'It's in your name.'

'But I don't know anything about it. That fucker Reynolds set me up.'

'And I suppose he took the pictures of the shed, too?'

'I don't know anything about those pictures. There was dynamite in the shed when I was at the cabin.'

Geddes swiveled his chair toward the window. The picture of the shed and the bank account were devastating. There had to be an explanation. He hoped it did not have something to do with being duped by Charlie Deems.

'Wait outside,' Geddes told Deems. Deems seemed only too happy to leave the room.

'What the fuck is happening, Neil?' the prosecutor demanded when they were alone.

'Either Deems was paid off to pin Justice Griffen's murder on Abbie Griffen or someone set him up.'

'Damn it. Reynolds is making me look like a fool.'

'What do you want to do with Deems?'

'Keep him at the farm until we figure out what's going on. If that son of a bitch lied to me, I'll have his balls.'

2

Raoul Otero was staring at the gray roiling clouds and sheets of rain that obscured the view from his penthouse apartment in downtown Portland when Bobby Cruz sat down across from him. Raoul's mood was as black as the weather and the fifth of scotch he'd been working on all afternoon had only stoked his rage.

'You want some?' Otero asked, holding up the bottle.

'*No, gracias,*' Cruz answered politely. Otero was not

surprised. Except for violence, Bobby Cruz had no vices.

'Well?'

'It don' look good, Raoul. Deems testified for the DA.'

Otero stared at the Willamette River. No ships were moving on its turbulent waters. It was so dark the cars crossing the Hawthorne Bridge were using their headlights even though it was only four o'clock.

'Why is Charlie doing this? He beat his case. The cops don't have no leverage on him.'

'What I think is, he's doin' it to get even with the Griffen woman for putting him on the row.'

Raoul nodded in agreement. 'That piece of shit was always big on revenge. Remember how happy he was when I let him do Shoe?'

'Sí, Raoul. He could barely contain his joy. Our problem is that Griffen isn't the only one Charlie's mad at.'

'How can he be stupid enough to talk to the cops about me?' Raoul asked incredulously.

'Charlie isn't stupid, but he's mean. He's also loco. Charlie does what Charlie wants to do. That's why I told you not to have no dealings with him in the first place. Remember I said you can't control Charlie, because Charlie is always out of control?'

'And you were right. José called from Tijuana while you were at the courthouse. The feds busted the two border guards we had on the payroll. Charlie knew about them, just like he knew about Lee Terrace and the rest area on I-5.'

'There's only one thing to do,' Cruz said calmly.

Otero knocked down what was left of the scotch in his glass. He did not like being in this position, but that fuck Deems had put him in it. Killing someone always hurt business, because the cops had to work hard on a murder case. Still, normally the risk was small with someone like Charlie, because the cops wouldn't spend too much time looking into the murder of a dealer who'd offed a kid. But 'normally' might not apply anymore. Charlie was on the side of the angels. The cops were going to work over-time if someone took out the key witness in the murder of a Supreme Court justice. But that shit-for-brains, loco son of a bitch gave him no choice.

'Do you know where the cops have Charlie?'

'They're hiding him at a farmhouse. I followed them from the courthouse.'

'Can you do it?'

'It won't be easy. He has two cops guarding him.'

'You need help?'

Cruz smiled. '*No, gracias*. I think I will handle this myself.'

Raoul nodded. A red mist clouded his eyes. He wanted to smash something. He wanted to smash Charlie Deems. If the situation wasn't desperate, if they had not lost three shipments already, he would wait and personally carve up Charlie Deems like a fucking turkey. But there would be no more shipments until Charlie was dead, so he would have to let Bobby Cruz have the honor.

3

Neil Christenson arrived home at ten o'clock Monday night, after spending all evening listening to Chuck Geddes scream at Charlie Deems. Christenson changed into jeans and an OSU sweatshirt, then he settled into his favorite armchair and tried to get into a sitcom his wife, Robin, was watching.

At a commercial, Christenson went into the kitchen to fix himself a snack and Robin put on some water for tea. It was quiet in the house because the kids were asleep.

'Are you okay?' Robin asked.

'I'm just tired, but I'm thankful for a chance to forget about the *Griffen* case for a few hours.'

Robin gave him a sympathetic smile. 'Is it that bad?'

'Worse. Geddes has been driving me crazy ever since Reynolds took apart Deems this morning.'

Robin put her arms around her husband and gave him a compassionate kiss.

'The trial will be over soon,' she said. 'Maybe we can get away for a few days.'

Christenson held his wife and kissed the top of her head.

'What did you have in mind?'

'I don't know,' she answered coyly. 'Maybe we could shack up in a motel on the coast for a weekend. Mom can watch the kids.'

Christenson froze. 'That's it,' he muttered to himself.

Robin pulled back and looked at her husband. He was staring into space. Christenson gave her a tremendous hug and kissed her on the cheek.

'I've got to go,' he said.

'What? You just got home.'

'It was the receipts, Robin. You're a lifesaver.'

'What did I do?'

'You may have won the *Griffen* case.'

Christenson walked back into the living room and put on his shoes.

'You're not going out?'

'I'm sorry. I have to check something to see if I'm right. If I don't do it now, I won't be able to sleep.'

Robin sighed. She had been married to Neil for twelve years and she was used to his odd hours.

As he laced up his shoes, Christenson thought about the afternoon he had watched Tracy Cavanaugh and Barry Frame sift through the state's evidence. He had never figured out what piece of evidence had intrigued Tracy so much that she had felt it necessary to hide it from his view. Now he thought he knew what she had been looking at. Some of the credit card receipts in the box of evidence from the bottom right drawer in Justice Griffen's den had been from the Overlook Motel. Christenson knew that motel. Three years ago, there had been a murder there and he had visited it during the investigation. The Overlook was a dive. What was a Supreme Court justice doing there on three occasions? Robin had given him the answer. He was shacking up. But with who? Geddes's guess was Laura Rizzatti, and Christenson was going to see if Geddes was right.

4

Charlie Deems paced back and forth across his small bedroom on the second floor of the farmhouse. The rain had trapped him inside and he was going stir crazy. Not even the game shows made this dump bearable anymore. To make matters worse, that asshole Geddes and his flunky Christenson had grilled him all evening.

'Why wasn't there dynamite in the photo of the shed? Where did the money in the bank account come from? Did he kill Justice Griffen and frame Abigail Griffen?' And on and on, over and over again.

Deems was certain he knew what had happened, but he wasn't going to tell Geddes. What he was going to do was take care of this himself. He'd been set up by that bitch Griffen. How else could Reynolds have made a fool out of him? According to Geddes, the whole case was in the toilet and that smirking whore was going to walk. Well, she might walk away from this case, but she was never going to walk away from Charlie Deems. When he was through with her, Abigail Griffen was going to wish she had been convicted and sentenced to death, because what he had planned for her would make dying seem like a fucking picnic.

Chapter Twenty-four

1

'As our first witness,' Matthew said on Tuesday morning, 'the defense calls Tracy Cavanaugh.'

Tracy could not remember being this nervous since the finals of the NCAA cross-country championships. She knew that she was only a chain-of-custody witness, but being under oath was nerve-racking.

'Ms. Cavanaugh, what is your profession?'

'I'm an attorney, Mr. Reynolds.'

'What is your current position?'

'I'm an attorney in your office.'

'Have you assisted me in defending Mrs. Griffen since she retained my firm?'

'Yes, sir.'

'On September thirteenth, did I ask you to do something?'

'Yes.'

'Please tell the jury what I asked you to do.'

'You asked me to go to Mrs. Griffen's home and pick up a Pentax camera and film from her.'

'Where was the film?'

'In the camera.'

'What did you do with the film?'

'It was late evening when I picked up the camera, so I waited until morning and took it to FotoFast, a commercial developer. The clerk took the film out of the camera and signed a receipt stating that he had done so. Then I brought you the camera.'

Matthew handed Tracy a slip of paper. 'Is this the receipt you received from the clerk?'

'Yes, sir.'

'Later, did you go to FotoFast to pick up the developed film?'

'Yes. And I had the clerk sign a second statement.'

Reynolds picked up the envelope with the photographs and Abbie's camera and walked over to Tracy.

'I am handing you what has been marked as Defense Exhibit 222. Is this the camera you picked up from Mrs. Griffen?'

'Yes,' Tracy said after examining the small black Pentax.

'I hand you Defense Exhibit 223. Is this the envelope you picked up from FotoFast?'

'Yes.'

'Did you give this envelope to me?'

'Yes.'

'Did you review the photographs?'

'No, sir.'

'Thank you.'

Tracy handed the envelope back to Reynolds. As she did, she noticed that the photographs Matthew had shown to Deems were still on the ledge in the witness box where witnesses place exhibits they are viewing. She picked them up and gave them to Reynolds to put with the other photographs.

Just before Reynolds took the photo of the shed from her, Tracy frowned. She was certain there was something odd about the picture, but she could not figure out what it was in the brief moment she had to view the photograph.

'Nothing further,' Reynolds said as he placed the photographs in the envelope and walked to his seat.

'Mr. Geddes?'

Tracy looked at the prosecutor. He was sitting alone this morning and Tracy wondered why Neil Christenson was missing.

'No questions,' Geddes said, and Tracy was relieved to return to her seat at counsel table.

'The defense calls Dr. Alexander Shirov,' Matthew said.

Tracy wanted to look at the photograph of the shed, but Reynolds had placed the envelope with the pictures under a stack of exhibits by the time she was back at the counsel table.

When Dr. Shirov entered the courtroom, Tracy turned to look at him. She had questioned Reynolds about the identity of his expert and the results of the tests on the metal strips, because she was dying to know what he could possibly do about this seemingly incontrovertible evidence, but Reynolds just smiled and declined to name his witness or discuss the results.

Dr. Shirov walked with a slight limp and carried his notes in both hands. He was tall and heavy, a man in his mid-fifties with a slight paunch, salt-and-pepper hair and a full beard. He looked relaxed when he took the oath and he smiled warmly at the jury when he took his seat in the witness box.

'What is your profession?' Matthew Reynolds asked.

'I'm a professor of chemistry at Reed College in Portland.'

'Do you hold any other positions at Reed?'

'Yes. I'm also the director of the nuclear reactor facility.'

'What does that job entail?'

'I'm responsible for the maintenance, operation and use of the research reactor and its licensing.'

'What is your educational background?'

'I obtained a BS in chemistry from the University of California at Berkeley in 1965. In 1970, I received a doctor of science degree from the Massachusetts Institute of Technology with a specialty in the area of nuclear chemistry.'

'Do you have any special expertise in the use of neutron activation analysis?'

'I do.'

'Would you please explain neutron activation analysis to the jury?'

'Certainly,' Dr. Shirov said, turning toward the jury box. His smile was light and easy and his thick glasses magnified the St. Nick's twinkle in his blue eyes. Some of the jurors smiled back.

'If we take a sample of any material and place it in a source of neutrons – atomic particles – the material will absorb the neutrons and become radioactive. There are ninety-two basic elements and fourteen man-made elements. More than fifty of the basic elements emit gamma rays when they become radioactive. We have instruments that measure how many gamma rays are given off by the material and their specific energy.

'A nuclear reactor is a source of neutrons. If I have material I want to analyze, I place it in the reactor. Once the substance is radioactive it is removed from the reactor and taken to a gamma ray analyzer, a machine that detects gamma rays and measures their energy. The information obtained from the analyzer is printed on a magnetic disk and stored so we can analyze the data and determine what elements are present and how much of each element is present.'

'Dr. Shirov,' Matthew said, 'if you were asked to compare two items which appeared to come from the same source, what could you tell about their similarities and differences by using neutron activation analysis?'

'I could tell a great deal. You see, materials in nature contain traces of other materials. Sometimes there are large amounts of one material in the other, but other times there may only be a small amount. Neutron activation

337

analysis is a very sensitive technique for determining the amount of minor elements that exist in a particular object.

'For example, if you filled a thimble with arsenic and thoroughly mixed it with four railroad tank cars of water, neutron activation analysis would be able to determine the amount of arsenic in a one-ounce sample of the water.

'Now, getting back to the comparison of our two samples, if the trace elements in the two are greatly different, it is possible to reach a conclusion with a high degree of certainty that they came from different sources.

'On the other hand, if we see no differences between the two samples, we can say that there is no scientific evidence to support an assertion that they are from different sources.'

'Dr. Shirov, I'm handing you what has previously been marked as State's Exhibits 36 and 37. Do you recognize them?'

Dr. Shirov took from Reynolds Exhibit 36, the charred and twisted metal strip with the notch that had been part of the bomb that killed Justice Griffen, and Exhibit 37, the clean metal strip with the point that had been found in Abbie's garage.

'You brought these two items to the college this weekend.'

'What did I tell you I needed to know?'

'You told me that you wanted to know if the two pieces of steel plate were attached at one time.'

'What did you do to find out?'

'There was no need to irradiate both exhibits in their

entirety, so I took samples of each. This presented a small problem. How to cut a sample without contaminating it. Most of the usual ways of cutting steel involve the possibility of contamination. For example, the steel of a hacksaw blade might transfer elements to the samples that would give off gamma rays when irradiated. I chose a silicon carbide saw because these elements do not give off gamma rays.

'You explained the importance of the two pieces of steel plate, so I took my samples from the middle of one side so as not to affect the end with the tool markings. I placed each exhibit in a vise and made a vee-notch cut that allowed me to obtain two one-hundred-milligram-size samples.'

'How big is that, Dr. Shirov?'

'Oh, say the size of a sunflower seed.'

'And that was enough for an accurate test?'

'Yes.'

'What did you do after you obtained the samples?'

'I put each sample in a pre-cleaned vial and washed it in distilled water to remove adhering material. Then I dried the samples overnight.

'The next day, I placed each sample in a pre-cleaned polyethylene vial and heat-sealed the vials. The sealed vials were then placed inside a polyethylene irradiation container, called a "rabbit," for irradiation in the nuclear reactor's pneumatic tube facility. This is similar to the pneumatic tube system used in drive-in banks, but ours ends up in the core of the reactor.'

Reynolds returned to the counsel table and picked up two lead containers, approximately two inches in diameter and four inches tall and handed them to Dr. Shirov.

'Dr. Shirov, I am handing you what have been marked as Defense Exhibits 201 and 202. Can you identify these exhibits?'

'Certainly. These are what we call lead pigs and they are used for housing radioactive samples.'

'Are the samples dangerous?'

'No. Not at this time.'

'What is in these lead pigs?'

'The samples I took from Exhibits 36 and 37.'

'If the state wished, could its own scientists retest these samples?'

'Yes, but they would probably want to use fresh samples from the steel plates.'

'Thank you. Go on with your explanation, Doctor.'

'I performed a five-minute irradiation on each sample. Then I retrieved the samples. Next I punctured the vials with a hypodermic needle and flushed out the radioactive argon gas produced when argon, which occurs naturally in air, is irradiated in a reactor. The vials were then placed in a clear plastic bag and put in front of a high-resolution gamma ray analyzer.'

'Explain what you did next.'

'When a substance is exposed to neutrons some of the atoms may absorb a neutron and become radioactive. These atoms decay differently depending on the identity of the original atom. No two radioactive nuclides decay with the same half-life and energy. Therefore, by measuring the energy of the gamma rays emitted during decay at known times after these samples were removed from the reactor, I was able to identify many of the elements in the samples by analyzing the data from the gamma ray detector. I counted the gamma rays emitted at one, five, ten and thirty minutes after the end of the irradiation. I counted the sample again at two and twenty-four hours after the end of the irradiation. The data for each gamma ray count was stored on a disk for later analysis. After the data was on the disk, I used a computer program to identify the energies of the gamma rays.'

'Dr. Shirov, what conclusions did you draw from the test data?'

'Mr. Reynolds, I have concluded, after reviewing the information obtained from the analysis, that there is no evidence to support a conclusion that the sample from Exhibit 36 and the sample from Exhibit 37 could have come from the same piece of steel plate. Furthermore, they could not have a common source of origin.'

Tracy was stunned and she could tell by the look on Chuck Geddes's face that she was not alone. The two metal pieces so obviously fit that she had assumed they were joined once. Now it looked like she was wrong and the state's case was in shambles.

'Are you saying that Exhibit 36 and Exhibit 37 were never connected?' Reynolds asked Dr. Shirov.

'I am.'

'What is the basis for your conclusion?'

'The fragments from Exhibit 37, the clean piece of steel plate, contained observable arsenic, antimony, manganese and vanadium. Exhibit 36, the sample that is charred and twisted, contains manganese, vanadium and aluminum, but no arsenic or antimony. It would not be possible for one piece of steel from a common plate to contain arsenic and antimony and another piece of steel from the same plate to be missing these elements.'

'Exhibit 36 was in an explosion. Could that account for the missing elements?'

'Mr. Reynolds, it is not possible that the explosion changed the composition of the steel by removing two elements. It would be more likely that an explosion would add material.'

'Dr. Shirov, did you conduct any more tests on the samples?'

'No. Since the observations were conclusive at this point, there was no purpose in further analysis.'

'Thank you, Doctor. I have no further questions.'

Chuck Geddes stood up. He was obviously fighting to control his emotions in front of the jury.

'May we approach the bench, Your Honor?'

Judge Baldwin motioned Geddes and Reynolds forward.

'Mr. Reynolds gave me Dr. Shirov's test results this morning . . . ,' Geddes whispered angrily.

'No need to go any further, Mr. Geddes,' Judge Baldwin said. 'I assumed you'd want to reserve cross. Any objection, Mr. Reynolds?'

'No, Your Honor,' Reynolds said graciously.

'Then let's take our morning recess.'

As soon as the jurors filed out, Tracy grabbed Reynolds's arm.

'How did you know the two pieces of steel were different?' she asked, unable to keep the awestruck tone out of her voice.

Reynolds smiled. 'I had no idea they were different, Tracy. When I'm dealing with the state's evidence, I follow a simple rule. I never assume any of it is what it appears to be. I thought I was wasting my time when I hired Dr. Shirov this weekend, but I couldn't think of anything else to do. Fortunately, whoever is trying to frame Abbie didn't know there was a foolproof method of telling if the two metal strips were once joined.'

Reynolds turned his attention to Dr. Shirov, who had walked over to the defense table as soon as Judge Baldwin left the bench. Tracy shook her head. Reynolds was astonishing. Now she understood why so many people, especially other lawyers, spoke of him with such reverence. And why so many clients literally owed him their lives.

Tracy saw Chuck Geddes rushing out of the courtroom and away from the humiliating events of the morning. Just as he reached the door, Neil Christenson came in with a big smile on his face. The investigator said something that made Geddes stop. The two men conferred. Geddes's back was to Tracy, so she could not see his face, but she could see Christenson gesturing animatedly and Geddes nodding vigorously. Then Christenson stopped talking and Geddes turned and stared at Reynolds and Abbie Griffen. There was a cruel smile on his face, an expression that was hard to reconcile with the stunning blow that had been dealt to his case moments ago.

2

Barry Frame lived in the Pearl District, an area of northwest Portland once filled with decaying warehouses that had been rejuvenated by an infusion of art galleries and an influx of young professionals and artists who lived in the renovated lofts. Some of the bare brick walls in Barry's loft were decorated with Matthew Reynolds's nature photography. A poster from the Mount Hood Jazz Festival showing a piano floating on a pristine lake with Mount Hood in the background hung above a low white sofa. Across from the sofa, a metal bookcase stood next to a twenty-seven-inch TV set and a state-of-the-art stereo system. Barry was listening to a CD of Stan Getz blowing a mellow sax when Tracy knocked on his door. She had called from the courthouse as soon as court ended. Barry had been in the field interviewing witnesses during the day and was anxious to be brought up to date on what had happened in the courtroom.

As soon as the door opened, Tracy threw her arms around Barry's neck and kissed him. Then she broke free and grabbed Barry by the shoulders.

'Matthew Reynolds is unreal. I mean, I'd heard he was

a grade A genius, but I didn't really believe it until I saw him this afternoon.'

'Slow down,' Barry said with a laugh.

'I can't. I'm on a fantastic high. You should have seen Geddes. He's such a pompous ass. God, the look on his face as soon as the jurors were out of the room. He went ballistic. It was priceless.'

'What happened?'

Tracy grinned wickedly. 'What are you willing to do to find out?'

Tracy was loaded with energy and wanted to expend it the same way they had when they missed the last half of *Casablanca* on Friday night.

'Jesus, I'm involved with a sex maniac. Is this the only way I can get information out of you?'

'Yup.'

'I feel like I'm being used.'

'Yup.'

'And here I thought it was my mind that attracted you.'

'Nope,' Tracy said as she started taking off her dress.

'Tell me what happened in the goddamn courtroom while I still have the strength to listen,' Barry said.

They were lying naked on Barry's king-size bed. Tracy rolled over on her side.

'I guess you've earned the information,' she said, smiling impishly. Then she told Barry about Dr. Shirov's testimony.

'Man, I wish I'd been there,' Barry said when she was finished.

'Didn't you know about Shirov?'

'No. This was Matt's baby. He's pulled stuff like this before. He gets in this zone only he can get to and comes up with these ideas. If there's a better lawyer in the country, I haven't heard of him.'

'Or her,' Tracy said, nestling against Barry's chest.

'Excuse me for being politically incorrect,' Barry answered as he kissed Tracy's forehead.

'It's all over but the shouting,' she said. 'Matt destroyed Deems and Dr. Shirov has wiped out Geddes's key evidence. The jury has to have at least a reasonable doubt.'

'I never like to get overconfident,' Barry said, 'but I have to agree with you. It looks like Matt has this one in the bag.'

PART SIX

THE MAGIC
TRICK

Chapter Twenty-five

1

On Wednesday morning, Tracy noticed that no one was sitting at the prosecution counsel table when the defense team entered the courtroom. The judge's bailiff hurried over to Reynolds as soon as he spotted him.

'The judge wants you in chambers with your client. Mr. Geddes and Mr. Christenson are already there.'

'Any idea what's going on, George?' Reynolds asked.

'Not a clue.'

Brock Folmer, the judge whose chambers Judge Baldwin was using, was a Civil War buff. A bookcase with volumes about the great conflict stood next to the door to the courtroom and a table covered with miniature blue and gray soldiers reenacting the Battle of Bull Run sat against the wall under the window. Judge Baldwin seemed lost behind a huge oak desk that stood in the center of the room. In back of him was a complete set of the Oregon Court of Appeals and Supreme Court reports and the Oregon Revised Statutes. The court reporter was sitting at Judge Baldwin's elbow.

There were three high-backed, brown leather, upholstered chairs in front of the judge's desk. One was empty and Reynolds took it. The other two were occupied by Chuck Geddes and Neil Christenson. Christenson looked nervous, but Geddes looked like he had just won the lottery.

'Good morning, Matt,' Judge Baldwin said. 'Miss Cavanaugh and Mrs. Griffen, why don't you have a seat on that couch over by the wall, and we'll get started.'

'What's going on, Judge?' Reynolds asked.

'Let's go on the record and Mr. Geddes can tell us. He asked for this meeting this morning.'

Geddes lounged in his chair. There was a smug smile on his face. 'I want to reopen the state's case,' he said.

Judge Baldwin looked a little put out. 'That's highly unusual, Mr. Geddes. We're well into the defense case.'

'I'm aware that my request is unusual, Your Honor, but Mr. Christenson has discovered new evidence that changes the complexion of our case.'

'And what evidence is that?' the judge asked.

'Evidence that Abigail Griffen also murdered her husband's lover, Laura Rizzatti.'

Tracy was stunned and Abbie bolted out of her seat.

'You sick bastard,' she started, but Reynolds was up, blocking the judge's view and holding out a hand to his client.

'Please, Mrs. Griffen,' he said forcefully.

Abbie caught herself and sank down onto the couch. She was clearly shaken by the accusation. And so, to Tracy's surprise, was Matthew Reynolds.

'Let's everyone calm down so we can sort this out,' Judge Baldwin commanded. Geddes had not moved during Abbie's outburst. Reynolds made certain that Abbie was under control, then he turned back to the judge.

'I object to Mr. Geddes's motion to reopen,' Reynolds said forcefully. 'The state has rested. Mr. Geddes had months to uncover evidence of this sort, if it exists. The introduction now of evidence of another murder would be untimely. I also believe it would require a mistrial or a lengthy continuance so the defense could prepare to meet this evidence. Both actions would be highly prejudicial to the defense case, which, as the court knows, is in an excellent posture at this point.'

Reynolds paused and cast a cutting look at Geddes.

'Frankly, Your Honor, I'm a bit skeptical of the timing of this motion, coming, as it does, right after Mr. Geddes's key witness and key evidence have been discredited.'

'Mr. Reynolds's points are well taken, Mr. Geddes,' Judge Baldwin said, 'but I suppose I have to hear the evidence you want to introduce before I can make a ruling. Why don't you enlighten us?'

'Certainly, Your Honor. That's why Mr. Christenson is here. Neil, please tell the judge what you discovered.'

Christenson shifted uncomfortably in his chair and faced the judge. 'Laura Rizzatti was Justice Griffen's clerk at the Supreme Court, Your Honor. She was murdered a little less than a month before Justice Griffen was killed. Mr. Geddes thought it was suspicious that the two murders had been committed so close to one another, but we had no evidence that they were connected, so we assumed that we were probably just dealing with a coincidence.

'Then, Monday night, I remembered that I had seen several credit card receipts to the Overlook Motel in evidence we had taken during a search of Justice Griffen's home office.'

Tracy's stomach tightened at the mention of the Overlook. She saw exactly where Christenson was going and she could not believe it. Until now, the defense was convinced that the prosecutors knew nothing about Justice Griffen's extramarital affairs. But it was clear that not only did they know about Griffen's trysts at the Overlook, they had drawn an unexpected inference.

'Initially, the receipts meant nothing to me,' Christenson continued. 'Then I recalled that the Overlook was a very seedy motel. Not a place where someone like Justice Griffen would normally go. On a hunch, I brought a photograph of Laura Rizzatti to the Overlook and showed it to Annie Hardesty, who is a clerk at the motel. Mrs. Hardesty confirmed that Justice Griffen used rooms at the motel on several occasions to meet women. She also told me that she had seen Laura Rizzatti with the judge more than once.'

Christenson paused to let the implications sink in.

'Then she told me two other facts that I considered

important. First, she told me that Miss Cavanaugh and Barry Frame, Mr. Reynolds's investigator, came to the motel well before the trial and learned that the judge was using the motel as a love nest.'

'Which will make it difficult for Mr. Reynolds to claim surprise, Your Honor,' Geddes interjected.

'Let's hold off on your argument until I've heard all of Mr. Christenson's statement,' the judge said sternly. 'Mr. Christenson, you said there was something else Mrs. Hardesty related.'

'Yes, sir. She said she started watching the news about the case after Miss Cavanaugh's visit because she thought she might be a witness, and she recognized the defendant, Mrs. Griffen, as someone she'd seen at the Overlook. She remembered the incident quite clearly because Mrs. Griffen and her husband were arguing so loudly that one of the other guests complained.

'Mrs. Hardesty told me that she went over to the room the judge was renting to get them to quiet down when the door burst open and Mrs. Griffen came flying out. Before the door opened, though, she heard part of the argument and she is willing to testify that Mrs. Griffen threatened to kill her husband if she caught him cheating again.'

'When did you discover this information, Mr. Christenson?' Judge Baldwin asked.

'Yesterday and the day before, Your Honor.'

Geddes leaned forward. 'I believe this evidence lays a strong foundation for our theory that Mrs. Griffen learned that Laura Rizzatti and the judge were lovers and that she killed them both when the judge did not heed her warning to stop his affair with Miss Rizzatti.'

'What do you have to say, Mr. Reynolds?' the judge asked.

Reynolds had carried a paperback copy of the Oregon Rules of Evidence into chambers. As he was flipping through the pages, looking for the section he wanted, the book slipped from his hand and fell to the floor. The pages crumpled and the cardboard cover bent. Reynolds leaned over to retrieve the book and Tracy saw his hand tremble as he smoothed out the pages. When he spoke, there was an uncharacteristic quiver in his voice.

'Rule 404 (3) states that evidence of other crimes is not admissible to prove that a defendant is likely to have committed the crime for which she is on trial simply because she committed another, similar crime before.'

'Yes, Mr. Reynolds,' the judge interrupted. 'But the rule also states that proof of prior crimes is admissible for other purposes, such as proof of motive or to show a plan involving both crimes. If there is proof that Mrs. Griffen had a plan to kill both victims or that she killed her husband because he and Miss Rizzatti were lovers, wouldn't the evidence of Miss Rizzatti's murder be admissible?'

'It's possible, Your Honor, but you've forgotten a step the Supreme Court set out in *State* v. *Johns*, the case that set up the procedure a judge must use to decide if prior crime evidence is admissible. First, you must decide if the evidence is relevant to an issue in the case, such as proving motive. *Then* you must decide if the relevance of the evidence is outweighed by the prejudice to the defendant that inevitably occurs if proof of another crime committed by the defendant is introduced at trial.

'In deciding the relevance versus prejudice issue, a judge must consider four factors, one of which is the certainty that the defendant committed the other crime. The burden of convincing the court on that point rests on the state and I haven't heard a single piece of evidence that connects Mrs. Griffen to the Rizzatti murder.'

'Does Mr. Geddes have to convince me beyond a reasonable doubt that Mrs. Griffen killed Miss Rizzatti before I can let in the evidence of the Rizzatti murder?'

'No, Your Honor. If I remember correctly, the cases hold that you must be "certain" Mrs. Griffen killed Miss Rizzatti, but that is still a high burden. There is a case, *Tucker* v. *State*, from Nevada that I would like to call to your attention.

'In the spring of 1957, Horace Tucker called the police to his home in Las Vegas. Tucker was unshaven, he looked tired and he had been drinking. A detective found a dead man on the floor of Tucker's dining room. The man had been shot several times, but Tucker said he found the body when he woke up and had no idea what happened. A grand jury conducted an extensive investigation, but did not indict Tucker because it deemed the evidence of Tucker's guilt to be inconclusive.

'Roughly six years later, in late 1963, Tucker phoned the police again. This time they found a dead man on the couch in Tucker's living room. The man had been shot to death. Tucker looked like he had been drinking. He said he awakened to find the dead man and had no idea how he got into his house or how he was killed.

'This time, Tucker was charged with murder. At his trial, the prosecutor introduced evidence of the first murder over a defense objection. Tucker was found guilty of murder, but the Nevada Supreme Court reversed because it found nothing in the record that proved that Tucker killed the first man. The court held that evidence of a prior crime is inadmissible unless there is proof that the defendant committed the uncharged crime.'

'That case is absurd,' Geddes said. 'I don't care what they do in Nevada. A Nevada case isn't precedent here. I don't think Oregon law requires me to jump through all these hurdles to get this evidence before a jury.'

'Calm down, Mr. Geddes. I'm not that impressed by that Nevada case myself. But it's clear that this issue is too complex for me to decide today. I'm going to dismiss the jury until we clear this up. I want briefs on the prior-crime issue from both of you by Friday.'

Judge Baldwin looked worried. 'One matter greatly concerns me, gentlemen. If I allow your motion, Mr. Geddes, I may also have to grant a defense motion for mistrial or a continuance because of the prejudice to the defense of reopening at this stage. I'm deeply troubled that the defense may not have the ability to investigate these new allegations against Mrs. Griffen during trial. I want this prejudice issue thoroughly briefed. This is a death penalty case and I am going to make absolutely certain that both sides have a fair trial.'

2

'Why didn't you tell me that a witness heard you threaten to kill Justice Griffen when we discussed the Overlook?' Matthew asked Abbie as she paced back and forth across her living room.

'I don't remember seeing her. I was upset. I just stormed out of the motel room. I was so mad, I don't even remember what I said to Robert.'

Matthew walked over to the French windows and stared out at the back lawn.

'I don't know if we can avoid asking for a mistrial if the judge lets Geddes reopen the case,' he said grimly.

'We've got to go on,' Abbie said, turning toward Matthew with a look of desperation. 'I couldn't go through another trial. I'd be trapped in this house again.'

'You've got to consider the possibility. If the jury starts thinking that you may have murdered Laura Rizzatti, they'll forget everything else they've heard. And the judge is right. How can we possibly investigate the Rizzatti murder while we're in trial?'

'But we're winning. If the case went to the jury now, I'd be acquitted.'

'Geddes knows that. It's one of the reasons he wants Judge Baldwin to rule that he can introduce the evidence.

357

It would force us to move for a mistrial and save him from losing the case.'

'That bastard. I hate him.'

Abbie stopped in front of Matthew. Her shoulders sagged and she began to sob. The pressure she had been under since her arrest was suddenly more than she could bear. Matthew took her in his arms. Tears streaked her face. She was so forlorn Matthew would have done anything to make her smile. Without saying a word, he stroked her hair and held her.

Finally, Abbie stopped crying. She rested her head against Matthew's shoulder for a moment. She felt as light as a feather, as if her tears had carried away all her emotions and left her hollow. Then she slowly tilted her head back and kissed him. The kiss ended. Abbie rested her cheek against his and he thought he heard her say, 'I love you.'

It was the voice of someone who had given up everything but one basic truth.

Matthew felt dizzy. He pulled back and felt pressure on his hand. Abbie kept hold of it, turned her back to him and led him toward the stairs. He followed behind her and walked into Abbie's bedroom in a trance, his heart beating so fast he was having trouble breathing. Abbie turned toward him. She unbuttoned her blouse and stepped out of her skirt. She was wearing a white lace bra and silk bikini panties. Matthew marveled at her smooth, olive skin, the hard muscle, the curves and flat places. The mysteries of a woman's body. Compared to Abbie, he was pathetic.

Abbie moved into Matthew's arms. He could feel the warmth and texture of her satin-smooth skin. She unbuttoned his shirt, then knelt as she slipped off his pants. Matthew kissed the top of her head and smelled her hair. There was a fragrance of flowers.

Abbie stood up and unhooked her bra. Her breasts were full and high. Her nipples were erect.

'Take off my panties,' Abbie whispered. Her desire paralyzed Matthew. How could a woman like Abbie want him? She read the confusion on his face and touched the tips of her fingers to his lips. Matthew began to shake. He had never felt such desire, had barely allowed himself to dream of it. Abbie's hand strayed to his penis and the fingers that had traced along his lips performed a different kind of magic. Then Abbie pushed him gently and he fell back onto the bed and into his dreams.

Matthew reached across the bed until he found Abbie's hand. As soon as his fingers touched hers, they entwined. They lay side by side without speaking. Matthew had never felt such peace. If this was all he could ever have out of this life, it would be enough, but he believed now that it was possible for him to have more than this single night with Abbie.

'If we win, will you go back to the district attorney's office?' Matthew asked.

While Abbie thought about his question, Matthew stared at the ceiling. With the lights off, the moonlight cast shadow patterns of the limbs of a giant elm on the white surface. The silhouette swayed gently in perfect rhythm with the calm pulse of Matthew's heart.

'It would be hard to go back, Matt. Jack and Dennis stood by me, but I don't know how I'd feel working there after being a defendant.'

'Have you ever thought about defending cases?'

Abbie turned her head and studied Matthew.

'Why are you asking?'

Matthew kept his eyes on the ceiling. There was a tremor in his voice when he spoke.

'I love you, Abbie, and I respect you, more than you can imagine. You're an excellent lawyer. Together, we would be the best.'

Abbie realized what he was asking her. Matthew Reynolds had never had a partner and his law practice was his life. She squeezed his hand.

'You're already the best, Matthew.'

'Will you consider what I've said?'

Abbie rolled over and stroked his cheek.

'Yes,' she whispered. Then she kissed him softly, then harder, then harder still.

3

Tracy went directly from the courtroom to the Multnomah County law library and started researching the law governing the admissibility of prior-crime evidence. The words on the page were starting to blur when Tracy began reading *State* v. *Zamora*, an Oregon Supreme Court decision that discussed the prior-crime issue. For some reason the case sounded familiar, but she did not know why. It had been decided two years before she started clerking, so it wasn't a case she'd worked on, and she did not recall reading it before. Then the names of the cases on Laura's yellow legal pad flashed in her head and she recognized *Zamora* as one of them.

Tracy skimmed the case. The defendant had murdered a clerk and a customer in a convenience store in Portland. A 5-2 majority reversed the conviction because the trial judge admitted evidence of a prior, unconnected robbery in violation of the rule excluding evidence of prior crimes. Justice Lefcourt had written for the court with Justices Pope, Griffen, Kelly and Arriaga joining him. The public defender had handled Zamora's appeal.

Out of curiosity, Tracy pulled the volumes holding the other cases that Laura had listed on the sheet from the yellow legal pad that Tracy had found in Volume XI of the *Deems* transcript. *State* v. *Cardona* had originated in Medford, a small city in southern Oregon five hours' drive down I-5 from Portland. Tracy did not recognize the name of the attorney who argued the case. Justices Kelly, Griffen and Pope had joined in Justice Arriaga's majority opinion reversing Cardona's conviction for distributing cocaine. Justices Lefcourt, Sherzer and Forbes had dissented.

The majority interpreted the search and seizure provisions of the Oregon constitution as forbidding the procedures the police had used when searching Cardona's apartment, even though the same procedures would not have violated the search and seizure provisions of the United States Constitution. There was nothing unusual about this. The United States Supreme Court had become increasingly conservative. Some state courts could not stomach its ideologically motivated opinions and had begun fashioning a jurisprudence based on interpretations of state constitutions that were frequently at odds with federal law.

In *State* v. *Galarraga*, Roseburg police stopped the defendant for speeding. After writing a ticket, they asked for permission to search Galarraga's car. According to the police, Galarraga consented to a search that revealed automatic weapons, money and cocaine. Justice Kelly reversed the conviction on the grounds that the search violated the provisions of the Oregon constitution. Justices Arriaga, Pope and Griffen had joined in Justice Kelly's opinion. Bob Packard represented Galarraga.

Tracy skimmed the cases again, but could not see a connection between them, other than the fact that all three cases had been reversed. One was a murder case and two were drug cases. They were from three different parts of the state. Two involved state constitutional law issues, but *Zamora* was reversed because of a violation of Oregon's evidence code. Different lawyers had represented the defendants.

The librarian told Tracy she was closing up. Tracy reshelved her books and drove to the office, where she dictated a memo on prior-crime evidence for Reynolds.

She placed the cassette on his secretary's desk with a note asking her to type it first thing in the morning. Barry was cooking her dinner at his apartment. Tracy called to let him know she was on her way and turned out the lights.

Barry served her spaghetti with meat sauce, garlic bread and a salad, but all Tracy could do was peck at her food. Barry saw how exhausted she was and insisted that Tracy sleep at his place. Tracy didn't argue. She staggered out of her clothes, collapsed on the bed and fell into a deep sleep as soon as her head hit the pillow. Soon she was lost in a dark forest. The trees were so high and the foliage so thick that only stray rays of sunlight were able to fight their way through the black-green canopy. In the distance, Tracy heard a muffled sound, strong and constant, like whispered conversation in another room. The dark woods terrified her. She felt trapped and her breathing was labored. Tracy struggled toward the sound until she broke into a clearing and found herself on the shore of a river that raged and swirled downstream toward an unknown destination.

As often occurs in dreams, the landscape shifted. The trees were gone and the land around the river was flat and barren. Someone called to her from the opposite shore. It was a man. She could not hear what he was saying because of the roar of the river. She strained to see him clearly, but his features were blurred by the reflected sunlight. To reach him, she would have to swim the river, and suddenly she was fighting a current that swept her downstream.

Tracy panicked. She sank below the surface, then bobbed up again. She was drowning, dying, when she splashed into a calm section of the river. She gasped for air, still unable to swim to shore, but no longer in immediate danger. The current spun her toward the far shore, where the man miraculously appeared. He shouted to her, but the water roared in her ears, baffling the sound. Then she saw that he was holding something. She watched his arms fly upward. The object sailed toward her. Tracy reached up to catch it and saw a ball rotating slowly through the air. The minute the ball touched her hands, Tracy bolted upright in bed, jerked out of sleep by a truth that frightened her more than any nightmare she'd ever had.

The offices were dark except for the reception area, where the lights were kept on all night. Tracy let them in with her key and Barry punched in the alarm code.

'It's in here,' Tracy said, leading Barry to the small room next to Matthew's office where they were keeping the defense evidence.

'I hope you're wrong about this,' Barry said.

'I hope I am, too.'

The evidence was arranged on a table. Tracy looked through it until she found the photographs and negatives in the FotoFast envelope. She set the negatives aside and shuffled through the photographs. There were shots of Abigail Griffen, pictures of the beach and the ocean, exteriors and interiors of the cabin and the photo of the shed

Matthew had used on cross-examination to destroy Charlie Deems. Tracy checked the dates stamped on the negatives. Some of the early pictures on the roll had been taken in June, but the bulk of the negatives, including the photo of the shed, were dated August 12, the day Deems testified that he had met Abbie at the cabin and the day Abbie claimed she had been attacked.

Tracy studied the photograph of the shed. Barry looked over her shoulder. The photograph showed the interior of the shed. Tracy could see the volleyball net, the tools and the space where a box of dynamite could have sat. In the middle of the space was the volleyball.

'I'm right,' she said dispiritedly.

'Are you certain?'

'Yes. While you were looking around, I walked over to the edge of the bluff and sat on the stairs. On my way, I looked in the shed. The volleyball was resting on the volleyball net. You had the ball when you found me sitting on the stairs, and we played with it on the beach. On the way back to the car, you tossed the ball into the shed. I have a very clear mental picture of the ball coming to rest in the empty space.

'We were at the cabin in September, Barry. The ball was on the net when I opened the shed door. If the ball was in the empty space on August 12, how did it get onto the net? And how can the ball be in the exact position we left it in September in a photograph taken in August? The only answer is that this photograph was taken after we were at the cabin and it's been phonied up to look like it was taken in August. Only I don't know anything about photography, so I have no idea how it was done.'

'Well, I know a lot about cameras. I have to on this job. Let me see the negatives and I'll try to figure this out.'

The negatives were in cellophane slipcases. Each strip contained the negatives for four pictures. Tracy handed the stack of negative strips to Barry. He held up the strip with the picture of the shed to the light. All four negatives were dated August 12.

Barry sat down at the table and picked up the Pentax camera. He turned it over and studied it. Then he looked at the strip of negatives again. Barry frowned. His brow furrowed. He examined the negative strips for all of the photographs. Then he laid down the strip with the negative of the shed and placed another strip directly above it. He studied the two strips, then he removed the strip without the picture of the shed and put another strip in its place. He repeated this with all of the negative strips. When he was done, Barry's shoulders sagged and he closed his eyes.

'What is it?' Tracy asked.

'You're right. The picture of the shed was not taken when the rest of these pictures were.'

'How is that possible if the negative is dated August 12?'

'That's the easy part,' Barry said, picking up the camera and pointing to a digital readout on the back. 'The Pentax 105-R camera has a mechanism for setting the date that is similar to the mechanism you use to set the date on a VCR or a digital watch. The person who took the picture simply reset the date to August 12, took the pictures he wanted, then reset the camera to the correct date.'

'But there are pictures of Mrs. Griffen on the roll of film. The roll had to have been taken before she was confined to her house.'

'It was. When FotoFast developed the film, it was in one strip. FotoFast cut the strip of negatives into several strips, each with four shots on them. The strip with the shot of the shed was the only strip that was not taken on the date stamped on the negative.'

'How do you know that?'

'When film is placed in a camera it's blank. It doesn't have any frames demarking where each photograph will be. The frames are formed when you take a picture. But each roll of film does have numbers imprinted on it that don't appear on the photograph but do show up on the negatives below the frames when a picture is taken. These numbers start at I and go 1, 1A, 2, 2A, and so on. You can see them here,' Barry said, pointing out the numbers.

'These numbers are spaced along the bottom of the roll of film at a set distance from each other. The distance doesn't change, because the numbers are imprinted on the film when the film is produced.

'Whoever did this went to the coast after we were there. He had the negatives of the film Mrs. Griffen gave you. He took out one strip that would be in the natural sequence on the roll for the shot of the shed to appear. In this case it was the strip with the numbers 15 to 16A. Then he took photographs with the Pentax using the same brand of film Mrs. Griffen used. When he came to the shot that would be numbered 15, he copied the shot Mrs. Griffen had taken at that point on the strip. 15A is the fake shot of the shed. He took the shot showing the shed without any dynamite. Then he duplicated shots 16 and 16A, finished the roll, had it printed by the same FotoFast store that printed the roll Mrs. Griffen took and switched the single strip.

'Look at the strips,' Barry said, holding up two he picked at random. 'Each row of film from the same company is manufactured like every other roll. If you take two rolls of film from the same company and lay them side by side, the numbers will line up. If you take a ruler and measure from the tip of one roll to IA and from the tip of a second roll to lA, the distance will be identical. But there's a little piece of film at the end of each roll of film called the leader that you place in the camera when you roll the film into it to get the film into a position where a shot can be taken. Every person does this differently. That means that the numbers will be in a different place in relation to the frames that are formed when each picture is taken on one roll than they will be on another person's roll.'

Barry put down one of the strips he was holding and picked up the strip with the shot of the shed. Then he held one strip directly over the other.

'On every negative strip but the one with the shot of the shed, the number is on the edge of the frame. On the strip with 15 to 16A, the numbers are slightly closer to the center of the frame. Can you see that?'

Tracy nodded.

'That's impossible,' he continued, 'if that strip was on the roll with the rest of the shots.'

Barry put down the strips. 'What I don't understand,' he said, 'is how Griffen was able to get away from her house, take the picture and make the switch without setting off the electronic monitoring system.'

'You don't understand because you don't want to, Barry,' Tracy said sadly.

Barry stared at Tracy. 'You can't think . . .'

'It's the only answer.'

'Bullshit,' Barry shouted angrily.

'I don't want to believe it either. But the simple fact is that Abigail Griffen could not have left the house. And even if she was able to defeat the electronic monitoring system, there's no way she could have known where on the roll to fix the faked strip. We had the negatives here along with the camera.'

'Ah, no,' Barry said in a voice so filled with grief that Tracy felt herself melt with pity for him.

'It was Matt,' she said softly. 'It has to be. He had access to the negatives and the camera and he's a great photographer. You would have to know an awful lot about cameras to come up with this scheme.'

'But why, Tracy?'

'You know the answer to that, too. You've seen how she's played him. He's so in love with her that she only had to whisper the suggestion and he'd do it.'

'Not Matt,' Barry said desperately.

'He's a brilliant attorney, Barry, but he's not a god. He's just a human being.'

Barry stood up and paced the room. Tracy let him work it out. When Barry turned toward her he appeared to have made a decision.

'What are you going to do?' he asked, his voice flat and cold.

'You know I don't have a choice. I have to go to Judge Baldwin. This is a criminal offense. If I don't tell the court, I'm guilty as an aider and abettor.'

'You can't do it, Tracy,' Barry begged her. 'If you tell Baldwin, Matt will be destroyed. He'd be disbarred. Geddes will go berserk. He'll make sure Matt goes to prison, for God's sake.'

Tracy placed a hand on Barry's shoulder.

'Don't you think I know that? But what else can I do? He broke the law. And you're forgetting something else. Griffen wouldn't need a fake photograph unless the dynamite was in the shed. Deems knew about the dynamite, because Abbie showed it to him, which means she asked Deems to kill her husband. If she convinced Matt to fake the picture, it's because she's guilty. If I don't tell the court, Abigail Griffen will go free. She's a murderer, Barry. She killed Robert Griffen.'

Tracy paused and her features became devoid of pity. When she spoke, her voice was hard as granite.

'She may have done something else, Barry. She may have killed Laura Rizzatti, my friend. And I'm not going to let her get way with that.'

Barry had not heard her. He was too overwhelmed by the facts he was forced to face. He looked at the floor and, in a voice on the edge of tears, he said, 'I don't believe it, Tracy. He's the most honorable man I've ever met. He would never fake evidence in a court case.'

'I understand how you feel, but I can't keep quiet about this.'

Barry's face fell. Tracy had never seen another human being so distraught.

'If you do this, you'll do it without me. I won't hurt Matt. And if you do . . .'

Barry couldn't go on. He simply stood in front of Tracy and shook his head.

'Barry, please. Don't do this to us.'

'Don't do this to Matt.'

'What about Griffen? Do you want her to walk away from a murder charge?'

'I don't care about Abigail Griffen. One hundred of her are not worth one man like Matthew Reynolds. Think of all the good he's done. All of the sacrifices he's made. Let her walk, for Christ's sake. Don't crucify Matt. Don't destroy him.'

'He broke the law. I'm an officer of the court. You're asking me to betray everything I believe in and to let a cold-blooded murderer go free.'

'I'm asking you to be human. We're talking about a man's life. And not just any man. Think about what you're doing.'

Tracy shook her head. She could not believe what Barry was asking of her.

371

'I can't let this go, Barry, but I'll talk to Matt before I go to see Judge Baldwin and I'll give him a chance to show me I'm wrong.'

Barry looked directly into Tracy's eyes. His own were dead.

'Do what you have to do, Tracy. But if you destroy Matthew Reynolds, I can never see you again.'

Chapter Twenty-six

1

For the sake of appearances, Matthew did not spend the night with Abbie. At four-thirty in the morning, he let himself into his house through a back door and climbed a staircase that went straight to his living quarters. Forgotten for the moment was the turn the trial had taken. Tonight, all of his dreams had come true. Not only had he and Abbie made love, but he had learned that she really loved him.

Before he went to bed, Matthew took out the manila envelope with the articles about Abbie and the photographs of her. This time when he looked at the photographs he did not feel longing or despair. In fact, they evoked no emotions. For the first time, he understood that the photographs were not Abbie. She was a warm, vibrant person. These two-dimensional images were as insubstantial as ghosts. He could not bring himself to destroy them, but he felt uncomfortable looking at them, as if by viewing the pictures he was betraying the woman he loved.

For the first time in a long time, Matthew awakened to sunlight. He showered and made himself his usual breakfast of toast and black coffee. One of his correspondence chess games had taken a peculiar turn. In a position where Matthew thought he held a slight advantage, his opponent, an architect in Nebraska, had made an odd and unexpected knight move that had him worried. Matthew carried his mug into the den and sipped cooling coffee until he was satisfied that he knew the architect's strategy. He addressed a postcard, wrote his move on the back of the card and descended to his office. Matthew's secretary was surprised to hear him humming.

A memo on the law of prior-crime evidence was waiting on his desk. Reynolds read the memo, then buzzed Tracy's office. There was no answer. He buzzed the receptionist.

'Do you know where Tracy is?'

'I haven't seen her this morning.'

It was nine-thirty. Tracy was normally in by eight at the latest.

'Please tell her to see me as soon as she comes in,' Reynolds said. Then he picked up the memo and walked down to the office library to read the cases Tracy had cited.

2

Tracy offered to drive Barry to his apartment, but he chose to walk the twenty blocks of night-time streets back to the loft. Barry cared for Tracy, he might even love her, but he could not bear to be with her and he desperately needed time to think. Tracy was relieved to be alone. The pain she and Barry had caused each other was too intense. She needed time away from him as much as he needed to be apart from her.

Tracy arrived at her waterfront apartment at two-thirty. She tried to sleep, but gave up after tossing and turning for half an hour. Whenever she closed her eyes, she saw the face of Laura Rizzatti or Matthew Reynolds.

Around three-fifteen, Tracy got out of bed and wandered into her kitchen. She poured herself a glass of milk and walked over to the sliding-glass door that opened onto her terrace. The terrace overlooked the Willamette. She pressed her forehead to the glass and stared at the lights on the Hawthorne and Morrison bridges. The ghostly glow of headlights swept over them like a legion of spirits aswirl in the night. After a while, Tracy was too exhausted to stand up. She curled in a ball on her sofa. Her eyes refused to stay open, but she could not sleep. The sadness of it all suddenly overwhelmed her. Laura and the judge dead, Matthew Reynolds's career on the verge of destruction and her relationship with Barry in ruins. She began to sob and made no attempt to hold back her tears. Her body shook quietly as she let herself go. When the dawn came, her tears had dried.

'There you are,' Matthew said with a friendly smile when Tracy walked into his office at eleven-thirty. Tracy could not help noticing how relaxed he looked. She, on the other hand, was exhausted and drained of energy. It had taken all of her courage to come to Reynolds's office to confront him.

Tracy shut the door and sagged into a chair.

'There's something we have to talk about,' she said.

'Can it wait?' he asked pleasantly. 'We've got to whip this memo into shape and I have some ideas I want to run by you.'

'I don't think the memo matters anymore, Mr. Reynolds,' she said sadly.

Reynolds frowned. 'What do you mean?'

'I know Mrs. Griffen is guilty,' Tracy said.

For a moment, Reynolds did not react. Then he looked at her as if he was not certain he'd heard Tracy correctly.

'What are you talking about?'

Tracy took the FotoFast envelope out of her purse and laid the photo of the shed on Reynolds's blotter.

'I spent last night looking at the negatives with Barry,' she said. 'He explained how it was done.'

Reynolds looked confused. He glanced at the photograph, then back at Tracy.

'I'm afraid you've lost me.'

'This photograph of the shed is a fake. It was taken in September. We'll have to tell Chuck Geddes and Judge

Baldwin. We'll have to resign from the case.'

Reynolds studied the photograph, but made no move to touch it. When he looked at Tracy there was no indication of guilt or fear on his features. If Tracy had not seen the way Reynolds controlled his emotions in court, she would have concluded that he was innocent.

'What makes you think the photograph was faked?' Reynolds asked calmly.

Tracy told Matthew about her trip to the cabin with Barry and explained about the position of the volleyball.

'It must be a coincidence,' Matthew said. 'The ball was in the position in the photograph on August 12. Then Sheriff Dillard or one of his deputies moved it onto the net when he checked the shed for the dynamite.'

'I hoped that was the solution, but it's not.'

'Then how could the negative have August 12 stamped on it?'

Tracy explained the way the fake was created, hoping that Matthew would drop his pretense and admit what he had done. As she spoke, Reynolds grew agitated and began to shift in his chair.

'But how could Mrs. Griffen have created the substitute strip?' Matthew snapped when Tracy was through with her explanation. 'It's ridiculous. She's been confined to her house since the last week in August.'

'She didn't make the fake. Mrs. Griffen had an accomplice. Someone who had access to the Pentax and the negatives. Someone who knows enough about photography to think up this scheme.

377

'How could you do it, Matthew? She's a murderer. She killed a good, decent man for money and she killed a good friend of mine.'

Reynolds tried to maintain his composure, but he failed. Moments before, he had been the happiest person in the world. Now everything was slipping away from him. His shoulders hunched and he slumped in his seat. He took a deep breath. When he spoke, his voice was barely above a whisper.

'I'm sorry,' he managed. 'I know how this looks, but, believe me, it's not what it seems.'

Matthew's chest heaved. It took him a moment to regain his composure.

'Abbie had nothing to do with the photograph and she didn't kill her husband or Laura Rizzatti.'

'I don't believe that.'

Matthew paused again. Tracy could see he was trembling. He closed his eyes and let his head fall back. When he opened his eyes, they were moist with tears.

'When you interviewed with me, I told you about several fine attorneys who have visited a prison after dark and left with their client dead. Then I told you that neither I nor any attorney who worked for me had ever visited a prison after dark. That wasn't true.

'When I was eight years old, I visited a prison after dark. When I left the prison before dawn, the man I had spoken with was dead. He was my father. I loved him very much. He was executed for the murder of a young woman with whom he worked. The prosecutor convinced a jury that my father had been having an affair with this woman and had killed her because she threatened to tell my mother about their affair. My father swore that he loved my mother and was only the girl's friend. The jury didn't believe him and he was executed in the electric chair.

'Two years after he died, the real murderer confessed. He worked with the woman and they were having an affair. My father had simply been the woman's friend. He was executed for a crime he never committed. If it wasn't for the death penalty, he would have been freed from prison and I would have had my father back.'

Matthew leaned back in his chair and closed his eyes.

'I know I must disgust you, Tracy. Preaching about morality and honor and dishonoring myself and my profession. But I had to . . . I was compelled to . . . I saw no other way.'

Matthew stopped again. He looked across the desk at Tracy. His eyes pled for understanding.

'She's innocent, Tracy. I'm absolutely certain. And I couldn't bear the thought that she might die. She doesn't know a thing about the photograph of the shed.'

'But how could you invent evidence?' Tracy asked, the words catching in her chest.

'I can't do it anymore,' Matthew said. 'Fighting for every inch, every minute I'm in trial. Having to be perfect, every time, because my client dies if I'm not perfect. It's worn me down. I've lost my confidence. I know I'm going to lose someday. That a client of mine will die.'

Reynolds paused again. Tracy could see him struggle to come up with the words he spoke next.

'You have no idea what my life has been like. I'm so alone. At first, my loneliness was a badge of honor. I had my crusade against death and I didn't need anything else. Then the crusade became an ordeal. So much was expected of me. I wanted someone to share my pain and there was no one. Then I met Abbie.'

Reynolds's face showed surprisingly little emotion, but tears rolled down his cheeks.

'I love her, Tracy. I couldn't live with myself if she was the one I couldn't save. I simply could not let her die. I just couldn't.'

'It's easy to fool yourself about a person you love,' Tracy said gently. 'What if Abbie did murder Justice Griffen and Laura?'

'It's not possible. I . . . I know Abbie too well. She's being framed. The metal strip proves that. And what about the money? Where did Charlie Deems get a hundred thousand dollars?'

'She could have paid Deems to kill Justice Griffen. She's a very wealthy woman.'

'Then why would Deems go to the district attorney and implicate Abbie? No. Someone else killed Justice Griffen and framed Abbie.'

Tracy was so certain of Abbie's guilt when she entered Reynolds's office. Now she did not know.

'What are you going to do?' Matthew asked her.

Tracy remembered Barry asking that very question.

'What choice do I have? I'll have to report you to Judge Baldwin this afternoon. Do you think this is an easy choice? You're one of the finest human beings I've ever known. If I go to Judge Baldwin you'll be disbarred and go to prison. But if I keep silent, I'll be abetting what you've done, I'll be opening myself up for the same punishment and I'll be betraying my oath as an officer of the court.'

'I'm not thinking of myself, Tracy. If you reveal what you know to the judge, he'll have to tell Chuck Geddes. Geddes will use the evidence in Abbie's trial and she'll surely be convicted.'

'But she didn't know. You said so.'

'Geddes doesn't have to believe that. If he finds out about the photograph, he'll argue that Abbie did know it was a fake and there will only be my word that she didn't. Geddes will use the fact that I used a doctored photograph to rehabilitate Charlie Deems. The jurors will believe he saw the dynamite in the shed. They'll believe that a prosecutor who kills, then tries to subvert justice by fabricating evidence, should die.

'If you tell Judge Baldwin what I've done, you'll be signing the death warrant of an innocent woman.'

3

The climb up the three-hundred-foot rock wall had been slow and relatively uneventful until Tracy reached a narrow ledge that stretched horizontally across the cliff face for sixty feet. The ledge was three quarters of an inch at its widest point, fading into nonexistence in spots.

Tracy had missed the sloping overhang that jutted out ten feet above the ledge and forty feet below the summit, because, from the base of the cliff, looking up, the overhang appeared to be the summit. Tracy stood delicately on tiptoes with her body braced against the rock and carefully studied the overhang. It covered the ledge like a canopy and the rock on either side of the overhang was too smooth for Tracy to work around it. It would be maddening to come this far and be this close to the top without being able to finish the climb.

Tracy had been studying the underside of the overhang inch by inch for several minutes when her foot dislodged a small rock. She paid no attention as it plummeted down, smashing into fragments at the end of its flight, because her concentration was riveted on a crack that ran through the middle of the overhang. The crack appeared to be wide enough to let her insert her hand, if her hand was open and rigid. Tracy thought about the crack and what it might let her do. Her plan would depend on split-second timing and the chance that the crack would widen as it worked its way into the rock. But Tracy's situation left her no choice. Her only alternative was to admit defeat and descend the cliff.

Tracy was dressed in a loose-fitting, long-sleeved white top and baggy black spider pants that zipped over her form-fitting rock shoes. The day was dry and cold. If it had rained, she would not have attempted the ascent. The solo climb was dangerous enough in good weather.

The maneuver she was contemplating was risky, but Tracy could not let herself think about the danger. Nervous tension is a climber's worst enemy, because it can make a climber's hands sweat and jeopardize the security of a good handhold. While she thought through her plan, Tracy dipped both hands into the chalk in a fat purple bag fastened behind her at her waist. The chalk would keep her hands dry.

Tracy stared at the crack and relaxed her breathing. Behind her, the wilderness spread out like a green carpet, but Tracy saw only the gray uneven surface of the rock wall. She scanned the area above her for handholds. When she was rested, Tracy worked her way up the rockface until she was just under the overhang.

Tracy turned and balanced on her foothold, then she extended her right arm slowly until her hand was in the crack. Please, please, please, she whispered to herself as her fingers inched upward. She breathed out slowly as she felt the narrow crack widen to form a pocket in the rock.

Up this high the air was as blue as the sky in a fairy tale and the clouds were pillows of white. To succeed, Tracy would have to float on the air. She watched the clouds until her body grew as light as one of them. She was gossamer, butterfly wings, puffballs blown from a dandelion.

Tracy made a fist with her right hand, increasing its width until it was wedged into the crack. She breathed in, then expelled violently, pushing out from the cliff with an explosive thrust. Her right hand was a ball of iron. For a moment it was her only contact with the world. Then she pivoted on it, swinging upward past the outer rim of the overhang. Her free hand reached high. It would only have a moment of contact in which to grip tight enough to support her body.

Tracy twisted and the fingers of her left hand found a hold just as the force of the swing wrenched her fist from the crack. For a second, she dangled in space, halfway between safety and oblivion. Then her fingers tightened and she drew her body upward in a one-armed pull-up. The right hand arced over the lip of the overhang and gripped. A moment later, Tracy was over the top, stretched out on her stomach, adrenaline coursing through her as she trembled with elation.

The summit was now an easy climb, not worth more than a casual thought. When she reached the top, Tracy turned slowly, looking across the evergreen forest at the peaks of rugged, snowdusted mountains all covered by a sky of the clearest blue. This was the world the way an eagle saw it. Tracy inhaled the sweet mountain air. Then she sat on the edge of the cliff, unhooked her water bottle and took a drink.

The climb had forced Tracy to forget about everything except the rock. Now that the climb was over, there was no way to avoid thinking about the conflict that dominated her every waking moment the way the Cascade Mountains dominated the skyline. Matthew Reynolds's life was an inspiration to every attorney who undertook a death penalty case. If Tracy did what the law and the Canon of Ethics required, she would bring him down. All of Matthew's good deeds would be forgotten, because of a single act committed for love.

Tracy had decided that she would never reveal the truth behind the photograph if she knew for certain that Abigail Griffen was innocent, because a jury that learned about the photograph would convict Abbie and probably sentence her to death. It was the possibility that Griffen was guilty that made Tracy's predicament so difficult.

Matthew was convinced that someone was framing Abbie. There was certainly enough evidence to support that conclusion. Griffen was brilliant. She would never use the same type of bomb Deems had used in the Hollins murder, knowing it would make her a suspect. If she did use a bomb, she wouldn't be stupid enough to leave a piece of it in her garage. The strip of metal Torino had found in the garage was not even from the bomb, making it likely that it had been planted to frame Griffen. Then there was Deems. If the $100,000 was a payoff for perjury, Abbie was innocent.

Which brought Tracy to the next question. If Abbie was innocent, who was guilty? Deems was the easy answer. But someone paid Deems $100,000 for something. Whether it was to kill Justice Griffen, frame Abbie, or both, there still had to be someone else involved. But who? And what motive did they have?

Suddenly a thought occurred to her. She had been assuming that either Abbie murdered the judge and Laura because they were lovers or the two murders were unconnected. What if Laura's murder and the murder of Justice Griffen were connected, but someone else killed them? That would put a whole new slant on the case.

Justice Kelly was a possible suspect. Had she lied when she said that her sexual relationship with Justice Griffen meant little to her? What if she was insanely jealous and killed the judge and Laura because Griffen had taken Laura as his lover?

Then Tracy remembered the transcripts and the cases on the sheet of legal paper. Laura had been upset about something for weeks before her death. It would have been natural for Laura to tell Justice Griffen what was bothering her, especially if, in addition to being his law clerk, she was also his lover. What if the transcript and the cases were evidence of something illegal? Were they what the murderer was looking for when he ransacked Laura's office and cottage?

The transcript was a public record that anyone could get, but Tracy had read the transcript and had no idea why it was important. It was the same with the cases. Nothing she had read in them had alerted her. Having the transcript and the list was meaningless unless you knew what to look for. If Laura's killer learned that Justice Griffen had the transcript and the list of cases, and suspected that the judge knew why they were important, he would have a motive to kill Justice Griffen. But how could she possibly figure out why the cases and the transcript were important or if they even had any significance?

Tracy wished that she could forget about the case and stay forever on this perch where she could be above it all, but she had to descend to earth. She felt defeated by the case but she had to keep going. She had no choice. If she could not solve the murders, she would have to tell Judge Baldwin about the fake photograph. Tracy sighed and took a mixture of nuts and dried fruit from a plastic bag in her side pocket. She chewed slowly and took another drink of water. Then she carefully checked her climbing gear and started her descent.

Chapter Twenty-seven

1

As soon as she woke up Friday morning, Tracy slipped into a heavy sweater and jeans and carried a bran muffin and a mug of black coffee onto her terrace. As she ate, Tracy watched the drawbridges rise to accommodate a rusted tanker with a Spanish name and a Liberian flag. She wished Barry was sitting beside her. Tracy missed him. He was a kind and considerate lover. More important, he was a kind and considerate man. She understood why Barry wasn't with her. She admired him for his loyalty. But she wished he was helping her and she knew that she would lose him for good, if she hadn't already, unless she could prove Abigail Griffen was innocent.

After breakfast, Tracy called in sick. It was not a complete lie. She was sick at heart and could not imagine being in a place where she would see both Matthew and

Barry. The receptionist told Tracy that Judge Baldwin was taking the prosecution's motion to introduce evidence of Laura's murder under advisement and had dismissed the jury for the weekend. Tracy hung up and called Bob Packard's office.

'I wanted to thank you for lending us the transcripts,' Tracy said. 'They've been very useful.'

'Glad I could help,' Packard answered.

'I was wondering if you could help me again.'

'What do you need?'

'Could you tell me a little about a case you handled in the Supreme Court? *State* v. *Galarraga*.'

'Is Ernesto going to be a witness in the *Griffen* case?'

'No. Why do you ask?'

'He knows a lot about Charlie Deems.'

'He does?'

'You didn't know?'

'No, I didn't.'

'Do you know who Raoul Otero is?'

'He's mixed up with narcotics, isn't he?'

Packard laughed. 'That's like asking if Babe Ruth is mixed up with baseball. Otero is a major Mexican drug dealer with a distribution network that covers large parts of the western United States. Charlie Deems was the Portland distributor for the Otero organization. Ernesto Galarraga worked for Charlie.'

Tracy thought about that for a moment. Then she asked, 'Do the names Jorge Zamora or Pedro Cardona mean anything to you?'

Tracy listened intently to what Packard had to say. As soon as she hung up, she made a call to Medford and talked to the district attorney who had prosecuted Pedro Cardona. When the call was over, Tracy was certain she had discovered the importance of the cases on Laura's list. She felt sick to her stomach. Coming so soon after her discovery of Matthew Reynolds's crime, it was almost too much to take in. If she was right, and could prove it, she could give the state Justice Griffen's killer and save Matthew Reynolds from disgrace. Tracy looked at her watch. It was only nine o'clock. She had time to do the necessary research at the law library and be at the Supreme Court by one.

2

Alice Sherzer gave Tracy a hug, then ushered her into her chambers.

'Are you surviving Matthew Reynolds's sweatshop?'

'Barely,' Tracy answered tersely.

'Is the job as much fun as you thought it would be?'

'Matthew is a brilliant man and a great trial lawyer,' Tracy said, avoiding a lie.

'How do you like trying a major murder case?'

'That's what I wanted to talk to you about. Mrs. Griffen's case.'

Justice Sherzer looked surprised. 'I don't think I can do that, Tracy. If she's convicted, there's a good chance the court will have to hear her appeal.'

'I know that. But I've discovered something that involves the court. Something you have to know. It bears not only on Justice Griffen's murder but also on the murder of Laura Rizzatti.'

'I don't understand.'

Tracy paused. Her stomach heaved and she felt light-headed. The full import of what she was going to say had not fully dawned on her until now.

'Judge, I think Justice Griffen and Laura Rizzatti were murdered because they learned that a member of this court is influencing the outcome of cases involving the Otero narcotics organization.'

Alice Sherzer stared at Tracy for a moment. Then she shook her head. 'I don't believe that for a moment,' she said angrily.

'Hear me out. I know how you feel. I've been sick with the thought of it, but I can't see any other explanation for what I've found.'

Justice Sherzer frowned. Then she pressed the button on her intercom and told her secretary that she did not want to be interrupted by anyone.

Tracy told Justice Sherzer about Laura's reaction when she had caught her reading the *Deems* transcript and the way Laura hid the names of the cases on the legal pad. Then Tracy explained how she found the transcript and the yellow sheet in the evidence taken from Justice Griffen's den.

'I'm sure Laura figured out a connection between the cases and told Justice Griffen what she discovered. I think

PHILLIP MARGOLIN

they were both murdered to prevent them from disclosing what they knew.'

'And what is that?'

'I still have no idea why the transcript is important. But I'm certain I know the significance of the cases.'

Tracy gave Justice Sherzer a summary of the cases. Then she said, 'Ernesto Galarraga worked with Charlie Deems and they both worked for Raoul Otero. Jorge Zamora was an enforcer for Otero. He murdered one of their rivals in a convenience store. He also killed the clerk to make the hit look like a robbery. Pedro Cardona was a front man for Otero in southern Oregon. He was trying to establish a distribution network in Medford when he was busted.

'Deems, Cardona, Zamora and Galarraga all worked for Otero. They were all convicted, but their convictions were reversed by a divided court. Justice Lefcourt was in the majority in *Zamora*, but he dissented in the other cases. Justices Griffen, Kelly, Arriaga and Pope were in the majority in every one of the cases.

'In every case but *Zamora*, which was reversed on an evidence issue, the court reversed on a novel legal theory. In *Deems*, the majority adopted a rule involving confessions that is the law in only three other states. In *Cardona* and *Galarraga*, the court interpreted the Oregon constitution in a way that ran contrary to the interpretation of the Fourth Amendment to the federal constitution. I talked with the DA who prosecuted Cardona. He was shocked by the reversal. There was a U.S. Supreme Court case right on point. He said the trial judge upheld the search without batting an eye and the Court of Appeals affirmed with no dissenters.

'I spent two hours this morning reading the criminal cases the court has decided in the past five years to see if I could find any other cases that fit this pattern. I think that's what Laura did. Justice Sherzer, those cases are unique. There are no other criminal cases with this exact voting bloc in the past five years.'

'How did Laura stumble onto the pattern?' Justice Sherzer asked.

'I have no idea. The cases are spread through a five-year period. The reversal of any one of them should have gone unnoticed. I think something in the *Deems* transcript tipped her off, but I have no idea what it is. What I strongly suspect is that either Justice Kelly, Pope or Arriaga is working for Raoul Otero to influence the other judges to reverse cases in which important members of the Otero organization are the defendants. Somehow, this justice learned that Laura knew what was going on and had told Justice Griffen. I think that's why they were killed.'

'How could one person guarantee three other votes?'

'There were no guarantees. But some of the judges, like Frank Arriaga and Justice Griffen, were very sensitive to defendant's rights and you know how an undecided vote can be influenced by a passionate advocate.'

'Tracy, listen to what you're saying. Can you honestly imagine a member of this court murdering Laura and Robert?'

'No, but I can imagine him paying Charlie Deems to do it. I think the hundred thousand dollars that Matthew found in Deems's bank account was the payoff for a double killing.'

'Tracy, this doesn't make sense. I know these people.'

'Did either Justice Pope, Arriaga or Kelly take the lead in trying to reverse these cases during conferences?'

'You know I can't reveal what goes on in conference.'

'You've got to. We're talking about a double homicide and the possibility of an innocent person being convicted for one of them.'

Justice Sherzer sighed. 'You're right, of course. But I can't remember the discussions of those cases. Some of them took place four years ago.'

'What about *Deems*. It's fairly recent. Who pushed for the reversal?'

'I believe Frank Arriaga was very concerned about the use of the informant. He and Stuart argued vehemently about the case.'

'Why did Justice Griffen write the opinion?'

'Frank was going to do it. Then he got hung up on a complex land-use decision and he asked Robert to write it. They were in agreement on the issues and Robert didn't have any outstanding decisions, so he volunteered to help out.'

'Can you think of any reason why Justice Arriaga would work for Raoul Otero?'

'Certainly not! And I cannot imagine Frank killing anyone. That's preposterous.'

'What about money? Is he in debt? Does he have a drug habit? Anything like that?'

'Frank Arriaga is a dear man with a rock-solid marriage and two children who adore him. I don't even think he drinks, for God's sake. You're way off base if you think Frank is your killer.'

'Then what about Mary Kelly?'

Justice Sherzer frowned. 'Money wouldn't be the motive. She was a very successful corporate attorney and has done quite well in the stock market and real estate.'

'Did you know that she and Justice Griffen were having an affair?'

'No, but I'm not surprised. Mary's marriage is not particularly happy.'

'If they were seeing each other when Laura was killed, Justice Griffen might have confided what Laura told him without realizing that he was alerting her. If Justice Kelly is the murderer, that would explain how she learned that she was in danger.'

'I'm afraid I can't help you, Tracy. I can't think of anything that would lead me to conclude that Mary is dishonest.'

'Which brings us to the most likely suspect. Arnold Pope is a conservative ex-DA. What was he doing voting to reverse the convictions of two murderers and two drug dealers?'

'Arnold is a peculiar man. He's the most obnoxious and contrary justice with whom I have ever served, but a lot of what he does is a pose. The man is very insecure and he desperately wants our approval. He knows he's seen as a buffoon and he knows everyone resents the way he ran his campaign and the fact that he replaced a brilliant justice who was well liked and widely respected. So to prove he is a legal scholar, too, Arnold occasionally takes positions that run counter to his image.'

'Do you know about Pope's run-in with Laura?'

'No.'

Tracy told Justice Sherzer about the confrontation in the library.

'I told Justice Griffen, the day I left the court. He said he was going to tell everyone about it.'

'He was very upset when Laura was killed. Maybe he forgot. What are you planning to do, Tracy?'

'I don't know. I was hoping you could help me. I thought that you might recall something that would shed some light on this if I told you what I'd discovered.'

'I'm sorry to disappoint you. But I'm still far from convinced that one of my colleagues is a killer who is working for a major drug dealer. It's too fantastic.'

'As fantastic as a justice and his clerk both being murdered in less than a month? It could be coincidence, but I don't think so. I've been thinking back to the night Laura was murdered. I was in the library working on a memo for you in the Scott probate matter. When I came downstairs, there was a light on in Laura's office, but there were no other lights on in the clerks' office area. I looked in Laura's office. I could see someone had ransacked it, so I reached for the phone to call Laura. That's when I heard the door to the clerks' area close.

'I wasn't thinking straight or I'd never have done it, but I rushed into the hall. There was no one there. I rushed to the back door and didn't see anyone in the parking lot. I was upset and I didn't want to stay alone in the building, so I calmed down and headed for my office to leave my notes with the idea of finishing the memo in the morning. That's when I discovered Laura's body. Do you see what I missed?'

'No, I don't.'

'Where did the killer go? I was in the hall seconds after the door to the clerks' area closed. If the killer left by the front door to the building, I would have heard it close. It's the same with the back door. And there was no one in the parking lot. A stranger to the building would have high-tailed it out, but someone who worked in it would have just as likely run upstairs.

'The person who killed Laura had to be familiar with the layout of the clerks' area to hide so quickly and to be able to get out in the dark without me hearing. I think the killer rushed upstairs, waited for me to go back into the clerks' area, then snuck down the stairs and left. This all points to the killer being a person who was very familiar with the court.'

Justice Sherzer mulled over what Tracy had told her. When she made her decision, she looked grim.

'I still don't buy your theory, but I'm going to discuss it with Stuart.'

'Thank you. And try to think back to the conferences. If

I'm right, the justice who's behind this had to have been working very hard to swing the necessary votes. If you can remember who the common denominator was in all four cases, you'll know the murderer.'

3

Tracy started back to Portland on the interstate as soon as she left Justice Sherzer. She was certain she knew why Laura and Justice Griffen had been killed. What she did not know was the clue that had tipped off Laura to the identity of the judge who was working for Raoul Otero. No one was going to believe a Supreme Court justice was on the take without proof and she had to believe that the transcript held the proof.

As far as Tracy knew, Laura had never heard of Charlie Deems, or his case, until Deems's appeal was filed in the Supreme Court. If that was true, then the information in the transcript had to concern the crooked justice, but Tracy had read the transcript and none of the justices were mentioned in Volume XI.

Tracy arrived home at 4:30 and went for a run along the river. She wore only shorts and a tee shirt even though it was cold. She was still sore from her climb, but the exertion soon warmed her. When she was into a comfortable pace, Tracy began reviewing what she knew about the Griffen and Rizzatti murders. She exhausted the subject with no new insights.

Tracy turned for home. A light drizzle dulled her enthusiasm for the run. She wished Barry was there to keep her company. She always felt so comfortable when they were together. Would Barry really leave her if she told the court what Matthew had done? The possibility was real and the thought of losing Barry frightened her. But would their relationship change if she sold out her principles to keep them together? Wouldn't the sacrifice kill the feeling between them anyway?

Tracy felt a tightening in her chest that had nothing to do with exertion. What she and Barry had was so good. Why couldn't it last? Tracy knew Barry was special the first time they kissed. She would always remember that morning at the beach below the Griffen cabin and the wonderful picnic afterward.

Tracy stopped in mid-stride. The Overlook. She bent over and rested with her hands on her knees. They had gone to the Overlook after their picnic and she had looked at the register. It had been right there all along. Tracy stood up, oblivious to the rain and cold. She followed her train of thought to its inevitable conclusion and knew she was right.

Tracy raced back to her apartment. She showered quickly and changed into clean clothes. She was impatient to look at her notes from the visit to the Overlook, but she wanted to wait until the staff was gone and, hopefully, Barry with them.

The rain stopped by 6:30. Tracy was relieved to see that the lights in Matthew Reynolds's living quarters were out

when she arrived at the office. She let herself in through
the back door and found her notes from the visit to the
Overlook in her case file. Tracy reread pages 1289 and
1290 of Volume XI to confirm her suspicions. Then she
went back to her car and drove to Salem.

4

At exactly 7:20 on Friday evening, moments before Tracy
turned off I-5 at the second Salem exit, Bobby Cruz parked
his car on a narrow gravel side road and walked across a
field that bordered the farmhouse where Chuck Geddes
was hiding Charlie Deems. The field was damp from the
rain that had stopped around seven o'clock, and there was
an ozone smell in the air. When he reached the house,
Cruz circled it cautiously, peering into windows so he
could figure out the number of targets.

The two cops assigned to guard Deems were watching
a Blazers game on the TV in the living room.
Unfortunately, Deems was not with them. If he had been,
Cruz could have held all three at gunpoint, shot Deems
and escaped without having to kill the cops. Now he had
to take them out. He couldn't risk Deems escaping while
he dicked around in the living room tying people up.
Cruz didn't mind killing cops, but Raoul was paranoid
about doing anything that would bring down heat on the
business. He knew he'd have to listen to Raoul scream at
him, but Raoul's ass wasn't on the line.

Cruz slipped through an unlocked side door into a short hallway that led to the kitchen. To the right was a stairway to the second floor. Cruz guessed that Deems was probably sacking out in an upstairs bedroom.

When Cruz stepped around the corner into the living room the cops looked shocked. One of them was drinking a glass of soda and balancing a plate with a sandwich on his lap. He jumped up. Pieces of bread, a slice of tomato and slabs of turkey went flying. Cruz shot the officer in the forehead while he was going for his gun. He was dead before his plate shattered on the hardwood floor.

The second officer had fast reflexes. While Cruz was shooting his partner, he was rolling and ducking. He almost had his gun out when Cruz shot him in the ear. Cruz took a second to check the bodies to make certain they were dead.

There was a silencer on Cruz's gun and both kills had been accomplished with a minimum of noise. Cruz moved to the living-room entrance and scanned the hall. He strained to hear any sound that would indicate that Deems was on the move. When he heard nothing he went down the hall to check the kitchen, before going upstairs to finish his work.

Cruz crouched low and swung through the kitchen door into more pain than he could imagine. The pain covered every inch of his face. It blinded and paralyzed him and it deafened him to the cry of animal rage that came from Charlie Deems's throat as he stepped out of the kitchen and turned the cast-iron skillet sideways. This time, instead of smashing the flat of the pan into Cruz's face, Deems swung the edge against his right shin. Bone snapped and Cruz collapsed on the floor.

When he swung the skillet, Charlie's face looked crazed, but a horrific smile transformed his features into a demonic mask as he watched Bobby Cruz twitch on the hall floor. The pan had smashed every part of Cruz's face, and it was hard to make out his features because they were covered with blood.

Deems caught his breath. Cruz's gun was on the floor where he had dropped it as he staggered back after the first blow. Charlie picked it up and put it on a hall table. Then he methodically crushed the fingers on both of Cruz's hands. When he was certain Cruz was incapacitated, Charlie looked in the living room. The cops were so obviously dead, Deems didn't bother to look at them closely.

Cruz moaned. 'Time to go to work,' Deems sighed. He went into the kitchen and traded the skillet for several sharp knives and a pitcher of ice water. When he came back into the hall, Cruz was looking at him with glazed eyes.

'Hey, Bobby. How you doin'?' Charlie asked with his trademark grin. Cruz sucked air.

'Sorry about the teeth.' Deems chuckled. 'It's gonna be tough getting dates for a while, amigo.'

Cruz tried to say 'fuck you,' but his mouth didn't work right. Deems laughed and tousled Cruz's hair.

'Sorry, Bobby, you're not my type. I'd rather fuck Abigail Griffen. But thanks for the offer.'

Cruz mumbled something and Deems smiled.

'I bet you just cursed me out again. Am I right? But that's not necessary. A smart guy like you doesn't have to resort to this macho bullshit. In a situation like this, you should be using your brains. Of course, you weren't using your brains when you came in the side door. Didn't you wonder why it was the only door that wasn't locked?'

Deems paused to watch Cruz's reaction, but Cruz wouldn't give him the satisfaction. That was okay. Charlie loved a challenge. He squatted next to Cruz and continued speaking as if they were friends seated in a bistro sipping a good dark beer.

'I knew Raoul was gonna send you after me sooner or later, so I've been watching for you. When I saw you creeping through the tall grass like a wetback crossing the border, I slipped downstairs and fixed it so you could get in.

'Now, I should be angry, because you just tried to kill me, but I'm not. You don't know it, but you've given me the chance to do some really naughty things without getting caught. See, I'm going out for a while. Then I'll come back and call Geddes. I'll tell him how you killed the cops and tried to kill me. You're gonna be my alibi. Is that some great plan or what?'

Cruz still stared defiantly. Deems looked amused.

'Don't be that way, Bobby. I don't know why you're mad at me. I'm not mad at you. In fact, if you tell me where you stashed your car, I promise I'll kill you quickly. What do you say?'

'Kiss my ass,' Cruz managed. Deems laughed.

'These offers of sexual delight are hard to pass up, but I'd rather play *Jeopardy!* The guards used to let us watch it on the row. It's my favorite game show and I'm damn good. Bobby, do you know how to play *Jeopardy!*?'

Cruz refused to answer. Deems drove a knife into his thigh. The scream pierced the air and Cruz's right leg shot forward, causing more pain in the fractured shin.

'Sound check,' Charlie told Cruz. 'I had to make certain that you can talk, because you can't play *Jeopardy!* unless you can answer the questions.'

Deems pulled out the knife and Bobby groaned. Deems splashed some ice water on Cruz's face and slapped his cheeks. Cruz opened his eyes. Deems slapped him again, hard, and said, 'Pay attention. Here's how the game works. I'm gonna give you the answer and you have to say the question. Like if I asked, "He was the first President of the United States," you'd say, "Who was George Washington?" Get it?

'Now, if you get all the answers, you get the grand prize. It's an all-expenses-paid trip to Hawaii for you and the wife and kids, plus a Buick convertible. Sounds good, right? But if you miss the question, uh-oh, there's a penalty. I'll keep you guessing about that.'

Charlie winked at Cruz and noted, with satisfaction, that the macho glint was leaving Cruz's eyes. Fear was their new resident. Cruz was tough, but Charlie was crazy and he was sounding crazier by the moment. If there was one thing tough guys like Cruz could not deal with, it was the unknown, and crazy people were the ultimate unknown.

'Our first category is American history. Here's the answer. "He was President Millard Filmore's Secretary of State." What's the question?'

'What?' Cruz asked.

'Wrong answer, Bobby. Watt was a Scottish engineer who made improvements on the steam engine.'

Deems grabbed Cruz's right hand and stabbed him through the palm, pinning the hand to the floor. Cruz fainted. Deems threw ice water in his face and waited patiently until Cruz revived. Then he leaned over and whispered in Cruz's ear, *'Jeopardy!* is a pretty violent game. It can hurt to get the wrong answer.'

'Okay, okay, I'll tell you what you want,' Cruz whimpered, his eyes wide with pain and fear.

'That's not how it works, Bobby. You have to wait for the question. However, it is time to play *Double Jeopardy!* There are two grand prizes. The first prize is a trip to Disneyland, where you get to meet Miss America. The second prize is you get to fuck her. Pretty good, huh?'

Deems smiled and picked up another knife. 'Unfortunately, there's also a double penalty for a wrong answer. It's both your eyes, amigo. Ready? Here's the answer. "He won the Pulitzer Prize for Poetry in 1974." What's the question, Bobby?'

'Please, Charlie, please,' Cruz sobbed.

'Buzz!' Charlie shouted in Cruz's ear. 'Time's up.'

Deems grabbed Cruz's chin and put the blade under

Cruz's right eye. Cruz began to tremble violently. He tried to shake his head from side to side, but Deems held it steady. Tears ran from Cruz's eyes.

'The car's by the field,' Cruz screamed. 'On the gravel road.' Deems smiled coldly. He shook his head from side to side in disgust.

'I'm disappointed in you, Bobby. I was sure you'd hold out a little longer. I guess you're not so tough after all.'

Deems picked up the gun and shot Cruz between the eyes. Then he took Cruz's car keys from his pocket, went upstairs and changed his clothes. When Charlie left the house, he was feeling good. Bobby Cruz had been a great preliminary and he was ready for the main event.

5

Arnold Pope's front door was opened by a short woman with leathery skin and a sour expression.

'Mrs. Pope, I'm Tracy Cavanaugh. I used to clerk for Justice Sherzer. We met at the clerk's picnic.'

'Oh yes.'

'Is Justice Pope in? I have something very important I need to discuss with him.'

'It's almost eight o'clock, Miss Cavanaugh. Couldn't this wait until tomorrow? Arnold's had a very hard day.'

'I wish it could, but it's urgent. I promise I won't be long.'

'Very well,' Mrs. Pope said, not bothering to mask her disapproval. 'Step in and I'll ask Arnold if he'll see you.'

The Popes lived in a modern ranch-style home in the hills south of Salem. The entryway where Tracy waited had a stone floor and white walls. There was a small marble table against one wall. A slender blue-gray pottery vase filled with daffodils stood at one end of the table under a mirror with a gilt frame.

'Tracy! Good to see you,' Justice Pope said affably, smiling at her as if she was an old friend.

'I'm sorry to come by so late.'

'No problem. Myra says you have something important to discuss. Why don't we go back to my den.'

Justice Pope led Tracy to the back of the house and down a set of stairs to the basement. To the left was a wood-paneled room where two BarcaLoungers were set up in front of a big-screen TV. In one corner was a small desk. A bookshelf with Reader's Digest condensed books, some best-sellers and a scattering of law books took up one wall.

The smile left Pope's face as soon as they were alone.

'You have some nerve coming to my house after telling those damn lies to the police.'

'I was very upset when Laura died. She was my friend. I wanted to help the police and it did look like you were making a pass at Laura.'

'Well, I wasn't. And I don't appreciate people talking about me behind my back.'

'That's the way it appeared to me. If I'm wrong, I apologize, but Justice Griffen told me you'd done something like that before.'

'What! I never . . .' Pope stopped. He looked furious. 'I'll tell you something, Miss Cavanaugh. I know all the clerks mooned around about Robert Griffen, the great protector of constitutional rights, but Griffen was no angel. He's the one who made passes at the clerks. I'm surprised he didn't put the make on you. Now, what's so important that you had to interrupt my evening?'

'I've come across some information that suggests that Justice Griffen's murder and the murder of Laura Rizzatti may be connected. Can you tell me why Laura was upset when you talked to her in the library?'

'I shouldn't give you the time of day after you started that damn rumor and I don't see how our conversation in the library can possibly bear on Laura's murder.'

'Please. I promise you it's very important.'

Pope frowned, then said, 'Oh, all right. I'll tell you what happened. Then I want you to leave.'

'Thank you.'

'That meeting was Laura's idea. When I got there, she asked me why I voted to reverse the *Deems* case. I told her that was none of her business. I must have sounded angry, because she got upset. I put my hand on her shoulder and told her to calm down. That's when you appeared. As soon as she saw you, Laura backed away from me. She looked frightened. I had the impression that she was concerned that you'd overhear us. In any event, I left and that was all there was to it.'

'Why did you vote to reverse *Deems*?' Tracy asked.

'That's confidential.'

'Justice Pope, I have reason to believe that one of the justices on the court was paid to influence cases involving the Otero narcotics organization. Over the past five years, four cases involving members of this group have been reversed. You, Justice Griffen, Justice Kelly and Justice Arriaga voted to reverse in each case. I think Laura Rizzatti figured out who was taking money from Otero. If one of the other justices put pressure on you to vote for reversal, that justice may be the person who killed Laura Rizzatti.'

Pope looked at Tracy as if she was insane. 'That's absolutely preposterous. Are you out of your mind?'

'No, sir. I have evidence to support my suspicions.'

'I don't believe it. And I can tell you that none of the justices put any pressure on me . . .'

Pope paused in mid-sentence, suddenly remembering something. He looked uncomfortable. When he spoke, he no longer sounded sure of himself.

'There is some horse trading that goes on among the justices. I felt very strongly about a fishing rights case, but I couldn't get a majority. One of the justices told me I'd get my majority in the fishing case if I changed my vote in *Deems*. Well, I was on the fence in *Deems*. It bothered me that the police used an informant the way they did. Deems deserved the death penalty, but I thought the law had been violated. I wouldn't have done things that way when I was DA.'

'So you switched your vote.'

'Right. And the other justice gave me my majority in the other case.'

'You also voted to reverse in the *Galarraga*, *Zamora* and *Cardona* cases. Think back. Did the same justice do anything to win over those votes?'

'My God,' Pope said, and suddenly grew pale.

'Which justice was it?' Tracy asked, certain she knew the name Pope would tell her.

6

Abbie had prepared chicken with apricots and avocado in a light cream sauce. The dish had been complemented by a fine Vouvray. It was one of several dinners Abbie had cooked for Matthew, who was beginning to appreciate cuisine more extravagant than the steaks he normally ate.

While Abbie was putting the finishing touches on their dinner, Matthew built a roaring fire in the living room. After dinner, they carried their coffee cups to the couch and sat side by side in front of the fireplace. Matthew had been distracted in court that morning during the hearing on Geddes's motion and he had been quiet all evening. Abbie was not surprised by his courtroom demeanor. They were both concerned about the possibility that Judge Baldwin would permit the state to reopen its case. But Abbie expected Matthew to loosen up when he was alone with her.

'What's wrong?' Abbie asked, putting her hand on top of Matthew's.

'Nothing,' Matthew answered, wishing he could enjoy

the evening but finding it impossible to be happy knowing that Abbie's freedom and his career depended on
whether Tracy Cavanaugh decided to tell Judge Baldwin
about the fake photograph.

'You've been so quiet. Are you sure nothing is bothering you?'

'It's the case,' he lied. 'I'm worried that I won't be
able to convince Judge Baldwin to keep out the Rizzatti
evidence.'

Abbie put down her coffee and turned toward
Matthew. She put her hand on his cheek and kissed him.
'Don't think about law tonight,' she said.

Matthew put his cup down. Abbie snuggled against
his chest.

'Very touching,' Charlie Deems said from the living-
room doorway.

Abbie jerked around and Matthew sprang to his feet.
Deems gave them his goofy grin and ran his finger around
his left ear to clean out some wax. He wore a pressed shirt
and ironed slacks. His hair was slicked back. He looked
like a farm boy at a 4-H meeting, except for the gun with
the silencer that dangled from his right hand.

'Looks like you two are having a real good time,'
Deems said.

'What are you doing here?' Abbie asked, standing
beside Matthew.

'I came to visit,' Deems said, walking casually across
the room until he was two arm lengths from them. 'I'll bet
I'm the last person you expected to see. Am I right?'

'I'd like you to leave.'

'I bet you would. Then you and Mr. Smart Guy here could do the nasty thing. Course, if I was in your shoes, I'd want me out of this house, too. And I don't blame you. Me being a previously convicted murderer and all. What did you call me during my trial? An animal, devoid of feeling.'

'What do you want, Mr. Deems?' Matthew asked.

'I might want revenge on the person responsible for putting me in that teensy-weensy cell on death row. I remember every minute on the row, Miss Prosecutor.' Deems smiled wistfully, like a man recalling a sweet summer morning. 'Did you know that the toilet in the cell above us leaked. Did you know we was double-bunked for a while. Man, was that cell crowded. I had to eat my dinner sitting on the crapper. That's quite an indignity. Some people put in that situation, finding themselves with the person responsible for it, might be filled with rage and an uncontrollable impulse to do the responsible person some type of outrageous harm.'

Deems paused for a heartbeat. Then he broke into a grin. Abbie's mouth was dry and her senses were more alert than at any other time in her life.

'Rape. Am I right? Bet it's what you thought of first. You're probably picturing it right now. Can you see yourself naked, tied up on the bed, screaming, with no one to help you? At my mercy? That's not a pretty picture.'

Deems let the thought linger. Then he took a step toward Abbie. She moved into Matthew.

Deems smiled again. 'I was hoping to get you alone

for a long weekend, Counselor. Unfortunately, I'm a little pressed for time, so I'm gonna have to do you now.'

Matthew stepped in front of Abbie. 'You will not hurt her.'

Deems laughed. 'What are you gonna do? Cross-examine me to death?' The smile disappeared. 'I didn't appreciate the way you set me up so I'd look like a fool. In fact, I don't appreciate either of you. So, first, I'm gonna have my way with the little lady, while you watch. Maybe you'll even learn a thing or two. Then I'm going to make sure you both die very slowly. And I'll watch.'

Matthew lunged while Deems was speaking. The move surprised Deems. Reynolds drove him into the wall, but this was the first fight he had been in since grade school and he had no idea what to do next. Deems brought a knee up between Matthew's legs. Matthew gasped and sagged. His grip on Deems loosened. Deems saw Abbie race out of the room and quickly head-butted Reynolds. Matthew staggered backward. Deems heard Abbie pounding up the stairs and shot Reynolds in the side. Matthew looked dazed and crumpled to the floor.

'We're gonna get to the good part soon,' Deems said, 'so you stay right here. Any objection?'

Matthew gasped from pain. Deems kicked him hard in the ribs and Matthew fainted.

'Objection overruled.'

Deems turned toward the stairs. He listened for a moment, then climbed them. At the top he shouted, 'Come out, come out, wherever you are.'

There was no response.

'The longer it takes me to find you, the longer it will take you and your boyfriend to die.'

Deems paused for an answer, but there was only silence. He looked down the hall. There were two doors on one side and three on the other. He eased open the first door. It was an empty guest bathroom.

The next door opened into Abbie's bedroom. Deems liked it. The bed had a headboard and a footboard to which he could tie Abbie's hands and feet. He smiled in anticipation. Then he dropped beside the bed and looked under it. Abbie wasn't there. But, he thought, she might be in the closet. He stepped to the side and whipped open the door. A wall of dresses screened off the back wall. Deems ripped the curtain apart and made certain Abbie was not hidden in the shadows. Then he stepped into the hall.

'You're pissing me off, bitch,' he screamed. 'Get out here now or I'll start cutting off your boyfriend's fingers.'

Deems waited, hoping the loud threats would flush Abbie from hiding the way beaters flush lions for big-game hunters, but the hall stayed empty.

Deems smashed open the door to the guest room. He heard a whimper from the closet and smiled coldly. He heard another muffled sob and relaxed. Deems put the gun on the guest bed. He did not want to risk shooting Abbie and spoiling his fun. Then he tiptoed to the closet door, counted to three silently and whipped the door open, screaming, 'Surprise!'

But the surprise was all his. Abbie was sitting on the

closet floor with her back braced against the wall. The handgun she carried in her purse was aimed at Deems. Her face was set and there were no tears on her cheeks. It dawned on Charlie that Abbie had lured him to the closet with phony sobs and whimpers. He felt a momentary flash of fear, until he remembered his dark angel.

Charlie straightened slowly and raised his arms straight out from his sides as if they were angel wings. Suddenly he knew his angel was in the room, a shimmering presence, ready to protect him from all harm. He did not fear the gun, because nothing could hurt him while his angel stood sentry.

'What are you going to do, shoot me?' Deems asked with a smirk.

Abbie did not answer. She pulled the trigger instead. Deems's eyes widened in disbelief when the first bullet hit him and he died with a look of utter confusion on his face.

Chapter Twenty-eight

1

Judge Baldwin took Abbie off the electronic surveillance program at Jack Stamm's request the day after she killed Charlie Deems. She was at Matthew's side on the Thursday morning after the shooting, the day the doctors at St. Vincent's Hospital permitted him to have visitors for the first time.

Tracy waited until the end of visiting hours and convinced Abbie and the others to leave on the pretext that she had a confidential legal matter she had to discuss with her boss.

'How are you feeling?' Tracy asked when they were alone.

'Okay,' Matthew managed.

'I brought these for you,' she said, holding out a vase filled with roses. 'Where should I put them?'

Matthew slowly lifted his right arm and pointed toward several other vases that decorated the window. The nurse had cranked his bed into a sitting position. There was an IV in his left arm and a breathing tube in his nose. He looked tired, but alert. Tracy pulled a chair next to Matthew's bed.

'You don't have to worry anymore. I'm not going to tell anyone about the photograph. It would have been the hardest thing I've ever done, Mr. Reynolds. You have no idea how much I admire you.'

Their eyes met and Reynolds nodded a silent thank-you. Even now, it was hard for Tracy to think about how close she had come to destroying this fine, decent man.

'Why?' Matthew managed.

'I know Mrs. Griffen didn't kill her husband.'

'Who killed him?' Matthew asked with effort. His voice was hoarse.

'Just rest. I'll tell you everything.'

Tracy summarized her investigation and explained how the link between the cases Laura had written on her legal pad led her to the discovery that a Supreme Court justice was fixing decisions for Raoul Otero.

'What I couldn't figure out was how Laura had discovered the cases. They were spread out over several years, she wasn't on the court when most of them were decided and there didn't appear to be any reason for her to run across all four at once. The more I thought about it, the more certain I was that the answer was in the transcript, but I came up blank every time I read it.

417

'After Charlie Deems was arrested for the Hollins murders, the police searched his apartment. On page 1289 to 1290 of the transcript, a detective explains the significance of several messages that were left on Deems's answering machine. One of the calls is from an Arthur Knowland. Knowland needed some shirts and wanted Deems to call as soon as possible. Detective Simon testified that people who deal in drugs rarely call the drugs by name. Instead, they talk about shirts or tires. That meant that Arthur Knowland was calling to buy cocaine from Charlie Deems.

'Remember when you sent Barry and me to the Overlook to see if we could discover the identity of the woman Justice Griffen was meeting there?'

Reynolds nodded weakly.

'Well, I checked the register at the motel for the day that Mrs. Griffen confronted her husband after receiving the anonymous call. Justice Griffen hadn't registered in his own name. I wrote down a list of the names in the register. An Arthur Knowland was registered at the Overlook on the day Justice Griffen had sex with Justice Kelly.'

Reynolds's eyes widened as he saw immediately the significance of this information.

'As a result of Neil Christenson's investigation, we learned that the judge was also meeting Laura Rizzatti at the Overlook. I checked the register again and I found an Arthur Knowland registered on several occasions.

'I believe Laura found out that the judge was sleeping with Justice Kelly. I know she was infatuated with the judge from the way she acted when she talked about him to me. Finding out that the judge had another lover must have driven Laura to make the anonymous call to Mrs. Griffen. She must have been racked with jealousy and furious with him, but she still loved him.

'Then Laura ran across Arthur Knowland's name in the transcript and remembered that the judge had used that name when he registered at the Overlook. When Laura found out that the judge was buying drugs from Deems, she must have become suspicious of his reason for voting to reverse the *Deems* case. I think she checked to see if there had been other suspicious reversals since Justice Griffen came on the court. She found the other cases and realized that Griffen was on the take.

'Griffen needed money. He was using cocaine, and we know he was living beyond his means. I don't think he would have been able to resist a bribe in the amount Otero could offer. Who knows, Otero may have had evidence that Griffen was using drugs and blackmailed him with it.'

'My God,' Reynolds said. His voice sounded hoarse. There was a plastic pitcher next to the bed. Tracy filled a paper cup with water and helped Matthew drink it. Then she eased his head back onto the pillow.

'Laura called me the evening she was killed and left a message on my answering machine. She said she was in trouble and needed my help. While she was talking, there was a knock on her door. That must have been Justice Griffen. Laura was so in love with him, I think she convinced herself that she was wrong to suspect him and told him everything she'd discovered. Then Justice Griffen killed her.'

Reynolds looked stunned. He closed his eyes and rested for a moment. When he spoke, it was with great effort.

'Who killed Griffen?'

'Charlie Deems. Remember the attack on Mrs. Griffen at the coast? She thought the intruder was Deems. This is all speculation, of course, but I'm betting it was and that Justice Griffen paid Deems the hundred thousand dollars in the account Barry discovered at Washington Mutual for a hit. It would have been worth the price. If Mrs. Griffen died before the divorce became final, Justice Griffen would have inherited all of her money. When Deems failed, Griffen would have wanted the money back. Maybe he made the mistake of threatening Deems.

'Deems was insane. He was also highly intelligent. Killing the judge and framing the woman who put him on death row for the murder is a truly twisted idea. And it's just the type of plan a maniac like Deems would devise.'

'I think you're right. You must go to Jack Stamm.'

'I will. But I didn't want to go without your approval. You're still the boss.'

Matthew tried to smile. Then, he started to cough. Tracy helped him drink some more water. Then she said, 'I'm going to go now. You need to rest.'

Matthew's eyelids fluttered. He was exhausted and medicated and staying awake was not easy. Just before

Tracy turned for the door, she heard him whisper, 'Thank you.'

Barry Frame stood up when Tracy left Matthew's hospital room.

'How did he take it?' Barry asked.

Tracy took both of Barry's hands. 'I think he's really relieved.'

'The poor bastard. He's been through hell. First worrying about what you'd do. Then getting shot.'

'You understand that I had no choice until I figured out that Abbie didn't kill her husband.'

Barry looked ashamed. 'I owe you an apology. You were always in the right. I just . . .'

Tracy squeezed his hands. 'No apologies, okay? Sometimes right and wrong aren't black and white.'

'What would you have done if you learned that Abbie was guilty?'

'I don't know and I'm glad I never had to make that decision.'

Tracy picked up her attaché case.

'Let's go to Jack Stamm's office and give him the evidence.'

2

That evening Abbie was sitting next to Matthew's bed, holding his hand, when Jack Stamm entered the hospital room.

'How is he doing?' Stamm asked Abbie.

'He's out of danger, but he'll have to stay here for a while. Is this a social call?'

'It is not. I wanted to tell Matt myself. I'm glad you're here. It saves me a trip out to your house.'

Matthew and Abbie stared at Stamm expectantly. Stamm broke into a grin.

'Chuck Geddes and I just spent an hour with Tracy Cavanaugh and Barry Frame. I'm dismissing the indictment tomorrow.'

'Does Geddes agree?' Matthew asked.

Stamm stopped smiling. 'He has no choice. His key witness is not only dead but thoroughly discredited, and his key evidence isn't evidence anymore. Chuck won't admit Abbie was framed, even after hearing what Ms. Cavanaugh uncovered, but I always believed in Abbie's innocence and I am now one hundred percent convinced of it. The Attorney General agrees. As of half an hour ago, Chuck Geddes is no longer a Multnomah County special deputy district attorney.'

Stamm looked at Abbie. 'I hope you know that I had no choice when I stepped aside and turned over the prosecution to the AG.'

'I never blamed you, Jack.'

'I'm glad. This prosecution has been very hard on me.'

'Matthew told me about your part in having me released from the jail. I'll always appreciate that. I don't know how I would have held up if I had to stay locked up there.'

'You would have done just fine. You're a tough guy.'

'Not as tough as I used to think.'

Stamm was embarrassed. He looked away for a second. Then he said, 'I want you to take a vacation with pay for a few weeks. Then, as soon as you're rested, I want you back at work.'

Now it was Abbie's turn to look away. 'I'm not coming back, Jack.'

'Look, I know how you feel. I've talked to everyone about this. There's not a soul in the office who doesn't want you with us. Hell, you're one of the best lawyers in the state. We need you.'

'I appreciate that and I want you to thank everyone. Hearing what you just said is important to me. But I've had an offer I can't turn down.'

Stamm looked back and forth between Abbie and Matthew.

'I'll be damned,' he said. Then he broke into a grin. 'I guess some good came out of this after all.'

'Will you be our best man?' Abbie asked.

'Hell, no. In fact, I'm going to jump up when the minister asks if there's anyone who objects to the wedding. If you think I'm going to let you two gang up on my office without doing anything to stop you, you're crazy.'

PART SEVEN

AFTER DARK

Chapter Twenty-nine

The way Tracy Cavanaugh was feeling, you'd think there was bright sun and a profusion of flowers outside her window, instead of a pounding downpour and predictions of solid rain for the rest of the week before Christmas. Tracy was humming while she worked and smiling when she wasn't humming, and there was more than one reason for her high spirits. The case against Abigail Griffen had been dismissed because of her detective work, Matthew was almost fully recuperated and would be released from the hospital in two days and her relationship with Barry was terrific.

A knock on her office door made Tracy turn away from her computer. On the monitor was a draft of points for the oral argument in the Texas case. Matthew wanted her to come with him when he argued before the Texas Court of Criminal Appeals.

'Tracy,' Emily Webster, Matthew's secretary, said excitedly, 'Dennis Haggard just called. They're dismissing the case against Jeffrey Coulter. Mrs. Franklin flunked the polygraph examination.'

'Fantastic. I'll tell Matt when I go to the hospital this afternoon.'

'The wedding invitations arrived,' Emily said, handing one to Tracy. 'Why don't you bring him a sample.'

'Sure.' Tracy grinned. 'He'll get a kick out of it.'

'Could you give him this, too. It's Dr. Shirov's bill. I want Mr. Reynolds to approve it before I write the check.'

Emily handed Tracy a sheaf of papers and left the room. Tracy set down the invitation and Dr. Shirov's bill and went back to work. Fifteen minutes later, she stopped typing and walked down to the library to check a case. She found the volume of the United States Supreme Court reporter she wanted and brought it back to her office, laying it on top of Dr. Shirov's bill so she could copy the passage she needed. When she was done, she closed the book, revealing the part of the bill that set out an account of the hours Dr. Shirov had spent on the case, the dates on which he had worked and the reason for spending the time.

Tracy frowned. Something was wrong with the bill. She picked it up and shook her head. It was obviously a typo. Tracy decided to straighten out the problem so Matthew wouldn't have to deal with it from his hospital bed. She was certain he would want Dr. Shirov paid promptly.

'Dr. Shirov,' Tracy said when she was put through to

the scientist, 'this is Tracy Cavanaugh at Matthew Reynolds's office. I'm sorry to bother you. I have your bill here. I'm going to bring it to Mr. Reynolds when I see him at the hospital this afternoon.'

'How is he feeling?'

'They're releasing him in two days. There's no permanent damage.'

'That's a great relief. Give him my regards.'

'I will. About the bill. There's a mistake on it. I'm certain it's a typo. I wanted to get the correct date, so we can pay you.'

'Good. I'm going on vacation and Matt's check will be welcome.'

Tracy laughed. 'I'll make sure we send it out pronto. Do you have your copy in front of you?'

'Let me get it.'

'Where is the problem?' Dr. Shirov asked a moment later.

'The first entry on your time records. It says Mr. Reynolds called you about the case in early October.'

'Yes.'

'We didn't know we would need you until the trial was halfway through. That would have been in mid-November.'

The line was silent for a second. Then Dr. Shirov said, 'The date is correct. I remember the call because Matt rang me at home.'

'Can you give me a summary, so I can refresh Mr. Reynolds's memory in case he has any questions?'

'Oh, it wasn't much. He said he was going to be in trial soon and might have a rush job for me. He was checking to make certain I would be in town. That was pretty much the whole thing, except for some small talk.'

'Did he tell you what he wanted you to do?'

'Not specifically, but he asked about the availability of the reactor.'

'Thanks, Dr. Shirov.'

'Remember to give Matt my regards, please.'

'I will.'

Tracy hung up and stared at the monitor. The words blurred. Her heart was beating so fast, it felt like it might blast out of her chest. Tracy walked out to Emily Webster's desk.

'Where does Mr. Reynolds keep his account ledgers?'

'I've got them.'

'I have to see if he wrote a check to Dr. Shirov in connection with the Griffen case,' Tracy lied.

'I'll look it up for you.'

'Don't bother. I'll do it. It could take some time.'

Tracy took the trust account ledger and check register to her office. She went back several months, but could not find what she was looking for. When she brought the ledger and register to Emily, the secretary was getting ready to leave for lunch with the receptionist.

'Who's minding the store?' Tracy asked.

'Maggie is sick. We're having the answering service handle the calls during lunch. You're the only one in. If you want, I'll tell the service to put your calls through.'

'No. That's okay.'

Tracy forced herself to wait five minutes after everyone left. Then she locked the front door and walked quickly up the stairs to Matthew's living quarters. She had never seen them before. At one end of the hall was a small kitchen. She went through the drawers quickly, finding only kitchen utensils. The next room was Matthew's bedroom. She hesitated before violating his privacy. The idea of searching his bedroom repulsed her, but Tracy steeled herself and entered.

The contents of the room gave no clue that it was the twentieth century. The oak bed was large, its head and footboards polished and ornamented with hand-carved floral designs. There was a standing mirror next to a chest of drawers that may have been part of a set some pioneer shipped around the Horn.

On the chest of drawers were several photographs. They were old. The first showed a man and woman standing together. The man was tall and solid. He had an easy smile and short steel-gray hair. The woman was slender. Neither person was handsome, but both were strong-featured with faces that radiated intelligence, humor and compassion.

The second photograph was of the man. He was dressed in a suit, walking down the steps of a courthouse, his back erect, his hands manacled in front of him. The photo was part of a newspaper story. The headline read: OSCAR REYNOLDS SENTENCED TO DEATH.

The third photograph was of Matthew and his father.

They were standing by a stream in the forest. Matthew must have been six or seven. His father held a fishing rod in one hand and his arm was draped around Matthew's shoulder. Matthew beamed out at Tracy so proud to be the one his father was honoring with his touch.

Tracy felt like she might cry. She took a deep breath. When she was back in control, she started going hurriedly through the drawers. Matthew's clothes were whites and blacks. There were no golf shirts, no tennis shorts, nothing that hinted at leisure. Nothing that hinted at anything but single-minded devotion to his cause.

Across from the bedroom was Matthew's study. Tracy glanced at the position on the marble chessboard. She had been bringing the postcards from the correspondence games to the hospital and recognized it.

Tracy looked up from the board. Around the walls stood collections of famous closing arguments, biographies of Benjamin Cardozo, Oliver Wendell Holmes, Felix Frankfurter and other great Supreme Court justices, a set of notebooks with every death penalty case decided by the United States Supreme Court and volumes on philosophy, psychology, forensic medicine and other topics related to Matthew's work. Tracy fingered some of the volumes, running her hands down their spines. This was Matthew's private sanctum, where he developed the ideas he used to save human lives. This was where he thought his most private thoughts. If there was a place in this house where Tracy would find the truth, it was here.

Tracy worked quickly, worried that the lunch hour

would end before she was done. She was halfway through Matthew's rolltop desk when she came to the bottom right drawer and found the manila envelope. She reached in and touched the bankbook. She had prayed that she would never find what she was looking for. Now that she had it, she was afraid to open it.

Tracy leaned back and the antique wooden chair creaked. There was $300,000 in the account after Matthew deposited the $250,000 he received for defending Joel Livingstone. There was only $150,000 the week after Justice Griffen's murder.

Tracy's hand shook as she emptied the contents of the envelope onto the blotter. She felt dizzy. She knew what she was seeing, but she wished with all her heart that it was not there. First were the articles about Abigail Griffen. She moved them aside and saw the photographs.

'Oh, God,' she whispered as she shuffled through them.

There were pictures of Abbie outside an office building in a business suit, talking earnestly to another attorney, and Abbie in the park across from the courthouse, resting on a bench, her head back, face to the sun, oblivious of the fact that her picture was being taken with a telephoto lens. Then there were pictures of Abbie at the house where Justice Griffen was murdered and the rental house where the metal strip had been found. One shot showed Abbie gardening in her yard in jeans and a tee shirt. There were several shots of Abbie inside both houses that had obviously been taken through a window at night.

Tracy picked up a set of 8½ x 11 photographs, taken with a telescopic lens from the woods on the edge of Abbie's property, which showed Abbie by her pool in a bikini. The first shot showed Abbie stepping through the French windows onto the patio and the shots followed her to the side of the pool. Several more photos showed Abbie in seductive poses: languorously stretching like a cat; lying on her side with her knees drawn up looking like a child; and resting on her forearms with her face to the sun. A final set, taken in extreme close-up, concentrated on every part of her body.

Tracy thought back to the wilderness photographs she had seen on her first visit to Matthew's office. Especially the shot of the doe and her fawn in the clearing. She realized, with horror, that Matthew had stalked Abbie with his camera the way he had stalked the deer.

But it was the final batch of photographs from the manila envelope that brought everything into focus. The shots Matthew had taken at the cabin on the coast. Abbie circling the cabin with her Pentax camera on the day she was attacked, Abbie walking on the beach, pictures of Abbie taken at night through the window. In several, she was naked, wandering through the living room unselfconsciously, searching for something. In the next group of pictures, she was terrified and racing through the woods.

Tracy could not feel the pictures in her hand as she slowly shuffled through them. In the next shot, a man in black was staring away from the camera. In the next, he was facing it. The man was wearing a ski mask but he had the physique of Charlie Deems.

The last group of photographs solved the mystery of the intruder's identity. Matthew had captured Charlie Deems, the ski mask removed, standing in the recesses of a deserted parking lot under a streetlamp talking to Robert Griffen.

Chapter Thirty

Tracy Cavanaugh sat beside Matthew Reynolds in his hospital room and imagined instead that they were in a narrow cell in the penitentiary after dark. The image would not hold. The concept was unbearable. The idea would not leave her.

'The outline for oral argument is excellent,' Matthew said as he reread the last paragraph of the document Tracy had prepared for the Texas case. Though Reynolds looked tired, and his pale skin seemed thin as parchment, a glow suffused him.

'Thank you,' Tracy answered stiffly.

Reynolds took no notice of her mood. He put down the outline and examined the wedding invitation again. He held it up and beamed with happiness.

'I think they did a good job, don't you?' he asked.

Tracy did not answer. Until now, she had been unable to tell him the real reason for her visit.

'Tracy?' Reynolds said, putting down the invitation. She was staring at the window. It was streaked with rain. Tracy shivered.

'Do you remember telling me about your father?' Tracy asked. 'The way you felt growing up. Losing him and loving him so much.'

Tracy paused. A hard and painful lump had formed in her throat.

'What's wrong?' Reynolds asked, his face clouding with confusion and concern.

'I tried to imagine what that must have been like for you,' Tracy went on. 'Knowing he was going to die and not being able to save him. Now I know how you felt.'

Reynolds cocked his head to one side, but he said nothing.

'It wasn't just the photograph, was it? You created *every* piece of evidence. You manufactured the bomb and the duplicate metal strips, then you lured Abbie to the rose garden so you could plant one of the strips and the Clorox bottle in her garage. You paid Charlie Deems fifty thousand dollars to testify against Abbie. You told him what to say and you created the account with the hundred thousand dollars, so you could destroy him on cross.'

Matthew's eyes were fully alive and focused on her. She had his full attention.

'What are you talking about?' Matthew asked evenly.

'When was the first time you knew the state thought

the metal strip was significant?' Tracy asked, ignoring his question.

'After Torino's testimony. You know that.'

'I also know that you called Dr. Shirov before the trial started to make sure he would be in town, and that the reactor would be available. What possible reason would you have to do that, unless you knew you would need his testimony to discredit the testimony of Paul Torino?'

'If I understand you correctly, you're saying that I murdered Justice Griffen and framed his wife for his murder.'

'That's exactly what I'm saying.'

'Have you forgotten that Abbie and I are going to be married?'

'No.'

'Do you understand that I love Abigail Griffen more than I love life?'

'Yes. And that's why you did this monstrous thing. For love. Bluffing won't do any good. I know everything. I've seen the pictures.'

Matthew's eyes widened. 'What pictures?'

'I was in your study.'

Matthew's face was suffused with rage. He rose halfway out of his chair.

'You were in my rooms? You dared to go through my private papers?'

Tracy was so drained that she could not feel fear or anger or even sorrow any longer.

'Was that worse than what you did, skulking in the dark, violating every rule of decency, because of your obsession? Peeping in Abbie's windows, raping her with your camera?'

Tracy stopped. Matthew sank back into his chair as if he had been slapped.

'Why?' Tracy asked, fighting back tears. 'Why, Matt?'

Matthew looked out at the rain. For a moment, Tracy was afraid he would dismiss her. Then, in a voice that sounded as if it came from a distance, Matthew said, 'She would never . . . It was my only chance. My only chance. And . . . And he would have murdered her if I hadn't stopped him. It was the only way to protect her.'

Matthew leaned back and closed his eyes.

'Have you any idea what it was like for me, growing up with a mother who killed herself, the stigma of being a murderer's son, and this face? I had no friends and the idea of a woman loving me was so alien I never ever let myself consider it, because I couldn't stand the pain it would bring me. My only escape was into my imagination and my only salvation was my mission.

'Then I saw Abbie. She was prosecuting Charlie Deems. I had dropped in to watch the trial because Deems wanted to hire me and I was curious to see how his case was being tried. She was so radiant I was struck dumb. I followed her that very first day. I couldn't keep my eyes off her. That night all of my defenses crashed and I saw myself for what I was. A pathetic little man so frightened of the world that I used my father's death as an excuse to keep from living. I was less than human. I was an animal burrowing deep into the ground, afraid of the light. And that light was life itself. And I realized that life was meaningless without love.'

Matthew leaned forward, desperate for understanding.

'Do you know what it's like knowing that everything you do must be perfect or someone will die? I never sleep peacefully. The fear that I'll make a mistake makes it impossible. Until I saw Abbie, I coped by fooling myself. I truly believed in my mission. I was like a religious zealot who can walk barefoot across coals because his faith shields him from the pain. When I saw Abbie, it was like losing my faith in God and suddenly seeing that there is only a void.

'I knew Abbie was my salvation. She was color in a world of grays. Only the thought that she was walking the earth kept me going.

'The week before we went to Atlanta, she told me she was going to the cabin. When Joel Livingstone accepted the plea, I flew home and went to the coast. I camped out in the woods and spent two days with Abbie.'

Matthew colored. He looked away. 'I know what you think. That I'm twisted, a monster. I am all that, but I couldn't help myself. It was something I'd been doing ever since I saw her. I never even bothered to rationalize my actions. She was like air to me. Without her I would die.

'Then Deems tried to kill Abbie. I saw him go in the cabin. I was paralyzed. I had to save her, but I had no idea what to do. When Abbie ran into the woods I followed.

'My father taught me how to move through the forest

without making noise. I waited and watched. I saw
Deems searching for Abbie. He was so close that he would
have seen her if he turned around. I did the only thing I
could think of. I used the flash on my camera to distract
him. He chased me, but it was easy for me to elude him in
the dark. He must have panicked, because he only
searched for a short time, then he went to his car.

'Up to this point, I had no idea that it was Deems who
had tried to kill Abbie, because he wore a ski mask. I followed him to find out his identity. Deems drove to a bar
and made a call. Then he drove to Portland to the far end
of a motel parking lot. The lot was deserted, but there
were streetlights. I took a photograph of Deems meeting
Robert Griffen.'

'I know,' Tracy said. 'I saw the photograph.'

'Then you understand what that meant, Tracy. *Griffen
had hired Deems to kill Abbie.*

'My first thought was to go to the police with my photographs. They would arrest Deems and he would tell
them about Griffen. But I couldn't do it. I'd have had to
explain why I was in the woods outside Abbie's cabin in
the middle of the night. The police would have told Abbie
that I was . . . was stalking her. She would have despised
me and I would have lost her forever.

'That's when I first considered killing Justice Griffen.
But Deems would still be alive and I wasn't certain about
his motivation. Was he helping Griffen just for money or
was it also revenge that motivated Deems? The problem
seemed insoluble until . . .'

'You realized that you could get rid of Griffen and co-opt Deems,' Tracy said.

'Yes.'

'And you also realized that you could be with Abbie all the time if you were her attorney and she was in jail or under house arrest.'

Reynolds nodded. 'I would be the only one she could confide in. We could meet and talk every day. I hoped that over time she would forget what I look like, and I hoped that when I saved her, she would be grateful enough to . . . to love me.'

'How could you be certain she'd hire you?'

'I couldn't. But I would have volunteered if she hadn't come to me.'

'What if she turned you down?'

Reynolds blushed. 'She would never reject my offer of assistance. I am the best at what I do. Everyone knows that. Abbie always knew that.'

Tracy shook her head. 'What if you misjudged? What if Abbie had been convicted?'

'I would have confessed. But I knew I could control the trial. Especially with Chuck Geddes prosecuting.'

'You couldn't know that Geddes would assign himself to the case.'

'That was my only sure thing,' Reynolds answered with the tiniest of smiles. 'Chuck Geddes would never turn down a high-profile case like this and a chance to have his revenge on me for his previous humiliations. No, that part of the equation was the simplest.'

'How did you know so much about the bomb?'

'The bomb was of simple construction and I heard Torino testify about it at Deems's trial.'

'And the strip?'

'Deems wanted me to represent him when he was charged with the murder of Hollins and his little girl. Before I decided against taking the case, I looked at the evidence. I saw the strip with the notch. I saw it again when Paul Torino explained its significance at Deems's trial.

'To fool the police the evidence had to be so convincing that they wouldn't think they needed to conduct more sophisticated tests. I took two pieces of steel from different manufacturers. I checked with the companies to make sure that the composition of the two pieces of steel was different. Then I put the pieces side by side in two vises and I cut them at the same time. I took the front part of the first strip and used it with the bomb. I took the end of the second piece and left it in Abbie's garage after luring her to the rose garden. I knew the strip I used on the bomb would be mangled in the explosion and that the piece in the garage would look enough like a match so that the police wouldn't bother with any other tests.'

'What if Jack Stamm hadn't called Torino to search the house and garage for explosive devices?'

'Deems was supposed to tell the police that Abbie wanted him to make the bomb in her garage. They would have searched it.'

Tracy shook her head. She could not help admiring

Reynolds's brilliance even though he had put it to such a twisted purpose. Reynolds was a chessmaster who had thought out every move and anticipated every possible problem.

'You knew how to get in touch with Deems by using the phone numbers in the old file.'

'Yes.'

'How did you convince someone like Deems to co-operate with the police?'

'I left copies of the pictures from the coast and from his meeting with Justice Griffen in a bus-station locker. We spoke on the phone, so he never met me. I told him that the police would arrest him for the attack on Abbie and the murder of Justice Griffen if I sent them the photographs. Evidence of prior similar criminal conduct is admissible, even if a person has been acquitted of the crime, as you well know from your research in Abbie's case, if the prosecution has evidence of a signature crime. The notches in the bombs were unique. I explained to Deems that no jury would acquit him once they heard the evidence about the Hollins murders.

'To sweeten the pot, I told him I would pay him fifty thousand dollars if he testified against Abbie and told the exact story I made up for him. I let him think I was someone Abbie had convicted. A criminal with a grudge. I convinced Deems that the best revenge would not be to kill Abbie, but to make her suffer on death row for a crime she did not commit.'

'Did you tell Deems to say that Abbie had shown him

the dynamite in the shed and suggested he use it in the bomb?'

'Yes.'

'Why did you do that when Abbie didn't tell you about the photos until after she was arrested?'

'I saw her take the pictures. I knew she'd shot some footage behind the house. If she hadn't remembered about the undeveloped film, I would have led her to remember it.'

'Just as you tricked her into loving you?' Tracy said, not meaning to be cruel, but unable to help herself.

Reynolds reddened. 'This was my only chance to let her see past this face. To let her know that I love her. To give her a chance to love me for what I am.'

'It was a trick, Matt. You brainwashed her. You arranged to have her placed under house arrest. You isolated her and made her dependent on you. You . . . you trained her, the way you train a dog. That's not love she's feeling. It's something you created. It's artificial.'

'No. She does love me,' Matthew answered, shaking his head vigorously.

'Love is something that comes from your heart. Would she still love you if she knew what you did?'

Reynolds looked stricken. 'You can't tell her,' he said desperately.

Tracy gaped at Reynolds. 'Not tell Abbie? My God, Matthew. This is murder. You killed a man. I'm going to have to tell the police. I came here to give you a chance to do that. If you confess, Jack Stamm may not ask for the death penalty. You can hire an attorney to negotiate for you.'

'No.'

'What choice do you have?'

'You can keep it a secret, the way you did with the photograph. I'll quit my practice.'

Tracy leaned forward until her face was inches from his. Was it possible that Reynolds did not understand the magnitude of what he had done?

'Are you insane?' she asked. 'Do you think this is some minor ethical violation like commingling funds? This is murder. You used a bomb to kill a Supreme Court justice.'

Matthew started to argue with Tracy, to use the powers of persuasion that had saved so many lives in the past, but he stopped and turned away, realizing suddenly that the moment he had feared had arrived. He was part of the case he could not win and the life that would be lost was his own.

'I'm going to give you two days to turn yourself in,' Tracy said. 'Then I'm going to the police.'

Reynolds turned back. He looked desperate.

'I'll destroy the evidence. I'll say you're lying. I'll deny we ever had this conversation. Last week you claimed Deems killed Griffen. This week it's me. Stamm won't accept your word against mine.'

Tracy wished she could just walk away and do what Matthew wanted, but that was impossible. She shook her head sadly.

'I have the pictures, your bankbook and the faked photo of the shed. If I give them to Jack Stamm, you run the risk that he will believe Abbie was in this with you. If you confess, you can save her from having to go through a second trial.'

'Griffen was a murderer,' Matthew implored Tracy. 'He killed your friend Laura Rizzatti, and he paid Deems to kill Abbie. Can't you let this be?'

Matthew's eyes pleaded with Tracy, but she stood up and turned away. As she did, she remembered the question Matthew had asked her the first time they met: 'Tell me, Miss Cavanaugh, have you ever been to Stark, Florida, to the prison, after dark?'

That image of visiting the prison after dark and leaving before dawn with her client dead had haunted Tracy. When she was with Matthew in Atlanta, when she was sitting beside him during Abbie's trial, when she worked on the brief in the Texas case, she had been driven by her fear that someday the image would become reality if she did not give her all every moment of every day.

Silent tears rolled down Tracy's cheeks as she closed the door to the hospital room behind her. In the moments she had spent just now with Matthew Reynolds, she had finally learned how all those brave attorneys felt in the prison, at the very end, after dark.

Epilogue

Abbie parked in the visitors' lot of the Oregon State Penitentiary, then walked down a tree-lined lane to the front door of the prison. On either side of the street were friendly white houses that were once residences but now served as offices for the staff. Looming over the charming houses and their neatly trimmed lawns was the squat, square bulk of the prison with its thick egg-yolk-yellow walls, barbed-wire fences and gun towers.

After checking in at the visitors' desk, Abbie walked through a metal detector, down a ramp, through two sets of sliding steel bars and down a short hall, where she waited while her escort unlocked the thick metal door that opened into the visiting area.

Abbie identified herself to a guard who sat on a raised platform at one end of a large, open room crowded with prison-made couches and wooden coffee tables. The guard called Matthew's cellblock and asked for him to be sent down. While the guard spoke on the phone, Abbie looked around the room. Along the far wall, a prisoner was waiting in front of a vending machine for a paper cup to fill with coffee. The prisoners were easy to identify in their blue jeans and work shirts. They played with children they saw once a month, leaned across the coffee tables toward their parents or stood in the corners of the room pressing against a wife or girlfriend, trying to steal a few moments of intimacy that would help them forget the dreariness that pervaded their prison lives.

'He'll be down in a few minutes,' the guard told Abbie. 'You can use one of the attorney rooms.'

On the left, outside the large visiting room, was an open area. Along two walls were windows. Behind several of the windows were prisoners deemed too dangerous to be allowed into the visiting room. Their visitors sat on folding chairs and spoke to them on phones.

Also in this area were two glass-walled rooms where prisoners could meet their lawyers. Jack Stamm had called the superintendent and obtained permission for Abbie to use one of these rooms. She closed the door and waited for Matthew, dreading the meeting, but knowing that she had to see him, no matter how painful the visit might be for both of them.

Abbie did not recognize Matthew at first. The starchy prison food had caused him to gain weight. His face had filled out and his hips and waist were fuller. She even detected the beginnings of a paunch. When he entered the room, Abbie stood up and searched his face for a clue to his feelings, but Matthew was keeping his emotions hidden. When he paused in the doorway, she thought he might change his mind and leave. Instead, he offered his hand. She took it and held it for a moment. Then they sat down.

'Thank you for coming to see me,' Matthew said. 'Aside from Barry and Tracy, I haven't had many visitors.'

'How are you getting along?' Abbie asked, not ready yet to talk about her real reason for visiting.

Matthew smiled. 'Quite well, actually. There's a real demand for my skills here. I was most frightened of physical assault when I came to the prison, but I'm under the protection of the prisoners. It seems I have many friends here. People I've helped. And there are many more who can use my assistance.'

Abbie laughed. 'I guess putting a criminal lawyer with a mission in prison is a little like letting a kid run loose in a candy store.'

They both smiled. Then Abbie sobered.

'You know why I didn't come sooner, don't you?' she asked.

'Tracy told me what you said to her.'

'I hated you at first, Matt. It was the pictures. When I learned about them . . . About the spying . . . It was such a shock.'

Matthew looked down. 'I wish I'd never taken them, but I couldn't help myself. I was so in love with you and there was no way I could tell you. To me, you were unobtainable. I just couldn't believe that anyone so beautiful would even look at me, let alone fall in love. I'm surprised you don't hate me still.'

'Tracy told me what you did when Deems chased me in the woods and that you killed Robert to save my life. She explained why you framed me for Robert's murder. She wanted me to talk to the judge at your sentencing, but I couldn't. It's taken me a while to accept that you did everything for me so I would love you.'

Abbie looked up at Matthew. He leaned forward expectantly.

'Jack let you plead guilty to manslaughter because of everything that came out about Robert and, mainly, because you killed him to save my life. You're eligible for parole anytime, since there isn't a mandatory minimum sentence for manslaughter. I've written to the parole board. I told them I want to be present to speak on your behalf when they meet to decide your case. I know that you never wanted to hurt me and I want you to know that I forgive you.'

Matthew slumped forward as if he had been struck in the chest. 'Thank you,' was all he could manage.

'Are you okay?' Abbie asked.

'Oh yes,' he answered.

Abbie noticed the guard announcing the end of visiting hours. She had intentionally come toward the end so the visit would be short, in case it went badly. Abbie stood up.

Matthew took a deep breath and composed himself.

'Will you visit me again?' he asked.

'I don't think so.'

'I understand. What are you going to do?'

'I'm not sure. I've quit the district attorney's office. I'm thinking about traveling for a while. I still need to put some space between myself and what happened.'

A guard knocked on the door.

'I've got to go now. I'm not going to wish you good luck. I don't think you need it, because I know you're going to come through this.'

'I'll always love you, Abbie. Everything I did was for you.'

Abbie reached out and touched his shoulder. 'I know that, Matthew.'

She took one last look at Matthew, then she opened the door and joined the line of people leaving the visiting area. Matthew knew that he would never stop loving Abbie and that he had lost her forever. He understood that there was no way she could love him now. Even so, he did not feel sad. He had saved Abbie's life and that made everything he had gone through and was going to endure worthwhile. And even if it was only for a little while, she had loved him and that was more than he ever hoped for.

And now he had been forgiven.